The Story of a Good, Kind Man

A novel in free verse

Dastan Kadyrzhanov

Translated by Simon Hollingsworth

CONTENTS

Author's foreword

Dear reader,

I dedicate this book to my contemporaries.

Not just those who, like me, were born in the 1960s, but those made to appear in this world in the once great nation that was the Union of Soviet Socialist Republics. Those made to take shape as individuals in a 'Godless' society, in the atheistic world of communism. And those who subsequently witnessed the collapse of this atheistic world.

What does the world know about us, about people like me?

In the 1990s, after the fall of the Soviet Union, the world watched on contentedly as fragments of the 'evil empire' marched away from socialism to what they called privatisation and democracy. All anyone was interested in was how our political systems, economic priorities, attitudes to human rights and property were changing. The world watched on as new countries became part of 'worldwide' processes and humanity became a truly global species, now that the Iron Curtain was no longer dividing it in two.

However, these events were only what the outside world could see; beneath the surface lay a layer of all that was happening and continues to happen in the spiritual rebirth of the former Soviet peoples. It is this layer that makes us so different and so unlike anyone else in the world.

You don't believe me? You want to know what makes us so different and unlike everyone else?

History knows many examples of entire continents becoming engulfed by antireligious and anticlerical views. One only has to remember Europe during the Great French Bourgeois Revolution. However, never has atheism taken such a hold of vast expanses and never has it been so fundamental as under the Communist Soviets.

About 286 million people lived in the USSR and, if we add the countries of the socialist camp, it's not hard to imagine the sphere of influence of the communist doctrine. This was more than a rejection of church postulates and institutions. As paradoxical as it may seem, communism became almost a new religion in itself, a religion asserting that the Kingdom of Heaven was entirely man-made and could be erected in defiance of God's power on earth, free of responsibility on Judgment Day, without the Good Books or any communication with God. This quasi-confession possessed its own temples, forms of worship and rituals, shaped over the course of many days and many generations.

However, it goes without saying that this was an antireligion, for the communist worldview had no room for God.

At the same time, communism was more than a simple ideology of power or a series of individual views; it was, in all respects, an entire doctrine, both scientific and popular. Not only that, but the victory of this teaching was generously sprinkled with the blood of millions, who truly gave their lives for its creation. Dialectical and historical materialism, coupled with Darwin's evolutionism, took on the features of an independent system of views, capable of providing answers to all questions concerning the world's creation. There were even communist commandments, collected together in a document named *The Moral Code of the Builder of Communism*.

My generation was raised under this system, a system which, by the end of the 20th century, had accumulated immense potential to influence the shaping of individuals.

At school they would tell us that Soviet cosmonauts had been to space and had seen for themselves that there was no God out there. From a young age we were taught not to believe that the Almighty was in any way involved in the creation of all that exists here on Earth.

I remember when, as a little pioneer boy scout, just three months after they'd tied that red neckerchief around my neck and pinned the badge with the young Lenin on my lapel, I had been goofing around with a pal near the Nikolsky Cathedral in Alma-Ata. We went up to the building and stuck a poster we'd made ourselves onto the gates, reading *There is no God!*. And I truly believed that what I was doing was right. It was nothing more than the foolish bravado of a child, but it embodied my involvement in the great teachings of Marx and Lenin, which proclaimed that we should believe in the force of our own reason and science, not in some irrational higher beings that the silly old women from the church so feared.

The grown-ups would tell us: *Before, the people feared nature and put its power down to the might of some God or other. Today, however, we are the masters of our own fate; we are materialists. Everything that mullahs, popes and priests have dreamed up is all lies.*

At school we were all *Octobrists*, *pioneers* and *Komsomol* members. Every Soviet child remembers that it was in these young communist organisations that the fundamental rejection of God, Allah and the Almighty took shape from a very early age.

At university, we were introduced to the subject of *Scientific Atheism*. Essentially, it had one objective only: to dress world religions as absurd, illogical and incompatible with dialectical materialism and to kill the notion of God in our perception of the world systematically and forever.

And you know what, people of the West and East? They did a damned good job of it!

That was the mighty Soviet Union, where the older generation (our fathers and grandfathers) were communists, defenders of its principal doctrine, not in quiet offices and temples, but on the frontlines of the Civil War and the Second World War. They continued defending it in their everyday life, in the struggle against 'global imperialism' and also against religion, seen as one of imperialism's main tools for enslaving human consciousness, from time immemorial and right up to the present day.

But then everything came crashing down. The USSR, I mean.

On average we were in our early twenties.

Suddenly, society needed to be something different politically, something that dawned so unexpectedly on the powers that be. The economy needed to be structured in another way; they realised that too. It turned out that relationships between people needed to undergo a root-and-branch re-evaluation as well.

But what were we to do about Faith? Here, things were a lot more complicated.

Did anyone from beyond what we call the Soviet space ask themselves, even once, about what really went on in our souls at that time? When we switched from militant atheism to Faith? When the communist doctrine simply disappeared and we remained alone with the realisation that it could never have stood up to scrutiny in the wider world and that we needed to find ourselves new day-to-day realities?

At first glance, it all seemed simple: those who believed in Allah before the Revolution would turn automatically to Islam and those once classed as Catholics or Orthodox Christians would turn to Christianity. Not much time had really passed, we thought, for us to have forgotten what they were all about. After all, many of our Soviet grandfathers and grandmothers had remained beacons of faith through all those thorny battles between the Marxist-Leninists and the 'religious heretics'.

That much was true, of course. And yet.

It was not simply a matter that we had to cross statistically from one social morph to another or just follow the path of restoring forgotten traditions. We were supposed to believe.

Actually believe!

Dialectical materialism explained everything, clearly and simply: the origins of the world, the Darwinian Origin of the Species and the connection between phenomena in nature and society. We had left one integral worldview behind, but had we acquired a new one? I don't mean officially; I mean truly? What had actually happened and how? Did we find God on our Path or only the formal signs of religion, without actually changing the essence of the way we view the Universe and the creation of the world?

All the world did was to 'rewind' this process on its control panel, the process of us finding our Faith. The world wasn't really that interested; democracies continue to be built, one way or another, countries are fully engaged with the international markets and other geopolitical gamesmanship. As for what happened and continues to happen in human souls is something very much behind the scenes. Or, at the very least, it is reflected in the chronicle of the struggle of confessions 'for canonical spheres of influence'. Plenty of people used to and continue to think, *As long as no hotbeds of religious extremism and terrorism spring up, the rest can just be exotic window dressing.*

My friends, relatives, acquaintances and I all started out on a Path toward awareness of our new understanding of life and the place we occupy in it. This search continues even now, with disputes ongoing about how to exercise our faith, what to believe in and which temple to visit. Is it acceptable for a Kazakh to be a Christian? Does a Russian have to be Orthodox? Do we have to perform *all* these rituals? How should we perform them? And so on and so forth.

Missionaries, mullahs and preachers then appeared, boldly taking advantage of our lingering *yesterday's atheism* ailment, often destroying lives and whole families in sects with dubious doctrines.

Incidentally, many of us asked why we should bother changing. There were plenty of atheists and people in the world without a religion as it is. So, what would change if I stayed as I was for the rest of my life?

It was on one of the turns I took on my own Path that I had a dialogue that inspired me to write this book. This conversation with a friend shone a heavenly spotlight on the main thing to which I resolved to devote the novel's pages.

One day my friend Naizabek said to me in the heat of an argument, 'You spend so much time thinking about how to perceive certain rituals and how you should relate to certain aspects of doctrine. Why don't you imagine another country, where the children, from an early age, are *naturally Muslim or naturally Catholic* and that this is their way of life, the system of their values, acquired and instilled from the very outset, from the moment they are born? And imagine that they never, ever doubt in the way that we do. It is not something new for them, just a thing they have naturally acquired from the very first days of their life, like their own name.'

It was then that I realised something.

This *something* comes down to this. Every religion has had its first champions: the first Christians, the first Buddhists, the first Muslims, the Muhajirun and Ansar[1]. They were truly the first, those who had to believe in the New Word of God from scratch. Those who were initially deprived of the comfort of simply following the established system of values, never thinking that life was preparing a wholly different, quite wonderful fate for them.

Just imagine, the Muhajirun and the Apostles were people who suddenly began believing in a new Message to the world, who were able to overcome their doubts, fears, conflicting interpretations and traditions of the past, reject everything that had come before, centuries of rules governing society and, most important, the traditions of their forefathers, which they had been charged with holding sacrosanct.

And yet they changed. They took to believing in Jesus Christ. They took to believing in Muhammad. They took to believing in Gautama Buddha.

They were the first to believe.

And I came to realise: we are just the same.

They began everything from the Beginning. We also carry the poetics of the pioneers and first followers. Like them, we tremble, we are afraid, we weep and we tighten our lips, we misjudge and we argue with one another until we are hoarse. We force ourselves to raise our eyes in objection, we keep our jaws from trembling, we laugh when we shouldn't, we lie when we say we believe and we believe we are sincere. Some of us are stubborn, some are conformists; some are logical, others, irrational. Every one of us makes their own first step, some in conversation with a remarkable individual, others in reading one of the Holy Books, others, under the influence of the example of friends.

We too begin everything from the Beginning.

It was *doubt* that made us like them, like the first ones. Our Path is paved with doubt and the struggle with it, victories and defeats of reason, conflicts of faith and the soul.

Of course, we could object, saying that modern-day neophytes have it much easier than their ancient predecessors. After all, society today encourages and welcomes the return

---

[1] The Muhajirun were the followers of the Prophet Muhammad who accompanied him during the *Hijra*, his move from Mecca to Medina. The Ansar were the followers who first converted to Islam in Medina.

to the spiritual roots of the past, only it doesn't set the lions on the people, stone them or crucify them.

Life tells us that this is a superficial understanding.

Both then and now, the Path to Faith within the human soul, within human consciousness, has never been a simple matter and nor will it ever be. This Path is always a process of fundamental transformation of the human identity, the tiny yet enormous universe, over which light and dark are forever locked in battle.

Then and now, society might bring the full force of its propaganda crashing down against the individual's genuine search for the truth, with its cynicism, careerism, hypocrisy, the power of its capital, its military might and police machinery all at the same time. After all, just as in ancient times, the world hasn't managed to organise life according to the commandments of the Great Books, and when is it ever likely to do so?

Both then and now, religion is dividing people more and more when they should be joining together, merging as a single human race in peace and harmony in the eyes of the Almighty.

After many years and centuries, history has created neophytes in us who, perhaps, might have to play a part in the final battles of Judgment Day. Perhaps not, but aside from the Main Day, every one of us will have our own judgment day, in a sense that knows no time.

Yes, we are the new Apostles and Muhajirun. Like the first followers of legendary, saintly and revered figures, we too must travel the same Path of doubt and torment, struggle with the same conventions and ingrained traditions, a lack of understanding and fear.

My dear contemporaries, do you think their fate is so different from your own? Do you think they journeyed to find Faith without the circumstances of the life you know? Do you believe it was a hundred times harder in ancient times, or in the Middle Ages, to tread the Path of Faith as it is now? Or do you believe that life in ancient times was easier than our own, more elementary and less saturated with emotions and worries, given, say, the lack of global knowledge networks back then? They were the same people as we are now, civilians and subjects, warriors and poets, fisherfolk and kings, relatives and debtors, brides and dealers, paupers, conformists and nomads.

When I understood this, I decided to look afresh at the famous tale of the Good, Kind Man and his Twelve Friends. To live the story again, to understand how these simple, young men became figures remembered for millennia, about whom knowledge is passed down from mouth to mouth. What happened to them before they stepped out on the legendary Path? After all, there were simply paths of ordinary folk before this, which still led them to those extraordinary events that peoples of different clans and confessions still remember and revere.

It struck me that there is one significant difference between them and us.

They were able to speak directly with the Great Prophets. They could get a sense of who they were, touch the hems of their robes, ask them questions about Faith and God and receive their eternal answers, take in the aroma of their breath and feel the husk of their divine charisma.

This interaction was the force that did away with their doubts and fears. They heard and saw the Great Prophets and they were fortunate enough to be their witnesses. They saw their struggle, not only against society but within themselves, and this was a priceless thing.

And what about us? Well, we can do that, too. We, too, can see and hear the Great Prophets. They will always be walking by the side of those who are genuinely seeking and trying to find them.

And I asked myself what I had to do to achieve this.
Oh, fellow believers!
Close your eyes and reach out your hand.
Touch the hems of their garments.
Just call the Great Prophets by name
And they will turn and look you straight in the eye.
And they will answer you
Just as they did back then
When, like us, they were surrounded
By doubt and fear,
And when Almighty God
Spoke with them, unhurriedly, in a way
Preordained for you and me.

Acknowledgments

If it hadn't been for my parents – Papa and Mama, if it had not been for my nearest and dearest, this book would most likely never have happened. Thank you for your support and your care, with which you surrounded me during this difficult time when these lines were being created.

I would like to express my gratitude to those I call my spiritual fathers *in life – Murat Auezov, Marat Sembin and those are no longer with us. If the Almighty had not given me such Mentors, my inner world would have been quite different and this book would never have appeared. In recalling Bolatkhan Taizhan, Makum Kisamedinov and Kalzhan Aitbaev, I say to them Thank you.*

Separate thanks must go to Gadilbek Shalakhmetov for it is to a great extent thanks to him that this work has seen the light.

It would appear that my student years are long behind me but, when I remember them, I cannot but thank my professors and teachers from the MSU Institute of Asia and Africa. It is they, the Maestros, who, brick by brick, laid the foundations for my outlook on the world. Thank you, Ferida Atsamba, Elena Sharova, Vyacheslav Moshkalo, Tatiana Markina and all those who guided me on that difficult path of knowledge, taught me to see the history and culture of the people of the world in all their varied beauty.

I would also like to devote the lines of this book in fond memory of my tutor and adviser, my Teacher – Ninel Belovaya.

Particular thanks must go to my friends Daulet Saudabaev, Murat Balapanov and Maxim Demin for believing in me and what I have created here.

Thank you to everyone who believed in this book and who patiently awaited its arrival.

And, of course, thank you, my dearest Nadezhda...

Translator's introduction

Dastan Kadyrzhanov's *The Story of a Good, Kind Man* is a journey. In every possible respect. It is a journey not only for the characters within, but for the author, the translator and the reader alike.

The author writes of a new understanding of life and the place we occupy in it, only not according to any single doctrine or religious teaching. Clearly a man of faith, Dastan found himself questioning the human obsession with our idiosyncratic approaches to worship according to one set of rules or another, and how these rules must never overlap. Dastan takes a step back and boldly questions this obsession. The result is *The Story of a Good, Kind Man*, a retelling of the story we are so familiar with, only with reference to all the great religious books at once.

The verses retell the stories of Jesus and the Twelve Disciples, only in a setting that is both ancient and modern, and which commence with citations from the Qur'an, Hindu, Buddhist and Jewish teachings and from elsewhere. The reason for this is simple: this story is for everyone, regardless of upbringing, time and geography. Dastan holds a mirror to humanity, showing us that there is no place for polytheism and that we can only really progress in this troubled world if we are truly united, if we find compromise and truly love.

People on Earth leave for Nibiru and leave governments behind, as such institutions are incapable of ensuring and maintaining unity, Gandhi tells Godse that he should not focus on differences, rather, he should talk of things that bring us together.

What was told before is told again and so it will continue. Our paths are a cycle of time; once a journey is made from *alpha* to *omega*, so the new *alpha* emerges and the journey continues. Where we are in history is irrelevant. Dastan writes of camel-mounted cannons and Abrams tanks, Serbs and Conquistadors, Gestas and Dismas with ballpoint pens, television commercials in Judea.

These circles of time are present throughout the book and the characters continually see themselves or others in unfamiliar guises.

> There was Golgotha
> And Gestas and Dismas had already been raised on their crosses.
> I saw that they looked just the same
> As the two lawyers, but this was
> Probably just my mind playing tricks.

Or:

> The Jew and the American believe we are speaking
> Not to the Creator, rather to some unknown neighbour of His?
> And this while rebuking us for denying the unity of God,
> To whom you are loyal yourselves?

Thomas Didymus strives to escape similarity, only to come full circle in architecture, and there are numerous instances of seeing ourselves in others, from Enver Pasha to the Hitler Youth, Hezbollah to Mossad.

The eternal subjects of unity and discord, giving and taking, hypocrisy and double standards clearly reflect the author's disillusionment not only with humanity as a whole but specifically with his native Kazakhstan, where he was a prominent political analyst:

> Why should our fates now be decided by those,
> Whose criteria is simply growth in consumption
> And a striving to elevate themselves
> Above those they once saw as brothers?

And yet, the overriding sense from this work is one of optimism, friendship and camaraderie. Dastan sees our journey, over and over, as a never-ending opportunity to better ourselves, even if this might only be achieved in a future cycle of time. Despite Dastan's untimely passing in 2021, his magnum opus is destined to remain true.

Forever and ever and ever.

***

Dastan wrote in Russian and his citations from the Qur'an come from particular translations of verses, mostly from the translations of Ignatii Krachkovsky and Valeria Porokhova. I have taken the approved translations of the Qur'an by Talal Itani and the *Tafsir al-Jalalayn*, the fifteenth-century Qur'anic commentary, translated by Feras Hamza (2007).

The novel is written in free verse, much like the major religious texts. Dastan himself wrote, 'As such the novel is a very eastern work, for it uses distinctly non-European, eastern dance rhythms and the poetic rhythm, *terme*, that is synonymous with that of the Holy Books. The free verse in my work is, I think, particularly eastern in style, either because of my education or my roots, but most likely both'.

I would like to express my thanks to Dastan's friends and family for their invaluable assistance in completing this challenging translation, and to Shelley Fairweather-Vega, whose initial translations of the Author's Foreword, and verses 1 and 39 proved very useful.

It is with great regret that my acquaintance with Dastan Kadyrzhanov came only after his early passing at the age of just 54. This translation ensured I spent many weeks and months researching and head-scratching, although the overriding feeling upon completion is one of joy that I have been honoured to tackle this masterpiece. Thank you, Dastan.

S.H.

(106) We never nullify a verse, nor cause it to be forgotten, unless We bring one better than it, or similar to it. Do you not know that Allah is capable of all things?

Qur'an. Surah 2, 'The Heifer'

Verse 1

(253) These messengers: We gave some advantage over others. To some of them Allah spoke directly, and some He raised in rank.

Qur'an. Surah 2, 'The Heifer'

I know you know this tale,
Everyone in the world knows it.
They know it and they judge it
As if they'd lived it themselves.
And they know it even if they didn't live it.

And I won't be telling you anything new.
Open the very thickest version
Of the book that you can find everywhere,
And there you'll read this tale.
Here it is destined to be told again.

This was all a long time ago, if I'm not mistaken,
In a country where war still rages.
A war which, despite the will of righteous men in their thousands,
Has torn asunder all that ought to have been united,
And which has no end in sight.

Well, as the Great Books say,
A man lived there, who was Good and Kind.
A man who enjoyed all his civil rights
And who voted, they say, in Council elections,
In the way his elders had advised him.

This man might not have even been a man, as such;
Everyone has their own thoughts on the matter.
For our simple story, it is not important
Who he was or when he died.
I will return later to *how* and *why* he died.

Some say he was a shepherd,
Some, that he was a carpenter.
That, too, is actually not important. Key, though,
Was that he had a special skill
That society found useful and needed.

Now, the Good, Kind Man was an original.
One day, he rose from a sound slumber,
Rose from his modest bed and realised
That a socially useful special skill was no goal
And no way of making people better.

But please don't go thinking,
Well, what would happen if we were all
To doubt our own special skills
And stop taking pride or enjoying them, eh?
That would hardly do the country much good, now would it?

The thing is, though, that this chap wasn't just anybody.
So, fate determined that, one morning,

15

The same morning I was just talking about,
After he had slept well and stepped out
Onto the scorching Nazareth street,

At that moment, God was walking by
Or, perhaps, it was some angel from the Divine Administration,
A minister of the angels for social affairs.
You know, it's not that often
That God walks the streets of Nazareth.

He hasn't walked there for so long, the people say,
But that's just idle speculation.
So, God said to him (God Himself or the angel, who can say?),
'And what am I to do with all this now?
With all that I've created here in Israel and throughout the world?'

And the Man, who was Good and Kind, replied:
'What so displeases You, Alahi?[2]
There are people with the skills they've mastered,
There are the officials, so patriotic in their conduct,
And, there, the priests, blessed, bearded and praying to You.

What's so bad beneath the shade of the palms You've created?
There, we even have insurgents, look,
Laying down their lives to liberate Israel
From the Romans whom the United States
Will later claim as their great-grandfathers.

What's so bad in this natural world?
Not enough knowledge? But Einstein and Voltaire haven't been born yet.
Justice? But isn't that a divine word, not an earthly one?
Surely it wasn't You who invented that?'
That was how the Good, Kind Man calmly replied to Him.

God stopped to think about it (or His angel did, depending on your confession).

'Yes, that's true; I didn't invent justice.
Surely some have to be richer and more talented,
Some with health insurance and some without.
Doesn't it all depend on the person,
The place they occupy in the world I created?

There must be hierarchy and subordination,
Like the bees and the termites and all God's creations.
Even the wolves of the Turkic tribes
Have Alpha males and Gamma opposition.
What do you expect from people with no tails?'

He wasn't cursing, don't think that. He was just thinking.
And this Man of ours was no fool. He went on:
'If that is the case, then all is well with the world.
So, what are You worried about, Father?
You could go to Europe, the best of Your creations.

---

[2] Aramaic for 'My God', from the Aramaic words *Alah* or *Elah* (God, in two different pronunciations); here, the first, less popular, version is used.

Why walk about this dusty Nazareth
And talk with a man with no higher education,
No rank, no monastic shackles, no throne or sword?
What's Your interest in human conversation?
What's Your business with Abraham's children?'

'With Europe, well, you're going too far.
That's not the best place in the world, but I get it:
You're a boy who can see the future.
After all, it was My idea that some can and some cannot.
You, for example. Now, you see things, it turns out.

So, here is something you can do for Me.
You ask the people: perhaps I conceived something wrong.
Perhaps this kingdom of man is a bad thing.
Perhaps they should build a republic, or a democracy.
Like the Greeks or the Romans, or the nomads with their horses.

Perhaps they should elect their Herods themselves. Why have me anoint them?
They even say there's communism, where they don't believe in Me.
What, you fancy a bit of experimentation, is that it?
For Israel is young and ancient at the same time.
It's even boring, somehow.

Or let there be global popes of some kind,
Dalai lamas, either universal or Roman;
You see, they've lingered too long in their national seats.
Men are not brothers, just sources of conflict.
So, off you go and ponder that thought. I'll appear

And we'll talk some more, if God... well, I mean, we'll meet again.'

The divine avatar then yawned and went on its way
Along the dusty Nazareth street
With a gait that all people imitate
When they're tired of pride and the burden of power, only with one difference:
People have no Eternity.

Those people who spoke Aramaic didn't know what had happened. Oh no.
They simply sensed something, probably. Oh yes.
Because at that moment such a sad song,
A Jewish song, flew over the town.
Someone's mother was singing it, so sorrowful and sad...

That was the moment when the world changed
Forever and ever and ever.
And the Good, Kind Man of ours changed too
Forever and ever and ever.

What were You thinking, You careless God, strolling whatever streets You wish!
What were You thinking, so nonchalantly and in passing,
Piercing the soul of the Good, Kind Man, with the idea
That You hadn't thought through, tossing it and watching him catch fire?!
What had man seen apart from the kingdom of man?

What was this young specialist supposed to say

To the magnates, worldly-wise from experience,
About how imperfect the world You made really is?
Oh my, how could he convince the powerful and successful?
Oh my, what have You done to the boy, Father?

Verse 2

(45) The Angels said, "O Mary, Allah gives you good news of a Word from Him. His name is the Messiah, Jesus, son of Mary, well-es-teemed in this world and the next, and one of the nearest.
(46) He will speak to the people from the crib, and in adulthood, and will be one of the righteous.
(48) And He will teach him the Scripture and wisdom, and the Torah and the Gospel. (49) A messenger to the Children of Israel...

Qur'an. Surah 3, 'Family of Imran'

No, no, the conversation that day didn't end like that!

God turned (or his sublimation did, I don't remember for sure) and He said:
'By the way, I will appear before you only three times.
So, if you need explanations or any systems consulting,
Don't hold back with your questions, my Son. Until we meet again.
For now, I'll admire the sunset over Galilee.'

And he left.

Our Young Man, meantime, lost consciousness.
You think it's a simple matter, chatting with the Almighty?!
I'd like to see what you'd do, if you see
Even a minor official from the Divine Administration,
What affect it would have on you!

He fell and his Mother came out and understood everything.
No, he hadn't hurt himself from his fall, oh no!
He had no temperature and no fever either.
Through her son's pale appearance, she saw
A familiar face, they say, of her beloved...

There is really much unknown in the story,
So don't go interrupting me, if you don't mind.
I don't know myself what it was she saw and understood;
She was a simple subject of Herod, but she wept.
They say that the waterfall in our hills are her eternal tears.

The Man awoke the next morning as if nothing had happened,
And he went off to do his day's work as intended.
Either he sheared sheep or made fancy furniture,
But his day was just like any other.
It seemed the dear man had forgotten it all.

Kind friend, go to the square and take a look!
Can you see the building with the tall spire?
What does it tell you? Does it speak of architecture?
No, my friend. It tells you that the Man did not forget his conversation.
By no means. And nor will we forget it.

Later, only later, there will be different people,
Emperors, Apostles and Martin Luthers.
Later, there will be Muslims, and other Muslims will come from them.
Later, there will be many fathers, but there will only ever be one Mother.
Later, there will be so many different events!

People will argue about what exists and what is transcendental,
About dogma, innovation, science and the creation.
Later, someone with the Man's name will even kill another.
Later, there'll be people who deny everything,
And fanatics who doubt nothing.

But, my friend, for now I don't really understand any of that.

Verse 3

(36) He [Iblis] said: 'My Lord! reprieve me until the Day they are resurrected.'

Qur'an. Surah 15, 'The Rock'

Now, this tale I remember well.
There is nothing odd in that for I saw it all for myself.
I was standing nearby when He fell on his back, so pale.
This was the second time, and not after the conversation.
It was when he said, 'I have found it – the Kingdom of Heaven'.

Just like that, without systematic consultation or any education,
Without the advice of his elders or the support of his friends,
Among whom, incidentally, I counted myself,
Until He was taken from me by, how to put it politely, that Passer-by,
Strolling along our street.

That was how He understood it all. Himself.

You think He went out into the desert alone? No.
I was nearby, beyond the next rock.
It was all very simple: He had started coughing and his Mother,
His Mother had asked me to take a warm blanket.
And so, off I went. To my own cost.

To be honest, I didn't see that passer-by on the street.
But, oh my, I got a right good look at the one out in the desert!
Terrifying, you think? No, sir. He was Bloodless. Greedy. Sad.
I have to admit that I listened in, but it's not that that bothers me.
It's that I cowardly wrapped myself in His blanket.

That was why he fell ill; that's why he caught a cold.
As for me, I took fright and hid in the blanket when that other one came.
The Bloodless One. The Greedy One. The Sad One.
Many BGs[3] now write a bit like Adonai
But another often responds instead of him –

The Bloodless One. The Greedy One. He is not always the Sad One.

Later, this all became the stuff of legend, but it actually happened like this.
The Bloodless One sat next to him. He sat there for some time. Quietly.
Then he said, 'You won't lose consciousness, will you?'
'No,' my Friend replied tentatively.
Three days passed. I was frozen through.

'You sure found a place to go bathing.' 'In the Jordan? I haven't been bathing.'
'Uh-huh. You're going to tell me you got baptised.
You believe that daft eremite, is that it?'
'What can I say?'
Three days passed. I got bored.

---

[3] The author takes the initials from Бледный (Pale, Bloodless) and Голодный (Hungry, Greedy) to make the abbreviation 'BG'. 'BG' can be seen as a substitution of the concepts 'God' ('Бог') and perhaps the Fallen Angel, when many values, spiritual and otherwise, have been altered and distorted.

'I got a new function. I'm now responsible for state structures.'
'Congratulations,' my Friend replied.
'Why do you care?!' The Greedy One grew angry.
'No. Don't you worry. I'm just thinking.'
Three days passed. I was no longer afraid.

'Perhaps you shouldn't have spoken with Him. It's dangerous.'
'I agree,' my Friend said with a shiver. 'I agree. Tell me this, Greedy One:
Are there many kingdoms in the world?'
'A great many,' the Bloodless One perked up. 'A great many! Why, you want to be a king?'
'I do,' my Friend responded, 'but can I be a heavenly king?'
'Hey, friend, that's above my pay grade.'
'No need, then.'

'Everyone thinks I'm an idiot and that I don't know the outcome of negotiations in advance.
But I'll try, what are the benefits: money, accounts, yachts, villas?'
The Greedy One's voice was languid. I began to feel unwell.
'Keep them.' I really had a temperature.
'You were left with love?' 'Nah, that's not for regular staff.'

I don't remember how many days went by.
All I remember are His mighty shoulders
When He carried me from the desert, and when He told me
That this meeting meant nothing
And that it was a mess up in the heavens, too.

I remember what I felt through the haze of my temperature.
I remember what I saw against the background of the heavenly eye.
O, Lord, I am only a little sick!
O, Lord, but how is He now?
How is He now?
For real?
Lonely!

Verse 4

(129) You will not be able to treat women with equal fairness, no matter how much you de-sire it.

Qur'an. Surah 4, 'The Women'

(35) My Lord, I have vowed to You what is in my womb, dedicated, so accept from me; You are the Hearer and Knower.

Qur'an. Surah 3, 'Family of Imran'

'Oh, Mary, it cannot be
That a young man does nothing, right?
That he lazes around for days on end. After all, he is not sick!
That he doesn't fulfil orders on time.
We don't pay him enough, is that it?

Well, if there were another carpenter
(Shepherd, hunter, cooper – delete as applicable) in the area,
Would we be bowing and prostrating ourselves so?
What is all this about, eh?
Were Joseph alive, what would he say about his son?

We hope our daughter's wedding will be soon.
We are relatives, after all.
What will the rabbi say about this if we complain?
After all, we should put ourselves in the shoes of the people!
As for you, you poor thing, take a look at yourself:

Once you had a son, a model worker!
The pride of the kibbutz, one could say!
But now? He doesn't pity his mother, his kin, no one!
Oh, that's no good! Oh, that's no good!
Perhaps the rabbi will have a word with him.

Somehow, we have to come together to do something.
You can't simply abandon a person to fend for themselves!
You think we won't find a case against you?
Shall we complain to the Romans?
When was the last time you paid your taxes?

You could have gone dancing at least once,
And spent time with your girlfriends.
You'd then have come to your senses a little.
The children, glory to Adonai, are tall and healthy,
If only you could live a little for yourself!

The Herods give no life to mothers! Tyrants, more like.[4]
How is that possible, I really don't know? Send him to Jerusalem.
He can work in the city where all our people are.
He'll learn life's knocks and then he'll at least know the value of a tetradrachm!
You simply can't go spending days on end doing nothing!'

'Sorry.'

---

[4] The Russian word for *Herod*, when used in the lowercase, means *tyrant*. The Russian first uses uppercase, then lowercase, thus forming an effective play on words.

23

That's what women would say about us to our mothers and the Man's Mother,
When they gathered round our Friend;
The one who is Good and Kind,
And they chose the Path of the search for themselves.
It's still not the same path, as when they leave home,

But it is when the day becomes filled with new meanings.
And who likes it when the new replaces the customary?
Nobody. We were destined to see this for ourselves
And quite quickly, too, for society reacts momentarily
When someone begins changing their customary behaviour.

No one remembers exactly when it was we got together.
Someone says that we knew one another from childhood;
Another, that some of us joined later.
There is no doubt, however, that we knew each other from our youth.
Our paths even diverged several times but then crossed once more.

It's just that no one can recall precisely
When this wonderful tradition came into being:
Getting together and talking, not only about this and that,
But to discuss issues that many people wave away,
Saying they are busy,

Or that others are even frightened of. We, however, were not afraid.

Verse 5

(111) And I do not know whether it is perhaps a trial for you, and an enjoyment for a while.

Qur'an. Surah 21, 'The Prophets'

One day He asked us. I am continuing the story
Of the Good, Kind Man.
What was the most complex feeling
Of all those that you experienced,
And of those that you are still to experience?

'Victory,' Judas said, 'and the joy it brings.
What could be sweeter and more powerful for a man?
How can we not be proud of the pyramid of influence
And the network of communities that we formed in Judea and Galilee?
Or the strength of our organisation?

How can we not be proud and happy
Seeing that Roman holidays
Attract fewer people than our meetings?
How can we not feel the muscle strength
That is sublimated into the power of the organisation?'

'Honour,' Simon said. 'What could be greater for a man
Than his sense of duty and the honour of an officer?
Honour runs through all our lives
And it is a factor in all our actions;
And it is the highest measure of like-minded people.

There is a maiden's honour, family and clan honour.
Honour for one's country and nation, and for one's sovereign.
What do we need rotten victory at any cost for?
No, only a sense of honour is what
Matters in a person's understanding of life.'

'Love,' John said. 'Victory is fleeting,
But love is complex, like the order of the world,
Like quantum physics; nothing is more resilient
And illusory at the same time.
Love, too, is multifaceted, from love for the Almighty

To love for a girl, for a friend.
One can love their homeland, unleavened bread and Shakespeare;
One can love one's uniform and philosophy;
One can love both physically and platonically;
One can love for an eternity and for an instant.'

'Fear,' Jacob said. 'Fear is the most important and complex feeling.
Fear drives everything – life and death;
Fear forms political systems and religious doctrines;
It rules on the battlefield and in the bed of the impotent;
It dictates root causes, designs and motivations.

Fear is made many times more complicated by man than it is by beast.
A stone house is the fear of what is outside and what is within.

25

State is the fear of the disappearance of a nation.
Poetry is the fear of not being heard in one's solitude.
Power is the fear of oppression. Victory is the fear of defeat.'

I remember how the argument became seriously heated.
It's because of them that they see us as idlers,
Wasting time for nothing and jabbering
Like the parrots in Baghdad about this and that.
But, Alahi! These were the best of times.

My Friend was silent but snickered; he was always snickering;
Few people know what about.
Not that he was quiet and mischievous.
It came from his pneumonia that he'd caught in the desert;
It gave him this quiet snickering sound.

Later, we went outside, the two of us (that's for the historians).
He was silent for a good while, only coughing quietly.
Then he saw a bright star up in the sky
And somehow, he was suddenly overcome with sadness,
And I recognised that expression.

'Doubt,' my Friend let slip. 'Doubt.
That is the most important feeling, equal in complexity to
The divine perception of the world.
Doubt as a triumph of the intellect, as the weakness and strength of one's faith.
Doubt as a search for a criterion, as a choice and fear of the Greedy One.

He who has no doubt in their faith is a fanatic;
This is what the psychoanalysts of the future will say.
He who has no doubt in the system of values
Is a conservative and a beggar.
He who does not doubt his actions is a fool and a castigator.

Doubt is a search, it is grief, it is war.
Doubt is love and marriage and a shareholders' contract, too.
Doubt is the ability to see the system from the outside.
Doubt is the three world religions of humanity.
It is a bunch of sects and movements, all looking for the One and Only;

It is this that makes us weak and so desperately strong.
Doubt is how honest folk will have faith in Me for two thousand years.
Doubt is existentialism and subjective idealism.
It is the Law of the absence of Laws.
It is His main feeling towards our world.

And finally... It is the most important thing that the Passer-by planted in me.'
I shuddered violently. I was afraid and realised he had no doubts here.
But my Friend laughed and said, 'He's not really sure Himself, right?
And I'm not sure that that wasn't the crazy old Rabbi Itzchak,
Who, they say, ran from Bethlehem
To see the sunrise over Galilee.'

He coughed and snickered and I felt awful.
But what if the Greedy One, too, was some artist from the Roman theatre?
As for me, I haven't been signed up at work for six months now,
And all because of some Rabbi Itzchak?!

And still, Jacob is right: fear will somehow be stronger.

'Doubt is the beginning of the mind, the beginning of the soul. And the beginning of one's faith.'

Verse 6

(22) Likewise, We sent no warner before you to any town, but the wealthy among them said, 'We found our parents on a course, and we are following in their footsteps.'
(23) He would say, 'Even if I bring you better guidance than what you found your parents following?' They would say, 'We reject what you are sent with.'

Qur'an. Surah 43, 'Decorations'

'You listen to me. Just listen.
You're, like, a normal person, right?
So you've come to work. Well done, you!
What would we do without work for the good of society?
Our kibbutz wouldn't survive unless everyone pulls their weight.

We can't behave like irresponsible people, you know!
So, you and your Friend went out into the desert; you're a whopping lad!
You caught a bit of a cold, while He got pneumonia
And lay prostrate for two months; we could have lost Him!
What would we have done then without the carpenter (shepherd, photographer, keeper of the Kaaba – delete as applicable)?'

'But, Rabbi, all of us go to work; I for one catch fish;
We all labour away for our daily bread.
Move over, Rabbi, I'll place my basket here...
Who cares what we do on a Saturday?
Why is it any worse than your discos and book clubs?'

'Now, I heard that you'd invented some baptism or other...
Some strange rituals or other... But we're Moiseev's children,
And we haven't invented any rituals for a long time.
I understand it's fun; I understand this is all the maximalism of youth,
But we need to protect the faith of our elders, don't you think?

You know how many Holocausts and persecutions our people will face?
It only takes one Austrian... You've read all that, right?
How would we get by without our principles? Without our customs?
How would we keep face, our name, faith and hope?
With what will we come to the new Israel? They say we'll even lose our language...'

'Don't go touching the baskets; your hands'll stink...
What, doesn't our faith tell us that the Mashiah will come?
Are there no prophecies? Did the Eremite not recognise Him?
So it's all futile, is that it? Just fairy tales about nothing?
But the Magi were real, the star and all that...'

'You're telling me... It was I who drove out those wise men of the Gentiles!
I knew that nothing good would come of this. Oh, I knew all right...
In they came, all jolly, wealthy and prosperous,
Said all manner of stuff to his Mum and dad,
Planting a seed in their minds... I knew it, I really did...'

'Rabbi, you don't believe yourself.
It was told, a Mashiah would come to the Judaic land.
All the signs and symbols are there; you of all people should know!'
'A Mashiah... they should be king! A victorious king, not some...

29

You, you're a boy and I'll give you what-for with my staff!

I didn't come here for a religious discussion with you,
But to knock some sense into you! Why don't you all just go and get married, eh?'
'Not all of us... I have a wife... so does Simon...'
'The Mashiah! You're so full of yourselves, you idlers!
You think, if you say it often enough, it will come true?'

'Then what is a prayer?' 'Take that you numbskull, take that!'
'Ow, ow! Get your stick off me, Rabbi, I am at work, I am!
What's all this about, eh?' 'Oh, so you're laughing, are you, you anti-social yob?! So, you're
mocking now, are you, you pipsqueak?!'
'Rabbi, Rabbi, what are you doing? Take it easy with us!

You're my uncle. I'll tell Mum... Hey, that really hurts!
I won't do it anymore, I promise! It's true, I won't laugh anymore!
You've made your sandals dirty, be careful... Hehe!'
'Hey, I love you silly-billies; you really don't know anything, do you?
You just don't know how precious you are to us...'

'Come on, Rabbi, don't go crying, please. I was only joking.
What Mashiah could there be in our age of nanotechnologies and gene engineering?
It's just that, well, we are used to chatting and talking about this and that.
My Friend really has the greatest of respect for you.
We love you too, Rabbi. Have a seat here, please.'

'But you... there are so few of you left. Everyone was killed then.
Shmul, Rabinovich, Shneerson... Everyone was beaten down then.'
'Rabbi, don't cry. Here's my hanky.' 'Thanks, but I have my own.
We smeared you in manure, so Herod's dogs wouldn't catch your scent.
We would cover your mouths, so you wouldn't cry out of turn.

Sigismund Yakovlevich's son, a babe in arms, ended up suffocating like that...
If it were the Romans or the Inquisition committing these pogroms...
But it was our own... and all because of these prophecies...
It's no laughing matter, kids. It's a serious thing.
They never did find that lad, Davidov's descendant.

I feel sorry for the Eremite, too. The females at court did him in,
And yet he lived by himself and never did anyone any harm...
All you *Yids* can do is tattle on about the Mashiah.
Oh, Adonai! There's so little hope left in people...
And here you lot are...' 'All right, all right, Rabbi, I've told you already.

We have all got jobs now.
Some have gone to Jerusalem; they're all our lads there.
Others simply returned to their families.
Well, had a chat, played at Maquisards[5] – you're zealots too, you know...'
'Keep it down, you!' 'I'm saying nothing... And here we are. How are we any worse?'

'All right, all right... You tell your Friend to come round and not be shy.
There's something I'll tell Him and show Him. He's a bright Young Man.
Only too obstinate. He could do with a decent education
In Jerusalem or even in Rome.
Pilate is now organising some colonial recruitment drive; now if one of our lot were to get in...

---

[5] French resistance fighters during World War 2. The word *maquis* means *dense forest*.

It's good for the community and, before you know it, someone will get into the administration.'

'Rabbi, Rabbi! Take some fish!'

Many people reckon
That, if you step out on the Path of the search,
Then bad people will bring their force crashing down,
Turning the seekers' lives into Hell on Earth,
For you dared to place society's founding principles in doubt.

It would be a mistake to think like that.
You'll encounter angry resistance before that, from those
You would never class as bad people.
Those who safeguard the emerald-like purity of their morals
Yet prove to be the sword of admonition that comes down on your heads!

Those who make up the nub of this tribe
And who are the true guardians of dogmas and traditions.
That's because, as a rule, others aren't trusted
With such an important, reverent yet, at the same time, solid mission,
In executing which they will make it perfectly clear to you

What the cruelty and uncompromising approach of society really is.

Verse 7

(79) Have they not seen the birds, flying in the midst of the sky? None sustains them except Allah.

Qur'an. Surah 16, 'The Bee'

Some say the Deed is nothing.
Some say the Deed is everything.
Someone performs the Deed daily.
Someone, once in a lifetime.
For someone, life itself is the Deed.

Together they are twin brothers.
They always go hand in hand.
They win together and lose together.
Doubt and Deed.
Soul and Faith.

Some spend years preparing for it.
Some think little and just do it.
Someone is glorified for their resolve.
Someone else is ridiculed because they can't do it.
There are a great many who have never done it.

There are a great many who have not reached agreement with themselves.
Who have failed to overcome Doubt and stepped back.
But they, too, are not bad people.
Everyone thinks that it is easy
To be a Good, Kind Man.

Some think that this is not an action,
Rather some world-outlook thing.
But not many know that being Him,
Simply being and not changing themselves,
Is what the Deed actually is.

Prophecies are nothing.
They are merely trappings for someone to do something.
The Deed, for example.
It can be years before it is done.
Sometimes centuries.

But everyone waits for it.
They wait for someone to overcome Doubt
And start living as a Good, Kind Friend.
In the end, you can simply be beaten with a stick,
Or you can become Immortal.

Verse 8

(7) It is He who revealed to you the Book. Some of its verses are definitive;
they are the foun-dation of the Book, and others are unspecific. As for those
in whose hearts is deviation, they follow the unspecific part, seeking descent,
and seeking to derive an interpretation. But none knows its interpretation
except Allah

Qur'an. Surah 3, 'Family of Imran'

Many believe that He disappeared for a time.
That he left aged twelve and returned at thirty.
Saying he left is just hyperbole, literature and symbolism.
No one ever left; it was simply a time
When we were all immersed in ordinary life.

We all returned, be it to our trades, to science or to business.
One of us passed away. I'm too old to remember who.
Then, I recall, Doubt had defeated us all.
It had defeated Him, too, or so we thought,
Because we calmed down, saying:

Here's some wine, some fish and some daily bread;
The family is growing without vitamins or a new outfit for Passover;
Father's getting older, mother cannot manage;
The Romans are building a new road;
Andrew has returned from Jerusalem – everything is fine there.

That means the clock is ticking of its own accord.
That means society is living with its everyday worries.
That means there's a place for youthful romanticism, and for getting things done.
That means it is simpler to grin and bear it, and live with fond memories
Of youthful, carefree, yet distinctive friendship.

At first, we forgave the one who got rich.
Well, we admonished him a little for, you know, selling our ideals.
Then we forgave the one who became a judge.
Well, we know he was mostly fair and so be it.
Then we forgave the one who succeeded our rabbi...

It's basically a regular story, wouldn't you agree?
Everyone's lives have the same kind of story
Of carefree youth and wonderful friendships
Of like-thinkers, brothers-in-arms and, simply beautiful young people,
Who, apart from nights out, also had spiritual interests.

You think our Friend criticised and reproached us? Not a bit of it.
He was himself very talented.
Work performed by His hand was discussed more than any other.
The only thing was that he remained unchanged;
He was Good and Kind with everyone

He worked with and those he worked for;
With those who asked him to complete an order and those who forgot to pay.
He did all this, smiling and coughing.
Everyone loved Him and came to Him with requests;
Simple requests, human requests.

Not for miracles; we'll come to them later.
Somehow, He did everything easily and light-heartedly,
And this in itself was a miracle
In this complex and multidimensional world,
Where it's either dog-eat-dog or do as the Romans do.

O, how the historians and myth-makers hate writing of this!
They'd be happy to hypertrophy and mummify everything,
And maximise it. But they're not young'uns anymore!
They want to present everything not as it is in real life,
Meaning not how things actually were.

I don't reproach those historians;
It was He who taught me to treat everything this way!
It's simply that leading an ordinary life
By no means indicates you are run-of-the-mill,
Destined to drown in subtopia or suburbanity.

If only you knew how boundless His sense of humour was!
The jokes He would tell!
How we all laughed at them until it hurt.
How can you, without jokes, unify people in a unit,
Be it a small one, but stable nonetheless? You'll see: it'll be stable for the long haul.

I once asked Him: 'Have You actually read what is written about us?
Is it true? It seems all too prim and proper
In the linguistic turns of phrase and unnecessarily forced...
What are they trying to prove, that God's Chosen One
Must live a fundamentally different life, is that it?

To stress this divinity
In the eyes of different peoples, both illiterate and erudite?
Tell me, perhaps all this hyperbole contains the fundamental value
Of the beliefs that people followed?
I really don't wish to be mistaken

In my judgements about this.'

He smiled with his intelligent eyes and replied:
'Don't judge by form or even by content.
Judge by essence. Actually, you know, best not judge at all.
You'll always be judging yourself but there is a certain hypocrisy in that,
As you're never objective in respect of yourself.

You ask, why there's such a big difference
Between what is written and what you know first-hand.
You ask why there are many differences
Between the canons and the apocryphal books.
You'll be surprised to hear that, in addition to the canons and the apocryphal books,

There'll be infinite interpretations, all different and all fascinating!
Take the book you're writing, for instance;
That, too, is merely your perception of what has happened.'
'I realised that everything is an outcome of the Almighty's Doubts about all of us,
So, He cannot talk about Himself in the same way.

After all, this is a story about Him, and certainly not about us.'

He smiled again, coughed and patted me on the shoulder.
'No, no, it's all much simpler; I am talking about these variant readings.
The meaning is simple and obvious, you'll see.
It's just that all these books are not legends.
They are prophecies, my friend, prophecies.

That's the whole difference, you see, for prophecies are a dream.
A dream of something wondrous, something that must inevitably occur.
This has all been before, but, at the same time, it hasn't happened yet.
But expectation is indeed Doubt and Faith.
A dream is, after all, such a varied thing, but it so often brings people together.'

I was taken aback and shuddered. I sat down on a bench that He had made.
'So, if it hasn't happened yet, what on earth am I describing?!
What... What am I to do now? After all, I don't want to be a liar.
Or an interpreter, or a theologian, or a remaker.
I just... Well, what should I do now?'

'Let's go to work, my friend, to work.
The time for books and deeds will come.
You'll understand this from the signs
That will be reflected in your soul,
So that you can become Good and Kind for a time. Perhaps even forever.'

Verse 9

(110) He knows what is before them and what is behind them, and they cannot comprehend Him in their knowledge.

Qur'an. Surah 20, 'Ta-Ha'

The day of our Deed and Choice came inexorably ever nearer.

The reason for this was the ever more frequently repeating
Hours of prophecies that rained down on our Friend in such a way
That He could neither drink nor eat; He would just take us from the house
And speak, addressing just one of us,
For He was still afraid of addressing many.

And so He said:

'Alif. Lam. Mim[6]. There is much I will tell you, while there is time, so listen up.
There are lands. There are peoples. There is geography and there is geopolitics.
You'll understand later what that is.
There is knowledge and there are predictions. You'll find what's where for yourself.
Just listen.

Many say that Revelation will come where it is expected.
This is a mistake, for, as ever, they are confusing the heavens with geography.
Therefore, the *Mashiah* is always a Jew, the *Mahdi* is always an Arab
And the *Maitreya* can always be recognised by the yellow cloak.
The King may be a stranger in appearance, but not the Messenger.

That is what people believe and will continue to believe for centuries.
And for more centuries after that. And then more again.
Where is the Wailing Wall? Perhaps it's in China and not in Jerusalem.
Where does power reside? Surely not only in Rome?
Where does the mountain path cross? Perhaps through the rocks of Afghanistan?

It will take a Jew a long time to realise that the Victorious King will be born
In a provincial shopping precinct, only next to the Kaaba wall.
His name will start with Mim, isn't that enough?
His name shall be Seal, isn't that interesting?
He'll bring not peace, but a sword, surely that can't be a coincidence?

Then Luther, the leader of the reformers, will come,
Such an earnest, honest fellow.
His name will start with Mim, isn't that enough?
His name shall be Friend, isn't that interesting?
He'll bring not peace, but a sword, surely that can't be a coincidence?

There are high-priest countries and there are legionnaire countries.
There are tailor, banker and tradesmen countries.
There are foolish countries where the people are thieves, thieves sit in power and the counties are dying.
There are countries, born to give birth only to one, but for centuries.
There are countries that represent Hell, but there are no countries that represent Heaven.

---

[6] Three letters of the Arabic alphabet, with which several surahs of the Holy Qur'an begin, such as Surah 32 'The Prostration'.

He says that perhaps it is a republic.
Or maybe some other social experiment?
You don't need prophets for that, just smart administrators,
To organise life, procedures and relations.
At the end of the day, you need kings; they can be presidents, but they must be kings in spirit.

How do we organise a life process effectively?
People will dwell on this for years and not just any people, but the best of them.
How not to fight, how to translate from one language to another, how to sing together,
How to bring rituals closer together, how to find compromise,
And how to gain fertile land (this will also be needed).

There will be the victory of which Judas speaks, and the honour
That the Zealot spoke of. And love, the dream of John.
And there'll be fear. Fear. The fear of Doubt.
To ensure there is none, there will be a war for faith, for faiths, in fact.
And there will be science. War and science. Science and war.

I will be drawn, duplicated, multiplied,
Circulated, stylised, French and Vietnamese,
Old and white, with a halo and driving a Mercedes,
With a sword and a yardstick, loved and hated, poor and,
You'll laugh... even rich!

I will roam lands with a landscape that is far from Israeli.
You remember, He said he would appear to me three times.
Everything that I am now doing is just expectation.
The expectation of a new conversation where I'm burning and He... I don't know,
When I need to ask, will He respond?

Alif. Mim. Ra. Some will say I am a prophet, others, that I am the Messiah,
Some, that I am Him and we are essentially one.
People will work on determinism for a really long time,
Mixing and blending the knowable and the agnostic,
Trying to relate everything in the language of science and logic.

This is also the Path, the Path of Knowledge and Doubt.
Some will actually say "Ana al-Haq" –
I am an individual, I am Him; I am Truth.
And what's the difference between Bodhisattva and the Anointed One?
Why is the doctrinaire more interesting to God than a girl who simply believes?

Hark. Alif. Lam. Mim. Faith will battle long with science.
Doubt with Doubt. Al-Jabr wa al-Muqabalah will come[7],
Solely in order to combine two doubts in quantum physics,
In its law of uncertainty.
Later, they'll combine all fields into one,

---

[7] *Kitab al-Jabr wa-l-Muqabala* (Arabic) (*The Compendious Book on Calculation by Completion and Balancing*). The famous work by the Arab scholar Muḥammad ibn Mūsā al-Khwārizmī, from whose name we derive the term *algebra*. An important milestone in the development of the science of solving equations. The significance of the book lies in the fact that it determined the development of algebra as a practical science many centuries before its time and without an axiomatic basis.

In an attempt to say that this is scientific evidence of Him,[8]
However, the essence of Doubt will not change even when placed in a formula.
People will seek his trace in genetics to understand once more
That a grandson looks like his grandfather,
But will they be able to understand what *in my image and likeness* actually means?

By the time you come to write your code,
Four great wars will pass.
In one of them, the disinherited will seek new lands.
The West will come to the East. The East will come to the West.
They will recognise each other in their quests for money and God.

Great Orders will emerge. And all the boys, old and young,
Will always play them, in the paladins of Islam and Christianity,
Copying their hieroglyphs and brotherhood until the day they die.
These orders will always be in place over countries and their borders,
Both as communities and special forces; you've heard the term?

People bearing the cross will gather from West and East
In the land of Abraham, to slaughter their son,
But the Angel Joel will be unable to stop them.
The children of the West will be cast out, while the Turks will fight among themselves
In Jerusalem.

There will be a second war, where the children, hidden between two oceans,
Will destroy children clad in armour,
To create a Babylon and prepare for a fifth war.
Hunters and astronomers will die in the Terranova
And their death will be futile and, hence, noble.

There will be a third war where the entire aristocracy will die,
Foolish kings will perish, so they will be noble,
The East will mix with the West for good,
But the understanding of this will not come quickly,
Not until Herod rises yet again to slaughter infants.

And there will be a fourth war of the New Religions, where
Two Romes will cross swords: the Roman Eagle with the eastern symbol in its claws
And the symbol of the family of Solomon in the red of the Kharijites.
The outraged Babylon, too, will enter the war,
And it will win, without even winning.

And, again, the angels will prove unable to
Stop the hand of the human
From rising up to kill its own son
In the name of faith, as we recall,
To defeat the fear of doubt, as is customary.

However a war worse than these will be fought in the hearts and minds,
When the major denominations despise each other so much
That there will be more and more unbelievers in the world,
Nevertheless residing in sets of axioms
Which they accept unconditionally as faith.

---

[8] Implies the so-called *Theory of Everything*, a hypothetical, unified physical and mathematical theory that described all known fundamental interactions. One direction of this 'theory' is an effort to unite into one all known fundamental fields of interactions: gravitational, electromagnetic and strong interactions.

People will seek Proof for a very long time.
Proof that cannot be proven, but which is obvious,
Proof of the correlation of Fact and Truth
Will drown in the chains of logic and mindless fanaticism
And will bestow me with all manner of names and life stories.

Hey, Babylon, you are eternal!
Not in your walls or corridors with nameplates,
Not in the figures on human brows, or the numbers
In their identity documents,
Not in its tower that speaks a host of tongues.

Not in the geography, bombed by hawks,
Not in its bull-headed gods and nefarious rituals,
Not in its greed and low morals,
Not in its exotic name or Breugel paintings
And not in its Rasta melodies.

A Book is on its way to you, written inside and out.
They will knock for you three times
And then grant access to their seals.
However, they will open it not seven times, but a million, a million!
And we will be witnesses to all that.'

That was how he spoke,
The one we call the Loved One in secret,
Only because He was, with us,
A Good, Kind Friend.
He did not fall weakly when such words came from Him.

How could we have helped Him in such moments?
We could not.
All we could do was drink in His every word,
Sensing that that would play
A critical, key role in our fate.

Verse 10

(33) O society of jinn and humans! If you can pass through the bounds of the heavens and the earth, go ahead and pass. But you will not pass except with His authorisation.

Qur'an. Surah 55, 'The Compassionate'

(25) To Allah belong the Last and the First.[9]

Qur'an. Surah 53, 'The Star'

'Why are you so sad, dear Friend?
Why are your prophecies so sorrowful?
Why does your face appear so dreadful when it speaks of war,
Is this not a regular thing for men?
Is this not control over the population in earthly kingdoms?'

I asked Him this with tears in my eyes,
As I had been frightened by all these terrible words,
Taken from who knows where,
But as if they had always lived within me,
Only they had suddenly taken shape in His words.

He laughed impishly and said,
'You need to read books, you silly philistine!
This has long since all been written
And it is no prophecy.
I haven't even got to the prophecies yet!

These events happened a long time ago;
Together we witnessed them, don't you remember?!
Together we followed the paths of Napoleons, Bismarcks and Tasunke Witcos![10]
But you were the one laughing, sitting there in Saladin's tent,
Loudly applauding Lobachevsky's theories!

You remember dying a Jew and a Zulu in the ghetto?
Weeping at the funeral of John Paul the Second?
Running in the ranks of the Red Guard through the streets of Shanghai?
Playing on Stradivarius' *Santa Maria*?
Building Columbus' *Santa Maria*?

You remember counting *riba*[11] on a calculator?
Or how a bullet pierced your Soviet Red Guard helmet?
Or how you shot Che Guevara dead with the words, "the Christian killed the infidel. And there's no sin in that"?
Or how you buried your sword but invented the rifle?'
And so, my Friend stung me over and over with laughter until I fell to my knees.

'Who am I, Rabbi? Who am I?' 'Well you're not Me, that's for sure', and he laughed again.

---

[9] The translation applied by Dastan (Sablukova) states 'To Allah belong the future and the present'.
[10] Tasunke Witco – Crazy Horse, leader of the Sioux, who headed the movement for liberation of the indigenous peoples of America.
[11] Riba (Arabic) – usurious interest, as such, any additional value from invested money. It is prohibited in Islam to levy *riba*.

Verse 11

(20) And the Trumpet is blown: 'This is the Promised Day.'
(21) And every soul will come forward, accompanied by a driver and a witness.

Qur'an. Surah 50, 'Qaf'

Yes, of course, I forgot to tell you in more detail
What each of us was doing back then.
When we were all in expectation of the Deeds.
Let them say that nothing happened in that period.
This, I think, is to shield our images

From what everyone understands by the word *Life*.
I'm not sure that's right.
How can you then understand how the Path
Led us to whom we have become?
How could we understand whom we didn't want to be?

Talking about it is pretty simple,
Because we have consequently told one another
A great deal about ourselves, without holding back.
Our Friend always listened attentively,
Never interrupting and never meddling with comments.

All he asked was this: 'Tell me, Simon the Zealot
(or Philip), what is your life? What is your Path?'
I'm not sure that everything was related in words.
It was more likely images of the feelings
That each given comrade had experienced.

However, the pictures of their lives were so realistic in my mind
That I can relay them today
Almost completely without error or omission,
Not forgetting the most important thing
And, basically not losing any of the finer details either.

45

Verse 12

Say, traveller, do you remember all
That happened with you on the Road?
Do you remember all who asked you a question?
Do you remember all who asked to borrow from you?
Do you remember all who instantly proved to be an outsider?

Do you remember all the paths you trod with fear?
Do you remember all the 'nos' that should have been 'yeses',
Twenty years ago?
Do you remember the first one you doubted?
Do you remember the last one you betrayed?

So, what makes you say 'I won'?
So, what makes you say 'I lost my nerve'?
Were you 'I' everywhere? And what about 'them'?
Do you love yourself in every instant?
Have you weighed every offence on the scales of your life?

Are there many songs you'd like sing in a new way,
And is there much that you'd like to experience over and over?
Do you see the Road in the new highway markings
Or in the tedious tutoring of the formal teacher?
Or simply in the traditions of those who have lived a life like yours?

Has there been a chorus in your life that regularly repeats itself?
Could you resolve into a woman who is your destiny?
Did you behave correctly with your employer
When you exchanged your bread for the folly of freedom?
Or, to the contrary, a yoke for the splendour of renaissance?

Is the 'I'm like everyone' always true because it is true?
Is the 'I'm not like everyone' always worthy of a classical novel?
Simply put, are you basically smart or stupid?
You know, there are very particular criteria for this assessment.
Come on, you mean you only learned this today? You have my sympathy.

You have my sympathy, for if you don't know these criteria,
You'll have to pick new ones of your own.
And this, brother, is either revolt or new religion.
Alas, though, it's more often nothing more than a news report
With a lifespan of two days at most.

So, we're not describing the life of commoners and cowards.
We're not writing about the drones of the intellectual periphery
Or of the fashionistas of the wheel of sophistication,

47

Or of the products of a global promotion,
Or of those who make capital on how dissimilar they are.

We are not writing about people at all, but about a path
That is joyful as it kisses their feet,
Because even a path can be sincere in its love
For those who don't trample it but drink it in.
Drink it in like a source of life.

So, Sufi, shall we practice the images of the Road?
Shall we turn it into a verbal *battle*
Of images, associations and adjectives
With but one objective?
Which one? I'll tell you which one...

So that even for just a nanosecond
You might stand on the paths that have been erased by the wind, by history and the indifferent;
The paths they walked – He and His companions,
For the chance of following the trail their weary limbs trod,
And the errors of their heel that hurt

From the concrete force of the sands of the desert of Galilee,
And from the indifference of those who *never*,
Not in those years and not in these,
Not in the interim and not in the periodic;
Never

Believed in what They say.

Verse 13. The Rock

> The temptation for evil grows in a position of power.
> *Jean-Jacques Rousseau*

'Tell me, Cephas[12], about your Path to this day.'
Quietly the fire crackled in the desert,
Quietly Judas of Kiriath jingled his coins.
Quietly the stars scorned us for not being at work.
We won't be going tomorrow, either; it's all been decided.

'My Friend, brethren... I don't know what is so interesting about my path.
I have yet to gain the talent of an orator
Which, as foretold, will awake with the coming of the Holy Spirit.
I'm not much of a storyteller... But... But I do know how to speak with people.
If I didn't, would I have become so successful in business?'

We saw Cephas's eyes light up,
Because ever-so-quickly, before his eyes, flashed
Pictures of his talented life,
When he was envied by so many;
There was a time when we did too, what's to hide?

The pictures were quick and vibrant,
But Cephas's speech was measured and slow; well, what was the hurry?
That Hour is still a way off, and we all
Have much still to understand
'This is why conversations are needed,' is what our Beloved Friend would have said.

'My Path is like the fate of many men.
I am a fisherman from a simple fisherman's family.
Everything was wonderful – our childhood and youth,
Until Dad received that letter
Which told us that our family no longer had anything.

Everyone understood all that was going on;
Only Andrew and I stood there, looking blank.
There was one thing even we understood, however: we were now poor.
How terrible that sounds: poor *forever*.
Not because we thirst for gold,

But because they had taken away from us
The life we thought we deserved,
Where everything was modest, yet sufficient:
Trendy clothes for me, computer games for Andrew
And meetings over coffee for Mum.

Dad fell ill... well, you see... he started drinking.
For men it is often the same thing,
As much of the problem is a sickness of spirit...
No, no, it's more from an assault on aspiration.
Like any other dad, he blamed himself for everything.

---

[12] Cephas (Ancient Egyptian) – *rock*, the nickname of the Apostle Peter. Peter also means 'rock' in Ancient Greek. Peter's real name was Simeon, or Simon.

And, as always happens, he left his wife.
No, no, no, he didn't get divorced or leave for another.
It's just that he wilted and left her to take care of the bread, clothes and books,
While he went on some internal emigration.
Only perhaps it was painful for him to see us.

Back then, I started smoking and getting into street fights.
I stole and sank our old boat
That now belonged to some corporation or other.
Dad sobered up, put on his suit
And went somewhere; he returned and I never served time for it.

Back then I didn't understand why those around
Would quietly whisper that "he had sold what was left of his name."
I don't understand what that means; perhaps, in the age of capitalism
There'll be those who understand how that is even possible.
They say that then everything could be bought and sold.

It was so painful for my brother and me to see
Our parents dying before our eyes, only not physically dying; this is worse.
We couldn't bear it, although we didn't know
All the socio-economic aspects of the problem.
But then this word Justice appeared.

And did it come from? I don't know – like out of thin air.
No one had ever taught us this. Unless it was the fights and the streets...
Unless it was our rabbi, but we didn't really pay him much heed;
Not because we didn't respect him,
Just because we were kids, which would explain it.

Anyway, this story is pretty typical, wouldn't you say?
People have already grown tired of shedding tears over such stories.
We all shrug our shoulders and say that it's logical,
When someone loses, another acquires.
It's simply the market, the rules of the competition.

Although those who push ahead are the genuinely strong
And capable of moving the nation forward.
These people (the strong ones, I mean) are the nation's elite,
In whom the nation is proud and who appear on television.
The rest are just social fodder for the winners...

These are not my words rather those of a Babylonian.
Back then, he called Dad a *loser*.
That republican so infuriated me that I drew my sword
(That's right, the same one that will appear in the Garden of Gethsemane),
Pressed it to his throat and roared:

"What makes you any different from the Spartans
Who threw weak children into the chasm?!
What makes you any different from the Nazis
Who killed inferior races?!
They, at least, just killed, while you

Condemn them to a life worse than a slave; a slave is at least a slave under the Constitution,
While on television you call them fellow countrymen,

50

At your villas, you call them the rabble, taxpayers and voters.
You devised an ideology of *also rans*,
To justify your own insatiable greed

And the world order that you have organised,
Where a person appears to be free but is in fact a slave.
Because, like a weak infant, they are tossed into the chasm.
Like a weaker race, they are shoved into ghettos
And occasionally shot at, to lessen the burden on the budget!"

I screamed so much at him that, I have to say, I nearly killed him.
However, this Babylonian was made of sterner stuff.
Evidently he was a member of the caste of winners for good reason.
I came to realise later that he had grown up in the Bronx
And that you wouldn't scare him by waving a little knife around.

He quickly gained his bearings and said:
"Listen. Look, you've spent time among the losers.
To judge life better, you need to try
Being one and the other; I can see from your eyes that you have a talent.
My intuition tells me you're a no-nonsense organiser.

I might be a wheeler and a dealer, but I have a gift when it comes to people.
This ability will help you many times in life
To reach the goals you set yourself."
That's what he said and I... I believed him!
I followed him and my life changed.

It became bright and beautiful!
Full of real emotions and the healthy competitive spirit!
It all began, how can I put it, not wholly legally.
I knew that everyone in our kibbutz was pretty, well, faithful,
But everyone had their weaknesses.

Everyone wants something important for themselves,
Which dilutes their weak spirit of naysayers and cogs in a social machine.
I organised the network in such a way, so that, in the blink of an eye
I could deliver to them, be it from Persia, Babylon
Or even from Rome itself (incidentally, it was back then when I was studying well)

That which distracts them from that idiotic word 'Justice',
Which was almost the death of me at the time.
Back then, you would often meet me with your brother,
Emerging from the night clubs and restaurants of our town.
By the way, back then I saw our town as an *also ran*.

All of it. The entire town...

Then I organised things in a way that made illegality a conditional notion.
How can I be against the law, when King Herod himself
Is writing scrolls to me at length and not altogether legibly
On his latest order to mark his birthday?
Well, and don't get me started on the Romans...

After all, they miss their homeland, so
They ask others to bring them something that you can get
Only in their factory outlets

And which you just can't get here in Israel.
And sometimes, hehe, all the decent Italian stuff

Can be made by those smart Chinese
With their odd philosophy on life,
Which, incidentally, is interestingly enough called Confucianism.
It is so unique that it doesn't even contradict
Communism... Well, anyway... I digress.

I got to have as many friends
As that soldier from Anderson's fairy tale about the tinderbox.
I stopped hating life and society.
And it's a wonderful thing, living in harmony with yourself.
And those Romans turned out to be very likable chaps,

Really amenable, I have to say,
And not at all greedy, like those from Herod's administration.
There were times when I couldn't understand which of them was genuinely the coloniser.
But that is another story,
To which you were all witnesses; they wrote about it in the papers.

It all began... No, no, not like that. And so, I believed that I,
That I was not a loser, but a winner,
That I was standing shoulder to shoulder with the world's strongest.
Everything that can be resolved is resolved with money.
All doors open for gold, even the doors to a temple.

If Pilate himself were to wish me a happy birthday
With a call from his mobile,
What could be unattainable for such a lad, eh?
I called the Babylonian Teacher...
Oh, sorry, not with a capital letter: teacher, chief, coach.

And here they caught this lad, the zealot.
He was in the same class as me and a fearless street fighter to boot
He received a hundred lashes and was sentenced to the cross.
Then they placed a crown of thorns on his head and roared with laughter:
"So you want to run the country do you, you scum?! Off you go then!"

I felt sorry for him; our mums were friends
And mine had passed away precisely a year ago.
So off I went, like an idiot, to ask the Romans
To let me into his cell; perhaps he'd come to his senses.
(Incidentally, the zealot endured his torture with courage).

The Romans laughed but, somehow, they looked at me in a peculiar way,
Like no one had ever looked at me before.
And at this moment I sensed that something new was beginning,
Something hitherto unexplained, I suppose...
Basically, I didn't go with my gut, which cried *danger!*

So, I went to meet the zealot.
What I saw was both terrible and somehow noble at the same time.
Beaten up and wounded, he was sitting by the cell wall.
Most important, he was clearly on his last legs and would drop to his knees at any moment,
But he was afraid of this and so used the last of his strength to hold it together.

His eyes were wolfish and proud.
Money does its job; I had brought bread and wine with me,
And herbal water to wash his wounds.
(I supplied these herbs to Herod to treat his awful disease.)
I approached him, kneeled down and, then...

Then he recognised me and... he burst into tears like a child,
Fell to his knees and started kissing my sandals.
I don't care now, but then I was cross with him for dirtying them.
(The sandals came from Rome and were really expensive.
The only other person who had them was Jerusalem's main tax collector

Levi, and you know what kind of guy he is.)

Anyway, he fell to his knees and started shouting, wiping his snot:
"Save me, Simon, save me! I can stand it no longer!
I repent! I will tell them everything, where my brothers are hiding,
What partisan forays they're preparing,
Where their guerrilla camps and stores of food and weapons are!"

He screamed so much that it hurt
To see a man so crushed by torture.
It was clear: a simple man could not endure such a thing.
I bowed and embraced him (carefully, of course, so as not to get dirty).
And... I made him a promise. I promised.

I left with the secret hope that, before I got to do anything,
He would die from the torture and I wouldn't
Have to keep my promise.
What was most interesting was that I wasn't thinking about him at all
Or how I pitied him as a fellow classmate.

I was thinking of myself and about the promise I'd made...
That's right, I even found it distasteful to see the image of
A fallen hero, all covered in snot. There was another interesting thing as well:
No one apart from me saw the zealot in this way.
All around, everyone would whisper: "Simon can do anything; he'll help our hero".

Then, I became overcome with inordinate pride.
Am I not, I said to myself, Chairman of the Board of Israel's biggest bank,
President of the Vacance Romani corporation,
Honorary Chairman of Galilee Football Club,
Son of a fisherman, a self-made man –
Am I not able to do this, save our hero?

Am I not the master of life and its systems organiser,
Deciding the fate of others and able, without faltering, to say,
"You're fired, you loser"; am I surely unable to handle this task?!
Am I not destined by the Almighty to be noble,
Generous and charitable?

And I saw my portrait in *Haaretz*
With the words *Hero Saves Hero*, where there was much written about me,
But merely a short bio on the young zealot.
These were the thoughts that overcame me.
Only once did I doubt,

When I decided to seek my brother Andrew's advice.
At the time, he had left business, saying he had to study,
That it wasn't enough to be rich and "what are the world's riches compared to knowledge?!"
Unfortunately, however, I didn't tell him what I was planning to do.
I ought to have done. After all, he is wise beyond his years.

What I asked him was this: "Can a man be deemed a hero
If he breaks down and weeps, dribbling snot?
Can he, even when no one else sees him? I'm talking about our friend the zealot, here".
Andrew was silent for a while and then said: "It all depends on you.
If you were the only witness, then it's up to you to decide
What is more valuable – the years of his irreconcilable struggle with an enemy of the State

Or a minute of weakness before his only true friend?
Just remember, he might not be an orphan, but out on the street, you were
A father to him. He came to you for advice; you're his beacon of light,
You are his measure of all that's valuable. I don't think this was weakness.
It was honesty. He was honest with you, as he would be with himself.

And he was in great pain, don't forget," Andrew said and wept.
I shuddered, recalling the many-tailed lash and the crown of thorns
And the freshly constructed cross in the yard.
And yet I failed to get the essence of Andrew's words.
About the hero's fate being in my hands.

I had fussed about, running from authority to authority,
Like some foolish Efraim[13], a spirit of Odesa, I ran into the hands of the powers that be.
I bribed, I parleyed, I drank wine with those I hate and fear.
One strange thing I noticed:
All of them, Romans, Jews and high priests –

They had all started looking at me differently.
Even Caiaphas once said, "Son, don't get involved in politics".
The sage Annas (they say he was the secret patron of zealots)
Actually tried to talk me round·
"You and your petty pride will be the death of that hero.

I met with him yesterday. He is steady as a rock.
Mercy for him is also death, for his friends
Will think that he is still alive because he betrayed them;
In battle everyone knows the rules; no one is under any illusion.
Live your life a prosperous subject

And forget this story; see it as just a bad dream.
Best you go and help your brothers who
Toil away diligently day and night,
Bringing you a daily profit while you are not kind to them.
All you do is exude the cynicism of joy at corporate parties.

Go, my son. It is not your job to save people from where
They've come after making their Choice.
You ask what that is? Your time will come.
Or perhaps it won't; there have already been generations like yours, like grains of sand
Washed to the bottom by the waves of Galilee".

---

[13] Reference to the Russian dissident writer Efraim Sevela, who emigrated to Israel in the 1970s.

What are you talking about, padre?! My soul screamed, albeit from within.
We had not been taught to answer high priests out loud.
I am all-powerful. After all, everyone says that Simon is a hero, that Simon will save him!
I didn't hear the advice of those around me. Even my partner from Babylon,
Seeing that my head was full of uncharacteristic thoughts,

Said one day, "Simon, you are stubborn as a rock.
But at the same time, you have no core.
You see, you aren't the useless kind of rock they toss onto the road.
You aren't the wise rock they place in the foundations of temples.
You and I are useful rocks. We are thrown into the well to gauge its depth.

This is how they give us the chance to fly a little, but no more than that.
So, you just fly while you still can. You think we have much time left?
For the powers that be, it's like this: while you serve them,
You are a great lad, talented and necessary.
Even essential, you could say. That suits everyone.

But the moment you stick your nose into how they run their lives,
Everything will change fundamentally. You become dangerous.
Because everyone sees that you now have new *thoughts*.
And that is not part of their plans. So, don't you go jeopardising
Our successful business that we've spent years building.

Take a look at how many of them have made a mistake in their lives.
Take a look where there are now, what they've become – social garbage.
And so it will continue for centuries; there is no recipe to counter it.
Well, if you suddenly come across a recipe... hehe, then we'll talk.
For now, though, get on with that contract with Persia.

You need to see to it while we're not at war with them."

However, I paid this advice no heed because I got another idea
That warmed my pride right back up: this is unfair!
This thought became an itch that I just had to scratch.
I started making mistakes in business.
First, I failed to dismiss two hundred rickshaw pullers, when I had to.

We lost, well, a considerable amount as a result.
Then I didn't dissolve the fish processing plant where my dad worked...
Although I should have; it would have gone to the wall in any event.
Then... well you all read about it in the books on the age of capitalism;
You've seen *Wall Street* and you've read *Martin Eden*.

But there was one thing I stubbornly refused to forget – I went from authority to authority
And that portrait in *Haaretz* became an obsession.
This young man, the zealot, had nothing to do with it.
They executed him, you know. Crucified him on that hill. What's it called? *Bald*[14], right?
He carried his cross and looked at me with hatred.

I thought it was because I hadn't helped him; only later did I realise
That he hated the only witness to his weakness.

---

[14] The author makes reference to *Lysa Hora* (Bald Mountain), which conjures images of witches and black magic. Bulgakov also refers to Golgotha as *Lysaia Gora*, suggesting Mussorgsky's *Night on Bare Mountain*. *Golgotha* in Aramaic means *skull*; it's alternative name, *Calvary*, translates from the Latin *calva* for *bald*. The location in Slavic folk mythology relates to witches and devilish sabbaths.

I ran after the man carrying his cross and caught his eye.
Everything inside screamed out: *It's me!!! Me!!! The one you saw as a father,*
Hating your real father all your life for

Being an also-ran and a drunkard.
I am your father! The true one, I am your flesh and blood! Love me!
I was the one who wanted to save you when your alcoholic progenitor
Just sat around at home washing his hands of you.
Not lifting a finger!

I was the one who ran around and belittled myself before the authorities. I made you a hero
With my silence! I never saw you and I won't tell a soul!
You owe me for the crowd that runs behind you and your cross,
Admiring you and spitting ire at the Romans,
United by an intifada, for whom you are now becoming the symbol!

Look at me!

They had nailed him down crudely, but accurately and professionally.
One of the Romans even said, "Hang in there, brother soldier, it will be over soon!"
Then I saw them raise him up, and with respect.
They expertly adjusted the cross, so it would stand straight.
Once they had done this, a centurion bellowed "Careful!"

Alahi, how foolish that sounds - careful! Can you imagine?
But there was a point to it and the Roman soldiers understood it well.
He had come to die, he was a warrior, taken prisoner.
Each of them could face a fate like this
Somewhere in the valleys of Dacia or Parthia.

Time went by... He never did catch my eye, so desperate
To catch his; I don't know why – perhaps for the sake of forgiveness,
Or for the sake of a valediction. Or... all my feelings by that time
Had become monolithic and unheard, like a sack of flour,
And they lay on my heart, not in my head, just like this sack.

And then, all of a sudden the young man on the cross burst into tears.
That boy from childhood and from the prison cell!
And the snot came flowing from his nose once more.
He raised his head and started looking for something in the crowd.
Then he cried out and, to this day, that cry

Rings like a curse in my head.

"Dad! Daddy! Where are you? Are you here?!"
Oh now, this wasn't like in *Taras Bulba*, where I too swallow my tears.
There was no *I hear you, son!*
I began looking around, scanning the crowd,
And then I saw his father. He was standing there in silence, his eyes devouring his son,

Eyes that screamed *I'm here, I'm here!*
I just forgot to mention that his father was mute.
He had cut out his tongue when he'd been captured by the Romans,
So as not to betray his comrades, and he'd been spared,
Only because he had not managed to kill anyone.

And he was no *Maquis* either. He'd only offered the zealots a place to spend the night,

Only the next morning wanting to run away with them.
And he *knew* where he was running.
Everyone has their Deed; back then I didn't know it.
For now, all I saw was that their eyes had found one another.

Father and son. Everyone somehow saw it and felt it.
The father's eyes spoke: *Don't be afraid, don't be afraid.*
I'm with you. Weep, son, weep. There's nothing wrong with that; we
Will be apart for a time, but we'll never see one another at home again.
Son, I see how much pain you're in. I feel it. I am taking on your pain.

And no one, can you imagine? No one: not the Romans, not the Jews,
Not the commoners, not the undergrounders, not the children nor the women
Doubted for a second that the young man's tears
Meant he was dying a *hero*. No one was ashamed of his tears
Or his boyish weakness, his snotty nose and bloodied lips

That whispered: *Dad, it hurts! Daddy, don't leave me!*
Farewell, Daddy! Farewell! And then I understood.
Everything as it appeared to me then.
My pride, glory, hypocrisy and cowardice,
My desire to buy myself a name by speculating on the hero's life.

A Roman sitting nearby suddenly shot up, rudely pushed me aside
And, without the order or instruction of a centurion, stabbed the young man in the side with a
spear.
I saw tears in his eyes. I was certain it wasn't sweat in the heat.
The young man let out a sigh and died. The soldier was suddenly afraid
And looked over at the centurion, but the centurion barely nodded.

Then there was an empty feeling. In my soul, all around and even on the noisy streets
Of Jerusalem al-Quds. For several days I just sat there.
Just sat. My hands on my knees. Looking ahead.
But you know all about what happened later. We had plenty on our plate.
Someone presented my letters and petitions

As evident endorsement of the zealots
And they used this against me and my partner.
Friends instantly disappeared... But, again,
This is a story like many others, so what's the point retelling it in detail?
I understood why they hated me so and why they'd begun to destroy me,
The moment they got the chance.

And why that young man, too, that zealot, had looked at me with hatred.
I am just a dealer of weaknesses;
And who likes dealers of weaknesses? No one.
Only my Babylonian partner turned out a decent sort.
He handed over a big lump of money so I wouldn't be handed over to the Romans.

We were left with one half of what we had had, and I decided
That he had spent my share. The Babylonian didn't really object.
What would he need a broken-spirited loser for now?
However, he left me and my father that fish plant,
Where you found me unloading fish.

Before I met you, my friends, I would chat at length with Dad
And tell him everything. So, what they write in their books is wrong:

57

He didn't object to Andrew and me leaving.
All he did was ask what we would live on.
I told him that we were on a pilgrimage and we'd see.

He stroked my head and said,
"Look for Him, son. Look for Him. Just don't make a mistake when you find Him.
You see, He's not out on the mountain paths or in the temples, but right by your side
Like that young man, that Good and Kind one."
I joked that he shouldn't take the Lord's name in vain and we left.

What might be the conclusion from my Path?
I don't know, my friends. I don't know, Beloved Friend.
As for the pride and the golden calf, it's obvious.
As for the hypocrisy and the egotism, again, I think
It's pretty clear to anyone with any sense.

As for capitalism, too, albeit a complex social structure,
Many people have long since realised that things are not quite right.
Although many communist countries collapsed some time ago, it is clear:
Well, the communists have gone, but what's left?
All right, well, too much thinking about the creation; that's also a kind of pride, I guess.

The main conclusion from my life is probably this:
Talent is a curse. If I were not a talented organiser,
If I could not persuade people, convince them,
Build an effective structure from their relationships
And networks of interests and needs, I would not have found myself in this cycle of malice

And mistakes on my life's path. We all have our curses.
I have my own. Talent is apparently a sophisticated means
With which the Almighty punishes a man,
Raises him up and then casts him down
When it would appear he has reached the peak of his powers and happiness.'

Don't you rush, Cephas, it's not a matter of what talent you have
It's much simpler, like the fate of Jerusalem.
The question is where and to what goal you direct it. That's one.
Will you find a true Path for its application? That's two.
Will you decide to take this Path? That's three.

And, most important, what will you see as a happy ending on this Path? That's one, again.

Verse 14. The Song

Beautiful music is the art of the prophets
that can calm the agitations of the soul;
it is one of the most magnificent and delightful
presents that God has given us.

Martin Luther

And the suffered verse, with melancholy keen,
Doth smite each heart with unknown power.

Alexander Pushkin

Our path, it is a hard one, Johanaan[15]!
Our feet, they are a-floundering, Johanaan!
The chlamys fibula
Is as sharp as a spear tip,
It chafes the skins and cuts it
Worse than an enemy's knife.
Sing a song, Johanaan,
Sing, for you are the youngest of us all.
Sing, so the path is jollier!
At least just to make it easier.
Our blisters are bleeding, brother.
Travel far, brother.
Where? Where is this distant objective?
The spirit is weakening, Johanaan!
The breathing is broken, for the hundredth time.
The legs, like the temple columns;
Broken and unwieldy at the same time.
So, how can we walk, Johanaan?
Brother, how can we make it through the desert?
Sing us a song, brother;
Perhaps life will at least gain a rhythm!

'But how do I become your strength, brethren?
But how do I become your staff, brethren?
How, in the noble but cruel desert
Do I become your camel, brethren?
How do I become your breath?
How do I nourish your legs
With the strength faith and joyousness,
If the rabbi says nothing, brethren?
For He is our Path, brethren!
For He is our objective at that end of the desert!'

Sing, sing, Johanaan,
I have no strength left, brother!
The spirit suffers from the body's weakness, brother!
What do we have left, apart from that?!
Sing a song, Johanaan!
Let it be our cup
Of water, sweet as heaven's manna,
Like the triumphal voice,
Like the cry of a lover

---

[15] Johanaan – Ancient Hebrew pronunciation of the name John.

59

Between the sheets, when the goal of the caress is reached!
Like the horn of victory,
Although we are no warriors.
But who are the warriors, if not us, the Militia Christi?
Our feet, they ache, Johanaan!
The body hurts and the spirit becomes but a shadow,
A shadow with no shade in the desert.
Give us shade and coolness, brother!
Sing a song for those thirsting for death,
So we might live!

'So, how can I lead you forward, brethren?!
How might I inspire you, Rabbi?
When you say nothing and we are but Your framework?
When only we see the desert, and You are its offspring?
How can I be first, Rabbi?
How might I stand before You, at least for a short while?'

Hey, John, child of that subtle world,
Weren't you the one given the voice that sings of heaven?
Weren't you the one given the voice that sings of rain in the desert?!
Of trees in the sea and of mountains in the steppe?
Is it not you who changes reality
With just one change in intonation?
Sing, John, sing.
We will not listen to you with our ears.
We will eat your song with our feet,
We will imbibe it with our body's pain.
We will breathe it in with our loins,
Aching not from the heaviness of our muscles,
But from the weight of a weary spirit!
The floor is yours, boy!
The floor is yours, brother of ours!
Sing, John, sing.
And don't go worrying that, for a time
You will become the faith and voice
Of our weak tribe,
Weakened by the leadenness of our step
And the fire of the scorched desert.
"Hey, mirages of the inter-temporal!
Hey, play-actors of the road!
Have I got a song for you;
You'll weep for this one.

He who talks with God dances in the twilight
He who talks with God twirls by the fire
He who talks with God is deprived of justice
He who talks with God laughs on Friday
He who talks with God eats ribwort
He who talks with God writes reports
He who talks with God doesn't remember His name
But follows logic most seriously
He who talks with God is tired of chemistry
He who talks with God writes a poem
He who talks with God changes profession
He who talks with God is contemporaneous
He who talks with God is a Croat

And an Uzbek, an Atlas and an ape-man
It's not important as whom you are classified
He who talks with God is beyond classification
He who talks with God has come to terms
That he is the only one who talks with God
While everyone else is convinced that
He is basically talking to himself.'

Hey, Johanaan the singer!
That is not a song to invigorate
And imbibe our tormented bodies with strength.
That is not a song to
Give us the joy of a clear rhythm,
To make us step more clearly and easily.
That is not a song to heal the wounds,
That macerate our legs with pain.
That is not a song to cement our
Our nails to be like they were in childhood,
Or before we stepped out onto this road.
That is not a song to remove
The pain of that wave of lactic acid,
That petrifies our muscles.
You have achieved but one thing and one thing only:
Despite this physiological sorrow
Our spirit has risen up in midst of the desert
And we hear the end of the road.
We've seen that our goal is attainable,
We've seen the finish line and this is glorious.
Oh, Rabbi! Is it the End of the Path or the Beginning?!
Oh, Rabbi, we will drink our tears!
Oh, Rabbi, we will declare our weariness
As the achievement of the righteous, parched in the desert!
We will create a legend
In which there are no convulsions of calves or brain;
In which the backs suffer no fatigue,
And there is no wind to roast on the oil of our sweat.
We will be beautiful in our robes of white
Depicted in the imagination of the foolish
In the pictures of virtual legend,
Where there are only profiles, faces and members,
A desert, an entourage and gestures,
Everything one could bow down before in ecstasy.
And yet, the most important thing cannot be heard: the song.

Verse 15

I do not seek to understand in order to believe, but I believe in order to understand.

Anselm of Canterbury

One day Thomas said,

'What I liked in Cephas's story
Was the allegory of human fate with a rock.
As far as I know, Russians have an expression
That sounds something like *the firmament*.
Any pilot or cosmonaut and, that means a school leaver, too, will tell you

That the sky is not firm.

Where does this delusion come from?
From basic Russian ignorance, as the
European lovers of stereotypes would put it?
Far from it. *Rock, kamen* in Russian, is *kaman* in ancient Sanskrit.
Then comes the Avestan *akman*.

Then the Persian *asman*, meaning *sky*.
Then, the Turkic *aspan-tengri – Eternal Blue Sky...*'
'And?' we asked Thomas.
'Well, that it turns out that *Cephas* is not a rock used to measure
The depth of a well

That is given the chance to fly.
He is something else. A heavenly-rock.'
'Okay, but what's that?' 'I don't know; that we'll have to find out.
Something like the Heavenly Spirit... or the Holy Spirit...'
'Right, something other than rain that can fall from the sky?

Anyway, and what's this pagan method
Of placing all images of God in the sky,
As if that's His place of permanent residence?
As if He's not here on Earth, not in the sea, under the ground or in the earth;
He's not inside us and not outside us either, is that it?

This doesn't tally even with our ancient convictions,
Not to mention the newly-forming doctrine.'
Thomas chuckled: 'I don't know, I tell you.
These are just musings on a level of semi-professional philology...
After all, not everyone can answer

The simple question, where does God live?'
'Well, any Babylonian or Achaean
Will draw you a load of images of where, how and with whom He lives,
On what Olympus, in what Shambhala,
On what *who art in Heaven*.'

'Beloved Friend of ours, give clarity
To our argument: to what extent is the Lord personified,
To live somewhere physically, and is there a place
For the doctrine of the rock in what we call Our Path?

Or are we simply splitting hairs here?'

Our Friend coughed, as he usually did, as if he wasn't expecting the question,
And looked at us with a gaze
That was helpless for a second, through John Lennon's glasses
(What, didn't you know that He had them before John did?)
And he put his Fender Telecaster down to one side.

'The sky, you say? Where does God live physically?
And you're the ones asking, the diligent students of our rabbi?
He is omnipresent according to the Jewish faith...'
'No, wait, we are kind of discussing and placing everything in doubt[16],'
We seethed, 'we are, sort of, on the search for our *own* vision,
Or... have we gone too far?'

Suddenly, and this was a rare event, our Friend became angry:
'You want to drown in anecdotal hair-splitting
About the personification and depersonification of the Almighty?!
Fight over His projections and images?!
Replicate His appearance and blow up Buddha in Bamiyan?!

You want to manipulate the fact that depersonification
Is personification in reverse?
Or reason about the golden age of ornamentalism as a consequence
Of it being impossible to depict the creation?!
Declare Him to be a total field and that He is inside all of us?!

Reduce Him to fire, a statue or thin air?!
A speaking bush, a dove or a voice
That broadcasts jibberish in Hebrew, Latin, Bengali or Arabic,
While, for some reason, not knowing or ignoring other tongues?!
Are you out of your mind?!

Or, by image and likeness, you're implying the style of your underwear?!
Your right tricep, the colour of your hair or something else?!
The number of legs or arms, or your IQ?!
Isn't the word *my* what lies behind all this, eh?
What are you planning to get your hands on, guys,

When you talk of "*our* new vision"?!

What do you want to talk about – the essence or the interpretations?!
You don't start a stupid haggling routine with a desire to communicate,
Without first having the resources to bargain with, do you?!
As the projection can argue with the Creator itself
And, moreover, can impose its own mercantile definitions, is that it?!

Shut up in an agnostic prison or flaunting the fact
That definitions can be found for everything?
What on earth can your poor tongue wag about, which
Is still a hundred times more meagre than the tongue of the Almighty?!
And, oh, Alahi, answer me this: how can a man who has not left death behind possibly talk of
Eternal Life?'

'What do you mean, *left death behind*?!'

---

[16] *Place everything in doubt* was a favourite slogan of Karl Marx.

'I don't know!!! I don't know,' he said, with tears in His eyes.
And, like an alpine wind but with the heavy step of an elephant, He didn't leave,
Rather, he rushed like a wall of wind into the desert gloom
That was especially black on this day around our campfire.

Everyone sat, frightened and in silence.

Peter said,

'Hm, even if we are on a common Path,
And we understood little from what our Friend has said,
This doesn't mean that someone's stealing a march on someone else,
Well, in certain aspects of knowledge...
And isn't our Beloved Friend the one, who...

Well, how can I put it? He's a special one...
Andrew, you always thought so, didn't you?
For now, he is unknowable, even for us.
But he who declares himself an agn... agnostic
As regards to what is happening,

Well, in this personal dispute, I'll personally smash their face in.'

Verse 16. The Resurgent Heart

'Tell me, Levi-Matthew, about your Path to this day.'
Er... well, my tale is not as emotion-filled as Cephas's
But there is something common or, rather, different, or I don't know.
Cephas, you said not to play with the powers that be in the world,
But I was those powers that be,

Who grant mercy on the merchants or grind them in the dirt for their misdeeds.
That said, it didn't start right away. Like any path to power for that matter.
Sometimes, you look at a pretty little boy and have no idea
That, one day, he'll turn into a cruel arbiter of fate
Or a tyrant, or an unscrupulous punisher.

Why am I painting everything so black, eh? Perhaps, he's an enlightened ruler;
Perhaps, a wise judge. The thing is that they all
Hail from those pretty little boys,
Who gaze at the world with the eyes of the one who'll forever
Be their guiding star, be it white or black.

When I stepped into my youth, I had everything,
In a material sense, I mean.
Well-off parents, an education, friends,
Favourite pastimes, collections and interests,
The look of the adults, as if saying 'what a lovely young man'.

Yet there was one vice, as yet unnoticed by anyone,
Which had appeared in the megapolis,
In the only megapolis the Almighty had yet given us – Jerusalem,
Where I studied and from where I didn't return home.
I loved life in the fast lane, loud company, big spreads.

And there was a strange balance in me:
My profession was a financier,
Yet money would disappear like water through my fingers.
However, I still managed to pull it in.
Ask me now how I did; I don't remember.

It wasn't that I wasn't working; I was.
It wasn't that I was foolish; I was very talented, in fact.
It wasn't that I was a squanderer; no, I was just generous.
Well, life was wonderful and its opportunities
Seemed as if to stretch out beneath my feet...

No, I did not commit the sin of gambling;
Well, basically, like everyone, I did a bit, in moderation, just a little.
Street walkers? Harlots? Not really.
To be honest, never at all. And don't you go laughing at me either!
I was shy, that's all... Shy – what's so funny in that?

However, back then, this is what happened with me.
Oh, a shame I quit smoking, for I'd light up otherwise.
You see, I might have been a squanderer, but I still always counted money
In my head: whom I owed, who owed me,
When I'd be paid my fee and so on.

I always had a voice in my head telling me to stop,
That that was enough for today. That would be all I needed, going out into the world;
I'd be ashamed to face my parents...
My relatives too; to a certain extent I was their great hope.
And, bang, what do you have but a financier who's whittled it all away.

The shame of it. Anyway, where was I? Oh yes, about what happened.

It was a splendid morning in Jerusalem.
The birds had only started chattering and the donkeys, their pattering.
The people weren't properly awake and so made little noise,
Travelling to work in silence.
I had emerged from a night club and was standing, taken aback

By the beauty of the dawn in my favourite city.
And there she appeared... *How beautiful you are, my darling!*
Oh, how beautiful! Your eyes behind your veil are like doves;
Your hair is like a flock of goats descending from the hills of Gilead.
Your teeth are like a flock of sheep just shorn...[17]

All right, all right, I won't sing any more... You just don't know
That this marvel of early-morning Jerusalem bore the name Sulamith...
Sulamith, my sweetheart! And now my heart sings the Song of Songs!
Over all those millennia
Could there be anything better than the song Solomon sang to his beloved?

That's right, Judas. A tax collector can be a lyricist, too, you know.
And come on, why are you always laughing?
No one was laughing when Cephas was telling his story!
What, is there anything funny in what I am telling?
You made the lad blush. Have you no shame?

Anyway, I'll go on.

Like the *Cutty Sark*, like a mirage in the desert of Canaan,
Like a *Zeppelin* against an alpine sky,
She swam past me, as I stood, dumbstruck,
Soaring proudly and with dignity, like a banner with stars and stripes.
Not ours, no, the American one.

I saw how small and frightful I'd become,
How ungainly, gnarled and fuzzy,
And how out of place.
And then a miracle occurred. Oh, what a miracle!
Her neck, like the tower of David,

Turned to me, like the Earth's axis
And... she smiled!!! A tender, modest smile
So pure and innocent that an angel
Flying by would have felt awkward
At fleeting flesh, peeking out from under his robes!

Your neck is like the tower of David, built with courses of stone;

---

[17] Text in italics throughout this verse is taken from *The Book of Solomon* (New International Version).

On it hang a thousand shields, all of them shields of warriors.
That's right, the shields of warriors, because I rushed to make enquiries
And I learned that she was no ordinary Jewish girl,
But the daughter of the head of all tax collectors.

(Yes, Cephas, the same one who wore the same sandals as you.
I gave them to him... But more on that later.)
I even learned where her window was and, now, every evening,
I would walk past, hoping to get
Another glimpse of that divine image.

In the end, I pondered and then made my decision.
Where was the shame, I thought.
I'm a young man from a decent family. And a noble one.
No Banu Hashin[18], but still.
Why not approach and introduce myself

To her father, as is right and proper? Not to declare my intentions;
Well, one has to start from somewhere.
After all, despite my riotous youth,
I had the reputation of a decent professional,
Properly trained in the latest management techniques.

Anyway, one fine day, I knocked on her door;
Well, her father's door... And I stood before him as was right and proper.
Come on, I had a decent mug! Stop laughing at me, you lot!
Philip, tell me, for you know what asking for someone's hand is all about.
You're not the same as these, single vagrants...

Pah, no, I'll say nothing! All right, all right, sorry,
My Beloved Friend. Just tell them... All right, I'm not offended.
Well, I violated certain customs. And, well, sorry for that;
It's what comes with living in the big city, you could say.
Anyway, I went that morning and made his acquaintance.

To be honest, I was so afraid, but I didn't hum and ha.
Thanks to Adonai, I know how to express my thoughts.
I didn't exactly ask for her hand, rather I just asked permission
To invite the young lady to some literary evenings or
To concerts of Roman celebrities.

Her father heard me out in a dignified manner and without thunder and lightning
He responded calmly, 'I see you are of a noble family.
Not the Windsors, but still.
You're a respectable young man, you have a profession.
Young man, I am going to trust you.'

And he called her into the room. Here I floundered and lost the ability to speak.
You have stolen my heart, my sister, my bride;
You have stolen my heart with one glance of your eyes,
With one jewel of your necklace.
That's an exaggeration, about the glance; she never raised her eyes once

During the conversation. All she did was reply with a nod and barely a whisper,

---

[18] Banu Hashim (Arabic) – the Hashemites, were descendants of the Prophet Muhammad, part of the large Quraysh tribe, which dominated the population of Mecca in the 7th century.

But I swooned from her voice and the Jerusalem heat
Became unbearable in my smart jacket.
But that was no torment, believe me! If it was, then it was
The sweetest torture that ever was. I wanted it to go on and on!

Several days went by and there I was, waiting for my bride
To go on our first date. The plan was that we'd go and watch a nice Indian film
Without any vulgarity, and then we'd take a stroll.
However, that evening, I was to realise
That my life would change forever.

We went outside, quietly and without fanfare, to my donkey,
We politely said goodbye to her parents, rode a couple of blocks and then...
I could see that my girlfriend had changed. Her eyes were now aflame,
Her red hair had broken free from under her shawl
And breathed in the fiery waves of the Sea of Galilee.

'Why's your donkey so slow, hun?
Why don't we hire a steed from that gent over there?'
'Hm... But... only Roman riders are allowed to ride steeds.
You understand, it's a matter of social class...'
'But the girls say that he'll give us a go for a couple of sesterces.'

Adonai! A couple of sesterces is my entire wage!
However, what wouldn't you do for your beloved?
It was good thing I could haggle him down to half a sesterce and a silver cigar case.
And I was lucky not to get punched in the teeth by the horseman
For encroaching on his class distinction.

That said, the fact of the matter is that she got her ride while this chump
Shuffled along behind on his donkey, wondering how she wasn't afraid.
What would happen if the national patriots saw us?
Oh, I just didn't know... Well, anyway, one thing at a time.
Something straight out of Bollywood it was.

I was livid, but then I thought that, once we were married, she would settle down.
I had to propose sharpish.
To be in a position to demand the correct behaviour.
I felt awkward facing her father, too. If he were to find out, I'd really know about it.
He would too; the city might be the size of the world, but it's actually pretty small.

So, we had a couple of dates and then I took control.
I took her away from prying eyes on my donkey and I said to her
That, well, that she would be my wife.
I noticed that I had already learned how to frown in her presence.
Before, I would go on dates and do nothing but smile like a statue, not knowing what to say.

And here everything became clear. 'Forgive me, Levi,' she said
(And she had her hand on my cheek, so tenderly
That I shuddered; I hadn't imagined what her first touch would feel like),
But I have a sweetheart. He's a Canaanite,
A partisan, and he's in hiding in the Białowieża Forest,

Fighting the colonialist enemies.
I have given him my heart. Dad doesn't know, although he suspects.
I am suffering and I am tormenting you now.
So, please take me out again on your donkey

And sing the *Song of Songs*, as you usually do.'

'What,' I said spitefully, 'I sing it well, do I?'
'No,' she replied, 'My Denis Davydov sang it to me.
You and I, we'll then go our separate ways, all right?'
I went cold. I had even had the *Song of Songs* stolen from me.
That was too much. I had already heard the words *we'll go our separate ways, all right?* from the
mist.

Alahi! Such banal platitude wasn't supposed to come my way!
Like a little boy, I had fallen into a trap of my own feelings!
'All right,' I said, 'I'll take you home then.'
And off we went. In silence. I could see tears in her eyes.
'Forgive me,' she said. 'I am not a cruel person and was not mocking you.

I didn't drag the money out of you either. These riders will leave for the mountains soon.
I just had to find out when and where.
You have helped a noble cause, by the way.'
It was then that I boiled over. Me?! A respectable citizen.
Who observes the laws of his homeland. And Rome!

It's not enough that my dream, the *Song of Songs*, had been taken from me,
But then I had to become the sponsor of bandits, too?!
How could you call that fair?! Is that fair?!
It was then that I hatched what I believe was the right plan.
I said to her, 'Okay, only I have one request of you.

I won't look at you like a bridegroom, but don't turn down my friendship!
I will help you when you need me.'
And... she kissed me! Only it was *another's* kiss!
Stolen from that Che Guevara! *It was not for me!*
But no matter, I thought. The time will come for *my* kiss.

Simon, you're very quiet. You think I planned to give up the zealots?
And be rid of her betrothed, is that it? No-o-o, sir. What were those *guerrilleros* to me?
I was thinking about power. Well, not about that kind for now... About power over Sulamith.
One thing I noticed. I'm a psychologist, you know.
When she was doing her secret intelligence,

With the horse rider or when we were in the restaurant,
Drinking wine with the Romans, or when we went to their opera,
To see Bocelli or Pavarotti, she was not really a secret agent at that time.
She liked all this frippery. She looked at it all and found some naïve joy
In those city lights. That's how it is with the daughters

Of parents who are not necessarily strict, but simply respectable.
Perhaps there was something missing from her upbringing?
I don't think so; the girls simply don't see what's behind all the showiness.
The Bloodless and the Greedy one stands there
And he devours those who... what, you're not ready?

So, anyway, my plan was simple. I would gift her this wonderful world
In all the finery of a modern civilisation.
With a grand gesture, I cast my coat of generosity at her feet.
And these walkways, the saxophones, the podiums and I
Will all eclipse the guerrilla image of the vagrant Commandant.

I won't go into detail about what I did...
If it weren't for you, I would hardly want to go back there with my memories...
I cast the entire night city at her feet.
She was not afraid, for she was with a friend (me, I mean)!
However, I merely wandered by her side, bloodless and greedy.

And I was not her friend.

I racked up serious debts.
You see, being a professional, people believed me and lent to me.
It ended when one day I raped her.
No! No! Don't look at me like that! It wasn't violence!
I just... placed my demand and she agreed.

All night long on my bed I looked for the one my heart loves;
I looked for him but did not find him.
I will get up now and go about the city, through its streets and squares;
I will search for the one my heart loves.
So I looked for him but did not find him.

I was triumphant! There's the victory! There's the triumph of Justice!
There's the conquered love, deserved, *mine!*
Later, I asked her, 'Do you love me?
You love me now, right, oh, my aching heart?'
But she said, 'No'. 'Then why?! ...Why?!'

And she says, 'You are so good to us.' Me?! Good?! To *us*?!
Hold on...

Hold on. I'll calm down.

Then, it all became clear. I understood everything. He, though, was laughing,
Bloodless, but Full and Satisfied!
My heart died then and I thought it was forever.
I didn't know that it would die several times, but now I do.
It can rise again. Can you imagine? Rise again!

However, at that moment, I died and turned to marble.
White-pale, rough around the edges.
Only then, I thought, don't be cross, Simon, just hand over
The lovers to the authorities. They met.
I knew where and when.

Only once did I ask her again: 'Sulamith!
Will your sweetheart forgive you?'
'I don't know,' she replied, 'but this is my gift to you.
For you are the only one among us whom I have met,
Who has shown me the evils of the world, but left me pure and vulnerable.'

That is what finished me off. And, well, I never did hand them over.
That was the work of other respectable fellow countrymen of ours.
I learned from the newspapers that the Romans captured them in the gardens.
The Commandant put up a strong resistance;
They had wanted to take him alive but he wouldn't yield.

They ended up killing her by accident; they didn't mean to. They pushed her in the heat of battle.
She hit her head on a rock and slowly passed away.

A centurion screamed that all they had to do was hand her over
Alive to the governor; everyone got a good shaking down for being idiots for what they'd done.
When Che Guevara realised that Sulamith had gone,

He rushed forward with renewed might and he had to be cut down.
He never did give up.
He wanted to join her.
They had spent too long
Living apart...

...But my tale is not finished yet. You want to hear more?
Then I died for a second time, but no one cared before...
I found I had a new problem.
As the saying goes, trouble doesn't come alone.
It all came down to my loose, riotous life

Which, obviously, was one I couldn't afford.
I've already said that I had got into debt.
I owed friends, neighbours, colleagues, partners,
Money changers, Romans and others. It snowballs,
Growing and slowly beginning to flatten you.

It's awful when you have to lie to everyone all the time,
Avoid people, don't answer the telephone,
Stand quietly by the door and listen to make sure people have gone away.
You're afraid to meet with friends, acquaintances and people in general,
Because everyone wants to ask: when?

Your imagination does the job up to a point;
You think up hundreds of reasons and the worst thing is that they believe you.
Then you run out of reasons.
Then you simply stop being a part of society.
Then you become an outlaw, when others start looking for you.

No, no! Don't think that everyone's mean as a dog or anything.
Some people are reasonably patient. The question is that *you* are no longer a person.
You've had an important social function cut off.
You even speak in conversations with yourself.
And you think of only one thing, rather that it's not there anymore.

Every day you think things cannot get any worse,
And then it turns out, they can.
At first, you believe in providence, then in success.
Then, all faith comes to an end. All of it.
You know what the worst thing of all is? It's that your Conscience starts dying.

And you sense it physically. That is awful.
Because Conscience is your faith in God Almighty.
It's not just your moral upbringing;
It is also a genetic thing and something you acquire.
It is the yardstick for yourself, basically.

You see the remnants of your personality begin to end.
However, I tell you straight, I held myself together. I even tried to do some work.
However, who believes a financier who himself is a problem human?
Any Jew knows that this is simply not safe;
That, with me, they are buying all my problems.

This is not a vicious circle, It's a chasm. A Bloodless, Greedy Chasm.

I don't believe stupid fairy tales of mice
Beating milk in a jug into butter.
St Nicholas the Wonderworker won't come knocking with cheque in hand,
To compensate your unholy debts and costs.
So how, you might ask, can a man actually survive?

You are bought, that's how. You are bought, if it's in someone's interests.
And, one day, one overcast day,
The door to my hole opened. I couldn't call my hideaway by any other word, really,
The hole in which I had hidden myself from the world.
And who do you think walked in? You'll never guess: Sulamith's father.

I was lounging on the floor like a savage. What else was I meant to do?
I no longer had a personality of any value.
He sat at length in silence and then, calmly and authoritatively, he spoke:
'Levi-Matthew! You and I are, to an extent, share the same misfortune.
But don't think I have come because I have feelings.

I knew everything about her, but I had hoped you would be smarter.
Well, it's all in the past now. I have paid off your debts,
But not because I am kind.
I am the main tax collector in Israel, and of all the kingdoms it has proved to be as well.
I need you, young man, for a job.

It's a serious and important job.
The people are not paying their taxes and exactions very well.
The Romans are unhappy. Herod is irate.
This could lead to geopolitical paralysis for us.
I need urgent reform to the industry.

You might ask why it's you I am looking for.
I don't care two hoots about your education.
I couldn't care less about your experience.
After all, I can always find a Jew in finance. Anywhere.
I have been watching you for some time. Observing your stories...

The stories about your debts
Or more accurately, how you got out of paying them.
This has given you priceless experience of inventiveness;
Thousands of ways of avoiding repayment.
You know all about them.

Your heart is as cold as marble.
Rough around the edges. For one, nothing gets by you.
Your dislike for national-patriotic rhetoric is also
Something I'd like to put to good use.
Forgive the tautology but this is precisely the thing I am looking for.

The Jews in our tax system, having heard their fill of zealots, and rabbis, too –
How can I put this politely – have gone soft with their people.
And there's one thing they don't understand:
If we fail to collect the budget revenues,
Rome will not be happy.

And who, then, will help us in the war with the Arabs?
Or the Persians; they say that could happen.
Our fate is being decided, sonny.
What are we to be? An imposing satellite of Rome?
Or a stupid outcast, like certain clueless nationalists?

So, this, my son, this is not Egyptian slavery;

It's geopolitics, so don't go confusing *corpus* and *curpus*[19].
Well, you think I didn't agree?
The very next day I was standing by the offices
Of the national tax department
Of the Ministry of Strategic Budget Planning!

And now I will tell you about power.
What is power over a woman? That is nothing but a tiny *corpuscle*
Of a great human control mechanism.
At our offices at the Ministry,
We would control giant waves, ebbing and flowing.

That means, if you take the allegory from physics, then power means light.
And let anyone just try to tell me it's the opposite.
Back then, we were a mighty order,
Standing between Roman and Israeli interests.
For that reason, neither side liked us much.

Their interests were pretty much identical –collecting money from the people.
But no, there were a great many nuances.
How much should they give to service Herod's palace?
How much should they give as an allowance to legionnaires?
How much for the Ides of March and how much for Passover?

How much should they send to Rome and persuade them that any more was impossible?
Hah, even war with the zealots was in my hands; it was simple.
Cut the budget for punitive expeditions and that's that.
You think Pilate wants to get buried under financial reports?
It has to be said that a certain problem did arise, however...

After all, he's not a simple young man and, despite being a warrior,
He happily counts silver talents, even after tiring bacchanalia.
But here, too, we showed our ingenuity.
Any order has its secret language,
Known only to the adept, so others won't understand.

So, we went and devised all these sequesters, deposits,
Excise duties, bills of acceptance and interdepartmental balance sheets
(Sounds like a song, right?), collections, offshore accounts,
Letters of credit, State Plans and accounting reports,
Payment instructions, credit managers and all manner of overdrafts.

Tell me, what Pilate is going to get to the bottom of all that Yiddish?
Hehe, and that is basically it, either in one's native Latin
Or in English
(even the residents of Jerusalem will have such a language).
So, this power is all-powerful and truly terrifying.

---

[19] Corpus et curpus (Lat.) – body and manure.

Releasing one bandit at Passover is not a tradition.
This is a cut in the budget of the penitentiary system.
Bear your own cross; that is no allegory.
This is the discipline of execution costs.
Herod Antipas was given more money for entertainment and he doesn't get involved in politics!

The best thing of all are the tax expeditions!
This is when you travel there on a donkey (not like the one I had, but a full, plump kind),
With two unladen camels,
But you come back with the beast bent double under the weight.
You take a dozen Romans with you; they are not greedy thieves like our lot.

The only thing was what happened to bring me here.
I had been sent to Bethsaida
(To your homeland, Cephas).
The expedition was an easy one – you just had to find the right approach for everyone.
But, well, I've already said, you won't get one over on me, which is why they took me on.

The merchants come running to us themselves.
The rabbis argue, trying to prove this and that, but I just say, for all to hear:
'What, my good fellow, you wish to skrimp on restoration of the Temple?'
So polite and yet imposing does that *my good fellow* sound,
That they moan, but they find the money; the people are watching, after all.

The kibbutz heads say that they'll complain.
You complain, dear Moshe, knock yourself out!
Only the grievance will end up on my desk, if you go complaining to the king.
And if you write to the Romans, it'll also end up with me.
So you'll end up building the road and the aqueduct yourself, okay?

Nothing is no good, the democrat fathers think, and so they keep bringing the money.
Or even various livestock or tableware.
Archaeological valuables are good too; Palestine has tons of the stuff.
It's worse with the common folk. The poverty there is terrible, what can I say?
And yet the state must prevail, right?
It cares for those people; they are all down in the State Plan.

That's what I thought back then, fanned by the Bethsaida breeze...

And it all occurred at a long-forgotten kibbutz on the outskirts.
I had entered a small, barely noticeable, rickety little house.
There was a woman who was getting ready to leave.
I looked around. Do know what *nothing* means? There was less than that in that house.
I caught sight of two coins there. There it was, that Jewish breeding!

Well, I said to her, to be fair,
She could keep one and give me the other
For the Jewish state and the Roman Empire, or *vice versa*.
She, though, through tears, pleaded with me not to take it. She was weeping uncontrollably.
I read her my lecture, that our state was surrounded by enemies,

Bla-bla-bla, citizenship, that security comes first, and all that.
And she said, 'Be a man and hand it over.' Well, I came over all Mr Nice Guy: 'But why?'
But she stood her ground and said nothing, just insisting that I, the good man, should leave it and that's it.
Well, I was well trained in all this. I pushed her aside and took the coin.

I came out, thinking, 'good job, for being so honest; I could have taken both.

The record probably states she's two months behind as it is.
Penalties and all that. But I'm kind and took only one.'
However, for some reason, I remembered that woman.
You see so many different people on those expeditions; you can't remember them all.
But I remembered her.

Several days went by. I had returned to Jerusalem.
I remember stepping out in the day for a stroll.
I could see this crowd heading somewhere. A familiar sight.
They were off to Golgotha to execute someone.
Everyone was shouting and raving.

I decided to have some wine and then I'd catch them up.
Then I realised I'd left my purse at home.
I could have presented my identification and they'd have served me for free.
(That's another great thing about power.)
Okay, I thought, I'm an honest chap, so another time.

Then, however, I felt that same coin in my pocket.
It had clearly been just lying around. No matter,
I'll add it to the coffers late, or not; what's in a penny?
So, I bought myself a glass of wine to enjoy.
It was so cool and pleasant.

Then I went to catch up with the procession.
I liked watching those ceremonies in the name of Justice, you see.
And of legality. That means there's order. That means there's power.
That means we have state control of the highest level.
You see, back then my heart was dead...

You see, Cephas, they were executing that young zealot.
That's right, I was there, only I didn't know you then.
I was there when he died. Only I was indifferent to his cries.
Then, something terrible happened.
Cephas, you exaggerate the people's love for him.

The young man died quickly; the people couldn't enjoy his torment.
Many onlookers simply shut up from the disappointment.
But you're right, at least they weren't indignant and grumbling.
Then a centurion called out: 'Are there any relatives?'
Suddenly, that woman emerged. I was dumbstruck.

The centurion went on: 'Anyone else? Come forward and take him from the cross!'
You know, my Beloved Friend, I think there were relatives.
Believe my experience as a cynic. It was just that no one came forward,
Fearing they were related to a terrorist.
And what is worse now in the Empire than being accused of terrorism?

Anyway, that woman was there, quietly weeping.
Then, one soldier pushed another, who pushed him back, saying he wouldn't take down that carrion.
The centurion roared so fiercely at him that the soldier shut up.
After that, the soldiers helped the woman take down the young man.
The one who'd talked about the *carrion* fussed about like a jackal.

77

And then, Adonai! The woman was weeping, saying farewell to her son...
And she placed a coin on one of his eyes. On the other, she placed... a... small stone.
You know, like I'd been given a shock. An electric shock... it's called
Here... at the kibbutz... soon... it'll be...
And she... a stone... One minute... I'll pull myself together...

....

It's all right. Thank you, I'm fine. That water tastes good. Ours, right?
I looked around and saw that those who could have given a coin had turned away.
Those who wanted to, didn't have one. The young man was evidently from a decent family,
Only he'd fallen into poverty... Perhaps because of me...
I just... I understand, when you haven't enough to live, but when you haven't enough to die?!

You know, brothers. I've had many debts in my life.
To be honest, you never want to give them back to anyone.
Like they say, you take from someone, but you return from yourself.
But at that moment, in that second, I so wanted to! I so wanted to repay that debt!
And I didn't have that coin for a wholly banal reason.

There and then. In that second. On *Bald Mountain*.
Where, who knows, may destinies might still come together.
From there I had entire state treasury just a couple of steps away.
And I understand that that coin had to be right there.
Or I should not have taken it when I was in Bethsaida.

Or I shouldn't have gone on that expedition!
I then realised that if she had told me back then
That the coin was for her son, soon to be crucified for terrorism,
That would have steeled my heart yet further.
SHE SAW THAT IN MY EYES, THAT MY HEART WAS DEAD!

No, Levi-Matthew, my heart is resurgent.
That's the way it is: we will learn much about the resurrection.
But that will come later. In its own time. In its own hour
That's right, my Beloved Friend, precisely that coin
Will be your debt, but you already know

That you'll not be repaying it in money.
There is no coin that bears the symbol of that Kingdom,
The Heavenly Kingdom. There is no tax collectors department there either,
Whatever your professional experience might tell you.
For now, my son, you weep, for soon you'll feel better.

Verse 17. A conversation between Thomas and the disciples about science and evolution

(91) And so it was. We had full knowledge of what he had.
Qur'an. Surah 18, 'The Cave'

At the end of the day, the value of dialectics is that it is forced to conclude
that everything on this earth is foolish.
Ryūnosuke Akutagawa

One carefree, peaceful, sunny day,
The Beloved Friend asked our Thomas:
'How do you think science came about? And what does it mean for faith?
And does it actually mean, well, many believe that these things
Are not only polar opposites

But they are set against one another?'
Thomas began to gabble, his eyes not even blinking:
'It's obvious: science appeared
When new inventions led to an increase in labour productivity;
These, in turn, led to a surplus in goods and foodstuffs;

In turn, this led to a social distribution of labour;
In turn, this led to the emergence of new social groups
That existed on account of these product surpluses;
Among these social groups there were people
Who were unable to manage or trade

And who likewise never made into the priesthood given their lack of loyalty to faith.
Now, these people, so as not to lose access to the glut of surplus produce
Found themselves something to do: grow a beard and think
About what bears no relation to normal people in life.
For example, about the speed of neutrons in the orbit of Alpha Aquarii.'

Everyone burst out laughing, but Thomas, as he always did, just smiled charmingly.
Our Friend waited for the joking and laughter to die down
And then he quietly asked again: 'But seriously, though?'
Thomas shot out his lips: 'Well, but it's obvious, Rabbi!
Science merely seeks an explanation for the world in a logical and materialistic way;

If you're talking about the natural sciences, that is.
There are different kinds of science, you see. There are even kinds that, in their very existence,
Involuntarily remind us of the surplus of produce.
There are all manner of pseudosciences that infest human ignorance like parasites.
And then there is the queen of all sciences: mathematics.

What else would you like to hear?'

'Well, I basically just wanted to share one thought.
I don't know if it's intelligent or not... If not, well, tell the Emperor Constantine
To delete it from our court journals.
Everyone knows how adept he is at that kind of thing...

Anyway, this is what occurred to me:
The monkey who invented the axe: that's a specific historical figure, right?'
'Well, that's if you believe Old Man Darwin.'

79

'But still, until the opposite is proven, they are no less valuable for humanity

Than I, you, Alexander the Great, Caesar, Napoleon, Mahatma Gandhi or John Lennon.
Let's give that monkey a name. Djamshid, say[20].
And who was Djamshid? Not from the point of view of an evolutionary leap,
Rather just because. Well, obviously, I am not talking about family status here...

I realised that Djamshid has many possible hypostases:
The first is that they could be a qualified professional worker,
Whose brain is always focused on finding an effective solution
To production matters that he
And his team face directly.

Now, let's say, they have to chop wood faster for a fence.
Add the expected arrival here of a group of Machairods[21],
And you get an external catalyst for development.
And, bingo! A certain historical phenomenon was triggered in Djamshid's head,
Which brought three simple ingredients: a rock, a rope and a stick

To combine in the only possibly, effective combination
Whereupon, most likely based on the principle of *go on, son, let's try it this way! So the little rock won't fly off.*
And, there you have an axe! There you have a fence to ward off predators.
There you have an evolutionary state. Or leap, call it what you will.

The second hypostasis: a design engineer who has noticed
That, during the manufacture of a fence based on the *break-and-then-tie-together* principle,
Trees often break in the places you don't plan them to,
Which means you can't get material of the same length.
And that's before we've even started on the big, thick trees.

Djamshid the engineer had the same three ingredients: a rope, a rock and a stick.
Only in the other situation there had been time to think and make drawings.
His thought process probably centred around the missing third ingredient.
Let's assume that he had a rock and a rope, but no stick.
Or he had the rock and the rope – but to what would he attach it all?

The most likely question, of course, would have been, with what could you
Fasten the crumbling Stone and the Shaft that enhance the impact?
And then his daughter walked up: Dad, Mum's busy; tie my pigtail!
Well then, well then! Young lady, could you possibly
Lend me one of your many pigtails, shall we say, in the name of progress?

And there you have the third ingredient! And there you have an axe! There you have evolution!

The third hypostasis is that of a scholarly analyst.
Djamshid looked at length at how his compatriots felled trees,
By chucking great big rocks at them. *You know, they either break or they don't.*
The scholar made no drawing and did not set the three ingredients in different ways.
He acted with nothing empirical; just all in his head.

He imagined the solution in theory. He sought in his mind a completely

---

[20] According to Persian legend, Djamshid was one of the first and greatest kings of humankind, who gave the world fire.
[21] Machairodus – the prehistoric sabre-toothed tiger.

Different principle and approach. Not a matter of huge stones against a tree,
Rather a small device that had the destructive force of a rock,
With enhanced accuracy and the capability of mass production.
It is even possible that two schools were fighting there.

One of them devised the following method:
An enormous rock was tied with a vine to the top of a tree to be felled.
People were then split into two groups:
One were the throwers and they climbed the next tree along;
The other were the servers, who presented them with the attached rock.

The throwers would then launch the rock with force against the tree, until
It fell to the ground.
It was not a productive approach, you understand why, right?
Try calculating the probability of accurate strikes and direct hits
And you'll get the picture. And so, our scholar got to thinking.

One version emerged: the rock would be small,
But there'd be only one person. He would tie it to the top and then draw it back
Before throwing it with all his might at the tree until it fell.
A great idea! However, laboratory observations indicated
That the rock would very often strike the tree on the side

Where the ropes pass.
They'll quickly be cut through and you'll never have enough.
A decent idea, but, well, not sufficient for the symbolism
Of a new culture, like the eternal theory of Marx and Engels.
There is no third ingredient. In this instance, there's no Lenin, just a shaft.

And yet the scholar's brain gathers so much information over time
On the empirical knowledge of his compatriots,
That is enough to be subjected to analysis.
Following this analysis, scientific conclusions and findings are made,
And the practical application is studied experimentally.

The scholar realised that a new tool had to be made
From a super-strength metal such as steel or a special alloy.
The shaft needed to be made from a flexible rubber blend, reinforced with synthetic materials,
And all of this would be secured using super-strong adhesive or soldered.
But, actually, the stone, the rope and the bit of wood would all come off!

You see, there is already an axe. But it's not actually there in reality.
However, thereafter, it all becomes a matter of technique.
The scholar goes to the design engineer and gives him the theory to read over.
The engineer produces drawings, undoes his daughter's pigtail
And gives it all to a qualified worker; the axe now exists!

The fourth possible hypostasis: a king.
King Djamshid was wise and thought strategically for the long term.
He realised that for his people to pull forward,
And outperform neighbouring countries by many years, in a historical sense, that is,
He would need a radical invention.

Such an important, serious invention, that would serve as a foundation stone of sorts.
The Persians believed that was fire, but that's not what we're not talking about now.
And so, King Djamshid gathered his Areopagus, his court, and he gave them a task:
Divide into three groups and in three days and three nights, think up

This radical creation that humanity would never forget.

The allotted time passed and the three groups
Came to the king in great excitement.
The first group began: "Oh, great King! Allow us
To show you what we have devised in this short time
And in the face of a severe shortage of source materials.

To be more accurate, there were only three: a rope, a rock and a stick."
The senior figure in the group pulled out a model and everyone gasped.
Such a terrible man-made creation required the immediate execution of the senior figure
And the entire group as well. (It was an axe, you guessed, of course.)
King Djamshid raised his hand, but...

The quaking voice of the elder from the second group interrupted him:
"Listen, Shahinshah, don't rush in!
Take a look at what we have created!"
It has to be said, this was a courageous act indeed:
He could see what awaited the previous candidates,

But he didn't hide away. Rather, he brought to light...
...Well, it was almost the same axe, only of slightly different proportions.
The rock was smaller and the staff, thicker.
At this point, the third pro-rector overcame his fear and also showed
The astonished king his vision.

Well, you guessed it: all three groups brought axes,
Only with different proportions; one had a part that was longer, another, shorter.
Then, the wise Djamshid realised that the objective had been reached:
The thing had been found that would glorify this people for centuries
And bring humanity the great joys of evolution!

All that was needed was just the sovereign matter
Of introducing the standards for the axe and handing it to the weights and measures chamber.
Only then would the invention be deemed created.
Well, of course, it was King Djamshid who received all the glory for its creation.
Who else? Was it not his monarch's wise mind and management ability

That enabled the axe to appear?

The fifth hypostasis: the priest.
In fact, this is the most probable version behind the creation of the axe.
Once upon a time there lived three different peoples
Who had been fighting one another for as long as they could remember.
They would do their utmost to destroy each other; you know, the same old story.

And, as with any war for mutual destruction,
All of them faced the question of basic survival; the greatest champions
Had long since laid down their lives, the best soldiers, only recently,
The leaders and their children, yesterday and, today, the boys were standing in line,
And they would perish without conceiving children of their own.

So, three armies stood in the field
And couldn't resolve to commence
The final process of mutual annihilation.
However, everyone understood that this would be the end;
Even the uncompromising *Likuds* and *Hamases* said nothing.

However, the first ranks of one of the armies parted
And an ancient old priest stepped forward.
Before speaking he began to sing in a low, cracked voice
A song about the times when war
Did not inflame and was not the raison d'être,

When women bore sons, not soldiers,
When you'd hear more *live honestly and with dignity*
Than *die with honour, but don't give up!*
When the silhouettes on the horizon are guests, not invaders,
When the borders were there to share across, not divide.

The song touched everyone. Then, *aqsaqal* elders emerged from the other two sides
And decided to conclude a strong and lasting peace
Between the three peoples.
And, as a symbol of this indestructible peace,
They proposed that the totemic symbols of each nation be united into one.

You guessed it: the totem of the first was the stone, of the second –
A tree, of the third – the rope[22].
A kind of cultural symbol resulted, which the priests preserved for a considerable time,
Until a spiteful young man dug up from the historical archives
The source of a personal blood feud,

But he failed to seek the blessing for its implementation
From the descendant of that elder, but also, for some reason, from the elder.
The true guardian of union and peace
Admonished the lad, saying that was not the way to do things,
That peace had to be preserved. In so doing, he pushed the symbol of that peace into the lad's
face.

The lad took offence, snatched the three-part symbol
And smashed it over the elder's head.
The three-part symbol instantly transformed into a battle-axe,
Like a tomahawk, *aybalta*, *alebarda* or *tabar*, and blood spouted from it...
The young man realised that this was a weapon and taught his friends how to make it.
His army held the upper hand for many years, until enemy intelligence

Stole the secret for the production of the battle axe
And introduced the weapon into its armed forces.
A hardcore war then raged
For so long that contemporaries thought it was a battle eternal.
All the fields and forests were strewn with the corpses of warriors,

Clasping in their decaying hands
What was yesterday a symbol of their peace.
Today, though, it had become a symbol of their savage hatred and death.
Only one hundred years later did the drunk, yet assiduous Russian bloke Miron,
Having found an axe in the forest, chop the first tree with it. So, there you go.'

The silence was so penetrating, that
A fly could be heard buzzing a hundred cubits away.
The sun shone brightly, but it felt that the light was fading

---

[22] The Russian uses the ancient Slavic word *verv'*, meaning a wound rope. The more widespread meaning of the word is *community*. The homonymous sound of these words is used here intentionally.

Compared with the light of love and deference,
With which the pupils gazed at the Beloved One.

Cephas's eyes were like two fires
That combined love and new knowledge,
From the joining of which, man becomes both better and more complete.
Only Thomas's smile, as it always was, remained
Mischievous and full of impish doubt.

John, timidly motioning with his hand, began slowly:
'Rabbi, your wisdom...'
'Hold on, wait, Beloved One,' Thomas broke the torpor.
'What was the point of what you've related, our Friend?
So that we would doubt the act of the materialistic and evolutionary origin of man? Is that it?

Well, not an act, not an act; they have a process.
I agree that the act of creating a rope is technologically no less complex than creating an axe.
And someone had to make this rope, of course.
And then what's with the fences, the priests and the war?
And, anyway, you told us about *people* who had already formed as a species, right?

Although, it's all, well, pretty logical really.
Most important is that the axe could have emerged only in the hands of man.
Which means that it was not the cause of the act (the process, I mean) of the creation!
But this is common knowledge. After all, the Marxists say that *labour made a man out of a monkey*, not the axe.
It's just that the axe, is, how can I put it, a historical allegory, I suppose.

A composite, three-section tool that enables man to do an awful lot.
Its variations (stick-rope-rock) are the spear, the plough, the arrow
And even, incidentally, the catapult and the trebuchet.
That also is clear; I mean, there are not many fools who really believe
That a monkey invented the axe and awoke the next day as some Klaus-Dietrich Schipke or a Jafarzade Niyazi.

And anyway, it is now understood that it was not inventions that lie at the heart of the evolution of the species,
Or technological breakthroughs; rather it was mutations,
As a result of which more species came about that were better adapted to life,
Species that had completed a difficult journey from the primordial soup and replication protein,
To the elephant, Absinthe[23] or Marylin Monroe.

Obviously, one of the problems in the logic of the evolutionists
Was mainly in that, if a higher degree
Follows a lower one
Then what is the very lowest degree?
Below cellular level? Below elementary particle level?

All of this is so obvious on the surface
That it is hardly likely to interest You as a subject for discussion...'
Thomas narrowed his eyes craftily and his smile became wider still:
'So, Rabbi, what *is* the thought that you
Wanted to share with us?

Remember, you spoke of this at the start of our conversation?

---

[23] *Absinthe* was the name of the legendary Soviet Akhal-Teke stallion, multiple winner of world championships.

And that, for some reason, you
Asked in advance to convey to Emperor Constantine
That, if anything happened, he would delete the subject from the classics?'

'I... Well, not so as to...
It's just that Judas is cooking *plov*[24] today.
And that would take him at least an hour and a half.
Everyone wants to eat; I can see it – they just can't wait any longer.
The same goes for me, incidentally.

I saw that you're risking wasting time on nervous and hungry waiting;
The usual internal squabbling and idle chatter.
And I decided: any time spent searching for the truth
Will reward us with a deeper knowledge of the world.
So that this knowledge, in turn, would help us take the right steps.'

'You were laughing at us, Rabbi,'
Thomas laughed loudly and said,
'But you've let yourselves get duped, you apologists!'
He patted the dumbstruck John on the head.
John had tears in his eyes.

Clearly, the idea hadn't filled him with joy
That, on this occasion, the conversation had been simply
To kill time.
Cephas was terribly upset. Actually, everyone was generally
And for some reason (why?) upset and began filing,

One by one out onto the street,
From where Judas's pot summoned them fragrantly.
Only Thomas laughed loudly and gleefully;
This conversation had clearly improved his mood,
Only, most likely, because he had managed

To have a good laugh at his friends.
Our Beloved Friend was also upset that things had worked out like that, but he laughed:
'Guys! Friends! But this was the idea from the very beginning!
Then, however, in the course of the conversation,
I understood the important thing about science

Is that you have to learn in order to comprehend properly what comes next!'
Either they took serious offence, or, more likely, I think, from the aroma of Judas's *plov*,
No one hung around and they all continued quietly to make their exit.
'After all, I wanted to get into quantum physics,
So, you would understand: how can things simultaneously

Exist and not exist?
A wave and a corpuscle?
Light and flesh?'
He became even more upset but even Thomas had gone outside by this point,
True, having first tenderly embraced his Friend in support.

The two of us remained alone. The Friend was silent.
I cleared my throat and asked Him:
'Erm, having seen what came to pass and what has been predicted,

---

[24] Central Asian pilau rice with lamb.

What interests me is how can this be existent and not...'
The Teacher suddenly put two fingers together over my mouth.

I raised my eyes and saw that the pain in His eyes had become an abyss
That only I understood.
'Now don't *you* rush in,' I heard the voice of Eternal Solitude,
Which always makes me uncomfortable.
'It's you who will understand it all when you have to.

When the heavens will gasp in terror when they realise what they have done...'

Verse 18. The Warrior

'Tell me, Simon the Zealot, about your Path to this day.'
But is that really necessary, my Beloved Friend?
Is that really necessary, my brothers?
You think you're ready to hear what won't be music to your ears
Or, more important, that my story won't put you off me?

I understand that you have walked a difficult path, too,
One that the churchmen will refuse to give you credit for.
After all, how, in their eyes, could the pillars of faith
Have ever committed misdeeds or have anything to do with evil?
However, I'm not interested in their opinion; only you are dear to me.

I've been looking for you all my life. Every one of us could say that.
It's just that... I fear for my tale, for a word can not only rouse;
It can also tear asunder, and for good, and I couldn't bear that.
I won't say that I've found peace in our society.
I won't say that we are at peace and in harmony with ourselves.

But, I think that, at this stage of my life,
A life that has been wayward and sinful in a way,
There is nothing dearer to me than our evenings and our meetings
Where we get together after doing the things that are asked of us,
Things that our Friend gifts us (that's right, gifts, not instructs!).

Well, anyway, if you insist.
Actually, there's not much to tell.
I am pretty typical, really.
There are hundreds of thousands like me:
Regiments, legions, tumen[25], brigades.

I was born into a family of military traditions.
Not because we are a dynasty of soldiers or anything,
Rather, when their peers would go to college
And learn a trade,
My grandfathers and great-grandfathers, with each generation.
Would loaf around after school, get some no-good job, here or there,

And then, they'd give it up and enlist.
We are no officers, military commanders or generals;
We are those who make up the 'acceptable losses'
Or to ensure no more than a certain number of prisoners;
Those same *les soldats inconnus*[26], whose names are more akin to numbers.

Then, from among the members of our class,
Talented leaders and individuals will emerge
To glorify us simple Simons.
It only takes one Son of the Star![27]

---

[25] *Tumen*, or *tümen*, was a decimal unit of measurement used by the Turkic and Mongol peoples to quantify and organize their societies in groups of 10,000, similar to the Ancient Greek term *myriad*.
[26] *Les soldats inconnus* (French) – unknown soldiers.
[27] Simon bar Kokhba (Aramaic). A Jewish military leader who led an uprising against the Romans during the reign of Emperor Adrian in 131–135 CE.

However, I say again, we are no Kshatriya, Mamluks or horsemen.

We are regular soldiers, troops, members of the ranks, mere elements of some tactical plan.

My grandfather swore allegiance to the Hasmoneans
And fought in the Patriotic War against Pompey.
But what kind of Patriotic War was that?
As always with us Jews, a civil war was
When Sabras fought against Sephardi

Or against the Ashkenazi, what's the difference?
They scrap as if we're not all the children of the Land of Israel.
As if we hadn't been born with the word 'peace' on our lips,
As if we had been chosen for such fights by the Almighty Himself,
As if history never teaches us anything.

Then, my grandfather told me, even the Arab King Aretas marvelled,
As he stood at the walls of Jerusalem:
'Hey brothers, sons of Abraham! To what end did you restore the Temple,
Only to burn it down because of some petty feuds?
Or haven't you read your history and you don't know

That they will make the house of the Hasmoneans wither away?
Or, for mutual peace, do you
Really need some external force
To come and remind you of times of slavery
And that, only then, you'd start seeing reason?'

Oh, the children of the Land of Israel, they paid no heed
To the King of the Ismaelites, who spoke the truth.
Pompey came, to all appearances, a civilised type.
And what did he give you? It was with him that everything started –
That story with the Romans, with their ecumenical national interests.

My grandfather fought on the side of Aristobulus.
He was the first to launch an arrow from the walls of Jerusalem and kill an Arab prince.
The Arabs and the followers of Hyrcanus were enraged;
They stormed the city day after day, night after night, and then the Temple.
The House of the Hasmoneans stood firm.

Only then Pompey appeared and the dynasty of the kings became no more.
The Arabs left for the desert with the words,
There's power for you, Hyrcanus, so, now sort things out for yourself;
Sort out your bronze Romans
And your people, now deprived of their sovereign.

I asked my grandfather when I was little.
'How many Arabs did you kill back then?'
He looked at his hand in silence
And uttered to himself in a whisper, 'Forgive me, Adonai, forgive me!'
I came to understand later: not one, only his compatriots.

Later still I was to learn that... All right, I'll come to that later.
My grandfather later fought the Romans long and hard,
And he died from thirst somewhere in the Syrian desert.
All he left were the words,
'The flag! The flag! Don't let the flag fall!'

His fellow brother-in-arms told me
That before his death, raving deliriously,
He had screamed and wailed before falling unconscious in expectation of the
Black vulture of the desert, who had no wish
To share its prey with the raven.

Then, in my homeland of Galilee,
The people only whispered about those who perished,
Seldom naming names, only number after number;
The number-names of those lost forever,
Raving about a flag...

My father wasn't like his father:
When his time came, he enlisted
With the Roman auxiliary forces,
Who headed off to the war with the Parthians,
How proudly the Persians had taken to glorifying themselves.

Our rabbi then said to him,
'You should be ashamed of yourself! Have you forgotten the memory of your father,
Who fought against his subjugators,
Who had burst into the Sanctuary and plundered the Temple?!'
To which my father had replied with a smile,

Adjusting his Syrian bow and Roman helmet,
'When you need to win a war with your neighbours
The one who's good for a Jew
Is the one who helps him in this endeavour,
Be it Rome or be it even Washington;

In fact, he was playing cunning;
He didn't give a hoot about geopolitical interests.
Being a soldier back then was a profitable business.
You were paid your wage in Roman denarii,
And there was never a campaign from whence he would return without spoils.

This Scythian sword, for instance, which I always have with me
Was what he brought from Armenia, where he had lost
His right ear and a toe.
However, he never complained; he only had to hear the Roman clarion call
And he would rush straight to the recruitment office, asking no questions

About where and with whom the next war would be.
To be honest, they're all the same; you must have seen them, right?
Those Roman veterans. Covered in scars.
And they're all, well, proud and serene.
Only sometimes at the tavern they'd reminisce about old victories

And smash the place to hell (oh, forgive me, Friend).
And smash someone's face in, for sure.
This is all followed by them fixing everything, much to their women's amusement.
I used to be amazed what soldiers' hands were capable of.
It was funny to look at them back then,

When they, headed by some centurion
Whose head was splitting after the night before,

Would work quickly and hurriedly, like a single organism.
And they would poke fun at their boss,
Saying something like, *is Bacchus playing drums on this head or what?*

Incidentally, they'd fix up the innkeeper's face
With some unknown soldiers' means,
And then they'd definitely bring him a gift
From somewhere in Azarbaigan[28]
Or Hellas. Where didn't father's destiny take him?

Then he disappeared for good.
I asked the Romans if they had seen Simon of Judea.
Would you believe it – they actually knew my father really well!
That surprised me. When I asked, the soldiers would perk up
And nod as if everyone knew him.

Only you're going a bit far with the Judea bit, sonny, they'd say.
He had the nickname, but it'd be hard to call him righteous.
And they'd giggle. *Son, he probably knelt before Mars and Bacchus, too!*
But what a warrior he was! So distinguished!
I cried when I heard the 'was'.

Later, I learned everything about him.
When in some Roman feuds
He took the wrong side, either that of Anthony or of Augustus.
Well, not the side that won, anyway.
The rebel legions then disbanded.

Of the Roman soldiers, some were demobbed, others transferred to another outfit,
While foreigners were either executed or sent to fight as gladiators.
My dad was one of those to become a gladiator.
Then, I thought that they were artists of sorts, much like Zinovy Gerdt[29].
It turns out they're not exactly artists.

One could hardly compare them in popularity stakes.
My father was even given the nickname 'The One-eared Lion of Judea'.
He fought Samnites, Gauls and Chinese Kung Fu fighters,
Murmillos, Retiarii[30] and even lions,
But he was never defeated. But then he died...

No, not under the wing of his patron Mars,
But above the cup of his other idol.
They say that, with a cry of *A soldier's woe comes not from his enemies,*
But from politicians!, like Iskandar Zulkarnain[31], he
He drained the cup of Heracles and died the next morning, freezing while asleep on a Roman
street.

'He died like a dog,' is what the priests say.
'A real man! And he died a real man!' the soldiers laugh into their beards.
And no one knows what remained of him in my soul.
Only the Scythian sword and a few memories

---

[28] One of the ancient names for modern-day Azerbaijan.
[29] Famous Soviet and Russian actor (1916–1996).
[30] *Murmillos* and *Retiarii* were types of gladiator that differed in the weapons used. *Murmillos* were swordsmen with small shields, while *Retarii* were armed with nets and tridents.
[31] Iskandar Zulqarnain (Arabic, Persian) – The Two-Horned One, a name given to Alexander the Great in the East.

Of brief conversations with him at home when he was on his latest campaign.

There were times when I hated him. Especially after the time I awoke in the night. I could see the
door was open, letting the wind in.
My father was standing in the doorway, ever-so handsome in his military apparel.
Mother was weeping, however. All he said was, 'Look, you see there is no place for me in this
world'.
My mother then wept for several days and nights.

I came to understand when I grew up:
He'll return from his campaign,
He'll booze it up for a week to celebrate his return.
And then, well, then he'll try and find work;
He has a soldier's hands, hands of gold, like the Russians say.

And what of it? He was thrown off the building of the Temple.
I was there at the time.
He had the foreman by the scruff of the neck and spoke to him, terribly and icily:
'I could put together a heliopolis with these hands,
But you, you son-of-a-you-know-what, you sold the Babylonians some polished rock.

And you say that *I* can't be trusted?! *You're* the one stealing from the Temple, you dog!'
The foreman screamed back at him, 'And you worship multiple gods;
You're nothing but a Roman henchman!'
My father spoke to the archpriest: 'What have you got going on here?!
You want to tell me a fasting thief is better than an honest man?'

But the archpriest replied, 'Off you go home, Simon.
Off you go, Nam-Bok the Unveracious[32], go on, and stop disrupting our status quo.
There's a good chap' you're just not one of us.'
The foreman then said, 'You've got blood on your hands, you reprobate!'
My father couldn't stop himself at that and, well, he throttled the scoundrel a little.

He would have throttled him to death and no one around would have saved him.
Only my father's eyes became kind of frightened, I suppose,
And he let the bastard go. And he walked away. I went after him. I only managed to notice
mischievously
How the archpriest struck the foreman with his stick, generating howls of pain.
But what was the point in this little act of vengeance?

Later I had one of those rare conversations with my father.
There were only three of them in total. I remember them all.
Those were the ones that took place when he was not on a campaign and fully sober.
Do I need to retell them?
I do? You're interested?

'Son, don't go taking an example from your dad. It's not worth it.
What is my life? What have I given you and your mother?
It can't surely come down to these Indian trinkets.
You know, son, that you only have one home,
Wherever your destiny might take you.

It is home alone that makes us alive; it is only thoughts of home

---

[32] Nam-Bok the Unveracious – the central character of Jack London's short story of the same name, about a
Native American who returns home after time among the 'white man' and relates yarns of 'flying birds' and
'giant iron boats', for which he is branded a liar and banished from his tribe.

That help us survive where others don't,
Where comrades perish as fast as a mountain brook
Washes away an ant trail in a second.
And the man who was just laughing by your side is no longer there,

And he who always called you his friend passes away.
It's one thing for us veterans: for our sins the Almighty
Leaves us here on this temporal earth and takes us not
Into His heavenly dwellings and sends us not to the slums of Hell,
So that we might drink from the cup of inadequacy of peaceful life.

And this young lad then signs up, before he's even started shaving,
And he takes his place in the ranks in a maniple[33].
He stands firm and doesn't let on that his knees are shaking,
Knees that mummy only yesterday rubbed with ointment.
He pales a little when the elegant

Ranks of the enemy march nearer.
Noise and hubbub bring no fear,
It's the silence and single-mindedness that stoke fear,
As if concentrated on one thought alone:
To drag you from the ranks and kill you dead. Kill you for all time.

Only yesterday, this lad tried on a legionnaire's helmet for size.
And here you are, fizz-thwish-thunk, a Hun's arrow
Strikes him in the throat and he leaves
This world, without even saying, *Farewell,*
Old comrade, sorry for being foolish and not using my shield as I was taught.

He looks at you with astonished eyes,
And you think why we all wept over him like that.
No, no, the ranks must not be broken, or other
Comrades will perish under Persian arrows.
And feet step over the lad. Many feet.

We march on, but he remains behind. They, too, remain behind.
Row upon row of maniples swallow them up like a wave
And pull them down, where faces are lost;
Faces, confused like new-borns
And their names are carried away into nothingness.'

I know that more or less
All war veterans talk of this.
But, more often, they talk of nothing.
You'll drag nothing from their vice-tight lips.
As if they are protecting us from something terrible.

'Call it what you will, son,' went our second conversation,
'Call it Vietnam Syndrome, call it Afghan Syndrome;
The meaning doesn't really change.
Only later does the essence reveal itself, only it's too late
And, to be honest, no longer needed.

We are soldiers and our faith is the faith in combat.
Faith in our comrade who, with his one remaining arm,

---

[33] A subdivision of a Roman legion, containing either 120 or 60 men.

Will, without fail, drag you, peppered with stab wounds,
If Allah so allows.
No doubt: it is on that that our faith is built.

Later we discover that in fact
We had come under fire from the *manjaniks*[34] of our own army,
Because when the legate was told
That our men were still out there,
He replied that the losses were acceptable, but the battle needed to be won.

But it's war, son, it's just war.
Well, so I smashed the legate's face in, but we did indeed win the battle
And we saved the Deiotarorum legion from annihilation
Because we intimidated the Parthians with our ammunition
And they thought twice about attacking.

It's another thing that's terrifying, son. It's terrifying that
All our Palestinian lads
Who went out to fight for the Romans against Parthia
Turned out to be traitors back home.
You know why?

Simply because public opinion
On our involvement in the campaign with Rome,
While we were gathering the remains of our friends in the Saka plains,
Changed fundamentally
And now we are outcasts, traitors of national interests.

You think we knew that the centurions, wearing the same clothes
As us, only in the colours of a colonial legion,
Were raping our lasses, and our lads at the same time,
Slowly taking away our independence
And actually recreating everything as Goya etched in his *Disasters of War*?!

And that old man at the elections to the Sanhedrin
Basically designed his election campaign against us
And emerged the winner because everyone now thinks
That we were some instrument of imperialism
And were implementing the will of Italian corporations.

And, to be completely honest, son,
Baal[35] be with it, with that politics.
It was actually not a matter of those around us
Rather in us veterans, who paid the price by,
Unlike their friends, remaining among the living as their punishment.

You know, there are plenty of jerks in the army and more than enough corruption,
Only there is the one, most important yardstick of Justice:
The battle, which puts everything in its place.
An honest, open and ferocious battle.
An iron archangel circles above the battlefield.

---

[34] Manjanik (Arabic) – an ancient and mediaeval siege weapon, similar to a trebuchet.
[35] Baal, Bael or Ba'al was an important Canaanite god, often portrayed as the primary enemy of the Hebrew God Yahweh, but sometimes seen as a demon in Christian tradition. Therefore, it is likely that this phrase can be seen as the equivalent as 'The hell with it, with that politics'.

You can see your enemy and you know who he is; there, right in front of you.
The criteria are simple, like the assembly and dismantling of a *Kalashnikov*.
And here, in a life of peace?
You don't know where the frontline is drawn.
And you have no idea when apparently normal folk

Will come up behind you and stab you in the back with a smile
For the cameras of public support.
They pierce your heart but, rather than dying,
You transform into a social animal
That runs about in circles, not knowing,

Not knowing from where the next strike will come;
However, you know that it will come for sure,
And, again, you cannot identify the enemy
And you don't know from where he'll come,
Or what laws force him to fight against you.'

'And another thing, son,' the third conversation began.
Yes, I'm getting to the point, guys, don't rush in.
We might be people who have given ourselves up fully to our faith,
But we are men, all the same, and what men don't like
To chat by the fire about their past military exploits?

'Another thing, son. I hate bureaucrats.
Never repeat the mistakes of the legate Cornelius,
Our commander. I wonder where he is now.
You see, I was in that same Legion of Crassus
That historians will later call the Lost Legion.

Anyway, our entire legion was captured; it was all so foolish, of course.
We were standing in reserve while the battle was being fought over beyond the ridges;
All we could hear were battle sounds and terrible wailing,
But our command was to stay where we were, like the Tien Shan mountains,
Unwavering and cold-blooded.

We sent a runner, but he tore off up the hill and never returned.
Half an hourglass went by and we found ourselves
Surrounded from all ridges on all sides, like the Terek,
By the Parthian Cavalry. All that was left for us
Was to surrender to the enemy's arrows.

And so, having not once interlocked shields in battle,
We found ourselves prisoners of the enemy, like Vlasovites[36].
The Persians are proud warriors and respect an enemy's pride.
Captivity was not belittling; at times it was even quite honourable.
They left us our banners and our weapons,

But they moved us *en masse* to somewhere near Isfahan.
It was there that Cornelius's mistake unfolded.
The Shah had passed a law, under which
We were left to settle freely,
Not as slaves, rather as free dehqans[37].

---

[36] Soldiers under Andrey Vlasov, who were captured by the Nazis in 1942. Historians are divided over whether Vlasov was a Nazi sympathiser or a freedom fighter.
[37] A term from Middle Persian, meaning *village farmer*.

They promised that, once the geopolitical situation had changed,
They would allow us to return home. We were much like hostages
And yet Rome had forgotten us; back then I couldn't understand why.
Later we were told that we'd been labelled traitors and fifth columnists;
We'd betrayed our oath and they called us the Turkestan Legion.

However, Cornelius knew nothing. The Shah died.
The Parthians reached an agreement with the Empire on borders, and yet there was not a word about us.
Later, Cornelius took to pestering the Parthian administration,
Saying that the Shah was no more, Peace reigned and they should let us go home.
But we said to him that we had all we needed: weapons and banners,

That we would break through to the West via the lands of the Greeks.
But he said that was out of the question, that they were treating us well,
And that we too should obey their laws. And that, well, we were in peacetime.
We'd get the court decision we needed and they'd let us go.
After all, there was no longer any reason to hold us.

And off he went to those offices and court authorities.
He wrote a mountain of letters in Latin, in Farsi and, when he had to,
In Aramaic, too, depending on what bureaucrat he came up against.
To the venerable Prosecutor of the Tabriz region
From the residents of the SPQR urban settlement. A declaration.

Or *To whom it may concern* or *To the Satrap[38] of the Southern District.*
All he received in response, however, was that the Shah had died and there was no one to overturn the law,
But, you know, there was some hope in the documents:
According to the International Convention on the Rights of Prisoners-of-War...
Or *Your appeal contravenes the statutory act*

On the Rules for Migration of the Northern Ostān[39].
Or *Officially, you cannot be deemed prisoners-of-war,*
Or *In order to apply the Law on Repatriation*
You do not have the required qualifying period of residence.
Or *The application requires the signature of at least five citizens of Parthia.*

Or *You have no right to remove military property from the country,*
Or *Present evidence of complete payment of all debts*
To the Iranian banks by all listed legionnaires,
Or *Your application expired the day before yesterday; where have you been all this time?*
Or *Prove that your departure is justified by good intentions toward Parthia,*

Or *If you have relatives abroad, please list them all by name.*

So it went on for many years, but it was eventually resolved in a matter of three days.
Huns came from the East and said
That a terrifying army was fast on their heels,
An army, a force like never before seen in the world.
The army of Khanate China, which not even the gates of Iskander could stop.

At that moment, the Persian military department got involved and declared

---

[38] A provincial governor in the Persian Empire.
[39] Ostān (Persian) – a province or administrative unit in modern-day Iran.

That this was a chance for us Romaioi[40].
That we should join them in their march
And earn our freedom with our blood.
And we'd resolve the regional conflict at the same time,
So that Chinatowns would start springing up only a thousand years later.

For many years we lived in Parthia.
The lands of Isfahan, *half the world*[41], became very close to our hearts.
And yet, there is nothing higher for a soldier than Home.
All legionnaires as one discarded their belongings
And stood the next morning in ranks beneath the sweltering Iranian sun.

The battle was terrible. The passionarity of the Chinese
Amazed even the battle-scarred veterans of Spain and Germany.
Against them stood three different peoples, shoulder to shoulder.
Huns, Persians and Romans. And our lads stood among them.
(Today they speak of them as some social problem.)

They say that no one emerged victorious,
But the Chinese dragon, nevertheless, proved unable
To make it over the Kazakh steppes
And break through in triumph to the Mediterranean.
And it won't for thousands of years to come, either.

I don't know where my fellow soldiers are now.
In that battle, I got shot in the chest by a Chinese cartridge
And I would have laid forever in the Turkic earth
If it had not been for that Hun lad
On his restless, shaggy little horse.

Shouting *hold on, hold on, Roman-aga,*
He fought off a dozen or so enemy foot soldiers,
Who had already started dividing my uniform.
In he flew like a whirlwind, but his blows were like those of Reuben the Blacksmith.
He strapped me to his saddle like a ram back at the homestead,

His cry was so fierce – it simply didn't tally with his baby-smooth young face;
It was at this point that I passed out for a good while.
So, you see, son, three days of battle
Gave us the Justice that the bureaucrats proceeded to steal from us in a matter of years.
Personally, I don't care, son, about being a number in military chronicles;

I do care, however, about being a number in bureaucratic reports.'

I remembered all my father's words very well,
But I can't say they helped me in life,
That they revealed some truth to me.
Clearly, in order to feel all this for myself,
I needed to have lived the life that my father lived.

All the same, however, telling you all this, about my father and grandfather was not for nothing.
Their lives, naturally, had an impact on the path I have taken,
The path to the tale I am now getting to.
I was a regular lout,

---

[40] Roman citizens.
[41] From the Persian saying *Esfahān nesf-e-jahān ast*, meaning *Isfahan is Half the World!*

A lout who hung around after the village school, not knowing what to do with myself.

Of course, I had no chance of getting a place at an institute.
I had neither the money nor, it has to be said, the desire.
Therefore, when I enlisted,
Mum and my relatives could breathe more easily.
It was an occupation at least.

And the army was no longer what it used to be.
For the most part it was populated by Hellenic mercenaries.
The Land of Israel was ruled by Roman governors;
Like any powers that be,
They were evil and fair in equal moderation.

Stupid drills and drunken brawls,
Studying the weapons of our probable opponents,
Political training in *Rome and Israel – Brothers Forever*;
Basically, all the idiocy of an army at loose ends,
With soldiers lapsing into indolence

And officers reading detective stories before bed.

Moreover, given who we were: *Peregrini*[42],
What responsibility could be expected of us?
We were second-class soldiers, not citizens, and that basically meant we weren't people,
Well, not Latins, not Latvians and not their underlings,
Just numbers; people with numbers assigned to them.

It seemed that the rule of the Emperor Tiberius
Was a time of stability of sorts.
However, one day, everything changed
And uprisings spread across the Empire.
Was this a syndrome or a symptom?

I'm not that good with all those Latin words.
So, forgive me, if you would.
Anyway, so these uprisings sprang up.
In countries that were previously unknown to me;
It was then that I became a punisher.

You think it's a simple matter for a lad to work out
That you're – it's such a bad word – a punisher?!
When people tell you every day that it's *us* here
And *them* there, people with a different approach and different values
When it comes to the sanctity of family, state and ideology.

Not that I really gave it that much thought;
It's just that one thing always surprised me:
How can that be? After all, *they* are initially in the wrong
When they make their demands.
After all, they are just freaks, enemies of civilisation, outcasts;

Those who try to undermine the world
That rests on foundations,
Tried and tested over centuries, great power and love for one's Homeland,

---

[42] Outsiders, not citizens of Rome, who had served in the ancient Roman army.

Values that I have built my world around,
With stable relations, relationships and basically everything!

Then, the Pannonian and Gallic legions revolted.
I don't know what they were protesting against,
But it was all somehow unfamiliar and alien; I mean, how can you rise up against the powers that be?!
Against the general order and harmony in which everyone has lived
In peace and goodness?

The Romans are smart people. They didn't set
Their citizens up against their own kind.
That was why they needed us, the Peregrini,
The outsiders, aliens to the honour of these Samurai-Roman-Rebels.
And they put us there to suppress the protest of the veteran legionnaires.

I didn't say at the start that I had been accepted into the Fulminata Legion,
With its fame and glory, but with a certain degree of rabble in its ranks.
And anyway, why did I, a simple boy from Galilee, need
To work out all the contradictions in those colonial goings-on?!
I had my soldier's ration and my share of the spoils – that I understood.

As for the rest, it's all Bashō lyrics and layman's gossip.
In short, back then, I didn't understand my grandfather's words, *Forgive me, Adonai, forgive me!*
I killed happily, fervently and with full justification.
I was awarded bonuses and they wrote articles about me at home,
About the glorious Jewish lads serving the Empire.

Back then, fate flung me from region to region.
We killed, punished and killed again.
I even saw Tacfarinas in Numidia
Just thirty seconds before his death
At the hands of three mutton-headed punishers from Bethlehem.

And you think only prophets
Come from that great city?!
Then I remember driving the nails
Into the hands of slaves who had lost their social graces in Italy
And who had risen up against the lords and masters of their world.

You want the truth? Well, there is nothing of significance
In the confessions of those lads I observed through the slit in my helmet,
Across the edge of my shield; lads who were standing up against the *ordnung*.
For lads, it is all about the thrill of the fight and the victory;
And did *we* do them today or *they*, us?

So, don't go moralising and inferring
About us, the tools of the regimes,
These rank-and-file Tonton Macoutes and *Federales*,
These Stasi, KGB officers and 1905 Cossacks,
Khmer Rouges and regular plain-clothes CIA operatives.

We were just doing our duty as we had been told
By the colonels in whom believed.
Well, and apart from them, there were no other grown-ups in the unit.
And you, reader, you think you can work out
What's black and what's white in this world?!

And you've got your mother writing from home,
Saying, you get on and kill those terrorists
And return home bathed in glory;
Your favourite apple pie will be waiting for you.
So, she is also involved in this concept, is that it?!

Just as with everyone, it all came to an end in the most banal way.
During the revolt of the Thracians, in Thrace, accordingly,
I was wounded in the chest, right below the right nipple,
And I was sent to the military hospital back at home,
Where, consequently, the Knights Hospitaller[43] was to emerge.

At first everything was hazy for several weeks.
Then the images of the sisters of mercy became clearer.
Then, a foolish optimism came over me,
As I walked about in hospital robes before the nuns and those sisters,
As if we were glad to have simply survived.

Joking, eating, smoking where we weren't allowed,
Stupid remnants of discipline on the part of the military physician,
Awaiting documents from the medical review board,
Letters from home about someone getting drunk somewhere,
The promises of a girl that she'd wait for me all her life, all full of lies of course.

Returning home. Emptiness. Then more emptiness.
Like everything is all the same. But emptiness.
The hell with her (forgive me, my Beloved Friend); her parents had forced her.
Well, and Baal with him, a friend builds a logical chain of reasoning in a new way.
And it's not important that, you know 'but we don't hire Chechens and the like'.

I'm at home. Everything is in a haze. I drink. They offer me more. I drink. I pay for it myself.
I drink. Turns out, the caretaker fought on Damansky Island.
I drink. A security guard is a noble job. I don't drink.
Prostitutes: that's not a vice – her mother's ill
And her little boy needs a new pencil case.

And there's no man at home. I drink. It's incompatible with one's occupation.

And you, you bastard, did you even once get your brothers... when...
You sniffed gunpowder outside the shooting gallery, just like your father?!
I try to dress formally and resolve the matter.
I am polite but principles are principles.
There are loads of cops. Where are you, brothers?!

I weep. In hysterics. It's really banal, like in *Rambo: First Blood*;
He's a soldier, but he's misunderstood, while the system is worse out of ranks
Than the enemy's honour, when he cries reverently in his own tongue that
Brothers, the Soviet is dying, dying a hero, the, djigit urus![44]
Oh, where are you, my enemy?! Oh, where are you, my beloved enemy?!

Oh, where are you, you red Afghan slopes?!
Oh, where are you, my tears of despair over putrid socks in the Jungle?!

---

[43] Means the Hospital of Saint John of Jerusalem, commonly known as the Knights Hospitaller, and which earned fame during the Crusades.
[44] The term *djigit* means brave fellow. Quoting the phrase found in Tolstoy's *Prisoner of the Caucasus.*

Oh, where are you... where are you... where are you... you who're left behind,
Like an eternal reproach for me, like a part of me, as I,
Dying along with you every minute,

Greeting you, saying farewell, but not forgiven,
Repentant, but not according to their system of values,
Weeping, but still strong,
Vulnerable, but not allowing himself to be hurt.
Alone. Alone, but there are many of us. But we are alone...

That's me, not overwhelmed with emotions,
Rather the contrary, insensitive and silent,
Sitting one day on the summer terrace of the tavern
Owned by a friend of mine whose soul died in Korea,
But who remained among the living. How so? You wouldn't understand.

And I overheard this idiotic discussion
Between a Hellene, a Jew and a Roman.
They were old, borderline senile,
But young people still complied with their opinions.
And this is the trouble with the reproduction of stupidity.

The essence of the argument is fairly simple:
Against a backdrop of a quiet, gentle, cool Galilee morning,
They engaged in a run-in, literally to the death,
As if their old wives wouldn't take them away in ten minutes,
As if they had to hammer out the truth on that day or never.

The Hellene said, 'You Jews are alien here.
And there's no need for pretence before the Arabs.
Everyone knows that you came here, according to different versions,
Either from Sheba, South Arabia, Yemen,
Or from Polish villages like nomads on camels.

However, while you were wandering about for forty years in the suburbs, *we*
Gave the Phoenicians a beating with Greek weapons,
And other native Americans too, using our military superiority,
Nourishing the bare local land
And dressing it in the fabric of Bourgeois prosperity.'

'Yes, that's right,' the Roman said with a face the colour of the Canaan earth.
'We forced the international community,
Despite your laughable prophecies,
To form a Jewish state,
When you hadn't even gathered your Twelve Tribes.' And he laughed.

'As for you, Romans, you're history's mistake,'
The smug Hellene went on.
'After all, you too are descendants of the Trojans,
Banished by our guys, Agamemnon and Achilles,
From the future resorts of Turkey.

You too, children of Aeneas, are alien in your own Italy.
What did you do with the Samnites, Etruscans and the Ainu?
The Delaware, Huron, Mohican and Shoshone?
The Celts, Incas, the Tibetans, Zulus and Sumerians?
Only we Hellenes are the most ancient, and the English, too.

But none of you are indigenous in your own lands;
You're not aborigine and you're not nation builders;
You have no historical roots and, at the very least,
No rights to these barren plots of land
That languish away under the microwaves of the Palestinian sun.

You are like the tenants of the will of Zeus,
And your inferiority complex
Will forever pass from generation to generation,
To give rise to fruitless aggression within you
And the stupidity of an imperial, ambitious perception of the world.

And you'll accuse anyone who has come here,
Of being temporary aliens:
Crusaders, Arabs, Turks, the English and the Romans,
When it comes to these scraps of land that your mythology
Declared was promised to you by someone else.'

'You're calling us aliens?!' the Jew replied indignantly.
'You say we're not indigenous aborigines, the salt of the earth?!
You might be a Greek, but it seems your ideology has been drawn up by Hamas!
You say it was Rome that gave us our nationhood?!
Have you even read our mythology, from the Scripture?'

'Yes, all right,' the Hellene said, quite at ease. 'I might not know modern history,
But, forgive me, the fact that we live here is a legitimate fact,
But you, let me say, be so kind as to clear off to your KwaZulu[45],
Go and live behind a wall or demarcation line,
Where the fruits of Roman civilisation never reached.

After all, only we and the Romans are not barbarians.
You, though, galloped about on camels,
Lived your lives in Arabia, like the Navaho,
In your pastoral, Hegelian paradise,
Like Kazakhs who knew neither dough nor vegetables.

What right do you have to this territory?
Who asked you to traipse around Egypt and the like
And lose yourselves *for losing your connection with the undertaking*, meaning with the Fatherland?
No, sorry, but it makes no difference what the protectorate promised you,
Beat the Jews, save the Eastern Mediterranean – it sounds clumsy but it sounds like a slogan.'

'Hold on a minute,' the Jew endeavoured to pull himself together.
'You want to tell me that ancient history with the First Temple
And the Great Kings means nothing?
You want to tell me that our most ancient calendrics,
The antiquity of our legends, is but an empty phrase?'

'Hehe,' The Greek snickered nastily. 'Calendrics...
Don't try and be clever: you started living on the threshold of the *Kali Yuga*[46].

---

[45] KwaZulu – a reservation for the black population of South Africa during the time of apartheid.
[46] Kali Yuga (Sanskrit) – in Hinduism, the fourth and final age, after which a new countdown of time begins. The Cycle of the Yugas is Satya Yuga, Treta Yuga, Dvapara Yuga and Kali Yuga. The further one gets from the first age, the greater the loss of morality, meaning that Kali Yuga is the most immoral of the ages.

I don't know what the future holds
And who the aliens will be: the Arabs, Turks or the Sephardi,
But one thing's for sure – today, you are invaders, Palestinians, Yasser-Arafatians.

So, make way for the Hellenes, Philistines,
Levantines, Samaritans and Romans.
Incidentally, for the Romans, it is their right as the powerful and civilised,
As civilisation is progress.
Walking around in fur hats in the heat is nothing less than barbarism.'

To confess, brothers, there's not much I understood from this discussion,
But, suddenly, I saw the light.
I don't know what *indigenous* means,
I don't know who came here first,
Or who's the barbarian and who has the myths.

It's enough for me to know that my grandfather and my dad lived here,
And told me that this was my Homeland.
Hey, Slavs! Put simpler, do I actually have another?!
And so, I stood up and squared my shoulders.
I knew now what I had to do.

My land was being trampled by outsiders; I didn't need myths to understand that.
They drive about differently, dress differently and speak differently.
I don't want them over here. Never. And nowhere.
Where I understand my home to be
Is where I don't want statues on my grave.

Anyway, so, I became a Canaanite or, as you like to put it, a zealot.
Having been trained in the best army, I got to thinking:
How could this military machine be defeated?
With their legions, manipules, aircraft carriers, mercenary Greeks
And the world's biggest military budget?

At first, several thousand of us got together.
I placed them in manipules and we moved on the enemy.
The Romans brushed us aside like we were children. I wept.
I knew why, of course: they had these high-accuracy weapons – Grads, Merkavas and Abrams[47],
While all we had were picks, four arquebuses, two camel-mounted cannons and our banners.

Later, we got even more people together, believing that our strength would come in numbers.
We rushed out into the open battlefield. And our army was no more. They suffered four minor casualties.
Later, wives of friends spoke to me, saying
You've sacrificed many, many people,
So why are you still alive?

We had to fight on; we couldn't surrender;
We had to retain our honour.
Wise men came to us and said,
Why not write to the UN; they'll pass the right judgment.
So, I wrote to them, in Latin, in Greek, in Arabic and in Esperanto.

And I received an answer: *Given the difficult geopolitical situation,*

---

[47] *Grad* – a truck-mounted missile launcher; *Merkava* and *Abrams* are tanks.

and so as not to create a precedent of a cold war, to preserve stability in the world and, heaven forbid, so that people will not perish, to avoid a humanitarian disaster, so the peacekeepers will not go hungry, so, oh my, there will be no ear-piercing rat-tat-tat firing of weapons, under a decision of the Security Council, to make many people weep that they have it bad, so the Romans and the Babylonians will take no offence, so tomorrow we might hold a normal meeting in fur coats, to ensure we are shown many times over on the television, so Hollywood stars will also weep that you have it bad, so China will protest about Taiwan, so your punishers won't hold back, so your warming will end in summer, so Russia will not Lego[48] all decisions, so cold cases will be reasons for an international holiday, so French will be used more than English, so fighters will stop using arms, if you are attacked, you're the guilty one, so there will only be a few dictators and so no goat will be crossed with a dinosaur during euthanasia, we are sending you one hundred sacks of rice, a conference on Jewish rights and three articles in the newspaper, titled 'UN gets angry', 'UN gets really angry' and 'UN moves to the next subject'.

Well?! So, what do you think I should have done?! Think. Think and search.

This happened quite by accident.
The Romans actually behave quite decently in the colonies.
They are dictated by the charter, failing which it's *castigatio*.
And this black sheep (you'll find one in any army)
Got blind drunk and wanted to rape Tsilya.

We were nearby and I couldn't control myself.
We cut him up like a sacrificial ram.
Later we noticed that the Romans had grown fearful of going out at night.
And we understood – they were afraid!
Fear is our ally, our weapon and our tool!

Then they started arresting everybody as a preventive measure.
I came to the police station and our lads from the Fulminata legion were there.
They say, 'Simon, *commilitio* [49], well, what are your chaps doing?
How can you cut up a soldier in broad daylight?
He was a right bastard, we knew that, as did you, but you can't go doing that.'

So I say, 'But let the lads go; by what right are you holding them?'
And they say, 'By the right of the powerful, *commilitio*, by the right of the master of law and order.
If every Jew starts proving something,
What will be left of the *ordnung*, eh?
You mean you've forgotten the uprising in Pannonia? And in Numidia?'

Well... Anyway, I became desperate. Not for long though.
Then came Munich, when we executed all the Roman charioteers.
We didn't want to from fear, but... the warriors of Arminia had started showering us with arrows.
And we said, your terror would multiply our fear tens of times over.
And we killed them...

Adonai! And you, my Beloved Friend!
You were witnesses to the fact that I wanted to stop it!
Only then, the Romans rolled out their catapults and ballistas
And bombed out the Palestinian zone.
I said, *Bardaran!* [50] There are no winners in this war! Let's put a stop to it!

---

[48] The author uses the name of the children's building toy *Lego* quite intentionally here.
[49] *Commilitio* – (Latin) brother in arms.
[50] *Bardaran* (Pers.) – the plural of *baradar*, meaning *brother*.

They didn't scream and shout. They said, 'All right, all right. Only, Simon,
Take this boy with his arms blown off
To his friends at the hospital, okay?
Ask them for mercy and love for us Jews, all right?
And speak Latin; perhaps they'll all go home tomorrow, eh?

They'll leave our land and leave for good; they're aliens here, after all.'
I said that we too were aliens here, that I had heard that from wise men.
'You, Simon, you're the alien. You studied at West Point.
You are alien to us and that's why you won't understand.
Take the boy. What are you afraid of? Aa-ah, no need, he's dead already...'

And here I was reborn. I'll become the Sword of Justice.
This is *our* land. Anyone who says otherwise
Will pay with their life.
Not face on, not in battle, not in attack.
But... But what else could I have done? How can you fight against the world's best military
machine?

We are zealots! We are the stronghold of faith! We are the witnesses of the Almighty!
Death is the wreath of our lives! We'll turn the lives of the Hellenes
And the Romans to fear and terror! To ensure there is nowhere they could feel
Safe from the Sword of Independence!
So that, not seeing the paradise of heaven, they would contemplate hell on earth every day.

May all world imperialism,
Having gathered the power of its capital,
Tremble before the pride of a small people,
Who, other than a will to win and their banner
Have nothing at all, and yet you'll see that this is really a great deal.

That is precisely how I was thinking
During that long period of holy war.
I remember every one of their faces,
Their names and, for the first time,
The losses stopped being just numbers for me.

We were the most implacable of the implacable.
We gained strength from our ancient faith,
That had given us the right of believers in one god
To kill any pagan worshipper of Jupiter
And a host of disgusting individuals that the Romans called gods.

And then It happened.
I have said that the problem for all warriors,
As my dad believed,
Lay in unscrupulous and cowardly politicians,
The dealers in human souls,

The things is we didn't know that Herod,
Your and my Jewish sovereign,
In exchange for a kingdom in the Land of Israel,
Sold out to the Romans, lock, stock and barrel.
And he sold us out too.

It turns out that he had agreed on everything,

And we zealots became terrorists, the Sicarii[51],
Thugs with whom no one wished to exchange
Even a word in the civilised world,
All wrapped as it was in Tyrian purple togas.

Now, Jewish tax collectors
Frequented Judea, Galilee, Samaria and all townships and kingdoms,
The scraps of which spread across
The sacred Land of Israel,
Bestowed upon us by ancient kings.

Well, we said to one another,
Traitors will receive the same sentence
As the Gentiles.
You think anyone in the world knows
How to stop the machine of terror?!

And here we devised an operation
To do away with the bloodsucking tax collector
Who, like you, Levi
Accompanied by the Romans,
Plunders our towns and villages.

Back then we had ranks of Fedayeens.
A great many boys perished
And young girls joined our cause.
These girls, loyal and strong of faith,
Were virgins, brides of angels.

So, we sat in an ambush near the highway,
Me and two Fedayeen girls, wrapped in blankets
And packed with Chinese bombs.
A detachment was approaching.
One. Two. Three. Alif. Lam. Mim.

I told them to advance and that they would behold the Almighty.
And then... One of the Fedayeen girls turned and said, 'Yes, Uncle Simon.'
I was taken aback; usually they were just a weapon,
But here... she knew me!
I never did recall how I knew the girl,

As they rushed out onto the road like two white martinets,
Or two seagulls, tousling in the sky
In their search for a large body of water like a sea.
One ran towards the Romans
And the explosion became an angelic, cleansing flame.

The second... The tax collector turned out to be a really young man.
He had clearly only recently earned his stripes.
He looked so proud and happy.
He was riding along on a donkey, singing a song:
For you, my love, from the oasis yonder

---

[51] Sicarii (literally *Dagger wielders*, from the Latin *Sica* for *Dagger*) – a terrorist group that operated in Judea in the first century of the Common Era. One of the most ancient terrorist groups in history. A radical, splinter cell of the zealots, which performed direct attacks and acts of terrorism.

I bring a wedding present so fine,
To call you the one with whom I'll grow old with
Viewing with failing eyes our grandchildren and great-grandchildren.
Out runs my martinet
And she froze, as if rooted to the spot.

I understood everything... Only a second went by,
But it seemed an eternity.
She was weeping and singing with a shaking voice:
My dear, I have brought you my gift.
To give the purity

I have saved for you only where
There are no Jews, Romans, Serbs or Conquistadors.
We will be together in the heavens,
Forever and ever and ever.
They say there's a kingdom up there,

Where there is no Hellene, Jew or Chechen.
Forgive me, dear, and accept
This gift that my uncle presents from our clan
As a sign of kinship and family love
Brought by him this very morning...

The boy understood it all too.
He jumped from his donkey, all pale,
And embraced the girl ever so tightly.
He said to her, 'You are my Homeland,
You are my truth. Let's go and be together for all time...'

Am I sentimental?! Do you know how many...
That was the next day, my Friend.
You had picked me up, stunned senseless,
By that road to my hometown of Galilee,
And you too said something about a Kingdom...

Sorry, I was shell-shocked and didn't understand all that was going on...

All I understood was that a miracle had happened
And the bomb strapped to me had failed to detonate and go off.
Evidently, the Almighty had prepared another fate for me...
Then, I just thought that this was the fate of a veteran outcast,
Who had been sentenced to suffer forever, for, instead of my lost friends,

It should have been me...

Well then, Simon, is a peacemaker really one
Who will see Almighty God?
Why did you demand an eye for an eye, a tooth for a tooth?
Why did you live your life with hatred as the essence of your being?
Why did you place hatred in the house of your heart?

You think I'll reproach you, my brother?
No, you are My pain, right here, look...
They say I forgive everyone, as I am all-forgiving.
But let me tell you this:
It's you who should forgive Me, My brother.

Forgive me; I take all the blame on myself.
That of you and the warriors on your path.
What have I done; how did this all happen?
How did this all happen under the heavens,
That I brought you not peace, but the sword...

Verse 19

(111) And I do not know whether it is perhaps a trial for you, and an enjoyment for a while.

Qur'an. Surah 21, 'The Prophets'

You ask what we called the thing
We spoke with others about?
A teaching, a doctrine, an opinion,
A religion, confession or something else?
It's difficult to recall.

At first, we simply remained silent and readily agreed
With our Beloved Friend, when he spoke so inspirationally
About something with the residents of Capernaum or Bethsaida.
For us, these were merely conversations,
Chats about life, nothing more.

We even doubted if we needed to
Divulge the essence of our intimate conversations
With strangers like this.
After all, the most important thing was not that these things were sacred to us.
It was the suspicion with which the people listened to us.

We sensed our *foreignness* and this was unbearable.
When you appear alien to other people
Who, together, had made your Homeland.
In other words, they are part of us and we, of them,
And what else do we have other than this?

Many times, we said to our Friend, let's keep it to ourselves
Without unwanted ears or prying, sidelong glances;
Just us, in our own little group;
We'll continue our quiet, intellectual conversation,
We'll discuss newspaper articles and science news.

After all, public conversations do have
A certain aspect where views are imposed
On others; surely, this lacks tact, does it not?
Well, what are we – a party of some kind or a political club
To influence electoral circles with our propaganda?

Let everyone see us simply as *unique*.
Well, it's now all the rage to get together like this
And create closed circles or communities around certain interests.
Like innocent Essenes, disappearing out into the desert,
So that no one can stop them building their narrow-minded Communism.

At the end of the day, fundamental self-improvement didn't start with us
And it won't end with us either.
We'll discuss books we've taken from the library,
New publications and even politicians' speeches,
But with one objective only:

To grow inside, respecting the foundations of society
And the rights of others not to have to be part of us and our ideas.

Surely, this is what social conduct should be like?
Surely, the objective of such societies is to nurture decent citizens
For the Fatherland and its progress?

And, basically, Friend, we said,
We find it so awkward and *uncomfortable* when you so heatedly
Argue with some innkeeper or fisherman
About the rudiments of our thousand-year-old world view.
What right do we have to impose on them anything that goes against

What our founding fathers formed over many centuries
In the minds of decent citizens of Palestinian kingdoms?
The high priests, too, are no longer so positively disposed
To us appearing at the synagogues and on the squares.
But they do have a lawful right to interpret

Our past, our present and our future, too.
Sometimes, we just want to let our hair down, go dancing...
Well, anyway, we shocked the public with our crossings on foot
From town to town, but we are also people
And, for the most part, we are young.

We want to see the boulevards in the town freshly painted,
The smiles on girls' faces, the greetings of colleagues, conversation
With prosperous and popular bohemian people.
Come on, Friend, let's see a little less selfless devotion.
A little more pragmatism and reliance on the realities of life.

Otherwise, you know, it starts to smell a bit like arrogant pride
When we reckon our vision of life
Is more advanced than the ingrained customs of the villagers,
Their wise old rabbis and petty town-hall bureaucrats.
In any event, life, with all that goes with it,

Will return us in no uncertain terms back to the day-to-day,
And it might even hurt...
Then... well, we did have a lot of fun, didn't we?!
Remember – especially when we had a good laugh at the Magdala rabbi!
Hehe, how hilariously he distorted the word *collider*!

We gave the town's residents so much pleasure!
What about when we sprinkled pepper under the tail of the money changer's donkey?
Or when we hid the service swords from the Roman soldiers?
Or when we handed out the money we'd nicked from the drunken tax collector?
Or when we sacked the site of the local Sanhedrin?

Now there's a protest that'll be to the local townspeople's liking!
In some places, we even became favourites, such as in Ptolemaida.
It's just that there is a time and place for everything, our Beloved Friend.
Thank You for tearing us away from the context of
A life so hard, ordinary and routine.

There was a lot that we understood; we managed to heal our wounds somewhere
During joint psychological relief.
However, the main objective of such group psychotherapy sessions
Was to return a normal civilian to society,
Help them collectively overcome the traumas of fate

And, with new-found vigour, become immersed in the harmony of society,
Balanced by a century-old history of development.
After all, there is no other evidence
That we have to move further somewhere, is there?
It's all rather terrifying, the fact that we just don't know

How things will unfold;
We might head off on a route that is perpendicular
To that which society politely
Pushes us each day in an ever more insistent manner.
And where is the evidence that it is we who,

Forgetting real life, have to head off into the unknown?
We haven't seen such evidence. Andrew... did you see
Anything extraordinary – anything that would set us apart
From the multitude of closed communities,
And which would give us reason to believe that our fate is somehow special?

No. And nor did I. Nor did I.

Only... You, our Beloved Friend,
Only You have this astonishing quality; it would appear that we are talking about ourselves,
And yet, experiencing our lives anew, we find
Some kind of appeasement, I suppose. By Your side and in Your eyes,
It's like You are not just speaking with us; it's like you're a healer.

That's right, a healer, overcoming the pain in our souls.
This is such rare thing in this troubled life of ours, believe me.
However, this too is nothing exclusive,
To see our community as something more
Than just a circle of friends who support one another

In the recreation of wounded hearts,
For an ongoing stable existence in society
Of which we are a part
And of which we want to be a part; what can I say?
Which is hardly likely to let us go voluntarily.

I can't say this was someone's coherent monologue;
A point of view as to the events that are unfolding;
Rather it was a unified opinion,
Which, slowly but surely, gained traction in our ranks.
And a sadness overcame our Friend.

And the shores in the sea of His eyes disappeared from view...

Verse 20. They're spiritually poor, those play-actors

(63) Have you seen what you cultivate?
(64) Is it you who make it grow, or are We the Grower?
(71) Have you seen the fire you kindle?

Qur'an. Surah 56, 'The Inevitable'

'Tell me, Judas Iscariot[52], about your Path to this day.'
Everything in Sima's story shines through with a hatred for politicians.
Friends spoke of the power of capital and finances.
But I want to tell you about the power of political people
Over human souls and over history.

Everyone thinks that politics is just intrigue and empty talk.
This is the opinion of the ignorant and the absenteeists.
In essence, though, politics is a sublimation of war,
With all its manoeuvres, attacks, losses and victories.
Only I think that better it be politics than war.

Shamil Basayev[53] once said,
'You know, I like politics – it's all talk and no action'.
That's more or less what it is, only with one distinction:
You're not fighting over money, like a merchant or tradesperson.
If you perform your politics right, the money will come in just like that.

I assure you, there is no crazy profitability
In any other field of business.
Of course, I am no king, *basileus*, prosecutor or consul.
These are all political personas:
They are in full view; everyone knows who they are, they are loved and hated in equal measure.

I am a political technician, a socio-architect, a PR-man,
A master of mass-psychology, a think tank and a communicator,
The brain trust behind any political victory.
I devise and I decide where, when and for whom
The sympathies of the plebs and the patricians shall shift.

In my own way, I am the organiser of the love of society.
Without love, stereotypes, traditions and interests
No one will ever truly adopt one side over another
And turn history in the direction that is beneficial to them.
Incidentally, I have no particular need for sincerity.

Everything consists of contracts, compromises and deals,
Cynical, seasoned and fundamental,
Where the nation's fathers are the same merchants,
Only the categories of the goods they peddle are completely different.
In essence, though, we are always talking of power and of money.

You think that any fool could work in this profession?
Oh, no, you need particular talents for this.
But the most important things are high professionalism, experience and far-sightedness.

---

[52] From Hebrew *ishq'riyoth* meaning *man of Kerioth* (a place in Palestine), also often used to denote outlying suburbs or small towns. Therefore, an alternative translation might be *the lad from the sticks*.
[53] A senior leader of the Chechen independence movement and a terrorist.

And excellent reactions. People aren't born with these traits;
They are acquired over many years of work in this field.

It all began when I made my first ad.
Well, it wasn't really an ad at all; what tv commercial could there be in ancient Judea?
We had a neighbour – Saul the cooper.
He made barrels for the wine that the Achaeans distilled
From the neighbouring Dionysian workshop in our village.

You see, a great many things in our world begin from barrels...
Anyway, what am I talking about? All right, you'll get it in time.
You see, the problem was that Saul's barrels were not that large;
Neither the Jews nor the Greeks were particularly fond of them.
It was simpler to have a large barrel, to fill it once

After the latest harvest, drink a little wine while it's still young
And then seal it for a good while and wait for the wine to age.
For small volumes there are the amphorae
And all kinds of other Achaean ceramic vessels.
Judea was not that rich in wood, you see,

So, Saul's barrels weren't that cheap either.
My foolish friends and I
Had not much to do during the summer holidays.
And we liked the cooper, because, in his spare time
He would whittle Roman soldiers for us from wood.

The rabbis would scold him like the blazes
If they ever found these toys on us! Ha-ha-ha!
He would say that he wouldn't do it again
And yet he didn't know what else to do with his hands.
In everything else he was a devout Jew.

Later I would arrange for the export of his toys to Rome.
Why should a skill be lost in the Homeland?
I would tell him not to worry:
'You think the Chinese play with what they sell us, or dress in what they ship over?'
Where was I? Oh yes, about the ad.

So, my friends and I devised this theatrical production of sorts,
Which we played out on market day
Right in front of Saul's shop.
Back then there was no concept of the costly nature of air time,
So the production lasted fifteen minutes.

In the first scene, Rosa played herself,
While Shmulik played an Achaean potter, turning an amphora on his wheel.
Ziama played a rabbi. He went up to the Hellene and asked what he was doing.
'Take a look at the girl,' the Greek replied. 'How slender her waist,
How high her breast and how long, her legs.

All the amphorae that I make are her portrait.
Look at her full posterior and her arms – they are the vessel's handles, resting on her sides.
The emptiness inside, that is the gaping womb that thirsts for the love of Dionysus.'
At this point, the rabbi Ziama would raise his arms theatrically to the heavens

And say, 'I will buy these portraits[54] from you, just don't tell my neighbours what they actually are.'

Ha-ha, what was to unfold! So, the thing with the amphorae was clear.
Then came the second scene, where two greedy Jews are visiting friends.
One says to his wife, 'Let's pour Isa some wine as a gift
From our really big barrel.'
His wife replies, 'Are you out of your mind? It's not matured yet!

You'll open it and, for the sake of one evening, you'll spoil the entire barrel!'
So, they go to their friends' house with empty hands.
In the other couple, the husband says to his wife, 'As a gift for Isa,
Shall we take a little wine?'
'Of course, darling,' his wife replies. 'Take one of the little barrels.'

So, both couples arrive at the house and drank wine from the barrel together.
Then, Isa says to the barrel's owner,
'The wine was wonderful, but that barrel is very expensive.
I cannot accept such a gift from you,
But I can't let you take it away empty; I feel awkward somehow.

Let me pour some honey in there for you.'
Well, so what would the Jews on market day make of an ad like that?
But this is not all. Then I went to see the affronted Achaeans.
(They were affronted because of the amphorae; now, no one would buy them.)
And I spoke to them amicably:

'You chaps might be ancient wine traders,
But you don't understand the simple charms of the small barrel.
Where's the charm, you might ask?
Well, it's in the fact that the wine is drunk faster;
The little barrel becomes, you know, almost empty psychologically.

You sell big barrels once a year, after the harvest.
During Passover, Shabuoth and Hanukkah, Jews drink their reserves economically.
Here, though, you'll sell more often and for each festival
The people will buy a new barrel
And buy two more as spares. Only, they won't really be able to store the smaller vessels.

So, you wait for a deluge of visitors,
If, of course, you place an annual order with Saul.'
And, here, our neighbour's business took an upward turn.
What was most interesting though, wasn't this.
Most interesting was that, for Passover, Hanukkah and the latest Communist Party Congress,

I always found myself with a small barrel of wine free of charge,
Bearing the inscription *From a grateful friend.*
How I liked everything that I'd done!
You see, I had done well and brought benefit for everyone,
And I hadn't lost out either!

That said, that Hellene went bust, the one who made the amphorae.
I saw him in tears with his sad and poverty-stricken family
When they were leaving our parts.

---

[54] Judaism prevented the depiction of living beings; that is the essence of the rabbi's exposure and the discrediting of the jug as a commodity in the eyes of the devout Jews.

Only then I didn't attach any importance to it,
As if to say, go on, you migrant worker, clear off back to Rhodes!

My troupe had become a hit
And our advertising services were in high demand.
The ads brought success to everyone.
I didn't care about those who went to the wall.
But what had stopped them placing an order with me for an advertising concept?

In time, I stopped putting on productions myself,
And I found a couple of talented lads from Bethsaida
To work on the creative side.
The market was slowly starting to appear a bit narrow to me.
What could I achieve in this little Kerioth?

Well, yes, the scope of our work had already reached
The other cities of Israel – Caesarea, Bethlehem, Nazareth...
But it had become, you know, boring for me; it was all the same:
Product – advert – money, product – advert – money.
I no longer even knew who the actors were.

One day, I was sitting all sad next to a rabbi by the synagogue at Passover,
Quietly observing the crowds of festival-goers.
And I thought, almost in disgust, about all those sandals I had advertised.
Benny had made them shoddily, but they were in fashion.
Even the Romans would eat the matzo that I had done a promotion for.

And then the rabbi said to me, 'You want to hear the parable
About the tax collector, the thinker and the woman?'
'An ancient parable, is it?' I asked indolently.
'I don't know, I read it online. What, am I not up with the times?
Or perhaps some wise man, a Sufi, say, told me. There are many of them here...

Anyway, there once lived a tax collector,
An honest type and a conscientious worker.
Every day, he would go from house to house, collecting taxes,
And he saw this as part of the world order that Adonai had created,
Stable purely because of the sanctity of the canons.

One day, he came to a woman to collect payment for the treasury
And she said to him, "You know what, tax collector, I'll not give you any money and don't you
ask for it."
"How so?" the official said, taken aback. "Why do you say that?"
"Because," the woman replied, "I have three children
And my husband died in the war.

My pension has been eaten away by inflation. My eldest has nothing to wear to school,
My middle son has nothing to buy a satchel with and my youngest hasn't enough
Even to buy Soviet-made infant formula.
So, don't get mad, collector-man, but I have a greater need for this money.
I won't give you a thing, so be on your way!"

The taxman was most disappointed and confused; after all, this was the first time
He had ever faced a situation so out of the ordinary,
When a simple woman cast doubt over
The world order and the rudiments of domestic policy.
He felt disappointed and confused, had nothing to say in response and left.

He continued walking and observed a thinker standing on the square,
With a crowd surrounding and telling him something.
He was talking them round with reason and logic.
The people believed him and, swayed, they departed.
The tax collector went up to the wise thinker and said to him,

"So, you're a thinker, I see, convincing and charismatic with it.
So, go on, fulfil my one request –
Convince one woman to pay me her taxes;
I'll give you half of her contribution in return.
That's my offer to you."

The thinker asked the man to tell him what the matter was basically all about.
The tax collector set out all that had happened,
Specifically detailing the arguments that the woman had put forward.
"No chance," the thinker said. "The woman is right.
She can barely feed her own family and you want her to feed me too?!

That is totally out of order."
The thinker basically turned him down. And the tax collector walked away.
He spent an hour in thought and then returned. "So, here's another offer for you:
If you can convince a great many people of what you say,
I'll give you a third of my grand total. What do you say?"

The thinker pondered a while and then, well, he agreed.'
The rabbi finished his parable and looked
Straight into my eyes as if to say, *you known what I'm getting at?*
But I didn't get the meaning straight away and I asked, 'Rabbi,
Is that some kind of symbolism or is there something you want?'

'What do you mean, symbolism, this is the reality of the day, so to speak.
The Romans allowed us to collect tributes
For the restoration of the Temple, but at the same time they refused
To make their own tax inspectorate available,
Reinforced with the spears and swords of legionnaires.

And so, I sit here and wrack my brains:
How can the people be turned toward spiritual rebirth?
After all, the Temple is not merely the construction of a cultural building;
It is our history, our future, the very meaning of our faith.
The people, though, are poor and bitter. They don't refuse out loud

But they're in no hurry to hand over their tributes.
A couple of rich folk came forward as philanthropists,
But then, only to build an electoral image for themselves.
What we need, however, is a proper system for collecting funds,
As, otherwise, the construction will grind to a halt and the Romans

Will gloat and say that the Jews were confident
That you need to have a practical approach to the gods (pah!).
The people, they say, need gods for things inherently human,
And not for anything abstract and messianic.
Accordingly, you barbarians with your culture are just fools.

And you have no thoughts when it comes to methods of state management,

Where there is no place for lyricism, rather a precise system of accounting and financial budgeting,
All designed for specific social and military programmes.
Learn from Rome or the Greeks, how this should be done.
An ideology without legions and fiscal systems is nothing more than book dust.'

In saying that, the rabbi looked sad, but I
Suddenly shuddered, seeing a new meaning to
My work. This was much more interesting
Than convincing another to buy some run-of-the-mill goods.
These were new horizons, for now unattainable but tempting all the same.

I basically said nothing to the rabbi, but decided to give it a try.
Then and there, while the people were still mingling about the festival,
I quickly gathered my best troupe and explained to them the task at hand.
The artists and other creative types looked at me with distrust:
'Judas, it looks like you're taking the wrong path.

Do we really need to interfere
In the systems created by our nation's fathers
And today by the colonial Roman protectorate?
What, were our lives and jobs so bad?
You think we're looking for adventures for the sake of karma?'

But there was no stopping me. I could even sense my eyes burning with the desire.
I am a pro and stagnation would be the death of me.
'Let's give it a go,' I said.
Here's an idea for a theatrical performance.
Come on, come on, let's get to it!'

The idea for the production was fairly primitive, to be honest,
But I thought it was clearly focused on the world view,
The stereotypes and superstitions of the ancient Jews
Who we all are, pretty much.
And so, the herald cried out that there would be a public service announcement.

The plot of the film would be based on two contrasting Jews.
One had handed over money for the Temple and the voice of Adonai
Sounded for him like the warbling strings of musical instruments:
'You, Moshe, have done well and your life be like heaven on earth;
After your death, you will make it to Heaven.'

The other refused to contribute and he heard a quite different voice,
One both threatening and angry: 'You, Isaac, have no soul.
You will live in hell-like poverty,
And when you pass, you will face torment and torture.'
The performance ended and... well, there was none of the customary laughter or applause.

The people dispersed without a word; the silence was deafening,
Like a curtain of dust in a cave with its tombstone moved to one side.
I had never experienced such a fiasco.
Still heated, I endeavoured to encourage my group:
'No matter,' I said. 'The people will go their own way and get to thinking.

The effect of an advert is not always unequivocal and instantaneous.
Tomorrow, you'll see, those fearful of hellish torments and lack of soul
Will head to the money changers by the temple.

My colleagues, however, just looked at me strangely.
They nodded in silence, demonstrating their cooperation and subordination.

It was then I realised that it had been a failure.
Then, some serious men, seven in number, came up to me.
They were the heads of the main workshops in Kerioth.
They were well-respected and reputable opinion leaders.
'You're a fool, Judas,' the eldest said to me.

'A fool and no mistake. There is nothing to say about your cynicism.
Who do you take us for, soulless Isaacs?
That's what you spell out so clearly in your performance.
You think we're indifferent to our heritage, is that it?
And that's why we're in no hurry to finance the construction of the Shrine?

We all loved you; you have done so much to help us, after all.
But you've got too involved. And you've gone too far.
What do you know about the hellish poverty in which your countrymen reside?
What do you, a bohemian lad, understand about the common people,
Doomed to scrape and beg by the colonialists,

The bourgeoisie and the Sadducee collaborators?
Do you even know the proportion of your comrades' income that goes on tax?
When we hand over money for the authorities, for the protectorate in Caesarea,
For the maintenance of all those roads and aqueducts?
You think the Roman civilisers build all that on their own money?

Even the zealot's cross on which he's crucified has been paid for
By the poor Jew from the money he makes from our sparse
Yet Promised Land, dropping like single tears into the hands
Of our children, our old folks, the women and the farm hands.
But poverty is not as bad, sonny, as

The poverty of the spirit, when dumb desperation
Clouds the eyes with a misty lack of faith,
When you, down in the dumps or atop a high hill,
Transformed by tyrants into a social animal, cannot even
Sprinkle crumbs from the table for your Temple, because there are simply none left.

When you bring down the world around you,
To a point when you stop seeing yourself as a divine creation,
When fallen morals, caused by impending doom, violence,
Hypocrisy, drug addiction, prostitution and natural baseness,
Dancing circles around you,

Scream each time in your face
It's not you! You were not created in image and likeness!
The hunger for knowledge and the thirst for discovery is not devoted to you,
For you there is only the poverty of spirit,
In a world, ruled by the Bloodless and Greedy One.

Do you know that, if it were not for the care and attention of the *tsekhoviks*[55]
The socially vulnerable groups of our kibbutzniks
Would simply never have survived. Physically. You understand?

---

[55] Shadow capitalists, owners of underground factories in Soviet times.

What can you tell them about heaven,
When even their imagination is unable to picture it?

Do you think that the penny the poor man
Gives the Pharisees, still believing in you,
Will go to finance the walls of the Temple, its vaults and its windows?
And not on the intrigues and the bribery of the Roman authorities,
The trinkets that Adonai himself probably deems

Unnecessary for rendering the cult a reality?
Son, your cynicism is more dangerous than the colonial oppression.
At least everything is honest there: I'm the boss, you're the slave.
You, though, are trying to manipulate values,
Which we are barely managing to preserve in our souls

For the generation who, in future,
Might actually see themselves as full-fledged people,
Who, in addition to an animal's struggle for survival,
Will also have a place in their hearts to love the purity of the divine,
The opportunity to respect themselves, their human dignity,

The opportunity to sense they are a creation of the Almighty,
But their feelings will be devoted to love and camaraderie,
Not the pain from the loss of loved ones, our Homeland and our future.
First, I wanted to beat you, Judas, good and proper,
For your lack of social responsibility,

But we think you have already punished yourself.
Life will quickly show you that and knock some sense into you, I hope.'
These words, like a slap round the face,
Flew from the mouths of these bearded elders,
And trampled me into the dust of Kerioth.

However... Perhaps it was down to my youth,
But more likely because you, my brothers, and I, had not yet met.
That was why I was overcome with quite different emotions.
Not repentance and not humility.
More a childish sense of undeserved affront.

I'll prove it to you, I would say to myself, I'll prove it
That you can't go belittling me before the eyes of honest folk,
In the sense of public condemnation.
You think you've beaten Judas, do you?
You think you've put him in his place, you smart alecs?

You just carry on living in your outhouses,
In your ghettos, and take pride in your community work!
As for me... I'll prove you all wrong! The time will come and you'll
Say, 'Forgive us, Judas, you are smart,
You are talented, and we did wrong by you, so, sorry!'

One thing I understood clearly, however:
A political ad is a completely different level,
A completely different field, which draws you in with its mystery and its opportunities.
I recalled the Pharisee's parable – that's where there's a lack of conformity!
There, the communicator was a wise sage and not just an advertising executive.

120

I don't have enough knowledge, that's what.
Knowledge about how the world is really manipulated
By these powerful men, vested in authority.
How they achieve popular love
And absolute support for their ruling methods.

Life gave me a fantastic opportunity.
I used my contacts in the Greek quarter
And I set sail with the very first merchant navy, to Achaea,
Where I had been promised a work visa and the post of
Student assistant in a Greek theatre.

Oh, the Greek theatre! This is no amateur hour in Jewish street markets!
This is a genre in itself! This is television!
Theatre is a critical platform for communication in Hellas.
I learned a great deal back then. I got to understand a great deal.
Primarily, the Hellenes were not the migrant workers

And drunkards in the colonial legion
Who, it seemed, Greek culture had kicked out, exported, if you will
To the shores of the Eastern Mediterranean.
This was the country that had devised democracy and the republic,
The most wonderful, well-balanced and harmonious
Social mechanism for politics, economics and culture.

The theatre is where it all happens: shows, courts,
Political and cultural discussions;
Where ads are displayed and Olympians are honoured.
This is the place where all social interests are projected
As concentrated rays

And, if you learn how to redirect these rays,
Pluck them like the strings of a cithara[56],
Illuminate what you need and burn what you don't,
Like the Garin Death Ray,[57]
Then you will discover the power of the political world

And the laws of how and by whom it is controlled.

What I could never stop admiring in a democracy
Was that, to achieve dominance in politics,
You need no violence or force.
Hellas hates tyrants and believes
That the people need to be *persuaded.*

And there it is: a nation without spiritual poverty!
There it is: a system of harmony and social accord.
Not like the Asiatic despotic governments,
Built on foundations of police batons
And on laws that the Hellenes call draconian.

Very quickly, I turned from student to specialist,
Whose services were much in demand.

---

[56] A 12-string ancient Greek musical instrument, similar to a lyre.
[57] *The Garin Death Ray* also known as *The Death Box* and *The Hyperboloid of Engineer Garin* is a science-fiction novel by Aleksey Tolstoy, written in 1926–1927.

The thing was that the key figures in the art of persuasion
In Achaea were seen as the orators –
The sages of logic, charisma and political charm.

My profession was called *speechwriting*.
What, you think the orators wrote their own speeches?
Far from it. All the theses, intermediate material and dramatic artistry
Were planned in advance by us grey geniuses
Of the art of speechwriting.

Every field, be it an advertising text,
Abstract of disputes, speech for prosecution or defence,
Electoral slogan,
National television address,
Or even *Commentarii de Bello Gallico*[58] and *Veni, Vidi, Vici*

Were never composed without our stylus.
At times I even thought that, if the Almighty
Had decided to address the people,
He too would have looked to the Heavenly Secretariat
For the best speechwriter.

You what, Cephas?! No, you're the fool!
You'll slap me round the back of the head next... Quit yelling at me!
I'm sorry, Beloved Friend, but I won't stand by
When he speaks for all to hear
That the shopworkers didn't beat me up back then...

I thought that *then*, back *then*!
All right, calm down and put your hands away.
Let me go, Simon, and sheath your stupid dagger.
I have no intention of fighting in front of my Friend.
And you too... But it's just a figure of speech!

There's no need, Andrew, to demonstrate an uncompromising stand here.
Who knows what you won't allow!
I'll decide for myself what I can allow myself or not.
And if you think I'm taking God's name in vain
Then that's your problem.

Pah, no, I'll tell you nothing! Go on, off you go...

Forgive me, brothers, I am in the wrong here.
I have to admit what I did was foolish.
Thank you, Friend; you are always ready to forgive.
And you, Andrew, you forgive me too. And you, guys.
I am not taking God's name in vain; I am just being figurative. Such is my work.

I get it that things are always like this with me. It's my stupid nature...
I always go too far and don't know when to stop... Forgive me.
I'll sit here, is that all right? No, it's fine. I'm quite comfortable.
What are you doing? You're waiting for me to continue my story?
Are you serious? Hm... Well... Where was I?

---

[58] Julius Caesar's first-hand account of the Gallic Wars, written as a third-person narrative. In it Caesar describes the battles and intrigues that took place in the nine years he spent fighting the Celtic and Germanic peoples in Gaul that opposed Roman conquest.

You are always smiling, my Friend, and I thought you'd be angry.

Aha, where was I? Greece. Hellas.
I was saying that politics was like war.
Only things unfold not so obviously.
It appears that nothing has changed in the world around,
But in fact something important has occurred unnoticed

That will go on to change the entire course of our lives,
That will alter the course of rivers to flow where deserts were expected,
And *vice versa*. That is how political campaigns go.
In addition to opposing sides,
There is also the Great Third Party – the crowd.

No, not the people, the crowd.
Taken separately, it consists of decent, intelligent and experienced individuals,
But, as a whole, it is an ochlocracy that can be controlled and directed,
Like Ortega y Gasset's *Revolt of the Masses*,
And it doesn't have to be a mass meeting either.

Rather the opposite: these are people who, they believe,
Uphold the values of society,
Carry forward the traditions, and think that the future
Somehow belongs to them naturally.
Therefore, they see themselves as custodians and the voice.

At the same time, we see a serious clash between
The representatives of different schools: the epicureans and two schools of stoics.
My patron was Zeno the Orator.
No, not the one who founded one of the schools;
That was simply his namesake.

He himself represented the school of Polybius,
Which had criticised the approaches of that same Zeno of Citium.
And this was not just a philosophical discussion either.
This was a really serious matter, which could determine
The future history of Hellas.

I won't go into the philosophical interpretation,
But the essence, let me tell you, was that, at the same time, in Achaea,
Resistance to Roman rule had begun to grow.
People everywhere were preparing for an uprising,
Readying weapons and singing hymns to Leonidus of Sparta.

Locked in battle with Parthia, Rome
Wouldn't have had the resources to combat a mass *intifada* of Greeks
Were it to arise. It was then that the wise Rome
Decided to put its democratic traditions to good use
And put the matter to the plebiscite

About the role of the government and the paths for the development of Achaea.
An important senator then arrived from Italy.
I don't know his name; being such small fry,
I wasn't let in on such details.
He came to a new wing of the school of stoics

And held a long discussion with Zenon the Orator.
We students sat around, bored and indolent.
Suddenly, Zenon emerged and gestured
For several of us to enter the room,
Where he was conversing with the senator.

We went in and I realised that they had called in the regular complement
Of the speechwriting and spin-doctor think tank,
In whom the patron had a particular trust. And I was one of them.
Zenon, without introducing the VIP there, briefly
Explained the task at hand and asked our opinion,

And if we had any ideas about its implementation.
What surprised me was that, although the other students were Greeks,
And the question related to the attitude to the independence struggle,
Not one of them stopped even for a second to think about the value of the idea,
And immediately set about creating a PR solution.

Now, I am really no patriot of Hellas,
Although I so loved this part of the world, displayed all that kindness by Helios,
But not burned to the ground so mercilessly as it had Israel.
Basically, the task was this:
Making use of the Greeks' admiration of the Roman *ordnung*,

Our school needed to persuade the population of Hellas
That Rome's colonisation was a good thing for the Achaeans,
While, on the other side of independence was the Asiatic barbarism,
Which risked the country tumbling down,
Having lost the union of two enlightened peoples.

A wonderful thought occurred to me and I voiced it,
For which I earned the approving nods of the Patricians
And a smug snort from Zeno the Orator.
This concept needed to be realised,
And the freedom-loving Greeks had to be persuaded

To pay additional tribute for the war in Parthia and Germany.
As the saying goes, trouble doesn't come alone.
The campaign culminated, naturally, in a public debate
In the arena of one of the finest Athenian theatres,
Illuminated by the watchful eye of the Almighty.

Here, the people will have to vote literally with their voices
For the concept by which they will then meekly abide,
Because these muddle-headed ochlocrats
Will instantly elevate it to a level of social value
And they, themselves, will protect it more effectively even than Cerberus.

Only when the Epicureans and the stoics of the old school
Emerged on the theatre's stage, illuminated by the strands,
They had no idea that they were actually
Defeated already, for
We had already warmed the people up with our professional propaganda.

An entire month before this day of dispute,
We didn't sleep well at all and our phones never left our ears.
We drank an inordinate amount of coffee,

Work was in full swing and not a soul outside knew
What campaign was being developed and implemented by our think tank.

What this was was a massive attack on Achaean minds.
At first, we put on three performances based on the themes of
What happened to the Seleucids when they took to wearing barbarian trousers,
The historical drama *300 Spartans Fighting International Terrorism* and
The Worldwide Persian Conspiracy to Destroy Civilisation.

Then specialists gave lectures:
Parthia has not Zoroastriansim, but fundamentalism,
Democracy and Asian despotism – what is more democratic?,
Thanks Rome, for your direct investment in our economy and, finally,
How much more beautiful the Roman eagle is than the Persian.

The news added what appeared at first to be, well, insignificant details.
For example, *Yesterday a man died in a drunken brawl. One of the instigators, incidentally, was a Midian, a migrant worker from Persia*.
Or *The Parthians are fleeing to Hellas to escape their despotic regime. We now have a lot of them. Incidentally, crime figures have now risen dramatically*.
Or even, *Roman cuisine has a predominance of vegetables and vitamins. In Parthia, however, they eat live monkeys*.

You think these little details don't have an effect?
Ha! They are the meat on the bones, the droplets of water on the forehead in Chinese torture.
We Greeks are the most ancient traders. The Persians have taken over all the market trading.
And then we show an Achaean granny saying how she didn't have enough to buy olives. 'How on earth can I eat *our own* inexpensive olives here in Greece?'

Every day in Hellas a hundred happy marriages are now being registered. But the leader in domestic violence against women, according to the latest statistics, is Georgia, the satrapy of the Persians.
Or this: *The German Proletariat thanks the Roman Paladins for the triumph of democratic values in their country*, followed immediately by *The Persian army has drowned the Mazandaran liberation movement in blood*.

And more: *Separatists have killed a thousand Roman peacekeepers in the Teutoburg Forest*.
If you trim a horse's mane according to the Asian Scythian custom, they'll go blind. This is not the accepted norm in Greece.
And so forth.

Other methods work better still,
Such as, when you put on theatrical performances
About love, thrillers and horror stories,
You have to name the evil protagonist Isfandiyar,
Artaxerxes or Alaric.

On no account should you ever call the hero Leonid
Or Epaminondas, rather Lucretius, Tarquinius or Lucullus.
Most important are not these routine processes.
What is most important is the shock therapy
That propels the consciousness forcefully forward in the necessary direction.

We purchased an entire Persian ship,
Hired a gang of miscreants and plundered an Achaean vessel
Of some peaceful merchant who later never left our screens,
Relating in the finest detail how the women had been raped

And the men, too, but, worst of all,

They had cut off the head of a statue of Athena and urinated
On what was left of her.
After that, they took a book by Aristotle
And used it... for purposes of personal hygiene.
(Of course, it was a copy; we had taken the original from the library and hidden it.)

However, then a Roman patrol turned up just in time
And sank the reprobates' ship.
The ship's captain said it was a pity that the Parthians had managed to escape.
If only we'd had a little more money:
We'd have raised an extra sail and caught up with everyone.

The Parthians themselves are no angels –
They would happily chop off an Armenian prince's head,
Or bury the Manicheans alive.
We are happy, you see, and yet you say that.
You see, and yet you object.

The occasional voice of the Achaean intelligentsia could be heard,
Telling us to stop with the dumbing-down of the nation.
That this is cynical propaganda,
Affronting our very civilisation!
We just say, yes-yes, our civilisation and that of the Romans too. Oh, that's no good!

Then, these new analysts, experts and congressmen appear,
This time raising the next question:
Let's compare the military wherewithal of Parthia and Greece –
Will we manage without the Romans to defend our outer limits from invasion?
Basically, nothing resolves problems better than the image of an external threat.

Then follow arguments on those Armenians who have launched an uprising;
What's left of their economy?
They remain pretty much naked and barefoot
Facing the steel hooves of the Persian cataphracts,
And they couldn't even fit out two cohorts by way of a resistance.

No, independence, of course, is a valuable thing to have.
Only, let's look at it from the other side:
What is stronger geopolitically – a large or a small economy?
What is more lucrative – a unified customs space
Or the Roman Navy refusing to get involved in matters of pirate attacks on our vessels?

At the end of the day, the masses voted for us, of course.
I was delighted: that was how we kept Achaea from spilling blood.
That was how the value of democracy was confirmed.
After all, the people voted.
And the people are always right.

Then I departed from Hellas.
I'll tell you now: I had been promoted.
I had no idea that the Romans later quickly and quietly proceeded to repress the people.
They arrested the Epicureans and the stoics from the old school,
They turned their wives and children to slavery in galleys and *latifundia*[59].

---

[59] Extensive landed estates specialising in agriculture.

I met one orator once on a trireme[60]
That was carrying me from Italy to Caesarea.
He had been an oarsman on the vessel for five years, in the upper bank of three.
This scholar, a refined philosopher and master in the art of discussion,
Wept uncontrollably and extended his chained hands toward me.

However, these were not tears of sorrow, rather of happiness
For having seen a former comrade-in-arms.
I had become some kind of ray of light for him,
Which had flashed unexpectedly against the background of those severe-looking veterans
Of the Roman Navy and their commanders.

Wiping away his snot and picking at his scabs,
He muttered as if in a fever, 'Hey, do you remember?'
Quoting passages from Plato and the doctrines of Cleisthenes,
Or the wondrous speeches of the orators of the time.
I removed myself from the stench and realised

That he was talking to himself
Without even seeing me through eyes that oozed with pus.
He was trying to remind himself that
In this stinking and stuffy ship's hold,
He had not become a mere beast of burden,

But continued to be a human and a citizen,
An educated son of a great civilisation,
A great democracy that he loved,
Without even realising that it had played such a wicked trick on him,
When the voice of the Demos becomes a fearful and cynical weapon,

Directing its barbs against its own archons,
Dicasts, aristocrats, strategists, demarchs and orators.
Rome, Babylon or Parthia are always nearby,
To push the ochlocracy to make the right choice
Either by the shimmer of the cassis[61] or the sharp blade of the shamshir[62].

More frequently, though, by the efforts of lads like us.
Which is cheaper and more effective.
They can always say that that's what you people wanted;
You're the ones who voted, so what have we got to do with it?
The people asked and we only satisfied their wishes.

Despite the doubts about my role
In this monstrous mechanism for manipulating human souls,
That had already begun to arise in my mind,
I left for Rome, confident that
The furthering of my career was a symbol of the Almighty's support.

The intensity of my work in Rome gave me no opportunity whatsoever to stop and think
About the moral aspect of my profession.
I continued with assurance to think
That communication and political manipulation

---

[60] An ancient ship with three banks of oars.
[61] *Cassis* (Latin) – military helmet.
[62] *Shamshir* (Persian) – scimitar.

127

Possess a colossal potential for humanism,

As they rely on the high values of public democracy,
The best human creation
In the field of social organisation,
Where we are ruled by the healthy competition
Not only in the sense of goods, but also of ideas and concepts.

Incidentally, back then I was noticed and invited to work
By that same Patrician from *The Case of the Epicureans and Stoics*
To the greatest city in the world,
The best Empire under the patronage of the gods,
Pax Romana, stretching from the East to the setting of the sun.

One of the most successful campaigns
That I ran in that Celestial Rome,
Was the victory of the legal scholars,
Who justified to the people of Rome
That the power of the princeps-emperors

Was far more humane and just
Than the patriarchal Republic.
This was all fairly simple:
I was using the mess and disorder in the minds of the stoics,
Who were unable to put the harm of absolutism into words,

Who were too obsessed with their moralité and the *wisdom of the wise*.
Haha, there was one thing I was sure of: when you limp about
In your search for compromise, hoping to please everyone all of the time,
Someone else comes in and, either by the strength of their organisation or simply by their strength,
Takes control of your life, clearly and confidently.

And control over your consciousness, too, it has to be said.

Everything on our part had been organised perfectly –
First the artistic design by experts, the finer details and the TV production,
Then the launch onto the Senate podium
Of all these monarchic jurist hounds.
All manner of Gaiuses, Papinians, Ulpians and Modestinuses.

And in a peaceful discussion in the shadows of the belvedere,
The foolish Roman man in the street, eyes agog,
Proves to *you* the decrepitude of the republican system,
Harping on about *your* propagandist formulae,
While you disingenuously give him a semblance of objection.

Basically, I lived in plenitude and popularity,
Genuinely believing that my art was *ars boni et aequi*[63],
Until that old feeling wormed its way back into my heart.
I really wanted to get even with the shopworkers of Kerioth,
Show them how prosperous I was and, accordingly, that I was right.

It was with this thought that, in early June,
I boarded the first Achaean merchant ship
And set off for the shores of the Levant.

---

[63] The Latin for *the art of goodness and equity.*

Incidentally, I had no sense of ever returning to my Homeland;
I merely bore my shaven face to meet its triumphant objective.

However, upon arrival in Caesarea, I had the feeling
That I didn't really want to set out on the dusty path
Through Judaic districts toward my home town of Kerioth.
A sense of comfort is often more important even than the strongest feelings,
And the night clubs and cabaret halls of Caesarea proved a great help.

It was then, though, that one thing happened
Which, I believe, is the very essence of my story,
Because, had it not happened, I would have remained in harmony
With myself, rapt in the surgery of society
And the consumption of the fruits of my success.

When you deal in the business that I do,
There will come a time when *they* will certainly appear.
It is almost unavoidable that *they* will not appear.
And who are they? Simple – the security services.
All of these CIAs, SAVAKs, Mossads, KGBs and ministries of public order.

He had asked to meet during one of those loud parties.
I recall that I had readily agreed.
I just had this hitherto unknown sense,
Like a sick feeling in the pit of my stomach.
A slight anxiety that you usually get when you meet *them*.

You know that you have nothing to fear as you've done nothing wrong.
But your anxiety keeps telling you, *but what if you have?*
Do they have anything on me? It's as if they know me better than I know myself.
However, I dispelled my fears and, once the cold sensation had passed,
I entered the booth where he had arranged for us to meet.

'Call me Titus,' he introduced himself, so to speak.
'You have been recommended to me by some very influential people.
I will not keep their identity a secret.
It was the esteemed Lucius Annaeus Seneca.'
He smiled without actually smiling, with his blue eyes and revealing snow-white teeth.

So he won't keep that a secret, but that must mean he will somewhere else, I thought.
Titus appeared somewhat strange.
He had a military bearing, but somehow different. Leopard-like.
He was wearing the uniform of the Gallica Third Legion for some reason,
And it looked brand-new, not like the uniforms of veterans.

He radiated good health, but occasionally
He would be shaken by a peculiar, sudden bout of coughing,
Which seemed to say that there was much I didn't and couldn't know about him.
Titus spoke simply and logically, with not a word out of place.
I rated that highly, as it spoke of a professional communicator.

'You have one fantastic talent that inspires me:
You are able to save people from death
At the very moment when they are walking happily to the slaughter, like foolish lambs.
You are able to prevent bloodshed,
And this is something your friends in Italy, Achaea and Judea value highly.'

I have to admit, I was flattered by how much he was devoted
To the twists and turns of my modest (modestly speaking) life.
'The Empire has achieved peace in Palestine,' Titus went on,
'And, you well know the monumental efforts
That made that possible. You yourself were involved.

Allow me to shake your hand; I have long dreamed
Of making your acquaintance. It is an honour for me.'
I extended my hand, quite enchanted, smiling with some embarrassment.
'However, forgive my display of emotion. Let's get down to business.'
At this point I had become quite bewitched.

'It's not even business, really, just a small service
You will do not for me, Jupiter forbid.
This is something the prosecutor and the sovereign of Galilee,
His Grace, the Tetrarch Herod Antipas, humbly requests.'
He held the required pause after these words.

'And so, my friend, a great danger threatens this peace
And, glory to Mercury for ensuring you are here in Caesarea!
Basically, one man needs saving,
A man who terrorists and extremists are leading to a certain death.
This man is incredibly important to us.'

I listened calmly and nodded in a business-like manner,
Recording the information in my mind.
'His name is Johann, known by the moniker Batista.
We simply cannot find him and inform him
Of the danger he is in.

Your and my profession are closely related in a way:
We both care about the same thing –
Security and harmony in our God-chosen state.
The only thing is that, how can I put it, we have slightly different capabilities.
We are better at one thing, but we cannot do another,

Which you handle so perfectly.
If only you knew how hard it is for us at the moment.
It seems everyone has gone mad; these days you just can't find
A decent person,
To discuss responsible issues in such a calm manner.'

Titus shook his head helplessly
And his face displayed the genuine sorrow of a lonely man.
'But never mind,' the Roman seemed to say to himself,
'We'll manage. If not us, then who?
Who, if not we simple folk, can distinguish good from evil?

The thing is that this Johann is an honest, genuine patriot,
And he possesses incredible charisma and charm.
He is a wise man and a stoic; he is the future of the Land of Israel.
I am forever arguing with my seniors,
And I tell them we need to give Israel more independence.

After all, they do have some decent individuals there.
No one listens to me yet, but I'm sure it's just a matter of time.
Common sense will prevail and your country

Will shine with the light of true sovereignty.'
Titus's intonation was calm but then...

His voice filled with rage
And grew louder and louder,
Rapidly building to a crescendo, until he was basically screaming:
'I won't let you, you leech, drink the blood of the Jewish people,
YOU VILE, DISGUSTING MOSQUITO!'

He slapped a mosquito hard on my knee and laughed out loud.
I shuddered, but Titus suddenly began speaking very fast[64]:
'You must find Johann Batista.
He is being hidden somewhere by a sect of terrorists and thugs.
They want to use his standing

And incite the Jews to revolt,
To bring unrest to the Empire
And spill the blood of peaceful residents,
Innocent women, children and the elderly alike.
Perhaps even on your street, in your home town of Kerioth.'

He paused to allowed to me to catch my breath, before continuing:
'Can you imagine what would follow then?
I'm not talking about how hard it will be for Jewish specialists
To have the chance just to work,
In the Eternal City, but to even get in.

And I don't think these honest chaps deserve such treatment.
Incidentally, I think you work there too, is that right?
It's hard for a Roman to arrange a search, even despite
Our broad network of, you know, friends of the Empire.
That *omerta*[65] law of yours is in effect all over.

You, though, are a professional and communicative lad.
Your task is clear and simple.
You have to find him; just speak to him,
Persuade him just as I know you can.
Tell him that soon Jerusalem

Will have a People's Friendship University,
Where he will be given the post of head of department
Or even dean of the faculty of Israel studies.
I'm telling you that in confidence, so don't you tell anyone, all right?
But the decree about the university's formation is already on the princep's desk.'

He winked at me amicably and conspiratorially.
'You have complete freedom to act as you see fit.
In any case, how could we force you to do anything?!
You know better than us what the score is.
We'll just meet up later and you'll tell me. How does that sound?

It's all very simple – there's no need to build Hadrian's Walls here.

---

[64] A technique used in neuro-linguistic programming (NLP), involving the sudden leading of an interlocutor into a state of shock, followed by a narrative that imposes certain conduct or actions on their part.
[65] The secret code of silence, cultivated by the Sicilian mafia.

Well,' he said with a laugh, 'how about we relax with a cigar?'
I don't smoke at all, but for some reason I fancied it.
'There you go. Wow, you like Cohiba like me?' he said in surprise.
'Well, if I'd known, I'd have brought more.'

Suddenly, he extended a purse of money to me.
'By the way, the Empire allotted me no money for this,
But I decided to give you a little of my own for now.
Come on, don't feel awkward! I'll get them back.
It's only for the matter at hand; you know, in case you need to pay for information.

They're not yours to spend at the end of the day, are they?!
This is a matter of state, so the state should pay. It won't go poor.'
He slapped me on the shoulder, like an old acquaintance.
Well then, so *they* were not so terrible after all.
And the assignment was not a matter of spy tricks and the setting of traps,

But noble deeds with noble goals.
It wouldn't be that easy to find this Johann;
I'd already heard that he was well hidden.
However, at the same time, it was like he wasn't really hiding, for he would appear here and there.
Those extremists were evidently sophisticated conspirators.

Perhaps, though, he was being held hostage?
Perhaps they were holding him under lock and key and blackmailing him?
No matter, we'd had to deal with worse.
And it wouldn't do any harm to make friends again with the Jewish authorities.
Who knows, I might have had to return to that hole sometime in the future.

Anyhow, we'd relax today, have a little wine,
Smoke a cigar and hear new jokes and tales,
Of which Titus had plenty. We'd have a laugh,
Me and those charming lasses.
Where did they even come from, those girls? I don't remember.

The next morning, I felt like a proper lurcher;
I always felt like this before an interesting assignment.
I slapped Tarquinia across her tight backside,
Although it turned out to belong to Sarra of Tyrus,
And an hour later my donkey was already trotting the road

Taking me to John the Baptist.

This was no simple search for a man.
On the way, I underwent metamorphoses,
Which, I think, changed me and changed my consciousness.
I never thought that such a simple task
Would transform into something so important for me, something so fundamental.

Much like Javert in his pursuit of Jean Valjean,
I came to sense a new meaning in my search,
As if behind every *tsabar*[66] in the land of the Jews
There were answers to the questions
That I had been unable to find throughout my wayward life.

---

[66] *Tsabar, tzabar* or *sabra*, from the Hebrew for prickly pear, a typical cactus for the Israeli desert. It also means Jews born in the Land of Israel, unlike immigrants who came to the country following repatriation (*Aliyah*).

As such, everything stemmed from the essence of the task at hand.
To find John and have the right conversation with him
I needed to find out all there was to learn about him and his followers.
Or were they extremists? I didn't know.
However, the picture became clearer with each passing day.

John's persona surprised me more, the more I learned of him.
It turned out that he was already very well known all across Palestine.
Like some mighty elm tree, drawing lightning from the heavens,
He would appear in different places,
Saying things that would shock people and change them forever.

Clearly, the Roman establishment and the court at Jerusalem
Lived so out of touch with reality,
That they had no notion of the true scale of this figure,
Viewing the world as they did from their chambers up high,
Protecting them from the world and protecting the world from them.

Many people even called him Mashiah.
And basically, a lot of it stacked up.
I might be a Jew by birth,
But I had forgotten many things in my distant wanderings.
I had to recover them, to be able to understand and properly perceive.

He hailed from a noble family and I finf it surprising
Why lads from noble families
Needed to condemn themselves to a life of ascetics and hermits.
For me, a simple kid from Kerioth,
This seemed like an awful waste.

If he, a descendant of the families of Aaron and David,
Could become the King of Kings, why would he want these rags
Of old wool? What was he, a Sufi, a dervish, an ascetic?
If his birth was indeed miraculous
And his salvation in the Bethlehem pogrom was too,

Then why did he not turn to the royal houses
And the international community
For help with military force or diplomatic skills
To restore the House of David to the throne?
Clearly, something was holding him back.

I could have organised a social movement,
Found support in Rome and Achaea, hey, even all over the Empire!
Basically, as they say, I would have placed a political stake on him.
And if he really was the Mashiah, then who was Elijah?
And who, the Forerunner, announcing the advent of the King of Kings?

And did he even thirst for a kingdom anyway?
The day before, the Hellenes said that he had called on them
To repent, as some Heavenly Kingdom was nigh.
What is that? Back then I didn't know and could not explain.
However, those words stirred something in me, even though they were retold clumsily.

One thing he said shocked me especially.

It was that *Anyone who has two shirts should share with the one who has none, and anyone who has food should do the same.*
I realised my disgrace in Kerioth
In the eyes of my countrymen even more profoundly,
And all the cheap cynicism of my social advertising.

Later, I learned of a new cleansing ritual,
That John had performed in the waters of the River Jordan.
They said you could be cleansed and repent;
All you needed was to be ready spiritually.
At that time, I had begun to feel that I was almost ready.

Ready to be cleansed
And to repent for my sins,
For my mistakes and wrong-doings,
For the trouble and the grief that I had caused others in my life.
My spirit sang: *I am ready! Ready, I say!*

And my understanding grew stronger
That John was being detained by some extremist forces;
They were hiding the diamond and the sword of Salvation,
So that, for their own illicit purposes,
They could use this wonderful person and national leader!

No-o, I would not allow political outsiders
To get their hands on such a trump card.
Adonai had clearly prepared me for cleansing in the Jordan's waters,
To later present me with a fabulous political career
For the good of society and the House of David.

All I had to do was find him,
Be baptised and persuade him
To escape the chains of the fundamentalists,
And begin his splendid rise
To the throne of the blessed Israel.

And here is where contacts would come in useful;
Contacts with the imperial and colonial establishment.
Oh yes, and *them*, those wonderful chaps,
Would likewise get in on the game;
There'd be plenty of victory spoils to go round!

Some strange news also forced me to hasten –
News that when John came one day to the Jordan with his flock
Something happened that changed him in a most peculiar way.
He became tight-lipped and pensive,
And the Forerunner's eyes stopped casting lightning bolts at the viper's offspring.

Hurry! Hurry! These are evidently competing forces!
Someone could take away my destiny from right under my nose!
And the wolf cub from the poor streets of Kerioth
Would not let anyone get away with that.
Never.

And I found him.
In a carefully hidden cave,

Two parasangs[67] from Ein Karem,
I caught sight of his powerful figure,
Wrapped in regal woollens.

My eyes burned with the anticipation
Of meeting my destiny...
Be cleansed and conquer! Be cleansed and conquer!
Our eyes met.
He smiled.

And that smile as if brought God's grace down upon me,
As if a mist of unnatural colour
Enveloped the land around the Jordan in wondrous mirages.
I wanted to shout out. No, sing. Sing!
Take me, oh King of Kings, to the river. I am ready! Ready, I say!

Such a blessed feeling overcame me
That I could see a host of angels.
They circled me, and yet...
I was surprised to see that the robes of the Heavenly Host
Were really similar to the armour of the Praetorian Guard.

The Praetorian Guard? In Judea? What visions!
Suddenly, though, I sobered up
When I saw that these were not visions at all!
The chief of the Praetorian Guard approached John,
Placed a heavy hand on his shoulder and uttered in a deep, lead-like voice,

'Pax vobiscum,[68] Johann Batista. Shalom.'

The Praetorians rushed to the Baptist,
They dropped him to his knees and began to tie him up.
Their commander removed his helmet and smiled at me:
'Shalom to you too, Judas Iscariot!'
It was then that I recognised him – Titus.

Only now he had become somewhat different.
Either the black Praetorian armour had made him somehow monumental,
Or his voice had gained the ring of forged steel,
Or it was the Bloodless colour of his face and the silvery Greed in his eyes...
Everything was new. Apart, that was, from the leopard's guise.

'Take him away,' Titus ordered weightily (or was it not Titus?).
'Let's sit down and have a chat, Judas.'
He slipped naturally and easily into Aramaic.
'Stop, stop!' I cried out and ran to the Baptist.
'Nothing should have turned out like this!

I was supposed to speak with you... How can this be?'
'Go on then, speak with him,' Titus said indifferently.
My words were lodged in my throat, however.
I tried to raise my eyes to John,

---

[67] A historical Iranian unit of walking distance, the length of which varied according to terrain and speed of travel. The European equivalent is the league. In modern terms the distance is about 3 or 3½ miles.
[68] Peace be with you (Latin).

But they only darted about, like panicked gazelles.

'Remember this, son of Israel,' the Baptist suddenly spoke,
And his voice rings in my ears to this day like an alarm bell,
'Every tree that bringeth not forth good fruit is hewn down, and cast into the fire.'
I fell to my knees and he was taken away,
Proud and upright, like an elm tree, gathering in the Lord's lightning.

'Well done, Judas, mazel tov, you did it!' Titus said.
'I have to admit, I was beginning to suspect that you had become infected with that heresy nonsense.
But you are energetic and single-minded.
My Hounds of Mars (he looked over at the Praetorian Guard as he said this)
Could barely keep up with you in these depths of the earth.

Is something the matter, son?
Tell me this instant. There should be no question left unanswered between us.
That wouldn't be good for you.'
'Who am I after this?
What have I done?'

'You? (Indifferent again, like he was discussing the weather in New Zealand)
You are a loyal hound of the Empire and an enthusiast,
A dutiful subject of the colonies
Who has completed his assignment with flying colours.
And here is your reward. Go on, take it There's a couple more cigars there; that's from me personally.'

'So, what, I was merely a cog in your plan?
A mindless weapon of betrayal and espionage?
Bait, a decoy, a lure? And no more? But we had an agreement...'
'So, who did you want to be?' he asked with a cruel laugh.
'Part of an imperial conspiracy?

We had an agreement...' he sniggered.
'This was no agreement, sonny, it was a plan.
You think I could allow someone,' he went on screwing up his face with disdain,
'To mess up the capture of a dangerous troublemaker and terrorist,
A criminal acting against the Empire and its faithful vassals?

Least of all a little boy, who had fallen under the spell
Of some idiotic, messianic fairy tales.
I've had it up to here with you Jews and your messianism!
You think I knew nothing and understood nothing about
What this lad's activities threatened?

Give me a break, I'll tell you your mythology better than any high priest.
You did a great job, thinking up that One God stuff. Ha,
Don't you think he's bored up there on his own?' A certain mischief flashed in his eyes.
'I couldn't care less whether there's one of him up there or crowd of them up on a Greek mountain.
The main thing is the foundations of the Empire; you can believe in Baal, for all I care.

Remember, son, I don't know what you were doing there in Rome,
But *we* are the ones ruling the world. And *we* will continue to do so.
None of that public opinion and unrest,
No wars, coups or changes of dynasties

Will ever take place if we don't want them and we don't organise them.

If needs be, we'll even mould you a Mashiah and perfect it for you.
But that is only if we decide it's in *our* interests.
Mars knows, perhaps you too will get into a sect
That we'll find useful and lucrative.
But we'll be the ones who take it on and adopt it as an official religion.

What? You think it can't be done?
In Rome? The faith of a Jewish sect?
Son, only priests have axioms and dogmas;
We have practicality.
And the eternal glory of Rome. Like that.

That, my friend, is grown-up stuff and not the trinkets of PR guys and spin doctors.
And you saw yourself as Mars knows who.
Let that be a lesson to you, a cog in the machine,
So that, sometimes, you might think a little about those
Who, thanks to your ridiculous creativity,

Now find themselves tearing about the Scythian fields
Or losing their human image at the oars of a trireme.
Oh, look at me getting all sentimental...
Better still, don't bother yourself about it.
Such is the fate of the plebs: to be social material

In the hands of the world's rulers.
All that you need is a king with a whip in his hand.
And we are that whip. Don't bother yourself; you were always good at that.
Don't go all mushy on me. You see, I've been watching you for some time.
Forget your search for the Heavens and live your life in this world.

Most important, see everything you encounter as a lesson.
Don't make yourself out as significant if that is not who you are.
Don't make yourself out as the master of the world; those seats are already taken.
As your new *idol* the Baptist says,
Collect no more than what is appointed for you.' With that, he laughed loudly and fervently.

'All right, farewell, Judas Iscariot,
I have no further need for you; I am being transferred to Britain.
They say there are these Irish cut-throats there,
Putting the stability of the throne in doubt.
Well then, so I'll have to learn some Gaelic.'

So, basically, brothers, it is for that that I asked your forgiveness
When I joined you. I related it all back then.
Only not in every detail.
However, the essence of my betrayal and pride
Is not something I have ever concealed.

I realised subsequently
That Adonai had indicated to me
That I was not ready to be cleansed and baptised.
Then, my pride and hypocrisy
Obscured the true nature of faith from me.

Now I sit among you, reborn,

And my past days seem like a dream to me,
As if it didn't happen to me
But with another person.
Only... just one thing remains unclear to me:

When false values and goals
Cloud my eyes and tear me away from all things divine,
Isn't this too a spiritual poverty of a sort?
Essentially, what's the difference between this and the content of maya[69]?
Is it a matter of need and oppression, or the illusion of glory, wealth and success?

No, Judas my brother, no.
You cannot substitute spiritual poverty with a lack of spirituality.
Those who are poor in spirit will come to know God's grace and will behold
The Kingdom of Heaven, and it will belong to them.
But others will have to make a long journey.

The difference is that the poor in spirit have no choice in the matter,
While those drunk with success, glory and power
Possess such a choice but they are just slaves to themselves
And the systems that they have elected voluntarily.
A great many people walk by the Jordan.

A great many dip their heads in its cold waters
However, the drops that fall from their faces are not drops of water of repentance.
The words they speak do not contain the power of the cleansing vow.
You know, to be perfectly honest,
We ourselves are only setting out on our journey,

And, we have yet to complete it, since we are all destined;
You won't find the full answers
To the questions you are not asking Me, in fact.
You should be asking yourself and from yourself you should be seeking the answers.
And you'll find them at the end of time,

When you too will be forgiven forever more.

---

[69] *Maya* (Sanskrit) – a philosophical category in Hinduism and Buddhism, meaning the illusory nature of the perceived world concealing the Brahman as the only reality.

138

Verse 21

(203) If you do not produce a miracle for them, they say, 'Why don't you improvise one.' Say, 'I only follow what is inspired to me from my Lord.' These are insights from your Lord, and guidance, and mercy, for a people who believe.

Qur'an. Surah 7 'The Elevations'

This all took place in the days of August,
Which were recently named in honour of the Emperor Octavian.
Once again, we were enjoying the river banks at Capernaum[70]
Which was always so welcoming to us.
More and more often, our friends would recall home;

More and more often, conversation centred around news from the television;
More and more often, they would call their nearest and dearest on their mobiles,
Promising that their creative search was almost at an end.
Phrases were heard such as 'I'll fix the shed' and 'I'll take them to school myself',
Or 'I'll speak with the foreman – that's a man's job'.

One evening, the Beloved Friend quietly went outside,
Avoiding an argument between Thomas and Judas Lebbaeus about
The government's new tax code being more unjust
Than the previous one. He left and the Sea of Galilee
Filled his ragged sandals with a desperate indifference.

Cephas, the Canaanite, and I lazily followed after him,
Simon grabbed his *navaja* knife in the event of hoodlums wandering the night.
Of course, there was no one out there; it was just his military habit of
Always being on guard. He and Cephas were laughing loudly
And waving their arms about, recalling the wine festival.

Later, they fell behind, seeing some large fish
Frolicking in silver against the blood-red sunset.
I continued after my Friend,
Gradually becoming absorbed in thoughts of the problems
That awaited me at home.

At one point, I even lost sight of him.
Only then, I heard a scream full of pain and despair
And I saw my Friend close by, down on his knees.
He was weeping. His fists were shaking from his debility.
And the force that came from that wailing,

Had me rooted to the spot as if dug in,
To the extent that my sandals slowly began to sink in the sands of the sea
That had grown unexpectedly restless and irritated.
I was about to extend an arm, but I sensed
The presence of another, whose breath

Paralysed me and made me tighten in fear.
My Friend, however, it seemed, did not sense what I did.

---

[70] An ancient fishing village in northern Israel on the shores of the Sea of Galilee. Today the town of Kfar Nahum stands where Capernaum once stood. Jesus lived in Capernaum after meeting temptation in the wilderness and it was here that he met several of his disciples.

His eyes were directed skyward
And I don't remember: either it was full of tears[71] or it was simply an illusion.
Or was it that my vision was clouded by a veil of pain?

At first, the Beloved One muttered something indistinct,
But then his words, like battle spears,
Pierced the sky with sharp blades.
They struck the clouds in a way
That made the gulls scatter, wounded...

I will remember those words for a long time;
What am I talking about? For a thousand years, many people
Will share this pain of the August lamentation.
He would repeat these words later, a little differently,
Would the Good, Kind Man as he transformed into...

But it's too early to speak of that.

'Abba! Abba! Father of mine!
Is Your name written in the heavens or is it, in our hearts?
Is it written in light or on scrolls?
I see Your Kingdom through the desert's apparitions
And the depth of the firmament!
I hear Your will in the myriad of souls, divided yet seeking unity!
I draw up the life You have given from the bread of the earth in my mouth and the bread of heaven
in my heart!
Allow us to be like You – to reward and give without demanding anything in return!
Make us complete, impervious to fear and temptation,
Doubt and faint-heartedness,
And, crossing the threshold of Your Kingdom,
Whose power and glory will return us forever to the place
Where, once again, we will
Find our true Father.'

Amen, I whispered, enchanted.
However, my Friend had not finished his dialogue with the heavens.
His call seemed to throw open the door to the Almighty
And through the light that descended from it,
His words shot up like arrows.

'Why?! Why do I have this dull, debilitating pain inside?!
This endless yearning which, despite all the merriment around,
Suddenly engulfs me and hurls me against the rocks of confusion
Of an unknown origin? I feel as if inside
An enormous cocoon is growing, laying waste to my innards?!

What is that? A punishment? A curse?
Simple schizophrenia?! Tell me!
Is there a point to it all? And what is the point, if I feel I am dying
Every day and every night under the weight of feelings
And thoughts that transform my mind into a bundle of nerves laid bare?

The instant this pain bursts out
Everyone around becomes genuinely fearful.
Can you imagine what I am feeling at this time?!

---

[71] 'It', meaning the sky.

When waves of mad yearning burn those close to me,
As they burst from me in streams of terror?

This pain is forever driving me somewhere.
There is nowhere for me to hide, not in my dreams and not in impetuous merriment,
Not in the daily grind, not in love and not in hate.
Why these prophetic dreams? Why these images and pictures,
As if deliberately revealing the gates of hell to me,

Or the faces of those who mere mortals are not supposed to see?!
Or the laughter of the Bloodless and the Greedy, hungry for my misdeeds,
Or a world of djinn, with voices like the trumpet of Azrael?
Is this part of a plan? Or am I just losing my mind?
If it is a plan, where is it taking me and my loved ones,

Now drawn into my circle of madness?
I just wanted to be a simple Jewish lad,
Enjoying the fruits of his righteous labours
And rejoicing in the successes of his children at school.
To what have you doomed me, Abba?

I thought that leaving on my journey was my Deed.
Indeed, for many of God's people, this is the *end of the journey*.
What is it for me? For my friends? Is it just the beginning?
What next? How do You see me before the end credits scroll up?
What else do I need to bring in sacrifice?

How many people can I lose around me,
Who say, "Sure, he's a decent, smart lad,
But there are times when it's quite impossible to hold a conversation;
So much bitterness and insane passion burn away all the positive
In our communication. Are things getting dangerous for us?"

And why do You bind me in all manner of signs,
Portents, symbols and far-fetched prophesies?
I only have to plunge into a serene life
And the latest portent or prophetic dream
Drowns me in the cold, clammy sweat of fear for the future!

Abba! Give me back my *integrity*! Give me back my harmony
With the world around, I beg You!
Do away with this incomprehensible pain from which I am even afraid
To look inside me, because I see
The cold shimmer of Eternity; this is beyond the power of any man!

Give me back the shores and destroy the desert and the abyss that live inside me!
Stop me running from myself!
Uproot the yearning I feel from every cell in my body,
From the secret rooms of my soul of which I am unsure if I am even still the master.
Colour over my fear with the colour palette of a normal human life!

Is that not the path of a simple, Good Man?
Is that not the fate of millions of great guys
From the quiet backyards of provincial towns?
Kill that wolf inside me – the wolf than runs hundreds of parasangs when I stand motionless,
Kill the eagle that soars restlessly in the sky of my soul when I have no desire to fly!

When I am simply trying to get to sleep!'

I had no idea from where that voice was coming,
Which came the next moment from out of nowhere.
I would have thought it had come from somewhere inside me
Had I not been sure that such a force would have ripped my body asunder.
All I did was frown; I didn't even manage to feel frightened.

'I told you that we would meet again several times.
I promised you it would be three times. Today is one of those times.
You want a long and meaningful discussion
About the whats, the whys and the wherefores? You want Me to explain the logic of what is happening?
But then it won't be yours, but Mine and what part would you play

In your own fate then? You ask why you need
This permanent existence[72], which lasts almost an entire lifetime?
I will tell you. Yes, you're welcome!
You want to wallow in vulgar philistinism?
As you wish! Have it your way!

Only there's one problem there!
It was not I who gave you this abyss and the pain of reason.
You decided that was my doing, right?
Everything you have told me originates in you and nowhere else!
So, don't you go asking me things that are beyond my control.

You are right that My will is omnipresent,
But not in this instance. There is much you still don't know
About the notion of *in His image and likeness*.
You'll understand later that it is not a matter of outward signs,
Rather about, I don't know, the range of responsibility, I suppose.

So, freedom of choice is exclusively a question for you humans.

Well, as a rule, er... But there is something I can
Do for you.' At this moment a dull thunderclap could be heard.
I thought through closed eyes,
Or perhaps it was just my imagination,
That someone had placed their hands on the Friend's head.

Someone standing next to him when he was on his knees.
The next moment, my Friend cried out and fell to the ground.
I opened my eyes and I saw that we were actually alone, the two of us,
And that the figure in my imagination
Had disappeared as if it had never been there.

And... It seemed that the Almighty had returned the Friend his *integrity*!
That this was His will and that 'something' that
He had planned to do for the suffering boy.
I had so worried for him! After all, his words
Resonated with bitterness and pain in my heart too!

---

[72] *Existence* is a central element of the existentialist teaching, one aspect of which is freedom of choice. An example of religious existence is given by Søren Kierkegaard, who cites the Bible story of Abraham giving up his own son Isaac in sacrifice.

Then, I heard alarming cries; it was Cephas and Simon,
Rushing toward us along the seashore. And, suddenly...
When I tried to raise my Beloved Friend to his feet,
Cephas's terrible scream burst into my ears.
I looked around and this is what I saw:

Although I didn't immediately realise what had happened,
In an instant I understood that it was something terrible.
Cephas was running, holding the Zealot's *navaja* knife, for some reason.
When he was close, he fell and in such a way that the knife,
Splitting open his forearm, pierced a vein and blood gushed out

Like from a sacrificial lamb, pouring a brown stream in all directions.
The Zealot rushed forward, awkwardly grabbed the *navaja*
And proceeded to slash his own wrists with deep, awful cuts.
Cephas instantly shed copious amounts of blood,
He turned pale and, frightened, fell into an abyss of unconsciousness.

Our Beloved Friend, who had
Overcome the debilitating faint, ran with me to our friends.
In that moment, something incredible happened.
Our Friend instinctively placed his hand on Cephas's wrist and...
The blood stopped and the wound slowly disappeared!

Our Friend cried out And His eyes suddenly revealed
A crazed expression.
As if in a feverish delirium, He turned sharply
And grasped Simon's hands, too and...
The wounds on the Zealot's hands also disappeared from view.

Without understanding what had just happened, we fussed around Peter
When our hubbub was suddenly broken by a dull, protracted moaning sound.
We saw our Beloved Friend fall to his knees,
Look in terror at his hands and, with closed eyes, he was moaning
Like an elephant at the edge of a perilous abyss:

'Alahi! Alahi! What have You done?! What now?! *What* am I now?!

Verse 22

News about Him spread all over Syria, and people brought to him all who were ill with various diseases, those suffering severe pain, the demon-possessed, those having seizures, and the paralysed; and He healed them.

Matthew, 4-24

But when the Pharisees heard this, they said, It is only by Beelzebul, the prince of demons, that this fellow drives out demons.

Matthew, 12-24

'Hold on there, young man! Don't be leaving so soon.
I have been observing your dispute for several days now,
My colleagues and I from the department of religion...
I think it is worth discussing everything in a calmer setting,
Rather than among so many people,

All crowding around the *knishta*[73] and preventing the normal perception
Of a discussion between two intelligent people... Allow me to introduce myself.
My name is Joseph, Joseph ben Caiaphas.
You are nobody, but I am a high priest,
A man who has achieved certain positions at his age.

Future historians will attest to the fact
That we never had this meeting,
But that is not important; what is important is that, today
We need to set a moment of truth,
From which future generations

Will then jump. You have no objections?
No, then here is my first question:
(Only please don't touch my clothes)[74]
You think that curing a centurion's servant,
Peter's mother-in-law and many lepers,

Possessed *from the crypts*, along with others, either impotent or demonical

Give you the right to consider yourself the Lord's healer,
A reproach to traditional medicine,
A wonderful doctor, healer and a kind of Kashpirovsky[75]?
Or are you trying to make us think that the miracle of healing
Was given to you by God Himself

For quite different purposes?
In other words, by means of some irrational healing,
You want to prove that you are somehow a messenger sent by God,
Whose mission is appropriate for our ancient Jewish level of understanding
Of the Messiah, a universal King of Kings and the saviour of our people,

And all other
Foolish and wayward peoples?
Who do you think you are? Let's just leave the fact that

---

[73] From the Aramaic for *temple, synagogue, knesseth.*

[74] For high priests, another person touching their clothes was considered a loss of purity.

[75] Anatoly Kashpirovsky is a Russian psychotherapist who claimed to be a hypnotist and a psychic healer. He enjoyed great popularity in the Soviet Union.

You are, perhaps the Mashiah whom the Jews
And, what can I say –

Many other people are awaiting.
Ambition is a normal thing; most important is
To where these ambitions are directed.
If they are directed towards mainstream politics,
Then, bravo, I'll do everything I can to make it happen –

Your influence over the minds of
The absurd and impressionable,
So they believe in the ridiculous miracles that you are demonstrating.
No, you'll end up being accused of using the
Spell of Beelzebub that you only just received

From the elders who are so inflexible when it comes to the modern-day changes
To consciousness, that has frozen from the fear of disrupting
The traditional values that have been cherished for centuries.
So, the matter is a simple one: basically,
You have certain superpowers;

We have the knowledge of to where this potential can be directed.
You simply need to decide,
Are you in the system of traditional political values
Or are you just a self-expressed one-of-a-kind,
The results of whose labours

Are not needed by anyone and which have no impact on anything?
You, young man, need to decide.'

'May I join the discussion...?'
I shuddered from terror,
For the Bloodless and Greedy One had joined the chat
Dedicated to our discussion of values.
However, for some reason, he had a sanguine and contented appearance.

'But I am always sanguine and contented
When official priests get involved in the discussion...
I don't know how it turned out that way,
But when the priests, imams and rabbis
Turn the conversation to the truth,

An awful lot of space opens up for me.
I will not miss my chance to stick my oar in, brutally and insistently,
Because, in vacuums that are created by a lack of faith,
There will always be a place for me...
What, you afraid, high priest?

Don't get me wrong, I am not refuting the power of the official church,
The official mosque and the organised synagogue...
Oh no... you don't have to appeal to arguments of the primitive...
There is no need to make an ally of me
In rejecting an organised religion; I am tired of all that.

It's just that a conversation started that is very important to me...
Come on, come on, let's continue talking
About those miracles, given by the Lord

In the service of certain political currents.
The subject is old news but, still, given the personae of those involved,

We'll elevate the degree of its importance
At least, to biblical proportions...
And so, little Jewish priest, what is it you're
Expounding your propaganda about to the Young Man
Who, in every sense, is exceptional?'

'Get thee gone, oh, fallen one and get lost,
Faced with the high priest of the ancient faith!'
'Oh, stop your showboating and let's have a normal discussion.
You see, that is very important for the Young Man,
For He is exceptional in every sense.

After all, I tempted him out in the desert,
But, unlike the earthly benefactors,
He did not succumb to the elementary charms of temptation;
And which of you materialistic priests
Could withstand that like He did, eh?'

'I can't see you and I can't hear you! Listen to me, Young Man!
For hundreds of years, this Bloodless and Greedy one,
Based on the errors of our work organisation and dedication,
Will make us out as idiots of an organised religion.
That's not news.

The conversation here, however, is on a completely different level.
In speaking about the spells cast by Beelzebub, we are speaking not about
The resurrection of Lazarus as an evil thing...'
'Ho-ho-ho! Not an evil thing?! Rip out the soul from *Saṃsāra*[76]
And sentence her to flee from divine fate; and that is not evil?!'

'Don't listen to him... basically, all these cures,
All these miracles mustn't simply hang in an ideological vacuum;
Rather, they should serve a specific purpose, you understand?
Now, we Sadduccees have been forming a resistance for many years
To face up to that hated Roman regime.

Why don't you focus your, shall we say, medicinal talents,
For the benefit of the national idea? The idea of national liberation?
How much could your irrational medicine
Advance the struggle against Rome,
So pagan and diabolical?'

'Hold on, was it not for the benefit of My ideas
That I directed this miraculous healing,
Gifted to Me by the Almighty, so that, contrary to your will
There might be a triumph of the New Vision
By people of the Kingdom of Heaven?!'

'Ha-ha-ha!' Caiaphas laughed nervously. You're such a naive Young Man!
What, you think this petty Aesculapianism

---

[76] A Sanskrit/Pali word that means *world*. It is also the concept of rebirth and cyclicality of all life, matter, existence, a fundamental belief of most Indian religions. Popularly, it is the cycle of death and rebirth.

Will pull people towards a true Divine Faith?
Your brother couldn't care less about the idea of organising a society
When he's pulling his sister from illness.

He is simply joyful to be pulling his sister from her illness.
Your wife couldn't care less about a just society,
When she sees her husband getting better.
All she sees is her husband getting better.
You are belittling the Pharisees and the Sadducees...

And they are only telling you one thing:
This is the work of Beelzebub, labelled as a family tragedy
To draw out some legitimacy from another social structure.
And that is all! And it is not, by any means, anything that can be cured or healed...
So, do your curing!!! Only don't go laying claim to some new moral and ethical doctrine.

There'll be plenty of doctors and quacks for the masses,
And non-quacks too. You want to join them?!
Go on, Young Man, make your mind up.
Are you relying on Adonai or Asclepius the Doctor?
The only thing is that I am telling you something quite different:

I am trying to persuade you to take your healing skills
And direct them in the right way.
It appears decidedly convincing
When you do a beautiful job of exorcising
Demons or whoever else it might be...'

'Demons...' the Greedy One interjected. 'You're just incapable of expelling normal, disciplined demons.
You exorcise all kinds of idiots, who throw their weight around
With their presence in a man,
With all manner of haphazard, scandalous behaviour.

Just you try to exorcise vanity, gluttony,
Avarice, contempt for others, ignorance,
Rampant hoarding of capital, Jesuitism,
Foolishness in Christ, imaginary religiousness,
Tyranny, hypocrisy, double standards.

You just try to exorcise loutish behaviour,
Division based on faith, fanaticism, egoism and indifference,
Drug addiction, prostitution – now, these, I understand, are a challenge.
But you're just walking around Galilee and Samaria,
Playing the miracle-worker,

Breaking Divine punishments with disease
And lifetimes, determined by the Almighty...
Listen, which of us is actually on God's side – me or You?
Who gave You the right to pass judgment until Judgment Day
As to who will fall ill and who will die?!

That said, mind, it would even work out in my favour
If you were to remain one of the simple healers.
Why do I need fundamental problems
When the price of the struggle is the souls of the masses? Now, that is valuable.
But your Aesculapian exercises

Actually play into my hands; they speak of God's injustice,
And I have pies to dip my fingers in, thank you very much...
Only, let me tell you this: don't you go serving two masters; it's just not right.
Either Faith, or political expediency.
If you follow the path of that priest,

You'll instantly replace the essence of what you do with a political environment.
I might be a rejected Satan, but I do live in the uppermost fabric.
I have no interest in having an elementary kind of opponent;
Just some psychic, healer and not even a doctor, rather an entrepreneur
In some pretend medicine that has nothing to do with science.

Lying – now, that is my fiefdom. Self-deceit is the rock on which my throne stands firm.
And if You are really so wonderful,
Then answer me this: why, when out in the desert I
Tempted you with a Divine miracle, you turned me down?
But today, you are walking around, tempting

Your patron with petty little cures?
And, every time, experiencing a crazy tension
And stress of the nervous system, and all that to cure some peasant
Who is not worthy of even a line in the Bible?
Is that the miracle that you

Promise humanity in Your Father's name?
You'd do well to get your doctrinal priorities right:
You want to improve the opinion of a couple of families
Or all of humanity? Then, well, accordingly,
You should devise something fundamental

To forever amaze the imagination
Of the people, their children, other people and their children too.
Die and rise again, for example... who did that before you?
Mithra, Osiris and a couple of other provincial deities.
Arrange everything correctly, create an atmosphere

Of sacrifice, put a couple of your daft apostles up to it;
Let them say things about you and hand you over to the Sadducees.
Just think about it – what a convincing show that would be!'
'Something has made me uneasy about what you're saying.'
'Caiaphas, but you'll never feel easy

About our conversation. Now, you listen to this, Young Man:
These chaps, the high priests...
They are the double standards we're talking about;
On the one hand, they built a system to enslave
Their people to Rome while, on the other, they are organising the Zealots

To fight them at the same time.
Their assessment system is merely an efficient aspect of the policy.
Where somewhere they are doing a great job, but in others, they are just hypocrites.
As for You, if you are going to set yourself universal assignments,
Then be so kind as to live up to them.

Don't go wandering about the Land of Israel with a heap of medical charts;
Create real propaganda instead.

You see, I'm bore in Tartarus – I have no decent opponents.
They're all just idiots with these Catholic ambitions.
Remember, you wretches, until Judgment Day comes, it's my time!

And if you fancy getting into scrolls of all manner of rare books,
Put on the corresponding show with all the shocks,
Where your patron and I will both warm our hands.
Well, Galilean, have I convinced You?
Mind you, what do I need all that for?

There'll always be plenty of the sick and weak;
So, go and heal them, seeing that Your Patron
Gave You the opportunity to do that.
What on earth could be more valuable to these
Wretched people than the health of their soiled bodies?'

'Listen, Bloodless One...' I heard the voice of Caiaphas.
Through me, you are insulting the ancient religion,
The ancient faith, using this story to portray it
As nothing more than petty political intrigues,
And not a fundamental understanding of the world.

A perception of how various phenomena are linked,
Rejecting the struggle of God's chosen people
For your own understanding of the truth,
For your own communication with the Almighty,
For your own particular history of the Temple,

The Promised Land and the mission of those who for years
Have been decimated by their enemies, so that we would lose
Our own language, our very image and even our Homeland,
But continued looking for an embodiment of prophecies,
Which should not simply be implemented,

But which should actually be of use to the rest of the world.
Where do you see national egoism in all that?!
For what can you possibly chastise us, after what we've been through
In our anticipation of Mashiah the Saviour,
Who will bring salvation not only to us Jews,

But to everyone who can be called people.
Surely that is our mission, isn't it?!
We don't simply veil ourselves as God's chosen ones for the sake of the privileges;
To a great extent we assume the responsibility
For everything that is going on!

Surely our fate is to be righteous, isn't it?
Surely our national character is a matter of piety!
Surely our moral foundation rests on virtue!
I am not dragging this Young Man into localised intrigues,
Rather into doing the right thing for the good of the people!'

'Ha-ha-a-a! Who do you think you're talking to, Rabbi?!
I am not the Central Committee of the Divine Party, you know.
I am the devil... The Devil!!! The Evil One! Satan!! Don't you see?
If you Jews have an exclusive God who is yours alone,
That means that *I* am also exclusive for you, right?!

Yours alone, only for you, you see?
How do you like that?!
Or are you unfamiliar with Zarathustra's *Doctrine of Dualism*?
I will always be the hardest to explain for you,
The most illogical for determining your place in the creation.

All you little people will deny my existence
But you'll actually be strengthening me; even the Iblis Stone...
Rather than removing it, you'll make it bigger and broader,
So as to – Ha-ha-ha! Pilgrims simply threw themselves at me like stones;
Such barbarism!

You can't privatise God and not take me on board,
For that is pointless. Am I making myself clear?
I say again, you cannot serve two masters simultaneously,
All that you do is either to me or to Him;
There is nothing in between!

And I tell you, Young Man, don't you listen to that high priest.
I am afraid of you, truly I am, because you aren't looking for personal gain,
Rather something on the verge of life and death.
You'll die, but I am simply suggesting we make a show of it,
So that everything base and mean will take fright and jump back.

You are currently walking about and waking all that is base;
You are curing these little people under a sign of abstract justice.
But there is nothing just and fair in someone being cured by a sorcerer
While another is not, just because they were not nearby.
What is the fault of the one who wasn't nearby?

That was Your Father who planted that ridiculous bravado in you.
If you want a Catholic influence, do something extraordinary.
Tell someone to betray you,
Play dead and then emerge like you're alive
And tell them that there's a miracle of resurrection for them! You only have to pretend!

Now, that I understand! Now, that will shake the principles of
A worldview and morality! And how!
Daddy took his son and, there: he resurrected Him!
Now, that is a shock for the ancient Jews.
Now, that is a miracle for me to warm my hands on.

How do I warm my hands? It's very simple –
Any universal deception is a matter of crowds of deluded people;
Crowds of fanatics, idiots and crusaders!
This is really my contingent of overly confident, narrow-minded fools,
Priests with burning eyes and inquisitors!

Most important is that deception lies at the heart of this show.
But this deception is for the good – You will get yours,
Ranks of fanatics; I'll get mine – ranks of the same.
And we'll go together, not squandering on trifles.
That high priest will come with us too.

He wanted politics? So, he'll get it.
Raze Rome to the ground? No problem, only why raze it to the ground

When we can just build a *knishta* right at its heart;
Let's have all of Rome believing in this phantasmogoria.
Not realistic, you think? And what is unrealistic for me? Nothing.

And later, Young Man, out in the desert, You
Asked for a Catholic Kingdom?
I'll give it to you here on Earth. It's simple.
The main law here is divide and rule.
We'll divide all the people in parts, many parts.

Let them forget the One name of God,
We'll give them many names and in different languages,
So that Your Daddy becomes as disorientated as possible.
We'll give them, say, ninety-nine, but the true, hundredth name, we'll conceal
So it is not called or shouted out.

Let the high priest forget any of the names,
Let him tie himself in knots in numbers and abbreviations.
Then we'll give a common, single substance;
Let it be used to assess everything – conscience, talent, labour,
Dedication, love, zeal and well-being.

We'll call it all a universal equivalent.
I think that's a great name, what do you think?
Cheer up, Rabbi, we'll give you the banks;
Young Man, we'll give You the weeping and the needy –
Let them wail and bow down to themselves.

And may everyone forget God for the sake of our universal equivalent.
Let the people dream about this more than they do, the Almighty. How wonderful!
And war! War! War! Never-ending and beautiful!
May God see only warriors, while we'll
Take the pogroms, the rape, robbery,

Annexations, contributions, the death of kings,
The burning of temples and libraries, the belittling of the defeated,
The captivity, repression and propaganda. What lovely words!
The hunger that affects the children of the dumps
And the poets of war and conflict; the geniuses of the word and of persuasion!

Young Man, You just think what
Such a show could create!
Most important is not that, but that, for all human actions
A worthy and well-ordered grading system will appear –
Our universal equivalent, something we can feel

With our hands, in our pockets, our social hierarchy;
Not some abstract statements by a priest
On unnecessary complications and intricacies of one's conduct.
We'll give tyrants plenty and the *Sudra*[77], very little;
We'll justify everything through the law, tradition and international treaties.

So, decide, son. You don't mind that I call You that?!'
Oh, how the Bloodless One's eyes burned!

---

[77] *Shudra*, also spelled *Sudra*, the Sanskrit term, denoting the fourth and lowest of the traditional *varnas*, or social classes, of India, traditionally artisans and labourers.

152

Oh, how beautiful he was and so terrifying at the same time!
And a fierce flame darted between the *knishta* walls
And its walls turned pale from the Devil's insult.

The Greedy One ceased looking like a simple interlocutor;
He had transformed into a dark angel of steel, in all its glory.
That is how his revelation burst forth;
That is how his will ceased to be a mystery,
And there was nothing that could control the power of his voice...

My Friend groaned and closed His eyes tight;
He and Caiaphas had fallen, vanquished
By the fire of the Fallen One's persuasion.
Both my Friend and the high priest began to spit up blood.
It was not within the power of human children

To listen to the wonderful steel king of the underworld.
The Bloodless one realised he was mistaken
In that limitless application of the irrepressible power of persuasion
On the two young men; I, meanwhile, was hiding nearby
With my quill and parchment to record it all.

The Fallen One realised that something had surely gone not according to plan.
He rose up and disappeared over the horizon in a rage,
Contemptuously kicking the bodies of two little people as he went,
Who had become so against his background;
They were the ruler of that era and the King of the Future.

He saw me on the way too, the witness
Of his fiasco, historical as it was in every sense.
He hissed at me in a whispering of the desert sands:
'When you meet the Almighty,
Don't reveal the mystery of our conversation,

Make sure He won't recognise you, even if you ask Him,
Even if He foolishly seeks your clarification,
Bypassing that Young Man and the high priest,
I will disfigure your face with scars.
Let that be a wicked reminder of me for you.'

The only thing was that I heard another Alpine Voice at that time,
Although my mind was verging on insanity:
'Don't be afraid. When I find I need to get to the bottom of all this,
I will bring up all details about what has happened,
And, lad, I'll seek you out specifically from your scars.'

I realised that I had a separate responsibility for everything.
There's the quill, there's the papyrus, here's my body and my brain.
Here is the night, here is my memory and here, the language of storytelling.
Here are my dedication, diligence and perseverance.
And here is Love.

Verse 23. The Three Sons of James of Zebedee

I have three treasures which I hold and keep. The first is mercy; the second is economy; the third is daring not to be ahead of others. From mercy comes courage; from economy comes generosity; from humility comes leadership. Nowadays men shun mercy, but try to be brave; they abandon economy, but try to be generous; they do not believe in humility, but always try to be first. This is certain death. Mercy brings victory in battle and strength in defence. It is the means by which heaven saves and guards.

Lao Tzu. Tao Te Ching, 67

Under Heaven all can see beauty as beauty only because there is ugliness. All can know good as good only because there is evil.

Lao Tzu. Tao Te Ching, 2

'Tell me, Sons of Thunder[78], about your Path to this day.' You go first, James.'
Well, it would be better to tell our tales separately.
My story and my brother's, I mean.
They are simply too contrasting.
And besides, he will tell you about himself in a far more interesting manner. He has this gift...

And anyway, we come from different generations.
The younger ones among you don't remember the olden days,
But there is much that I encountered, back when everything was still...
Well, it's not about the age difference.
It's just that I thought my tale would be easier to understand that way.

My words are a little muddled, but don't be cross;
I'm just nervous. But anyway, we have plenty of time.
Well, what else do we have that's good?
But is this the true treasure,
When you sit like that, reminiscing and thinking...

Guys, in my life I have never encountered either politics, business
Or public service.
You, my Beloved Friend, place that log beneath your head to be more comfortable
Here, let me square it off a little, or your back will go numb.
It's no matter; it's actually easier for me to talk when my hands are busy.

Forgive me for my lower-class speech;
We don't know Hebrew and the like[79]; we express ourselves more simply.
Well, I'll start by saying that we have the simplest origins.
You have seen for yourselves that, when we first met,
My father and I were out fishing.

It's only during international crises that anyone can go out fishing;
Those who have lost everything or have gone bust at the stock exchange.
Everyone needs to eat, so they turn to their grandfathers' methods to find food.
Nowadays, a fisherman catches fish,

---

[78] Sons of Thunder or Boanerges – this is what Jesus called the brothers James and John, sons of Zebedee and Salome, evidently because of their impetuous nature. This nature was displayed in full when they wanted to bring fire down from heaven upon a Samaritan village and also in their request to be given seats to the right and left of Jesus.

[79] In the ancient kingdoms of Israel, Hebrew was presumably spoken by the upper classes and the clergy, while common folk spoke mostly in Aramaic. In Galilee, from where Christ's disciples hailed, Aramaic was the main language in use.

Meaning the simplest of the rural proletariat.

Only the thing about fishing – that's the end of the story;
Well, and the start, too.
Alpha and *Omega* – is that not what you say, my Beloved Friend?
Right, everything started from the *alpha* and everything came to it in the end.
That's how it goes... Well, then, try to lie down like that; is that better?

I'll just hide my knife; you don't want to cut yourself by mistake...
Right, then. About politicians.
They're the only ones who look down on us;
You know, like we're all rabble and electoral fodder;
People of a lesser culture and coarse biological interests.

You think it was only Karl Marx and Lenin
Who taught the proletariat to take pride of itself as a class?
Oh no. We are professionals. Skilled craftsmen. The salt of the earth.
The foundation of any society and its prosperity –
We have known this about ourselves since time immemorial and without that Marxism-Leninism.

We are the creators of those material comforts
Without which there can be no growth, progress or exchange of goods.
We are both the foundation of society and its gluten,
Which glues relationships together and gives them meaning.

It's all very simple – whether I build a train or a car,
It makes no difference, for the owner will come along and take possession,
Or a statesman responsible for the rules of how they move around.
Or a bank will appear to take these things as collateral, and the passenger,
Who hurries each day to work, to make their contribution to society.

I am that Protestant labourer, the Chinese worker,
The Russian artisan, the honest Catholic and trade union member,
Who all, however the swirling waters of history might seethe,
Will never fold their hands idly,
Will never alter the beauty of their work

For the sake of the hunters of easy prey and the speculators,
For the sake of empty demagogues and troublemakers
And those who like to warm their hands on working shoulders.
Who builds a house better and stronger, the liberal or the social democrat?
The correct answer: the professional builder, that's who.

That's right, I understand that it is the workers
Who have often, during historical cataclysms,
Become the social cornerstone for various revolutions.
This is not evidence of our rebellious nature,
It's just that the working people are a terrifying thing when enraged.

After all, one's simple origins
By no means bear witness to a lack of pride
Or a sense of one's own worth.
Quite the contrary in fact – is it not us, the cornerstone of society,
Who are the main bearer of its moral and ethical values?

Only the Romans believe that the slave is productive.
Ha-ha, that's why they are still sitting in their backward

Socio-economic formation,
Where democratic wordplay
Concerns only dimwits with a civilian number in their passports.

Those who rely on slaves are prepared inside to become slaves themselves.
Those who rely on people with their own dignity
Will never lose face
Simply because they are not allowed;
They support, advise, entrust, sympathise and forgive.

Is it not us who will open the door to a stranger at night and offer them food?
Is it not us who refuse to shake the hand of the vain and greedy non-entities?
Is it not us who, hearing a call for help, won't close our windows or block our ears?
Is it not us who say 'here, take it, for you have the greater need'?
Is it not us who love when we say 'I love you' and believe when we say 'I believe you'?

Oh, you ask why I sigh so heavily when I say this?
And why my eyes gaze vapidly into the night
And don't shine with pride?
You see, my history is still to come.
And the entire night lies ahead... Pass me the kettle or you'll go and smoke it through again.

There's something I'd like to say straight away;
I think it's very important, so you give it some thought.
There is much that is tragic in the tales of our friends –
Genuine life dramas
That are worthy fodder for storytellers and writers.

One gets the impression that all of us gathered here
Have experienced such drama in their lives,
That only that high note of anguish and tragedy
Have made us come together.
Like a club for the unfortunate (hehe).

Yes, and what did you think?
Losers, as my youngest son likes to call them –
Those who think about the essence of life only
When it gives them a good kicking.
Who think about God only

When they find themselves helpless and crushed
Either from a set of circumstances,
Or from people's treachery, it makes no difference.
What is important is that, having experienced deprivation
The unfortunate start thinking about

Who is the master and controller of fates.
Only then do they remember God, true meanings and Justice.
No, no, hold back on your objections!
If things had actually been like that, then you would be of that sort
And I would have nothing to do with you. That's it.

I understand, I do, that, as the Marxists say,
There is a reason and there are preconditions.
I see, brothers, that you are remarkable people.
The only question is did the Almighty assign this to you
Or did you choose your own path?

You know, I believe it is most likely both.
One thing I know for sure: you are one of those who,
What is the best way to put it...
I read in one good book that
What is the End of the World for a cocoon is a beautiful butterfly for others.

You are those who see the butterfly
Or themselves as the next evolutionary stage.
What allows me to think that way?
Well, the fact that we didn't gather here to moan about our fate,
And our eyes are burning with a flame of some kind.

Which kind? I can't say for now. I don't know. I'm not sure.
Perhaps you, our Beloved Friend, know the answer?
Or perhaps we don't need to talk about our goals,
Rather we ought to arrive at something ourselves.
Only the haziness in our consciousness,

So overwhelmed by the pain of loss, is something we really don't need.
Life is what it is, guys.
Every one of us has our own drama, not necessarily obvious
But, still, one that has formed our entire life's path.
The people who view the future with a bright sense of Hope

Form the majority, that's what I mean.
We are seeking answers to the questions
Not only because we've received a good kicking from fate and other people,
But because that is the Path that you and I are taking,
Our outlook, if you like. Indeed.

And we still don't know who is destined in the end to come out on top.

Pass me that bit of wood, would you, Philip?
Well, that was like a preface to my story.
I, too, spend a lot of time thinking if there is a difference
Between human Justice and Divine Justice.
How do we judge it and how does He?

Is the same scale of values used,
If the values have come down to us from His scrolls and tablets?
Are we disobedient or just bad students?
Or perhaps we are actually decent students?
Will human judgment ever be even similar to the Eternal Judgment?

Is being poor fair or is it the result of injustice?
Is being rich the result of cunning or is it a reward?
Is it true that I so enthusiastically asserted
That only poor people are the true bearers of moral values?
And that only the wealthy have access to earthly joys?

I began to reason in this way only recently;
I had always thought about it but only during those brief moments of idleness.
There weren't that many such minutes in my life.
As I've already said, we are representatives of the working people, after all,
And idleness really doesn't suit us.

My father Zebedee was not a simple fisherman,
Pulling his nets from the waters of the Kinnereth[80].
My grandfather had noticed that, in his early childhood, his son cared more
Not for the fish, but the boats in which we went out to sea.
One day, Zebedee made a little boat from planks of wood.

My grandfather realised instantly that the design of the little vessel was quite different
From those that the men had made in the village from time immemorial.
My grandfather thought long and hard and sent Zebedee to stay with his brother for the holidays
In Acre[81], the father of the Palestinian ports,
To look at the large ships there.

'What do you want that for?' my grandfather was asked.
'Don't you see?' said my grandfather, his entire beard grinning. 'Take a look at the design
Of the little boat he's made!'
'No, we don't see.' 'What good's a keel like that on a lake?
The lad's destined for the sea and not our flat-bottomed punts. The sea.'

It stands to reason that my father remained in Acre for good.
Back then, the Phoenicians built their best ever ships.
You think they managed that without our Jewish hands? Far from it.
The world's best docks launched such beauties onto the water
That Poseidon roared with laughter at the Achaean triremes.

Naturally, I have spent all my time since early childhood,
Carrying on the family tradition.
How else could it be? Zebedee was a man bred in the bone. He would teach me by saying,
'Son, our town is fed by the port (mine, factory, plant, delete as applicable).
It gives jobs to everyone. You see, your mother works in the port canteen,

Your sister, in the port hospital.
Neighbours, friends and relatives – the port gives them everything.
Love the port. But not just because of the work it gives you.
Go to the embankment early in the morning and look at the ships.
With those eyes on their hulls we see a boundless world.[82]

The port lives, so we will live.
The thread will live that joins us with the world,
Passing through our hearts and working hands.'
Zebedee was right, but the truth was confirmed not through the joy of prosperity,
Rather the opposite, as is often the case.

The Romans came and moved the construction of their navy
To the newly built gateway to the seas at Caesarea.
Acre began to decay. The Romans had intentionally abandoned the Acre docks
To cut us off from the Phoenician influence.
It was a sensible decision on their part –

They wanted to decide the fate of the Mediterranean themselves
With their aircraft carriers and destroyers.
The Phoenicians were an obstruction to them in this.

---

[80] The Sea of Galilee.
[81] A port city in northwest Israel, on the Mediterranean coast.
[82] In the ancient world, the hulls of ships were often decorated with enormous eyes. The Greeks, Romans and Phoenicians all did this.

After all, the poor Lebanese and Palestinians will always
Stand proud, like a splinter in the eye for imperial plans.

It was then that the now elderly Zebedee
Made the only decision that was right for me.
Exploiting the respect he enjoyed in the trade unions,
He got me a job at the port of Caesarea,
The new gateway to the seas for new marine ambitions.

And that is how my working fate began to unfold.
The fate of a simple lad from the Sea of Galilee,
Who swapped the shifting sands for the dunes of the sea's emerald waves,
The proud masts of camel necks for the bowsprits
Of daring ships that tormented Neptune's very flesh.

My whole life, like the expanses of the sea,
Lay before me, far and wide.
Only one sadness overcame me, though,
When I sometimes visited my parents in Acre.
The old port was as if shrouded in cobwebs

And the people there had gradually turned grey,
So in contrast with the blue of the sea.
The port hospital had fallen into disrepair,
The noisy canteen had burned down because of a lack of care.
There were no young people and no kids could be heard.

Only the old men kept up their spirits with their far-sightedness,
Sitting on dilapidated benches, looking
Out on to the horizon in the search for ghosts of a past life,
That had forever left for somewhere new...
I think it was what you could call a depressed town.

However, I didn't have much space for sadness
In my heart; isn't that typical
For a fine lad of my age?
Of course, I would tell my father that he only had to wait a little longer,
I would find my feet, get a mortgage on a new apartment,

And move them in with me; they just had to be a little patient.
'Come on, son, what do we old folk want to move for?
You need to start a family
And it would become cramped in that new apartment.
You have to provide us with grandchildren after all, right? (he said with a sly expression)

You know, new shipbuilders and their little brides?
Better to tell us how Samuel's getting on; has he already mastered
That installation for a new navigation system?
And what about the manoeuvrability of those Roman triremes?
And why didn't the Phoenician oblique sail meet the customer's requirements?'

The conversation would switch in an instant to news about the industry.

My father would instantly brighten up, nod or speak angrily:
'What idiots, it's not adapted for boarding!
They'll suffer heavy losses when taking an enemy ship!'
Or he'd speak approvingly: 'Now, that is the right thing to have done;

In our time, we never thought to use such materials.'

I'd just feel a little sad, leaving Acre, the legend of future crusaders;
I only had to turn a little, grumbling about Why would I need so many pancakes
When I only had a short way travel;
I only had to dally in embracing my mother
Under my father's disapproving gaze.

And then, it was back to the noisy cauldron of the working week,
Once more, the image of the grey, rickety old house
Supplanted by the proud rows of frigates and battleships;
The noise and excitement of a new galleon launch
With the clapping of rigging and the clinking of anchor chains.

The work had taken a complete hold over me.
You see, I had to relearn the new engineering methods.
The Romans, like all young imperial nations,
Ravenously mastered the experience of others
But, in so doing, they strove to create their own, better versions.

Then, after the naval battle of Octavian with Anthony,
The Roman strategists realised that most of the problems
For the navy of young Augustus
Was created by the enemy ships
That the Phoenicians had built.

Their high manoeuvrability and strength,
Their ability to tack through narrow spaces,
Their nimble combination of oars and sails –
All this ensured they could hold out longer than the rest,
Faced with the onslaught of Octavian's triremes.

The Roman naval commanders and skippers,
Casting aside their Patrician arrogance,
Came themselves to the docks and gathered the shipbuilders together,
Spoke with them at length, making sketches and drawing drawings,
Ensuring they spoke with every master there.

They studied everything at length and to the finest detail,
Then disappeared for a while, before returning
With a confident plan of action. Instantly
And, importantly, in an organised and precise manner, they got work,
Simply and clearly setting out their new goals and objectives.

Now, that is management! Those are the right approaches!
That is how you work with people!
You see, then all the workers and shopfloor foremen went to their places,
Scratching their heads and muttering to themselves
And sometimes even expressing dissatisfaction.

However, their eyes were already burning
With a flame that could not be extinguished
Until they had found solutions to the tasks they'd been set,
Until they had shown the customer, proudly and excitedly.
And the customer would slap himself across the thigh, exclaiming, 'Oh yes, Shlomo!

Great work! I knew it, I knew it!

How did you get those blocks... That's... I don't know what to say, Shlomo!'
That was how new shipbuilding concepts came about,
Based on the shared experience of the Achaeans, Phoenicians and Romans,
These ships were destined to conquer all the world's seas.

Everyone thinks that the most important thing in a navy's combat readiness
Is to have a whole bunch of warships built.
No-no, one of the most important things is their repair and maintenance,
Technological improvements
And timely rearmament.

How beautiful the *Santissima Trinidad*[83] had become
After we had reinforced its broadsides,
Changed the rigging and installed a hundred guns!
It was a true masterpiece, but it was not the result of the work of a lone artist,
Rather that of hundreds of master craftsmen, loving their work more than their wives...

Well, about the wives, I am, of course, you know...
Then I got married and my three sons were born,
The foresail, mainsail and mizzen-mast of my frigate.
Gradually, my dreams somehow
Turned from being for myself to being about their future.

It is to these dreams I wanted to dedicate my tale, so listen up.
When the time came to build a large number of
Warships for the naval battalions,
Brigades of colonial residents appeared in our port,
Hellenes, British, Spaniards, Tajiks and many more.

These chaps are all linked by a common history
Of slaves and free labourers.
Perhaps you'll find something familiar in it too.
I'll tell the story and you'll know about my *first dream*.
Back then, things happened like this:

The Romans introduced us to their public relations.
I am talking here about classical slavery
Which for some reason really caught on in the East.
Or perhaps it existed but then disappeared,
But only scholars and historians know about that.

This was the first time we had encountered such a relationship.
Previously, only freelance civilians were employed at the port.
Their working hands were more than enough to launch
A couple of merchant vessels and one warship a year.
The Romans needed a full-fledged Eastern Fleet.

So, in other words, mass production.

Therefore, the managers of the young empire
Herded thousands of slaves from all over the Mediterranean into the docks at Caesarea.

---

[83] *Santisima Trinidad y Nuestra Señora del Buen Fin – 'The Holy Trinity* was the flagship of the Spanish Navy during the Napoleonic wars of the 19th century. At the time it was seen as an outstanding achievement in shipbuilding. After the Battle of Trafalgar, it was captured by the British and sunk.

For the most part, they were (Lord, forgive me) good-for-nothings –
Shepherds, nomads, people from the Eurasian Heartland[84], simply petty thieves,
Or sometimes the soldiers of conquered nations.

It wasn't that the Romans cared only about quantity.
Absolutely not: they demanded quality, power and longevity from their ships,
Fewer losses in battle and a flawless execution of *decursiones*[85].
It has to be said that this was a very ambitious assignment.
Previously, the Achaeans coped well with the task,

But one could hardly compare their feather-light navy
With the heavy rigging of the Roman triremes,
Even though they had absorbed many of the traditions of the Greeks in this.
This crowd of slaves was not rated in terms of their qualification;
It was rather a matter of how many there were.

Every craftsman, be they a native of Acre or a Phoenician,
Were given a dozen haggard souls,
Who were forever hungry and indifferent,
With no interest in the results of their labour.
To be honest, they were basically animals...(Forgive me, Alahi!)

All right, we said, quantity can sometimes turn into quality
Under some law of philosophy or other.
So, let's try to give the customers
What they want, we decided after some deliberation.
Oh, and what choice did we have, to be honest?

However, almost immediately, all the problems became clear.
What could we have expected from such a level of productivity,
When climbing the ropes, secured any which way by steppe children,
Was a terrifying matter, with continuous concerns of breaking and falling from the very top of the mast?
How could you place your trust in rigging and tackle

Made by slaves in a half-starved delirium?
We needed to introduce quality control,
To check and recheck all that had been crafted
By our wards.
More often than not, this meant that everything had to be done all over again.

Our work, so beloved and traditionally honoured by generations,
Had become a hell on earth and one that continued round the clock.
The worst thing of all was that, at first, it was done voluntarily,
For we could not have allowed the quality of our brand to slip
Even in our worst nightmares. That was that.

Why at first? Because the biggest problem
Was not the volume of work done for the same money,
Rather the system that stipulated all-round responsibility
Which was maintained by a motley crew of bureaucrats,

---

[84] A large area in the north-eastern part of Eurasia, bordered to the south and east by mountain systems, although its borders have been defined differently by various researchers. The central notion of the geopolitical concept, raised on 25 January 1904 by the British geographer and Oxford Professor Halford John Mackinder in an article submitted to the Royal Geographical Society and later published in his famous article *The Geographical Pivot of History*.
[85] From the Latin *decursio*, meaning *attack*, *manoeuvre*.

Controllers, inspectors and supervisors,

Responsible for the safety regime,
Plus bookkeepers, accountants and auditors.
It was no longer the total love for one's work that reigned supreme,
Rather the cruel system of fines and *castigationes*[86],
That would be applied to everyone, be they a freelancer or a slave.

And, if the commission concluded,
Based more often than not on the reports of operators in the field...
Hm... meaning skippers and military men,
That a failed *decursio* during battle or, Heaven forbid,
The death of people out of battle,

Was the fault of the manufacturer, then *decimationes*[87] would be applied,
When we stood in the same ranks as the slaves,
The craftsmen of Palestine and Levant.
Needless to say, hundreds died
And not only from execution and punishment;

Occupational safety had turned from a professional culture
To something that people couldn't care less about.
Probably because life had ceased to have any value,
The profession was no longer a matter of pride,
More a punishment served from hell itself.

A punishment that could not be avoided.
After all, what made us any different from the slaves?
Only one word: freelancer.
When you see the grey slums of Acre before you
And the children who have forgotten laughter and indulgence for all time,

You start to understand that the notion of slavery is not linked with property and salary,
Rather with the lack of choice and the inevitability
Of death, injury and poor health.
Most important, the loss of one's own professional dignity.
What can I say – the loss of human dignity itself.

You could leave your job at the port only in theory.
You knew what would follow: poverty and death by starvation.
Before death, however, you would have to experience something more terrible:
The destruction of the very foundations of your family and the lovingly created world
That was based primarily on the standing of the breadwinning father.

Now, just imagine the morals that reigned in such an atmosphere,
When an accusation of guilt was equal to the loss of one's entire life.
Instead of a working fraternity, we witnessed whispers,
Intrigues, informing and undercover operations.
Quite different values were now at the forefront.

Shopfloor solidarity was a thing of the past; it was every man for himself.
The smarter and more successful were no longer the open and the honest,

---

[86] Physical punishment.
[87] *Decimatio, -ionis* (*decimationes*) – the punishment of an entire military detachment, when every tenth man, drawn by lots, would be executed.

Rather those with *decursiones* hidden in their pocket –
Hypocrisy, envy and the manipulation of another's common decency.
The smart man was he who survived whatever the cost, while the fool was the one thrown by the wayside of life.

So, Cephas, those were the ships we built.
Take a look: made from a piece of wood.
This is not a trireme, rather a bireme with two banks of oars.
This is how we attach a piece of parchment
And, there you go, a sail. Off you go to sea, then, fisherman...

Only one thing prevented us from become mere social animals:
Hope. They say that animals can't remember the past and cannot picture the future.
But we could. The one thing we didn't know was how to change the present.
All sorts of politicians came to us from Jerusalem,
Asserting incomprehensible things and too afraid to soil their tunics.

They seemed to be decent-enough lads, only looked like the panicky kind on-board ship.
In the event of a storm, they would run about with arms flailing, crying, 'A storm! A storm!'
But when it was calm, they would sleep in the affectionate embraces of Aeolus.
Why the panic and the heightened passions?
Take the rigging and lower the sail with everyone else.

Or don't be afraid – take the wheel, hold it tight and don't let go.
Or, if you can, give out commands, clearly, intelligently, quickly and fearlessly – they'll believe you.
Actually save people's lives; you are on the same ship, after all.
We don't need you to tell us we're living in hell; we sense it very well for ourselves.

Why do we think they're decent-enough lads? Well, at least they were somehow striving for something...
We supported them, shared with them and empathised.
Only, then they come when they've received what they want and they talk about something different,
About the challenges of our time and about the budget,
Only now they're calm and confident. And they, too, are afraid to soil their tunics.

No, I don't blame them. Quite the opposite.
They gave us Hope, after all, at least for a while. At least for a while.
So, you stand there at the rally and listen to what they say.
Then you approach a guard and ask for a smoke.
You stand there with him for a bit, chatting about this and that.

'How are things, Naum?' 'Not bad, nothing new, Jacques[88].'
'How are things with *The Thunder-Bearer*? You heard anything?'
'Aha (spitting indolently). They say the port is at fault again. Dock Seven.'
'Shlomo again? Will there be *decimationes* again?'
'The deuce knows (lazily adjusting his baton). I'm fed up with the whole thing.'

'They say they're going to introduce a new law on migration. You not heard?'
'It's all lies, Jacques. What would the port do without the immigrants? All they're ever saying is gimme, gimme.'
And, you know, he's somehow closer to me, this lad in his Roman uniform.

---

[88] Jacques (from the Jewish name Jacob) – in the Middle Ages, this was the name given in France to the hoi polloi. From here we get the word Jacquerie, the French peasants' revolt of 1358.

One of my own, from my world. However, that lad in the toga and under the spotlights,
He was a quite the opposite and then became even more distant.

And that sensation put the wind up me.
This is what my world looks like now.
We are all tied down here, with one and the same hemp rope.
The guard, the slaves, the craftsmen and me.
It matters not who loses their human form:

The one with baton in hand, or the one
Whose back the baton frequents.
And all this circulates in the one biocenosis,
In one cycle of affairs and events
In an eternal wheel, like the coal mines of hell.

It is during such periods of depression and despondency that *they* appear.
No, Judas, not your *they*. But those ones.
The ones who alter lives
And force them to change course at their bidding.
The lads with the unusual fate.

The lads who were becoming for a great many the image
Of a dream that became a reality and one that would become a reality in your children,
If you had already left the greater part of your life behind,
But never lost Hope,
That life is actually a wonderful thing.

That's Naum. That same Jewish lad from the coastal watch.
His parents also hailed from Acre.
He had appeared at the port when the
Great construction of the Eastern Imperial Navy was in full swing.
Another offshoot of the shipbuilding dynasty of Palestine and Levant.

True to say, he had dreamed more of a career in the military.
But the navy of any nation is always the elite,
So, even if foreigners were accepted into the infantry, the *Peregrini*,
The imperial sailors zealously maintained a purity in their ranks
Excluding dubious immigrants from the colonies.

This explains why Naum entered the port security force,
Thinking that his talents would prove his right
To the life that he had wanted for himself,
And not the one which had unfolded owing to the yoke of circumstances,
And one which was in his nature to reject.

However, he was never indeed intended to become a military man.
Who knows to where the fate of such lads with the unusual fate would lead?
The involvement of the coastal watch in executions, surveillance and informing
Spawned a sense of protest in him, first silent and dull,
But then one that came out into the open.

When Dock Seven was punished for *The Thunder Bearer*,
He refused to beat Shlomo to death
And event beat up the warrant officer who had tried to force him.
Naum should have been crucified for his rebellious act,
But for some reason the warrant officer amended his report,

Saying that this was a simple argument over cigarettes.
Naum was whipped and thrown out of the service
Because the heads knew the reason all the same.
However, the Romans are often slaves to their own procedures,
So, they could not punish him anymore.

As for Naum, when he handed back his uniform and was leaving,
He simply went up to the warrant officer in silence and shook him firmly by the hand.
They looked one another directly in the eye for a long time and understood what was going on.
That said, by the by, the warrant officer was a Roman,
And for one hair falling from his head, the penalty for the foreigner should have been death.

When Naum was serving in the watch, we all noticed
How his shipbuilding origins
Would often rise to the surface.
Unlike his colleagues, he
Never played cards at his post and didn't chat up the girls either.

Often, leaning on his spear, he would watch with close interest
All the work going on in the docks.
Sometimes he would even interject with a valuable comment;
Everyone would express surprise for not having seen the simple solution for themselves.
We would often joke, telling Naum to swap his *cassis* helmet for a wood plane.

A couple of times he did just that –
He'd look round to make sure no superiors were around, take off his cape, helmet and baton,
Push away a clueless Persian or Turk,
Pick up some hemp and twist it into a rope, saying,
'You can make a lasso; this is pretty much the same.'

Then he would slap the lad next to him on the shoulder, saying, 'come on, make an effort,'
And for a minute, the lad's troubled and lingering yearning would leave his eyes.
Naum would already be back, all handsome in his full uniform, in no time.
For the sake of form, he might say, 'Get to work, you rabble!'
But he would remain smiling throughout. So, there you go.

Therefore, when he was kicked out of the watch,
We dressed up, clean and tidy, and went to see the bosses on the board.
'Would you look out for Naum, see to it that he comes to work with us at the docks?
Look, the lad made a mistake; it happens.
We're not asking for a particular inspection and control post,

Just a place with us on the shopfloor. The lad has parents to feed,
And we can't have him losing his way. He has the hands of a master craftsman too, that's clear.
We know his father too; he's given life to more than one naval ship.'
You know, heads of the board were actually delighted to hear this
And the matter was quickly resolved. They even told us that the authorities had to be sweetened,

But that was resolved too. Everyone loved him. The only thing unclear was why, precisely.
Well, he didn't display any evident mercy or
Open care and involvement.
He never beat his chest with speeches about justice,
He wouldn't fuss over a soul come to grief and he'd never wipe mothers' tears.

He never interrupted his elders to prove a point;
No one really ever turned to him for help,
They probably loved him because he was honest...

167

Although no, he could also keep silent and conceal things.
It was simply that he wasn't afraid to be himself. That was probably it!

Actually, he didn't manage to remain a shipbuilder for long.
After a couple of months at the docks, we began to notice
A fire in his eyes.
Sometimes, he would drag a sailyard with the Tajiks and then talk with them about something,
Gesticulating, nodding and then falling into thought.

Or he'd sit next to the foreman and ask him questions.
The guards wouldn't chase him away; they were former colleagues after all.
They would only ask him, 'Naum, we'll not make it, will we, eh?'
And Naum would reply, 'Just one moment, bro,' with a broad smile.
The guards would shake their heads and walk off.

Don't get me wrong, he never held anyone back; quite the opposite.
If he distracted anyone, he would apply double the effort and spirit back at work, exclaiming, for example,
'Get to it, you orangey children of Spain!'
Or, 'What's with you, you British driftwood – make an effort, would you?!
Or your great-grandchildren will never become shipbuilders!'

The *driftwood* weren't angry, just muttered,
'No way, no way! Why do our great-grandchildren need these troughs?'
Somehow, they quickly and efficiently got down to work.
We sensed that somewhere inside, in the docks of his heart,
He was building his own kind of wondrous ship, unbeknownst to us.

You know, we started singing while we worked. Singing!
The Persians would raise voice like doves about the gardens of Isfahan,
And the Turks would see waves in the feather grass of their steppes;
The dashing German would jump up onto the sailyard and yodel in full voice.
And every time these songs were heard, Naum's eyes would shine.

He was where the song was and the song was where he was.
He clumsily pronounced words in foreign tongues
To the approving laughter and joking of the migrant workers.
They would ask him, 'Hey, Naum, how do you manage to be so happy
And carefree? In the face of all that's going on?'

His eyes would grow as cold as steel,
But his lips would smile. He would say:
'I am the spirit of Flanders! The ashes of Claes beat upon my heart!'[89]
Everyone believed that this was the latest foreign joke and laughed,
But he cried out, 'Long live the Beggars!', jumped up onto the sailyard and looked up to the heavens.

And the heavens looked at him.

No one spoke to anyone about Naum,
Only to say *'Zhaqsi zhigit! Keremet zhigit!'*[90]

---

[89] The words of Thyl Ulenspiegel in Charles de Coster's novel *The Legend of Ulenspiegel*. Ulenspiegel's father, Claes the blacksmith was burned at the stake by the Inquisition. Thyl carried his ashes in a bag on his chest. 'Long live the Beggars!' – the slogan of the Flemish and Dutch protestants who rose up against Spanish rule in the latter half of the 16th century.
[90] Kazakh for *What a fine young man! What a splendid young man!'*

Somehow, everyone gathered around the dock of his heart
In expectation of when that wondrous ship with its proud form
Would emerge on the slipway in all its dazzling beauty.

No one thought if it would be a battleship
Or a pleasure boat but the fact things would change
With its emergence was something that went without saying.
And Hope was always with us
And Hope now never left us.

It all began with news that somehow
Got all hearts pounding among those working the docks.
It became known, from individual words, phrases and rumours,
That some Committee had appeared,
Or it could have been a union, or a strike commission.

They said that straight after three Slavs
Had fallen from the ropes of the new cruiser *Minerva*,
For violating safety standards, the Romans
Decided to punish the builders severely
And, uttering the word 'unprecedented', they executed twenty people.

And fifteen of those twenty were freelance workers.
The Romans said that this was in order to enhance the *level of liability*.
A great many people gathered for the funerals in the worker's settlement.
Everyone was morose and reticent, merely shaking one another firmly by the hand.
Among the workers, once more, political gulls flapped about, squawking, 'A storm! A storm!'

However, the real storm didn't occur there.
They later said that Naum had raised his head
And quietly uttered *basta*[91] and, for the first time, named us *comrades*.
Shlomo's little house gathered together not just Jews
But also our comrades from among the migrant workers.

Arriving the next day at the docks
I couldn't hear the banging of mallets or the roar of the circular saw.
An uncustomary silence reigned.
On the way, I met a fighter from the
Coastal watch, hurrying somewhere. I asked him what was going on.

He said, 'I don't know'. For some reason, he was fully armed.
He frowned and, grunting, 'Sorry, I'm in a hurry,' he rushed off.
Near the unfinished hull of the ship *Mercury* in Dock Five
We met the guys and they told me
That a *strike* had been called at the port.

What is that? It was devised by the Committee,
And the Committee was headed by Naum.
I went cold. This was an uprising! They'll crucify the lot of us!
No, comrade, they said to me,
They won't crucify us if we all stick together.

They cannot replace an entire staff of thousands
Of port workers overnight, everyone understands that,

---

[91] From the Italian for *Enough!* Or *That will do!* From where the Russian *zabastovka* meaning *strike* is derived.

Be it the board's management or the customers.
They need to deliver on time
And they won't get a pat on the back from Rome for being late.

And if they want to kill us, well, you're hardly going to scare us with that, are you?
Death no longer scares us when it is inevitable in such conditions.
That means, they will have to meet our demands;
The comrades from the Committee will tell you what they are.
So, you go, Jacques, to your dock. Naum himself is there.

From among those hurrying cautiously to work
A small group of us had already gathered.
Walking around the repair shop, we found ourselves
On the broad square at the port
And we gasped at what we saw.

The square was full of workers and slaves, all interspersed,
And they were sitting on the ground
Or on their haunches in the Asian manner.
I had never seen so many people, even when the new prisoners
Had been brought in in their swathes.

We pushed the confused soldiers of the coastal watch apart
And sat down nearby ('Come here, comrade, sit closer'),
Instantly asking, 'What? How? What about them? And him?'
A Turk by my side told me excitedly
That, early that morning, the Committee had called a *sit-in*.

At first, the elder comrades told everyone to sit in their docks
But then Naum had come and called everyone to the square,
Speaking heatedly; all the Turk could catch was,
'Together they can't break us'.
First, the guards beat up three slaves

But the workers got them back or, it would be more accurate to say, the crowd squeezed them out.
They wanted to give the guards what-for, but Naum wouldn't allow it.
He said, 'We are not murderers, so keep order and maintain strict discipline.'
Well, that is something we are well accustomed to!
'Now look over there – Naum is talking with the heads of the board.'

'But does the Naval Administration know about it?' I asked and looked back in fear.
'Oh yes,' the Turk replied, 'and let them; we can't be broken.
Tie this red cloth to your forearm, brother.'
People continued arriving through the half-hearted ranks of the coastal watch.
I could see faces across the square as far as the eye could see.

They were vibrant and open-looking; perhaps the fresh morning wind had cheered everyone up?
And then I looked over at Naum...
There it was! There it was, his magnificent ship!
There were its sails playing on the breath of Aeolus!
There were the sailyards, proud and slender like the arms of a ballerina!

There was its bow, ready to dissect the waves with its power!
There were the muzzles of the mighty guns, looking out with a calm dignity.
There it stood, like a flagship, proudly swaying on the roads,
Full of serene power and assured valour,
Alongside the *Santissima Trinidad*, the Battleship *Petropavlovsk* and the *Mikasa*.

Naum's conversations with the heads of the board
Could not be heard from our distance away.
Only fragments of phrases reached us from the centre of the square.
Suddenly, the world seemed to shake from a rhythmic noise
And everyone instantly realised what it was.

This was not a noise at all, rather the clear, crisp step of legionnaires.
In the northern part of the square, a fair distance from where we stood,
The red plumes on their helmets came into view,
Trembling from the marching
Of the sovereigns of the world who know no doubt.

It wasn't that everyone took fright;
The strength of the new spirit had washed that away like a wave.
However, to say that excitement shook through our ranks
Would be an exaggeration, even a lie.
After all, the faces of the legionnaires

Breathed a cold inevitability of retribution from the stronger force.

A centurion with three guards
Pushed his way brusquely through the crowd
And walked up to Naum, firmly and steadfastly
Placing a hand on his shoulder:
'Would you be Noam from Acre?

You and your main instigators
Are ordered to appear immediately
At the Naval Administration. You have thirty seconds
To decide who will come with you. Hurry up!'
With that, the centurion adjusted the sword on his belt.

Not even a seagull dared flap its wings
To break that silence that engulfed the square...
However, Naum was as calm as a cruiser
In the serene Boston Harbour.
'Comrades, the time has come to sort this out once and for all!'

Believe me, it was not from curiosity, rather from some new sensation
That I made my way through the ranks of comrades
And joined the small group
That, murmuring 'don't go, Naum, don't go – you won't come back!',
Moved in the direction of the imperial office of the Naval Administration.

We were led into an enormous hall, in the centre of which,
Bent over charts and rolls
Stood none other than the Commander-in-Chief of the Eastern Fleet!
Timidly, we came to a halt at a respectable distance
Under the watchful yet indifferent professional eye of the centurion.

Naum stepped boldly forward, when suddenly...
'What else have you got there, Naum?'
The Commander-in-Chief asked in a measured, calm and assured voice.
'He knows Naum!' came the whispers from our ranks.
'Shut your mouths!' the centurion commanded, quietly but with authority.

'You kicking up a fuss again?' asked the Commander-in-Chief. He walked over and...
Shook Naum by the hand, sat in the armchair directly in front of him
And, calmly folding his arms, smiled.
'We should have crucified you back then.
You're a Jew – where did you pick up that restlessness from?'

'Hear us out!' Naum said firmly, as an equal to an equal.
'You cannot be indifferent to the fate of the fleet,
So give a thought to the people that are building it!'
'The people? But they're slaves, rabble for the most part.' And so on.
Why and so on? Because, to be honest, I don't remember

The entire conversation. Because my thoughts drifted to another steppe.
And my feelings, too. Because I instantly realised that something important
Had already occurred. Something had changed.
No, I am not talking about the fact that the approach had fundamentally changed to
Who should work in the docks and how.

I am not talking about how the Commander-in-Chief, equally calmly,
Agreed with all of Naum's reasoning after a little thought.
Even I put my penny's worth into the conversation,
Nodding and saying 'Yes, yes, that's right' out loud,
For which I received an indifferent clip round the ear from the centurion.

It must be said that the Commander-in-Chief did add
That 'an uprising is an uprising, but I will not execute you.
But I will give you a good leathering, oh yes. Incidentally, Naum, you'll get twice the number of lashes
Of your numbskulls here. That's fifteen lashes from Rome
And fifteen more personally from me!'

However, we laughed when they lashed us, because this was a victory!
Naum laughed loudest of all, although he was carried away
And it took him a good while to recover.
The victory was in this...
I won't overburden you with the details of the organisation of labour

But the idea was this: slaves were now admitted to qualified work
Only after they had undergone training with a craftsman.
For his patronage, the craftsman would receive a bonus.
And the same if he incurred no industrial injuries or had no emergencies.
And here's the best part: those students who particularly distinguished themselves…

Would be freed from slavery! This, however, was on the condition that the craftsmen would accept their guarantee
That they wouldn't run away for three years. In all the time that I worked there,
I only recall two occasions when released slaves rushed immediately away.
One of them was from the Caucasus; you can never really know what's going on in their heads;
Two others were Turks. They are quick to learn but, for the sake of their horses,

They are always ready to flee to their own steppes.
People even say that they have a fear and hatred of walls!
But how can anyone live without walls? I don't understand...
But this is not the most important thing, brothers, oh no!
I want you to understand correctly why

Why I'm telling this story about Naum to you.

172

There are such people in the world
Who possess a character and a strength of spirit
And who are capable of making the world around them change.
Certain fundamental shifts, if you will, take place.

And everyone who is by their side
Also senses these changes and they change as well.
They even say that the procurator wished
To punish the Commander-in-Chief of the Eastern Fleet for easing up on the slaves
And demanded that the old regulations be reinstated.

And so the Commander-in-Chief sailed quietly to Rome in the middle of the night
And asked for someone to intercede before Caesar.
Caesar forgave him but, it seems that this cost the patrician[92] a fair amount of money.
However, when the Commander-in-Chief returned, he was pleased
And, when he descended from the trireme onto the shores of Caesarea,

He admonished Naum and with affected anger said to him: 'I'll still crucify you one of these days.'

As for the ships... Well, you know for yourselves how mighty the Roman Navy became!
And there was no need to crucify Naum. He worked with us for about a year
And then he lost interest and departed on a Roman minesweeper
To no one know where. Some say he went on a kind of expedition.
There are those who say he perished, having reached Scylla and Charybdis;

Others whispered that they'd seen him in Persia, others, in Scythia.
Others still say that he never sailed away at all,
But remains in hiding with the zealots in the caves
Near Magdala – they say there are such people there.
But one thing I know for sure –

Wherever he ended up, his soul was never at ease,
For he always wanted to change, improve and help others.
So, my dream was that my eldest son
Would become a great leader like him.
Only with one difference: without wafting around the world like the wind.

I also want him, upon becoming a professional and a specialist,
To become a person, around whom others
Feel both happy and strong,
Confident in themselves and of their ability
To alter the order of things, because they have a leader like him.

Hey... Philip, put that blanket back; that's not what it's for.

Uh-huh. That's right. For my middle son, I asked Adonai
To ensure he also became a man with a useful profession,
But (children are always different, after all), one that suited his character, right?
My middle son is a different kind of boy.
I saw in him the makings of an architectural engineer.

I saw engineers like that in our docks
After the Romans took Syracuse
And there was this stubborn old Greek man

---

[92] A noble person with respected social status; any of the ancient Roman citizen families.

Who alone had killed a host of their soldiers and sailors.
Back then, I didn't understand how an old man could be capable of such a thing, even if he was a Greek.

But then everything soon became clear
When an additional workshop was opened at the docks
For the production of all manner of wonderful machines and devices,
Designed for military operations on land and at sea.
Not only that, but new design requirements were placed on the ships.

It was then that these chaps appeared at the port.
Where did they come from? They were either followers of that mathematician from Syracuse,
Or the pupils of demons, or madmen.
Why madmen? Well, their brains are somehow set up wrong.
Not like us ordinary Palestinian artisans.

It was then that I came to learn this word – *engineer*.
It was a kind of technological priest, a leader
Who sees a ship down to its every detail
When it does not even exist,
When you have no concept of its shape and see nothing but pine ship's timbers.

These smart chaps invented such things! Thanks to them, the triremes
Now had three-tier boarding towers and *corvus* ramps.
One even wanted to change the steering oars
For a device that you turn
To make the ship change direction. I think it's called a *helm* or a wheel of some kind...

Thanks to Adonai they didn't accept the idea
And whipped the lad as a warning
Not to suggest such nonsense
That goes against all shipbuilding traditions.
But still the lad persisted.

One day, he took the oblique sail and pulled it
From the foremast to the bow.
The oddball said it was for manoeuvring...
Perhaps this invention would have worked,
If he hadn't wrapped a sheet around the neck of Minerva,

The figurehead on the new cruiser.
They didn't flog him for insulting the divine being,
But they did say to throw out that oblique sail.
But I saved it. By the way, Philip.
I sewed your jeans from it.

I still admired them, you see.
I realised that it was chaps like these
Who would pull scientific and technological progress forward
And, if we Jews didn't come to understand this,
We would remain forever on the margins of innovative development.

Oh yes, our downtrodden people are not at all disposed to this kind of stuff;
We were never destined, it appears, to have a technological mindset...
But I dreamed. I dreamed that my son would become such a lad
Who would introduce technical engineering ideas
Not only to our docks, but as a valuable asset for all our people.

After all, the engineers were mostly Hellenes or Norwegians.
And they were not simply inventors; they were artists, too
And Architects! You should have seen
The porticos, the columns and the overall design
They brought to our vessels – such a sight for sore eyes!

Sometimes you think how incredible it is that the mind of a *homo sapiens* like you
Could give rise to such images and solutions.
These chaps are also changing the world in their own way.
You see, it's not just the industry that's changing, but the way of thinking.
Under their influence, people begin to search and invent for themselves.

Even Shlomo sketched an idea for a mechanism of some kind
That enabled... well, yes, I didn't really understand what it was even.
What was it? Oh yes, I remember – it's called the splitting of a nucleus or something.
'You idiot, Shlomo,' I told him back then, but I was delighted
That such complex thoughts come to the minds of simple Jews.

And who knows – maybe this idea
Will also come to change the world, like Naum and the engineers did?
That said, Shlomo didn't keep the drawing and sold it to some German, I think,
Who attached it to his shield as some decoration. What a barbarian.
He said he'd use it to scare the Franks and the Poles

And he called his shield Radium. They're odd, those barbarians;
They give names to their shield and sword, as if they were living souls.
Let him scare them if that's what he wants.
At least no harm will come from it –
Those Germans are never likely to become engineers, let alone civilised.

And I'm not offending a soul when I say that! Well, all right, sorry, my Beloved Friend.
That was the dream I had about my middle son. Ye-e-es...
But I didn't see my youngest as a person
Destined to change the world and its qualities.

Quite the contrary, he was so well brought-up, quiet and such a mummy's boy
That I saw his future in teaching.
I saw him teaching schoolkids the invariability and consistency of our traditions
And storing his accumulated knowledge in libraries and books.
What is it that children need? Consistency.

Life will throw them the twists and turns of life later.
That is how I saw the future for my sons.
So dearly I cherished my dreams and how happy I was
When those capabilities that I had wanted to see in them
Indeed began to develop and strengthen in my boys.

And later, when they were strapping lads and, then, as young men.
Anyway, I won't stretch it out – my children never did become
Who I imagined they would.
That is because the elderly are right:
You cannot be overly-democratic with your children.

You need to instil your plans and values in them,
Not tolerating self-righteousness, for what society would we be living in then?
Not a society, rather non-stop conflict of the generations...

That's what I thought then. However, to be honest, I never did adhere to these arguments.
Because my sons became decent lads all the same.

And, to be honest, I couldn't have been happier with them.
I might have muttered at times – *so you've left the docks; what new generation is this?*
There's no continuity. No respect for your father's opinion.
But that's just an old man grumbling. And why should I resent the fact
That my sons became worthy subjects of Herod and the Empire in any event?

Let them live and grow as people and as specialists in their field.
They can expect a long life and work for the good of the people.
And my good family name will live on, even after I die.
Oh!
That was what I thought then, you know, when joy for one's children...

It's quiet somehow. The night is so quiet;
Even our cricket is silent. What could that mean?
It probably means it'll be hot tomorrow...
John, did you wash your hands before touching the pot?
Go on, get the water and bring some for your brothers!

Well, my eldest became a policeman.
A good policeman, too. Kind, strong and sympathetic.
Most important, he was fair and wise beyond his years.
Every dispute and quarrel in our district ended with the words,
'I'll tell Aaron!' 'I'll tell him myself, I will!' 'Let's go see him; he'll decide!'

He wasn't really that kind. He could dust down a scoundrel and no mistake!
I remember the bruising he gave Shmulik for beating up his wife!
'This is for you, Shmulik,' he said to him, 'and for the sake of your children.'
Shmulik yelled back: 'I'll get you for this!', but later
Sat Aaron next to the rabbi at his silver wedding anniversary, the most honoured place.

Oh, and how the criminals feared him!
They would keep a good parasang from our block.
My middle one, Moshe, became a doctor and a surgeon.
Also an architect of sorts.
Only of the human body.

And my national pride didn't suffer,
Because the Romans at first didn't trust him;
I mean, a Jew becoming a doctor? Hadrian's Wall would sprout legs and walk
Before the son of a camel herder became a healer.
But he changed this opinion and, I hope, for good.

Now the procurator's secretary, for every trifle,
Runs straight to Ephraim. And Ephraim, by the way, is a pupil of my Moshe.
So there you go.
My youngest, Isaac, was initially a good-for-nothing lazy bones.
I couldn't even pronounce the words *rock musician*.

For a long time, my better half and I battled with him to come to his senses.
However, when we saw his posters and realised how people love and listen to him,
How the entire town sang his songs to themselves, we understood
That our boy was talented. Evidently, Adonai had determined his path.
After all, he glorified the Zebedee family; how could we not feel pride?

I realised then: if it is your destiny to change people
And their lives for the better, it doesn't matter if you're a docker or a police sergeant.
It turns out that my dream had indeed come true.
It turns out that the Almighty had heeded my nightly prayers;
My boys were growing and the world, prepared to change for the better,

Was awaiting my lads, laying prostrate at their feet...

So immersed I was in the sensation of my happiness
That I proved ill-prepared for that bitter day
When it all happened.
It was a cool, sunny morning,
A time when the persistent Caesarean flies

Have yet to start pestering the people rushing to work.

Now I wonder if I had had a chance to do things differently
And avoid what followed.
Perhaps I was at fault for it all – my stubbornness, stupidity
Short-sightedness and excessive pride?
Most important, was it logical, what happened,

Or was there an element of chance in it?
After all, not everyone has to face a test such as this.
Not everyone has to face such a categorical choice.
Not everyone is fated to experience such a thing, but it's something else that's important –
Then carry on living, going over the events in one's mind.

I'll get back to my story; we can discuss everything
Later, if you want to, of course.
Or perhaps you'll just judge me and say,
'You, you old blockhead, you've let your bird of happiness go
For the sake of some incomprehensible principles and convictions. You only have yourself to
blame for it all.'

Anyway, back to that wonderful Caesarean morning.
It was particularly happy for me, because,
On that day, we had decided to celebrate an event
Which, so I was convinced, was evidence
Of the highest divine justice

In relation to me, my family and all my dreams associated with it.
On the day before, my middle son Moshe received a quite wonderful gift.
He had cured the seriously-ill daughter of the procurator's secretary.
For two long months, my son never left the bedside of that poor girl,
But he finally defeated that vile disease that had clung so long to her young body.

The proud patrician had wept when he saw his child,
Seeing the sun shimmering on her cheeks and sparkling in her eyes.
He embraced Moshe and said, 'Forgive me, Moshe, for earlier
Not believing in you and for the way I treated you. You see, only my wife believed in you
While I was lost and believed that no Jew could

Know the depths of the divine craft of Aesculapius.
My wife and you emerged victorious while I, in my patrician swagger
Had been led into clouded thoughts by Jupiter,
Punishing me with madness and faithlessness.

177

Forgive me. As a sign of my remorse,

Take that new whaler that sits at the docks
And was made by master craftsmen for my amusement.
You know I am a keen fisherman and that is why the boat was made
According to my carefully planned design.
That is why it turned out so handsome!'

My son began to refuse, saying it was wrong
For a commoner to possess such riches:
'Why give me a whaleboat when I am not a fisherman at all?'
'Don't you worry, son. You're the son of a shipbuilder, after all.
Your dad will see the gift for what it is. I just wish every happiness
Not only to you but to your family as well.'

Moshe left the secretary, thinking that *his noble sir* would come to his senses
And keep his whaler for himself; it was such an expensive thing!
Not even Herod's pleasure cruisers looked quite as wonderful,
Not to mention whatever the simple Jews might have had.
But the secretary had not tossed idle words to the wind

And the next morning, moored at the little jetty opposite our house
Was that proud-looking little seabird,
The whaler *Lucretia* (the secretary had so named it in honour of his daughter).
As a specialist, I couldn't take my eyes off it;
I could see the hand of the Achaean; yes, we still had a while to go to catch them up.

Joy is particularly sweet when it is unexpected.
The Roman was right – I really did appreciate the gift for what it was worth.
In my eyes it appeared to symbolise that
I had raised decent sons and for the good of society,
And so I was overcome with joy and pride.

But that was not the only thing that made the occasion the brightest ever.
Moshe and I were standing on the shore when, from round the corner
Came a group of Roman soldiers in full dress.
They were being led a stately-looking warrior.
I took a closer look and, would you believe it? Were my eyes deceiving me?

It was my very own Aaron, so imposing in his military uniform!
So, how... how did he find himself among the Romans?
'Dad, I wanted to surprise you,' my eldest son
Said with a smile and looking embarrassed at the same time.
'My dream came true... An exceptional case, of course,

But... I was accepted into the Imperial Army.'
Moshe and I, looking apprehensively at the soldiers,
Jumped about like children around Aaron.
'But how?! And what a uniform!
But they don't take our sort, right? How did you pull that off? Have you told Mum?'

'That's right, dad, they don't take our sort, but there are exceptions.
And these guys are my friends, my *contubernium*[93].'

---

[93] Contubernium (Latin) – meaning *tenting together*, is the smallest organised unit of soldiers in the Roman Army, consisting of eight or ten soldiers.

'Oh! You're an officer!' 'No, no, just the *decanus*[94],
A bit like a prefect, I suppose, the first among equals.
It's not even a title, really...'

Ooh-la-la! What did I care about all these finer points of subordination?!
'Dad, I'm now a full-fledged soldier of the Empire and a citizen of Rome,
And this, in sixteen years or so, might give me the chance
To retire and receive a plot of land
Somewhere in the expanses of Europe...'

'Oh, son, what joy!
Moshe and I were just about to put this gift to the test
And, just like in the olden days, like our forefathers, to go fishing,
And catch something for a modest dinner.
Why don't you let the lads go until the evening and then they can join us at the table!'

Aaron hadn't yet managed to let his colleagues go and admire the whaler,
When a black motorcycle of my youngest, Isaac, drove onto the jetty.
And it wasn't just Isaac gracing us with his presence!
A beautiful girl was behind him, her arms around his waist,
Smiling modestly from under her lashes.

'Dad, I'd like you to meet Gila, my bride!
If you gave your blessing, I'd be the happiest man on earth, no...'
I threw him an affected look of sternness and said,
'No, no, young man – you'll ask this evening, before me and mum.
For now, say goodbye to Gila until evening; we're going to catch fish

For a feast for the soul. Oh, glory to You, Adonai, we have something to celebrate!'

Brothers, do I need to tell you that in those minutes, I was not a man,
Rather a bird, soaring over the sea's waves?
Do I need to tell you that the colours that day were brighter
Than any I had seen in my life, not before and, unfortunately, not after?
How beautifully the Almighty makes apogees

That then become a trial!

We caught a good deal of fish that day,
Sufficient to feed the entire family, guests and my son's *contubernium*.
The spray from the waves, bright and radiant,
Interspersed the words and phrases of the conversation
That so joyously flowed between my sons and me.

We didn't notice the storm clouds that had gathered over our whaler.
It wasn't actually a storm cloud at all, rather the shadow of a coastguard patrol vessel,
Which had approach from the starboard side. It sounded its siren, telling us to stop.
Heavily armoured, the boat was in such contrast to our happiness
That I couldn't help but feel a wave of anxiety in my heart. And for good reason.

The boat came closer still and the captain leaned over to us.
However, I noticed a more distinguished bird, lounging
Behind the trierarch[95] in a comfortable chair,

---

[94] *Decanus* (Latin) – head of the unit.

[95] *Trierarch* (Latin) – the commanding officer of a trireme.

With an extremely displeased look on his face,
As if he was seeing something utterly obscene.

'Who are you? What is the reason for you being in port waters?'
The boat's captain asked in a cold voice
And it seemed to me that he looked back at the distinguished figure
Behind him, as he asked this; personally he didn't seem particularly interested in
Who or what we were; he was just fulfilling orders.

Fortunately, Aaron, although he had removed his uniform, acted clearly and in military fashion,
Saluting and reporting what was what,
That we were simply out fishing. This was a private boat, our intentions were peaceful and we were civilians,
That we were residents of Caesarea and all our documents were in order,
So, mister Trierarch, allow us to move on.

The captain was satisfied with how my son had conducted himself and, with a salute,
Allowed us to continue on our way.
However, at that moment, the patrician interjected from his comfortable armchair.
Something wicked flashed in his eyes.
With an unexpected energy, he jumped up and ran to the side.

'A private vessel, you say? And where did an old hooknose like you
Get your hands on such a whaleboat? Stolen, I suppose? I don't ever recall
Any of the indigenous people having such a bird
In their private ownership.'
There was something ominous in the way he moved his fat fingers.

'Ora maritima[96], sir...' Aaron was about to begin, but the patrician
Barked back at him: 'Shut your mouth, private! This boat is registered
In the name of James of Zebedee, is that right? Let him do the answering!
How did you get your hands on this vessel? Who supplied it to you
And for what purpose? And for what is this fish for?'

'Senor, it's a simple fishing trip. The boat was given to me and my son Moshe
By the procurator's secretary himself. You must know him...'
'Of course I do!' the prefect roared for some reason. 'I also know that,
According to the coastal regulations
It is forbidden in a state of emergency

For high-speed boats to be provided to the indigenous peoples.
This is a gross violation and the vessel is subject to seizure
And then, by court order, to confiscation in favour of the coastal prefecture!'
He ended on that dramatic note and returned to his chair,
Nodding to the captain to act on his order.

We were dumbstruck, as if a bolt of thunder had come down upon us.
What state of emergency was he talking about and why did we know nothing about it?!
The captain of the patrol boat was himself taken aback by this turn of events.
He called Aaron over to one side and began talking to him quietly.
The distinguished man darkened and his jaw began to tremble.

We only heard the captain's last phrase:
'You, guys, do as you are told

---

[96] *Ora maritima* (Latin) – coastal prefect, one of the highest ranks of officer in the Ancient Roman Army.

180

Everything will work itself out. He'll scream and shout and then he'll calm down.
It'll be fine, believe me.
You just crossed his path. It happens.'

At that moment, two ladies fluttered out from the cabin out onto the deck,
And exclaimed with affected voices, 'oh, what a lovely little boat' and 'oh, how slender;
Will the old man let us ride it for a while?'
It was then that I decided to approach the prefect myself (Isaac followed behind me) –
Two grown-up men could always reach sensible agreement.

'Senor Prefect, but we haven't violated any regulations;
This is nothing but an innocent fishing trip. My son here was accepted into the army
And we are celebrating. Why don't you join us this evening?'
The ladies then said, 'Oh, Lucius, we can just see you
Chewing matzo and that lovely aromatic fish, yuk!' And they spluttered with laughter.

The prefect suddenly roared and, spitting filthy words,
He rushed at me as if I were some impish youth:
'You little mother..., you little bastard, you ought to know your place!
You...' And so on, with other obscenities not for your ears.
A cold anger shook within me.

I am a working-class man and I've heard all manner of things at work.
And my bosses have had to give me a dressing down at times,
But never before ladies and my sons
Had I been so insulted with
What could not even be called a speech.

However, I was experienced enough not to flare up,
So I said in a composed tone, 'Come now, Senor,
That is hardly befitting a *caballero* before ladies and children, is it not?
I have every respect for you and your Emperor...'
There and then, sparks flew from my eyes

As I received such a shattering slap from the Roman
That the sun faded and tears rose up.
Everything slowed, like in the films, and was split into long frames.
Things were in such slow motion that I saw in great detail
The *navaja* blade in Isaac's slender hand.

He thrust his arm forward
But only managed to cut the capacious toga of the patrician
And lightly scratch the hand that had slapped me.
Soldiers rushed upon us and pressed our faces to the deck.
Oh, the screaming and shouting that then ensued!

I saw them strike my Isaac with the butt of an arquebus
Before I too was knocked out cold in the same way a moment later.
I awoke in the dungeon of the coastal prefecture
Sharing a cell with some criminal rabble. Isaac wasn't there.
I imagined remembering that I had simply nodded off out fishing

And that I had had this nightmare,
Which simply had no place
In the vibrant colours of that wonderful day
When, naïvely, I had decided that all my dreams had come to fruition
And that that was all down to my correct path through life.

Then, however, everything came crashing down in an unstoppable landslide,
Down and down, away from the regular logic of life.
Just as life had previously, day by day, accumulated droplets of positivity,
It was now pouring out irreversibly into a bottomless well,
And nothing could reverse its course.

Evidently, it was already evening when Aaron came to the bars of the cell.
His colleagues had let him in, although, I sensed, it had not been easy.
I said to him, 'Get to the truth of the matter,
For there is no state of emergency
That would have restricted fishing, that's for one.

As for Isaac, use all your contacts, and get Moshe to do the same,
To ask for leniency,
And let's give that damned boat to the prefect,
Maybe that will be the end of it, eh?
Get recommendations at the docks, too. There are plenty of people who would speak up for us.'

Aaron laughed ominously and somehow angrily and said,
'Dad, the boat has already been confiscated anyway.
And the charge is a terrible one:
That we were conveying provisions to the Edomite zealots from Gaza.
There's an uprising in the blockade and anyone caught helping them

Is executed without delay. Isaac is imputed with
An act of terrorism against the prefect.
After such a charge nothing and no one will help us.'
'How can that be? What terrorism? What provisions?
Can you really feed a rebellion with ten little fish?'

Aaron was silent and, with the words, 'Wait a while, Dad,' he left.
The Almighty alone knows what I felt in that dungeon.
How could I, such an old fool, have allowed this to happen?
What was I thinking, going fishing? Why couldn't we have sat quietly at home and not
Showed off something a simple docker had no right to boast about?

Later, Aaron informed me
The prefect had good reason for being as irate as the devil (forgive me, my Friend).
Until recently, he himself had been the procurator's secretary,
But he had been demoted to the coastal watch, suspected of taking bribes,
And based on information from Jewish high priests.

The procurator, by way of punishment,
Had confiscated two whalers from him, similar to our *Lucretia*.
Oh, those games that the powerful play! How frightening it is for the simple folk
Who, without knowing, fall into their awful nets
And flail about, failing to understand where it all comes from!

A big delegation arrived the next day, headed by Shlomo
And a lawyer. They took me from the dungeon
And, accompanied by the scowls of Romans and countrymen, they took me home.
'Now listen, Jim,' Shlomo said sternly
When we were alone.

'Things are really bad,
We have sought the advice of everyone we could;

After all, this all casts a shadow over the port, too, you understand.
Basically, the outcome is this, and you just listen carefully.
Don't boil over; unfortunately, there are no other alternatives.

Isaac can't be got off outright. A terrorism charge...
It doesn't get any worse. He has the death penalty looming.
The only thing we can do is to get the charge lifted
Specifically as regards organising aid to the insurgents in Gaza;
Say, he was young and foolish and decided to help them.

Then he'll get about eight years as a galley slave, but his life will be spared.
Hold on, hold on, let me finish!
We got you out not just on bail but on the promise
That in court you'd testify that you heard
Isaac saying something about helping the zealots.

As for the slap round the face, just forget it ever happened, all right?'
'Wait a minute, Shlomo,' I said, startled. 'What terrorism? What zealots?
The lad has no political views whatsoever!'
'Listen, Jimbo, being a Jew and having no political views...
There's clearly no such thing and there never will be.

You want to keep your son alive or what?'
'But that is totally outrageous! Can this really not be explained to anyone?!'
'Basically, Jim, if you don't agree, you'll bring everyone down.
Moshe will have his doctor's licence revoked and Aaron
Will end up sent to dig trenches somewhere out Berdychiv-way.

Think about it; you're the one who has to decide.
Adonai's my witness – we've done all we could for you.'
I said nothing for a long time. Shlomo waited.
'How could this happen, Shlomo? Why does such injustice reign over our people, eh?
Have we ever done anything like that to anyone just because we had a position of power?'

'Don't you go generalising about the people. Who knows how things will turn out in history.
Think about yourself, about your family.
Don't do anything stupid, Jim, I beg you.
Then, they'll start repressions against the lot of us.
So much effort has been directed to resolve this matter.

Give up one son and everyone will survive; this is the wisdom of the ages.
Don't give him up for execution – he'll return; many return...'
'Who has returned?' And so Shlomo and I continued talking until morning.
Aaron sat motionless on the other side of the door, smoking.
Moshe helped his mother out somewhere in the kitchen, in grave-like silence.

It was up to me to choose.

At dawn, the weary Shlomo rose up and, embracing me tightly, he said,
'No one has ever emerged victorious from wars with the state, with the Empire.
Don't go kidding yourself that you'll be the first.
It's just that you've been unlucky. This time, you pulled the short straw,
Like a deer in the hunt – such is the fate of us simple folk.'

My children! I had dreamed that you'd grow into lads
Who would *change life for the better!*
I dreamed that each of them would do so much good on their paths through life

That people of all kinds would honour you
As good doctors, poets and enforcers of law and order!

You would scatter like tributaries all over the world,
And the glory of the Zebedee family would progress and progress.
Later, your children, becoming agriculturalists, bakers, academicians and so on,
Would multiply your good deeds thirty times over
And life would become more beautiful than ever!

We just got together in one fateful place,
And there appears to be a way out, only there is a cruel price to pay.
For what am I paying with you, Isaac?
Where is that knife of Abraham that I will hold above your head?
Where is God's voice to tell me to 'offer this sacrifice?'

I'll go to court and seal your fate with my own lips.
But will the Angel Joel appear to shut me up
With words that it was only a test of my faith, Jacob,
And your execution will be overturned?
Doesn't Shlomo know that being a galley slave is the same inevitable death,

Only a long way from my cowardice and with *no right to correspondence*?
And what, the icy jaws of eels will be your grave, son?
Come, Adonai, and just tell me that this is all in Your name!
Give all this some higher meaning, let it at least be that!
Or tell me to build another ship

To dash away to the thinning grey top of Ararat, like our forefather Noah,
Far from human courts, prefectures and empires!
Is one human life really not worthy of divine attention?!
Is it the case that only a select few can hear Your voice,
Hark Your angels?

What will I betray tomorrow, and what will I save?
Oh, Angel Joel, give me your hand for support!
Let me hear the beating of your wing,
So I might understand that God is with me, that he has not deserted me!
Place the words in my mouth that the Almighty will understand!

Who said that three sons is a lot and if I lose one
I will still have a lot? How much is it enough for a father to betray one of them?!
How much is enough for a father if he condemns one person to their death?!
Who will I be after such a sacrifice?
Will the lives for many improve if Isaac departs it?

Where is his crime if he defended his father from affront?
How was I to safeguard him from what happened? Hide him away from the public eye?
Teach him to remain silent, lack any pride and life in a permanent state of prostration?
Not reap the fruits of his labours?
Where did I go wrong yesterday and what will tomorrow bring?

Oh, Angel Joel, I hear the breath of the land of Moriah[97],
What choice do I have, regardless of
Whether or not God deigns to pass comment on what has occurred,

---

[97] The name given to a mountainous region in the Book of Genesis, where Abraham is said to have bound Isaac.

184

Or, as always, will he say nothing and leave me alone
With my sacrificial knife in hand, raised over my own son?

No matter, Adonai, no matter. I will make my choice.
I will squeeze my hand even without the angel's return handshake.
I'd like to see what you'd have done if You had Your own Son;
What You'd do when surrounded by such dark human wickedness,
When You are faced with the choice, and I hope such a thing never comes to pass,

But, all the same, I would like to see what You'd do.

You know, my Beloved Friend, I got the impression
There was something strange in Your eyes, as if
You'd seen the abyss. It wasn't my story that
Caused that, was it? Perhaps...
Okay, I will continue my tale.

Everything was resolved in a single burst and, completely spontaneously.
I won't say that we had a clear plan or anything.
I emerged the next morning from the room, where I had been abandoned with my thoughts,
And there were Aaron and Moshe, waiting for me in silence,
But with a certain decisiveness. We understood one another without words.

And my wife, the mother of my sons, understood too.
We gathered quietly and went up into the hills, to the maquis,
Concealing our *navajas*, swords and other combat things.
That night, we lit a fire outside the city,
Beneath the aurora of which certain faces began to appear.

Benzi and the son of the Rabbi Akiva were there,
As well as Shmulik's son Menachem, the Ishmaelite Maruf and some other chaps.
What surprised me most was when, under the cover of night,
Aaron's companions-in-arms quietly joined us
From his *contubernium*, and silently drew their Syrian bows.

Aaron had planned everything wonderfully.
Like agile and ferocious spirits of wolves we descended
Upon the guards of the prefecture's dungeons.
We brushed them aside in an instant and brought Isaac out.
Only when we were leaving, the irreparable occurred.

A young soldier from the watch rushed at Moshe,
Who, without thinking, thrust the cold steel of his *navaja*
Up to the hilt into the soldier's neck.
Aaron shuddered and said,
'Now there is definitely no way back.'

Isaac looked over at him with a frown
And suddenly dipped his finger in the man's blood and quickly
Drew the six-pointed Star of David
Like a gaping wound on the white skin of the wall.
We gasped from the unexpected advent

Of this ancient symbol in such a bloody context.
However, everything happened so precisely and so rapidly,
As if angels had led us by the hand through this nocturnal affair.
A moment later, from just the tsabar, swaying in the desert,

One could understand that people had just run by this place.

The second sortie was more daring,
For it was an attack on the well-defended residence
Of the coastal prefect himself, my old 'friend'.
We put paid to the guards quickly; there was no longer any point
In safeguarding men's lives; we had crossed that line when we spared that old renegade.

Then, under the light of the fire, we sat him back-to-front on a donkey
And, before sending him into the town,
I gave him a good punch on the face, and for a particular reason:
Before doing this, I dipped my hand
Into nut-oil paint, the kind they paint ship's sides,

To ensure that my fist brought joy
To the Jewish population of Caesarea, and the Romans, too, for a good week.
And once again, on the walls of the prefect's house,
Like a flame of vengeance, freedom and sheer audacity,
Blazed that star of Jacob[98].

That was how our destiny became so clearly defined.
Word of our daring attacks spread quickly
And people came to see us.
As God is my witness, we only wished to seek revenge and free Isaac,
But often fate decides instead who you will be.

To be honest, word of our feats was greatly exaggerated.
We launched only three attacks after our assault in Caesarea.
I don't know why, but we selected three fortresses for these sorties:
Yodfat, Masada and Beitar.
Our attacks were swift and daring; not a military storming, of course –

That was something beyond our powers,
But our sabotage operations were a great success!
So many captive zealots passed under that burning star
To their freedom, past the heavy gates of these mighty fortifications,
Built according to Roman military artistry!

It was only at the third fortress of Beitar where we were caught in a trap,
And that marked the end of our military path.
Well, 'military' would be putting it strongly, for we were simply
A well-organised gang, no more than that.
It was later that people blew this up as if it were almost a mass uprising.

The garrison at Beitar did not scatter in all directions,
Rather, emerging, it regrouped and took up positions
So that not even a sparrow could fly through them.
They held us until help arrived,
Sent by the procurator with the specific objective

Of destroying every last memory of us;
So that, from that moment on, not a single Jewish soul

---

[98] The rising star of Jacob, according to a messianic prophecy, was to settle on the rebel, who was destined to free Jerusalem. The fulfilment of this legend was ascribed to Simon bar Kokhba, Son of the Star, who headed an uprising against the Romans in 131–135 CE.

Would ever contemplate rebellion or uprising.
We were ill-prepared for battle
According to that Roman military artistry.

Our ranks were mixed up, each defending themselves where they stood
And each dying where they stood. It was essentially just a massacre
Of our little squad, which fell under the stinging rain
Of the Roman arrows, so ruthlessly accurate.
When the Romans ascended the walls

There were only a handful of us left.
They say that someone broke our ring and left –
Perhaps the young Akiva, with two Romans.
I stood on the wall of the citadel and saw
Aaron with a severed ear and a wound in his side.

He was making his way towards me like a mighty elephant.
I saw Moshe, carrying Menachem on his back and attempting to close his gaping wound
From a spear. What was he hoping for?
I saw Isaac, fierce as a lynx, snapping and howling
And instilling terror in those battle-scarred legionnaires;

He was making his way toward the citadel, the last stronghold.
And there we stood, my sons and I together, just like we were on that jetty.
We stood, wounded, but alive and our feet planted firmly on the ground,
Like the roots of Lebanese cedars.
It seemed that nothing could fell us, but I was wrong:

An arrow screeched and pierced Aaron's chest.
The light in his eyes faded and his lips barely whispered, 'It wasn't for nothing, was it, Dad?'
As if I could answer such a question,
But I said, 'No, it was not for nothing...'
With a smile on his face and with the word 'farewell', my Aaron departed into the distance, from where

He will watch down on us from up on high.
Moshe, pierced by a spear, was trying
For the last time instinctively to wipe the blood from his glasses.
So childlike and naïve was his gesture,
That the soldiers held back from finishing him off, and just waited

For him to look over at me in farewell and give up the ghost himself.

I saw Isaac too, with no sword or spear, but with his *navaja*,
Rushing at the Gastati[99] in full attire.
At the last moment, he rushed to me and, for an instant,
He escaped his pursuers only, in the next second,
To fall, struck by a dart, right into my arms.

With a wicked smile, he began drawing his symbol with a blooded finger
On the rough wall, losing his nails as he did;
There was that blazing star which, just like my boy,
Was slowly fading away, turning from crimson
To brown and then to black – the symbol of the death of heroes.

---

[99] *Hastati* (Latin) – heavy Roman infantry.

My eyes, too, were closed by a powerful blow to the chest.
I thought that was the end and I said farewell
To the smell of my native desert,
Where, by the will of God, or simply my own will,
I had lost all my dreams irrevocably...

That is how I would have ended my story
Of my sons and the dreams I associate with them,
If it had not been for one episode that occurred
Shortly before our meeting on the shores of the Sea of Galilee,
Where you met me in the guise of a fisherman.

Who found me and took me north, and how,
Where they left me in the care a simple fisherman's family, without asking
Who I was and where I was from, I simply don't know.
I remember how long it took for me to emerge from that haze of nothingness
And gradually return to life;

A life that now I had absolutely no need for.
Completely automatically, based on nothing but genetic memory, I helped the family weave their nets,
Casting them and, at length, pulling the supple fish
To shore, so strewn it was with sharp stones.
Every day the death of the fish

Reminded me of the futility of life,
A life that my children lost because of a fateful accident,
Because of my pride and obstinacy,
Because of my inability to find compromise and smart solutions,
Because all of my experience gained from life proved to be a hollow noise.

I thought of the futility of my faith,
Which wailed to God and the angels only for them to remain indifferent
To the world that was falling apart; a world that meant nothing to them but everything to me.
How meaningless the sacrifices, the diligence and the commitment
To observe social norms and traditions.

Everything. Everything had lost its meaning in an instant,
Destroyed by some alien force.
But the use of its force, too, proved to be just as futile,
Leading directly to the voids of hell,
A hell that was as silent, indifferent and cold as the rest of my life.

So, one day, I overheard the conversation of that old fisherman
Who had nursed me back to my feet
With his three boys. I still remember their names, for some reason.
Two of them were called Simon, the other, Joseph.
They were sitting by the fire and the father, in a cracked voice,

Was telling them about some *Children of the Star*, legendary rebels
Who had achieved fabulous feats.
I didn't immediately realise that he was talking about us, about our gang
And I simply sneered bitterly, for they couldn't have a meaning.
What was all the hyperbole and exaggeration for?

I said out loud, 'What is this meaningless sacrifice for?
What did these chaps achieve other than their death,

188

At the swords of the colonisers?
They could have become pillars of society
And be of benefit to the people, but here...

What will become of them, other than being the subjects of
Silly stories of dubious accuracy? They probably don't even have a normal grave.'
The boys' eyes blazed with rage.
One of them, the youngest of the three, clenched his fists and cried out,
'What are you saying, you crazy old man?!

When we grow up, you think we'll break our backs for your Romans?
No! We'll dress the fortresses of Yodfat, Masada and Beitar
In new, glorious attire,
And you just sit here and stink of fish!'
The old fisherman struck the boy painfully over the back of the head.

'I'd show a little more respect, Ben Kosiba[100], when addressing your elders!
Go on, off with you to the village. I'll finish off later.
You hear me?! And you, Bar Giora and you, Josephus[101], get out of here!'
The boys rushed off into the gloom of the night
Casting withering, contemptuous eyes on me as they went.

I sat for a long time in silence with the old fisherman,
Listening to the crackling fire. I didn't know if he had guessed who I was or not.
Well, it wasn't really important. Finally, I said,
'Tell me, old man, what is it, after all, in these rebel lads
That so enraptures the boys?'

'Not only the boys, but the grown-ups too
Tell one another the stories of the glorious and daring victories
Of the lads from Caesarea.' 'But they say that they didn't actually want
A rebellion, that it was just circumstance.
And if it were not them, those lads would still be sitting

At their workplaces in Caesarea
And wouldn't be thinking about a struggle for national liberation.'
The old man thought a while and then said,
'Things could not have turned out differently for them,
It's just that these are *the lads with the unusual fate,*
Changing life for the better... '

---

[100] The actual patronymic of Simon bar Kokhba.
[101] Simon Bar Giora and Josephus (Flavius) were heroes of anti-Roman uprisings of ancient Jews in Palestine. Flavius Josephus consequently wrote the famous book *The Jewish War.*

Verse 24. The Mountain

(49) 'I have come to you with a sign from your Lord. I make for you out of clay the figure of a bird; then I breathe into it, and it becomes a bird by Allah's leave. And I heal the blind and the leprous, and I revive the dead, by Allah's leave. And I inform you concerning what you eat, and what you store in your homes. In that is a sign for you, if you are believers.'
(50) And verifying what lies before me of the Torah, and to make lawful for you some of what was forbidden to you. I have come to you with a sign from your Lord; so fear Allah, and obey me.

Qur'an. Surah 3, 'Family of Imran'

(51) Allah is my Lord and your Lord, so worship Him. That is a straight path.

Qur'an. Surah 3, 'Family of Imran'

'I love the truth...'

From the final words of Lev Tolstoy

And so He emerged and set foot on the Mountain,
He looked at the world with menace,
He looked at the world with tenderness,
He looked at the world and wept,
He looked at the world and laughed.

Those who stood nearby said,
'He's mad.'
Others standing nearby said,
'No, no, the man just got emotional,
So, go on, brother, don't hold back.'

And He wept at the mundanity even of such
A triumphant moment.
He was joyous that nothing
Had changed in the world
For many thousands of years, glory to Adonai.

He set foot on the Mountain

But no one noticed,
And no one understood.
And even if they had understood,
That would have meant instant death
From the contemplation of Eternity.

The one thing that saved everyone from the flames of that greatness
Was that the depth of the teachings does not
Reach the depths of every human soul straight away.
Not straight away, far from it...
How much has gone by, you ask – two thousand years?

He was mighty yet spindly at the same time.
He was silent and he was chatty.
He was the voice of God and simply of one's neighbour.
He was right there, outside and inside everyone.
He was many *Is* and, separately, the one sole *I*.

At first, there was silence; just the wind
Played with its dark curls, as if it wished to soften
The Divine Wind

191

That had come from the East
To colour His brow a chalky pale hue.

Then, the most impatient people began to whisper,
Saying, *where's the promised performance?*
They said he was one of a kind.
They said he'd say something new,
Something we haven't heard before, something unknown and in a strange tongue too.

Only, when His voice, coughing lightly,
Trickled down the mountain slope,
The onlookers were simply overcome with terror, for
This was indeed a strange and new tongue,
But one that caused a pain in recognition.

'With whom am I talking?!
Is it only with Jews, Edomites, Galileans,
Samaritans and other tsabars of antiquity?
With personalities or with people?
Am I talking today

Or many centuries ago?!

With those with knowledge and those who are well-read,
Who have heard much from priests,
Those who boldly enter a debate on religious matters,
Who defend their faith,
Those who live or who have already fallen for its sake?

With those who are persuaded, being persuaded or doubting,
With die-hard fanatics
Or with those who love with their hearts, minds, education and tradition?
Who are you – people of information,
Sapiens, homo-erectus?

Or those created in image and likeness?
Are you slaves voluntarily or forced?
Are your eyes closed as you think they are?
Do you need the Word as you so exclaim?
For you, do God and society live in the one place?

With whom am I talking?!
Is this the first time or the last?
Am I your sacrifice or you, Mine?
Is your prayer really to Me
Or are you simply unhappy with the way things are?

No, no, I see the people are all different
But the personalities are the same as before!
Hey, you tyrants and despots, breeding spiritual poverty!
Hey, you worshippers of calves who trample over the weeping and the inconsolable!
Hey, you evil warriors who gnaw at the flesh of the meek!

And even you, the scholars who try to combine
The Theory of Relativity with quantum mechanics.

You here, who thirst to find M-theory[102],
So that, once you find it, you can just see My face in the morning.
What 'M' are you seeking? Is it not the Messiah, Mahdi

Or Maitreya with the Great Arab?
Which 'M' will reassure you?
What answer would sate you?
Do you really need a purely logical justification for the unity of the world?
Most important, do you want to convince Me of this as well?

So, here you are, the organisers of world order,
Who fail to consider the merciful and the pure of heart!
How subtly you handed the sword to the peacekeepers!
Who have you expelled from your model of social harmony?
The victors, the successful, the ruling classes

In all modern kingdoms – you're all here.
And you priests, apologists and scribes,
Who have pulled apart the earth and the human race
To make odditoriums of canons and rituals,
False images of prophets and their followers

And to make war between them all – here you are too.

And so are you communists and socialists of all denominations,
Who have promised the Kingdom of Heaven here on earth,
That would function on account of ideal organisation
Of the lives of people but who would fail to realise
That the *Moral Code of the Builder of Communism*

Can hardly replace the commandments of the Great Books
And the laws of Abraham, Noah
And the others who have spoken with the Almighty.
Listen, if people haven't wanted
To fulfil *these commandments* for thousands of years,

Then you have to ask what is the root cause
By which they can change their very essence,
So overloaded with vices, avarice and a lust for power,
Only on the basis of directives from some collective ochlocracy?
In other words, you never did find that cherished lever

That would need to be pulled within the human essence
For the human world to find harmony
And step out on the straight path, not with fanaticism, but for real.
But for real, you understand?
Reason and constitution have proved incapable

Of fencing off human needs.

Capabilities haven't increased much either.
You see, instead of capabilities, sophistication is what flourishes more.

---

[102] In modern science, the so-called *theory of everything*, which attempts to find a universal explanation for the world. A major problem with this theory is the search for a platform to unite Einstein's Theory of Relativity and the Standard Model, based on quantum physics.

Now, here, as they say, man progresses in many ways.
You could even say every day,
Making wonderful use of all that the brain and nervous system are capable of.

So here you are, the central characters –
Onlookers, indifferent philistines and commoners,
Witnesses of the crucifixion of prophets and viewers of wars on television,
Central characters, long-since deprived of your faces;
Let's face it, you gave them up voluntarily.

So, anyway, I say hello to you central characters,
But I am not talking to people.
I stand here high on the Mountain top, but I cannot see.
I sing with the voice of the sea and the wind, but I am not heard.
I weep and I laugh, but these emotions are alien to the rock.

Do not kill, do not steal, love your enemy and your neighbour,
Don't succumb to temptation, stop the machine that churns out evil...
What other language could I devise
So these words actually reach the people
Who are so engrossed in their social role play

That they are no longer the salt of the earth and the light,
And who have once and for all become personalities
Of what is now a global information world,
Which pushes forward impetuously, based on a truly
Universal substance – that inconsumable instinct for consumption.

Oh, that vice is as simple as it is terrible!
And its essence is far from being a simple striving to have some
Legally protected private property.
You fools took the words *in His image and likeness*
Quite literally, it seems,

I mean, figuratively, simply ascribing to the Almighty
Legs and arms, and even a mournful facial expression.
But you need to look inside, in the essential plane,
In the state of mind; and what will you all find in yourselves?
Power. A god-like desire for power.

Over an object, objects, a universal equivalent,
Over a woman, children, a flock, the mind of the taxpayer.
Over the past, the future and the present even more so.
All of your godliness has been sublimated into this
Awful substance that permeates

The entire meaning of your existence as personalities,
As mere statistics, as standard and exceptional
Consumers of all manner of configurations,
From the consumer of the throne to the consumer of hand-outs,
From the comic-book reader to the writer of constitutions.'

'It's all right for you to say,' the sceptics objected,
Worldly-wise from their experience of life and dusty universities,
So, what will you order now – so that seven billion homo sapiens
Will scour the world in a chaotic search for food
Like wildebeest in the Serengeti?

That is what the birds of God are like, tireless in their social responsibility.
You see, the whole motion picture (and this, incidentally, is a reflection
Of the collective mind and mass sentiment)
Tells us that people who are brought down to their quintessence by circumstance
Are terrifying without the chastising hand of the law hanging over them

And they simply begin physically to devour one another.
Isn't that the case? Does society not hold
This animalistic essence in a cage and fail to give this same
Passion for unbridled power
For a man to lose his last traits of civilisation?

Is it not the rules of international law
That prevent people with Kalashnikovs
From simply taking the world with a force no less terrifying
Than in ancient times and middle ages; we haven't really changed, have we?
Surely it is hunger that will take over the world,

If you don't sow, reap and distribute what you create?
These ideas of Kropotkin and Bakunin
That a new order will arise from anarchy – we are long past that.
Their apologists are now old, sit chewing popcorn
And dress according to the latest revolutionary fashion from a couturier.'

Other sceptics objected, saying, 'They're not altogether fair, those words of Yours.
You see, we have long-since departed from tyrannical administration
And society, in the form of representative democracy now
Conjointly resolves all issues by agreement,
Which they call a social contract and constitution.

And, indeed, what have they devised that's any better?
Even God's servants, with their priesthood and their inquisition
Went down in history as failures and were removed from power.
Well, perhaps in certain other places...
But give us time: we are fighting this effectively.

We are actually pretty successful
In our struggle not only with basic crime,
But also with various diseases of the consciousness, such as racism, Nazism,
Genocide, Holocaust and human rights abuses.
And all that, by the way, without any particular help from You.

Why? You said "Don't judge", but how
Are people to achieve justice
If there's no judicial system, from district courts to international courts?
How do we rein in disorderly animals
If not by legal punishments, the law and regulations?!

Well, these systems are still not perfect;
Well, case law doesn't take all nuances of,
As You put it, human sophistication, into account.
Well, the courts, states and even entire nations make mistakes.
However, first of all, even nations are now apologising

For their sins in history.
Second, everything is still under development and still being sought.

Well, it won't be our generation that achieves perfection;
Let that be the lot of the future children from the Age of Aquarius.
Well, even Capricorns, but humanity is evolving.

And noticeably so.
Now no country can
Simply slaughter two hundred thousand rebels on the banks of the Yellow River
And not have severe sanctions applied
And be left in international isolation.

So, forgive me, we are improving our human race
With each passing year; we already see the light at the tunnel's end.
What would have been if it weren't for the organisational talent
Of the fathers of various nations and human geniuses?
After all, in addition, we don't just go shopping and fight each other.

We write books, we have opera, poetry,
Classical music and a varied folklore.
You're wrong to rebuke physicists too. Okay, so they devised
This terrible bomb, but what about the genetics?
Or the medicine that saves swathes of them every day?

The problem is simple, really – what we need
Is simply to bring the backward nations up to our common denominator
Of culture, healthcare and social justice,
Level the overall index across the world;
Well, not one index, but about two hundred of them.

Then an age of sustainable development will begin,
An era of ecology and enlightenment;
A golden age of eugenics, with equal access to the benefits of civilisation,
No war and a caring approach to nature.
And that is what we, Your wards, have been doing

Diligently, from one century to the next and from one year to the next.

So, there's something a little unfair in Your words
When you talk of human world-builders.
Was it really worldwide chaos and disorder
That lay at the heart of Your Great Plan?
And are we not the guides of Your order here on earth?

And you are displaying a certain injustice
To the popular masses of onlookers and simply citizens.
They are not just witnesses of what is happening.
World order is based on them, our relatives;
Primarily, the legitimacy of our mandate to govern.

Now, we're not talking about the others of God's chosen ones
And those anointed onto the throne, incidentally, by your will.
And are not the popular masses of television viewers
The truest of Your disciples?
Is it not their voices you hear every night

And every day in Your Heavenly Secretariat?
Take a look: the number of temples around the world has grown by the thousands,
Yet the neophytes and the God-fearing have grown by the millions.

Those interfaith conferences on religious tolerance
Are now commonplace around the world.

So, what are we to do – reverse all these positives?
Turn the other cheek to terrorism and the drug lords?
Not bless the soldiers of the fatherland for chastising pagans?
Not buy goods, cars and property?
Stop caring for our daily bread and break down the principles of distribution?'

This is the sort of thing the sceptics said,
And, I must say, they didn't hold their tongues back then either,
Two thousand years before this conversation.
This was always a heated argument, even on the Mountain.
Only I've got myself muddled up again.

What was I talking about, that conversation on the mountain path
That was described earlier,
Or was it something else? After all, He remained unchanged
As for *them*, I don't remember; it's very hard to get to the bottom of
The twists and turns of the temporal dimension.

However, my duty is simply to recall and record,
And certainly not to get my head around the paradoxes
Of how the future and past intertwine,
Of the legends and the prophesies and which of them came first,
What was the *alpha* at the outset and what described the *omega* of what's to come,

And what remains forever in ancient Palestine.

The only thing I remember for sure was that it had started raining
And the deep-blue look of the rivers flowing from the Mountain
Clouded over and the wind threw handfuls of dust into the faces of those listening.
And yet no one stirred, as if turned to stone;
You see, I realised that on that day the tightly-closed gates

To the house that seldom open
And for some, never at all, had opened.
And everyone understood that, beyond the cold streams of rain
And henceforth, they would see God's providence
Feeding good fruits with life, but oh, how can we see them?

He coughed a little; the sky responded with thunder.
His eyes flashed and we saw
That, with the dust of the mountain slope, all doubts were dispelled
Of what He would have to do again
And again, or perhaps for the first time. But it was inevitable,

That path, written not by the pen and not even with ink.
And not by me, not by them, not in words and not in any language.
It was inevitable. It was inevitable. It was inevitable.
It wasn't God who formulated it for him once more, rather those
Who again surrounded the Mountain in confusion.

He said:
'I will tell you. Listen.
Forget for a moment that you are personalities.
I'll tell you, so listen, Homo Man.

197

You think this is accidental, this Mountain?

You think it is simply a convenient minbar[103],
So that I might rise above you?
Above you, the people of the world around, with your desires?
You think it is just part of the landscape,
Decorating a storytelling routine?

Look *from above* at everything that is this world around.
After you've been expelled from Eden, are you able to do this?
And are you still My partner in conversation
Or have I long been conversing with an absorbent of information
And petty emotional and physiological entertainment?

Look *from above* at all that is man-made.
You think that I condemn order, human judgment,
Social relations and international law?
You think that I am simply voicing indignation
Against the profound and deepening social differentiation?

You believe it's injustice I see
Through the prism of when for one it is not enough and another, too much?
Or even when one has everything and another, nothing?
Should I show you the essence of human judgment through the prism of *may you not be judged?*
Please, but in Mind's eye, you only just

Saw but a speck of injustice of reproaches and judgments.
So, have you actually learned already to remove the beam that is in your own eye?
You know, but how is it my concern, how God devised the rudiments
Of the creation so many years ago; am I to
Stop and think about their rearrangement?

You know, I'm not the root cause, rather I am a part of His plan, right?
And is it not on Your behalf that the priests and propagandists explain
How harmoniously everything is arranged in the world around?
The question is not *how* they judge, *how* they rule and *how* they submit and conform.
The question is *who* does all this and what is the qualitative subject of the creation.

And the answer is that for Me you are not *a separate I* person,
Rather a *I am all people* person.
I am Homo and I don't care if you are Sapiens or Lyricus.
Say the phrase *Ana al-Haqq*[104] and pull yourself together.
If you say it for yourself, you will burn in a flame of arrogant pride.

However, if you say it on behalf of all people,
You can become a companion in conversation. And now, answer this:
Could many do that? Have many been given that ability?
It might be given to many, perhaps even *to everyone,*
But who was actually able? Who was able to take the responsibility

Without plunging into the sin of vanity?

---

[103] An Arabic word for a pulpit in a mosque where the imam stands to deliver sermons.

[104] *Ana al-Haqq*, translated literally from Arabic, means *I am Truth* while, figuratively, it means *I am God*. The phrase, according to legend, that was uttered by the Sufi Mansur Al Hussein al-Hallaj, who was executed for heresy in Baghdad in 922.

Remember.
They say: I am not everyone; I stand apart from the Muslims, the Japanese and the mime artists;
I stand apart from the Africans, children and republicans;
I stand apart; I am not responsible for them. *I am a part.*

I am a part of that part, of which I am also a part.
And so it was from the children of Adam and Eve, and then from the children of Nuh[105].
We are dividing, dividing and splitting apart all the more.
I am but the stalk of the tree that apparently yields fruit;
Only I don't know what fruit; I don't live in the crown, rather in the humus.

And I am actually performing my part faithfully –
Incidentally, I supply water from the trunk to the branches,
From where the fruit later forms.
I am part of the process, perhaps even the most important part,
But the quality of the fruit, sorry, is not really in my remit.

What I mean is, of course, I worry about the results of our common labours;
I can even send a supervisory committee up the trunk
To obtain an exhaustive report
About whether or not the harvest is a decent one.
And I hate the weeds that suffocate my root system.

I'll strangle them myself.

You grumble, saying, "O Lord! Cast your eyes upon me!"
I reply, "Man! And you cast yours upon me!"
And you reply, "I am a part! I am speaking only for myself,
But not on his behalf; not on his and not on theirs either!"
I give you fish but you reply with a forked tongue.

You say, "O Lord! You abandoned me! You forgot me!"
I implore, "Homo! What about you? Isn't your day and your year divided
Into a time *for God* and a time for *don't take his name in vain*?
Isn't your day divided into the *I am righteous*
And the *Well, that's the way of the world, what can you do?*

Can you serve two masters at the same time?
Then who is your *second one*?
Who takes up the other hours?
You see, you are yourself divided *into parts*,
While being a part yourself. So, answer me,

What part of you makes decisions in court?
On the throne? In love? In the stop, at the end of the day?
Or is it your parts one after the other?
You memorise *The Lord's Prayer* and *Al-Fatiha*; they are lines of verse.
But you are tired of the complexity of the perception of poetry.

What you want is clear instructions on *this is down to faith, this is against it,*
To have a more specific understanding of the compartmentalisation and where each part is found,
Who is on that side of the line and who is on this.
Homo! Where is your *Integrity?*
Tell me, did you ever actually have any?

---

[105] Noah in Islam.

Why do you store legends on the intricacies of Egyptian executions,
On every slightest little grim war,
But you've forgotten about the Golden Age?
Tell me, did this age ever actually happen? Well, let's start from the beginning:
Is there a God?'

The silence was soft and kind.
The wind quietly dropped off on His shoulder.
The sceptics' tears turned to salt
On the infant faces
Of bearded men.

With a placating, even breath, the night
Lulled to sleep all
Who had surrounded the Mountain.
Somehow, the arguments abated.
We, we at least, had merged into a unified whole;

You see, He had placed His hand on our (my) head
(Does He not have a thousand of them, after all?)
And, with the quiet voice not of a prophet,
Not of the heavenly sword and not of a Superbeing,
But of our Friend, who,

From this evening on, we'll call The Teacher;
He actually asked us to call him The Poet,
But we specifically wanted The Teacher for some reason...
Anyway, so, with his quiet voice,
He said to me (us) sadly,

'Go to sleep. How quickly you grow tired, Human.
What is strange is that you sleep as if you have an eternity before you.
But I am in such a hurry,
As if all I have left in life
Is just a few rhythms.

It's like I want to have time to ask,
But why do you, Homo, need questions on the creation?
Perhaps there is no need for them at all?
And perhaps I'll go spend the night
On a bench or even, say, in the thorn bushes?

The only thing is that thousands of voices each day,
Despite the calmness of those building the world order,
Call to the heavens with their ancient lament.
This is clearly not the will of the Heavens,
These are clearly those particles of the whole

That form their desire
To return to the conversation once more,
To be a companion in conversation once more,
To see again that
Which we, it turned out, had been deprived of for years.

To see that a peaceful Palestine
Is a fantastic symbol of *Integrity*.
This is a sublimation of the world from within,

And not just some geopolitical act;
It is the return to Me of a certain debt...

Well, my son,
Sing praises to yourself, you have been reborn;
Sing praises to yourself, you have made that step,
And to yourself for trampling the Mountain,
By my side.

Take it easy.
Don't cry.
You're alone,
But then so am I.
Love.

After all, that's what I do.
I LOVE.
Can you understand that?!
I don't kill, steal or trample others.
All I do is LOVE.

If My path was (or will be) a road to death,
It's just, so you know,
It's just something inevitable.
Can you find
A more unrequited love than Mine?!

Then what new thing can you possibly be waiting for
Other than what your mother and father bequeathed to you?
Get up.
Lift that leg.
There's the Mountain.

Put it down here.
No, Mine is here; put it here.
And now, shut up,
For now, give me Palestine.
Give it to me – you're already dead there.

Or, resurrect yourself and take it for yourself.
Just place your foot on the Mountain.
You don't know how?
I'm waiting.
I'm waiting. There's an eternity in front of me.
What's in front of you?

Then at least start to love.
And remember, no one has killed more than Me.
What, and you'll wreak revenge on Me too?!
Take a look around.
Find something that you'd place close to your heart and believe in.

You have to rise up again as you are dead.
Then I'll split Palestine with you.
Then I'll understand, that I don't LOVE for nothing.
And now leave me in peace.
You fool,

Son.

You're blocking the sunrise for Me.
You're blocking Me out for Me.
You're blocking yourself out for Me.'

Verse 25. The Architect

> There are four Ways in which men pass through life ...
> ...Fourthly the Way of the Artisan, or the Way of the Carpenter (Architect).
> The Way of the carpenter is to become proficient in the use of his tools, first
> to lay his plans with a true measure and then perform his work according to
> plan. Thus he passes through life...
> ...The Carpenter must know the architectural theory of towers and temples,
> And the plans of palaces, and must employ men to raise up houses. The
> Way of the Architect is the same as the Way of the Commander.
>
> *Miyamoto Musashi, The Book of Five Rings*

> Jesus said to his disciples, 'Compare me to someone and tell me whom I am
> like.' Simon Peter said to him. 'You are like a righteous angel.' Matthew
> said to him, 'You are like a wise philosopher.' Thomas said to him,
> 'Master, my mouth is wholly incapable of saying whom you are like.' Jesus
> said, 'I am not your master. Because you have drunk, you have become
> intoxicated from the bubbling spring which I have measured out.'
> And he took him and withdrew and told him three things. When Thomas
> returned to his companions, they asked him, 'What did Jesus say to you?'
> Thomas said to them,
> 'If I tell you one of the things which he told me, you will pick up stones and
> throw them at me; a fire will come out of the stones and burn you up.'
>
> *The Gospel of Thomas, Verse 13*

'Tell me, Thomas Didymus[106], about your Path to this day.'
I will tell you the story of my Business.
You think this won't be enough
To relate about life, my view of the world, the power of feelings and suffering
If I only tell you about my Business?

For many men Business
Incorporates the full understanding of life.
Not to the detriment of the family, one's relatives and harmony between them,
No. The thing is that Business, a man's profession,
Is a kind of pivotal element in assessing everything that goes on in the world.

In a world that embraces us so passionately with its problems,
Circumstances, feelings, struggles and multitude of obligations
That, with a haze of hustle and bustle, often overshadow
The path that becomes part of the *I*,
And I mean its main part.

What is more, not every man can find the strength, the courage and the determination,
Even over the course of his entire life, to admit
That specifically this is your Business.
Enslavement to relationships and circumstances,
Frequently a splitting of systems of values into two

Allow some of these men to live
Without even knowing the true nature of their vocation,
Unable to find their Business, which, according to the degree of love for it
Stands on a par with such significant concepts
As *family, love* and *Homeland*.

What does such a man become?

---

[106] *Didymus* (Greek) – literally meaning *Twin*, was Thomas's nickname, as he was probably the spitting image of
Jesus. Thomas is also translated as *twin* from Aramaic.

No, not necessarily a messed-up and grumbling, self-righteous hypocrite.
Perhaps his tragedy passes unnoticed by those around him.
It simply sublimates into different escapes –
Hobbies, collecting, dreams at night and so on.

However, a true calling never, *ever*
Leaves a man's soul or his mind in peace –
That gigantic place that it initially occupies,
Either because of the predestination of the Lord,
Or through the genes in one's DNA, or because of daydreams,

Which never did become a reality.

And then... could he really be called happy,
Even if he lives a life that is worthy
Of a positive verdict on Judgment Day?!
No, he could not. The death of a dream is the same
As the death of one's mission, the death of one's spirit,

The death of Man, as a divine unit,
Not only of society, but of that abstract
Divine design
That you nevertheless believe in. For another logic is somehow weaker
Than the notion that life is arranged

Completely in line with the laws of theatrical drama and is not possible
Without overture, plot development, apotheosis,
Epilogues and striking endings.
It's as if a biography must be like
The intrigue presented in a series or a graphic parable.

I am fortunate, as I have found my Business in life.
I dreamed of being an architect, I taught myself to be an architect, I bettered myself to become an architect,
I became one and then sought recognition;
I went through ups and downs, misunderstanding and intrigue.

I knew poverty, believing I could see a new objective after my triumphs;
I tossed my diploma to the ground,
Only to return it to its place of honour.
Basically, I went through the entire gamut of emotions
In what it is customary to call professional growth.

Only there was one word that became my enemy...
It is a terrible word and one that destroys the whole meaning
Of what it is to be an artisan and not a run-of-the-mill bit-part player,
Of being called by name
In a number songs of glory.

And that word is *Similar*.

That cursed word *Similar* has followed me around since childhood.
When I was born, it was at first warm and amicable,
Mostly because I was a child,
And little children like all that *coochi-coo, isn't he just like his father?* or
Coochie-coo, he's the spit of his grandfather.

To be honest, it didn't sound that bad when I was a teenager;
You see, fortunately, I was lucky with my ancestors...
The problems started when the hormones
Began forming an individual male of the species in me.
Back then, of course, I wanted the girls to like me,

Not because I was *similar in appearance to Forrest Gump* or *your dad*
Was just as charismatic when he was your age.
I wanted the young belles to talk about that Thomas,
He's an individual, one of a kind, and not simply
Just one of the gang of kids at school.

Later I quickly rid myself
Of the teenager's understanding of what *similarity* meant.
Not right away, I have to admit. For a long time, I was controlled
By my parent's standards for managing personal motivation,
Like, *but your grandfather when he was your age,*

Or *you're ashamed to lag behind the family name.*
Or *we so hoped that you'd become like so-and-so.*
Or the most sophisticated of all: *so much*
Work, genetics and upbringing,
And sleepless nights thinking of your future;

Everyone would be so disappointed
If you ended up not justifying
All that's been invested in you.
After all, look at the others; they've had things far harder.
All you need to do is conform.

I quickly rid myself of that teenager's *classification*.
And no, it wasn't easy. Simply one's first love
Opens the doors to one's first self-assessment;
My first love simply loved *me*,
Preferring my modest self

Over those university wannabes and supermen.
It wasn't that I was lucky; there are those who live life
And never meet such a girl.
That's not what I'm talking about. I quickly realised
That this hormonal-family programming of the individual

Has nothing in common with the *real* choice –
The choice of one's profession in life,
The real focus of dreams, desires and ambitions.
Yes, my friends, that is a good word – ambition,
Especially when we're talking about conquering the steps

Of self-improvement in a specialist field, in one's Business.
And I make no appeals to vanity here.
They would be out of place. Am I being overly opinionated? Possibly.
But let me tell you...
The flames of the fire are so wonderful, my brothers.

The meaning of today's stories are,
I believe, so as to relive one's Path.
Therefore, let me be frank,

Particularly when describing the ideas
That had a hold over me on this Path.

Basically, as a young fresher
I turned up at the door to the Jerusalem Institute
Of Ancient Architecture... Why ancient?
Friends, and what was it actually like back then for us Jews?!
It was only ancient then, for such names

Like the theatre builders Oscar Strnad or Kaufman,
Or all the Kaufmans, or Iofan with his Palace of Soviets
Were still concealed in history or forgotten
Under the layer of our lack of understanding of the cyclical nature of history.
Incidentally, unlike historians and philosophers, architects

Have a good understanding that the real creation of the Parthenon
And the lighthouse at Alexandria are still to come.
Just like it was for the Russians in the 20th century,
For whom the Cathedral of Christ the Redeemer is the future
And not a forgotten past.

I will continue. Anyway, when I thought, having decided on my profession,
Let's say, a fairly rare one for that time, and a respected one,
That I'd finally rid myself of that terrible word *similar*,
Things could not be farther from the truth. Here, in this real and cruel creative work,
The word acquired a different and even more terrible meaning.

Night after night, you chop boards,
Slice polystyrene with a red-hot blade,
You paint, draw and create your own little world of a project
Only to hand it in the next day and hear, *Excellent, it's so similar to*
Early Hippodamus of Miletus.

Or *That portico so reminds me of Ictinus and Callicrates*[107],
Only fresher. But, yes, it's generally very good.
This is much in the spirit of the urban-planning ideas of Persepolis
And this is where your influence comes to bear, Mister Shmoel,
This is wholly in the spirit of the ideas of the Assyrian architects.

It wasn't that the professors were saying I wasn't talented, quite the opposite.
It wasn't that they were saying I came second in terms of my ideas.
I was actually pleased to be compared with the very best,
But that was not where my doubts lay.
That was not the cause of my sorrow.

Perhaps I would have remained among the diligent chaps,
Who create those hybrids, wonderful and functional
And the eclectic nature of our towns and streets.
After all, not everything erected in yesterday's desolate wasteland
Is a sure-fire masterpiece, sculpted from the heart by the project's author.

Not everything is a unique and unrepeatable image of the intertwining
Of divine inspiration and engineering thought,
Embodied in simple components – walls, roofs and doors,
And in window apertures and tile cascades.

---

[107] Ictinus and Callicrates – the architects of the Parthenon.

More often than not, it is just a functional arrangement,

Dreamt up by a hungover prom student[108].
Or it is simply the copy of a building, made on a whim, like
I want my country too to have an Erechtheion
Or an Eiffel Tower. The fancies of sovereign idealogists
Will always dominate the work of artisans.

Today, the role of the architect often fades into the background
When we actually talk about architectural achievements.
More often, the image of great builder monarchs feature.
As if Shah Jahan himself devised the lines of the cupolas
On the Taj Mahal, or the Greek Basiliuses could

Describe in detail the rudiments of Chryselephantine sculptural techniques!
Who today can name the architects who drew
The first outlines of Mohenjo-Daro or Machi Picchu in the sand?
Or who calculated the length of roads and the remoteness of wells?
Or the dependence of wall breadth on its stability

Against Manjanika ammunition?

I don't speak now of one's envy of monarchs.
To put it more precisely, this is a building block in understanding
What could become the embodiment of *my* ideas in stone.
Why, when describing architecture, do people so often talk about kings?
This was a question that tormented me greatly, until I realised the most important thing:

A king doesn't see the binding of reinforcement elements or the exactness of gable ends.
He sees the design of a common objective, the philosophy of the building.
His place is not on a particular mountain, rather in the hearts of the people,
Who quail on their donkeys
To work past the grandeur of the stone's eternity.

You see, it's just not for nothing that they go through life together,
The kings and the architects. Are we but a vehicle for their greatness?
Or a reflection of the dominant philosophy,
Or their way of communicating with the Almighty,
Before whom kings stand in fear and reverence.

You see, when you trample over peoples and empires
With feet that fear neither enemies nor uprisings,
You feel like the ruler of the present.
What, then, could be better than the architect's stone,
To launch the memory of yourself into the future?

But, let Allah be my witness, I had no ambition
To become a Basileus myself
And express my political aspirations
In the outlines of artificial leaves of Corinthian column caps
On the façades of royal chancelleries.

No. Back then, I was unfamiliar with the concepts of kingdoms and the Kingdom.

---

[108] In this instance, *Prom* refers to the abbreviated slang name for the Industrial Construction Faculty of the Moscow Architecture Institute.

I merely realised that a cornerstone of architecture
Is the relationship between the client and the artist.
The client (king or house owner) always thinks
In two categories: functionality and beauty.

And, the higher the client's level,
The more beauty becomes all the more functional,
As I've already said, from an ideological point of view.
If sculptures and high reliefs do not intimidate or relate tales
Of Imperial victories on the Trajan or Trafalgar columns,

Then the beauty becomes superfluous and there is no call for it.
Time, though, is generally an impartial judge.
Often, what once appeared unshakable
When the first brick went down,
Is later covered cold-bloodedly in a dust of needlessness.

The wise monarch strives to maintain usefulness and beauty in a state of harmony.
You see, if a chancellery is beautiful but inconvenient,
It means the king couldn't care less about its principal purpose.
Kings like this, for as long as the stone remains in place,
Are doomed to ridicule by the people, as slaves to ambition.

Now, if buildings are overly functional
At the expense of their beauty, the eyes of generations to come
Will not stand such ugly stone monsters and will pitilessly
Pull down such foolish boxes, with the name of their creator,
Both the architect and the king, it must be said.

Like a number of lads from Galilee,
I was lucky enough to continue my studies
At the best architecture school of the time,
In Rome, that austere yet true megapolis,
Where not only the walls serve as a source of inspiration,

But the seething Bohemia, with its chequered views of the world,
Its ethnic diversity and the pathos of the creators of history.
It was a wonderful time to learn,
When the subtleties of various solutions,
Both technical and visual,

Help you comprehend the greatness of a man who builds,
Each so different but all captured by a single emotion –
With a single objective of proving to the Almighty
That the man-made can be as equally beautiful as His mountain
Or His tree. Better still would be to gather all this together,

And erect a *yamadziro*[109] inside the walls, embracing the rock face,
A rock garden or bonsai world, as evidence that
Man is also powerful enough to change the natural laws of growth
For his own aesthetic whims
And enthusiastic views of the historical age.

---

[109] A *yamadziro* is a medieval castle in Japan. It differs from other types of castle, such as a *hirayamadziro* (built between a hill and a valley) or a *hirajiro* (built on a plain) in that it was literally built into the mountain, ensuring it enjoyed particular impregnability.

At metropolitan universities, we mastered the skill
Of retaining the status of art for architecture
While achieving a triumph of strict functionalism.
To be honest, however, no one really teaches you
How to overcome the eternal conflict between the artist

And those who restrict his flight with questions
Of financing and feasibility.
Another important aspect for me was how to do away
With my ever-present enemy *similarity*.
To rid my work once and for all

Of those awful expressions such as,
I want it to look like the Alhambra,
Not like Gaudi, but a little reminiscent of Giotto;
I want the grandeur of my pedimental compositions
To be no inferior to the ancient classics or Renaissance traditions.

The matter of similarity no longer plagued me on the level
Of the artist's personal ambitions, rather as a third cornerstone criterion
For appraising the work of architects, pushed by the masses into the periphery
Or, worse still, to the mass-produced and the generic, when fashion
Is not actually fashion, merely a dumb imitation.

Until the advent of cinema, architecture would for centuries
Be the most high-value of all art forms.
It would be architecture that would combine the grace of painting,
The magic of sculpture and the symmetry of carpet weaving;
Even the stamp of science in substitutes for stone and torches.

At first, I thought my individuality
Would be saved by knowledge and awareness.
After all, there were some true breakthroughs
In Renaissance architecture or Art Nouveau, right?
There were some fresh trends, weren't there?

Follow events, seek something new; what, you'd think, could be simpler?
But do you know how many powers, great and small
Are now being erected in the expanses of their natural landscapes?
How many rocks, taken from the body of the Mountain,
Are becoming parts of man-made fantasies?

I never stopped drawing, sketching, searching,
And went through tonnes of ink, card and wax.
Books, treatises and photographs
Became my friends, acquaintances, relatives and brides.
My house became a creative battlefield

Where fanciful shapes, ideas and designs
Swallowed up every free space on
Tables, beds, walls and furniture.
The only thing is that the mechanical and systematic search
Is not always where you'll find the power of true inspiration.

It was later that I realised that the most important thing was practice.
Involvement in the most varied of projects

In different parts of the world and among different peoples
Would give me an acute understanding of
What the *I* is in this art and whether it would ever even exist!

I erected painted porticos in Hellas,
Inhaled marble dust when grinding caryatids in the colonies of Asia,
Calculated the proportions of stadia and aqueducts,
Organised hundreds of teams of stone cutters in Egypt
And mixed the blue glaze of Babylonia.

When on Crete, I fell in love with a girl, a beautiful island nymph
And, inspired by my feelings,
The night before submitting my project,
Without permission or the knowledge of the chief architect,
Adorned the roof of the model of the Navy Chancellery

With a slender, air-like belvedere pinnacle.
It was completely unnecessary and superfluous
And, moreover, out of place with the building's harmonious logic.
And yet, what a creation it was!
As if limestone and marble had lost all gravity

And, rushing upwards, they were hanging, suspended, between the mountain and the cloud!
This was not a construction, rather the embodiment in stone
Of love, desire and passion, and contempt for any triumph of reality!
As if someone had sung a tender confession in a military formation
In place of a courageous triumphal march over the defeated.

The next morning, the stern Roman trierarchs,
Along with the chief architect,
Gazed in surprise at this madcap creativity,
Asking, 'And what is that? Why?! Where?!'
I kept my cool, even under the withering gaze of my superiors.

'It's, er, a pavilion for Contemplation of the Sea and Yearning for Rome,'
I blurted out, completely off the cuff.
'After tiring battles, one must return
To higher matters and incentives
And dedicate time to thoughts of the might of the Emperor and of Neptune!'

One elderly trierarch had even raised his whip,
And his distorted expression told me that such blatant irresponsibility
In military office was simply criminal.
However... the prefect, for some reason, suddenly spoke: 'And what of it?
Let it remain. A great idea and a new one.

Perhaps this lad is ready to receive orders himself,
Only... Only not from the Navy,' the military commander concluded, this time more sternly.
The tetrarchs bowed the plumes on their cassis helmets;
The chief architect finally breathed out a sigh.
Basically, the design was accepted and I avoided punishment.

Then I thought: so that's when things work out!
Only when your hand is guided by the song in your heart,
By your sincere, true emotions
And genuine feelings. Specifically, it is spirituality
That can overcome the discipline of practicality.

Only then is dissimilarity born,
Something new and genuinely unusual!
From then on, I let my imagination run free
And my fear of experimentation simply disappeared.
And love? I saw it as being merely an ingredient.

I continued my journey through the building sites of the Empire
And then beyond its borders, too.
I asked myself: which buildings, more than the rest,
Present genuine inspiration and freedom of spirit?
Well, in the temples, of course!

Temples reflect the striving of the human race
To break away from the shackles of earthly things.
Only the subtle mystery of communication with the Almighty
Can reveal the incomprehensible in you,
That which is locked up in the artist under the pressure of everyday life.

Thousands of draughtsmen toiled away in my imagination,
Drawing new building outlines and new shapes.
Thousands of engineers set about addressing
The integration of materials and spirit.
The lancet arches of my eyes shone with the flame

And shadow of galleries, flights and stairways.
Mighty towers shot up into the sky
Like a stone-clad plea of man
About our eternal striving for perfection,
For that which we call faith in the beautiful.

I sped like the wind to the yellow plains of Palestine,
Where my origin would present to me the opportunity
To implement most completely the flight of my imagination.
However, I was so cruelly mistaken.
There is no building more conservative than the construction

Of a temple of religious worship in any confession.
The moment I suggested altering the configuration of
The Ezrat Yisrael and the Ezrat Kohanim[110] based on the fact that
The elevation of the priests' courtyard broke the symmetry
And that the Corinthian order of columns could be replaced with Ionic examples, more of the day,

I was expelled from the Temple and banned from taking part
In any Jewish religious construction
Accompanied by the words of the high priests, 'Young man,
This is no place for naked self-expression!
Every stone here reflects the traditions

That have been gathered here for centuries, piece by piece.
Better you go and work in residential construction instead!'
However, I had no wish to accept this fiasco and, believing
That the Greek pagans were more democratic and receptive,
I rushed to the cities of Achaea.

---

[110] *Ezrat Yisrael* – courtyard for simple Jewish folk; *Ezrat Kohanim* – the priests' courtyard. Compulsory elements of a Jewish temple.

Well, anyway, Apollo's oracle told me
That he predicted a sad ending to my opportunism even without Apollo.
I decided to direct my feet to the peoples
Who were not so burdened, I thought, with so many conventions
And traditions, meaning they would be less sophisticated in their architecture,

To be able to put the brakes on my self-expression.

So, I went to Germany to see my old friend Arminius,
For whom I had once built a simple
Residential district for some unpretentious forest warriors.
Arminius was actually in need of a building
That would identify both faith and power simultaneously.

However, when I showed him the models of my idea,
This is what he said to me:
'You know, Hamlet[111], let's sit down here
And have a quiet chat.'
Incidentally, I got the nickname *Hamlet* from the Germans after

I had built them this drab district
Of identical-looking, five-storey blocks[112],
Like twins. I have to say I was deeply offended at this nickname,
As if it reflected my affliction
From that terrible word *similar*.

Anyway, I'll carry on about the conversation with that German leader.
'I have two important things that
I'd like to tell you today. The first is this.
And it's good news – I won't chop your head off,
Although I have every right to do so.

These here... solutions,' he said waving his hand at my canvases,
'Are things that only crazy monarchs
With no sense of responsibility to their people
Could ever afford. I hope you
Don't see me as a madman.

And then, your work as an architect of the Imperial School
Displays a certain lack of respect for us, as if we were barbarians
With no understanding of the nuances of architecture.
You see, my friend, I receive you and hear you out not because
You're a jolly and smart lad,

But because I have a detailed dossier
On your successes with grand construction projects,
Where you have shown yourself to be a wonderful artist.
And, you know, you're getting a bit famous;
Perhaps paradoxical, but it's still celebrity of a fashion.

So, son, you yourself are a child of the colonies.
Never fall for the charms of the metropolis,

---

[111] *Hamlet* – old German for *twin*, *double*.
[112] Called *Khrushchevki*, as they were designed and built in the time when Krushchev was First Secretary of the Communist Party of the Soviet Union.

212

Striving to elevate oneself at the expense of others.
I advise you to remember the words, *Di provenza il mar, il suol*
Chi dal cor ti cancello[113]...

After all, you are striving to create something eternal, isn't that so?
But empires are not eternal things.
The second thing. I really don't want to kill off your thirst for the search,
But I still really must say this.
My people are saying that Hamlet is imitating madness

Because he is concealing his true objective.
You understand I am talking about creativity here.
Why madness, specifically? Because, despite the fact that
You are seeking an embodiment of the spirit,
You are still obsessed with shapes.

And if you only experiment with shapes,
Forgetting such nuances as spatial perception,
The philosophy of communication with the elements,
Conversing with the heavens, at the end of the day,
Then you will inevitably slide into two things:

Either to dumb eclecticism,
Or the superficial mechanics of Feng Shui.
But the worse thing is not even that, but that
Your escape from similarity,
Which results in an imaginary dissimilarity,

Will surely become your mirror,
Similarity only in reverse, you understand?
Because the elementary nature of the *a contrario* method
Always sticks out and the fact that it is secondary
Offends the true connoisseurs of the art.

Most important, it results in fragility.
Building construction is not calligraphy with water on asphalt,
Encouraging us to think about transience and mortality.
Quite the contrary, this is a striving to insert into the picture of eternity
At least something man-made; to present, so to speak, to God

Their naïve right to the Earth.
Then, once again, you missed something really important:
The most paradoxical thing in architecture.
That's when, by limiting *space*,
You are still striving to create *space*.

Is it even possible to comprehend this when studying
The variety of shapes and methods of construction?
Of course, this is not enough.
After all, even troops are not just a formation and a battle cry.
An army, first and foremost, is an idea.

A common understanding of the totality of all that is valuable,

---

[113] Lines from Germont's Aria in Verdi's *La Traviata. What has vanished from your heart*
The dear sea and soil of Provence? Only the name *Provence* is used here nominally to mean *Province.*

213

What it protects, defends and irradiates, too
Across the expanses of geographies, both our own and often the spaces of others.
I hold no grudge against you, *Hamlet*.
And don't take offence at our elders talking about madness.

It's just that they see in you a search for an idea and a goal,
But for now they don't see the connection between your spirit
And what you're doing. And that is dangerous.
You know, the way anger in battle can replace courage,
So madness can be a reason for enlightenment.

However, we are not talking about a madness of vapidity;
I am talking about a protest against the strict walls of consciousness.
However, you aren't old enough for that yet, sorry.
Therefore, we'll go our separate ways today. I, the master,
You, my interesting guest, no more than that.

Tomorrow, if you are able to comprehend more.
Then come back and we'll talk about temples;
There are several ideas I am thinking about,
As to how we Goths could create a style
That would be called by our name.

Not in honour of military ferocity,
Rather in honour of our striving to the Lord,
For a love of order, symmetry and validity,
A desire to fly high and look down from on high
At our land, which tomorrow we will defend against the Romans...'

I left Germany in sorrow,
But this was not a sadness from rejection.
I knew, I sensed, that my friend was right,
That the merry springtime rainbow
Might hold a natural phenomenon for one person

But a stairway to Heaven Eternal for another.

What is most interesting is that, upon my return to Rome,
I was amazed and shocked by the news
About what was happening in the world of imperial architecture.
Pax Romana had grown by this time
To a scale previously unimaginable.

The streets of Rome had seen
A many-fold increase in the number of immigrants from the new colonies.
A multilingual hum filled the ears
And the variety of people in the crowd was amazing
With their many different faces, clothing, mannerisms and customs.

What is most interesting is that what
Prevailed over this variety was a stupid eclecticism of shapes,
Which for me were already a thing of the past,
But here, they were blooming with tempestuous colour
On the streets and squares of the Eternal City.

And this madness of the geopolitical reality
Was embodied in the architectural styles

That simply devoured with a mad hunger
All that had once been inadmissible and harmful,
But which had now acquired the traits of major trends.

In somewhat of a stupor, I looked at
How the classical Hellenic tradition
Was now mixed with Assyrian bulls and Persian bas-reliefs,
How slender columns and galleries
Now neighboured Egyptian obelisks.

The temples now combined Etruscan gods
And mystical profiles of Anubises and Baals.
Jupiters crowded together under the onslaught of idols,
Cult figures and images of Asian satraps[114].
Statues of Isis shared forums with the resurrected Mithra.

Stunned, I made my way to the university,
Where the latest surprise was waiting for me.
It turns out I was now recognised as the founder of the fashion for mixing forms;
I was the ideal, an example for the new generation
Of the Empire's architects.

While I had been traipsing around the back alleys of power,
Glory had been patiently waiting for me at home;
With a laurel wreath and specially-cut togas,
To evidence the fact that I was of particular value to Rome,
Its science and practice of architecture.

They say that fame and recognition
Are the pinnacle of an artist's career.
Well, a very fair statement, I suppose...
I confess, I greatly enjoyed
All those receptions, seats of honour at feast tables,

Conferences, the doting gaze of students,
Who awaited my approval, even if only fleeting.
However, for some reason, this time of bathing in the rays of glory
Now seem lost to me,
For this tinsel of public popularity

Forced me then to place progress
Toward my cherished dream to one side for a good while.
A dream to which I had strived personally, with my inner spirit,
My abstract contract with my creative muses;
A contract unwritten but recognised by all those parts of my *I*.

Unfortunately, drinking is a frequent
And even unconditional companion of fame and recognition.
It appears quite innocently
In the form of a glass of wine 'for the outstanding role, bla-bla-bla',
Growing into violent boozing

With the limits of what is accepted
Unexpectedly cast wide open.

---

[114] Governors of the provinces of the ancient Median and Achaemenid Empires and in several of their successors, such as in the Sasanian Empire and the Hellenistic empires.

215

Offences that ordinary folk cannot forgive
Are transformed flatteringly into delightful pranks of a genius,
Which might even become an example for others to follow.

Speaking of imitation. That word *similarity* had caught up with me again,
Only in an inverted incarnation.
In architectural circles it had now become fashionable
To brand new, rising stars
With the dubious compliment of being similar

To my 'incomparable architectural style'.
However, becoming a criterion for primacy
Didn't make things any easier for me. In fact, quite the opposite.
Remembering the words of my wise friend Arminius,
I felt even more fully how vicious that circle was

Round which my talent was galloping like a circus horse
In blinkers and with daft plumes of glory
On its head, laid to waste by society's obsequiousness.
I would respond only to those who had become
More tightly embraced in the arms of the supple priestesses of Bacchus...

From time to time, I felt the impulse to 'give it all up',
And become, as before, honest with myself
And return, in the assessments of surrounding events,
To a basic understanding of myself and my work.
But, oh, Alahi! How tenacious and pleasant that vice is,

Nurtured as it is by vague pagan values!
How pleasant, the unrestrained consumption of female bodies,
Wine, exotic foods and relations
That are remarkable in their easy lack of commitment
And general acceptance of the triumph of primacy

Of the cult of satisfaction of all base desires
Over notions of morality, integrity and dialogue with the Heavens.
At times, something itched within me, calling to break out
From the fog, but this torment of incoherence
Merely served once more to drag me back to those fauns,

Dancing their devilish dances on my remains
And the remains of my soul which I was already ashamed to call
A particle of God in His creation.
Hm... there really are not that many people who know what to do with
Fame and glory and all that goes with them.

That said, I do sometimes think
That those who do know how to do this
Are usually the ones who don't deserve this fame and glory, but we won't digress
From the essence of my story for the sake of a discussion.
There is a time, it would seem, for everything.

The most dangerous embraces in fame are not
Those of Bacchus. I'm talking of the box
Into which you are gradually dragged by the notion
Of the social status of a Bohemian.
More precisely, a standard of consumption that is varied in a million little things.

216

You are no longer wandering coolly around the Palatine,
Rather, you travel in an expensive carriage
That has become not simply an essential accessory but worse –
A habit, as natural for you as waking in the morning.
You've got your slaves, admirers, your gadgets and a cute little mansion,

Stuffed with furniture, art-deco bells and whistles,
Servants, Chagall originals and Turkmen rugs,
All called to demonstrate the fine taste of the master,
A true indulgent man of leisure and trendsetter in architecture,
Nurtured by the adoring crowd and 'useful acquaintances',

Who are able to solve your problems in ways not like those forced
Upon commoners and apprentice geniuses.
There comes a time when you realise
That the selfishness of your vain pride might tear you away from Bacchus
Into other embraces, such as that of the elite *Aesculapius*,

A fashionable psychologist or a press-attaché.
But what you really can't do now
Is break out of that box of consumption.
Why a box? Well, because, despite all the multifaceted nature of your life,
It loses the one most important thing – *space*.

It's like you see yourself screaming from a fear
That watches as, ever-so-slowly
The box lid closes over you.
And you are drowning in the depths of the tinsel
That fills the giant box more and more,

The box you customarily call *life*.

Indeed, from time to time, I allowed myself
Cultural leaps into the past,
Getting properly drunk on cheap apple liqueur
With old friends or apprentice geniuses
In shoebox-sized student cells.

At the same time, exclaiming falsely,
'That's what I love you for; because you're genuine!
And I am genuine with you! Tomorrow, I'll do away with this feigned,
Painted-on social success.
They know where they can get off!

I will never belong to *them*, not on your life!
In your dreams, Thomas the Unique
Will dance a jig to your fanfare of hypocrisy!
I am *yours*, brothers! I am your flesh and your blood!
I will never betray you for any earthly blessings!' and so on.

You can even mess about for five days or so
Saying 'I am the son of these slums and lowly yards',
In obscure hostelries with obscure people.
But then... Sorry, friends, but it's so damn nice...
(Forgive me, Rabbi,

For my unbridled language. I am ashamed of myself)
...To then stand under a warm shower,
Dive into my own pool in a shaded garden,
And then, weary from my massage,
Stretch out on a sun-lounger facing that landscape

That you so skilfully and so long
Selected when purchasing your big house.
It's great to laze around, thinking of the
Immorality of superfluous comforts,
Which I am certainly not ready to give up in life.

However, the dull, silent pain remained with me,
When I had to create, make and design.
Creativity has its own algorithm of feelings,
Which you can't eclipse with any benefits of a satiated life.
It burns within you with a cruel flame,

Burning the hands that carry the stretcher-frame,
On which a hotch-potch of shapes dances
The wild jig of that mad faun,
Triumphant on the fields of your mediocrity.
Now, mediocrity is what is many times worse

Than even the curse of similarity. It destroys
Your very essence, irrespective of the delighted cries of your hangers-on.
The pain accumulates and burns, searing
Worse than soulless self-indulgence and alcohol.
There's nowhere to run and hide from it.

In desperation, I suddenly remembered that I could find
A celebration of traditional space back in my Homeland.
I stretched out my hands for salvation
To Judea, recalling the strict intransigence of the elders,
Guarding the ancient canons of the Temple.

And what do I learn? That Herod,
It turns out, had also forced the high priests
To alter the configuration of the Temple courtyards,
Like I said before, in favour of Roman symmetry.
And the column heads were replaced with Ionic designs...

But one day, the pain exploded like a naphtha shell,
When I learned that my friend Arminius
Was killed as a result of a conspiracy among fellow tribesmen.
His conclave of sages, too, was executed
By the victors of a military detachment.

I wept and it seemed that the words *Farewell, Herman, my friend, oh, great leader of the Cherusci!*
Just hung there, in a gaping void,
Addressed to no one in an instantly empty world.
Suddenly, however, as if in reality, I heard
Arminius's actual voice, mocking with the words,

Farewell, my friend, Thomas of Galilee!
Are you no longer imitating insanity, by protecting

Your search for the true *space* from the ignorant?'
I shivered and I so wanted him
To call me *Hamlet* once more.

However, that was apparently a name from some other life.
Something broke inside me, somewhere near my heart.
When the order was brought from the consuls of Rome
For a new temple, a new concept,
I locked myself away in my workshop

And forgot all my Bohemian diversions
And set about creating, as if in a fog.
'You want eclecticism? You'll get plenty of that.
Why limit oneself to one master of a temple?
You'll get a temple to *all* gods and then, perhaps, you'll get your fill...

I'll erect such a monster
That it will terrify you, your children and your children's children for centuries
With all the senselessness of my design,
All the melting pot of your pagan views.
Pagan, not because of the nature of your faith,

But because of the true barbarism of your way of life!
Because of the foolish snobbery in your regard for those you see as barbarians,
Just because you haven't looked in the mirror for so long.
It is this mirror that I'll be erecting
To your horror and the curse of generations to come!'

I was as devious as a Libyan cobra,
So that, until the very end of the construction,
No one saw a full picture of
What was soon to blot
The landscape of the Great Metropolis.

Both when defending the design or at the construction site,
Everything was concealed by shrouds, half-words,
Tricks to distract
And even blatant dummies.
And all this, for the sake of one day: The Grand Opening.

The birthday of the monster to spoil the snow-white face of Rome,
A monster with an agglomeration of outright Asiatic flavours,
Sculptural pandemonium, a rebellion of light
And pictorial designs, all wholly alien
To the Roman view of the creation.

Why was I wreaking vengeance on the Eternal City that had raised me?
That had taken a provincial builder
And made him an architect with a name lauded like thunder across the Oecumene?
My vengeance was for the fact that any megapolis
Always gives rise to monsters on a wave of glory,

Which, here, is deafening and immensely, wickedly generous,
Yet wholly devoid of love and tender affection
When it comes to talent. And, well, basically,
That does everything to ensure its neutralisation and death,
Casting the seducible and weak into the arms of the ever Greedy One.

For the fact that, for geniuses and artists
In the cold walls of supercities
Either a loud death of the spirit is programmed, in agreement
With the triumph of commercial mediocrity,
Or drunken death from a powerless protest.

For the fact that luxury and vice of the Great Cities
Carry such a corrosive, artificial light in the colony,
That the local guardians of tradition and ancient spaces
Are dying out and disappearing with greater efficiency
Than if there was simply a war on.

For the fact that I was basically a part of all this evil.

I called this monster the *Pantheon*,
Disguising in this harmonious title
The name of the goat god Pan,
Who rejected the depravity of the Olympian gods
And escaped forever from them into the dense forests of Germany.

Only... Only Eternal Rome proved stronger than me.
Once again it chewed up my *I* and spat it out,
Only this time in a far more sophisticated manner.
The entire beau monde of the Empire's capital
Gathered for the opening of the new miracle,

Which promised to take shape from the trowel of the 'great' architect.
I skilfully covered it with canvases and scaffolding,
So that no eye could grasp the whole picture of my plan
Until the time was right, to ensure the effect would be more stunning.
And so, to the fanfare of the consular lictors,

The veils fell back and my stone monster
Reared up before the onlookers in all its barbaric beauty.
In utter silence, the consuls, senators, vestals and plebeians
Went inside the building, not knowing how to react.
They went inside and stopped in their tracks, for every whisper

Carried all round the interior space of the hall.
Before the eyes of this prim-and-proper high society
Was more than just a mix of genres – Hellenic,
Barbaric, Asian and God knows what other kinds – of architecture
All blended into a frankly eclectic form.

Against all the rules and Roman traditions
A monstrous dome rose up to the heavens,
Suppressing the natural arrogance of Aeneas's descendants.
Most important, though, was
The open mockery of the Roman deities,

Which, despite the fine symmetry of placement in a circle,
Appeared crowded under the mighty vault of the sky.
Atop this picture of humiliation
Hung a simple, open hole,
Symbolising that above the ridiculous Olympian ambitions

There hangs but a crystal-clear *void*,
Suppressing them all with its true might.
All of these ideas hung so plainly and nervously
In the inner air of the monster
That the silence merely emphasised the helplessness

Of Jupiter and Co., who gazed in awe at the Romans
And sought patronage from the barbarian,
Who had so shamelessly smeared them over the walls of the creation.
Over all this reigned the light of truth from the hole in the dome,
The pillar of which was more powerful than any pillar of Hercules.

I was triumphant and rubbed my hands together.
There you go, you cruel, emasculated Rome, there you go!
However, an unexpected, quiet *Bravo!*
Came from the harsh lips of the consuls.
The occasional and timid applause suddenly transformed

Into a loud, madcap ovation.
I could even see tears on the cheeks of the consul Marcus Agrippa,
Who was in fact the lead customer.
'Bravo, Thomas! Bravo! Your creation truly
Encapsulates all that represents

The cultural and political diversity of the Empire!
You have forgotten nothing; there is so much symbolism, gathered in one place
That the plebeians will wander here for years and then centuries,
Endeavouring to work out even just a tiny part of what has been conceived here.
And, Jupiter be my witness, the aristocracy

Will line up before leaving for Orcus[115],
To reserve themselves a spot for their ashes to rest.'
The consul raised a crater of wine and, in a loud voice
Proclaimed, shaking the hall's acoustics:
'Today, we will do away with the injustice

That has unfolded due to circumstances beyond our control.
Thomas, no more shall you be called 'similar' and 'Didymus'.
Oh, greatest architect of them all, allow me
To henceforth call you Apollodorus.
You see, for our city, you are a true gift from the gods!'[116]

The senators present grasped this idea
And with cries of *Bravo, Apollodorus, Bravo!*
Enthusiastically began pouring the nectar of Dionysus down their throats.
A little while later, the now inebriated Gracchus
Approached me with slurred speech:

'Allow us, Apollodorus, this day,
To elevate *Justice* to perfection!

---

[115] *Orcus* (Latin) – in Roman mythology, the underworld of Hades.
[116] *Apollodorus* (Greek) – a gift from Apollo. This is a reference to the name Apollodorus from Damascus, an engineer, architect, builder and sculptor who, it is assumed, worked in Rome in the 2nd century C.E. Apollodorus was Aramaic by birth. He designed the Roman Forum, Trajan's Column, the triumphal Arch of Trajan in Benevento and in Ancona, among other achievements. Some say that Apollodorus was involved in the construction of the Pantheon. He was executed by the Emperor Hadrian for mocking his desire to see himself as an architect.

Let the pediment of this architectural wonder
Decorate the name of its main ideologist and customer –
Consul Marcus Vipsanius Agrippa!'

I nodded and everyone applauded, loudly and drunkenly.
Oh, Adonai! Take the throne, oh, you crowned architects!
That's what it's like, your perfection of *Justice*!
To be known for centuries as an artist
There's no need to burn at the stake of inspiration.

All you need is to be the master of stone and timber
And, at the end of the process, after settling up with all your contractors,
Scrawl your signature
Onto paper and, hey, why focus on trifles? Sign the building's pediment as well.
And enter Eternity with this signature.

This is how the Eternal City deceived me
And laughed wholeheartedly in the process.
'What, Thomas, you're sad?
It's hardly for you to decide what from all this crazy irrationality
Of whims of the mob and the Bohemians

Will end up being a masterpiece and what will perish for all time
In the sands of non-recognition and oblivion.
You thought you'd have some fun and get your plan to subjugate
Such a powerful substance as the collective mind of the megapolis to your plan?
Well, there's a decent answer to your insinuation –

What you thought was a monster and a freak
Henceforth found itself among the masterpieces.
You cursed and lashed out at the merits of glory, didn't you?
Well, then, you held it for a moment
And there and then lost it before Eternity.

Incidentally, you're wrong to think what you've made is monstrous!
After all, you dreamed, as Arminius of Germania advised,
Of creating your own new space, right?
Well, it is this that you have achieved, architect.
In many things, your spatial solution

Predetermines tomorrow's architecture,
So, chin up, Thomas, or how should we address you now?
Apollodorus... Off you go; return
To the embraces of your admirers, including those more ardent.
Or has Bacchus already depleted his soul-healing springs?'

To be honest, after the Pantheon, I was despondent for a long time.
Nothing – entertainment, the attention of the Bohemians, the press
Or the powerful in the world around could
Pull me from the clenches of depression.
And, well, you know bad it can get among us creative types...

But, as often happens,
It is the factor of the search for the unknown and the undiscovered
That becomes that thread of Ariadne
That pulls a person, step by step,
From the dark labyrinths of their depressive nightmares.

I was continually tormented by the words
Of the ancient Germanic sages from the Cherusci clan
About my *imitation of insanity*. What did they mean by that?
I could ask only their silent ashes,
Scattered by the Romans across the Teutoborg Forest.

Then, I decided to visit the one
Who had long enjoyed the reputation of a true madman.
Not in the sense of banal insanity,
Rather in terms of the unpredictable breadth of creativity
That stretches from mathematical knowledge

To the predictions, from which, in terror,
The priests' hair around the tonsure would stand on end.
We're talking about the mysterious old man Leonardo,
That antisocial Tuscan genius –
A true nightmare for the paparazzi but a favourite of popes and kings of Europe.

Moving north, I learned that the *Master* was not in Tuscany.
In the end, ditching my nice new carriage,
I made it on foot to Mediolanum,
Where I found the old man, although he was actually quite the opposite;
Only his eyes were full of what

We call the consequence of contemplating Eternity.

'A-a-ah, so the Roman darling has appeared...'
It was like he had been expecting me, at least that was how it seemed,
When I entered the temple of the ancient order of ascetics,
Where the Master was painting the wall
With some ancient and mystical subject.

Incidentally, rumours about this subject,
Somewhere between curiosity, inspiration and terror,
Made it across Italy at the time –
Leonardo was supposedly creating something hitherto unseen;
Something monumental and beyond the comprehension of the human mind.

When I stood before him, the Master smiled, his eyes sparkling.
However, I felt embarrassed, for the situation in which I had found Leonardo
Spoke of a tense and important moment.
I had clearly entered while the artist had been conversing
With the monastery's prior, who was evidently irritated and unhappy with something.

'Leonardo,' the prior merely nodded slightly in my direction and continued his speech,
'Please, please finish it! Please!
What do you mean "I can't find three heads?"
Where can't you find them? Is it not in your imagination that you're seeking them?
Aren't there enough prototypes around already? I don't get it...

You want to find them? So, look! If you want, we'll roll all of Mediolanum
Past you on the orders of the Duke!
After all, that's how people search, right?
For days and nights you stand in front of the wall
Looking, looking, saying nothing and looking!

Sorry, but that looks like some kind of sabotage!
We've missed all the deadlines; the duke is beside himself... And I'm not talking about...
One mustn't abuse the goodwill of these excellent people!'
This admonition must have been going on for a good while,
Because Leonardo suddenly lost his patience

And slapped his hand down on his knee: 'All right!
You'll have your three portraits, friar! Just give me a little more time,'
Suddenly, he cast a cunning look in my direction.
'At the very least I can already see one portrait.'
The prior departed, muttering as he went, but the Master

Suddenly saddened and tossed his brush into the pail with the paint.
'You see, *Tommaso*, things occur here fairly typically
In the relationships between art and its customers.
You were probably thinking that you'd see something fundamentally new, eh?
No, my dear man, here's the very same Rome only in miniature,

Because all people gradually
Become children of the walls of their megapolises,
Only as if delegated to the provinces and even the villages
To mutilate the pastoral landscapes out there
With silhouettes of dark walls. But that's only half the problem.

Walls carry morals with them; customs change.
And we artists are forced to flee urbanisation,
The factory chimneys, the slums and the dubious romanticism
Of lightning flashes on trolleybus wires,
And even fauns and maenads now walk about in denim...

I think, and you, architect, will agree with me,
That when beauty and utility have an argument,
Like they do in architecture and inside a person,
Unfortunately, you always end up with a fortress,
While it could have turned out to be a temple of free art[117].'

'So, what is this free art?'
I asked timidly, trying to get myself nearer the wall,
To get a view of the Tuscan's mysterious work.
However, to my disappointment, the wall was shrouded,
Which was somewhat of a surprise; where was the scaffolding?

Leonardo noticed my movement and gave a wave of the hand:
'You'll have a chance to see it, you will...
Starting tomorrow, we'll be spending a lot of time here.
I simply covered it up to annoy the abbot a little.
He's actually a decent man; it's me who's the troublemaker...'

He smiled so knavishly, that, in an instant, all those
Rumours of being a cantankerous and egoistic narcissus were dissipated.
I have to admit, for the first time recently,
I felt somehow at peace in my soul.

---

[117] This verse presents interpretations of many of Leonardo da Vinci's comments and proverbs from his famous notebooks.

Alahim alone only knows, perhaps this was from the customary smell of the paint?

'You know, Thomas, what is sad is not even that vulgar contradiction
That has formed over centuries between the artist and his customer.
For example, there's something else I'm afraid of: often, painting
In the hands of these painter-colleagues of ours
Becomes simply an imitation of forms, transforming

These, if I may say so, artists
Into pitiful builders of historical subjects
That pursue but one objective - to achieve simple congruence
Of an object's image with its prototype,
Be it alive or imagined, as in the case of this fresco.

I know you came to ask me
About accusations of imitating insanity.
Well, they grow from far more complicated things
Than simply accusations of rampant eclectic creativity.
A profound understanding of this matter in art

Is associated with the fact that many painters
Possess a segmented talent in the portrayal of particular features,
And in that they have succeeded.
The power of such talent is reduced ultimately to a small space for success,
Deprived both of growth and expansion.

The result is a systematic or, worse still, a straight-out
Disregard for the general for the sake of the particular,
Which leads to a catastrophic contraction of judgments
Once more, in favour of particular features, to the detriment of the general idea.
And, as a consequence, as a reflex,

We see that everything that
Goes beyond the framework of such a limited judgment is accused of insanity.
An insanity that, in their eyes, is something like those Moorish dances;
In other words, something alien and repulsive.
What's there to say about when this approach is applied,

Not only the overall vision is lost,
But the most important thing too: the *meanings*, the fundamental idea.
The integrity of painting is lost, like the windows of communication
Of the Created with its Creator and everything that He created.
Love, focused on particular features is segmented.

As a result we break our understanding of the world
Into fragments and will this philosophy of disunity
Bring us much good in our communication with nature?
People with people? A culture with another culture?
Man with the Almighty?

There is this proverb about the spider who battled with flies.
The spider found a convenient *space*, a hole
Where it could weave decent webs
To catch the flies and then eat them up with relish.
The spider peered out and waited, watching. However, one evening

It heard a noise and, as was the custom, hid itself away deep down

225

Into its new, comfortable hiding place.
The noise was a human who, inserting a key into the keyhole,
Squashed and killed the spider. Such was the story...
Our friends the prior and the duke think in a similar way.

They've built this useful building to
Catch human souls from here, those same Moors as well.
Everything has been designed with a use in mind; even the frescoes
With the image of the Almighty Creator
Should follow the idea that they see

Through the prism of their understanding of the world, in its specific features.
As a result, what they do is divide the world into segments.
Here are we, the righteous; over there, the Moors in their raving dance.
And, well, from the standpoint of integrity and unity of the human race,
Let those Moors dance if they want to, right?

Anyway, Thomas, let's take a break. Today you're tired from the journey.
Share your spread with me and my students.
It's late already; We'll continue our conversations tomorrow.
After all, you came for them, so that we could search together, right?
Right then... By the way, might I ask you to pose for me?'

I awoke the next morning from a terrible din.
It turned out that the quiet of the previous evening
Was deceptive because of the late hour.
The noise was coming from many different workshops,
Where the Tuscan genius had been expressing himself in every possible way.

You should have seen his flaming eyes
As he rushed about the workshops, like a mighty ship,
Steered by a smart pilot in a way
That avoided crashing into the piles of parts, materials and other odds and ends,
That filled the multitude of studios.

Here, surrounded by mysterious machines and structures,
I found Leonardo, astride a peculiar monster,
With its wings spread, like the mythical Simurgh bird.
'This, Tommaso, is the *Ornitottero*[118],' the Master nodded to me.
'Either I'm an old fool, or it will take flight!

Neither conclusion of the two would particularly surprise me.
Here, hold this!' Leonardo thrust a wooden mallet into my hand.
While I held it he pulled something from his pocket
Like a notebook with meaningless scribbles.
'No, not that. The angle should have been increased here...

Come on.' I hammered fiercely at some pin or other.
I looked round, curiously, taking in the workshop.
There they were, all the famous *invenziones*[119] of the great Master –
Examples of his genius, his eccentricity and, according to many, insanity.
They were of weird and wonderful shapes but none looked ugly,

---

[118] *Ornitottero* (Italian) – an ornithopter, a flying craft based on the principle of flapping wings.
[119] *Invenzione* (Italian) – this is how Leonardo called his machines and various craft. At that time, such a word was innovative.

As it had seemed at the start. Across everything, there was a kind of new
And unattainable harmony of a new age,
The age of engineering thought, the beautiful combination of functionality,
Design and technical magnificence,
Which in future would turn men into the slaves of the aviation industry.

However, what drew my attention most was a different harmony –
The spirit of free and even joyous creativity
With which da Vinci and his students
Created, drawing, nailing, screwing and cutting,
All the while laughing, shouting and swearing in ways that were unbecoming to a monastery's
walls;

They were in concentrated silence if seeking a solution,
They drank wine and danced when they achieved success,
And they were genuinely disappointed if they hit a proverbial wall.
Later, I even started a notebook,
Imitating Leonardo, and I started jotting down my own ideas.

I was accepted very simply and without particular deference
Into this amazing brotherhood.
Although, when he introduced me, Leonardo stammered with ceremony,
'This is Senor Apollodorus, the famous architect and master of his trade,'
During our subsequent work, he simply called me Tommaso.

Quite intoxicated, I plunged into a world of all possible *gatti*,
Briccole, intrabucchi[120] and various military equipment.
In time, my notes became my own collection of
Inventions of various apparatus[121]
That I was extremely proud of. What could you do when the main demand at the time

Was specifically for military equipment? Has much changed today?

'Tell me, *Maestro*,' I once asked Leonardo,
'This... engineering, is it simply something to keep you busy or is there something more going
on?'
'What is it that interests you, Tommaso? Tell me straight.'
'You see, you are a multifaceted man and you criticise those
Who are locked into a single field of business,

Which restricts them in the field of particularity.
But I am, after all, an architect and I want to make my mark in my Field.
It's harder for me... how can I put it... to move in many directions.
In your own way, you are unique...' 'Stop, stop!

When I spoke of the loss of generality,
I didn't mean the obligatory nature of universalism.
There is by no means an obligation to succeed in all genres
Of science and art, grasping at every field of knowledge.
Although you have already achieved success in engineering...'

---

[120] *Gatti* – literally *cats*, a type of battering ram; *Briccole* – a machine for launching arrows; *Intrabucchi* – catapults.
Names taken from Leonardo's notebooks.
[121] This refers to *Poliorcetica* (the Greek Πολιορκητικά), or *siege mechanisms*, the works of Apollodorus from
Damascus.

'Hold on, Maestro, things are far more complicated.
I am not striving to create many things. My dream –
And I came to understand this only very recently –
Is to build *one* Temple. One. But a real one,
An embodiment of harmony, light, love and everything else

That is implied in the supreme act of addressing a creation
To one's Creator, and you understand that this is not a matter of confession.
Architectural style or approach to facing stone.
At first I thought that I needed knowledge
And I did very well in my studies at the best schools of architecture.

Then, I gathered experience by studying the technology, faiths and traditions
Of many different peoples and countries, embedded in the landscapes of various natural zones.
Later, I grasped the magic of forms
In their exactitude, diversity and even in the mixture of styles.
Then, I discovered space and its allegories,

And I filled my creations with hosts of gods and idols.
And yet I never did find my own harmony...'
'Hold on, Tommaso... go on! You so gesticulate with your hands.
Would you mind if I made some sketches on paper?
Go on, my dear man!'

'Your words about if someone achieves success only in a specific thing,
Then their picture of generality will never be whole...
They really scared me.
Is it really the case that, to present to God your creation, something proper for Him,
You need to create something that simultaneously comprises

A *Kunstkammer*, an Academy of Science, theatres, a library, a factory, residences,
A cathedral, Knesset, mosque and monastery,
A stadium, bath house, office block and everything else,
So as to comprehend and invent humanity?!
In one place?! I seem to be confused again...'

'I'm confused to a certain extent myself, Tommaso, believe you me.
Before, I sincerely believed that truly great love
Comes about from great knowledge of the subject
To which you have dedicated your life, and it responds in the same way.
All of my searches were linked with this one objective, just like you:

A true understanding of all the figures that are inherent in works of nature
Will lead to knowledge of the world in detail and that, in turn,
Will create an opportunity, through depictive methods,
To convey not only fleeting movement or emotion,
But also certain *higher meanings*, so much higher

That all the minor details of human strife will fade
Before such a level of the understanding of existence.
I got carried away with an unbridled accumulation of experience
And a study of the workings of hidden mechanisms
In human anatomy and machine engineering.

I thought that simple and pure experience was a true teacher.
This was my struggle with the scholasticism and spiritual inquisition,
The triumph of dogma and an axiomatic perception of the world

228

That reigned supreme in the minds of my time.
And so? Where have I come? Well, almost to the same place as you.

When the world around me has reached a mighty decision
To move irrevocably towards the Renaissance,
I basically went back to where I had started.
The more specifics prevailed over the abstract in my mind,
The more generality in my understanding of the world

Became lost in a vague haze.
Come, Tommaso, the time has come for you to see the fresco
And say what you think; after all, it's unclear
For whom the subject will prove more important, you or me.'
When the curtains fell back, my eyes fell on

Something that would leave such a lasting impression,
That would haunt you your entire life as a single emotion,
Seemingly hanging in the air but, all the same, having
Very clear contours within your imagination.
And this emotion, like all true beauty,

Would contain a distinct feeling of inexplicable anxiety.
The fresco was unfinished; there was a lack of completion
In the three portraits. Leonardo climbed up the scaffolding
And, looking at the sketches he had only just made,
He decisively depicted one of the missing images in charcoal.

One of the central characters acquired my features,
And it turned out to be so harmonious, as if this space, next to the central figure,
Had just been waiting for my arrival at Mediolanum.
'Look, Tommaso, there are no problems with two of the portraits.
One is you. And this lad, on the Creator's left-hand side,

Has already acquired a distinct outline in my likeness.
He will be dark as treachery, but we are not talking about official treason.
What's implied is a certain fundamental, ethical rift
Specifically in the *end point* of the concentrated essence,
From where something new will disperse

In circles around the world. However, with the central figure
I have big problems; the prior is right.
It's true that I spend days on end standing in front of it
And I see that there no understanding of all the mechanics of the universe
And no experience garnered in the workshop and laboratories of life

Will give me the opportunity to complete this image...'

'Perhaps, it is purely a matter of ethics?
After all, Maestro, you know that my ancient faith
And the views of the Muslims, too, forbid the depiction of all living things;
And when it comes to its Creator, that has long since been the case.
Perhaps Alahim is hence building a deserved framework for you?'

'No, Tommaso, we're taking the conversation to a completely different plane here.
Well, all right, if you want to hear my opinion
On this matter, here it is:
There are two levels here. One is in the depiction of all that exists;

229

The other is in attempts to depict the Creator.

As far as the former is concerned, compare painting with philosophy and poetry.
Or even with medicine. What do they have that depicts the world of things existing?
This is a striving to understand the world around in all its complexity.
What makes painting any different? Well, nothing,
Apart from the fact that it presents an opportunity to see the world

With the help of the most sophisticated mechanism – sight.
After all, in your faith you bow not to the Book and not to its cover,
But to what's written inside, right?
Therefore, if you don't read the world with your eyes,
How can you understand the magnitude of its Creator?

From the very moment when humans first
Endeavoured to draw round their own shadow in the cave,
There has been a desire to achieve that *eternal* objective
With which the Creator placed His child in nature,
And He gave painting as the best way to comprehend this.

Therefore, painting is not a process of a simple
Congruent reflection of silhouettes and an imitation of colour.
That is nothing more than a banal and meaningless *similarity*,
From which you've been running your entire life.
After all, *impressione* might turn out to be not an impression-sensation,

Rather an elementary stamp-impression of a shape, reflected in a mirror[122].
Painting is a continuous stream of knowledge, a *science*,
And you have realised that over the time you have spent by my side.
There is no point drawing a hand if you don't know
What the minutest muscle and joint tensions

Are that force it to grasp a sword or lay peacefully on a cloth.
How can you convey the natural flow of a river
If you don't know the first thing about hydrodynamics?
How can you depict a lightning strike
If you haven't the remotest understanding of electricity?

Scholastics and dogmatists believe that, in depicting nature,
Painters come over all proud, likening themselves with the Creator.
If any artist likens themselves to the Creator, that is just foolish.
The artist's true objective is not to depict other worlds,
Rather to understand the world that the Creator has already created.

All illuminated objects are accessorial
To the light of that which illuminates it.
Darkened objects retain the gloom of the object
That darkens it. We are not talking about paints here.
Both philosophy and literature have plenty of those

Who serve the darkness with dark objectives and excessive pride.

However, a dogma that would forbid foolishness,
Platitude, mediocrity, pointless imitation, photographic portraiture and poster art,

---

[122] *Impressione* (Italian) – as in the impression left by a stamp on paper.

Unfortunately doesn't exist and it would be impossible anyway.
I sometimes think, though, that the existence of such a dogma wouldn't actually hurt

And would help cleanse the science of painting from the chaff of ignorance (I am off again).

But cleansing a human's life of fine art?!
Then, you'd have to take the books on philosophy and the collections of poetry
And delete all descriptions of bodies, natural phenomena and everything
That makes up the world of all living things. That would be absurd.
Let's remove the description of the human organism from medicine

As an encroachment on the perfection of the Lord's creation.
Let's remove music that so fascinates with its sounds of rain and the sea.
Let's dispose of the dying swan from dances,
All mention of birth, death and happiness from song,
And, while we're at it, let's rid our dreams of physical images of kin and the land of our fathers.

Sure, it may be possible for a short while, as it did
At various times in the past, until some shepherd called Modigliani
Once more finds a piece of charcoal and
Tries to draw a perfect line round his shadow in a cave,
While a beautiful Cro-Magnon woman nearby experiences *impressione* as a result.

And now for the second aspect: the depiction of divinity.
Here, unfortunately, I have to say that my thoughts and views are not as complete
And, paradoxical as it might sound, they coincide to a large extent with the dogmatists.
You're surprised, Tommaso? Yes, that's right.
If you discard the axiomatic taboos in the spirit of *you can't and that's that*,

But you take my extensive experience in painting as a basis for science,
Then this experience tells me that all attempts to depict the Creator
Have three fundamental enemies.
Incidentally, in your striving to attain the pinnacle in architecture
You, too, will come up against them, and some.

The first enemy is *the extrapolation of faith.*
This enemy is the least dangerous, because it is the easiest to understand.
The point of extrapolation is that the created image,
For the ignorant and the simple-minded, itself becomes
A thing to worship, eclipsing the greatness of God.

This is not just the legacy of paganism in the form of idol worship.
It's all about the striving of the simple man to achieve universal simplification,
A pop-culture that dumbs down the complex and multifaceted
To a point where it is simple for common perception;
An elementary nature of sensations and vulgar specifics.

In such a perception, the image
Is endowed with every imaginable divine property,
Among which power is brought to the fore,
Along with the ability to change the course of events.
In particular, to change the fate of man and his living circumstances.

An image, designed only to draw the attention of the believer
To the Everlasting and the Almighty relegates the knowledge of faith
To a simple, self-serving conversation with an idol
That is not even able to move itself from its place.

And this approach inevitably gives rise to hypocrisy,

When a person says, "What are you saying?
Of course, I understand this is just a symbolic image
Of our Lord. It's just that it's easier when in conversation
You see with whom you're speaking, even if they are only imaginary."
Can you imagine, Tommaso?

Such a delusion is never-ending, because
When one art form is popular, they are told,
"That's God!" pointing to a sculpture, say, by Botticelli.
However, when the posters and comic book stickers appear on the wardrobe
They find it easy to believe that "That's God!" this time in

A different depictive culture.
And yet, why think about heaven when it's so hard to do?
Just give me a god to look at; what could be simpler?
Oh, Lord! At this rate, I wouldn't be surprised if tomorrow
Someone were to bow down before a mobile phone gif

With the words "That's God!" You're right, Tommaso, I've drifted back to my grumbling again.
The real challenge here is *how* not to lose
One's way in the depictive knowledge of the Creator, so that crowds of madmen
Don't turn images into objects of targeted worship.
Is that possible? My experience tells me not yet.

As soon as you write or sculpt something,
According to the accepted dogmas, it might be defined as a *That's God!*
Which corresponds with a canonical description of divinity
And everyone around will *recognise* Him and fall to their knees.
So who, then, is the artist?! The creator of the Creator?! That is just absurd.

If I have called painters God's grandchildren,
The creators of knowledge of the riches of the world, nature and humankind,
Then certainly never those who aspire
Even just a little to eclipse the Creator.
How can you even fit the Creator into a man-made object?!

How can what comes first trade places with what comes second?
The monastery prior reasons by saying,
"Finish the central portrait, Leonardo!
Find the canonical prototype and place the symbols that say Worship Here!" Did you see,
Tommaso,

That I didn't place those customary symbols on the fresco?
The halo, crown, the divine light and all that?
Alas, I said myself that painting must give rise to *the sense of God*,
Not his pseudo-projection with arrows pointing
To where the believers should direct their enthusiastic faith.

In this work, I depicted the Creator as one among equals
But, nevertheless, it is already clear that I went the wrong way with this.
I have not escaped the extrapolation of faith and the dark Judas
Will state for all my life that a choice is often
Not simply erroneous, but final as well.

And... well, I will never be able to complete the central portrait...

The second enemy is *giving what is universal the features of the particular*.
We have already spoken of this, when we recalled the spider
That died in the keyhole.
Only here will we look differently at relationships
Between the universal and the particular – through the prism of an image of God.

Imagine that I have taken it upon myself to paint your portrait.
Time passes and you get an exquisite and quite magnificent
Image of your index finger.
And I have taken all the complexities of its organisation into account –
The joints, the fluctuating fabric, the flows of fluids

And everything that, I believe, defines
The scientific background of your finger.
You say, 'Sorry, but what about my portrait
Being my image and my likeness?'
And I say, 'Look, it's an identical image of your finger.'

Next time I bring you an ear, then a buttock; they are all parts of you!
The point is not that I don't see the entire you, but only a fragment;
That would be too simple for our reasoning here.
The essence is that, each time, I create boundaries of you;
I enclose your image in an outline that *I* understand,

From which I do not allow myself to venture, either intentionally or involuntarily.
And then I distribute this image among my audience.
Look at how wonderful Tommaso looks, say.
In so doing, we are in constant dialogue, you and I.
A dialogue about what your image is and what you are like.

I explain to my viewers that they shouldn't personify Tommaso in the form of a finger,
Rather, they should engage their imagination; he's not a finger! Not a finger!
People then appear who rebuke me and say,
'Don't say *finger*, say *digit*, for that is more dignified.
Be that as it may, you are perceived through images

Of scattered body parts and, sooner or later, you'll get fed up with it.
Then, you'll come to me all angry. I'll open the door
And your fist will come through the doorway
And knock me unconscious.
Coming round and wiping my Sodom and Gomorrah,

I continue to depict you, by inertia, as a fist,
But this soon passes. Our dialogue continues.
I suddenly grow smarter and radically change my approach.
I paint a large canvas with an image of all of you,
Only with the addition of your home, friends, servants, your car and your dog,

Your children, office, stamp album, wardrobe and other minor things.
When you see this nightmare of a painting, you understand two things:
First, once again, I have failed to encompass everything.
No, for example your wife's relatives; and there's a hundred of them.
However, second, I have still contrived to lose *you*; you simply cannot be seen

Behind all that associative frippery, direct or indirect.
Do you grasp the essence, Tommaso, through this pile of stupid examples?

You see, we are not talking about an understanding or a knowledge of you,
From a standpoint of religion or philosophy.
We are talking about conveying your image using fine art.

You could also gather together absolutely every picture from the very beginning –
Fingers, fists, buttocks and ears – all in one place.
You could make five thousand identical copies of you and place them in a line.
You could put on a paradoxical performance and add punk music.
There is so much more you could do and never stop.

In the end, you know, you'll even end up with a full portrait, top to toe.
You'll appear and say, 'I am Tommaso!'
But the response will be, 'No, Tommaso is actually flat!'
You order a marble sculpture by Phidias
And you'll stand next to it and say, 'I am Tommaso!'

But the response will be, 'No, Tommaso is actually white!'
You order someone to paint the sculpture a flesh colour
And dress it in your favourite suit and tie.
Standing next to it, you say, 'I am Tommaso!'
But the response will be, 'No, Tommaso is actually cold!'

And, once again, you understand two things: first,
From the very advent of that finger, everything that was created
As a direct copy of the real you
Becomes wholly irrelevant. All of that is not you.
Second, you are like *the cosmos* which, despite the diversity

Of fine art forms
Cannot be encompassed by any artist or even an entire stellar grouping of masters.
For many years, from various angles and in different proportions,
The bottomless pit of labour was directed to what?
Only your external appearance, *of one simple man!*

The search for your correct boundaries and true contours.
Needless to say, no one bothered themselves with your inner world.
And then, on an early, warm July morning
The Duke of Sforza comes to you and says,
'Tomasso, paint me God!'

Of course, my friend, what I have described is merely
The emotional side of the problem's perception.
Now, if we return to my beloved, orderly
Scientific research of the matter,
Even if our fellow physicists

Actually come to comprehend *The Theory of Everything* and clothe the knowledge of the universe
(And of the Creator, too, as it turns out) in a certain harmonious,
Uniform and well-structured mathematical formula,
Then the question of how to approach the depiction of the Universal,
Without enclosing it in boundaries of the particular,

Will still remain unresolved.
What was it that Malevich portrayed in his square?
Perhaps, this is not a geometric shape at all,
But the depiction of the unified field theory?
Or perhaps it's just the Kaaba?

Physicists will create a model of the universe that explains everything,
Perhaps even the physical basis of the soul in the form of the Higgs boson[123]
Or something else, no less sophisticated.
But how will this knowledge transfer to the science of painting?
And will painting be able to retain its status as a science?

Sometimes, I think that a simple line,
Drawn on a blank canvas,
In the instant that it appears
Becomes the boundary of two spaces,
Immediately losing the divine sign of universality.

Shall we continue?

Speaking of the third enemy, we need to turn to the objections of those sceptics
Who might have been following our conversation
About that overly vulgar approach to the essence of a portrait
And how to convey the uniqueness of an image and likeness.
They might object by saying we have distorted the principal meanings,

Which come down to the fact that, essentially, when first drawing a portrait,
The artist is not actually faced with
Tasks of informational universalism. On the contrary,
The artist's skill is indeed manifested in being able,
By recording a fleeting, passing moment,

To convey the depth of emotions and the features of an individual.
And also even to recreate stories and back stories in the viewer's imagination,
Associated with that brief instant that is depicted in the painting.
Movement and spontaneous impulse might create unique dynamics of the moment,
Anticipating the next second or perhaps even an entire life

Or death, as in Bryullov's *The Last Day of Pompeii*.
A true master can convey smells, music,
Serenity and even fear of eternity,
All encompassed in the chilling gaze of a vanquished demon,
Such as emerging from the strokes of Vrubel.

A canvas is like a thin stratum between the ages,
Connecting past and future in a short flash,
With inimitable yet wholly tangible images that are frozen in the present.
And so, Tommaso, it is time to meet the third enemy –
The fixation of God's image in time.

Take a look at the fresco and ask me the key question:
What does it depict? When you get the answer, ask this:
How did it take place? Or when will it take place?
If you start looking for answers in familiar notions,
You'll get lost in a host of other questions,

Which will stem over and over from these three.

---

[123] Higgs Boson – the last, still undiscovered particle of the Standard Model. The Higgs Particle is so important that Nobel Prizewinner Leon Ledermann called it the *God Particle*. The media, too, describe the Higgs Boson as the *God Particle*. On the other hand, the failure to discover this boson might compromise the current implementation of the Standard Model.

And these questions will take you further and further
From the truth. From the truth of the key answer to the key question.
This whole process of the emergence and geometric growth of questions
Is what science, physics, mathematics and philosophy are all about.

They will reach tremendous depths and breadths of knowledge,
Compared with which my humble dabbling in engineering
Will prove to be no more than a course at elementary school.
Yes, I agree with you that everything has to start somewhere
And if it were not for my research, where would quantum physics be today?

On the other hand, however, the theory of relativity
Turned away from the direction of time only in the twentieth century,
While centuries before it, the Incas
Already had their notion of *Pacha*, which means space and time simultaneously.
In Pashto, nouns can be in the past,

The present and the future; what's the point of that
If there is no movement in time of an object and a body
Which might meet and need somehow to be distinguished?
So, where on the axis of time is the discovery that it is not an axis?
In the past or the future?

Knowledge will develop more and more
But today, being a man of natural science and an apologist
For painting, as a science, I cannot answer the question of
Whether faith and science will ever converge at one absolute point
Of understanding of all that exists, or will they forever run in parallel?

What is the Creator – the lord of entropy and fluctuations?
Or is He the Lord of inviolable static systems?
The critical point of thermodynamics concerns liquid and gas,
Or is it also found between life and death?
And does this mean it's in the phenomenon of the Resurrection, too?

Is there a demon that tempts or is there only Maxwell's demon?
An absolutely rigid body has six degrees of freedom,
But how many does an absolutely rigid spirit have?
What does the sound of my lyre have to do with quantum string theory?
Is dualism a matter of corpuscles and waves or Ahura Mazda with Ahriman?

And how do we create the image of the Creator in the
Space-time continuum, avoiding the charms of the simplicity of determinism?
After all, you understand that the matter
Is not simply the fixation of a moment in time,
Not the creation of its simple imprint.

Rather, it's so that all the power of the universe,
In all its known and unknown,
In its static and its chaotic,
Can be implemented so that the contours and visible boundaries
Speak of the complete opposite:

That knowledge and faith are identical
And do not contradict one another, even in the presence of dogmas and axioms;
They have no boundaries, not in time and not in space,
That *Omega* is the start of *Alpha*,

And that there was a crucifixion but it is genuinely still to come.

It transpires that a painting or a fresco, or any image
Of the Maker, who has made and continues to make,
Or of the Creator who still has to create
Must give man a burst of energy
To create an infinite number of degrees of freedom,

At the same time depriving humanity of certainty and peace.

I have this feeling that I don't know, Thomas, *what* I painted today:
Your portrait or a figment of my imagination and my prophesy.
This very day, my protest,
Which bears witness to the temporary helplessness of painting,
Will be expressed through

Me leaving the central portrait forever unfinished.

And I don't know if I can ever return to
This image in future or not. Let's put it this way, I am not yet ready.
Or perhaps it simply means that painting, as a science, is doomed to come to an end and die.
But as to whether you are ready to implement all that I've said
In your architectural creation is for you to decide.

What makes a temple not an address to the image of the Creator?'

That is what Da Vinci said and what do you think remained in the head of this old Jew
From this monologue by the Master?
Of course, total chaos. Most importantly, however,
I received such an injection of *impressione*,
That, as far as my search and I are concerned,

Leonardo certainly achieved his objective.
There was not a trace of my depression.
Obsessed with the search for answers to the questions
That burned brightly in that Tuscan's workshop,
I turned my feet to the East...

There, on the border of Ethiopia and India[124], many years later,
I learned from a Hellenic traveller
That Leonardo had created a picture
Which, in its level of sensations and *impressione*,
Makes one lose their mind with its mystery and, evidently,

It will make future generations lose their mind for many years to come.
I asked him to explain what he meant by this.
And this is literally what the Hellene replied: 'You know, Thomas,
When you look at it, you feel more than when
You study its content.

Actually, you forget about the content almost the moment
You first set eyes on it.
Then the wonders begin. You understand

---

[124] The ancients believed there were two Ethiopias and several Indias. The second Ethiopia, unlike the African Abyssinia, was situated in the Far East, beyond the gates of Alexander the Great in the Caucasus (now Derbent in Dagestan).

That you are seeing a very specific character;
A woman, but you *see* that this is by no means about her.

You view landscapes that disappear in the haze,
But you understand that the picture has no frame
And you appear to freeze at the door to infinity.
You observe the calm and the movement of the moment
But you are unable to see their beginning and their end;

Either the calm is eternal, or it's the movement of the lips and the face
That are in constant and elusive repetition,
Compared with which even the waves on the shore
Will one day come to an end and fade away, but it's not that *emotion*.
Is the subject about life or about death?

It is so beautiful yet simultaneously terrible.
Is it about beauty or madness? About canons or their destruction?
How frightening are these infinite degrees of imagination,
Ranging from 'it's just some woman' to 'it's something beyond our understanding'!
However, my friend, this might be blasphemous, but I think

That the Tuscan was able to present us God,
Avoiding his vulgar portraiture.
You know, Thomas, they say that the technique used for painting landscapes
Is called *sfumato*[125], but I don't think we are talking about landscapes at all.
The entire picture has been painted as if its essence consists of three things:

The ambiguity of the image, which tells us
That one does not have to draw a portrait version of the Eternal;
It can be seen in any of his works...
Second, *the incomprehensibility of the image*, which tells us
That the universal might be presented in sensations through the particular.

It is completely impossible to understand Leonardo's feelings for his subject.
Did he love her? Did he hate her? Was he just working to order?
I have never seen portraits, painted
With such ambiguity when it comes to the painter's attitude
To his heroine... Or, perhaps, eternal understatement?

Like a phrase, cut off in mid-flow,
When one is unable to express the boundless power of love
Or a boundless indifference, perhaps?! Like the symbolism of prayer
Or the blurred nature of excuses,
Or the interjections of delight, along the lines of *Oh! Matsushima, oh!*?[126]

What is most incredible is that Leonardo was able to achieve
A *sfumato* of time, *an elusiveness of the moment*,
That is continuous and simultaneous in its emergence
And its disappearance. Happiness! Perhaps this is what happiness
Looks like in its transitory essence?

---

[125] *Sfumato* (Italian) – shaded or, literally, *disappearing like smoke*. In painting this is the softening of a figure's or an object's outline, helping to convey the air that envelops them. It is generally thought that Leonardo da Vinci devised the *sfumato* technique, both in theory and practice.
[126] The famous *Matsuo Basho* haiku dedicated to the beauty of the Matsushima Islands in Miyagi Prefecture, Japan:
Matsushima!
Matsushima!
Oh, Matsushima!

Serene... Although... You know, Thomas (and, with that, the Greek smiled mysteriously)
Perhaps it really is just a painting of some woman;
Someone specific with a place in history.
Well, all right, you can't describe in words
What you simply need to see.'

The Hellene had no idea how his words would echo in my soul,
For his description was a precise repetition of those enemies
Of which the great Master had spoken of to me.
Suddenly, I became acutely aware
That art is far from being doomed to die,

Whatever the physical constraints of shape and contour
That have forged it. And that meant I had to
Find my own *sfumato* in the Work that I had chosen for my Life's Work.
Failing that, I thought, life itself would lose all meaning.
And so, in my search for my Temple, I set off for lands unknown,

Lying to the north of the towns of Sogdiana and Bactria,
To the land of the Turks, to their boundless and frightening steppes.
It seemed to me that out there, amid the naïve nomads,
In their state of barbarism,
And, hence, inexperienced in architecture,

I could find the inspiration and the circumstances
That would allow me to build my life's Temple.
That is how I found myself in the court of the steppe monarch Mahdi Kagan[127],
Who united the children of Touran and Altai
Into a single Hun ulus, as extensive as the Ocean that washed the world.

Throughout my entire journey in the empire,
I never saw a single stone building or homestead,
From which hope and the anticipation of work
Beat in my heart like a free bird.
It was in this mood that I arrived at the seat of the Great Kagan.

For several days, distracted from the worries of governance,
Mahdi Kagan, in the presence of his *kam* priests,
Listened to the long tale of my search for the Perfect Temple,
Although I saw, for some reason, that the priests' eyes often
Shone with anger and a total rejection of

What I was setting out to the lord of the steppes.
However, I now had nowhere to go
And, in my desperation, I continued to insist on the need
To build the Temple within the Hun Empire,
As evidence of its might and divine protection.

To my great surprise, at the end of the seventh day,
The Kagan invited me and gave his consent!
What is more, I could not believe the metamorphosis that had overcome the priests:

---

[127] *Mode Shanyu* – the founder of the Hun empire. The precise transcription of his name, following the Turkic manner, is unknown; in Chinese historical literature he appears as *Maodun*. There are various alternatives -- *Mete*, *Mode* and even *Dulu*. There are legends linking the name of *Mode Shanyu* with Oghuz Khan, a legendary figure among the Turkic people. The transcription *Mahdi* is suggested here with a particular meaning implied.

Their eyes smiled and their thin beards swayed to and fro in time with their approving nods!
'Build your Temple, Thomas,' Mahdi said, 'with but two conditions:

After all, you are no missionary, forcing your views
Upon us against our will; you are an architect, an artist.
That means that we will learn as you build,
From one another. You will give us your experience and your knowledge;
We will give you our vision of the universe as we see it.

After all, this building will serve our society, will it not?
Second, however barbaric you may imagine us to be,
We are well versed in the achievements of world architecture,
And we understand that you are building something secondary for us.
The horses of our kin, the sons of Touran and Altai,

Have raced all over the Oecumene, so we have a sufficient understanding
Of the pyramids, the pantheons and the triumphal arches of other empires.
So, this is the second condition. You, though, it seems, want in any case
To create something original, something *not similar*.
So, get to it, look around, do what you do... and another thing:

As far as our view of the world is concerned, any of my subjects,
Be they a *kam*[128] or a warrior, or even me – we are all happy to talk with you.
And now, off you go and select a site.'
'One moment, Great Kagan, what about protection of the idea, of the design?'
'No, Thomas, no constraints.

Why start the construction of a Temple of an elusive form
From finite obligations at the initial stage?
Perhaps the creative process itself will be the meaning behind our mutual evolution?
After all, they say that Gaudi spent 30 years on his expiatory cathedral[129] and still never finished it,
Not because he didn't manage to, but perhaps he didn't want to?'

And so, I set about my search.
First, out of habit, but rather out of inertia, I began with a basic shape,
A basic idea. For days on end I made mockups
And sketches, before going into finer detail
In my search for the overall idea.

However, every time, all my ideas ended in the same way.
With disappointment, you think? No, with laughter!
I have to say that the Turks are a very good-natured and straightforward people
And because I had no walls in my workshop,
For the simple reason that there are no walls there at all,

I was always observed as I worked
By a loud crowd of nomads who were not idle, no;
Every one of them brought me something to drink or eat,
Or a gift like a griffon carved from wood.
I had already grown accustomed to this noise.

---

[128] *Kams* – ancient shamans and also, presumably, Tengrian priests. The word is the root of the word *kamlanie*, meaning shaman incantation.
[129] *Temple Expiatori de la Sagrada Familia* in Barcelona. Antoni Gaudi worked on its construction from 1882 to his death in 1926.

The only thing that upset me was how directly and quickly
They would destroy my ideas, leaving no meaning to them whatsoever.
Not a stone, not a chip. And all without the slightest scientific spiel,
Just with the power of their laughter, bringing the naivety of the nomad
And the sophistication of the city's architect to the same level of meaning.

'Oh, Thomas, you've made a pyramid! You plan to bury someone
Or are you dying?
Thomas, what's that dome for? Will it just be a great big yurt?'
And they said that about my model of the Pantheon! Oh, how naïve those nomads were!
'Hey, Thomas, what are these bow-shaped arches for? You trying to shoot Heaven?
What a tower! Aren't you ashamed to think that the earth has a phallus coming out of it?

To whom and why are you likening yourself, Thomas? The Creator? Make a fish instead!'

And so on and so forth...
You think I got cross? No, I laughed just as much as these children of nature,
And the next shape lost all meaning, transforming into a mountain of rubbish.
One day, in total desperation, I simply erected a wall,
A tall one, several fathoms long and two men high.

And then it dawned on me that for thousands of parasangs,
This was the only wall in the Empire.
Why?! This stone was always laying beneath the feet of the Turks;
They had seen their city neighbours putting walls up
Many times over. Why had I built the first wall here?!

'That's a good question, Thomas,' I heard the Kagan's voice above my head.
'Take to your horse. Let's have a ride around the ulus.
Take a look at the people, my friend, from a totally different standpoint
From that taken for many centuries by the city dwellers
And other residents of the Empire who build walls.

Listen to our legends and our tales.
Perhaps you'll find in them what you'd like to display in your creation?
And you'll understand why we have no walls or stone houses,
What our way of life means to us
And why we hold it so dear and why we take such care of it.

I'll get our *kam* storytellers together for you, and you listen.
Listen and then do as we've agreed – what you deem appropriate.
In the meantime, take a look at the Mangi El[130], outstretched before you.
I recall you asked why we don't sow or reap,
Why we eat only animal food.

Anticipating the age of universal vegetarianism,
I think your question is both legitimate and relevant.
You asked why we are embraced in the arms of barbarism.
Well, we view all this with slightly different eyes.
You decide for yourself; you're the one building the temple.

---

[130] *Mangi El* (or *Mangilik El*) (Turkic) – *The Eternal Nation*, the ancient name for the Turkic world, *Pax Turcica*, which is far broader than the name of any state that the Turks have ever formed.

Let the first *magus* relate his legend to you.'
The first *kam* came forward. He remained silent for a very long time
As if he were remembering what he had not endured himself,
Enduring what is not written in any books,
Until silence reigned in the steppe and the *magus* began his tale.

THE FIRST LEGEND OF THE TURKS

A-a-ah-o-o-o-oo-oo-oo-oo-oo!
Hello, Tengri with your Eternal Blue Sky!
Lord of worlds, Creator of everything!
Master of Justice in Heaven and on Earth!
Guide on the straight path and the people's way!
Kagan of destinies, Kagan of the word,
The Master of the Beginning and the End!
Lord of all things!
Pointing to the head of the House
And instructing him!
Hello, you creations of Tengri,
Yer-sub – The Expanses of Mangi El,
And other peoples who possess and take pride in the name!
The master of mountain paths, the Great Steppe, the rivers, forests and the mighty Ocean!
Hello, Umai our foremother, the protector of people!
Mother of all mothers; is there even a sense of God without a Mother?!
Hello, Erlik, Lord of the Dark World,
Who does not rule over us unless we decide otherwise for ourselves,
Who watches for every deviation from the truth,
For every deviator falls into your eternal embrace!
Hello, dear ancestors, who safeguard us from
Becoming slaves of anyone or anything!
To ensure we take good care of Mangi El!
So that men remember that they are men – warriors and protectors!
So that women remember that they are daughters of Umai –
The keeper of Honour, Beauty, the Hearth of the Home and the Mother's Song!
Hello, you living children of Mangi El!
Remember to return to Tengri soon!
Our *kösh*[131] forever and everywhere moves to Him!
To Him, our eternal *kösh* heads East!
The thirsty one and the seeker will find their peace by His side!
Until we achieve our peace

Let's be merry and fearless, as all warriors should be!
Let's be kind and open-hearted, as our ancestors told us to be!
Let's be just and gentle, as we wish and dream!
Let's be honest and generous, for otherwise our daughters will not forgive us!
And let us not forget that between us and the return to Tengri[132]
There is a brief yet never-ending Life!
A-a-ah-o-o-o-oo-oo-oo-oo-oo!

I call you to witness
What my story is about.
And allow me to call Erlik a friend,
If but one word is imbued with lies.

---

[131] *Kösh* (Turkic) – nomadic migration.
[132] In Kazakh, the word for *died, passed away* is қайтты, which literally means *returned*.

242

Never mind Erlik; Allow me to become the laughing stock of all women!

Long, long ago, during the Golden Age of Altai Zaman,
All children of Tengri lived like kith and kin.
There was Buffalo, the mighty son of the prairie,
Who came merrily for the festivities of spring.
There was Horse, the handsome lover of freedom,

Who danced under the summer rain.
There was Snake, the wise teller of tales,
Who sent you to sleep with his age-old songs.
There was Antelope *Saiga*, dazzling with its grace.
Rushing in to see her brothers and sisters.

There was Monkey, whose agility and strength
Was an example for all young men.
There was Man, whose perseverance and hard work
Evoked the delight and admiration of Mother Umai.
There are Fox, Leopard and Eagle;

They all came together for celebrations
And parted with tears of joy,
For, you must agree, family festivities
Are when you always view your kith and kin in new ways
Even though you have lived many hundreds of years together.

All of Yer-sub lived in a harmony
That today we cannot describe in detail.
You see, if we could, would we not have restored
Those same traditions from the life of Altai Zaman?
(Oh, memory mine, how cruel you can be at times!)

But one day, everything changed under the Eternal Heavens.
The wolves gathered at the foothills of Tarbagatai
And said to one another, 'A-a-ah-o-o-o-oo-oo-oo-oo-oo!
Are we not the strongest and the smartest?
Are we not the greatest creation of the Almighty?

Are we to beg for food
When the might of our swords and armour
Mean we can take it for ourselves?
Take a look at our race,
How perfect our fighting spirit and our sense of brotherhood!

Let us conquer this world of carefree creatures.
Is this not our historical purpose?'
And the wolves said, 'It is time to stop speaking in a common tongue.
We will have our own language of higher beings,
So that the Sudra, the plebeians and the low-lifes of this world

Cannot understand the imperial way;
This will become a symbol of their enslavement.'
So spoke the wolves and, several moons later,
An enormous army of new fearsome warriors
Spread like lava across the Great Steppe.

The wolves boasted, 'We were made for battle and conquest,

For legends, splendour, power and song
To laud us. We have it all –
Intelligence, beauty and noble standing.
Are we not destined to rule the world?!

Was it not thrown to us at the feet of Tengri?!'

Their former kith and kin all fled in terror,
Like seagulls, frightened by thunder over the Aral Sea,
Closer to their ancestral home in Altai,
Where they gathered in council amid noise and uproar,
Forgetting the nobility of their conduct and their innate civility.

They gathered in council at night, too, in hiding like thieves.
Experiencing quite new, hitherto unknown feelings.
What were they to do? How could they stand up to such a terrifying army?
In line with the Tengri covenant, no one entertained thoughts of slavery.
Who could create even a semblance of that

Terrible army that was coming from the West, and how?
The first to come forward were Tiger and Lion:
'We will defeat the enemy; are we not symbols of strength and power?
Are we not the heroes and knights
To take this opportunity

To die for the glory of our kith and kin?'
The Tengri children watched with alarm
From the mountainside as the metal-clad army of wolf archers
Showered the mighty Pahlevans, Tiger and Lion, with their arrows.
And the clan of valiant protectors was no more.

Then Antelope *Saiga* spoke: 'Are there not many of us?
Can our light cavalry,
Armed with our sharp horns, not
Scatter the ranks of wolves like wormwood across the steppe?
We will enter battle tomorrow!'

Yet only three saiga, soaked in blood,
Returned from the Battle of Hattin.
So badly were they torn apart by the wolf pack
That it was clear that numbers were irrelevant.
Kith and Kin fell mournfully silent

And, although accustomed to merriment,
They moaned with anxiety and songs of loss,
Like the Nogai dombra over the silence of Edil.
Then the mythical Simurgh, the strategist and saviour, spoke up:
'My fellow kin! I will fly high and ask Tengri

If there is a Great Warrior in the world
And a Great Weapon capable of standing up to
This army of wolves, or whether we are doomed.'
On the third day the Simurgh returned and said,
'I have received a response from Tengri. Here it is:

Far, far away in Azerbaigan
There is a great weapon that you need to take

244

And it shall be the Great Warrior who shall take it, only
The Almighty did not reveal who this was. That means we have to find this Warrior
From among our kind.'

'I know,' said wise Snake.
'This weapon is called Fire but, from time immemorial
No one has succeeded in reaching agreement with it,
As it has its own language, which
None of us speak.'

The kin fell once more into a gloom, but Eagle then spoke up:
'I will go to the Fire and try to bring it here.'
Eagle left but returned with nothing.
'Brothers! My keen eye found it in the mountains of Azerbaigan!
And, it seems, I was able to find an understanding,

But it scorched and stung my wings so badly that I could not fly off.
My claws were unable to grasp even a fraction of it.'
Then Monkey spoke: 'I have strong and nimble hands!'
And off she went to the mountains of the Caucasus, but returned empty-handed, saying,
'I was able to take some of it in my hands, but it burned me badly.

The problem is that I don't speak
The language of this creature.' Then Man spoke: 'All right,
I will go and speak with this Fire, if I am able.'
Eagle exclaimed, 'Man, take my keen sight!'
Snake whispered, 'Take my intelligence!'

Monkey cried, 'Take my agility and make it happen!'
Since that time, Man has possessed all these qualities
In which he surpasses his other kith and kin.
However, he still lacked the most important thing:
He knew not the language of Fire.

Man departed for the mountains of the Caucasus
Where he met with Fire. He saw it with Eagle's keen sight.
Fire danced and sang at length before him,
But Man was unable to discern a single word.
And then he prayed to Tengri:

'Oh, Eternal Blue Sky, help me persuade Fire!'

And he heard a voice within: 'All right.
Only Fire will demand a sacrifice for knowledge of its language
And you have simply no idea
How you will be delivering it, for years, centuries and all eternity.
Are you ready for that?'

'Oh, Almighty Tengri! What is greater for a Turk that his kith and kin?
Nothing!' And Man agreed. And he approached Fire once again.
And he spoke in its language. Only Fire said,
'This will be your sacrifice: some day you will
Call me powerfully in my dialect.

At that moment, you will forget all other languages of your kin.
But that is not all. After that, you will reach immeasurable heights
In your knowledge of the world and the physics of the universe;

You will own me. You will use me for warmth, to admire and even to kill,
But you will never-ever be able to comprehend me alone;

You'll just take me for granted
As a flame, no more. You will know light, fields and the smallest particles,
How waves crash on the shore, anatomy and the splitting of the nucleus,
But you will never comprehend me, do you agree?'
Man objected: 'Are you not likening yourself to Tengri –

Know you, but leave your essence as unknowable?!'
Fire replied: 'This deal concerns not just you and me,
You understand. Agree.' And Man agreed.
Fire extended its hand and set the trunk of a sacred saxaul alight.
'Take it and go,' Fire said. 'Use Monkey's agility.'

'Are you not coming with me?' Man asked.
Fire replied: 'Out of a part of me, all of me will arise.'
Man began to leave but then stopped and asked,
'Who else does this deal concern apart from me?'
Flame grinned. 'You are growing. Clearly, Snake's intelligence

Is helping you. I will say only this:
When you ignite me, you will always think,
That you are holding only a part, a piece, a single episode
Or a part of the overall idea.
I think you have understood who else this deal concerns.'

Man was unable to understand it all at once; he needed time
And time was something he didn't have.
Rumours reached him from the blessed Altai
That he was surrounded by the wolves and that the final assault would soon begin.
The son of Tengri hurried across the steppe plains to his kith and kin.

Soon he arrived at the besieged camp.
At first his native ulus was confused,
What this wood was and how it would save them.
However, when the bonfire flared up, first fear and then hope
Grasped the souls of the Almighty's children...

Early one morning, the kith and kin ventured out onto the plateau
And gathered a war council.
Below them the wolf cry
A-a-ah-o-o-o-oo-oo-oo-oo-oo!
Shook the foothills, turned the rivers and made the trees tremble.
The battle was that day. A fearsome battle.

The buffalo spoke: 'Man, you have comprehended the language of Flame;
Today you will be commander-in-chief.
We will march forth in one formation and we will perish if needs be.
Today will decide everything. Lead us into battle.'
The elk sounded the trumpets!

Into battle! Into battle, the might of the Turks!
Like waves of steppe wormwood over the hills
Came the light cavalry of antelope.
The bows of the martens, foxes and lynxes rang out like dombra strings.
The wind played with the bears of the rhinoceros infantry.

The mighty buffaloes flooded the valley in a fearsome stampede.
Ferocious camels joined cheetahs
In troop formations. Darts and slings whistled
In the hands of monkeys and turtles.
Oh, listener! Are you prepared to stand up and defend your kind like this?!

The troops of beasts and people froze...
And then, from out of the silence came the iron clash of a fearsome army.
The hills began to cover with a grey shadow.
The wolf army advanced unhurried
Across the valley, calmly yet cruelly.

There came the cataphracts in their chainmail,
Then the heavy infantry with their sun-like shields.
There were the military machines, scorpions and ballistae.
There was the wolf army, in all its splendour, in its appearance alone
Speaking of the superiority of the *Bozkurts*.

Over all other children of Tengri.
The troops stood at the ready. Silence reigned. No one thought that
Things could be any other way. Death!
Everyone had asked for a worthy death. Fear!
Only of the fact that it would pass them by.

A nervous tremor suddenly ran through the ranks.
This was a matter of warriors setting off on their final journey to meet one another.
The wolves howled for they had never tasted defeat.
Beasts and men howled, demanding vengeance for their previous humiliations!
The wheezing sound of the wolves' *karnais*[133] and the battle drums of the wild boars

Provided the music for this first battle.
The wolves fought with ferocity, pushing through the centre of the enemy's positions.
Zebras and onagers flinched on the flanks
As the enemy's *Bozkurt* grey wolves crushed them with iron teeth.
This, though, was the moment when the battle turned.

A cavalry attack from the right flank
Launched the mighty Fire into the ranks of wolves.
Man ran in front, but the flame was prepared to swallow him too,
If it had not been for the horse offering its back for flight.
With a relentless blow of doom, the horseman and fiery dragoons

Tore the ranks of the grey army to shreds.
From this point on, Wolf was powerless in the face of Fire,
If you, listener, haven't forgotten his language!
A terrifying wail rose above the valley,
Accompanying with a fatal symphony

The death of the best army in history; the wolves trembled.
They took flight, in tragic desperation.
The assembled people and beasts stung, beat and tortured
The remains of the once brilliant and glorious military might.
The jackals and the hyenas had triumphed...

---

[133] A copper woodwind folk instrument, considered a national instrument in a number of Central Asian countries

On the third day of the decidedly patchy resistance
And the flight of the now rudderless great army,
The armies reached the waters of the Ocean.
The wolves now had nowhere to retreat. Man prepared himself
To finish off those guilty of the death of the Golden Age.

They did not stop, but the soldiers collapsed in exhaustion
On both sides of the front line. Man stepped into the middle.
With a formidable cry and a crack of his whip
He drove the jackals and vultures
From their nefarious beating of prisoners and deserters.

The wounded wolves gathered themselves and lined up
In preparation for the last battle of their lives.
They were surrounded by the army of beasts
Who could not find the courage to strike the final, fatal blow.
The ranks of the victors became confused. A murmur passed through their ranks.

Brothers, remember that, when all is said and done, we are kith and kin!
Would the world really be perfect without the tribe of wolves?
Are they not children of Tengri as we are?
Elk then spoke: 'We have no experience of battles and their resolution;
This is the first war in history, after all. How can we find a solution?'

Noise and uproar rose above the assembled ranks of beasts:

'We won tactically and strategically...'
'Let's tell the wolves not to emerge again from their lairs.'
'Let the leaders battle it out,' someone cried from the ranks.
And so, Man and Blue Wolf Kokbori[134]
The leader of the wolf race, stepped out onto the plain.

Their shields clashed and the steel of their *akinaka* daggers rang out.
The battle lasted seven days and seven nights.
On the eighth day, badly wounded but unbroken,
The *Bozkurt* fell before his enemy and said,
'Farewell, Man. From now on, all beasts who display cowardice

Will forever fear us wolves, but our tribe
Will forever fear you, avoid you and hide in the steppe.
Only don't you rejoice in killing me for you, as before with Monkey,
Eagle and Snake, you will absorb *our* spirit, the spirit of the hunter, for all time.
The destruction of our army will not leave you unscathed.

You will inherit the stomach and the fangs of predators,
You will kill and devour your own kith and kin.
But that's not the worst thing. In the hazy pride for your services
You'll think you wear nature's crown,
That you can trample over her freedom; that you're a *Comprachico*[135], disfiguring her face.

Your kind will multiply and settle all over the world,
And their ranks will feature not only your valour,

---

[134] Translates as *Heavenly Wolf* – one of the principal totemic animals for the Turkic peoples.
[135] A word coined by Victor Hugo in his novel *The Man Who Laughs*. It refers to various groups in folklore who were said to change the physical appearance of human beings by manipulating growing children, in a similar way to the horticultural method of bonsai – that is, deliberate mutilation.

But the features of snakes, jackals and monkeys, too.
But you are a great warrior. And a victor. Therefore, I bequeath you
And your tribe our princess.

One day, when your fellow tribesmen, the jackals and hyenas,
Drag your kind to paltry nooks and destroy the warrior's spirit,
You call in your debt and our union
Will give rise to a great tribe, which will be the stuff of legend.
Only don't go losing it again behind words, a lack of will or fear.'

Man then shouted angrily at the beasts: 'Here is the fruit of your doubts, you cowards!
From this day on, when remembering the past,
Everyone will talk of only battles and victories,
Instead of remembering Altai Zaman!
The world will never be the same.'

He turned to Blue Wolf:
'Farewell, warrior. This was a worthy battle!
Because of that, a wolf's head will henceforth adorn my banner,
As a sign of respect for a worthy adversary,
Only we will never end the war with you.'

The leader of the wolves closed his eyes and returned to Tengri.
The two armies scattered across the world, and Man left
To the slopes of Alatau in search of peace and tranquillity.
However, he never found it.
A year later, Buffalo came to him and said,

'You know, we are afraid to live without protection.
Out there, somewhere in the steppes, what is left of the *Bozkurts* still roams and torments
Our frightened tribe.
We are kin; take me under your protection!
I will lift some of the burden of the hunt from you

And every three months I will give you
A sacrifice from our ranks as food,
As payment for our right to feel safe and secure.'
A month after that, Saiga came and said,
'We are tired of saving our skins

From the remnants of the wolf army with our feet.
Take us under your protection, as we are kin.'
Horse came with recollections of the great battle
And he also remained forever with Man,
Creating the tribe of riders of the Great Steppe.

Then other kith and kin came...
Oh, listener! That is how the duty of the beasts,
Children of Tengri, to feed and warm Man came to be,
But that is not the whole story.
In time, the beasts lost their wild appearance

And became mollycoddled and cowardly.
One day, when a terrible frost had gripped the steppe expanses,
The animals wept bitterly from the cold and frost
And asked Man to warm them.
Man thought long and hard about how to do this

249

Until he remembered the terrible heat of Fire,
Which had almost burned him alive in the Great Battle.
Then he spoke in the language of the flame and...
He lit a fire. He lit it not like a battle legion,
Rather to warm himself and his relatives.

It was then that Man heard Fire's laughter,
Which appeared to rush from Azerbaigan itself:
'Oh, ho, Man! So this is how my prediction is destined to come true!
Now you will remember by language for all time,
But you will forget the tongue of your kith and kin!

Let's see if you can preserve your relationships!'
And it laughed out loud once again. In terror, Man ran to Buffalo,
And called his name but, in response, Buffalo merely mooed and shook his head.
Man rushed to Saiga, but Saiga simply bleated timidly.
Since then, we have lost the language of our kith and kin, who have become simply livestock for us.

They say that the animals once decided to review
Their agreement with Man.
They came to him and spoke, only... no one understood a word from the conversation.
Often, an inviolable agreement is nullified from a simple
Inability to talk...

They say that just one horse approached Man in trepidation
And whispered, 'Don't give me away, but I can speak and understand you.'
However, neither will say which of them it was,
But every son of Tengri knows
With which horse he can converse.

Oh, listener! Even now you can hear the wolves' songs
Of their former power.
They still sing them in that same ancient language
And their lament of defeat in the Great Battle
Frequently tears the night asunder with longing.

A-a-ah-o-o-o-oo-oo-oo-oo-oo!

And just as Blue Wolf had predicted,
Man was left all alone
With no one to talk with.
It was then that he thought of his uniqueness
And he began to think that he alone was speaking with Tengri.

After all, he had stopped hearing his kith and kin.
He saw himself as wearing nature's crown,
And that meant he had the right to change it
As he saw fit.
He began inflicting wounds and scars on her face.

You see, none of those who remember Altai Zaman
Could reproach him in a way that he would hear.
Knowing this human weakness,
Erlik sent new armies to face the human race:
Black rats and iron locusts.

Man fights them alone
But no one hears his groans or his fear.
Oh, listener! Our song calls not to apportion blame
And calls not for vengeance or judgment.
For there is one Judge over us all and He is but one.

Remember, being only *a part* of the human race,
Of what other lost *integrity* does the lark sing to you?
Does the Siberian salmon dance in the depths of the Irtysh?
Does the buffalo low when looking at the endless Ergenekon?[136]
Does the snake whisper when it strokes the skin of the Karakum?

Who determined that you were the pinnacle of all on earth?
Could it have been Tengri, looking down to earth from above in springtime?
Or was it not you, like the ancient wolf,
Who proclaimed yourself to be unique and, therefore, alone,
Having forgotten the language of your kith and kin?

****

The *kam* storyteller fell silent. As if in confirmation of his words,
A *Bozkurt* sang in the deep of night. I shivered, either from cold
Or from the impression that I had heard a legend.
The next morning, we said goodbye to the *magus* and, taking to our horses,
We set off further along the ulus.

'You see, Thomas,' Mahdi Kagan broke the silence,
'What views these people hold.
I understand, legends are legends, but it is on this that our state is based.
We are all Humans; kith and kin from the very outset.
There is no Hellene or Jew among us,

For we are all children of the Eternal Blue Sky.
The Turkic states are enormous because they unite those who are close to them.
From time to time, the Spirit of the Blue Beast
Might awaken in some tribe. This tribe is sure
To come up with a new name for its new empire,

Such as *Huns, Mongols, Kushans* or *Qara-Kitai*.
And yet they still contain the same families who prefer
To recall the name of their own clan, for empires come and go,
While you always remain with your relatives,
Who you need to go on protecting and caring for.

Hence Mangi El – transforming but essentially unchanging.
One has only to raise the blue heavenly banner, bearing the *Bozkurt* head,
And declare that a threat is coming from West or East
And you'll always see that you have kith and kin, ho-ho,
Often more than you'd like.

Are you a Persian, Thracian or Han? Do you need protection from wolves or hyenas?
Come in, take the seat of honour, be our brother.

---

[136] *Ergenekon* – in Turkic mythology, a mythical place in remote Altai valleys, where the Turkic peoples are said to have originated and united.

Even your Engels said that a form of government such as that of the steppe people,
Based on assignment of the duty to protect
Onto a part of society, is more ancient than that of the townsfolk.

We actually don't care if its more ancient or not;
This is the prerogative of others to state that we are pioneers or barbarians.
We know one thing: we have the spirit of the wolf warriors
And we are the best starter culture for all empires
That have been and will be in history.

Probably, because we carry with us the spirit of the *Bozkurt*
That we have inherited and we will pass it on to those
Who actually want it and not be a buffalo or an antelope.
But this is if we leave with our nomadic settlement to distant lands.
Here in our steppes, Thomas... Have you noticed that we have no poor folk?

No, no, don't be fooled. We are talking ideologically here,
That we have the fairest state.
To a greater extent this is actually a specific feature of life
In the arid zone of the forest-steppes. Well, how can I put it more simply?
A person basically won't survive here

If they don't have fifty or so breeding sheep,
Ten bulls and three dozen horses.
He'll simply starve to death during the severe frost;
He won't be able to feed his offspring and that'll be the end of him.
The townsfolk think that the steppe dwellers are wealthy,

And why should we in authority plunder the family once again?
You let someone off around the world and when war comes you find
Yourself a couple of warrior trios short. And I'm not just talking about soldiers
But warriors, arriving on the front line in full battle gear.
Everything, Thomas, has its pragmatism.

So, as Sigmund Freud puts it,
"The intention that man should be *happy* is not included
In the plan of Creation," and we are no exception.
And yet, we cannot have an excessively high level of social differentiation
Like they do in the city.

But more on that later...

The family and family ties, as you've heard from the legend,
Bind together a far greater universality
Than just a human one.
Perhaps these are views of a very primitive nature.
Well then, if primitive means a closeness to the primordial

Then perhaps this is no bad thing.
However, true primitive types live in somewhat closed societies.
We have too many enemies
To enable ourselves the luxury of living in a state of contemplation.
And today tells us

That we have forgotten the languages of our kith and kin, and not only from the world of Animal Planet.
Is it not your Jewish epic tale that relates

Of the linguistic crisis that arose not so long ago
In regard to a certain, well-known construction project?
Well, Muslims basically say

That when shepherds start building towers
In the steppes and the deserts,
This is a sign of Judgment Day approaching.
Perhaps it will be global man who is judged
For his over-zealous invention of languages.

Thomas, you know, those who don't believe the legends
Will more than once fail to believe that a prophet stands before him
,
Perhaps even the one sent by Tengri himself.
Maybe we are already speaking with the prophets in different languages?
Who knows, someone might suddenly think that Tengri speaks

Only in his language. Naïve, don't you think?
Why is that when the wolf howls in its ancient tongue,
I know for sure that it is speaking to Tengri.
So why, then, when we address the Creator in a Turkic tongue,
The Jew and the American believe we are speaking

Not to the Creator, rather to some unknown neighbour of His?
And this while rebuking us for denying the unity of God,
To whom you are loyal yourselves? Okay, let's say it's not a Jew
And not an American. Let's say it's a Spaniard
Who kills a Fleming for reading the Bible in a language other than Latin.

We are not talking about the specifics of examples here.
What I think is that if the most important thing that divides us is the name of the Almighty,
What destructive force, then, do the words
Spoon, cart, selva and *kangaroo* have?
Or *wrong, friend, oath* and *nation,*

When spoken by different people or their leaders
For no particular reason or for a specific objective?
Was it not Erlik who sent the languages of men to earth,
To convince them that they are not related,
Not brothers and not children of Tengri? That they are *strangers to one another*?

Hm, I am predicting how the Roman would not scream out,
"I am no child of Tengri, I am a child of Jupiter,"
While the Jew will find it hard even to say whose son he is, hehe.
There is only one language that everyone understands without question
And for all time, and that is the language of Fire...

What am I getting at? Ah, right! We are talking about the lifestyle of those
For whom you are planning to build your Temple.
Yes, we are very jealous when observing our *modus vivendi.*
It is enough just to recall the Scythian King Scylas,
Who was executed by his own brother for his love

For the Hellenic way of life.
The wise man Anacharsis, who lived many years among the Greeks
Returned home and was also killed.
Was that cruel? Yes. But you should listen to another legend

253

That they'll relate in that aul way over there,

To understand the origin of this uncompromising approach to things.
Let's go, spur your horse and don't go worrying about the time.
You already know too much about it today as it is.
What about the construction? Well, I know a fair few creative people;
I can see you're listening to my chattering but inside you are already busy building.'

And so, with a leisurely conversation, we approached the next nomad camp.
The Kagan only appeared to be slow and carefree in his conversation.
By some strange coincidence, we arrived at the aul at the moment
When he was actually desperately needed there.
Everywhere we went, he introduced me to his relatives, his kin, his brothers...

It seemed never-ending for this chap with a Roman's view of the world.
Although we Jews were once nomads, too,
I even began to look for signs of the Blue Beast in myself.
You know, I found them, too, particularly when I was presented
A Scythian steel sword; that was when I was transformed.

However, when I returned to my bricklayer's trowel, the itch of creativity
Took complete hold over me, leaving no space
For the genes of ancient Yemeni barbarians to awaken in me.
In the new aul, another storyteller was once more waiting for us.
This one appeared well versed in the subject

That the Kagan and I had, I thought, discussed by chance.

THE SECOND LEGEND OF THE TURKS

A-a-ah-o-o-o-oo-oo-oo-oo-oo!
Great Kagan, when it seems to you
That your greatness reaches the
Eternal Blue Sky, stop and think:
What can be higher than Khan Tengri?[137]
When you are sure you can comprehend the abyss of the sea
With the depth of your knowledge, stop and think:
Could the sea not turn to salt dust?
Great Kagan, when you imagine
That the power of your very word
Can change existence itself, stop and think:
The breathing you think you control, can it be compared
With the breath of the Great Steppe?
When you, mighty ruler, decide
That Turan and Altai
Hold no warrior your equal, stop and think:
Is one not galloping from the lands of Iran and China
To make you a thing of the past?
Great Kagan, when you count your riches
For three days on end, stop and think:
When you return to Tengri,
About what will you talk to Him for even just a minute?
Lord, when you vent your anger,
And a hundred nomads leave for Edil as a result,
Stop and think, Great Kagan:

---

[137] A mountain of the Tian Shan mountain range. Roughly translates as *Lord of the Skies*.

Who will remain an orphan? Will it not be you?
Mighty ruler, when you hear the voice of your ancestors,
Leave your vanity and arrogance behind,
Bow your head and listen.
Standing before the greatness of Mangi El,
Perhaps you are nothing more than a dervish,
Heading out on the Road
In the search for Perfection?[138]

****

Once, long, long ago,
On the wondrous Night of Revelations,
Oghuz Khan had an incredible dream
That two sons had been born to our forefather Adam
Who were called Kazak and Zhatak[139].

When Zhatak grew up, he became a farmer,
Sowed wheat and awaited the harvest for the holiday.
His brother chose the path of the shepherd, tended sheep
And awaited young lambs for the holiday.
And so, when sounds of joy announced the day,

They appeared before Tengri
With the fruits of their blessed labours.
It was a truly great holiday.
All kith and kin noisily, with laughter and dancing,
Rejoiced together, glorifying the Creator.

The brothers presented their gifts to Tengri.
The Creator was delighted with the crop
That Kazak's herd had yielded,
But, for some reason, He was wholly indifferent
To the harvest that Zhatak had presented.

The older brother harboured a grudge, but he didn't show it,
While the carefree younger brother failed to notice a thing.
The holiday passed and the year rushed on full circle once more.
As before, the brothers went out into the valley,
Each working on the path they had chosen.

As before, the brothers talked
And helped one another.
Only the grudge revealed itself
More and more often in Zhatak's actions.
More and more, the cup of affront was filled.

One day, Kazak's sheep wandered into his brother's plot.
Zhatak was terribly offended, even though his brother had asked for his forgiveness.
In the morning, when the shepherd awoke,

---

[138] This verse has been rearranged by the author from the song of the Turkmen poet Makhtumkuly *Bolar Sen* (*'Perhaps you are destined to be'*).
[139] *Kazak* in Turkic languages means free man, a nomad, who is subject only to the laws of free men of the steppe. The word *Arab* is translated in much the same way. It is the self-designation of the Kazakhs. *Zhatak*, translated literally from Kazakh, means *recumbent* – sedentary, agricultural and urban people, the opposite of *Kazak*. For the Arabs, these are the *badii* or *badawa* (Bedouins, people of the desert) and the *hadara* (sedentary people).

He saw something he had never seen before.
Zhatak had built an enormous, black fence overnight,

Shielding his field from the sheep's hooves.
Kazak came to his brother and asked,
'What have you done, Zhatak?
That will hardly save your crops from the sheep, for the wall will have to end somewhere.
They will stupidly walk around it; perhaps it would be better

Simply to trust me. I did promise you
That this wouldn't happen again!'
Zhatak became angry. Indeed,
The wall had no ends and however long he made it,
Somewhere, if not the sheep, then wild onagers

Would get round it and trample his field.
While Kazak was driving his herd to the wintering ground,
He created a ring from his wall and was satisfied with the result.
When Kazak returned he was as surprised as before
And once again he beseeched his brother:

Zhatak, why have you cut yourself off from me and the rest of the world?
From whom are you shutting yourself away behind such tall walls?'
Zhatak answered angrily, 'From now on, know this, brother:
Everything inside this circle is mine.
And don't you dare enter, under any circumstances!'

Kazak was confused: 'But doesn't everything here belong to the both of us?
Why have you taken such a small circle
And called it your own?
Are you not robbing yourself in the process?'

'Listen, boy, when I say *mine*, that means there are rules
That exist within this property.
And you, be so kind as to follow them and force your stupid sheep to do the same!'
Kazak shook his head and walked away.
Only once did he appear again at Zhatak's walls.

'Brother, I understand now. Forgive me, for not seeing
How our Father Tengri offended you!
That appears to be the root of all this misunderstanding!
I have brought you a lamb as a gift, let's dine on it together,
Like before, as friends. I also wanted to tell you

That when you built this enclosure
The reason for your offence no longer had meaning –
Your occupation, I mean. Other meanings appeared
In that you are now shut off from the world.
Locked inside, you unfortunately not only lose

Your place in the vast world outside.
Your rules within those walls, do they not mean you are running from Tengri?
Are there any other rules other than His?
And how can they coexist without conflicting with one another?
Is the appearance of such a small *mine* really worth

Losing the greater *mine*, tell me that, brother?'

Zhatak was furious and the cup of his resentment was now overflowing.
'Were you not told not to cross this threshold?!
Yet you come to *my* house and trample over *my* rules,
Expressing your contempt and lack of respect!'

In his anger, Zhatak grabbed his hoe and struck his brother.
Kazak fell and breathed his last
With an expression of naïve surprise on his face.
At that moment, Tengri's formidable cry could be heard:
'Hey, Zhatak, what have you done to your brother and under what law?!

Be you forever banished from Ergenekon!
Let your deeds and your name be consigned to oblivion!'
Zhatak was afraid and saw that within his enclosure
The ire of the Judge Most High had laid his land to waste, for no man-made walls offer protection,
And he disappeared in the mists of the distance far away.

That was the dream that Oghuz Khan had seen and, when he awoke,
He felt a burden of unease on his chest.
But he did not disappear beneath the rays of the day's sun or even after a week.
Oguz Khan summoned his heavenly sons –
The princes Gun-Tegin, Ay-Tegin and Yildiz-Tegin

And, relating his dream to them, he ordered them to seek wise men from across the world,
Who would be able to interpret the khan's dream.
Perhaps then the sorrow of worry would leave the ruler.
The sons dispersed across the world and soon appeared anew before their father,
Each of them accompanied by wise men from different countries and peoples.

Yildiz-Tegin was brought by the star in his name to Israel
From where he brought the protectors of the Law and the Testaments.
The Sadducees and Pharisees listened to the khan's dream and said this:
'We know of this story from ancient legends and books.
This is the legend of Abel and Cain, one brother rising up against the other.

We ourselves are unable to interpret the meaning of this tale.
It is not for us to reason about any given decision of Adonai,
All the more so for He adopted it Himself
As regards the fruits of the labours of the two brothers.
However, we think we can find an explanation for why

You dreamed of this legend, oh, Great Khan.
Many nations, large and small, consider you their sovereign.
These include the *kazaks*, free inhabitants of the steppes,
And the *zhatak* farmers.
Your Lord appears to be telling you to pass fair judgment,

So as not to cause affront to one or another,
For, failing this, a major feud may break out between your sons.
And great sorrow will befall Mangi El.'
The khan thanked the Jewish sages
And saw them off to their motherland with gifts.

Only the sovereign was still plagued by sorrow.
Gun-Tegin was brought by the sun in his name to ancient Iran
From where he returned with most wise mobads.
They stood before the khan and listened to his dream.

257

They thought for a long time and then Mobedan Mobad said this:

'Your dream, master, is to tell you
That the world, as before, is divided into black and white.
The eternal struggle of the principle of light – Ahuramazda
And dark – Ahriman, the king of evil and sin.
Not a single human being can

Overcome this eternal partitioning of principles,
But much lies in the hands of the sovereigns of the earth, the human kings.
All human children are cursed with *similarity*,
The likeness of their nature either to the Spenta Mainyu,
Or the Angra Mainyu[140] but each has a moral choice.

We believe, Your Highness, that with this dream,
Your Lord Tengri is commanding you,
When you build the walls of the empire, its borders, laws and its army,
Not to forget the spiritual development of your people
Who, locked within the walls of the state,

Should not forget moral principles,
Good thoughts, words and deeds.
Failing this, Ahriman, the ruler of the Black House, will enslave them.
And, forgetting about the great battle that the whole world is waging,
Brother will destroy brother coming from outside and, thus, will destroy himself.'

So spoke the mobads and then fell silent.
The khan thanked them and saw them off to their motherland with gifts.
But the sorrow continued to gnaw away inside him
And the ruler thus realised that the true answer
Had yet to be found.

On the third day, from the remote and mysterious India
Came Ay-Tegin, accompanied by wise Brahmans
The listened to the dream of Oghuz Khan, pondered in silence and then said,
'Oh, Sovereign Khan, there can be no doubt
That you are as great as a *kshatriya* in the management of your people.

We have no doubt that you will
Define the moral path that your people must take,
Worthy of divine approval!
However, we believe that this dream did not concern a state or a nation,
Rather your personal spiritual prosperity.

The wall that one of the brothers built
Symbolises that your *ātman* might find itself locked
To merge with the Eternal and Indivisible Brahman,
Sovereign of Worlds and your essence as well,
If you, in your enthusiasm for management, forget the search for the Truth.

Shut away behind your walls of your *I*,
You risk not allowing the Universe in
And you'll squander your opportunities,
Not seeing and having lost your divine originality,

---

[140] *Spenta Mainyu* in Zoroastrianism is the Holy Spirit, created by the Wise Lord, Ahura Mazdā, to oppose the Destructive Spirit, Angra Mainyu.

Your *dharma*, your path of piety,

Replacing its law with rules of governance through weakness,
Meaning government through the vices of men.
What does the loss of Truth mean for a person?
How different is this loss for a simple Turk, compared with
His sovereign? Not different at all.

You see, despite the differences in birth and class,
Everyone communicates with God individually, making their own choice,
Either building a wall in one's soul, dividing oneself and Brahman
Or seeing oneself *as an integral part* with him.'
The twice-born[141] fell silent and Oghuz Khan thanked them.

Giving them gifts, he sent the wise men back
To the shores of the sacred Ganges,
Much had been revealed to the great sovereign
After his conversations with wise men of different peoples.
Nevertheless, anxiety still remained with him.

And all the doctors and quacks were powerless.
Worry and sadness took a hold of the khan's entire quarters.
However, one day, the curtain of the khan's yurt was raised
And in came a tall, white old man
With a long beard and rays of sun around his eyes.

Oghuz Khan rose up in joy to meet his guest,
For it was Khydyr-ata himself who had come to visit him in the heart of the Great Steppe.
The khan told him about his dream and the sorrow that never left him.
The wise man pondered a while and then asked for three days.
He spent many long hours watching over the ulus.

On the fourth day, the Great Traveller appeared
Before Oghuz Khan and slowly began to speak.
'I have heard all that the wise men have told you.
Do not ask me how, for that is not the most important thing now.
Each of them was right in their own way.

But one of the main things
Nevertheless escaped their attention.
And this thing is not a thing of joy for us, rather a great sadness.
For your dream is not simply a retelling of a biblical legend,
Rather a prediction, a prophecy that

Centuries will pass and the nomadic world we know so well will die away.
The harmony of man with the mountains and steppe will end,
The eyes of Yer-sub will darken in a sad haze,
The mighty Altai will be shrouded in a fog of mourning
And the deserts of Touran will shed arid tears.

The wall has been built and there is no way back.
Time cannot be turned back; this is beyond the powers of people and djinns alike.
The Kazaks, Bedouins and Sioux will disappear
Under a tsunami of what is now being forged
Quietly and imperceptibly beyond the walls of big cities.

---

[141] *Dvija*, meaning twice-born, is name given to the caste of Brahmans (Brahmins) in India.

259

This will not take place imminently; while they are still able,
The mighty khans will venture to the *Zhatak* world
And crush walls and fences there
That separate kith and kin into those within and those without.
Defeat, however, will not come from the sword.

Ever so quietly, the daring nomads
Will be lured by the charm of the cities
Where they will be defeated by the noise, the shimmer and the power
Of what will be called the new god –
Fair trade and the hoarding of gold.

The naïve and unsophisticated children of the vast prairies
Will try on new laws and rules for size.
Slowly but surely, the worms of wealth and bliss
Will change their appearance, their *dharma* and their moral choices.
The Tengri cross will be tightly covered by a roof,

The Family will scatter like shards of a smashed China vase
And no khan or sudra could put it back together.
And the people will believe that we have no other way.'
Oghuz Khan was greatly saddened and his head dropped to his hands.
'Is it really the case that

Our life's path and our search for Truth is all in vain?
Can it be that the only motive that remains in
The building of a nation is the intoxication of power?'
'Don't be sad, Khan,' Khydyr-ata went on.
There is a continuation to this story.

Perhaps one day the children of men will understand
That one cannot live in war with nature.
Perhaps they'll come to their senses and will seek a way of life
That would allow them to preserve the riches of Yer-sub
Not only for the many, but for the long term, too.

The only thing is that, if you don't save Mangi El,
Then where will they find the answers to their questions on how to live?
If those who see the world as a unified whole vanish from its face,
Where will the Zhataks and the Cains then take Tengri's children?
This task, you understand, is largely in your hands.'

With those words, Khydyr-ata vanished as if he had never appeared at all.
That is always the way he comes and goes, that eternal traveller.
The khan then summoned his three mortal sons –
Gök-Tegin, Taq-Tegin and Tengiz-Tegin[142] – and he told them
How the white old man had interpreted his dream.

And he asked them, 'What do we need to do, my sons?'
The princes pondered and then Gök-Tegin stepped forward.
The young man's eyes flashed with anger and he said,
'Khan Father! Should we warriors of the *Bozkurt* tribe

---

[142] Legend has it that Oghuz Khan had six sons. Three heavenly sons from a heavenly wife – Gun (Sun), Ay (Moon) and Yildiz (Star) and three mortal sons from a mortal woman – Gök (Sky) Taq (Mountain) and Tengiz (Sea).

Weep and wail in fear of the weak peasants and merchants?!

Do we not have a powerful army; are our warriors not the best in the world?
Does anyone really have such heavenly horses as ours?
Is our wondrous damask steel to be compared with any other?
Summon your army, let's march to the West and the East
And wipe the cities and walls of the Zhataks and Cains from the face of the earth!

Let terror be their master;
Let them run to the forests and deserts in fear!
It is we and not that force of nature Yer-sub
Who will become the divine scourge that will destroy
This corrupt, petty tribe to its core!'

'No, no!' the brother Tengiz-Tegin interrupted,
'It would be foolish to start a war that will then prove endless
And will bring neither peace nor final victory to any people.
The expanses of Yer-sub are great; let us travel far to the East.
They say that bountiful land is aplenty beyond the Ocean,

Land where the experienced and sly feet
Of urban-dwelling merchants and charmers have not trod.
It is there that we shall find our new Ergenekon,
And there, in new expanses, we will set our yurts
And continue our nomadic life in the spiral of winters and summers!'

'Khan Father, I believe,' said Taq-Tegin, entering the conversation,
'We need to deceive and confuse the *zhataks*.
We need to adopt their customs, build similar walls,
Erect fortresses that look like cities
And set out enormous bazaars for trading there.

Learn to work the land, irrigate the fields,
Dig channels and live all year round
Amidst the cramped, stuffy walls and fences.
We will ride out this dangerous time
But we'll cherish the memory our own lifestyle and customs!'

Oghuz Khan heard his sons out and then said,
'I will think on this for seven days and seven nights.
Then return to me and I will tell you my decision.'
The sons departed and the khan left his yurt
And climbed the hill nearby.

At first, he looked at length over to the East
Where the grey-topped Altai rose up from the misty haze.
Then he turned to the North
Where he saw the dark caps of the sombre forests.
After that he gazed long and hard at the West,

To where an enormous, living sea was raging.
The ruler's gaze then swept at length
To the yellow expanses of the deserts of the South.
On the eighth day, the khan came down from the hill
And, donning his ceremonial dress, he ordered that all his kith and kin be summoned.

The Turks gathered around the khan's enormous yurt.

Oghuz Khan raised his hand and began to speak:
'Kinsmen! We often think
That the Lord Tengri created us as grains of sand in the deep waters of the Onon,
And that the force of destiny, like the course of the river,

Carries us meet the inevitable!
At times, Tengri's revelations about the future are sad
But do they mean that we should
Be like that powerless grain of sand
That rushes headlong to the promised peace of the sea?!

The happiness of the Turkic people lies in the fact that
Through dreams at night and insights gained in the day,
Through the rich minds of wise men,
Who come from peoples and lands far and wide,
The Almighty helps us understand the strength

And the dignity with which we will live our lives
Until the moment comes for our return.
The happiness of the Turkic people is that we have raised sons
Capable of seeking the truth both in distant lands
And in their own minds.

And that we have mothers and daughters,
Who tend our hearth and who give us the strength
To believe what we believe and to champion
What we believe is right,
Just as our noble ancestors bequeathed to us.

We knew then and we know now, and we will carry this knowledge through the ages,
That submitting to the force of destiny is for slaves,
While the strength of faith and integrity in faith
Require more than just a mindset,
But the courage, always and everywhere, to abide by it, never recanting.

It so happened that Tengri has spoken with us
Through my dreams, the words of sages and our own kinsmen.
Now, we sense we are armed with knowledge,
But most important, though, is
If we'll be able to use this knowledge correctly.

I have had time to think this through and give it my consideration
And now I would like you all to listen to
What I command you and all those to be born in future
In the steppes and valleys of Ergenekon
And, perhaps, also in other lands where the Turks' destiny may take them.

For now on, no Turkic khan, from his very first day of rule,
When Tengri and the nation raise him on the white rug,
Shall have nothing that he cannot call his own.
From this moment on, he shall possess
What the Turkic people determine for him,

For he must stand before Tengri
Unburdened with saddlebags of gold
Or of thoughts of riches left on earth.
Rather, he must be pure in his nakedness, meaning

That his worries and thoughts were of Mangi El alone.

From now on, any ruler of the Turks
Shall bear full responsibility for the moral choices of his people,
To believe in the One and Only and turn away from the charms of the dark Erlik.
May he be the high priest and master of the temple,
To stop vice and sin from prevailing

In the minds of the nation that Tengri entrusted to him with his decree.
May the khan stand alert on the boundary of black and white
As a father or with all the force of the law,
As is befitting for the Head of the House,
Preventing Tengri's children from crossing this line.

The same goes for the heads of clans and tribes
To whom the Almighty pointed his finger, and the decision of kith and kin.
Our traditions are powerful, ancient and stable,
But, from now on, all families must know
That, in observing these traditions, each person not only lives as the Good, Kind Man,

But personally bears responsibility for the destiny and the freedom of Mangi El.

From henceforth, every ruler of a Turkic throne
Must gather around him wise men from different Houses of this earth
To ensure his intelligence and spirit are always growing.
To ensure we not only feel part of the Universal,
But also have a true sense of its wholeness.

Only then will a ruler be able
To pass just and fair judgment,
Not tainted by petty interests.
Only then will enlightened people have faith in this judgment
And shall address the Almighty not with prayers and requests,

But with song and verse, as befits a free tribe.

From now on we will erect no walls
And if we come across any, we will destroy them, to prevent such walls
From giving rise, at the site of a lone El,
To a myriad of disparate and petty details,
To prevent any rules from hiding behind these walls

That differ from the laws of the Almighty,
Concealed from the people's eyes and its fair judgment.
To prevent brother from rising against brother and for there to be no strife,
For strife is like a narrow gorge
That only accelerates the path of a grain of sand in the river to its demise.

I instruct you to prepare for great wars,
Only not so much on the battlefield; this is something we are familiar with.
Wars of reason, faith and endurance are what await us.
And not with those who simply plough the land and build cities,
But with evil, lowlife erliks suffering from spiritual poverty,

Who are the product of that first wall.
Tengri's predictions might be sombre
But a great many centuries will pass and the day will come

263

When the Kazaks will kneel near Lake Alka-Kol,
The Great Famine will devour people in the steppes,

And Fire will lose its mind in the green valleys of Ergenekon[143].
And then my people will cry out, groaning and screaming:
'Mangi El is no more; the nomadic wheel has stopped turning!
There are no more nomads in the world, no Kazaks, Bedouins or Sioux!
Bloody wounds have slashed the face of our foremother Umai!

Farewell Touran and Altai! Farewell, steppe grass!
Farewell, Great Plains and Black Hills![144]
Our feet are tormented, our knees, wounded!
Our hearts say farewell to our native pathways, lakes and streams,
When the walls and fences so pitilessly closed forever around us!'

I can see the destruction of princes and *kams*,
And men from foreign lands making golden cups from the heads of khans.
I can see the heads of the Houses competing with one another
In money-making and riches, falling from the sleeves of the *zhataks*,
And then hide it carefully behind their cold walls.

I can see the loyal Turk, frozen in slave-like prostration,
Without his own name, without memory of kin and living on handouts.
I can see the ancient commitment of our warrior now trampled in shame,
While the banner of the Eternal Blue Sky
No longer bears the head of the noble Blue Beast.

And yet, I believe, children of Ergenekon,
That when our enemies believe
That Mangi El has become cold nothingness,
And we have dispersed across the world like the *Bozkurts*,
Destroyed on the shores of the Edil,

Then Yer sub, at the behest of the Almighty, will reveal its secrets,
Give us its blood and bile, to sate us full,
And the Wolf Clan will rise up again in a new greatness.
So, we must preserve all the strength of body,
Mind and, most important, faith, strain every sinew,

Maintain our desperate valour and, most important, love Mangi El,
Yer-sub and Umai forever and ever, to save ourselves
For these days, when the khans of the Great Steppe
Will once more cast aside all temptations of the *zhatak* world
And will lie with their relatives by the fires of their ancestors,

To relates tales to one another in laughter,
Tales of wolves and the Simurgh, of wise men and warriors,
Of the East and the West, of Khydyr in white

---

[143] The three great tragedies in the Great Steppe *when we lay with tormented feet by the shores of Lake Alka-kol*: the death of Kazakhs during the Dzungar invasion; the *Great Dzhut* famine of the Volga peoples in Kazakhstan in the 1920-30s; nuclear weapons testing at the Semipalatinsk Test Site during Soviet times.

[144] The Great Plains – the plateau in the United States and Canada that was home to several Native American tribes, including the Apache, Sioux and Cheyenne. The Black Hills War (1876-77) was a series of battles involving an armed uprising of Native American tribes against their white colonisers. The Wounded Knee Massacre was a deadly battle at Wounded Knee Creek, where Chief Big Foot (Spotted Elk) of the Miniconjou died in the last armed conflict between the Lakota Sioux and the US Army.

And how Zhatak attempted to create *space* within walls,
Where the laws of Tengri have no force.'

****

I had failed to notice that, from the moment the *magus* had fallen silent,
Mahdi Kagan and I were alone around the fire.
'Allow me, my Lord, to say,' I broke the silence tentatively,
'But I saw a certain contradiction
In the testaments of the revered Oghuz Khan...

It turns out that the Turkic tribe
Was instructed to wage an uncompromising war over centuries
With the settled tribes, so how then
Can you speak about achieving the unity and wholeness
Of the entire human race when it comes to the relations of kith and kin?

And then... not all settled peoples are the descendants of Cain,
As the legends of my people state,
Rather, for the most part, they hail from Seth, Adam's third son.'
'That is all correct, Thomas,' the Kagan replied, throwing a twig into the fire.
You are right; there is no need to be categorical here.

We are not talking about war with peaceful farmers;
Just like the nomads, they too depend on the ecosystem –
The natural circle of life of nature and society.
Their harvests fear the might of Yer-sub or the flooding of the Nile
To the same extent as a nomad's life in the winter and summer pastures.

The intelligent farmer will not leave unhealed scars
On the fertile steppe plains.
You must have noticed, Thomas, that all our things,
Even our yurt homes, are made from things that quickly rot
And disappear into the ground without trace: wood, leather and plant materials.

We don't even cover the wheels of our carts with metal,
Although we produce it to a higher standard today
Than many of the settled peoples.
You ask why? The scar left by a metal wheel
Will not heal on the steppe's hide for fifty years or more. So, there you have it...

So, when we migrate to the wintering grounds,
We hope to return and find the steppe in the way we left it,
Whatever we dropped into the soil the previous autumn.
As for Cain's descendants... The farmer is not our enemy and nor is the city dweller.
Thomas, did you know that it was Cain

Who built the first city of Enoch.
It was there, in that city that a new god and idol settled.
The dark rays of his power emerged
From that city as if from a dark sun,
Subduing steppe and mountain, tribe and race.

You know better than me, Thomas, about the sins of the metropolis...
Beyond the walls there, a space is created
Where deities with other names rule.
And if the believers of the world are divided in their address to the Creator

By their many different languages,

Then these gods and idols devour these languages and the people that speak them.
How many more prophets have to appear, Thomas,
To nail the golden calf and its priests who lend money to earn interest
To the board of oblivion?!
And then to chuck this board back into Erlik's dark kingdom...

That is the true enemy of the wholeness of the human race.
And that enemy lives in cities, surrounded and demarcated by walls.
You know, Thomas, I used to think that the engine of capitalism
Is greed and a striving to rise up
The ladder of consumer standards.

But, you see, the problem is far more deep-rooted, on an unconscious level.
People are driven by a fear of poverty, all created by the city
With its slums, dirty canals and rubbish dumps.
The constant contemplation of the beggars, the poor and the social non-achievers,
Who are all below you on the ladder of consumption

Force man to erect walls ever-so-quickly
Inside and around the spaces that he calls his own.
Fear breeds the conviction that poverty is fair for *them* to have,
But it's not for *you* and this is already a reasoning
On a level that replaces the law of Tengri with the law of the city corpuscle.

Is such a standalone *ātman* really able
To perceive itself as a part of a Brahman who is the same for everyone?
No. It is the city that creates such a level
Of social division of labour and property
That a nomad could only dream of.

Is it not a city like this, a museum of spiritual architecture,
That you and I wanted, Thomas? I don't think so.
Against a background of the Jesuitism of the townsfolk, justifying the poverty of spirit and body,
The Indian division into castes appears simple and wholly unsophisticated.
You might say that my reasoning is sanctimonious.

So, what about scientific and technological progress and its fruits?
For this is the pure fruit of an industrial city is it not?!
Let me tell you: this matter has a moral side to it, too.
What is the expropriation rate of people around the world
From the achievement of this progress? (If you take everyone as a whole and not the Swedes
separately, I mean.)

After all, the majority of technical innovations are, again,
For the most part, focused on improving comfort and consumption.
And to a much greater extent than back into science
And to the military! You can learn all about
This moral aspect

From the residents of Hiroshima and Semipalatinsk and from Academician Sakharov.
Lately, it's been very noticeable
That development of the military machine of urban civilisation
Is directed at repressing the last of the free -
Those who don't wish to submit to the new capitalist *varnas*.'

'So, we are talking about an eternal Babylon, Great Khagan?
Eternal and moving in space and in history?'
'Well, something like that,' the steppe ruler chuckled.
'But... let's move to a level that's more practical,' I interrupted the khan.
I am talking about the building of the Temple in Mangi El.

How can it be built faced with such an uncompromising rejection of the notion of walls?
Of course, I understand that the image of a wall is largely allegorical,
But, all the same, this is a very specific testament, one of the key ones,
And for violating it I might pay with my life, right?'
'Thomas, I suggest you avoid unnecessary dogmatism.

I am talking about approaches, concepts and reasoning.
On the one hand, a wall is no allegory.
Just look to the South – the Han have built a huge wall there
Without even knowing why, as, for hundreds of years
Not one nomad has ever even tried storming it, preferring just to pass it by.

On the other hand, we are talking about a temple, not a fortress
Or some solid enclosure around a correctional facility.
Of course, you were right to notice that, at the very beginning of our acquaintance,
That the *kams* were beside themselves from such a direct breach of the ban.
However, they now see the other side, of which I have managed to convince them.

When a wise man comes to the Turks from outside,
Allowing him to express his opinion freely
About us and what is happening with us
Is something we recognise as an historical *mirror*,
Into which enlightened people should occasionally gaze

To understand if we are on the right path
Or if we have lost our way by deviating from ideals.
Can we really be objective
In our assessment of ourselves, what do you think?
I think we cannot and let me take this reasoning

As the basis for our cooperation.
That is why the *kam* magi actually cheered up;
You see, is it not a happy thing to be there
When the most important moral rulings
In history are passed?

Thomas, I think that the free creativity you have been presented
Will increase your objectivity many times over,
Because there is nothing more wonderful than the truth,
Filtered through the spirit and mind of a talented, wise man
And revealed, through this work, to those who seek and thirst for it

In all its original glory.

So, Thomas, my friend, don't be put off
By our traditions and dogmas.
Be sincere and open, and keep a keen eye on where you're going;
Perhaps, we'll prove to be that mirror for you,
In which you'd like to look into and understand who you really are.'

Inspired, I set about the construction of my creation.

Each day, I drew inspiration
From the simple, honest
And even somewhat rough-hewn
People of Mangi El.

Over the many years of my life among these people,
I came to see that which is not immediately apparent
To an admiring stranger.
As Mahdi Kagan said, it was not worth exaggerating
The just nature of the steppe kingdom's state structure.

I saw grief and sorrow, reproach and resentment.
I saw the Heads of the Houses, languishing over the mountains of city riches;
I saw the 'just' Kagan, with fire and sword,
'Forcing peace' on entire camps and even peoples.
I saw the guile in conspiracies and the lobbying for mercenary deals.

However, all that surrounded me,
One way or another, was the polar opposite of Rome
And even the desert Palestine with Jerusalem at its centre.
No one would kneel here
If they had not chosen the path of Erlik for themselves.

Even if they were crushed by the punitive power of the state,
The people would die nobly and with dignity
And no one dared to take that opportunity away from them.
Mangi El could have been called
Noisy, multilingual, even cacophanous,

For it was here that people flocked, who saw themselves as free Kazaks
And who acknowledged the covenants of their ancestors as regards the societal structure
And the right to die for one's freedom.
To die dashingly and with an expression of love for their God,
For a true warrior would always be prepared to meet their maker with joy.

The memory of my nomadic ancestors even stirred within me,
Those who departed back then to wander the desert expanses
From the high and mighty, self-evident cities of Egypt.
However, this recollection by no means made me want to sit on a camel
And rush out into the steppe with rash young Turkic lads.

Quite the contrary, I recalled the role that
The Temple played for my people, becoming the focal point of the universe.
I had hoped that, for the Hun Empire, perhaps,
I would be able to create something that would
Not so much alter the attitude to walls,

Rather would reveal the riches of architecture,
Like science and art of a *dastan*[145], embodied in stone.
And that, with the end of summer, there would be no need
To take everything with them to the wintering pastures.
The Temple could be left in the very centre of the sacred Ergenekon,

For it to serve forever as a spiritual,

---

[145] *Dastan* in Persian, the same as the author's name, means an epic work in folklore or literature, based on heroic myths, legends and fairy-tale themes.

Historical and even geographical guide.
Quite unlike the approach taken in building the Pantheon,
My take on the matter of
Preventing anyone from entering the building site

Was quite different; it would be boring to have no laddish grins or
The shaking of heads of the *kams*, prodding the materials,
Their beards shaking amusingly and their tongues clicking;
After all, children of the steppe see boredom
And loneliness as bad form.

Now, the freedom to visit the site at any time
Anyone so pleased
Was what decided the fate of the best temple
I have to date ever built
In the expanses of the Oecumene.

One peaceful and warm afternoon,
Having returned from a punishing war with the Qing,
Mahdi Kagan gathered his *kams* and ruling kin
And came to my construction site,
Perched atop a majestic hill,

From where fabulous views of Ergenekon stretched out below.
By that time, I had erected the main walls
And raised the first level of the roof.
The cavalcade of horsemen drew near
And I came out to welcome the ruler of the Turks.

'Hello there, Thomas,' smiled the khan and the *kams*,
As if they had not arrived to conduct an inspection,
But were anticipating letting their hair down.
Suddenly, I felt a particular lifting of my mood,
As if I had just welcomed a close friend,

Whom I had missed greatly and would share a really old bottle of wine
That I had been saving just for his return.
'Go on, tell us about the basic idea behind
Your new creation, even if just the basics.
What will please or intrigue us?'

The riders dismounted and entered the unfinished building.
It struck me that the magi and the khan's retinue
Were too high-spirited,
So emphasised was the admiration with which they viewed
The incomplete shell of the building, as if their eyes were so sophisticated

That they were able to see this early
What would stand here upon completion.
The khan himself was serene and, placing his hand on my shoulder,
Pointed, as if to say, *go on then, tell us*
About how tomorrow we'll have the world's greatest ever creation.

I hesitated and, in the expectant silence,
I heard the chirping of grasshoppers in the grass,
The cry of a falcon high up in the sky,
The beckoning neighing of horses, the distant rush of a waterfall

And the tender whistling of unseen quails.

What could I say now about my Temple?
That, for the first time in my life, I was not building to completed drawings,
Rather according to some divine intuition,
That each time drew the curtain
On a new step only once I had completed the one before?

That only my vast experience protected my brainchild
From errors in the strength of materials and design solutions?
That, for the first time in my life I had not seen the final shape,
Rather, I was merely following an anticipation of *impressione*,
Floating in my imagination as a vague, yet

Whole and complete picture?
That this was a feeling of infinite freedom,
When your step is attributable not to some dry drawing,
Rather the opportunity to make decisions at every
Moment of the creative process?

And that my professional pride was now
Complemented by an understanding that
Only a true master of his Craft
Can work in such an adventurous way,
When every moment is not a link in a chain, rather a minute of freedom?

'Tell me, Thomas,' one of the *kams* asked, interrupting the wave of my emotions,
'Are you sure this will indeed be the best Temple
You have built your entire life before?'
He smiled approvingly, but I blurted.
'My entire life before? Yes, I am prepared to accept

That this could be seen as the only one I have ever built!
Look,' I sang. 'There is the roof.
It personifies the boundless beauty
Of the Eternal Blue Sky and that is why it has been made
From this thin blue tile.

When viewing it, a person will be carried upward
In a slender web of thought, a euphoria of dreaming and
A boundlessness of imagination!
They will look into this mirror and see Tengri,
But, at the same time, they will see themselves, both tiny and gigantic at the same time!'

'Oh! Oh!' Mahdi Kagan suddenly applauded.
'Thomas, you are not talking, you are as if singing to us!'
Someone cried out approvingly, another applauded.
This outburst of admiration was suddenly penetrated
By the fine, tender voice of a *syrnai* flute.

Then, quite unexpected, a drum joined in with a
Rum-tata-tum! Rrrrum-tata-tum!
A dombra shook into song and a member of the retinue,
Still in full battledress,
Slowly floated into a smooth, imposing dance.

Everyone laughed and shouted,

'Go on, Thomas, don't stop now!'
'Take a look at the site I chose for the Temple!' I went on in my inspiration.
'Look at the noble beauty
And the perfection of the vista!

You won't find an elevation better or more monumental
Anywhere, as if this is God's own overturned chalice,
From which the rivers, streams and waterfalls have poured out onto the earth!
From here all the beauty of Mangi El can be seen,
Not in a flat painting of the steppe

Or in the noble poise of a mountain range.
Yer-sub has gathered absolutely everything in one place!
There's the mystical forest, concealing the cautious boar!
There is the strip of sea, like a heavenly mirror!
There is the expanse of the steppe, broad as wings frozen in flight!

It is from here that I so want to whisper softly
And then scream out at the top of my lungs:
Hello, El! Hello, Home!
And, closing my eyes, soar to the heavens like an eagle,
Afraid of the height yet out of my mind with happiness!'

Rrum-tata-tum! Rrum-rrum-tata-tak!
Everyone was spinning in a dance of unbridled, pure joy
And my feet just couldn't stand still.
'Go on, Thomas, sing us your song!'
Oh, the simple nomads, trampling over Rome!

How strange those fearsome, thin-eyed faces look
When music paints them in childlike innocence.
Even the Kagan himself had started dancing like some frivolous young lad,
Twisting his shoulders, slapping his thighs
And copying the graceful gallop of the pacer!

'Thomas! Thomas! But where's the sky? Where?
You sure that's not stone above us, Thomas?
It certainly looks like the sky. But are you sure it's not stone, Thomas?'
The Kagan sang, breathless from all the excitement.
'Show us the sky about which you formed that beautiful verse!'

It was then that something happened to me,
As if the wave of inspiration had transformed into a giant tsunami
That swept over me with an incredible energy,
Filling my loins, arms and legs
And agitating my mind.

Without breaking the quite incomprehensible dancing,
I took an enormous sledgehammer
And, with all my might, I smashed the tiled roof to smithereens!
All the dancers then took whatever they could get their hands on
And, laughing as they went, they took to clobber what was left of the roof.

Literally several moments later
The stone had gone, as if it had never actually been there.
In that instant, light flooded in,
The light of the genuine sky, not a manmade imitation!

271

The dancing continued with even greater verve. *Rum-tata-tum!*

'What's this here, Thomas? There, on the northern wall, Thomas?'
'That wall is made of wood.
I plan to depict the ancient forest on it –
The master of mystery and secrecy,
The hidden friend of hunters and lovers!'

'But why paint it, friend?
There's the forest! Right there! Ask the wall
To show us the forest right now!'
I laughed out loud and took my sledgehammer to the northern wall.
And the forest burst in with its thousand aromas;

Hundreds of eyes stared out at us – wild beasts,
Perplexed pines, dignified firs,
Capricious maples and pristine birches,
And moss-covered rocks deep in the thicket.
'Come on in, forest! What a beautiful wall it's turned out to be!'

The beams of the northern wall had collapsed,
Disappearing in a moment, to be replaced by juniper and cedar,
As if those beams had never even been there.
'And this is the southern wall, which looks out over the desert.
Man will come and will want Tengri

To speak to him; they say that only in the desert
Can you most likely hear the voice of God.
There'll be dunes and sands painted here
As a symbol of total solitude and contemplation,
When in emptiness and silence you can hear the Almighty sing!'

'You know, Thomas, there's something we'd like to tell you...
But there's the desert! It's right there. Ask the wall
To show it to us in all its original glory!'
The southern wall had been made of clay
And it, too, crashed down in a single instant

Under the cordial clobbering of the other dancers and me!
The clay disappeared there and then, melting away at the top of that hill
And flowing away in vernal streams as if it had never been there at all.
And the desert, too, entered the Temple,
Burning us with dunes blowing imperious.

Snakes slithered, taking with them into the depths of the sand
The secrets and tales of antiquity.
Powerful camels ran by,
Inviting us to follow into the mysterious and unknown distance.
My heart was breaking from love for my Homeland, so far away.

A flock of young girls on horseback then rushed in,
Having heard the merriment and dancing from afar.
They sang, moving their arms in dance like the wings of swans.
'Girls, take a look over here! This is the western wall!
It is made of reeds and it will

Depict the sea, whose shores

272

Are surrounded by an army of reeds!
This is a wall of love, both tender and beautiful,
And as dangerous as the coastal undergrowth.
It is not only the white swans who call to one another on the shore.

The Turanian tiger and the fierce cheetah roam there;
They might take you and carry you off to a remote, strange aul.
Girls, don't you go down to the sea!
It's beauty deceives, only, if you don't go there,
You might never meet your true love.

And what is life without love? Just lonely wandering in the reeds!'

Rrum-tata-tum! 'Thomas, tell the wall to show us the sea!
Where is it? What does it look like? We want to tremble in the embrace
Of its waves, both cool and bitter,
Yet so caressing at noontime!
Thomas, show us the sea and we'll sing you a new song!'

The wall of reeds came crashing down and
In one second its stems disappeared from the slope;
In an instant it became overgrown in innocent, carefree flowers,
From which the girls wove garlands for themselves.
The sea then entered the Temple in a myriad of salty droplets.

Some it embraced and caressed,
Others it whipped palm-like waves across the cheek;
It took the breath away for some, frightening with its sheer force and power,
While it whispered a prayer to others.
Others still it simply passed haughtily by.

'And what does this wall talk about, Thomas?'
The Kagan asked me sonorously.
'The one that looks to the East.'
'This, my lord, is where the mountains will be painted,
Which is why the wall is made of cold stone.

Cold as the icy peak of Khan Tengri.
This wall will not only talk to us of our ancestral home;
It will remind us of Altai Zaman,
Hidden from us for a time,
But promised to us once more!

This wall will also tell us
That prophets will come from the East,
They near the rivers and the rivers recognise them;
They climb the mountain and the mountain listens to them,
After which they descend from the mountain and speak with us.

Then they depart into the distance, but we will be waiting for them.
It's just that the human life is a short one;
We live and return to the Eternal Blue Sky,
While only the mountains, patiently and silently,
Await the return of the prophets, but the time will come.

'We know, Thomas, we know,' the *kam*-magi exclaimed.
'We have already seen one boy,

Marked with the heavenly Tengri cross!
And now, you know...' 'I know, I know!'
I cried out and struck the eastern wall with my hammer.

In an instant, rocks flew in all directions and,
Crashing down, they disappeared into the hillside, as if there had never been a wall.
They became overgrown in moss and merged into the peak.
And the mountains came into the Temple and they spoke with us
In the language of eternity and the patience of old.

And at that very moment, the mighty Sun
Emerged in all its glory from behind the backs of the magical mountain peaks!
With its might and its benevolence,
It promised us that we would see
The return of the magical light from the East.

So strong was this mystical insight
That everyone was launched into the apotheosis of a dance,
Heads titled to one side, one hand welcoming the sky
While the other seemingly caressing the earth, and uniting into something whole and complete.
With that, the Universe trembled inside everyone[146].

Suddenly and simultaneously, everyone collapsed, exhausted,
Lying side by side on that magical peak.
The *syrnai* flutes and the drums at once fell silent,
The laughter, joking and hooting all subsided.
All that could be heard were the people's hearts, beating from excitement.

We lay there quietly, like naughty and now tired children
Who felt not guilt, just the joy of their mischief.
The Kagan himself lay there reclining, his arms outstretched,
And I was by his side, then the magi and the warriors,
The boys and girls, and the musicians.

Once again, I could hear the grasshoppers.
The Tarbagan marmot whistled cautiously and carefully.
Up in the sky, the eagle announced it could see everyone from up above.
A waterfall once more murmured in the distance and the grove rustled.
Unseen beyond the pines, the elk boomed its call.

As if from a great distance away, I could hear the faint voice of the Kagan:
'Oh, Lord! Look, Thomas. Look at what a beautiful Temple you have built!'
I raised my head and looked around.
Oh, Adonia, everything around me was shrouded in a fine haze of true *sfumato*.
The vision all around me was everything that Leonardo and I had dreamed of.

The true grandeur of the shapes and the incomprehensible nature of eternity,
The *staccato* of the moment and the breath of infinity.
Time had stopped and, with a groan, it had rushed off somewhere.
The light altered with a million imperceptible changes;
Smoke and clouds were transformed.

At the same time, everything remained absolutely, universally still
And unalterable. I saw myself, many thousands of parasangs

---

[146] The dance style of whirling dervishes of the Sufi Mevlevi Order.

Away in the distance, standing as a lone blue fir
Atop the mountain. It was like my reflection in a mirror.
That fir tree looked back at me with equal surprise.

I felt a lump in my throat and the tears that flowed were of delight.
I wept and no one interrupted my emotions.
One *kam* quietly placed a light, almost unbodily
Hand upon my shoulder.
This faint touch

Simply and directly turned to dust the thousands
Of spotlights of the glory and applause of artificial admiration
That had accompanied me throughout my work
Like a sticky glue of falsehood
Under the shade of endlessly progressing megapolises.

My tears seemed to cleanse me, and I thought
Where else, if not in a true Temple could such cleansing be possible?
When divine grace descends upon you
And tells you that, yes, Thomas, I, the Lord of Worlds,
Have always been present and I have spoken with you in your creative throes.

When I parted from my new steppe friends,
I too wept, but these tears were now different – simply tears of life.
When a heavenly horse carried me away,
Further and further was that blessed El,
My Temple remained in sight for a long, long time.

It looked at me as I did at it
And I remembered my friend Arminius, and the great Tuscan.
Before me flashed images of Oghuz Khan and the wolves,
The wise men from the different Houses and the boys from the Kagan's aul;
And ever-so slowly, a yearning crept into my soul, like Erlik's very shadow.

What next? Stop there or start over?
Freeze in a stillness of contemplation
Or, to the contrary, develop some dynamic activity?
Quit architecture altogether or open my own school?
One thing I knew for sure: I was returning Home.

To keep myself busy, I took a job
With the fishermen of Capernaum, concealing who I was
And from where I had come to avoid unnecessary questions to distract me.
In other words, what I did was blend in just by being there.
Do you know why the fisherman took me on?

The first time I went out, I caught more than they
Did put together.
The fisherman pointed at me and said,
'When he mutters like that he's talking with the fish
In its own language, asking forgiveness and begging for food

As if he were a relative or something, come visiting.
Then, he studiously seeks out the fry, the females bearing roe
And God knows what else and on what basis,
Then throws them back into the sea.
And the fish, before swimming away, appear to nod to him.'

Well, let them say what they want;
I simply laughed about it.
It seemed that life had frozen still...
That was, until I heard about this lad, Rabbi Johann,
Who said, well, that the Kingdom of Heaven is upon us.

Then, ever-so slowly, a thought began to crystallise inside me:
Would it be possible to erect a Temple there?
It seemed that I had been reborn in the Great Steppe...
So, *who* and *what* would I need to be
To be able to erect Heavenly Temples?

I became afraid that things were beginning to look
Like I was losing my mind. And I really began to get desperate,
For I had no one even to discuss such a thing with
Without fear of being locked away.
Well, brothers, it is in these thoughts that you found me.

It can't just be a matter of excessive pride, can it?
Can it really be just the scandalous behaviour of someone who's had his fill of creativity?
I know this is not the case, because, to build a Temple that is so *different*,
You yourself have to be just as *different*.
You see, just as I will be the mirror of this Temple, so it will be mine.

Tell me, Rabbi, are we meant to build Temples in the Heavens?

Thomas, my wise old friend!
The day is near when we will know everything
About the Temple and about temples, both of this world and of the heavens.
As we have not only to build it
In three days but destroy it too.

And in these difficult days, will it not be you
Who'll be my support in my construction?
And am I not yours?
Won't you be seeing your reflection in My eyes?
And will I not see Myself in yours?

Will it not be you and our brothers
Who will be our new windows and doors?
After all, you didn't come here just to build,
But to be My word,
And if needs be, my sword and cleansing fire, too!

We will search together for the site to erect the Heavenly Temple, my friend,
And we won't stop until we find it.
When we do find it, we will get through the distresses you know so well.
With it will come wonder,
Because, at last, it will help us see Our Father

And that very light that had hidden Him from us.
Wonder will come, because we will build our Temple
From the stone that, before you and me, all architects
Discarded for being unnecessary.
And this stone will be the cornerstone.

Verse 26. Go, Apostles, Go!

(104) And let there be among you a community calling to virtue, and
advocating righteous-ness, and deterring from evil. These are the successful.

Qur'an, Surah 3, 'Family of Imran'

Go!
Go and be!
Who will you be? That's for you to decide.
You want to be a propagandist? So be one.
You want to be a healer? So be one.

Right now you are unable to realise
What Salvation truly is.
Is it salvation of purity in thought?
Or a purity of intentions?
Is it the salvation of one man from pain?

Or a terrible disease?
From a fever or leprosy?
You can do this.
I order you.
You can do this.

No, no. You are simply people.
Simply, that's right, simply people,
Only those who can, who are able, who are gifted.
That is your mission.
You can heal and you can teach.

How?
It's not important.
What's important is that you can.
I don't know how.
I don't know why.

I am the same freak
As you'll feel
Healing your first patient.
This is a different matter.
Is our mission to treat and heal?

Then you're magi,
Then this is our command.
You say *Rabbi*.
You say *we believe*.
You say *miracles are undeniable*.

But make your own choice
Between healing
And Teaching.
You sense the difference? Not yet?
Well, off you go and sense it.

First, though, get a sense of this joy of healing.
It's a lot.

277

For you, that's seven minutes.
For them, it's an entire lifetime.
Hold life in your hands.

That's the point.
Hold it.
Pass it from one hand to the other.
Seven minutes, that's it, and you move on!
Seven minutes, while they remain and are happy for all time.

The point?
There's only one point:
I give you the power to heal and save,
I give you the power to exorcise demons.
In essence, though, I give you *power*!

But you have to decide yourselves,
Holding the Lord's miracle in your hands:
How do you carry on living?
Do you become popular healers,
Using this gift of Mine?

Do you know how much you can inspire people
When you have such a gift?
You can inspire them in everything.
That's because for you, it's a matter of seven minutes;
For them, it's a lifetime.

It is a challenge.
We break up here.
We meet up there.
The one who'll come here
Is the one who understands

That what's out there is more
Than that
Wonderful thing you have in your hands.
He who dedicates himself to medicine
And the healing of the many

Might never return again.
He who believes that here is strength and power,
Might never return again.
It's all just and fair
And I am giving it to you.

Go, apostles, go!
I am giving you the strength,
And the opportunities.
These opportunities have the power.
I give you the ability to heal and teach.

And to control human souls.
But not only souls. Control their fears, too.
There you go – almost limitless power!
There you go – a competitive edge.
There you go – crowns and chests. So, off you go and rule.

Off you go,
Those who'll transform their capability into power,
Let it be so!
Those who'll transform their capability into money,
Let it be so!

You now have everything.
Off you go. I love you.
I will be here, in Galilee and in Capernaum,
In three months from now.
Don't be idiots.

Transform what I've given you
Into power, influence and prosperity!
Go on, get out of here!
You stupid fools!
I have always had to carry you.

If it were not for that ridiculous Jewish tradition
Of having twelve students
To be called a Rabban;
I don't need you any more for anything.
You are no more than an entourage, window dressing.

Get out!
There is nothing in what you say!
You are nothing, just a middle class,
And there is no more insignificant social definition, believe me.
You are the proletariat

And under no circumstances will
You ever have a chance to climb higher
Than the bottom rung of all the world's societies.
This is a chance, a gate to a new life.
Out, I say!

I'm giving you everything that I had!
Exorcise demons,
Cleanse lepers,
Even resurrect some Lazarus!
You have that strength!

Off you go and know that!
Many centuries will pass
And Babylon will say,
The world belongs to the fortunate and the deservedly successful!
And the losers will be just pariahs and outcasts!

This philosophy will say:
Take this chance and rise!
Enter the ranks of rulers,
Only understand and realise that this chance
Comes to you but once; that's what the intellect is for!

Well, I'm giving you some start-up capital in the form of an opportunity
To work miracles: heal, exorcise demons, speak the Word of God.

Well, you're now fully armed and you will win.
You now have the strength to walk all over
Those who didn't make it,

Those who didn't get up in time,
Those who weren't convincing enough,
Those who were out of place at the interview,
Those who didn't radiate self-confidence,
Those who failed to speak up and say, *I'm the one you need!*

Thousands, millions and thousands more
Would give so much
To be able to compete
With such conditions at the start,
When one has not only an impeccable reputation,

A resume, work experience and self-confidence,
But also the ability to work wonders.
Off you go! Out, I say! Get out of my sight!
Make a career for yourselves!
Walk on water as if it were land!

You can't?
Come on, Cephas, you row out to the middle of the lake.
Stop! Look, I'm getting out and I'm walking on water!
Don't be afraid! Out you come and do the same!
A-a-ah-h! You're drowning,

Drowning because you don't believe!
Only Thomas here is a specialist in doubting!
There you go – stand like that on the water. Do it!
Well done!
Well, and now you get out! Stop! As ever, Thomas manages best of all...

Well done, all of you! And now, get out of here!
All that I've given you is start-up capital.
How long can you go on wandering around like this, poor and hungry?
Off you go and take the opportunity!
Set up your business, your influence and your wealth.

When you do a good deed for ten people,
Hundreds more will follow with their pockets full.
For that is how all those economic sects and
Charitable hypocrisy societies are built:
To suppress the mind when it sleeps and is wounded;

To suppress the soul when it awaits a miracle.

So, I am giving you the ability to heal, judge and resurrect.
Off you go and make a name and a future for yourselves.
This is all that I can give you,
But it is far more than some Harvard degree,
Because what you are holding is the ability to work genuine wonders.

So, I will be here, on the banks of the Sea of Galilee,
Waiting for precisely three months.
He who comes will come,

But they will be fools, losers and numskulls.
I will not be waiting for those who achieve success.

Well, who else has had such a chance in life only to ignore it?
Well, who else has been given such might, eh?
You'd have to be a complete idiot or
At the very least, a wholly impractical person
Not to put what I have given you to good use.

Well, how will other people laugh at you?
How will those apologists for success, the Americans, despise you?
What will you answer your children when they ask why Daddy was such an idiot
And failed to take his opportunity?
When he failed to understand his key competitive edge?

And later, all this needs to be transformed into a tangible,
Material success; how else?
And yet, there is still power.
So, take the power, the realms, kingdoms and dictatorships,
To rule and be the criterion of truth.

Become kings, presidents, dictators.
Gain the opportunity to draw up the rules
By which millions will live.
Hold court, for this is the measure of the righteous choice of the Head of the House.
Comfort yourself and your people with doctrines and ideas.

You'll see that supreme power
Gives you far more than divine and wonder-filled treatment!
It gives you the opportunity to make even the Lord a secondary element,
Running errands for geopolitical expediency.
And to speak on His behalf, casting Him down in the dreams of the weak.

And there are other peoples, too,
For whom you'll be able to become Mashiahs
And save them from fear and perhaps also the pleasure
Of being godless and without one God,
Without historical responsibility of any kind.

And replace what is perhaps their current heavenly paradise
With one that is theoretical, fictional but righteous all the same.
You could be the first among them
To confuse their worldview for the good of the Almighty,
And bring them the light of holy war and Faith.

There are so many opportunities that I am giving you. Off you go. Farewell.

****

Hello Cephas.
Hello Andrew.
We haven't seen one another for three months. Hello Simon and John.
Hello Didymus. Hello Nathaniel.
Hello Judas. Hello Philip,

Hello Jacob. Hello James, son of Alphaeus,
Hello Thaddaeus. Hello Levi Matthew.

Hello.
You've all returned.
Lord and Father of Mine, what idiots they all are!

Verse 27. Me, Family and War

(175) That is only Satan frightening his partisans...

Qur'an, Surah 3, 'Family of Imran'

(48) ...Had Allah willed, He could have made you a single nation, but He tests you through what He has given you. So compete in righteousness...

Qur'an, Surah 5, 'The Table'

'Tell me, James, son of Alphaeus, about your Path to this day.'
I have never told this story to anyone.
First of all, I am no storyteller.
Second, I am unable to speak in a way
Where I can remain impartial...

Meaning not to take sides.
Well, it's unavoidable – you always end up taking sides, right?
Especially when you're talking about war...
Did I promise to talk about the family?
In this case, it's one and the same thing.

Because there's a curse on our kind...
Recently, however, it seems to me
That it's not a matter of some clan-focused curse.
It's just the way things go in the world,
Or, more accurately, how things go in wartime.

That's because war is the principal controller of destinies.
War and hate. Mutual malice.
But not peace by any stretch.
Peace tries to build something, gradually, step by step.
But then war comes along and destroys it all.

It divides the world into the *us* and the *them*,
And it often turns out that,
For some reason, you find it hard yourself to work out
Who's where, and that's even despite the fact
That in wartime, the front line does that for you.

Sometimes you get the impression
That peace is merely a period for in-depth preparations
For the latest war;
So acute do motives and differences in views
Become at times like these

And, during war time, they are fated
To divide people, clearly and fully,
Into two factions, which stand against each other
And view one another through rifle sights
Or the narrow arrow-slit of the fortress.

Simon noticed the subtle matter
Of thousands and thousands of individuals during a war
Transforming in an instant into a military statistic,
When, after the disappearance of whole universes,
Which, in regular times, are formed by individuals,

283

All that feature are the numbers of military units,
But more often the losses, in the tens, hundreds, thousands
And then the millions.
Then you get the impression
That there's little point investigating the fate

Of one person alone, for where would be the interest in that,
When many souls perish and hundreds of destinies are broken
In a bloody conflict?
What lessons could such tales teach people
Who are planning the invasion

Of a neighbouring country,
To bring it to its knees,
Force it to accept a point of view,
Which it would never have entertained before the conflict,
As its own, even through the use of violence?

So, when does this *us* and *them* actually begin?
In early childhood? The time in life
That I know as carefree and happy
Contains no recollections for me
That the image of an enemy

Or simply an outsider was forming.
Perhaps I was too young
To remember any words or intonations from my parents,
Capable of making me understand
That there are others in the world who are not like me.

All I can see is a blissful yet blurred picture,
Where everything was full of smells, colours and mysteries.
Back then, the world was uniform and enormous,
Unknown and wonderful,
Bit by bit revealing its secrets and mysteries to me.

This cloudless period in my life ended, oh, so quickly,
For I lost both my parents too early.
One evening, my father didn't come to collect me
From school as he normally did.
Nor did my mother, which also happened on rare occasions.

My older brother didn't collect me either,
Which is not to say that didn't happen –
When Nathan did do this,
It meant the evening ahead would be wonderful,
Because we would spend it with our kind neighbour Hanna Barukhovna.

It meant that our parents were celebrating something
And they would share this joy with us
By leaving us with Auntie Hanna,
Where we would turn her house and backyard into a veritable bomb site,
For which our kind neighbour would dish out not the slightest reproach.

On that day, not one of them came for me.
The only people who came were a man and woman, dressed

As if they had been forced to appear black and menacing to children.
They came and spent an age talking about something,
First with my form tutor, then with the headmistress.

For some reason, my tutor and the head both appeared distressed
And looked over at me oddly.
Then, the woman in black came over to me, bent down
And, enveloping me in the smell of unpleasantly sharp, unfamiliar perfume,
Told me that we needed to go somewhere where I'd be fine.

I asked where my dad was and why we weren't going home,
But they replied that we would pop home
Just to collect some things
And that Daddy and Mummy wouldn't be coming because they...
Well, I would be told later where they were.

I was calm and just had a sense of anxiety
That, if my dad and my mum couldn't come,
Where had Nathan got to?
I would spend the evening with Auntie Hanna on my own without him.
And that was so much more boring and, well, unusual.

When I was in the car with the man and woman,
I asked about Nathan. Where was Nathan?
They just looked at one another and said nothing.
It was only then that I became anxious;
Nathan would always tell me where he would be,

Even if he had run off with friends
Without telling our parents.
On his return, he would always bring me something, without fail:
An enormous apple or a bag of sweets.
Once he even brought me a teeny little tortoise.

Strange as it seemed, it was our kind neighbour Auntie Hanna,
Who brought the burden of grief crashing down on me.
When they brought me home, she rushed to hug me
Crying and wailing something terrible and unclear.
Then she calmed down and told me what had happened.

That I was now all alone,
Because the car with my dad and my mum,
With my favourite brother Nathan on the back seat,
Had crashed at full speed into a fuel truck,
Exploding instantly like a giant bomb.

I didn't cry, rather I did the opposite and calmed Auntie Hanna down.
I probably hadn't comprehended the full terror of what had happened.
I wept only later, in the thick of night.
Auntie Hanna had stayed over at our home for the night,
But I simply couldn't get to sleep.

After many sleepless hours, I went up to the settee
Where she was sleeping and asked her,
'Auntie Hanna, so, does forever mean forever and ever and ever?'
She leapt up and, in her fright, pulled me so tightly in
That, for some time, my tears were unable to make it out.

The next morning I didn't go to school.
The man and woman all in black came
And took me and Auntie Hanna
To some other institution,
Where there were other children, only there were fewer of them and they were all

Somehow not the same as those at school.
For some reason I looked at them in fear,
Because it seemed that those bad words were written all over them:
Forever and ever and ever.
Because of that, they appeared cruel and unwelcoming.

The institution to where they'd brought me
Was our town's children's home,
Where children would study, spend the night and even stay for the weekend.
Later, I learned that not all of them were orphans like me.
Many of the children's parents simply lived a considerable distance away.

Later, I also discovered that the children's home
Looks for new families for children who have
Lost their parents, where they are given the chance
To be happy again.
However, before I learned about all that,

I was destined to live in this foster home
For the best part of four years,
Not because no one wanted to take me,
Rather that everyone was in a very difficult time.
Moreover, the teachers at the home didn't want to give the children away to just anyone.

Nevertheless, children would continue to leave,
While they simply couldn't find the right family for me
And another couple of teenagers.
I have to admit that this began to prey on our minds,
We got this chronic sensation of being unwanted.

Auntie Hanna didn't desert me.
She would often come, bringing something tasty
Or some things. She would also cry all the time, saying she couldn't
Adopt me because she herself was a widow
And she earned so little as it was.

I won't tell you about
What a child experiences when it loses its parents.
How he misses them, how the word *mum* is like an unspoken pain,
Not something soft and gentle.
How you become afraid, not of solitude,

But of the memories of your father, brother, mum,
Of playing with them or simply spending time with them in silence, only together,
Gradually erasing; it is the fear of this disappearing
That is the most terrible, because no one will come in their place,
And you'll be left with that unspoken and harsh *forever and ever and ever.*

When we came outside into the yard
To see off the lucky ones leaving for a family,

The headmistress, it seemed, would raise her hopes and mine
When she encountered my sad expression
And, with a forced cheerfulness in her voice, she would say, 'Not to worry, James the Less,[147]

Adonai is simply choosing and pondering
Your fate with great thoroughness.'
To which I would blurt out in reply, 'But I'm not the Less, I am Alphaeus!'
'All right, Alphaeus, I got it,' the headmistress would agree apologetically
And instantly get on, fussing about her business.

I don't know where that nickname *James the Less* came from.
At the children's home, they simply tried not to call the children by their surnames,
Evidently in an attempt to ensure we didn't stick to them.
Therefore, when we would be taken into new families,
The idea was that we would adapt faster to new surnames.

That's where nicknames *Less*, *White*, *Moor* and even *Doctor* came from.
I most likely acquired the name *Less* after playing soldiers,
When, given my age, I would have to play the more junior ranks.
I would run about, screaming, 'Young officers, report in!' Or,
'I am no boy, but a junior officer in the army!'

Or something like that.
Yet we never took offence at these nicknames.
The staff at the children's home were always very kind to us.
I don't know if that was natural for folk from Galilee or if all people were like that.
At that age, I had nothing to compare.

As for those terrible stories of teachers' brutality in such institutions,
They had yet to be drubbed into us via the television.
Or perhaps the world was simply different back then?
Perhaps it was still a kind place,
And preparations for a new war hadn't yet started?

And then the day came
When the headmistress, unable to conceal her excitement,
Called me into her office and, with the words, 'There you go!'
She plonked a thick file down in front of me
With the details of a family.

I opened it, but in my excitement, I couldn't see anything inside,
Despite there being photographs of smiling people,
With their names in big letters,
And their life stories, all proving their right
To make me specifically a happy boy.

For some reason I quietly burst into tears, although, not really.
It was just that tears had filled my eyes and the images on the photos
Seamlessly became those of my mum, dad and Nathan.
I didn't know what to say, but it seemed that the headmistress hadn't expected any
Other emotion from me.

She quietly stroked my hair

---

[147] James the Less, the Minor, the Younger or the Little, was the nickname given to James, son of Alphaeus, by Christ's disciples, to distinguish him from James, son of Zebedee.

And then said,
'Every time when one of you leaves for a new family,
I make three prayers to the heavens.
To the Lord, to give your new parents

Courage, kindness and patience,
Wisdom and love for this small child.
To the Almighty, to give you a strong heart,
Capable of growing a tree of happiness and joy of a new Home
On the infant scars left by your cruel fate.

My third prayer I direct
To your real, deceased parents.
I ask them to protect you as ethereal angels
And leave the fears, pain and yearning of regret
Down here.
With me.

The days spent waiting for new parents
Cannot be compared with anything. Regular children,
Who have grown up in regular families,
Will never understand this, and nor do they need to.
These are not worries you'd wish to share with everyone.

And yet, all the same, spirits were high
And close to joy, because
It had somehow turned out that the other two long-term fixtures at the home
Had also been found suitable parents.
That feeling that you're sharing your joy with someone else

Intensifies the joy many times over.
Are we, the pupils of shelters and boarding schools
Not meant to understand this?
Grievances big and small were forgiven, quarrels forgotten.
This was a time for dreams and imagination.

However the day I met my new family
Proved nothing like I had imagined it to be.
For me, in any case.
Early in the morning, we looked out of the window
And saw several cars approaching the building of the children's home;

Different colours, different makes,
Each evidencing the different levels of prosperity of the occupants.
With some hurrying and skurrying, three couples emerged from them.
Then, the headmistress appeared.
They would stand five minutes or so in the yard,

Before entering the home itself,
Embarrassed, excited and clumsily letting one another go first.
We knew the procedure by the minute.
A good half hour would be spent signing the paperwork
And completing the various formalities.

Then the children would be called in one by one,
To meet the parents.
We knew that *they* had already studied us from afar

Or unnoticed, but the acquaintance was arranged only
When *they* had decided, so as not to traumatise the child

By rejecting them after meeting them. Well, of course! We're not talking about goods in a shop.
In any case, these were the procedures.
Arthur, Lera (my fellow long-termers) and I
Hid ourselves in a corner of the sports hall
And lit up a concealed cigarette in our excitement.

This was not careless on our part;
We knew for certain that in thirty minutes the smoke smell would dissipate
And would have no impact on *their* first impression,
While it would give us the opportunity to put paid to the jitters.
After sharing gum and drops of aftershave,

We returned to the boys' dorm,
Where the kids, with noses to the windows, were admiring and discussing the cars below.
We used to do the same thing ourselves,
But we weren't up to it that day; why torment ourselves guessing
Which of them had come *for you*?

Steps were heard on the squeaking stairs
And that was it! Everyone at the boarding school knew that these were special steps!
The door opened and the loud voice of Aunt Tsili the nurse
Called out, 'Arthur Feltsman, the head would like to see you downstairs!'
Of course, at that moment, everyone expects to hear their name;

That expectation becomes something unbearable in fact.
Why couldn't everyone be called together?
Everyone knew, because the head's office
Tried to turn this process into a little festive occasion of sorts,
With everyone given individual treatment.

Oh, well, Lera and I would sit it out.
Arthur jumped up, quite forgetting about us,
Spitting his gum into a napkin, grabbing his rucksack,
Kissing us hurriedly on the cheek
And rushing off after Aunt Tsili.

We knew he had more on his mind.
He was looking at his future life; he could almost see it,
After going so many years unable to see it this close.
We forgave him, of course. Before leaving,
He would definitely return to say goodbye and Lera would cry,

While I would slap him on the back and wish him all the best.
We'd tell him to call, come visit, to keep in touch.
At the same time, we knew he wouldn't do that any time soon.
And it would be good if it weren't soon,
For that would mean everything was going well.

If he were to call or, worse still, appear in person,
The opposite would apply and alarm bells would ring.
So, pray God, we wouldn't see him for some time.
Somehow, we'd find one other without fail.
Without fail! You see, we were a *family* for a considerable time.

289

This would have been a normal course of events, only today,
When Arthur was called first and not me,
A sixth sense told me
That it was far from being just like that.
I tried to put it all down to nerves

But, I have to admit, I failed miserably.
As if in confirmation of my fears,
Half an hour later, Aunt Tsili returned to call
The name Lera Voinovich. Now, I was almost completely sure
That my path in life would not take me that day to where I expected.

They were now supposed to call me, but this didn't happen.
Arthur and Lera later appeared, radiant with joy.
It was hard to call it happiness at that moment,
But certainly joy from the expectation of a new life.
They came to say goodbye, radiating from within, and only then did they realise

That I was still in the dorm and hadn't yet gone to meet anyone.
Their faces suddenly displayed anxiety,
But I decisively forbade them to feel that way;
I kissed and embraced them tightly, fighting off the other noisy kids,
And I accompanied them to the door, to their new lives.

A little while later, I heard car doors shutting
And the noise of engines as the cars drove away.
Only after these sounds had died away
Did I forced myself over to the window and looked down.
A dark-coloured Mercedes stood silent

And still with its lights off.
Submissively awaiting its masters, it anxiously shone
Bright side mirrors, as if understanding that
Its masters were stuck inside the building
And not for any pleasant reason either.

So what on earth was my status?!
The front door to the children's home opened,
Preparing to let someone out; a pupil perhaps?
Perhaps it was our cleaner, my namesake James?
Or perhaps... I didn't have the strength to look any more and stepped away from the window.

Clearly, something wasn't going according to plan. But what?!
Several moments later, I heard
The doors of the Mercedes shut weightily;
Unlike the sounds of the previous doors,
These were heavy from the weight of grief.

The car nervously started and reluctantly pulled away.
At that moment, someone's heavy hand descended onto my shoulder.
I shuddered and turned to see the headmistress before me.
With unexpected firmness, she said, 'James, it's not what you think.'
She knew that we had learnt the procedure down to the last second

And she could imagine what was going on in my heart.
'Have a little more patience, son. Everything will become clear *today*.
I promise you that, very, very soon,

You'll be turning the new page in your life
With our children's home on it.

Have a little more patience,' she repeated with equal firmness.
'And for now, off you march to class and pack up your prize books
That you forgot to put in your rucksack.'
'I'll leave them there,' I said more in a sniffle than a voice.
'No, James, they are named, so you have to take them with you,

Because you'll have someone to show them too,
So they can be proud of you.'
She went back to her office and shuffled off to the classrooms.
On the way back, walking past the head's office,
I sensed the smell of cigarettes, which was really unusual.

I slowly continued past without stopping,
But I caught sight of the headmistress through the crack of the half-open door;
She was standing by the window, smoking,
And all of her tense figure indicated that she
Was waiting nervously yet persistently for something.

The day turned unexpectedly dark beyond the bedroom window
And rain busied itself against the eaves.
I pressed my forehead to the glass and looked out.
I like the rain; I see it as a visible work of God,
But now each droplet seemed to pepper my soul with buckshot.

Suddenly, a dirty yellow taxi entered the yard,
Clumsily splashing through the puddles.
Turning its clumsy frame sharply at the door to the children's home,
The car came to a stop. The rear door flew open,
Releasing the tall, thin figure of an unfamiliar old man.

The old man straightened to full height and entered the home most decisively.
I managed to catch sight of a distinctly military step,
Despite his advanced age.
Before entering, he cast his eyes over the home's windows
And, for some reason, I sensed that in that second,

He had seen and assessed everything he saw,
Including my own astonished look
Over which his grey eyes had clearly scraped.
On this occasion, Aunt Tsili's usually measured step on the stairs
Became a clatter that was unable to hide her excitement.

Breathing heavily, she blurted, 'James, son of Alphaeus!
To the head's office, Right now!
Don't just stand there,
This instant, I tell you!'
'James, James, what's going on?' the little ones jabbered.

They, too, knew the procedure by heart
And this latest occurrence had been so unusual
That they were fussing about, all excited.
'Oh, a taxi!' Someone cried near the window.
'I dream of riding in a taxi! James, what's up?'

'I don't know,' I muttered. 'Everyone, be quiet! Do your homework! I'll come back and tell you!'
I began to gather my rucksack, books and whatever else I could get my hands on.
'James,' came the voice of little Mos',
Handing me a dictionary I had dropped in my hurry,
'Don't come, James! Better you go home instead! Don't come back...'

I was taken aback, then hugged Mos' tightly,
Before rushing down the stairs. I could have told him I wished him the best.
I could have told him I wouldn't forget. I could have said that one day, his time...
But that is not the done thing here.
You can't talk about the future.

That would be bad luck. Everything I didn't say, however,
Went without saying,
Because we were talking about what, for me and these kids,
Was the Most Important.
And this is something you can't put in words. It's a sacred dream.

'...I have to admit, after such searching,
That your call was wholly unexpected for us,'
I heard from behind the door of the head's office.
'I managed to explain everything to that family.
Of course, it came as a shock to them, but...'

At that moment, I pushed open the door and went in.
'And here is our James,' the headmistress announced triumphantly.
I looked round and, in a large armchair in the corner of the room,
I caught sight of the tall old man I had seen earlier
Through the window.

The headmistress paused,
As if she didn't want to dispel my confusion,
But then she announced solemnly,
'James, I'd like you to meet your grandfather,
Solomon Izrailevich Kogan.'

'Hm, it's actually Shlomo ben Israel Kohan,'
Came the cracked baritone of the mountainous old man.
'Yes, yes,' the headmistress replied, embarrassed, 'Of course.'
'Not to worry,' this newly-sprung grandfather smiled back at her,
'You see, I am from the old guard, so that means I can say it in the old way.'

Grandfather? What grandfather?!
Memories flashed through my head like lightning.
'Dad, why don't Nathan and I have grandfathers and grandmothers?'
'My parents died in the war, son.
They were martyred in Poland.'

'And what about Mum's parents?' 'Mum's also died in the war, son.'
'Mum, who's picture is this? It says Slo-lo... So-lom...'
'Solomon Kogan, honey. My maiden name is Kogan.'
'So, that's your dad? But why do you always hide his picture?'
'I'll tell you when you grow up, James, honey.'

'Auntie Hanna, Mum hides the picture of my grandfather.
Do you know why?'
'Oh, James, I don't know. They say he disappeared during the war.'

'I'll grow up and I'll find him!'
'Hm, maybe it's not worth it, James?'

'Why is that? Why can't I go looking for grandfather?'
'Oh, James, honey, bad people say that he was a traitor...'
'A what?!'
'Oh, well, I don't know. You'll grow up and work it out for yourself!'
'I'll still find him, if he's still alive!'

So, that's where those grey eyes came from! They are Mum's eyes!
That's where the height comes from; Mum was tall and slender, too,
In a way that made all heads in town turn as she walked down the street.
Well, not as tall as this... grandfather;
He is simply huge!

The old man was sitting in the armchair, but his eyes
Were on the same level as mine,
But I was standing upright!
I shuddered when I realised that, as per the usual procedure,
I was supposed to remain alone with this giant.

However, the old timer suddenly clapped his hands on his knees and said,
'Well, relatives probably don't need to get to know one another in someone else's home,
So why don't my grandson and I head home, if you will allow!'
He stood up and in that instant the headmistress became quite tiny.
However, the old timer kissed her hand so gallantly

That she clearly felt anything but.
'I am so, so grateful to you for everything!
If it weren't for you, I would been unlikely to have found my boy.
You see, it is so hard from such a distance away.
People manage to lose one another even in the same country!'

'Oh, please! This is our duty, our work.
And as for... You know, I am sure that flesh and blood
Will find their own even across great oceans.
All the very best to you!'
'Merci, and the greatest of happiness and success to you and your children!'

And so, without uttering a single word in acquaintance,
I shuffled after my new-found relative.
Lightly holding his powerful hand,
I sat in the taxi and, only when the old timer gave the driver the address of *my own* home,
Did I quietly burst into tears.

My parents' house was similar
To the stage of a fairy-tale performance,
After the show has ended and the performers have gone.
The all-conquering dust seemed to have engulfed
All that I once saw as the flowering garden of my childhood.

The only things of bright colour were my large
Rucksack and the bag by the door.
I guessed these were the old man's things.
'In you come...' The old man stopped short and fell silent,
And then sat down in the armchair by the door and pulled me towards him.

His eyes were directly opposite mine.
It was as if I had dived into his bottomless grey eyes.

'Listen, son... er, Grandson!
You and I are now alone in this world. Me and you.
There's no one else, you understand?
At least as far as I know...
I have been looking for you for many years and now I've found you.

You are now my entire life,
Everything that God has left me in this world.
If you tell me now that you'd prefer a new family,
Well, I mean... a new dad and mum, you just say so...
Then, I'll... I'll...'

Then, I don't know how it happened,
But then my hand rose of its own accord
And touched the old man's, no, Grandpa's lips.
And, looking straight into Mum's grey eyes, I said,
'No, Grandpa Solomon, I don't want anyone. I will stay here with you.

And... I won't let you down, believe me.'
His eyes suddenly filled with tears.
'What do you mean, James? How could you ever let me down?
It is I who are in your debt!'
He embraced me tightly and I.. well, I had yet to experience adult emotions

To be able to describe them to you.
I can say only one thing:
From that moment on, Grandpa and I became a unified whole.
And what does that mean?
It's a family, my friends, albeit not a full one, but a family nonetheless.

Or, as Grandpa called it in Latin, for some reason – *familia.*

We lived a short while in my parents' house.
One day, though, I told Grandpa it was not easy for me
To live so close to all those memories.
He understood that oh, so well for himself.
And so, we moved to Jerusalem.

I learned much about Grandpa in that city.
At first he related almost nothing at all about himself,
But over time we became, I don't know, close friends, I suppose
And he slowly began to draw back the curtains
That concealed the secrets of his life.

And, by all appearances, there were oh, so many of them!

At the least, we could start by saying that everyone,
Beginning with the young IDF lieutenant[148]
Who met us in a jeep at the airport,
Called him Colonel
And saluted him with emphatic displays of respect.

---

[148] IDF – Israel Defence Forces.

It wasn't hard to see from Grandpa's poise
That he was once in the military.
But when? And in what army? Where had fate taken him?
There was much that interested me:
Where are our roots, what was my grandmother like?

How was my mother born? You see, I had been deprived all of that.
I knew everything about my father and his parents,
But almost nothing of my mother and her family.
The only thing I remembered was that
Dad sometimes joked with her, saying,

'There goes your Russian obstinacy again!'
But my parents would brush aside my questions,
Saying they'd tell me when I grew up.
But they never got to a point where they could tell me anything.
If it were not for Grandpa, I would have remained in the dark

Forever and ever and ever.

So, what can I tell you about the years we lived in the Holy City?
I enjoyed school and going boxing,
And I achieved pretty good results, too.
That said, to be honest, I put the effort in for Grandpa, for I could see
How proud he was of my success.

This joy for my Grandpa's pride
Gave me far greater comfort than my personal ambitions.
I asked Grandpa why Dad had called Mum Russian.
'You mean, you're from Russia?'
'In a manner of speaking, I am,' Grandpa replied, but then said,

'Hey, shall we go to the beach on Sunday?'
I felt that the day would surely come
When he would tell me everything.
Somehow I came to realise that it wasn't that I needed to grow up
To be ready to hear his tale,

Rather that he needed to resolve himself to tell me everything.
That is why I waited patiently, confidently anticipating
Tales full of adventure,
Would be no less enthralling than
The stories of *The Fifteen-Year-Old Captain* or *The Three Musketeers*.

By that time, however, something had become clear.
Grandpa had come for me from distant America,
Where he had served in the army, genuinely reaching the rank of colonel.
He had been numerous times in Israel;
At any rate, his command of Hebrew was impeccable.

What was he doing there? And why didn't he visit his daughter or grandchildren?
It was unclear. What was most surprising was
That when I asked how old he was, he would always answer differently –
Either it was sixty-five or sixty-nine,
Or he would screw up his face, grin slyly and end up just brushing me off.

I realised from the few photographs he had

That he had retired some fifteen years before.
But what had happened with him then? Where?
In the United States? In another country?
And why did he let slip on several occasions,

'When I was allowed to return here again'?
Why was his most secret notebook,
Covered in diagrams, circles and tables
All written in Arabic?
Did he write it himself? Or was it not even his?

Why did he, a retired colonel,
Dislike watching military news,
Always quietly switching channels?
I had thousands and thousands of questions brewing,
And I came to understand more and more

That the Colonel was no ordinary man.
I would definitely soon learn what it was that made him so singular.
This extraordinary man was *my familia*,
My *familia's* history and property,
And that meant it was my history and my property.

One sunny Sunday morning
A quite wonderful thing happened –
Auntie Hanna, our old neighbour, came to visit!
It transpired that her son had moved from Russia to Israel.
This was now commonplace

But before, they say, Jews had not been allowed back to their historical Homeland.

Now everything had changed fundamentally
And he had come to Jerusalem with his entire family
And, naturally, he had brought Auntie Hanna with him.
They invited us round for dinner
And I still laugh when I recall that evening,

Because they were all gabbling away in their unfamiliar Russian,
Of which I knew not a word.
Sometimes, Auntie Hanna would interpret for me,
But she was clearly so happy with her *familia*,
That I realised her attentions were directed elsewhere.

The only time I really wanted to speak Russian
Was when I met her granddaughter Masha,
Who so clumsily concealed beneath that girlish importance
That repatriate's perplexity that we know so well.
However, we instantly discovered

That we both had an excellent command of English,
And I returned from that night, very happy in my own way.
Grandpa had been really touched by conversing with *Russians*,
But I noticed that he didn't speak the language that well,
Constantly trying to recall forgotten words.

What was most interesting
Was that he would ask Auntie Hanna's son to remind him... in German,

Which he knew so very well.
Learning that Grandpa knew *Deutsch*
Was for me yet another big surprise

And it merely served to fan the flames of my curiosity.
Grandpa was in no hurry to douse them, either. Oh!
It was also great news that
Auntie Hanna's *familia*
Had moved in not far from us,

Just a couple of blocks away, which meant
That I could see Masha frequently,
Under the guise of just happening to be visiting Auntie Hanna,
Simply passing on the way to school
Or the sports hall.

'James, you should speak in Hebrew with Masha!'
Oh, Auntie Hanna, in Hebrew, in Yiddish, even in Maori!
Just to see those large, slightly surprised-looking,
Grey eyes, seemingly slightly slanted because of her high cheekbones
And so completely fathomless!

At about the same time
I started having these strange dreams
For which I could find no explanation at all.
More likely, an experienced psychoanalyst would probably find one,
In my orphaned childhood or somewhere else like that.

However, I am not inclined to think that dreams
Are simply an extension of an individual's psyche,
His conscious, subconscious experience and much more besides,
That give rise exclusively to this body
And the brain placed inside.

Although, perhaps what comes to light is information
Contained in our genes.
Or perhaps coming from previous reincarnations?
I don't know for sure, but I don't want to view dreams strictly
Physiologically or from a viewpoint of memory coming from another body,

Even if that body was once my own,
And I think that many others would
Support this simple opinion.
Although, you know, dreams are so varied
That they could arise for various reasons.

Let's put it this way: as regards the dreams that I'll tell you about,
I believe they were the precursors of many events
That I was destined to experience in the future.
That means that they came to me from other times and other worlds,
Travelling in the space where

We are not fated to wander in our waking hours.
Or not fated for now, who knows?
These were particular visions and not just regular dreams.
I could say that they were vibrant,
If it were not for the fact that they were full of the harsh hues of pain.

Once I dreamed that, wailing wildly,
I had burst into a huge city,
In a chariot,
Harnessed to two fierce war horses.
Fires raged all around and a street battle was in full swing.

Enemy warriors were dying, appearing like aliens.
My warriors were prevailing,
With cries of, 'Let this be the end of you, Babylon! Die, you Aramaic dogs!'
My chariot flew onto the central square
And I saw the enemy leader, a tall, stately prince,

Fighting off my guards.
Catching sight of me, he cried, 'Traitor,
Come and fight an honest battle!'
Seething with inhuman hatred, I leaped from the chariot at full pelt,
Motioning to the guards and signalling them to step away.

With one true, heavy blow,
I pierced the prince's chest!
In my rage, I drew him close, to look him in the eye before,
Defeated by me, he breathed his last.
And I froze in horror...

His face... It was me whom I had just killed!
Not a doppelgänger or a twin, but me!
Lowering my eyes, I saw the same bloody
Wound flowering on my chest;
The wound I had inflicted on the enemy prince!

In another dream I saw myself, standing in a line
Of several soldiers, their bayonets at the ready.
I was in a strange uniform, surrounded by an unfamiliar mountain landscape.
Up ahead were some unknown people,
Dressed in all sorts,

As if they had been awoken at night and cast out into the snow,
Given the chance to throw on whatever came to hand.
We were at a railway station. Beside us, a train groaned with measured breathing.
Suddenly, a biting and malicious command was heard
And a terrible hatred broke into my heart.

I hated those people up ahead with their alien and frightening appearance.
Their men rushed upon us, howling like wolves,
But this desperate wailing merely served to intensify my hatred.
One of those outcasts, with a sharp dagger's blow,
Slit the throat of the soldier standing by my side.

I lunged forward and thrust my bayonet
Deep into the terrible outsider's heart,
While screaming, 'Die, you Chechen beast! Die!'
The outcast pressed his entire body down onto my blade,
As if he wanted to terrify and bring me down with his own death.

I could see his face up close...
Oh, Lord! But it was me! I had just killed myself!

In terror, I looked down at my clothes and my hands –
For some reason the odd uniform had gone;
I was now clad in gazyrs[149], while, between them

An enormous red patch of blood was spreading...
My third dream was saturated in the brightest flowers,
Splashed over wondrous mountains and valleys.
Somewhere in the distance I could hear the beating of war drums,
But the troop noise was unable to disturb the beauty of the landscape

Spread around us.
By *us*, I mean me and the giant Turanian warrior
I had been in single combat with for many hours.
Around us were broken swords and spears and shields smashed to splinters.
Helmets and armour lay discarded, banners trembled with fatigue.

'Are you ready for death, Rustam?' the Turanian asked
And launched his bare hands on me like a mountain leopard.
'Die, you Turkic carrion!' I grunted like a predator
While plunging my curved Iranian knife
Right into the heart of the mighty *pahlevan*[150].

Down he came like a felled oak,
But I stopped him from falling,
For I wanted to enjoy the look of agony
On the face of the best warrior of the tribe I hated so bitterly.
And... that's right, the same again.

I could see my own eyes fading away like a mountain sunset.
Death was entering me with an Arctic cold,
A terrible weight was befalling my eyes,
Paralysing my arms and legs, my throat, mouth and tongue.
An awful scream broke this state of paralysis and I woke up.

I told my grandpa about these dreams.
I held back at first; after all he might think and deem me
An over-excited little girl who had read too many novels before bedtime.
However, Grandpa listened to my stories in silence and turned pale,
As if he had heard his very own nightmare.

The circumstances and the storylines in the dreams were different,
But they always contained two identical elements:
A sense of fierce hatred for some *outsider*,
Followed by my murdering myself.
No, no, this was not an act of suicide!

There were no suicidal thoughts,
You know, like saying goodbye to life or a desire to inflict
Irreparable harm on myself. Quite the opposite.
There was a specific desire to kill, to destroy something terrible,
Something unfamiliar, united in the single word *outsider*.

---

[149] An implement to hold a rifle charge: a tube with a bullet and a measure of gunpowder or a paper cartridge. They were carried in *gazyr* bags or in rows of small pockets on the breast. Later, *gazyr* pockets became a distinctive element of national dress of the peoples of Caucasus.
[150] An Iranian wrestler and also a title of honour granted by Shah of Persia to men who, in addition to their athletic stature and honesty, were brave warriors

This wasn't some latent hatred for certain people either,
Because one night,
I was a Frenchman from Napoleon's guards,
And I killed an Englishman. In the next dream
I was an Englishman with a blazing hatred of the Zulus.

Grandpa acted as an exemplary modern parent;
He took me to see a psychoanalyst. And not just one either.
One of these analysts dug long and hard into my orphanage past,
Looking for a reason why I might hate some part of myself,
Or struggle with something inside.

I did what I had to and told them everything.
The sessions continued but so did my dreams,
As if there had never been any therapy at all.
The next psychoanalyst, with a long beard and wearing a hat,
Told my grandpa that, aside from any psychology, this was possibly

Something surfacing in my genetic memory
About the *galuts*[151] of the Jewish people –
Babylon, Persia and so on.
The first dream is very reminiscent of the death of Belshazzar of Babylon
At the hands of the traitor Ugbaru, who had crossed sides to the Persians.

The death of Belshazzar and His father Nabonidus
Is linked with the end of Assyrian rule over the Land of Israel.
The image of the Persian legendary hero Rustam
Might have surfaced linked with the time of Persian rule.
The other dreams are packed with allegories

About the *Shoah*[152] and other persecutions of our people,
Of which there have been many in history.
And the killing? Whose hatred had been resurrected in me then?
Perhaps, the follower of Jung and Freud went on,
This was an allegory of the desire of Jacob the Forefather, your namesake[153]

To protect himself from killing his twin brother Esau,
By killing whom you yourself desire the disappearance
Of all incarnations of evil and grief for the people of Israel
And to prevent the longstanding *galut* of Edom.
Well, that's an entertaining inversion,

I must say, for did Esau not want and threaten to kill Jacob?
And then, I did not kill a twin or a brother, meaning another person;
I killed myself.
And another thing: what's with the Chechens or Zulus,
And the masses of other peoples who bear no relation to Jewish history?

---

[151] *Galut* (Hebrew) – literally means *exile*, the forced settlement of the Jewish people out of their native country, the Land of Israel. The age of deprivation of the people of Israel during various conflicts. The first was Babylon, then Media (Persia), the third Greece and finally the ongoing *galut* of Edom (commonly identified as Rome).
[152] *Shoah* (Hebrew) – catastrophe, or disaster. A term that means the systematic destruction of the Jews by the Nazis during the Second World War. It is the same as the Greek *Holocaust*, only the *Shoah* is seen as the more accurate term.
[153] The Russian uses the name *Iakov* and its diminutives, which together translate both as James and Jacob (Jim, Yasha and so on). For ease of reading, the name James has been used throughout.

The thing is that I knew nothing of the existence of most of these peoples,
Until I heard about them in my dream.
Then, of course, I researched books and magazines,
To find out more about these mysterious tribes.
Of course, there was much that was similar in meaning to the *galuts*.

For example, the Chechens were displaced from their homeland
And exiled to all corners of the world.
The Zulus lived many years, segregated in Bantustans,
Like the Jews were segregated in the ghettos.
But the French, Japanese, Russians and Dutch?

What's the genetic or associative connection there?
Given that psychologists found no other signs of
Evident schizophrenia in the rest of my life,
Grandpa gave up on the doctors
And said, 'I think I know the reason for these dreams,

But you'll learn about this a little later, Koppel.'
Again that *a little later*. So, how long can you drag it out, Shlomo?
How many more do I need to kill and hate in my dreams
Before you decide to share with me
Those secrets you are so intent on hiding?

I can see that it's not me who's not ready for the story, but you.
When will you finally get it done?
Time went by and, you know, the dreams somehow began to fade.
The horrors of war and hate visited me more and more seldom.
Perhaps this was helped by the advent of other feelings?

For instance, my love for that delightful,
Grey-eyed granddaughter of Auntie Hanna, *Masha*?
How I was thrilled by the cooing of her Russian dialect,
From which all I could understand at first was the 'Jim, Jim'?
Evidently, that was where the real Freudism was hiding,

For it was Grandpa who grumbled, 'But her eyes are grey,
Like your grandmothers and mothers!'
'And like yours, Grandpa,' I said with a laugh. 'Just like yours.'
'The same but not the same,' the old Colonel muttered,
But grinned mischievously for some reason.

Then, however, the day came
When I actually heard Grandpa's story of his life.
To be more precise, it turned out to be not just one day.
We had travelled for Saturday and Sunday especially to Lake Kinereth[154],
To stroll around Capernaum, chat, listen and chat some more.

It actually all began with an unexpected argument with my grandfather.
Not so much unexpected,
As one that had me simply stunned.
The thing was that I was preparing a surprise for the Colonel,
And I thought that he'd be happy when he heard what it was.

However, as it turned out, I was wrong.

---

[154] *Kinereth* (Hebrew) – an alternative spelling of Kinneret (the Sea of Galilee).

The everyday delight of having the Colonel as my grandfather
Led me to decide
To choose the military life as my destiny
And I would join the cadet corps

And study at the preparatory college.
I was proud of my decision
And expected the same pride in me from grandpa.
Therefore, when I announced that I dreamed of devoting my life
To the service in Tsva ha-Hagana le-Yisra'el[155],

I was literally swelling with joyful excitement, but...
The Colonel's reaction was, to say the least, unexpected.
His face suddenly turned pale
And his eyes widened as if in horror.
He jumped up and began pacing the room in silence.

Then he stopped and said hoarsely and importantly,
'Never. No. Never.'
My eyes darkened and I felt sick,
So unexpected was the reaction.
A second later, the darkness was replaced with flashes of lightning.

At first, I still managed to display a calm demeanour
And, finding it hard to hold back my feelings,
I asked him, as calmly as I could,
'Why? I don't understand. Why?
Is it not the act of a true patriot and grandson of a military man?'

'I said no,' my grandfather interrupted me, his voice shaking a little.
'Because... because you can't.
Because you don't know yet...'
It was here that I snapped. My head span with
Questions, feelings, indignation, doubt and expectation!

'But when am I to find out?!' I literally screamed.
'And what is it I have to find out?!
You will go on putting it off, but what about me?!
When am I to make a decision?!
Now, that's when! My life is happening now! Now is when young men make decisions!

When will the day come when I will learn everything you're hiding?!
That's just what my parents said:
We'll tell you when you grow up.
Well, I've grown up. And what about them? Can they tell me anything now?!'
I suddenly began crying and a lump appeared in my throat.

My legs felt wobbly And I fell into the armchair and wept.
Somewhere in the corner of my mind, a thought stirred indecisively:
All right, cadet, act like a man.
But the image of my parents meant I couldn't stop;
They had gone, concealing their secrets from me

Forever and ever and ever.

---

[155] *Tsva ha-Hagana le-Yisra'el* (Hebrew) – Israel Defence Forces, abbreviated as Tzahal.

Through my tears, I could see that Grandpa had silently left the room,
But then he reappeared in the doorway in his usual military cap
And with our two favourite backpacks.
'Let's go, Koppel, the time has come
For you to hear it all.'

When we were in Grandpa's car,
Speaking through my departing sobs,
I asked him, 'Saba,[156] but when… you sometimes…
(I could have said, *in a fit of particular warm of feeling toward me*,
But back then, alas, I couldn't find the words)

Well... why do you sometimes call me Koppel?'
Without turning, Grandpa said,
'Koppel is a diminutive of James in German.'
'German?! Well, Grandpa, I won't rest until I have shaken
It all from you, Adonai be my witness!'

ISRAEL BEN ARYEH. FATE. WAR.

It was a wonderful time, not because of the warm weather in Capernaum,
Or the gentle waves of the Kinnereth,
But because there was an enormous world all around us,
And we were side by side, next to one another,
The two of us, grandfather and grandson, *la familia*.

So, there were just two of us and an entire generation separated us,
But we were here, walking and enveloped by the secrets
Of the history of the ancient Sea of Galilee
And of our family – ours and no one else's,
The only one in all this enormous world.

The waves murmured at our feet,
But Grandpa could still not bring himself to start his tale.
It was then that I took the bull by the horns
And asked the most sacred of questions,
Which would have tormented any young boy more than any other.

'Saba, is it true... well, that you were a traitor?'
I was a little frightened, but, to my surprise, my grandfather reacted calmly:
'Yes and no, Koppel. Yes and no.
Now is no longer the time for justifications;
I'll just tell you how it was.

You are a grown lad and you should understand it all.
If you don't understand it today, you have your life ahead of you;
You'll understand tomorrow. I'll do my best not to hold anything from you.
What you are about to hear
Is something I have never told anyone.

But I have no one else but you,
Who I could call *la familia*.
So, you will not only hear,

---

[156] *Saba* (Hebrew) – grandfather

You'll share the burden not only of my fate,
But the fate of our entire ancient kind,

A kind that is truly cursed.'

'What curse is that, Saba?'
'Koppel, please, hear me out as I tell it.
That's because if I tell you about that straight away,
You're not likely to understand the essence.'
'Why do you refuse me in understanding?'

'Because I can see that, not only you, but the whole world
Is not able to respond to the lessons
Given from on high.
So, God has given you one storyteller, and that's me.
That was His decision, while I, acting on this command,

Will implement His will.'
'So, it's not just the two of us, Saba?
So, God is here too?'
'Evidently He is always present,
But you leave those arguments to the theologians...

You were asking if I was a traitor?
That is not exactly the right question,
For it is not something that I can answer;
That would be for you to do.
You see, I will never be objective.

What's most important, though, is how you'll define me in the end.
What is important is what does God wish to convey to you?
For I have lived my life; yours is still ahead of you.
I will give you everything that perhaps will enable you
To make the right choice in life.

Although I have seldom met people who have achieved this.
Most often, people simply follow the corridors
That open before them in life, no more than that...
However, that doesn't mean you should listen to my story
As just a story, you know, when they say that's how it was.

There is a particular meaning hidden in all this.
And this meaning is not only yours, but that of all other people.'
'But how will all the other people learn of my fate, Saba?'
'You know, when you asked me
What *it's not just the two of us* means,

For some reason, I thought not of the Almighty.
I imagined a certain subject plodding along behind us,
Awkwardly clutching pens and sheets of parchment and papyrus
And stopping from time to time
To write down the main idea.'

'Yes, that's funny, I imagined him like that too!'
We stopped, looked round and imagined what this
Person would look like. We grinned at one another and Grandpa went on:
'Well, anyway, let him complete his mission; we'll finish ours.

Listen to my tale.

I don't know if it was the Almighty who created hatred on earth
Or if it's purely the product of the human mind.
I am not talking about hatred for one's neighbour;
That is a separate matter.
I am talking about hatred between peoples, between nations.

Who invented the *galut*? And when?
After all, you understand you can't understand where it came from
If you don't know the history of other tribes,
Dispersed all over the world,
In all corners of the Oecumene.

No one knows what it started from either.
Perhaps from Cain and Abel, or Esau and Jacob,
Or from Nimrod's Tower of Babel,
Which split human unity using a simple method:
The separation into hundreds and thousands of languages.

After languages came customs, culture, history,
Rules governing how to live, eat, pray and praise God.
However, nothing is as effective in tearing people apart
As the history of wars, civil and domestic,
Between nations, countries, empires and colonies.

My life unfolded in a way
Where the separation into nations and peoples
Were, for me, never actually the true boundaries, marking differences.
What were the *galuts* for me?
What, for me, was the *Shoah* of my mind and my faith?

The answer? The *galut* of my family,
The only thing that served as a system of reference.
Family is the only thing that I strove for,
And, given all the circumstances of my fate,
The thing I was deprived of.

Some will say that am not patriotic enough,
That I don't have what lies at the heart of
The main human values – a feeling of national community.
Possibly. Only those *some* are not the judge for me.
The judge for me today is you.

Ironically, members of our family
Have had an incredible ability to pick up
Languages quickly, so there are few who would suspect us
Of not being compatriots.
The curse of Nimrod's Tower never concerned us.

As for the rest...
I was born into hate from day one,
Into one of its most incarnate nightmares.
You were right to notice that I often confuse my birthday.
This is not from a normal course of events in my life.

I was born in a quiet Jewish town

Near Zhytomyr, then part of Soviet Russia.
It's actually Ukraine but at the time it had acquired new meanings.
This was 1922, when the Civil War
Was already coming to an end.

The First Cavalry, distinguished not only
By its outstanding military history but also by its pogroms of the Jews,
Had already been disbanded.
However, some units were still carrying out
Certain military missions or, let's say, cleansing,

As per the more commonly used term.
To the honour of the First Cavalry, the pogromists were convicted and shot,
But when the Civil War had only just come to an end in the country,
No one could assert that
Order had been established once and for all.

The fires from the crushing of the Makhnovists[157]
And the Russo-Polish war still smouldered
There were still gangs operating in the Zhytomyr environs,
Whose political convictions
The local Jews found it hard to fathom.

All they knew was that they had to survive.
After so many years of White Guard, Polish,
Red Army and Makhnovist pogroms, they needed to survive.
So, on the day I was supposed to appear on this earth,
A Red Army attachment had arrived in our little village,

In their pursuit of the latest gang.
The residents, Jews and Ukrainians, welcomed the Red Army
As you would expect, with bread and salt and with long, laden tables.
They brought out the *horilka*; what hospitality could there be without it?
They had put on a joyous spread, understanding

These authorities had come to restore order.
On every corner one could hear, "Comrade, do try these pies,"
"Take this fresh milk, pancakes and meat" or
"May the Lord help you; find those thugs – we are so fed up with them."
Commissars and Cossacks alike became tipsy and relaxed.

But then a terrifying scream broke through the beauty of the festivities.
On the square before the building of the local Soviet
A commissar with a couple of soldiers appeared,
Dragging two men in nothing but in their undergarments,
Bandaged and bloody.

"Rabbi!" the commissar screamed terribly. "Ephraim, you old bastard!
Where is the rabbi?!" Everyone froze in terror; something awful was happening.
Old Ephraim jumped up from the table, his hands shaking.
"Comrade Commissar, it's... it's not what you think!"
The commissar, without stopping, rushed at

---

[157] *Makhnovshchina* was an attempt to form a stateless anarchist society in parts of Ukraine during the Russian Revolution of 1917–1923. It existed from 1918 to 1921, during which time free soviets and libertarian communes operated under the protection of Nestor Makhno's Revolutionary Insurrectionary Army.

The old rabbi like crashing waves.
"Who is that, you fucking old Jewboy?!"
Everyone rapidly realised that these were wounded thugs.
"Comrade Commissar," the rabbi babbled, "just look at them.
They are simply dying kids. I beg of you, Comrade Commissar."

Indeed, the lads were no more than nineteen years old.
Tears and snot mixed with the blood on their faces.
Only yesterday, these "warriors" had been prancing on tall *donets* steeds,
Playing with their sabres and rattling their cartridge belts.
Today, though, they were like naughty teenagers.

Only they weren't teenagers. They were warriors, enemies;
Perhaps it had been they who had shot Petr Mironych and Antosha dead,
Whom the Red Army soldiers had just been praying for.
This was the enemy. Who would object?!
"You have just killed us, Rabbi," the blacksmith Reuben uttered in doomed resignation.

And he was right. Unsheathing his sabre,
The commissar slashed the men down,
His eyes burning with an ominous flame.
With a frightening voice he whispered to Ephraim in a lethal threat:
"You're hiding enemies of the Revolution, are you, Yid?"

Ephraim fell to his knees. "Comrade Commissar, Com...
Just look, they're wounded kids, show mer..."
An awful blow of the sabre cut his babbling.
And his life. Forever. Even the Red Army soldiers froze in horror.
Have you ever had the feeling

That something terrible has happened but that there is no way back?
A summary execution had clearly taken place before their eyes.
How were their souls supposed to react?
Adonai knows, if this power had not been so young at that point,
Perhaps they would have stopped their brother.

But it never happened.
The young sons of the Revolution had not learned
That in a choice between law and military brotherhood, you should choose the law,
Putting up the right boundaries between what is yours and what is not.
Oh, Adonai, is it really in this ability that the right decision is concealed?!

The tipsy or, let's face it, drunk Red Army soldiers,
And I don't mean the warriors from the pictures,
But people who had seen the horrors of the Civil War,
During which they had had to sear counter-revolution
From among their brothers, their kith and kin,

Flared up in righteous anger in a second.
What was the life of a Jewish traitor to them?
Collaborators, hiding their mortal enemies?
Someone overturned a table and the terror began.
The realisation that there is no turning back

Strangely leads people to a need to
Intensify their sin many times over, as if,
If you leap over the boundaries of reason,

You can jump over the boundaries of values, too,
And run from them beyond the tempest of one's own anger.

The professional hand of the warrior soon remembered
What the meaning of killing is. And of punishment.
Not from the notion of *God's punishment*, rather from the word *punisher*.
Anyway, in a matter of moments,
The small village met its Armageddon.

Like a feather, floating lightly upwards,
The customary cry for these parts rose into the bloody sky:
"Kill the Yids! Get the traitors!"
You think the Red Army was any different from the Whites?
Why argue; it was often the very same people,

Who had switched sides to the Reds.
And did war improve their spirits over the years?
Did the ideas of revolution cleanse
And transform them there and then
Into apostles of proletarian internationalism?

Let the descendants live in myth and legend;
We had not a single chance to live in them.
And later, whatever any authority ever says
To any nation about creating a new approach
To love between nations, well, that will always be a great exaggeration.

My father was not present at the festivities
For one important reason:
I was being born in one of the huts.
When he heard the shots and screams,
He ran outside and then attempted to close the gates to the house.

However, falling under the Cossacks' whips,
He fell and crawled to the stream.
And then the irredeemable happened. My mother,
Who knew first-hand about the pogroms,
Instantly cottoned on to what was happening

And tried to run from the hut and hide in the shed.
And that was moments after she had given birth to me!
With incredible effort, she wrapped me in old rags
And, grabbing warm clothes and blankets as she went,
We went out into the yard. It was there in the yard

That she was struck down by a Red Army sabre.
Not all the Red Army soldiers were overcome with this drunken
And bloody madness.
It was that that saved my life.
It was saved by an old, bearded Cossack

Who noticed that small infant
Whining and wheezing near the prostrate body of its mother.
"Herods, heathens, what are you doing?!
Stop this instant! This is not our way! This is not the revolutionary way!"
He cried quite desperately but he was unable to control the madness.

The Cossack looked back and, seeing the village in flames,
He made a decision. He picked up the bundle of rags with the body inside
And jumped up onto his horse. "I won't let you, you bastards,
I won't let you kill a small child, you animals!"
Barely had I appeared in the world,

And on the very same day and hour,
I found myself in a soldier's saddle.
That was how I was born, on the line between hatred
And human compassion.
That was how my time began.

Whom was I to love, and whom to hate?
The irresponsible but merciful rabbi,
Whose foolishness sealed the fate of the village?
The Russians running amok or the Russian
To whom I am obliged for being alive and speaking with my grandson today?

Incidentally, my father wasn't a villager.
He simply hailed from this place
And, for some reason, he had wanted for me to be born there.
What's this unnecessary symbolism for, you might ask?
He was an exemplary Zhytomyr citizen

With the highly respected profession of postman.
Either it was because of his job, or our familial features,
But he spoke Polish, German, Ukrainian,
French and, of course, Russian fluently.
After the tragic events in the village,

My father, having survived the massacre, headed to Zhytomyr in the tracks of that squadron.
Probably, his professional pedantry
Stopped him from succumbing to emotion and
Losing his only son in
That dark abyss of time and events.

He arrived in Zhytomyr and headed straight for the local revolutionary committee.
There he learned that there had, in fact, been no pogrom at all,
Rather a special mission to liquidate the thugs
Who had dug in at the village and, thanks to the connivance of the locals,
Had put up fierce resistance to the Red Army troops.

These degenerates, fleeing from the Red Army,
Had murdered a large number of the local population.
But they would receive the harshest revolutionary punishment for sure.
Where was that squadron? It was on its way to the front lines at Turkestan.
If he hurried, he might still manage to see them at the station.

And so, my father set off for the station
And, in the crowds heading both West and East,
Of troops, civilians, refugees and migrants,
He learned that there was a squadron that had yet to depart.
It was not far from the station and it could be found if he wished.

Comrade Srul' (that is how they pronounced the name Israel in Poland and Ukraine)[158]
Headed directly off in search of the squadron.
But how would he find that unknown Cossack
Who had saved his child?
He had neither name nor surname, just that he was an elderly Red Army soldier with a beard,

And nothing more than that.
So, what would my dad do? What do you think?
He went to the revolutionary committee and... signed up to join that same squadron!
"Comrade Srul'," said revolutionary committee member
Comrade Berkovich incredulously.

"So, you... You really have immersed yourself so quickly
And so much in the revolutionary ideas,
That you're prepared to shed blood for them?"
The commissar reacted unexpectedly to my father's meek nodding.
He suddenly jumped up and grabbed my father by the lapels.

"I know you, you sly hooknoses!
If you're up to something, you Polish spy,
I'll get you in Turkestan, you understand?"
Then he abruptly stepped back and straightened his tunic.
"But, Comrade Berkovich, are you not a Jew too?"

My father challenged the committee member in horror.
But Berkovich just burst out laughing merrily.
"Comrade Srul', Soviet power is international in its essence.
Soon, there will be no such notions as Greater Russian, Little Russian or Cossack.
Yes, I am basically a yid too... Anyhow, bugger off now, *Red Armyman* Srul'!"

And so, with such a proletarian blessing,
My father set off
For the Turkestan front lines.
While he was being issued his tunic and rifle,
He quickly sought out the Cossack

Who had saved his little yid. It was a Red Cossack called Semyon Mitrofanov.
You think my father rushed to him with questions?
Far from it. If his new brothers-in-arms had found out
That he had witnessed that bloody massacre in the village.
It wouldn't be a case of whether he'd make it to Turkestan, rather would he make it alive to the
next station.

However young Soviet law might have been then,
It endeavoured to deal with murderers and pogromists
Swiftly and severely.
One testimony from my father at the revolutionary committee would be sufficient.
He was later to discover

That the Red Cavalry had not left a single witness alive.
My father had been saved by that unknown stream.
Or it was fate, which had prepared many more trials to come.
You ask how a new-born like me could have survived

---

[158] The name *Srul'* is a diminutive of the name *Israel* (pronounced *Isruel* in Ashkenazi Hebrew in the Polish and, to an extent, Ukrainian variants) but, if read in Russian, it stems from the word for *to shit*. This form of address would or would not have been offensive, depending on the language spoken.

In such harsh military conditions.

The army, Koppel, is not just a crowd of soldiers.
It's a transport column, a kitchen, a medical unit. And what do these words mean?
Women, that's what.
And these were not your girls of today's Tzahal,
Who go on a visit home with automatic weapons.

These were women who had lost their homes in the flames of civil war
And who wandered after the unit
Where their husbands and sons,
Perhaps even their betrothed, were serving. So, it was the breast of women like these
That saved me from certain death.

You see, I could hardly have been called a person back then,
But the Red Armymen took care of me
Like I was a living reminder of the sin of murder.
They say that any man strives for redemption,
And perhaps that is what saved your grandpa in the end.

You know, I didn't get my name from my father,
But from the Red Armymen who had destroyed my family.
They say that they named me Solomon because
Of my round cheeks and quiet demeanour. Why?
My father never managed to tell me that.

Note that my name is not Russian, not Orthodox
And not neo-proletarian, but Jewish. So, there you have it...
They said that I'd grow up and would live in a new Kingdom,
Where there was no war; they were fighting for me for now,
And I would go on to build a new society

Where there would be no Hellene and no Jew,
Where everyone would be equal and the main feeling between people
Would be not simply love, but love on a high, civilian level.
Where there would be no bourgeoisie with their mercenary interests,
No cruel rulers, and where everyone would be as one.

Later, this unified people
Would unite the entire world and never, ever, ever,
Would a small boy from a village near Zhytomyr
Cry to the roar of gunfire.
Nor any other boy or girl, too.

That's how strange those Red Army types were,
Who killed and meted out punishment, yet who believed in a bright future,
For which they would sacrifice themselves, their life and soul.
However, all of this was supposed to take place only in the future,
While on that day, they didn't deny themselves

The chance to have their fun with my Jewish father,
Calling him either *Sral'* or *Zasrul'*,[159]
Or basically even *the shitty red jew.*
Apparently, there was nothing more for them to do
On that long journey to Turkestan.

---

[159] Other offensive names that are Russian forms of diminutives stemming from the word for *to shit.*

My father, however, was not a simple man.
He allowed them to have their fun at his expense while on the train.
When the train stopped at the border with the Great Steppe
And the unit began to unload,
He was able to show them what a Zhytomyr postman was capable of.

There were many Kyrgyz crowding the station
(that's what the Kazakhs were called back then).
The Red Armymen, for the most part Cossacks,
Were gathered round
A harnessed horse of singular beauty,

The likes of which had rarely been seen before.
The Cossacks and Turkmens were laughing and arguing about something.
One Cossack jumped up onto the Akhal-Teke,
But the steed bucked so sharply
That the son of that congenital tribe of horsemen simply couldn't hold on.

To the laughter of his comrades, he flew from the saddle,
Losing his sheepskin hat. The Turkmen tutted condescendingly.
At that moment, my father, amid the noise and the bustle,
Adeptly flew up into the saddle and, spurring on the black demon,
Galloped out into the steppe, to the crowd's hoots and cries of admiration.

There is no secret here.
It was just that postmen often had to deliver
Urgent mail, in any weather and at all times of day and night...
From that point on, his colleagues had great respect for Red Armyman Srul'.
They replaced his nickname with the respectable Arevich,

From my father's surname, Ben Aryeh.
Koppel, I'll tell you a separate tale about that surname,
But for now we'll continue following the fate of Israel Arevich
In that remote, unknown region of Turkestan.
Well, and my fate, too, as it happens.

The squadron commanders immediately noticed my father's riding talents.
When Squadron Commander Zabolotsky learned that Israel
Had been a postman, assigned him there and then as *aide de camp*.
You see, Koppel, it is really important to have knowledge and a profession.
The position of *aide de camp* or more precisely, an orderly in the Red Army,

Held one very serious advantage.
Residing in the command carriage, you were not so limited by discipline,
Like the other fighters, so
At each stop on the way, my father was able
To run to the medical carriage and see me.

Imagine the jealousy he must have felt
When Mitrofanov came to the medics!
He fussed about, scolded the girls and the women,
Washed and, if he could, even fed little Solomon,
That was me, while my father had to

Observe all of this in silence.
One day, he took me in his arms; I squealed and reached out to him.

312

Just look how a nation senses its own, the women snivelled.
Semyon Timofeich enviously took me away from my father.
'Come, come, little Cossack, don't you go to that dirty man,'

The Cossack grunted at my father in reproach.
If only he knew what was going on in Israel Arevich's heart!
It is hard for us to understand today
How he could have travelled silently in the same carriage
With the murderers of his people and his family.

This is not something we could understand or will ever know,
But we can say for sure what made him act in that way.
War. A war that isn't waged on the front line alone.
A war that cuts through the fates of city dwellers and villagers,
A war that is like a way of life and a way of thinking.

The train carried the cavalry regiment and my father's squadron
Deep into the steppes of Kazakhstan, somewhere to the south.
The Red Armymen grew despondent when they saw the flat and yellow steppe.
For some reason, however, Israel Arevich rather liked the landscape.
He told me why.

This reddish desert and light, hilly terrain,
Dissected in places by the beds of now dry rivers,
So reminded him of something he had never seen before,
But which reveals to every Jew his blood:
The deserts if his native Canaanite land.

It might be a hundred times smaller than this endless plain,
But it often seems that it is here that the
Great prophets, fleeing, aspiring for and seeking the tribes of Israel crossed paths.
As if in confirmation of my father's dreams,
Camels appeared in the hot haze of this bleak place.

It became noticeably easier for the orderly with the *Jewish question* too,
For most of the commanders were fellow tribesmen
And the commissars – well, almost all of them.
That said, it was not the done thing to
Speak about their nationality –

All these people saw themselves as part of the new nation.
That said, my observant father did notice
That the Cossacks and Russians didn't really understand what it was about;
What, they were suddenly to become someone different?
However, all national indicators were confidently replaced with terms such as

Comrade, Red Armyman, fighter of the Revolutionary Army and the like.
It has to be said that, in their persuasiveness and insistence, the commissars
Were superior in many ways to the rabbi preachers.
They were so convincing, in fact,
That my father arrived in Turkestan a confirmed soldier of the Red Army.

At one of the stations, the unit was dressed in a new uniform
Of the Turkestan front; the regiment was supplied with additional weapons.
The equipment and uniform spoke most convincingly that
The new army and, hence, the new authority
Was now established and was standing firmly in place,

313

Not only in a military sense,
But in the sense of the revolutionary
International conviction as well,
Under whose charms not only the Russians and Jews had fallen,
But also the residents of the distant and now close-at-hand Turkestan.

Upon arrival at Perovskoe, the regiment was met by none other
Than Commander of the Turkestan Front himself, Vasily Ivanovich Shorin.
From staff conversations, my father understood
That, when they reached their final destination,
The regiment would have to fight the Basmachi Army

Led by a certain Enver Pasha,
Of whom even the Red Army commanders spoke
With evident respect.
This could mean only one thing:
A serious struggle lay ahead, with a powerful opponent.

From that point, the regiment needed to advance south by itself,
Toward the lands of the Tajiks and the Uzbeks.
However, leaving the Kazakh lands,
The regiment had to complete one further mission,
Which initially appeared rather odd

Given their new, impeccable equipment and rearmaments.
To the regiment commander's question as to how things were doing with provisions,
The staff representative at the front sniggered oddly
And, nervously retorting, "Comrade Zinoviev will explain everything
And show you," he turned away.

Commissar Zinoviev ordered the detachment of two
Dozen fighters for an expedition, which included Israel.
The commanders assumed that the detachment should
Advance on horseback to some remote warehouses
Or the army provisions depot.

But things turned out very differently.

That evening, my father approached the nurses and cooks once more,
To torture himself with the view of his son,
Or to be more accurate, the son of the regiment,
Being caressed, fed and entertained by a bearded and attentive Cossack
And alien women.

The very next morning, he went, Mitrofanov too,
With the detachment of twenty-five cavalrymen,
Taking three carts with them,
Having first removed the machine guns,
And set off into the depths of the still-sleeping Kazakh steppes.

"Here we'll top up our reserves of provisions
And here we'll get some more horses,"
The experienced Zinoviev chattered to our squadron commander,
Pointing to somewhere on the map.
It was incredible how he found his way

In these plains and occasional
Grey hills.
Zinoviev babbled without stopping for the entire
Journey, about the stupid heat, the wayward morals of the Kyrgyz,
About how he hailed from Ukraine,

Like the majority of the detachment's fighters,
That he should soon be transferred back west.
My father didn't listen to him,
For he was deep in bitter recollections of the past.
Zinoviev came to an abrupt halt by a chain of hills.

"Right, men, everyone listen up.
We are now going to act according to a decree
Of the Turkestan Central Executive Committee
And the order of the frontline command
Regarding the supply of provisions to the Red Army.

On the other side of this hill is the aul
Of Basmachi's Daulembai, who hasn't been finished off.
He's not even a merchant *kulak*, a *bai* in their terms.
But a serious counter-revolutionary element
Who is treacherously sabotaging the policy of military Communism.

So, comrades, his property needs to be confiscated
In favour of the revolutionaries
As represented here by the gallant Red Army. Any questions?"
He spoke as if he were relating leisure plans at a holiday resort.
Israel saw the Cossacks frown.

"Is it not the people's militia
Who do this?" Squadron Commander Zabolotsky raised his eyebrows.
Zinoviev laughed as if the cossack had told a witty joke.
"My dear man, what people's militia? What people?
These are the Kyrgyz-Kaisaks! Every other one of them is a thug.

Basmach! By day they crowd round the Council yurt,
While at night they cut the Red Armymen's throats.
And that Daulembai is just getting fatter
While his fellow tribespeople are starving to death.
Do you know what famine is like in the Steppe?!

But this famine mustn't stop us
From doing away with this Basmachi snake once and for all.
And, you know, Comrade Tobolin[160] once said,
This tribe would not survive in the struggle for Communist ideals,
Because it would not find a way out of its feudal past.

Right! That's enough! You soldiers are not here to
Discuss orders from the decision-makers!
Or do you need explaining another way?"
Zinoviev took out his polished *Mauser*
And began shaking about above his head.

"Put your *Mauser* away, Commissar!"

---

[160] Ivan Osipovich Tobolin, Chairman of the Tashkent Council of Workers' and Soldiers' Deputies.

Zabolotsky hissed, politely but menacingly.
"Say, you know... how you do things around here.
Prepare for battle! Two-line formation and face the front!"
The Red Army soldiers silently assembled

And set off in the direction of the top of the hill.
What I am telling you, Koppel,
Is how the old Israel told me of the horrors of that early morning.
Home for the Kazakhs is a felt yurt.
My father saw how, before his very eyes, these yurts crumbled

Along the stream, hidden behind the line of the hills.
The hearths smoked peacefully and it smelled of something tasty and new
But, strange as it may sound, it did not seem alien.
The detachment quietly approached the aul.
Suddenly, an awful, terror-filled female scream broke the silence:

"Oybu-u-uy! Kyzyl asker! Kampeske-e-e-e-e!"[161]
The aul instantly came to life.
Half-dressed children and women emerged;
Men rushed out, belting themselves up as they came.
Zinoviev kept his *Mauser* raised.

The detachment slowly came out onto the square before a large yurt
Which was evidently the central dwelling;
A dirty red flag hung above it.
An elderly Kazakh leaped out of the yurt,
Donning his gown as he came and, for some reason, clutching

A sheet of paper.
"Gracious me, so much livestock!"
Israel heard a quiet exclamation from Red Armyman Vyatkin behind him.
"Shut it, you idiot," Mitrofanov interrupted him.
"Apart from beasts, these breeders here have nothing."

At Zabolotsky's signal, the Red Army soldiers
Dispersed across the valley in businesslike fashion,
Having cordoned off the seething aul.
"Ba-a-a! Salamatsyzba[162], Sarybai-myrza!"
Zinoviev shouted to the old man in a half-mocking tone.

"Aron, and what *myrza*[163] am I to you?"
The old man replied in Russian, unexpectedly almost without an accent.
The morning sun was looking out from behind the hill
And it began to bake a little.
"So, what should I call you, then? Comrade?"

The commissar chuckled in satisfaction.
"Still serving Daulembai are you, *aqsaqal*?"
"What gives you that idea?"
"So who gave him two carpets that third day, then?"
"You see, he had a party to mark His daughter's wedding.

---

[161] *Kampeske*, during the time of the surplus appropriation system, is what the Kazakhs called the confiscations which were essentially pogroms, dooming the people to certain starvation. *Kyzyl asker* is the Kazakh for *Red Army*.
[162] *Salamatsyzba* is a Kazakh greeting, literally meaning *How's your health?*
[163] *Myrza* is a Kazakh form of address, literally *Sir*.

And if you class them as carpets,
(the old man nodded at his rough felt mats,
Decorated with a large, lurid pattern)
Take any one you like."
Zinoviev opened his folder and retrieved a piece of paper.

"You've been in town? You've read this order?"
"Comrade Zinoviev, under the requisitioning, our aul
Has already handed over livestock three times, and our horses too.
Look around and see what we have left;
Have you no pity for our starving children?"

"Don't you go looking for pity from me, you peasant!"
He turned to the Red Armymen:
"Well then, you three, what's cooking? Verstiuk!
Get over to that hill over there and drive back here
Everything you see. Now!"

The Cossacks whooped and ran off over the hill.
"You calling me a peasant?" the angry Kazakh began.
"Aron, don't forget I have two sons serving in the Red Cavalry."
"Yes. That's right. Two of them. And where's the third?!" Zinoviev screamed.
"Where's Kazangaziy?! You're not saying, you sonofabitch?!"

He shoved his *Mauser* under the old man's nose.
"You say nothing because you know, you scum!
He buggered off to Junaid Khan in Khiva!
The traitor wounded the commissar at Perovsk[164]
And deserted! With his rifle!"

"Aron, that is not true, you know it. No one saw..."
At that moment the Cossacks appeared from over the hill,
Driving a small flock of sheep,
A few skinny horses and two cows.
"Here we are!" Zinoviev looked pleased.

"Huh! Skinny, aren't they?!" one of the Cossacks whistled.
Zabolotsky glared at him and he shut up.
"Well, what do you say, Sarybai, where d'you get this from?
These aren't on our list."
For effect, he tapped the paper with his *Mauser*.

"That is Daulembai's livestock, Aron,"
The old man said with a frown, as if cornered.
I went to see him at the feast with a request.
The children here are bloating out from hunger.
What the hell does he need my felt blankets for? It was out of courtesy...

He didn't refuse us. You know how many people I have here.
And what's this? If the drought doesn't end, they'll drop dead as well.
That's to feed the entire aul for the summer.
I don't know what we'll do after that..."
"What are you jabbering on about, Sarybai?

---

[164] Now Kyzyl-Orda.

The Soviet Government has given you your freedom,
But you are herding Daulembai's livestock, like a farmhand.
This is what it means. Since it's not yours but the *bai's*,
It is subject to confiscation,
As an object of the exploitation of the working people."

Zinoviev gestured the Red Armymen toward the livestock.
"Take it away!" "Stop, Aron!"
The old man croaked and grabbed the reins of the commissar's horse.
The Cossacks stood stock still.
"Take me if you want. Do what you want with me,

But don't take the livestock... I only herded it here yesterday.
They look more like death.
The children have only had milk the once...
And what can you milk from skinny cattle?
Aron, what will I tell Daulembai?"

"Here's what! Your Daulembai has shoved his cattle about
Around his relatives like you on purpose," and Aron prodded him with his *Mauser*.
"And he pretends to you that he's all kind,
While to us he pretends he loyal to the Soviets.
We know these charlatans well!

Lads, take it away as per the list!"
In desperation, the Kazakh babbled a plea in Kazakh,
Addressing the Red Army soldier Badmaev.
"I'm not a Kazakh, but a Kalmyk," Badmaev replied sullenly,
Lowering his eyes and shuffling away.

The old man turned limp and fell to the ground.
Zabolotsky nodded to Israel to count and record the heads of cattle.
Suddenly, the women began to weep and wail.
It was awful to look at them.
They were not looking at the soldiers, but were looking to the skies for their God.

The Red Army soldiers drove the livestock in businesslike fashion to Israel.
Someone found a branding iron with the regiment number
And began heating it on the nearest fire.
Israel heard the soldiers' quiet conversations.
"Just look, that's plenty of livestock.

Lads from the Russian provinces told us
They should leave them one cow, like at our village,
Or that gelding over there. They'll get by.
Our peasants back home don't have that much."
"Oh, shut up, would you?!" Verstiuk shouted at them.

"Comrade Commander," he addressed Zabolotsky quietly.
"You know, they'll all die, those Kyrgyz.
At the stations they said they were dying in droves.
They are our Kalmyks, see.
They live just like cattle.

Don't we Cossacks know that?"
"Hey, quiet over there!" Zinoviev said, as if he'd overheard.
Zabolotsky turned to the steppe with a wave of the hand.

Zinoviev busily dismounted and, whistling, went from yurt to yurt,
Lazily lifting the flaps of felt.

Suddenly, someone cried out, "Look, he's running, look!"
A lad had jumped from one of the yurts
And, jumping onto a horse, had galloped out into the steppe.
"But that's... that's Kazangaziy the deserter!" Aron screamed.
"Grab him! What are you standing there for? After him!"

Three soldiers rushed off in pursuit.
The Kazakh would have escaped, but Badmaev, with a clever
Toss of his lasso, caught him and pulled him to the ground.
"Gotcha!" said Zinoviev with boyish glee.
"Come on, bring that snake over here."

Right then, a shot went out.
Everyone looked about them and saw
An old woman in tall headdress on the threshold of Sarybai's yurt.
She had evidently shot up into the air
And now she was slowly approaching the commissar,

Angrily shouting something in Kazakh and threatening him with her rifle.
Zinoviev lifted his *Mauser*.
"It's not loaded! Commissar! It... it has no cartridges left in it!
Don't shoot!" Zabolotsky cried.
But then the unthinkable happened.

The old woman had so furiously set upon Zinoviev
That he shot her right in the chest in his fright.
She flew back like a doll, dropping her rifle.
It wasn't clear from where old Sarybai got the energy,
But he jumped up like an agile argali and rushed to his yurt.

An instant later and he was back,
With sabre in hand and, running up to Aron,
Chopped off his ear with a single blow.
Everyone gasped from the unexpected nature of it all, but the events
Had already begun to spin in a totally different way.

"Fricking hell," I heard Verstiuk by my side.
Now we'll have to raze them all down, like in Chervonytsy"
Israel shuddered when he heard the name of his village.
At that same second, another shot rang out.
The bullet flew between Verstiuk and him.

The shot had come from the yurt opposite us.
The experienced Verstiuk quickly took his gun and fired back in response.
Someone threw up their hands and fell.
The Cossack rushed over and, in an adroit turn,
He picked the person's rifle up from the ground.

"Prepare for battle!" Zabolotsky's baritone boomed.
Zinoviev, having fired three shots at Sarybai,
Wailed and fell to his side.
An ominous noise rose up. Shots rang out.
Men starting running out of the yurts,

Wielding long sticks like clubs.
Whooping wildly, they rushed at the Red Army soldiers.
Israel took to his horse and, unsheathing his sabre,
Swept between the felt tents,
Looking out for armed Kazakhs or, perhaps, fleeing from them.

A lanky type jumped out at him from behind a fence,
A dagger in his hand,
But when he saw Israel, he threw his knife to the ground in fear
And ran out into the steppe.
My father rushed after him.

Catching up, he raised his sabre and brought it down on the lad's back.
"Let me through, you fricking postman," came Verstiuk's voice from behind.
Stretching out, the Cossack slashed the lad to the ground.
There was a crash and the young man groaned his last.
The Kazakh slumped to the ground like a sack.

Verstiuk looked back mischievously and winked at Israel
As if to say, *you see how it's done?*
About twenty minutes later and the resistance was crushed.
The aul's residents dispersed into the steppe, the hills and undergrowth.
The Red Armymen chased after the men, caught then and chopped them down.

"That's it! Stop now!" Zinoviev screamed hysterically.
"Let's get out of here like the hounds of hell!"
Zabolotsky looked incredulously at the commissar and,
Pointing his sabre out into the steppe, asked, "And them?
They'll report us and a court martial is inevitable!"

"Who are those sheep going to report to?" Aron hissed maliciously,
Pulling out a scrap of fabric and pressing it to his wound.
"They'll go to ground like marmots and be dead in three days.
Take everything you can find!
Grain, cereals – take the lot and get back here!"

The aul's residents had indeed fled without a backwards glance,
The children had disappeared into holes like steppe creatures.
The Red Army soldiers gutted all the yurts
And then set a couple alight as a warning.
They knocked another two to the ground with lassos.

Israel watched all this in a stupor.
Later, he would tell me his feelings and thoughts:
"I am Israel Ben Aryeh, a Jew, and I have become a pogromist and murderer!"
In an instant, the Red Army soldiers changed;
Just half an hour before, they were prepared not to fulfil the order

And spare these poor Kyrgyz!
Prepared to leave them their skinny livestock and challenge their commander,
But not to have their death on their conscience!
But all that was needed was one shot and there was the line,
Across which there is just an enemy, just a war.

And war requires precision and professionalism
In suppressing resistance and destroying the enemy.
It all came down in an instant to simple formulae,

And the notion of *civilian* was relegated to the background.
Everyone had become a participant in the battle

And this *enemy* had suffered a deserved defeat.

Israel couldn't bring himself to look
At Mitrofanov dragging a
White goat kid, saying,
"And here's the milk for little Solomon!
That little Cossack will be happy!"

That was his son, Israel's son they were talking about!
But the realisation that his son would be drinking milk
Taken from these poor, dirty natives,
From their children, black from fear and clothed in rags,
Made my father sick from the horror of it all.

Well, and he wasn't the only one as dark as storm clouds.
However unfeeling a soldier's heart might become,
After many years engaged
In just the one thing, day in, day out:
Murder, war,

Plunder and violence over civilians,
Even if they had been
A counter-revolutionary hotbed of resistance to Soviet authority,
It still felt like a low thing to have done.
This was something to keep well away from,

Zinoviev's wound meant a report was unavoidable.
Orderly Arevich got to read it:
The requisitioning had been completed,
The armed counter-revolutionary *Basmachi* element
Had been destroyed, including one deserter (that old *Basmachi* woman!).

The civilian population had come to no harm.
A regular, concise report from war time,
Without emotion or detail,
Which conveyed that, despite the difficulties,
The Red Army was successfully fulfilling its combat missions.

Meanwhile, my father's regiment continued its march south,
Away from the Orenburg-Tashkent railway,
Crossing the Hungry Steppe
(Which was what they called it back then).
The local guides said it would soon come to an end

And with it, all its horrors.
Red Army soldier Arevich would have to attend
Many more requisitions.
As a rule, they met with no resistance.
The Kazakhs would often even drive their skinny livestock themselves,

Just to avoid encountering those *angels of military Communism*,
Like that highly experienced Aron Zinoviev.
Only once did Zabolotsky's Red Army soldiers
Get caught in a real shootout

With *counter-revolutionaries*.

This was at just another aul amid the red hills, like any other,
Approaching which the military requisitioning detachment
Had been met with weapon fire
From rifles and antiquated flintlock guns
(Known as *multuk* among the Kazakhs).

However, this shooting was erratic at best
And no one got hurt.
The Red Cavalry soldiers had by this time gained experience
And they left one machine gun on one of the carts.
This machine gun was used to suppress the aul gunfire.

When the fighters entered the village,
They realised that only one family had been shooting –
A grandfather, father and three young lads,
While the yurts contained nothing but dead bodies.
The women, children and the elderly had all starved to death.

The Basmachi had been firing so erratically
Because they were so exhausted from their hunger.
It transpired that they were merely protecting the graves of their *familia*.
And that was it.
No bread, no livestock, just the bones of a chewed dog in the fire...

Up ahead, the regiment faced the blossoming Fergana Valley
Where the farmers managed better with
The drought and the *dzhut* famine.
However, before reaching this Asian paradise,
The Red Army soldiers endured another night of terror in the Hungry Steppe.

Once, during a night bivouac,
Badmaev was on watch
When he heard screams ringing out in the black of the moonless night.
He raised the alarm and the soldiers, with torches and weapons,
Sped out into the night.

Israel found himself out in front
And when he reached the scene,
A terrible picture appeared before him.
There in the middle of the steppe, pressed close to one another,
Were two dozen Kazakh women and children,

More like wizened mummies
Than human beings.
They stood in a pyramid, pressed tightly together,
And, hiding the children in the middle,
Were fighting off a pack of wolves,

Among whom there were two enormous
Feral wolfhounds.
The animals howled and wailed, grabbing the women by the arms and legs,
In their attempt to pull someone from dense formation
And devour them.

The women had been fighting back, silently and powerless and, when

322

The soldiers had driven the wolves away with rifle shots, they stretched their arms to them,
Shouting and muttering words of gratitude,
Only to fall to earth dead.
The soldiers dragged only two teenagers and

Three infants alive from that pyramid.
The children were covered in scabs and lice.
The soldiers picked them up
And carried them to the women at the medical unit.
Israel had heard a noise some five metres from that place.

He and Badmaev approached and saw
A withered man lying on the ground,
Grappling with a lifeless wolf.
He had gnawed open the beast's throat and was drinking the gushing blood.
Seeing the Red Army soldiers, he fixed mad eyes on my father

And croaked, a bloody finger pointing: "Azrael! Azrael!"
Followed by several words in Kazakh; after that he breathed his last.
In horror, my father asked Badmaev,
"What did he say? What did he say?! How does he know my name?!"

Badmaev replied that it wasn't *Israel*, but *Azrael*,
The Muslim angel of death.
What he had said was something like,
"Azrael! Angel of death! When you see Allah,
By whose side my ancestors will be standing,

Don't tell him that you saw *how* I died.'"

Grandfather Solomon fell silent and stopped,
Poking the sand on the Kinnereth shore with a twig.
'You know, Koppel, everything happens for a reason, right?
Israel was no over-excited city girl.
Quite the opposite; the Jewish commissars, from the outbreak of the Civil War,

Encouraged him to join the Red Army because
He was clever, young and strong, and everything about him
Spoke of a warrior with an ancient genetic heritage,
Despite the fact that only very few Jews in Tsarist Russia
Could ever enjoy a military career.

However, he actually always avoided taking this path,
Because he knew from his father
That nothing good would ever come of it.
He knew of the family curse.
Koppel, I won't digress from the story,

But I want you to know that our kind is cursed.
We are destined, from age to age, to repeat the same things...
But wait – listen to the story to the end first...
No, *all* the stories to the end, to understand
Why I don't want you to choose the military path.

The sun is soon setting, grandson, so I won't
Go into great detail about how my father's regiment fought in Turkestan.
You'll read about that for yourself in your great-grandfather's diaries.

323

That's right – the same notebook that is full of
Arabic writing.

You'll learn Arabic, won't you, James?
Learn it without fail. That said, those writings are not exactly Arabic.
They are *totenshe* – Turkic but written in Arabic script.
Israel studied the Turkestan dialects
And he was helped in that by our family's talent for languages;

Truly, either a gift or a curse of the Tower of Babylon.
On the eve of the decisive conflict with the forces of Enver Pasha,
A battle took place that was to have special significance.
Koppel, I am talking about significance for my father,
For our *familia*, not for the historians.

Essentially, it was not even the battle, but one insignificant military event.

When the Red Army took Dushanbe,
The army of Enver Pasha retreated for the most part
In total disarray.
The Reds pursued them only sporadically,
But during one such pursuit,

Zabolotsky's squadron was caught in an ambush
Organised by the retreating
Troops of Davlatmand-*Biy*, a Basmachi leader.
A dozen Cossacks stood their ground to the last,
But the squadron commander, Verstiuk and Badmaev perished.

Vyatkin and Mitrofanov also fell,
But my father and three Red Army soldiers managed to escape,
Although they lost their horses and their uniforms,
As they had needed to cross a raging mountain river.
This is an important detail, because they later came into the hands

Of the 16th regiment of the 8th Bashkirian Cavalry Brigade.
The Bashkirs had repelled the Basmachi of Davlatmand-*Biy* from the Red Army men.
My father and his fellow soldiers were enlisted in the 3rd Squadron of this brigade.
So, the important detail is that my father was dressed
In the regiment's uniform – a Circassian coat with *gazyrs*, a *papakha* sheepskin hat and a *bashlyk*
hood.

Therefore, during the decisive conflict
With the forces of Enver Pasha at Baljuvon near the village of Chagan,
Israel had the appearance of a Bashkir cavalryman.
The fate of this battle had already been decided.
The Red Army succeeded in cutting Enver Pasha's central staff

From his main forces, who had been delayed
When celebrating the holy Muslim festival of
Eid al-Qurban[165]. The general's staff hastily retreated,
And the Bashkirian squadron rushed
In pursuit of the Basmachi.

I've told you that Israel was an excellent horseman,

---

[165] *Eid al-Qurban, Qurban Bayram, Qurban Ait* – the principal Muslim feast of sacrifice.

So, in one moment, there proved to be
Only two riders rushing across the yellow Tajik mountains.
My father caught up with the Muslim leader,
Who, seeing that this Red Army soldier had broken away,

Boldly turned his black horse
And raised his sabre in readiness for battle.
The Red Army Bashkirs had been left
Far behind while, up ahead, the riders
Of Davlatmand-*Biy* were looming.

My father flew like the wind at the legendary general,
Who repelled the first strike and laughed.
He turned and then himself attacked,
But... raising his sabre, he froze.
At that moment, too, Israel managed to see his enemy.

They were... the spitting image of one another,
Like twins, like the children of the same mother!
Perhaps the poise of Enver Pasha was a little more noble and proud,
But in all else, the nose, moustache, brows and eagle eyes,
They were like two drops of morning Kulob dew.

The Circassian coat and *papakha* hat had merely intensified the similarity.
"Who are you?!" the general exclaimed in surprise.
Israel himself had been taken aback.
Their horses snorted and twirled in a furious rage,
As if they and not their masters were locked in mortal combat.

Bullets whistled over the warriors' heads,
From both the Basmachi and the Red Army.
At that moment, my father remembered why fate had cast him here
To this unfamiliar region of Turkestan.
Because of his son, whom he had to find. Find and raise.

How much more killing, grief, war and hunger
Would there be between him and his son?
"I am Azrael!" my father cried darkly and slashed back with his sabre.
He removed Pasha's head and part of a shoulder
And the legendary hero of legend, inspiration and regret

Fell to the ancient Tajik earth
Like Sohrab, defeated by Rostam,
Like Takeda Shingen, after losing his most important battle.
At that moment, two bullets flying from different directions
Knocked Israel from his saddle.

He lost consciousness and fell to the ground,
Landing face to face
With the head of Enver Pasha,
Whose eyes had frozen in an eternal look of astonishment,
As if giving him the chance

Once more to get a good look and remember
Whom he had only just killed.
Killed, hesitating only for a second
But nevertheless doubtless in his conviction that he was right.

A horseman jumped out from the side

And, calling the name of the general, dismounted.
He surveyed the field of single combat for a second
And then decisively grasped Israel by the belt,
Cast him across the saddle of his steed
And galloped off towards his own men...

That had been Davlatmand-*Biy* himself who had rushed to save
His brother in arms and had confused him with my father.
During this frantic galloping
Israel had come round for a moment just once
And he had attempted to reach for the Basmachi's *Mauser*,

But at that instance a shot struck Davlatmand-*Biy*
In the back and Israel lost consciousness once more.
He came round several days later
In a house, fitted out as a hospital.
When he came to, he felt overcome with horror.

Unknown people were walking about,
Saying something in strange tongues
And, by all accounts, taking him
As the Enver Pasha he himself had killed.
"This is the end," Israel thought,

"As soon as they discover that I am not him.
They will realise straight away that I am his killer."
My father had no doubt that this would soon be revealed.
He didn't speak their dialect,
And they would soon detect that he was coming round.

Israel had begun to say goodbye to me.
To whom else? Everyone else had died
While an orphan's lot was what awaited me,
Having lost, in the depths of Civil War and
Thousands of kilometres from home, his precious *familia*.

However, fate kept an eye on this Jew Israel Ben Aryeh.
The next morning, a man appeared by his bedside,
Dressed in secular clothes with a fez on his head.
For some reason, he spoke to my father in French and German,
As if he found it more customary to converse that way.

My father muttered something indistinct in reply
And, to the great joy of the Basmachi, he returned to the world.
The man in the fez now never left his side.
The fact that Israel didn't react to most of the Turkic
And Tajik phrases was attributed to his serious injuries.

Two days later, the man in the fez
Spoke to him excitedly and heatedly.
"Enver," he said, "I understand that you are very weak,
But the army is demoralised.
I have a request to make and I ask for just a few minutes.

We will dress you in military uniform.

Stand for a few moments on your threshold.
Let the Mujahideen see that you are alive;
They will take inspiration from that,
For you know, Enver, that rumours are circulating...

Please, just a few minutes!"
What was left for Israel to do? Just nod
And then think of a plan for how to save himself.
The next morning they brought in Enver Pasha's
Parade uniform, with all its medals and regalia.

Several men dressed my father and led him to the mirror.
Whom did he see there? An imprisoned, mixed-up Red Army man?
No. He saw an unfamiliar man,
Worn out by war but burning with an inner flame
Of desire to fight for something very important in life.

And Enver Pasha looked back at him from the other side
And appeared to smirk and say, *Well then Azrael?*
Who actually defeated whom in that battle?
My father was led by the arm to the awning before the house.
What he saw took him totally by surprise.

It was not simply a crowd of thugs;
In a neat formation in front of the house,
To the sound of drums and *karnais*,
Marched the troops of the Turkestan Army,
Saluting him, this imposter.

This was a triumph of war,
A triumph of the beauty of doom,
For orderly Arevich knew
For certain that these magnificent regiments
Would the following day be crushed by the Red Army,

Who had already set their trap.
He saw these smiling faces, young and old –
Uzbeks, Tajiks, Kyrgyz, Kazakhs
And other tribes of Turkestan,
All destined to meet their death

But inspired today
By the false image of their legendary general.
Adonai, what else does a warrior need to die with dignity?!
And stand before Allah or Christ,
With a green crescent or a two-headed eagle on their hatband,

Or even with a red star on their sleeve?
Nothing. Only a clear awareness that he is right.
Awareness of the justice of war and its illumination by a higher ideal.
An understanding that the *us* are us
And the *them* are them and that they need simply to be killed.

Or to die oneself and see the Lors with a pure heart,
Saying to him: this is me. A warrior. Here is my simple truth.
On the night after the parade, my father, subduing the pain,

Climbed up onto the karabair[166], tethered by the house,
And galloped into the darkness, towards Red Turkestan,

Standing on the threshold of the creation of a new world.

People say that the disappearance of the false Enver
Gave rise to a host of legends.
As if the great Turkic general had never died at all and still
Gallops about somewhere on his black karabair,
Calling the Turks and Sarts to a holy war...

However, back then, my father had no time for legends.
He broke through into the Red units,
Where the commanders hastened
To declare him a hero,
Because he was living proof

Of the death of the Basmachi general.
And so, through an irony of fate,
Israel found himself both the inspiration for legend
And its destroyer.
Is it not this, Koppel, that tells us that war

Is so insignificant, stupid and absurd?
Of course, the Red Army soldiers and the Muslims
Fought for their ideals back then.
A flame burned in each of their eyes, speaking of a just fight, but...
But we are not talking about them today,

Rather about our family and its fate.

My father found me in Tashkent,
A year later, for he had to continue
Paying his dues to the war.
In that time, I had quietly been growing up
In the family of a Russian commissar,

Who knew that I was a talisman of sorts
For the squadron that had perished in Kulob.
Somehow, my father managed to persuade the authorities
That I was his son, and he came for me.
My new *familia* said their farewells, tears in their eyes,

And, for some reason, we knew that the Russian page in our
Family history would not end there.
We returned to Ukraine, to Zhytomyr,
And it is here, Koppel, that I end my tale of my father
Israel Ben Arych.

You see, it's night already, but tomorrow
We will come again to the shores of the Kinnereth
So that you may hear the story of my own fate.
Grandson, have you recognised some of the things
You've dreamed about?

---

[166] An elite breed of Central Asian horse. A mix of an Akhal-Teke and a Kyrgyz horse.

Now you understand why I was so charitable
To what the psychoanalysts say.
In addition to the physiological, empirical or gene-based mentality,
There is evidently something that comes to us
From other worlds, protecting the memory of the past

No less than genes or the pages of books.
Today I'll tell you something else as well –
I dreamed those same dreams.
I saw not only Turkestan and Zhytomyr,
But the history of other tribes and their war heroes too...

Look, Koppel, the first star is rising!'

THE WAR, PEACE AND LOVE OF SOLOMON BEN ISRAEL

The next day, my grandfather and I didn't go to the shore,
But to the ruins of ancient Capernaum.
There was no specific objective in doing this;
We just wanted to talk about
Our *familia's* history there.

'Koppel, you now know the history of our family's
March East. Now listen to the western stage.
It is connected with me, your grandfather.
Arriving in Zhytomyr, Israel decided not to remain in Soviet Russia.
Either because Ukraine was seeing the start of a new,

Terrible famine,
Or because, having seen the Babylonian cauldron of Turkestan,
He had no belief in the new Soviet people.
Perhaps it was that simple Jewish mind
That forced him to flee, first to Bessarabia, to distant relatives

And, from there, through Romania and Poland,
To prosperous Czechoslovakia.
At that time he couldn't have suspected that
Another steely ideology was coming his way,
Which his son would have to face.

I have to say, in defence of Israel the soldier,
That he was simply trying to provide for me,
While he actually changed his mind and resolved to return to Russia.
But the political situation
Was changing rapidly at that time,

The borders had been slammed shut and Israel Ben Aryeh
Died somewhere on his way back
To the Red Kingdom of proletarian internationalism.
It is not known if he died a Jew, a deserter, a soldier
Or simply as a border trespasser,

But from that moment on, I heard no news of him at all.
As for me, I grew up happily with my relatives
Until my fate forced an encounter with
War and that sophisticated deceit

With which it cuts short human destinies.

As a Jew, Koppel, and having heard the story of my childhood,
You should have known that, in my life,
I was deprived of one of our main rituals:
I was never circumcised.
I often think that, perhaps because of that,

I was not exposed to the full "delights" of what it is to be a Jew
And was not protected from what was later to happen.
However, in Czechoslovakia, this proved to be a guarantee of my survival.
You see, Koppel, my appearance means
It is hard to define who I am.

This Israel was black-haired with dark, burning eyes,
Making him look the spitting image of Enver Pasha.
Evidently, I was like my mother's side of the family.
My hair was red and I was grey-eyed, too,
Only back then I was not tall; my childhood in famine-hit Turkestan saw to that.

All of this meant my fate could take me like a whirlpool,
Carrying me on its waves to meet the unknown.
I had already turned sixteen,
But I was short and puny, so
I didn't look my age.

As you know from history, in 1939,
Czechoslovakia was occupied by Fascist Germany
And it transformed into the Protectorate of Bohemia and Moravia.
In September of that same year, the world was hit by
The Second World War.

In October 1939, my friends and I joined
The large demonstration of Czech students.
I remember the enthusiasm and how it had grasped hold of us
Schoolkids, who had joined the march, not really understanding
What was awaiting us around the corner,

Be it the corner of the street or our fate.
I remember walking along, under the evil eyes of the
Metal helmets of the new world order –
Soldiers of the Great and Invincible Reich.
I remember the shots ringing out

And how that lad called Jan fell right nearby[167].
He was marching right by my side and he even turned and smiled at me
When the bullet passed through his neck,
The second striking him in the chest,
Right before my eyes.

The November days that year witnessed awful acts of persecution,

---

[167] Refers to the Czech student Jan Opletal, who died during the student uprising in Czechoslovakia on 28 October 1939, on the anniversary of Czechoslovakian independence. Opletal died of his wounds on 11 November. His funeral was held on 15 November, which transformed into a major protest march. On 17 November the Nazis closed all Czech universities. Students were executed and sent to concentration camps. From that time, 17 November is recognised as International Students Day.

Against the students and anyone else
Who came out against Fascist occupation.
So, what then did we teenagers do?
What lads my age usually do –

We united in vengeance squads of boys
And, applying every backyard method we knew,
We did our best to inflict maximum damage on our enemies.
Of course, this damage was more amusing
Than any real contribution to the struggle against the brown plague.

We'd beat up a corporal who'd fallen behind his column,
Or we'd let down the tyres when motorcyclists were not paying heed.
Once we even tossed a grenade into a convoy cart,
Where a fat sergeant was sleeping.
Once we stole two machine guns and handed them over to the students.

Once, though, some real
Carnage went down.
It took place because we had met our peers –
Young lads from the Hitler Youth,
Running errands at one of the German headquarters.

Iozhik and Vladi tracked down this young Nazi offspring
On the streets when they were out of the watchful eye of
Their senior *parteigenosse* comrades.
They were about 13 or 14, but they behaved shamelessly and with excessive bravado,
As befitted young Fascist lion cubs.

But lion cubs need to learn how vulnerable they are
When the lion leaves to patrol its territory,
Leaving the red dogs of the savannah as masters of the night.
There were about fifteen of them.
First, we lured them out onto wasteland,

Chucking stones and badgering them
As street tearaways do so well.
My knowledge of German and Yiddish came in handy here.
When we were out in the open,
The Yugends saw that there were a little more of us, about twenty.

They stopped in orderly fashion and,
With impudent grins and displays of contempt
For us *slav mugs,*
They removed their brown uniforms and caps.
Oh, the Aryan arrogance: they even folded them.

Remaining in just their T-shirts they assumed the pose, ready for a punch-up.
Many of our lads were equally well trained,
Having attended the *Sokol* Patriotic Physical Education Club[168].
Therefore, without the slightest embarrassment, we also stripped to the waist.
And, puffing hot steam,

We rushed into battle.
The first blood spattered. Someone fell into the cold autumn mud.

---

[168] The youth sporting movement, founded in Prague in 1862 by Miroslav Tyrš.

Gradually, the fight began to lose the yardboys'
Rules of the game.
Several Yugends were finishing off our brother, down on the ground.

Our lads were kicking the shaven head of one of the Fritzes.
Despite the excellent physique of the young Nazis,
We gradually began to gain the upper hand.
However, there was one thing we hadn't taken into account:
Two of the Hitler Youth's leaders were carrying pistols.

They were unlikely to have been service weapons,
But *valkyries* always fly in the sky of war,
Handing out weapons to whomever they wish,
Not guided by any means by staff list or military rank,
Logic or common sense.

When the first shot rang out,
Yozhek groaned and fell onto his side,
Thrusting a hand to his chest for some reason.
When he removed his hand, we realised why.
There was blood.

The lads howled like genuine savannah dogs.
Two further shots had no meaning and went nowhere
Because of the lava-like rush upon the young Nazis.
Vladi took one of the pistols and, without hesitating,
Opened fire on the *enemy*.

One of the Hitler Youth leaders who had held
A second pistol
Kept his cool, despite our onslaught
And despite the loss of a pistol.
He nimbly evaded single combat and, moving across the battlefield,

Worked out who the leaders were and shot at them
From almost point-blank range.
Death didn't frighten us, rather, it made us lose our minds a little.
With a desperate yelp, someone threw themselves at the Yugend's legs, pulling him down.
I flew on top and we rolled downwards.

There was a dark stream
And we were quickly covered from head to toe in mud.
The battle continued somewhere up above us;
We could hear the muffled cries of the boys
And another two shots rang out.

The leader of the young Nazis and I
Had become locked together,
In an attempt either to strangle one other
Rip each other's throat,
Or drown each other in the liquid mud.

I was a little older than this *world conqueror*
And, evidently, more experienced in fights.
Therefore, I gave him no opportunity to use his pistol,
Which, to my surprise, had never left his hand.
Although would the gun have even worked after such immersion in mud?

I had had no time to think.
This was no longer a fight, but a battle not for life, but to the death.
At some point, I let a terrible blow through to the head with the butt of the pistol.
I began to lose consciousness when I suddenly sensed
How weak my opponent was also becoming.

With all my strength I pushed him with my body into the slurry of mud and blood.
In the end, all that was left on the surface of that mush
Was a hand grasping this *Walter*.
After several convulsions, the boy went still
And I suddenly came to realise that I had killed a man...

No, a boy...

I was sick into that filthy mixture,
In the depths of which a human body was turning cold.
For a moment, I lost consciousness.
I don't know what brought me round –
Either the cold of the night, or the sound of crisp automatic gunfire.

One thing was certain: had I not come round in time,
I would have been drawn into that bog along with my victim.
Forever and ever and ever.
To get out of that turbid embrace,
I discarded my heavy shoes and trousers

And, pushing off from the enemy *Walter*, I climbed up.
The automatic gunfire I had heard from below
Had come from German soldiers
Who had been near the wasteland and
Who had come unexpectedly to help the Hitler Youth.

I didn't know that I should have hidden in a hollow
Until the soldiers had gone and my consciousness
Was completely fogged over.
I realised my mistake once I had completed the climb,
For I saw forged boots of Germans approaching me.

It was too late and I fell back into unconsciousness.

Koppel, I think you have enough imagination to understand
What happened next with me.
Yes, indeed, the same thing happened to me
As with my father in Turkestan: they mistook me for another,
For the lad I had killed with my bare hands

And of whom I had been the spitting image.

His name had been Dietrich Reutermann.
Now it would be more accurate to say
That that is what they now called *me*.
I remained unconscious for some time
And, what a miracle, I somehow managed not to give myself away.

I can't imagine what would have happened,
If just once in my feverish delirium

I had sworn at the medical staff in Yiddish.
If it had been in Czech, it wouldn't have been so awful.
Because Private Reutermann was a Sudeten German.

My Jewish physiological feature didn't give me away either.
Well, the one I told you about;
The one that I didn't have...
I got into the National Political Academy,
Or NaPolA for short, in Ploskovice in Sudetenland.

Now the evil *valkyries* of war had seen to it
That I became a member of that same Hitler Youth,
Fighting whom has been where my military path had begun.
Israel's stories had taught me
That there was no need for panic.

Evil fate, moving a man paradoxically
From one value system
To one that is its polar opposite,
As if laughing and having fun at my expense,
Would most certainly present me with another chance

To survive.
And so it happened. I had never had problems with German.
A slight Slavic accent merely confirmed
My origins from the Sudetenland.
Despite the fact that I was older than Dietrich Reutermann,

I was still the puny little son
Of the Turkestan and Ukrainian demons of famine.
Therefore, when I saw my new identity card,
Confirming that I had been born in 1926,
I took this date as my second birthday.

I have already told you about my appearance.
My portrait hung in the ward at the NaPolA unit
Where I was recovering; a young man in a black cap
With the inscription
Our schoolmate and hero of Great Reich battles in Bohemia.

And, do you know, Koppel? I was even put forward for an award!
The story of the heroic battle of the lads from the Hitler Youth,
And particularly about the one who was wounded
But never lost his weapon,
Reached the Reich Protector of Bohemia and Moravia

Konstantin von Neurath,
And he petitioned for my inclusion in the list of
The 1 October 1938 Medal winners![169]
They say that an award like that raises the spirits
Not only of the soldiers, but the new stock of the NSDAP!

---

[169] The 1 October 1938 Commemorative Medal, commonly known as the Sudetenland Medal, was instituted on 18 October 1938. It was awarded to those involved in the annexing of Sudetenland in Czechoslovakia and the creation of the Protectorate of Bohemia and Moravia. On 1 May 1939, an additional series of medals was released.

After my recovery, I was given
A bronze plate depicting the Prague Palace,
Along with the infinite respect of the officers and pupils at NaPolA.
D'you hear, Koppel? For me killing myself
And for conquering the country that had been the cradle of my youth!

Only one main problem remained – my memory.
My memory of the past, of my fellow-student friends,
The knowledge gained at NaPolA;
All that I didn't have and couldn't have had.
Yet this problem resolved itself at the hospital.

Perhaps the fact I'm uncircumcised (sorry, Koppel)
Means I have lost part of my Jewish essence.
But I hadn't lost my Jewish good fortune with it.
Demonstrating my lack of knowledge to the doctors in my stupor,
I had been waiting for fate to deal me its blow.

But it wasn't to be like that,
For the staff weren't there to incriminate me;
I was a hero, you see,
And so, finding out why I remembered nothing and no one
Was not a job for me, but the Third Reich's doctors.

Strange, but no one suspected for a moment
That they had found the wrong guy.
Nevertheless, the medical boards all remained lost.
I was convinced that one of the doctors
Would reach a more sober explanation, but...

You know, Koppel, when knowledge and
Conviction become powerless,
Delusion steps out in all its glory.
This role in my fate was played by a Professor Steiner
Who dealt with the finer features of the Aryan brain.

He told his colleagues that,
Well, they were really dealing with an instance
Of what would appear to be irreversible amnesia,
And that, if he were given the opportunity, he would prove
That the outstanding Aryan brain

Possesses such incredible abilities to restore memory
That it can not only recover the past,
But even advance forward.
Just give it time and the opportunity
And give him the chance to work with this heroic patient.

The doctors shrugged, for they could hardly object.
They of course agreed.
I quickly worked out how to support Doctor Steiner's theory
And, stocking up on dictionaries and phrasebooks from the library,
I quickly proved to him (and his colleagues)

The truly outstanding capabilities of the Aryan brain
To learn Russian, French and English.
And, to the utter horror of the doctor's colleagues,

The Turkic and Iranian languages too,
Which, as you might guess, Koppel,

I had been taught by the Red Army's Israel Arevich
And the mysterious Babylonian code of our kind.
As for my active memory,
I had no problems there –
I quickly restored my acquaintance and even friendship

With the guys from NaPolA.
In essence they were just boys, really.
Shouting joyfully, "Till! Till!"[170]
They greeted me at the barracks as their best friend,
And it was this and not Doctor Steiner or that Aryan brain

That "restored" my current memory,
My memory of human relations.
As I mentioned to you, James, I was really not that tall before.
But in the two years I spent at NaPolA, I shot up
To where I am now.

It was all down to the swimming, volleyball and boxing.
And, Koppel, it was the *diet*. A good diet
That I'd never seen the like of
Since the day I'd been born.
And so, after several terms of study,

Doctor Steiner presented his colleagues with a true marvel
Of an Aryan brain: the brain of Dietrich Reutermann,
Born Solomon Ben Israel,
Who spoke several languages,
Excelled in sport and his studies, an erudite, a giant, a hero

And a wonderful friend to his Hitler Youth comrades...

So, there you have it, James, the true story of my "treachery".
What do you say to that, grandson?
Of course, it's a terrible thing for a Jew to realise that his ancestor
Not only wallowed in the whirlpool of war,
But bore on his uniform those awful symbols of *Galut* Edom.

I am not trying to justify myself either.
What is the use of superfluous words? You'll understand it all for yourself.
The only thing I'm grateful to Adonai for
Is that I never took part in the *practical execution*
Of the *Shoah* of our people.

But I don't know how much that might sound like an excuse. I did fight.
One thing I do know is that I must simply tell *you*
What might possibly safeguard *you*
From the wicked embraces of the *valkyries*,
Rushing frantically over the fields of battle.'

My grandpa fell silent and, seeing the
Ancient ruins of the Capernaum Synagogue before him,

[170] *Till* (German) – a diminutive of the name Dietrich.

Came to a stop. The wind over the Kinnereth fluttered his grey hair.
I don't know if he was asking forgiveness
Or praying, but it seemed to me

That the tranquillity of the Israeli landscape all around
Had ever-so slowly come to recognise in him a son...
Or perhaps not, who could ever really know?
Grandpa embraced me but his arms did not encounter the warmth he expected,
Although they were not insisting on this.

I was as yet unable to determine
How I could take all that my grandfather was telling me.
I wasn't ready.
Solomon knew this
And refused to hurry things.

'So, Koppel,' he continued.
'1943 came.
What did it mean for me?
Only that this year saw the formation of
The 12th SS Panzer Division *Hitlerjugend*.

And that, little James, meant that my peers and I from 1926
Had to step from the theory of war
Into the very heat of battle.
I won't tell you about how I fought for *them*.
You will learn from your history that this division, like wild boars,

Crushed and destroyed its *enemies*
On the other side
Of that simple line of values known as *the front*.
All I will say is that, in 1944,
I escaped from the Falaise cauldron[171]

And joined the Belgian partisans.
No, this time there was no miraculous transformation
Thanks to an absolute similarity to someone else.
It was just that three other traitors and I brought and handed over to them
Our commander, Obersturmbannführer Meyer.

You think this ensured we received immediate and limitless trust?
Far from it.
My three comrades and I had to prove in blood
That our Nazi past had been an error of fate.
How did we succeed in this?

You know, grandson, success is not usually achieved.
We can forgive betrayal in love, in politics,
Sins of gluttony, adultery, vanity,
Hatred for our fellow man and even proselytism.
But one thing that is hardest of all to forgive

Was that, once, you were not *one of us*, you were from the other side of the front line.

---

[171] The Falaise Pocket was a decisive engagement of the Battle of Normandy in the Second World War between the Allies and Germany, waged from 12 to 21 August 1944. This engagement, in particular, saw the capture of Commander Kurt Meyer of the 12th SS Panzer Division *Hitlerjugend*.

All the same, I am an Officer
Of the Belgian Order of the Crown.
So, there you have it, grandson...
Incidentally, at that time, in those unsanitary partisan conditions

I transformed myself into a full-fledged physiological Jew.
Well, you understand... I read out a prayer
That I had written myself and... I did it!
I wanted to be sure that if I were to fall into enemy hands again,
Fate would not play any more transforming games with me.

So there would be no turning back.
I knew that if I had been able to escape capture that time,
It would be better never to get caught again.
Most likely my cup of good fortune was also running dry
Just like everything else in this world.

Therefore, my defector friends and I fought like
We had a death wish.
After all, what is captivity? You know, grandson.
Most players in this big man's game
Called *War,*

Who found themselves on the other side of the line, not on the winning side,
Consequently formed new armies,
In the GULAGs and prisoner-of-war camps,
On the building sites of Moscow, Kiev, Alma-Ata
Or in the American PoW camps on the Rhine.

Just as many died there from disease and malnutrition than in battle.
They died of hunger and malnutrition just like
Their *enemies* died, in the death camps on the *other* side.
You say this was a matter of different ideologies and different motives?
In different ways and for different reasons?

Yes, you're right again, my young James, son of Alphaeus.
Only tell that to Azrael
The angel of death, gathering his bountiful harvest from war
And not asking if you're a Communist or a Nazi,
Or if you were killed by the gas chamber or camp typhus.

I am a Jew, Koppel,
And I have my *Jewish essence.*
I know the value of the word *vengeance,*
And I understand when it will be just and fair.
I know that Adonai punished our enemies, but...

But, as the son of generations from the military, let me tell you:
Grief befalls the defeated!
He is culpable for all the madness of the *valkyries* of war.
And he will carry that guilt until
The lot of the vanquished befalls a new victim.

You know, grandson, that when there was a war
In the heavens between the black angels and the white,
They *all* thought that they were fighting for God.
Meanwhile, Satan not only managed to confuse half of them,

But he got his hands on many victory spoils,

Because he assumed different guises,
Including that of the Lord of Worlds.
They say that even the Almighty had himself tied in knots.
The Greedy One so confused Him that, to this day,
In all stories of wars and their consequences,

The winner, revelling in his just victory,
Slowly begins to acquire the same qualities
That he most hated in his enemies.
And all because the purity of his assessments
Are overshadowed by the sweet and then trumpeted voices of those wonderful *valkyries*.

Therefore, when you meet fierce and determined types
Who deliver verdicts in peacetime,
Demanding vengeance for past wars, know this:
They are calling you to a place where very soon that
Line of the simplest of truths will flare up – the front line.

That means they'll call you to where war is.

Now you'll ask where I was after the war.
This is no shorter a story.
And it is far from a tale like a *family history*,
But if you want to learn about this in detail,
Then you can read about this *tale of vengeance* in my diaries.

You'll find everything in there.
About my move from Europe to the USA,
And about how, one day, I went to the authorities and revealed my past,
About how I was tried and sent to prison.
About how I thought I'd sit in that cell until the end,

Without ever sowing the seeds of my family.
About how *they* came and persuaded me
That I could atone for my sins another way.
It's all there, Koppel, in those thick notebooks.
You'll even learn things in them that no one knows and no one will ever learn.

But you'll be able to learn if you learn languages.
How else will you be able to read it all?
No, James, you are destined to continue the tradition of your kind,
And so...' Solomon sat down on the rocks,
As if he'd once more become exhausted from his life.

'It took me so long to find you,
Because I could not enter Israel.
Not because my Second-World-War past was running after me.
I had atoned for my sins, rather I had been redeemed...
No, it wasn't because of the Hitler Youth that I had been deprived the right to enter.

They had arranged it so that no one really knew about my past.

I was denied entry for another reason
And this, God forbid, is the story of my last war.
They had no interest in my atonement in blood,

Which my comrades and I had ensured in Europe.
They knew that my Jewish pangs of conscience wouldn't be silenced by prison,

Belgian awards nor the testimony in court of fellow partisans,
Asserting in unison that only a miracle
Had saved me from death because of that reckless heroism
That we had demonstrated in battle with the Nazis.
They needed me as a controllable tool.

And, well, *they* got it.

In the autumn of 1972, analysts from US military intelligence
Concluded that Mossad was conducting an unprecedented
Mission to eliminate PLO activists,
Guilty of or privy to the bloody massacre
At the Munich Olympics.

Back then, I was given the chance to atone before my Motherland
By taking part in this as an embedded American agent.
You think it was to help Israel?
It would be ridiculous even to assume such a thing.
It was to control the situation.

The Americans always want to control everything and everyone.
That's the truth. You see, the Chinese sage Sun Tzu,
One of the greatest war strategists, once said,
Victorious warriors win first
And only then go to war,

While defeated warriors go to war first
And then seek to win.
So, how can you win in advance?
Only if you have complete control over the situation,
You have true knowledge of *what* is going on.

If we're talking about organising a group for elimination purposes,
Then Israel demonstrated
That it has sufficient might and political will.
The only thing there wasn't enough of was information.
And that is what the American Sun Tzus put to use.

And so, in the autumn of 1972, I joined
Operation *Za'am Ha'el*[172] as an information gatherer
And a designer of special operations.
I won't tell you all of it, Koppel,
Just one episode.

After the murder of Basil al-Kubaissi[173] in Paris,
The guys returned, dragging one of the shooters with them.
They were all pale and the shooter himself (we'll call him Avner,

---

[172] *Za'am Ha'el* (Hebrew) – *Operation Wrath of God*, a mission by Israeli Mossad to destroy terrorists from the Palestinian Black September group, who were involved in organising and implementing the terrorist act at the 1972 Munich Olympics, and members of the Palestine Liberation Organisation who, according to Mossad, were responsible for the taking of hostages. The operation was launched in the autumn of 1972 and lasted more than 20 years.
[173] Basil al-Kubaissi was a member of the Popular Front for the Liberation of Palestine (PFLP) and a professor of international law at the American University of Beirut. He was shot dead on the street by two unknown gunmen.

340

Like in the film *Munich*) had lost all self-control.
For some time, no one was able to explain what had happened.

Only some days later, I went into Anver's room.
He was lying on his bed, staring blankly at the ceiling.
 "You know, Slomo (well, as if he were addressing me by name),"
Anver said a few minutes later.
"He was the spitting image of me..."

My heart missed a beat
And I thought he must be feeling the same
That Israel and I had felt,
When taken by the angels of war into their mindless whirlpool.
"Do you regret anything, Anver?" I asked him.

"Are you kidding? No way. I am an Israeli, a Jew.
More than that, I am a weapon of vengeance in the hands of my people;
I will never have a single doubt of that.
And I never thought I would kill myself or someone like me anywhere.
The Palestinians are our *enemies*. There might be a Paris Spring out there,

But I saw that red strip of blood run through the city
Like a front line between *us* and *them*."
"But Anver, if you are convinced you are right,
What then threw you into confusion?"
Anver paused, then got up and poured himself a whisky.

"You know, just for a moment...
Simply for one moment, I thought
That the me of today
Was killing the me of tomorrow
Forever and ever and ever."

The Mossad group operated extremely secretively.
Naturally, it didn't actually exist at all.
Therefore, to be on the safe side, those who joined the group in Europe,
Were prevented entry to Israel for a considerable time,
As if there weren't any such people in the first place.

That, grandson, was why it took me so long to get to you,
Not to mention arrange all the guardianship papers.
But *they* helped me
I wouldn't have managed it on my own, Koppel.
But all's well that ends well, right?'

Solomon stopped and closed his eyes.
'Saba, but who is my grandmother? Well, mum's mum?
Is there an awful story behind that too?'
'Don't clown about, you rascal,' Solomon said with a smile.
That story is not awful at all; it's actually quite wonderful.

You asked why your father
Often joked at your mum's expense when he spoke of her Russian stubbornness?
You remember me telling you
That it's not with my Tashkent family
That the Russian page in our *familia's* history ends?

341

So, listen up.
In 1957, a wonderful event took place.
It was called the *Moscow World Festival of Youth and Students*,
And I had travelled there as a delegate
As part of a youth group from the USA.

They say that this festival brought
Together some thirty thousand foreign guests
And another hundred thousand from all corners of the USSR,
While two million Muscovites came out
Onto the streets of the Soviet capital to greet them!

The last time I had seen that many people at once
Was during the war, but then there had been blood,
Shells were going off and terrible machines were advancing.
Thousands of soldiers, engulfed in a single outburst of madness,
Taking life, losing life or a part of life.

But here...

Koppel, I saw the whole world and peace simultaneously[174]
It was an enchanting celebration of love,
Friendship, light and an indestructible human faith that
Wars, be they cold or hot, are simply a relic of the past,
Which is destined to sink at any moment into oblivion

Forever and ever and ever.

There was no belief that humans had already achieved that
Level of development, that social behaviour,
A development of spirit, heart, humanism
And thousands more wonderful words like them,
To ensure mutual hatred and murder would never happen again.

Naturally, I arrived in Moscow with *their* mission.
My partisan past and knowledge of Russian
Couldn't have come together at a better time.
However, this mission swiftly vanished from my mind
When I travelled in an open-top car along the Garden Ring and wept

The tears of a little boy, a soldier, orphan and simple lad,
For whom the phrases *Peace to the World!*, *Friendship!* and *No to War!*
Struck me right in the heart.
My tears then doubled when
I remembered that once I'd been the *enemy* of these people,

But it was then that I first began to think
That I could be truly forgiven.
Seeing the banks of European medals on my jacket, the people
Embraced me and wept.
Former Soviet partisans offered me cigarettes,

And dedicated heartfelt sounds of the accordion
And Soviet military songs to me.

---

[174] The author uses the pre-revolutionary *міръ* which means the world, society, the people, and then *Мир*, which is the modern Russian for peace. Both are pronounced *mir*.

Girls gave me flowers and bright pennants.
Lads shook my hand and pinned the festival's five-leaf
Badge or a Komsomol red flag to my lapel.

Two days of festivities and socialising went by
And they seemed to me a joyous and warm-hearted eternity.
And yet a dull pain suddenly began to rise inside.
Burning ever stronger within me was
My Nazi Prague Medal.

The black SS runes choked me
And doubts of ever being forgiven
Or ever finding redemption
Stifled me more and more
And quite overwhelmed me.

The reason for this lay in the recollections of veterans,
Of which there were a great many among the festival-goers
And from different countries.
This inevitably led to memories of the days
When we, America and the USSR, were allies.

The subject of military brotherhood often put paid to discussions
And heated arguments, even though they were well-intentioned.
No one wished to cross that invisible line.
When discussions got close to the line, you would generally hear,
"What's all this arguing for, friends, we're brothers-in-arms after all!"

This would be followed by embraces, recollections,
Hearty feasting and get-togethers
In cramped yet cosy Moscow apartments,
Occasional cafés and, most often,
On benches in parks and boulevards.

One day a large group of us were strolling in the Lenin Hills
Near the main building of Moscow University.
We were standing by a bench and were probably singing our heartfelt
Rendition of *Podmoskovnyie Vechera* (*Moscow Nights*) for the hundredth time.
I still remember it by heart, Koppel.

We hear not a rustle in the garden,
All has frozen here till morning.
If only you knew how the Moscow Nights
Are so close to my beating heart.'

Old Solomon fell silent and I chose not to break this silence.
He was elsewhere. He was *not now.*
'You know I told you
How we sang this song hundreds of times back then,
And I would always be happy to sing it a thousand times.

At the moment when the lingering melody
Was stretching over the slopes of the Lenin Hills,
Somewhere up there, to the enormous star
Atop the spire of the university,
I was dealt a terrible blow...

No, it was not a fist or a lightning strike.
It was blow dealt from my inner pain.
Nearby, countless young people were out strolling,
In couples and groups.
From one of these groups, a cry in German rang out:

"*Till! Till!* Dietrich! Get over here!"
A young man darted out,
Dragging two others by the shoulders.
"Dietrich, do you know who this is?
These are the lads who freed us back then"

I turned pale but in an instant I realised
That the young German was speaking not to me
But to a lad standing to his side.
"Look, Till! This lad is a veteran, too."
The first German said with a smile, nodding in my direction and pointing at my medals.

"Come, comrade, come with us!
These lads have a bottle of scotch hidden!"
Somehow, I overcame my stupor and, muttering something, I agreed.
The four of us sat down on a bench and introduced ourselves.
The young Germans were anti-Fascists from East Germany,

And the lads they'd brought...
Were infantry highlanders from the Nova Scotia Highlanders,
Which whom fate had brought me together;
And I am talking about the SS Hitlerjugend Division
In Lower Normandy near Évrecy.

I remembered this battle not because
The SS tanks had grenadiers had almost completely
Destroyed the Canadian divisions and the
Nova Scotia Highlanders,
Rather because, furious from the opening of the Second Front,

Our command had given the order to take no prisoners.
That meant that, after a bloody battle
And not even wiping the blood and tank soot from their faces,
The brutal Jugends had shot
The captured Scots and Canadians dead.

I had not taken part personally in that shooting,
But I had always felt the blood of that merciless murder
Was on me, on my hands.
After a couple of burning shots of whisky,
I quietly walked away. My departure had not been noticed;

The Scots and the Germans had been joined by
A group of Russian and Uzbek war veterans.
What was going on inside me, Koppel?
Operation Wrath of God had yet to take place,
And Avner's words had not been spoken.

However, I realised what had happened in that second
When I strangled that boy from the Hitler Youth –
I had killed not only Solomon Ben Israel,

Reincarnated as a young Nazi.
I had killed myself, a lad from the beautiful, peaceful

And brightly coloured Moscow summer called *the future*.

Slowly I shuffled off, following my nose,
When I suddenly saw a dim light before me
Over the entrance to a Christian Orthodox church.
Something stirred within me
And I realised the time had come to speak with God.

Pushing open the heavy door, I went inside.
Inside it was quite unlike what was going on outside:
An almost total silence reigned.
A smiling priest darted out from the darkness
And gestured how to light a candle and where to place it.

I nodded my thanks to him
And went up to one of the icons.
It was the *Blessed Heaven* Icon of the Mother of God.[175]
James, I don't recall what I said to the heavens,
How I asked for my penance to be accepted.

Words and images were jumbled in my mind,
While my shoulders shook from the weeping.
Sometimes, when I raised my eyes, I noticed that, somewhere behind me,
That priest had stopped still, deciding
There was no reason to bother me or to comfort me,

For it was evidently clear
That I was holding a difficult conversation with the Almighty Himself.
I wasn't praying to God – I didn't dare.
I didn't ask him for anything, for I saw myself as unworthy.
I asked for forgiveness and the gift of penance

From the host of images that passed before me.
They included Dietrich Reutermann and the Scottish highlanders;
There was that Russian lieutenant with the Molotov cocktail in his hand,
Which our tank had run over and cut in half,
There were the trembling Bavarians whom I had slaughtered

With my broad-bladed partisan knife,
There were the black eyes of a black sniper from the 1st Canadian Army,
Who had terrorised our positions for several nights,
For which his body had been ripped to shreds
From us almost emptying our automatic weapons into him.

These images also included the burned faces of the young men
Who were crawling away from the burning Kangaroo[176],
When we had showered them with grenades,
The shocked faces of the young men from the Feldgendarmerie[177],

---

[175] An icon in the *Zhivonachalnaya* (Live-giving) Trinity Church on Vorobiovy Hills (formerly Lenin Hills) in Moscow.
[176] Kangaroo – the general name given to improvised, heavy, armoured personnel carriers used by the allied forces during the Second World War.
[177] *Feldgendarmerie* – German military police, assigned to assist the occupying forces in Belgium.

At the sight of me on the threshold of their barracks, grenades in my hands –

The last thing they ever saw on their journey through life.

I saw the little Mosya from the Jungvolk,
Who had confided in me,
"*Till*, I really like our uniform, but, you know...
I really don't want to go to war. I dream of making barrels,
Really big barrels like we have back home."

Then I saw this Mosya, or, more precisely, Sturmmann[178] Moritz Büttner,
Looking open-eyed at his gaping innards and saying,
"Dietrich, am I going to die now?"
I saw boys and girls from the Resistance, all so young,
But who had already seen the 20th Convoy operation[179].

I stood in the church for about an hour.
The acute pain in my soul gradually gave way to a dull yearning.
I was afraid to think that God hadn't answered me,
That I hadn't sensed His reply.
Nodding silently to the priest, I wandered out.

And you know, Koppel, God did in fact give me a chance,
Because, several moments after that,
On the observation platform at Lenin Hills,
I met my *Lyubov*[180],
The only Love in my life.

That's right, James, the Soviet student Lyubov Vorobiova
Is indeed your Russian grandmother,
To whom you and your mother owe their Russian lifeblood.
I heard that the Lenin Hills have now got
Their old name back - Vorobiovy.

Can you imagine the symbolism in that for me?
So, when you go to Russia,
And you'll definitely have to go there, grandson,
Make sure you go to the place
Where I met my Lyubov.

Some bright sparks consequently
Liked to speculate about the wanton morals
That the Soviets openly displayed
During the youth festival.
As if the Soviet girls had been overcome by some insane debauchery.

You know, Koppel, I have not met girls
More chaste anywhere.
If we are talking about love, real love,
Then, for sure, the air was full of it back then.
Although... Perhaps that was just an impression I got?

---

[178] A *sturmmann*, in the SS forces, was the equivalent of a corporal.
[179] The 20th Convoy was the name given to the special train, transporting Jews to Auschwitz. The operation, organised by the Belgian Resistance, helped 115 prisoners escape. The youngest members of the operation, Simon Gronowski and Régine Krochmal, were both 11 years old.
[180] Means *love* in Russian.

After all, for the remaining eleven days
She was the only one I had eyes for, my beautiful nymph of peace.
We walked the vibrant Moscow by day.
We strolled the mysterious Moscow by night.
We stood on Manezh Square, holding hands

And singing, *One great vision unites us,*
Though remote be the lands of our birth,[181]
And I thought there couldn't be another person in the world
Who could sing these words more sincerely than me.
I taught my Lyubov to pronounce, clearly and correctly, the tongue twister of the lines,

One, two, three o'clock, four o'clock, rock,
Five, six, seven o'clock, eight o'clock, rock,
Nine, ten, eleven o'clock, twelve o'clock, rock,
We're gonna rock around the clock tonight.
When she slipped up, we would laugh out loud together!

And you know, Koppel, she became the altar
That accepted my penance.
One day, after some raucous event
That our Latin-American comrades had organised,
We were walking back along a Moscow boulevard.

It was then that I told her everything. Well, almost everything,
For I left out the most gruesome details
In my description of the bloody carnage of the war.
I told her about the Hitler Youth, the Scots and the church.
I even told her about Arevich from the Red Army,

About how I perceived her arrival as a chance from God,
To be forgiven, as nothing other than love
Has the strength of purity and revival.
Of course, Lyubov was a Komsomol member
And, probably, she had been raised an atheist.

But she never once made my appeal to the Almighty
A matter of doubt or discussion.
She probably sensed
That it would be hard to explain the twists and turns of my
Cursed fate through dialectic materialism.

She only asked quietly, "But do you... see love only in this,
From the standpoint of your forgiveness?"
"No, no, my love," I answered with passion.
"It's just that I have always spoken with God about pain,
Thinking that, apart from this, there is and cannot be anything in the soul.

I don't know how to speak about love.
I cannot put into words that mighty ocean of feelings
That engulfs my heart in warm waves.
I have never experienced anything like this,

---

[181] Lines from the hymn Democratic Youth. Music by Anatoly Novikov, words by Lev Oshanin. Below, the famous verse from Bill Haley and His Comets' *Rock Around the Clock*, also popular during the International Youth Festival.

So... so, the only thing I can do is show you!"

"How?" she asked warily.
I turned and saw an enormous poster,
Depicting Picasso's *Dove of Peace*.
"I can... fly!"
I jumped up and began prancing and jumping about like a madman,

Flapping my long arms like wings.
"Wait for it... wait for it – I'm about to take off!"
I screamed, while Lyubov laughed out loud.
The noise awoke a fluffy white dove, sleeping
In the branches of a tree; thousands of them had flown over Moscow back then.

It first flitted crazily from branch to branch,
Before, having seen my vain attempts to
Master its native elements,
Soared over Lyubov and me in businesslike manner,
While the two of us stood looking into one another's eyes,

And soiled Lyubov's dress and me
With a long white stream.
We saw that as a sign from the heavens.
In torment, I counted the days before I had to leave,
As if foreseeing a long separation.

One evening, Lyubov took me decisively by the arm
And, leaving a rowdy company of friends,
We came to that church up on Vorobiovy Hills.
The very same young priest
Secretly married us, uniting our souls in heaven forever.

That's right, Koppel: I am a Jew and she was a Komsomolka
But we simply knew of no other house of God.
Indeed, the priest who had seen me that terrible night, too,
Didn't particularly follow the formalities of the rite,
Saying that he would assume all the responsibility before God for any violation.

Only then did we come to belong to one another...
Hm... Koppel, I won't fill you in on all the details here.'
Solomon took a mighty breath
And, smiling at something, he stepped out quicker than before.
Catching him up, I heard his creaking baritone:

'Why are you dear looking so askance,
Bowing down your head so low?
It's so, so hard to say and not to say
All that is here in my heart,

And the dawn is already coming into sight,
So please be so kind,
And don't you go forgetting, my dear
These summer Moscow Nights.'

After a pause, Solomon continued his tale:
'When we parted, we vowed to one another
That it would not be for long,

For the world had changed and would never be the same.
How wrong we were!

Very soon afterwards, an iron wall rose up again
Between our countries.
Rainbows of peace were once again replaced with military banners.
I managed to receive just a few letters from Lyubov,
The first full of words of love and eternal fidelity.

I received the second much letter and not by post,
Rather in various, unthinkable ways.
I realised from that that
Only one of my letters had reached my darling.
The most important news I learned from the second letter

Was that I now had a daughter, Maria.
Yes, Koppel, your mother was born in 1958.
Lyubov was not forgiven for her *disreputable connections*
Of which her so-called friends had reported in detail to the KGB.
She had not denied anything.

She was thrown out of the Komsomol and her institute,
While Maria was born in the virgin lands of Kazakhstan,
To where Lyubov had gone, leaving not only her "friends",
But also her strict, Communist parents.
Later, I learned that she had gone from there to Tashkent,

Where I found my father and my *familia.*
It's really a small world, Koppel.
When I tell you about the curse on our family,
You'll understand it even more.
Like a fierce tiger I tried gnawing through

The bars of the steel cages
That separated me from my love
But to no avail.
The Iron Curtain had become a new front line,
Dividing the world into the *us* and the *them.*

I left no stone unturned and,
Making use of the fact that the USA was fighting hard
For the rights of Soviet *refuseniks,*
I established contacts among the Jewish emigre population,
Enabling me to receive news from Lyubov.

I discovered that, like me,
She had never broken the vow
We had made to one another at Trinity Church on Vorobiovy Hills.
In 1976 we were able to exchange letters
(Well, hardly letters – more like little notes).

In hers, Lyubov told me
That Maria had got into a college in Moscow,
But had been unable to study for some reason
And had returned to Tashkent.
Lyubov and I agreed

That I would do all I could to bring them over to me.
A year later I learned that Maria was returning to Moscow again
And that she was getting married. Her fiancé was a Jew.
Lyubov implored me to do everything for the children
And only then look after her.

I began actively to arrange
For Maria and her husband to come over under *Jewish Emigration.*
As you might guess, Koppel,
That Muscovite Jew is indeed your father Alphaeus,
Who knew first-hand about that so-called *Russian nature.*

In late 1978, I finally succeeded in
Bringing your parents out of the USSR.
However, despite their leaving through an
American immigrant aid society[182],
Once in Vienna, Alphaeus decided to travel not to the USA, but to Israel,

To his historical Homeland,
To where, by that time, the door had been firmly shut.
Your parents were not ever that keen to meet with me.
Later, I learned that your father had for some reason decided
That I was a Nazi criminal,

On the run from just vengeance.
For that reason, information about me was taboo in your home.
Naturally, they had been kept in the dark
About my active involvement in their departure.
Well, in 1979, Nathan came into the world.

And then, two years later, so did you...'
'And what about Grandma? Did you see her later?
Is she still alive?'
Solomon lowered his eyes, bent down
And picked a long blade of grass.

'No, James, she died,' he said sadly.
'She died having never got to meet with me again.
After Soviet troops were sent into Afghanistan
Aliyah[183] from the Soviet Union became considerably more complicated,
Especially given that Lyubov Vorobiova was Russian.

Only with the launch of Gorbachev's *Perestroika* in the USSR
Did the situation change fundamentally.
But Lyubov never made it to that moment.
My darling passed away in 1986.
She died in Tashkent from cancer,

Just three weeks after learning of her diagnosis.
Several months later, I received her last letter,
Where she was full of hope that she would see me.
However, a certain sadness betrayed her forebodings.
She sent me photographs

---

[182] Implies the American Hebrew Immigrant Aid Society.
[183] Aliyah – the repatriation of Jews to their historical Homeland.

That I now carry with me; I am afraid to part with them.
Look, James, that's Lyubov way back in 1957.
That's me next to her. Can you see how alike we are, even though you're son of Alphaeus?
And this is her last photo.
Look, grandson, how the years have graced her beautiful face.

Look at her poise and pride,
That nothing but an evil disease could ever break.
Well, there's the front line, the war
That man fights long to overcome and beat.
And what about this. Do you recognise it? Your mum when she was really little.'

'Saba, and why did my parents never speak with me in Russian?'
'I don't know, Koppel. You see, I've only seen my daughter the one time,
When they travelled on holiday to Europe.
You and Nathan were very young at that time.
I arranged a meeting so Alphaeus didn't know.

After that, Maria almost never left Israel.
I think that, in addition to me being a *traitor* in their eyes,
She also blamed me
For her mother's unhappy fate,
Which was basically not so far from the truth.

And then, of course, I don't know what Lyubov told her about me
Or under what circumstances.
So, you see, I wouldn't dare hold it against my daughter.
All I dreamed of was to see my
Lyubov Vorobiova once more,

That beautiful student, standing on her own
At the observation platform on Vorobiovy Hills.'
'I see, but what is that curse on the family
That you keep talking about in riddles
And which is preventing me joining the military?'

'Hold on a minute, Koppel, let's pause for just a moment.
You see that Christian church over there?
Let's go and see it and then
I'll tell you everything to the end.
To be honest, I am a little tired,

But I promise to finish my tale today.
After all, you have to go to school tomorrow.'
I read the inscription above the door, informing me this was
the Monastery of the Twelve Apostles,
A Greek and, coincidence or not, an Orthodox church.

We went into the main temple of the monastery.
Solomon went over to an icon and fell deep into thought.
Looking at the frescoes, I raised my eyes to the dome
And saw the images of Christ's twelve disciples.
In my attempt to remember their names, I ran my eyes

From one portrait to the next.
Stopping on one of them, I tried to work out who it was.
Suddenly, my eyes darkened and then flared up.

351

All I could see were multicoloured circles.
With a gentle gasp, I fell to the floor of the basilica.

TWO LETTERS

By all accounts, nothing terrible had happened with me;
It was something like heatstroke or sunstroke,
Which wasn't surprising after those long strolls
Under the hot sun of Capernaum.
After a day, I was fully back to normal and returned to school.

I came to regret my collapse only a week later.
Solomon and I had wanted to go somewhere again,
Where we would be alone,
And he could continue his story
About our family and its mysterious curse.

Only this was not destined to happen.
The mighty Shlomo was admitted to hospital with a heart attack,
Where he passed away, on the eve of Jerusalem Day.[184]
The heart of this wandering warrior, with his incredible yet
Controversial fate could take it no longer.

Perhaps his strength had been undermined
Because, through his tales, he had once more lived his life with me,
With all its experiences, both wonderful and terrible.
After Shlomo's death, I still had many unanswered questions,
But the most important was how was I to carry on?

I was accustomed to relying on myself for everything
And I decided that I would enrol at the
Preparatory college all the same
And I would choose a military career.
This was my reasoning:

First, this would remove the problem of guardianship,
As I could easily live in the college's dormitory.
Second, the secret curse of my family was something
I would not come to face now,
Although it was probably related to the fact

That at some point I would come face to face in battle with my double.
I saw nothing supernatural in this.
Who knows – among the some five billion people on Earth,
There might well be people with a face like mine.
I was not as similar to Solomon as he had thought.

I had the typical features
Of the *Mediterranean race,*
Which, using the Italian, was *una faccia una razza.*[185]
So, people like me could have been born in Lebanon, Turkey,

---

[184] *Yom Yerushalayim* – an Israeli national holiday commemorating the reunification of Jerusalem and the establishment of Israeli control over the Old City in the aftermath of the Six-Day War in 1967.
[185] *Una faccia una razza* (Italian) – One face, one race. A phrase that once referred to Italians and Greeks as representatives of the same source of ancient heritage. Later, this spread to all peoples of the Mediterranean, which gave rise to the somewhat unscientific expression *Mediterranean race.* From a scientific point of view, there is the notion of a *Southern European group of the Europeoid Race.*

Greece, the Maghreb, Southern France and even in the Caucasus.

Third, I reasoned, I was not in danger of repeating
The military fate of Israel and Solomon.
That was the time when the Jew had no Homeland,
Which meant that the notion of an enemy had become somewhat blurred,
Just as the notion of *us* would have done.

Today, everything is as clear and understood as it could be.
There is our small but proud country,
Located in a hostile Muslim and Arab environment.
Now, every man knows quite definitely
Where the front line runs, for it has never really ever disappeared.

While I was at college
I had neither the time nor the opportunity
For an in-depth study of Solomon's diaries.
Moreover, this would have required a knowledge of Arabic,
Yiddish and Turkic dialects.

I didn't get to visit our home in Jerusalem that frequently
And, if I did, I would spend most of my time
Warding off various suitors for Maria.
Of course, it was Auntie Hanna who did most of the work for me;
She dreamed that we would be together with her granddaughter.

Actually, my Maria grew up a modest girl.
Despite that, I would still fight off suitors,
Approaching from the most distant of tacks.
At the age of 18, like all lads my age, I joined the army.
It was there that I was proudly given my yellow badge bearing the olive tree

Of the famous Golani Brigade.
And near the Wailing wall, I was presented
The coveted brown *kumta*[186].
Successfully completing *tironut*[187], advanced and sergeant's training,
I was recommended for the officer's course.

Six months later I enrolled at the Tactical College.
Over my time of my training there, I did what
Solomon had instructed me –
I completed serious language training,
In particular and among others, focusing on Arabic and Turkish.

And, after several years of dogged training,
Now a deputy company commander, a *Golanchik*,
This young *segen*[188] of the elite combat unit,
James, son of Alphaeus, proposed to
The young Maria Levinson, granddaughter of a delighted Auntie Hanna.

I formed my *familia*, and I could not have been happier.

---

[186] *Kumta* (Hebrew) – the beret soldiers are awarded after the *Masa Kumta* March of Glory. The Golani Brigade beret is brown, symbolising the soil of the Land of Israel. *Golanchik* is the widely used term for Golani Brigade soldiers.

[187] *Tironut* – young recruit training.

[188] *Segen* – the second officer's rank, corresponding with the rank of first lieutenant, given in the Israel Defence Forces to career soldiers, who have received a purely military education.

For the first time in many years, I had
A sense of fulfilment that cannot be put into words.
This feeling will most likely be outdone only
By those who have endured a childhood in orphanages.

Bursting with these new feelings, I sought out Arthur
And Lera Voinovich (now Shatz), who had also started families of their own.
We met, rejoiced and shed tears,
But the feeling of peaceful balance and belonging
To such a grand concept as Love and Family

Prevailed over any sad thoughts.
When twins were born into our family a year later,
The boys Nathan and Ariel,
My sense of fulfilment transcended
Into a new stage, which I could even call a stage of Perfection.

I could.
But you can't be a soldier in a country like Israel
And not encounter that which we label with that customary
And terrifying word –
War.

12 July 2006 saw the start of
What subsequently became known as
The Second Lebanon War.
It was a somewhat strange war.
Despite the fact that the military campaign was called

Worthy Vengeance, we came to call it among ourselves as
Embarrassed Vengeance.
The IDF soldiers burned with a flame of holy punishment,
But the general impression was
That we had come to Lebanon more to retreat than to attack.

Of course, some of the officers tried to convince us
That the reason lay in the barbaric tactics of Hezbollah,
Which relied on using a *human shield* of civilians
For their units and rocket launchers.
However, when there is a front line between us

And there is that notion of *us* and *them*,
Does war not infer acceptable losses
Among those *others*, even if they are seemingly peaceful and yet, all the same, enemies?
Do they not share a common political responsibility?
For giving those monsters from Hezbollah their support?

Are not the lives or *our* civilians on the line,
Who die every day under terrible rocket
Attacks by terrorists?
Should our response not have been commensurate
With the evil grimace of those Muslim thugs,

Who refuse to spare even their own children?
One way or another, entering the battlefield,
We left all our doubts and resentments behind.
So, when our command sent us

354

To comb the streets of Bint Jbeil,

We never complained of a lack of air cover,
But prepared ourselves properly
And set out on that fateful raid.
We knew that there were still many civilians in that town,
But we counted, with good reason, on our experience

And professionalism, not to degrade either the combat
Or the human face of the Israeli soldier.
As we paced the deserted streets of Bint Jbeil,
I felt another special responsibility, for
By my side walked *turai*[189] Moshe Huberman.

It was none other than little Mosya
From our children's home,
Who now bore the new surname of his new family.
Mosya had grown into a tall, handsome man with the muscles of steel
Of a soldier from an elite army unit,

Only with that same naïve,
Almost childish, embarrassed smile on his face.
'Mosya,' I had whispered at the very beginning.
'You always keep close by my side
And don't ever think of lagging behind!'

'All right, James! I mean, yes sir, Segen ben Alphaeus!'
This was the last way seniors would have been addressed in our company,
But that was Mosya down to a tee.
We moved through the town from block to block,
Noting everything that moved and anything that might have seemed suspicious.

It has to be said that Bint Jbeil was really not that empty at all.
Here and there, concealed behind walls and peering out carefully,
Barely visible, women and children occasionally flashed by our eyes.
The sight of these simple people relaxed the young,
Inexperienced soldiers a little.

They had to be continuously kept in check.
Beyond one corner we even saw a large group of Arabs,
Hurrying to the mosque.
Seeing us, they were visibly afraid, but continued on their way.
That was because, we realised, they were not going there to pray.

They were going there to hide from us and a possible air strike.
It was not easy to discern suspicious men among them;
There were many children, an old man and a pair of imams, meeting them at the entrance.
Keeping them in our sights, just in case,
We waited until they slammed the mosque door shut.

We moved on.
We had not walked more than a couple of blocks
When we were attacked at full pelt
By soldiers from Hezbollah's elite special forces,
Who opened heavy fire.

---

[189] *Turai* – a private in the IDF.

In a matter of moments, several of our fighters had fallen to the ground,
Wounded or possibly even killed.
I kicked open a nearby door
And, grabbing Mosya and another young fighter by the scruff of the neck,
I pushed them into the house.

Pressed up against the windows, we saw our
Fighters had smashed in other doors with rocket launchers
And were now hiding in adjacent buildings.
Tracing the direction of enemy fire,
We realised that we were almost completely surrounded.

A fierce exchange of fire went on for several hours.
Our command gave the order several times over the radio to get out,
Only we were unable to do so.
Not because we couldn't break the blockade –
The battle was being fought pretty much so as not to hand over

Our guys to the enemy, alive or dead.
From time to time we would dash out to save the wounded.
Our commander died during one of these sorties,
Diving onto an enemy grenade.
When the helicopters arrived, the fighters were completely exhausted.

However, no one but us could have brought our guys out of that slaughter,
So we had to return there, over and over,
To where hundreds of shots
Continued picking out men from our ranks,
One after the other.

Not only that, but we were also afraid of falling under fire from our own artillery,
Who were providing fire cover for us.
Our lads, though, were extremely accurate and professional,
Delivering precision strikes to the points from where we were emerging.
The place filled more and more with Hezbollah militants.

Then came the final battle march. We brought out not only the wounded
But the bodies of the dead too.
All that remained was to leave this hellhole with the group
That had covered the evacuation throughout the mission.
We coordinated things over the radio with the artillery

Who couldn't wait to transform the former battlefield
Into a genuine *Armageddon* for the terrorists.
'Get out fast,' we could hear over the radio.
'There's going to be a strike on block N, one hundred metres to the Northwest!'
'Hurry, hurry, that's right behind us!'

We hurtled towards the helicopters
And it was then I sensed an unaccustomed void behind me.
Mosya! it suddenly struck me.
Looking back, I saw Private Huberman
Standing stock still by a concrete wall of the Lebanese fortifications.

His automatic weapon raised, he was peering into the depths of the street.
'Mosya, what the hell are you doing?! Let's get out of here!'

He raised his hand and pointed into the smoke. Then he shouted,
Attempting to make himself heard over the shots and explosions:
'There... block N. It's there! It's the... the mosque! There are people in there!'

'Mosya, all hell's about to break loose...
You planning to save them? Are you nuts?! Are you out of your mind?!'
Pretending not to hear, Mosya turned away from me
And, diving into the smoke, rushed to the mosque.
I turned and screamed at the radio operator: 'Stand down! Stand down on block N!

Huberman's in there!'
Several fighters stopped and rushed towards me.
A bullet scratched above my eye
And my eyes were instantly filled with blood/
I tried to wipe my face as quickly as I could, to not lose sight of Mosya.

Seeing him already at the door,
I released a volley of shots somewhere down the street
And rushed towards Mos'.
He was already dragging an imam out and screaming something at him,
Pointing to the building opposite.

At that end of the street, someone gave a sharp order in Arabic
And the Hezbollah fighters, seeing people running out of the mosque, one by one,
Stopped shooting.
Pushing the last man out of the mosque,
Who was carrying two lads under his arms,

Mosya tore towards me.
His face was illuminated by a mischievous and happy smile.
I let off a few shots over the roofs
And was waiting for him, my arms out
To usher him to hide behind the pile of rocks I was hidden behind.

When I had shouted out, requesting that the artillery stopped firing,
The soldiers hadn't heard me, either from all the explosions
Or from the noise of the helicopter blades.
Mosya was extending his hand to me
When a terrible bang went off, followed by an explosion.

In an instant, the old mosque was transformed into rubble.
Mosya fell from the shock wave but quickly got back up again
And, jumping over the rocks, collapsed by my side.
He was breathless from the joy and excitement,
But I grabbed him by the collar and shook him as hard as I could.

'Have you any idea what you are doing?!
I'll have you court-martialled for this, you idiot!
You've placed not only yourself in danger, but the lads, too!
Get to the chopper. Now!!!'
Before racing after Mosya, I looked back down the street.

It seemed that, amidst all the dust and smoke
A man was kneeling and screaming silently,
Shaking his fists up at the heavens.
By his side, someone was lying prostrate.
I could remain there no longer

And so, I ran to my guys.
In the chopper, Mosya pressed up against my shoulder and,
Looking into my eyes, from the bottom up,
Just like in our distant childhood, he smiled, happy and at ease.
Then, quite exhausted, he closed his eyes and fell into a deep sleep.

I embraced him and looked over the lads. No one had been forgotten,
No one had been left behind.
I secretly took a deep breath and relaxed a little.
A few minutes later I got the feeling
That my arm around Mosya was filled with something warm.

I looked down. At first
I thought it must be dirty water from a broken pot or something.
Then I lifted my friend's head sharply and realised.
There would be no need to reprimand Moshe Huberman for his crazy act.
Private Huberman was dead.

Israeli society later discussed at length
What had really happened during that war.
Someone spoke of a military defeat,
Another, of a psychological defeat.
Even the officers gave vent to their emotions.

I took no part whatsoever in any of that –
Not rhetorically and not emotionally.
The pain I felt for the death of my fellow soldiers,
Naturally, gave me no peace.
However, I knew that a real officer

Must be psychologically prepared,
Even for the loss of friends at the front.
Otherwise, come the next threat to the Homeland,
His approach would be soured and
His personality, unstable.

It was then that I sincerely hated all
That wartime propaganda,
Where that conflict between *us* and *them*
Takes on particularly cynical forms.
I also found my anger stifling me

Because it had been concocted by squeaky clean
Journalists and military ideologists
In the same impeccably ironed uniforms.
The hostile press talked about brutal murders
That we had committed.

Our press reported about the cynical and cold-blooded
Shooting of our peaceful districts by Hezbollah militants.
'Grief befalls the defeated!' I heard Solomon's voice.
I was outraged and shocked to my core most of all by
The appearance of photographs in the world press

That someone had taken in Bint Jbeil.
Two in particular,

Where one depicted
A fierce, giant Israeli soldier
Angrily pushing an Arab man in the back,

Who was carrying two small boys under his arms.
The other showed that same Arab man, his face covered in blood,
Embracing the corpses of his two dead sons.
'All right, you bastards,' I said to myself.
'You've turned Mosya the hero into a murderer,

You propagandist jackals.
Well, hang around here some more
And you'll *all* get your share of lead,
Which won't distinguish between soldier,
Accomplice and provocateur!

I will no longer allow people like Mosya
To venture to the front lines with soft, unprotected hearts!
You're hiding behind your stupid civilian status, right?
Well, you'll reap your sacrifice to the full!'
That was what I said to myself but what did I actually feel?

I sensed that my heart,
Like a *Merkava* tank, was coated in a layer of stale armour.
Only one image prevented this armour
From forcing its shell shut for good,
However hard I tried to drive it away.

This was the expression of complete, boyish happiness
That Turai Huberman had had on his face
When he saved those people from their death.
Finding no emotional outlet anywhere
From this contradiction,

I started, for some reason, to delve deeper
Into reading the diaries of Israel and Solomon.
I could do that now, for there was no longer
Any language there that I didn't know.
Moreover, one day, I decided that I wanted to learn more

About my grandmother Lyubov Vorobiova.
Her parents were probably no longer alive,
But perhaps someone would remember something.
Perhaps there were still some of my mother's relatives alive.
Six months before the war, I went onto the Internet

And began an intensive search for correspondence with the authorities
In Russia and Uzbekistan, the capital of which
Was now that mysterious and distant Tashkent.
And what do you think? I discovered much that was of interest!
The senior Vorobiovs had indeed already passed away,

But Mum, it turned out, had an older sister, Aunt Marina.
She was delighted to reply and she told me
That Lyubov's parents were by no means such dyed-in-the-wool Communists
And they didn't want their daughter to leave
For the virgin lands of Kazakhstan at all.

Lyubov's father, Sergey Konstantinovich,
During the campaign to admonish his daughter
Was even forced to denounce and publicly condemn her,
But he categorically refused to do it,
For which he paid with his brilliant career as a scientist.

Lyubov's parents always kept in touch with their daughter,
But they saw one another fairly seldom
For obvious reasons.
That said, they still managed to play a role
In my Mum's destiny. How? Now, this is very interesting.

Unfortunately, Aunt Marina, had no children,
So all hope of me finding any cousins
Was dashed there and then. However, some time later,
I discovered some incredible news,
Marina told me why my mother

Came to Moscow in 1976 and then returned
To Tashkent. It had nothing to do, as
Solomon had thought, with the fact that she 'couldn't study'.
It turned out that my mother's marriage to my father
Had been her second!

Maria Vorobiova, finishing school in Tashkent,
Had come to Moscow and gained a place at MSU.
Where, at one student party,
She had met some foreign students from
The Patrice Lumumba University.

Two months into a passionate affair with an international
Student Marina didn't know,
She married him, having asked no one for permission!
Then, angry Grandma Lyubov came to Moscow,
Wanting to bring some order to the daughter's life,

But, to her surprise, she finds the daughter wretched and abandoned.
The foreign student, without completing his studies,
Had run off back home,
Leaving my mother all alone.
Grandma Lyubov was oh-so familiar with this situation.

She took the strong-willed decision to take her daughter from Moscow,
Because... because she was expecting a baby,
Who was born in 1977.
Grandma decisively recorded the child (boy or girl, I don't know) as her own
And drew up a plan with Solomon to save their daughter.

As we know, this salvation came about thanks to the Jewish Aliyah.
Lyubov approached her father for help
And he acquainted his granddaugther with the young, talented
Scholar Alphaeus (or Fedya, as Aunt Marina calls him),
My father in other words.

Mum was very lucky. For some reason, my father really loved
Mum from the outset. I remember this myself from certain recollections.

The ideologist behind the *all things Russian* taboo turned out to be my mother,
Who had wanted to forget her first, unhappy, love once and for all,
And not my father at all.

But then, if Grandma Lyubov had died,
Where was her child or, more precisely, Maria's child?
For he (or she) would be my uterine brother (or sister!).
Can you imagine the excitement I felt?
Unfortunately, Aunt Marina didn't have an answer,

Because Grandma Lyubov had done her best to
Conceal this page of her life and her daughter's unhappy liaison.
I spent almost a year corresponding with the Uzbek authorities.
In the end, I managed, by way of social media,
To find the people who knew Grandma – her neighbours.

I found a woman who was the daughter of a friend of Grandma Lyubov.
The only thing she remembered was that there had been a boy in the yard,
Who they believed was Vorobiova's little son.
However, neighbours always know everything about everyone. They gossiped about
Him actually being her grandson,

The child of a Jewish *refusenik* who had *run off to her precious Israel*.
However, this boy then disappeared somewhere
Because hardly anyone remembers who he was, what his name was and what he looked like.
The neighbour's daughter (Anya) promised to write to her mother in Voronezh,
Where she now lived with her son, but she did warn that

Her mother was very old and would not be likely to remember anything.
I rummaged through old photo-albums and, just in case,
I sent her some pictures of Nathan and me as children,
In the secret hope that the old neighbour
Would find some common features and remember.

After some time I received a short message from Anya,
Telling me her mother remembers it all really well
And would write me a letter herself; she loved my grandmother.
Anya told me not to worry that letters take so long
As she would ask her brother to scan a copy and email it to me.

However, it was then that the Second Lebanon War broke out
And I stopped corresponding for quite some time,
Quite forgetting about my Facebook page,
Which I had used to chat with Anya.
It was only having returned to reading my grandfather's diaries

That I gradually resurrected my interest
In seeking my brother, lost somewhere out in those boundless expanses
Of the former Soviet Union.
I had just the last of Solomon's diaries,
After reading which I had hoped

To solve all the mysteries of my ancestors
And relate them to my own sons
Once they had reached the appropriate age.
The postwar wounds on my heart
Slowly began to give way to the more ordinary emotions in life.

One day, my family went to the seaside
For the weekend.
I had asked my bosses to add a day to the weekend
Giving me the Monday as well,
To spend more time with the children and Maria.

On the way Maria asked me,
'James, how is your correspondence on your brother coming along?
You haven't said anything new about that for ages.'
I muttered something, but she replied both strictly and tenderly,
'That won't do. More than a year has passed

And you're still holding all those emotions
Like in some stone sarcophagus.
I don't think you need to focus on your grandfather's diaries alone.
There is so much awful stuff in there,
That, rather than distract you from grave thoughts, actually does the opposite.

So, listen to me, matey.
Pick up your correspondence with Russia again.
After all, you applied so much effort before the war.
And people have genuinely helped you,
But you seem ungrateful and a bit rude, really.

James, we have a never-ending war going on;
Unfortunately, it's just our customary way of life.
There's lots in Russia that's different and people might misunderstand you.
So, keep corresponding and, when you find your brother,
You'll take some time off and we'll visit my first Homeland.

I show you where I spent my childhood
And we'll all get together round one table;
Our big family, our *familia*.
After all, your brother probably has children too.
So, your sons will enjoy

Meeting their dodans.[190]

I'd like you to hold on to all that is bright, James.
And you have to do that for your sons.
Despite the fact that war is your profession
And a continual state of affairs for our Homeland.
After all, if we Jews lose that bright light

What, then, is the point of all those losses
That our ancestors incurred for our sake today?'
I stopped the car and tenderly embraced my darling.
She was right and I made a vow
That I'd do everything that she had said.

I promised her always to be bright and merry,
Whatever the hardships that might become us.
During that weekend, I had a real sense
Of the soothing effect those words of Maria,

---

[190] *Dodan* (Hebrew) – cousins.

My one and only love, had on the soul.

On the journey home, we decided to stop off in Dimona
To buy some provisions,
To arrive home and spend the rest of the day
Simply lazing with the kids in front of the television,
Leaving the outside world alone and enjoying our own world inside.

I pulled up near a retail centre,
Told Maria that while she was shopping with the boys,
I would pop into an Internet café.
Maria smiled, realising that I could wait no longer
To fulfil my vow, and she disappeared into the store.

I went onto Facebook and I felt truly ashamed.
There were a dozen or so messages from Anya
That I had not replied to.
However, I sensed no offence in her letters.
Quite the contrary, in fact – more a concern that everything was well with us.

We did have a war going on, and she understood perfectly well.
I was particular happy to read one of her last messages,
Although it was about three months old now.
It said that, while I had been offline,
Anya's mother had actually succeeded in finding my brother!

Anya asked me to send her my email address as soon as I could
To where she would send her mother's letter.
She would also forward me a letter
That my brother, not knowing my address,
Had emailed to her to pass to me!

I understood that the lack of detail
Was only down to me disappearing off the radar.
I quickly sent my email address to Anya,
Praying to the heavens that she hadn't stopped using Facebook
For whatever reason.

I didn't run to my family, I flew,
To tell Maria all about it.
I could already see her through the store window.
She was waving to me.
One moment, darling, I'm coming to help with the bags,

I'll sit both you and the boys on my shoulders and we'll fly home!

It was the town of Dimona. 4th February 2008. 10.30 in the morning.
The shock wave from the explosion threw me into a car
And I smashed into it at full force.
Everything went dark, but my military training ordered me
That I mustn't lose consciousness.

Through the haze I caught sight of a mobile phone that had fallen
And there was a person crouching down by my side to pick it up.
How cold-blooded can you get?! flashed through my mind.
I saw the person was trying to dial a number,
But the phone had clearly been damaged from the fall.

363

Right then, a terrible thought struck me.
He was trying to set off another bomb with the phone!
I tried to shout out, but my mouth was full of blood.
I had been seriously shell-shocked by the explosion.
At that moment, as if from a distance, I heard gunfire.

The man discarded the phone and in the next instant
Our eyes met.
He yanked me up and leaned me against the car.
Up close, I could see his cruel, grey eyes.
That gaze of his bored right into me.

I began to lose consciousness and my eyes fell to his arms.
On his right wrist was a small tattoo of a scorpion.
In that instant, a picture flashed before me
From my course in anti-terrorist training.
An image like that was not sported by ordinary militants,

But by a special avenging unit,
Which recruited only those who
Had personal scores to settle with the IDF and Israel.
Those who had lost close friends and family,
And who was prepared to dedicate his life to retribution.

The scorpion indicated that they would never surrender,
Because that would threaten them with a cruel reprisal
From those who, in turn,
Might wish to charge them in blood
For their cold-blooded murders.

A commotion had kicked up, which was why the man had picked me up,
To pass himself off as someone helping the victims
He bared his teeth at me in a cold and pitiless grin
And slowly, without drawing undue attention to himself,
Walked away.

I tried in vain to tell the police what I could.
But my blood-filled mouth merely emitted a tormented gurgling.
Everything inside me was screaming, 'That's him! Stop him!
That's the man behind the act of terror!'
Desperate, I closed my eyes and it was then that I came

To the awful realisation of what had happened with me personally.
For some reason, I remember the day
When that man and woman in black had come,
To inform me that I was now all alone.
I could see them before me once again.

They were looking at me, while my dad and my mum were standing behind them,
Nathan.. Little Maria, and...

I didn't lay around in hospital for long.
Having barely managed to bury Maria and the boys,
I asked to be transferred to
The special anti-terrorist group

Of Flying Tigers – Sayeret Golani[191].

We were redeployed to the south
To take swift and decisive retribution
Over those who were involved in the attack in Dimona.
We scoured the borders of the Gaza Strip,
Like the fierce dogs of the savannah,

Destroying anyone capable of holding a weapon.
I didn't keep my promise to Maria,
For I was black, black in everything –
In thought, in deed and even in appearance.
Most important, I had not a shred of Doubt.

One day at noon, we received a tip-off
From the guys at Sayeret Matkal[192],
That two cars with terrorists were
Travelling along a particular road.
'This is your day, James,' the Matkal intelligence officers said to me.

'They tell me they are your sworn enemies, the Scorpions.'
I had never prepared for a parade like
I did for this incursion.
Loading the magazines, I prayed to God for one thing only,
For each bullet to reach the enemy and for Azrael to call to them.

We lay on the red plain,
Concealed behind the folds in the terrain
No higher than the shoots of the fluffy tsabar.
Two 4x4 vehicles were approaching us at speed,
Each with large-calibre cannons mounted on their chassis.

The battle was short and decisive.
Having blown up both vehicles, we fired continuously
Until those inside
Ceased their rapid gunfire.
The surviving terrorists responded

Merely with occasional pistol fire.
I didn't wait for the snipers to pick out the last of them.
Running from clump to clump, I drew nearer to the cars
From a blind spot for their defences.
I wanted to *see* them dying and finish off those who were still clinging to life.

Circling one of the cars,
I took out two terrorists.
There was now just one of them, still shooting
From the second vehicle.
I leaped out from my cover and

Found myself face to face with an Arab.

---

[191] *Sayeret Golani* is a special unit of the Golani Brigade, known as the *Flying Tigers*, from the badge on their berets, depicting a winged tiger. Interestingly, the Russian refers to *Flying Leopards*. It is one of the most famous special units of the IDF.
[192] *Sayeret Matkal* – A major special unit of the Tzahal, Under the direct command of the General Staff of the Israel Defence Forces.

That's right, face to face,
Because I instantly recognised the face.
It was... Me!
He was just a little thinner and taller.
The Mujahid extended his hand with his pistol and he too froze in amazement.

All that was left in the world was our eyes,
Speaking in words only we understood.
The expression in the Arab's eyes changed to curiosity.
We stood there for what seemed an eternity,
Our weapons pointed at one another.

It was obvious that thoughts and words were spinning like mad
In that lad's head, as if he were trying to remember something,
Sorting through pictures, words, images and recollections.
I think I probably looked the same.
The tension in our hands, clutching our weapons,

Slowly began to subside.
It seemed that we were about to address one another with words...
Of greeting? Questions?
The Arab began to examine me with curiosity and then...
His gaze fell onto the olive-yellow emblem of the Brigade.

The Mujahid's grey eyes
Filled first with an intolerable pain.
And then with hate.
I, in turn, had seen the small symbol of the scorpion on his arm.
I raised my eyes and recognised the grey eyes,

That had pursued me in my dreams every night
After that fateful day in Dimona.
Our brain instantly awakened a host of images.
I saw Mosya, Maria, Nathan and Ariel,
I saw Roi Klein and the lads who had fallen in Bint Jbeil.

What did the Arab see in that instant?
I don't know and I'll probably never know,
Because, in the next moment,
We squeezed the triggers of our guns.
Each squeezing their own.

I was grateful for my military training,
Completed in the Golani Brigade,
Because the round in my automatic weapon
Proved faster that his pistol.
The *scorpion's* shot struck me in the shoulder,

But I managed to release a long round into the *enemy*
And he fell flat on his back.
At that moment, my guys and lads from Maskal turned up...
'James,' A *seren*[193] from the General Staff intelligence asked me later,
Do you feel avenged?'

---

[193] *Seren* – captain in the IDF.

I was lying in a hospital ward and, emotionally,
I looked more like the tree on my insignia
Than a human being.
'How many more years or decades will pass, Saul,
Before Israel will feel avenged...'

Saul crumpled his beret in his hands and spoke:
'So, this war will go on forever, James?'
'For our lives, for sure, Saul.'
'And what do you reckon – is there anyone capable of stopping it?'
'I have no idea, Saul, what would need to be done for this.'

'Okay, Saul, war or no war,
Forever or not forever.
Just promise me this, brother:
If one day you suddenly realise how it can be done,
And I don't mean with any of that pacifist or namby-pamby stuff...

You let me know, all right?
After all, you'll know where to find me;
I'll be right nearby, *at war*.'
He donned his beret and left.
But I remained black at heart.

When I left the hospital,
The hardest thing for me was to return home.
I walked past the children's rooms and the bedroom,
Pretending that I couldn't see if they even existed;
I went straight to my study

And sat in my chair.
I closed my eyes and sat in silence.
You think I was deep in recollections? About the children?
No. That was too tormenting.
I could see only Maria and her alone.

Somehow, my darling's image calmed and pitied me,
Spoke with me and asked me again to become bright again.
But where?! Where could I find a source of light?!
My eyes fell on Solomon's last diary.
I removed it from the bookcase

And began turning the pages without much interest.
Several sheets of paper fell from the notebook;
They were clearly newer than the diary's yellowed pages.
I opened them with shaking hands.
A rush of blood went to my head,

For it was Solomon's letter to me, written in his own hand.
I unfolded the letter and began to read.
This is what he wrote:
Dear James,
In telling you about my life,

I came to sense that each episode was accompanied
By a further fading of my life force,
And Azrael is prowling very close now.

You are so busy with your lessons
That I won't bother you until the weekend.

However, when you fell unconscious in the church,
I suddenly realised how thin the thread of life is
That binds us.
I have also come to understand that I have no right
To leave you, as fate has usually treated you,

With words omitted or unsaid.
This particularly relates to the matter
That you always hungered to hear
And which, what can I say, this old fool
Never got to tell you.

That's right, Koppel, about our family curse.
As you have already guessed, my surname is not Cohen.
I took that name to somehow rid myself
Of the fact that you and my descendants would inevitably choose
A military destiny.[194]

You have already realised that, like a red line,
The inevitability of meeting someone who is our spitting image
Runs through the fates of our men.
That's right, the curse affects specifically the male side
So, it is unimportant

How halachic a Jew
Any given representative of our kind might be.
You might think,
And it is probably that you have,
That I am talking about a simple outward resemblance

Of warriors from past and present.
This is not the case.
I'll start from the beginning.
Our family hails from Omar,
Grandson of Esau from the Bible,

Who once, in a fit of passion, killed his own brother,
Your namesake Jacob.
The descendants of Esau gave birth to the kings of the Edomites,
But the family branch of Omar did not.
Instead, it created a dynasty of warriors

Who guarded the Edomite throne for centuries.
They also served Antipater of Edom,
Who wanted to intervene
In the feud between the Hasmonean brothers,
Aristobulus and Hyrcanus.

This terrible feud,
In the end, led to the fall of the Hasmonean dynasty,
Which gave way to the Edomite kings – Herod and his descendants.
During this civil war,

---

[194] *Cohen, Kogan, Cohanim* – priests. *Aryeh* – lion.

And you know from my tales, Koppel,

That there is nothing more terrible,
The Romans came to the country
And laid siege to Bet YHWH[195] *together with the supporters of Hyrcanus.*
Pompey's military commander Gabinius
Took the church by force.

When the Romans, the followers of Hyrcanus and Antipater's guards
Burst into the temple, they encountered
Cohanim priests holding a service,
Paying no heed to the military action going on outside.
Our progenitor Ariyeh, commander of the

Edomite guard, was among the captives.
The incensed Romans set about executing the priests.
Before killing the last of them, they gouged out his eyes.
This priest, before accepting death,
Extended his hand

And uttered the terrifying words of a curse,
Which stated that every warrior
Representing this cursed family
Will be doomed to seek his brothers, kill them and eradicate them
Until all wars on earth have come to an end.

Or until their family has disappeared from the face of the earth forever and ever and ever.

The priest was placing this curse on fighter-brother Hyrcanus,
But he had been blinded and pointed at General Aryeh as he spoke.
And that is how we became the eternal Jews of war, Koppel.
Now you understand why I was so against
Your desire to become a professional soldier.

As if, in spite of the priest's curse
In one period of history,
Our family had grown and spread all across the world.
It was later that I realised why:
So that its decline and disappearance

Would be all the more telling and terrible.
This is what I called the galut *of our family, James,*
And now you know that this is
Not a literary comparison at all.
The biblical family of Esau and his grandson Omar

Spawned many generations of warriors.
They all perished and destroyed one another with an inspiration
That any teller of tales might envy.
You have no idea, James,
The size of tree into which one family could grow.

In my last notebook
You'll find those family tree parts that I've managed to recover.

---

[195] *Bet YHWH* is the name of the church in Jerusalem, corresponding with the rules of Judaism as regards pronouncing the name of God.

Most interesting is that the trunk of this family tree
Has moved across countries, nations and continents
In such a way as to make it hard to believe

That in the 20th century, it returned to the Jewish line.
The charting of the family tree shows traces of the great empires of Persians,
Greeks and Assyrians, Turks and Arabs, Anglo-Saxons,
Slavs and Germanic peoples. Everywhere our seed has penetrated,
It has carried the stamp of that cursed feud.

However, any nation, like treating a disease,
Has always and instinctively strived to rid itself of our kith and kin,
So, not only did we destroy each other, but we were
Driven away by the immune response of new peoples
For survival in the historical arena.

Even when peacetime came,
And wars no longer scythed through military ranks,
Fate still found ways to
Rid itself of those troublemakers –
Of that family tribe of ours.

And so, by the 20th century, enriched by war and violence,
We arrived like a pitiful little branch,
Where you, grandson of mine, are most likely
The Last of the Mohicans.
What will happen if the family line stops with you? I do not know.

When the branch of my cousins Nathan and Ariel faded away,
All that was left was my family line.
Perhaps that's why fate looked after and didn't kill me.
Nathan, a member of the Jüdischer Ordnungsdienst[196] *in the ghetto of Warsaw,*
Executed his own twin brother Ariel,

Who was a member of the underground resistance.
Ariel actually outlived his brother by a little –
He disappeared without trace in the hell of Auschwitz.
And so, in the nineteen-forties,
The one to continue the family line of Esau

Was a lad from a SS Hitler Youth division.

And now for some explanations associated with those stories
That I told you in Capernaum.
Dietrich Reutermann wasn't just a German who looked like me.
His ancestors hailed from a family
That arose after Roman peregrini *from*

Syria intermixed with warriors of Alaric.
It would appear that, at some point,
They even lost the last bloodlines
Of the people from the Land of Israel.
However, the story of the Germanic descendants,

---

[196] *Jüdischer Ordnungsdienst* (German) – The Ghetto Police, a body formed to ensure order in every Jewish ghetto during the Nazi occupation of Poland.

Who shared the views of Jan Žižka and his Taborites,
Or, more accurately, their cruel feuds,
Tells us that Galut *Edom is a problem not only of the Semites.*
The descendants of the Taborites settled much later in the Czech Sudetes,
From where Reutermann hailed.

It would seem to be a very thin thread for a complete likeness.
What was most interesting though,
Was that Dietrich had the bloodlines of the Ashkenazi
Who were the descendants of the fierce Khazar warriors.
His own grandmother had been one such Ashkenazi.

As for Israel's resemblance to Enver Pasha,
It's all much simpler.
Israel's wife came from Bessarabia,
Where the great Turkish adventurer general was born.
Her grandfather was called Omar, he was the purest Gagauz,

Meaning a Turk. He even had the nickname Turk,
Which found its way into the archives.
Most interesting is that some of the best units
Of the Basmachi Davlatmand-Biy and Enver
Were Khazars – Turks from Afghanistan who had lost their dialect.

So, basically, Koppel, you understand,
We have been killing our blood brothers, always and everywhere,
Nothing short of that.
Read the diaries – you'll learn much from them
Not so much interesting as seemingly paradoxical,

And at times even impossible.
For example, like the descendant of the Altai people,
The Japanese officer Nakamura
Died in Manchuria at the hands of his blood brother Li Zicheng,
A descendant of the Altai guards of Qubilai Khan.

And they were very much alike in appearance,
A mirror image, in fact.
Or the Cossack Ermak Timofeevich stopped his sabre
When he saw that the Tatar batyr *warrior*
Was his spitting image,

For which he received a spear to the throat.
Koppel, I never believed that the brave chieftain
Had died without honour in a Siberian river.
My last notebook contains many such stories.
Simply continuing Israel's tradition,

Whom life forced to learn the Turkic and Iranian dialects,
I continued to write in Arabic letters.
So, I'll say again, learn Arabic. Learn languages,
While Babylon hasn't joined people into one
Once more.

You'll learn that, before, in different times, there are so many
Representatives of our familia *all over the world,*
But the galut *of our family, in the end, has brought us to a point*

371

Where we will soon disappear from the face of the earth.
Well, rightly so, probably, if War is to disappear with is.

And yet I implore you, James!
Don't enter the military.
According to my information, you are the last of your kind;
You no longer have anyone to raise your sword for,
And no one else's sword is rushing to meet you either.

Someone has to stop all this, right? I don't know.
Only if you find out one day,
Be sure to let me know. You know where to find me.
If I am not by your side at some war or other,
I will be watching you from up in the heavens,

Signed: *Your grandfather Solomon Ben Israel from the fading Aryeh family.*

I jumped up and fussed about the study excitedly.
'Stupid old man!' I shouted inside.
'Last of the Mohicans... Yeah, right!
And what if I have sons?
But I do have sons, twins – birth brothers!'

I collapsed in the armchair,
Because I realised
That now I didn't have sons any more.
I dropped my head into my hands and sobbed,
No, more like I wailed!

Perhaps this was the human race cleansing itself of our tribe?
Perhaps we're a symbol of something for someone?
So that people might realise something?
But seriously, do people still not understand
The senselessness and cruelty of war?!

Or perhaps my family is that bearer of this obstinate
Code of misunderstanding,
Which, time after time,
Pushes nations into taking up the sword?
Suddenly I remembered,

It had come to me and I rushed over to the computer.
No, no, old Solomon is mistaken.
I'll go to Russia and I'll find my brother.
My own brother!
After all, I am not an Aryeh, I'm an Alphaeus.

Maybe I'll have to give up my military career. Maybe I will!
I have to see my brother,
To... well, even if I don't get to sit at the same
Table to celebrate,
Then at least to warn him of the grave curse of the Cohanim of the Second Church.

I saw a message come up on my page from Anya.
Anya, you're my angel!
You were most certainly not sent to me by the black demon of war!
The message read,

James, at last!

I am so pleased to hear you're doing well!
I am forwarding a letter from your brother.
Mum's letter got lost somewhere,
But, while waiting for your reply,
I read Jacob's letter (that's your brother's name).

You're not angry with me, are you?
Anyway, in his letter, he says everything
That Mum wanted to tell you,
Only more accurately and in more detail.
It was written a long time ago

But I don't think that, since that time,
Things could have changed that much.
The letter contains all Jacob's addresses and contacts,
So I don't think you'll lose one another now
Forever and ever and ever.

I truly hope that you'll meet
And, when you do, be sure to come visit us in Russia,
So we can get to know one another,
Seeing as fate has dictated we find each other.
I am sincerely happy for you. Anna.

Impatiently, I clicked on the link to the letter
And sat down to read.
Hello, dear brother James!
This is your... I wanted to put 'uterine',
But I think I'll use 'birth' brother.

My name is Jacob, the same name as yours,
Only in Arabic. Incredible, isn't it?
I had no idea that I had a brother,
Although I never ruled out the possibility,
Because when I was very small, 'kind neighbours'

Revealed the secret of my birth to me,
Telling me I was not the son of Mama Lyubov, but her grandson,
While my real mother had left for Israel with her new husband.
I guessed that somewhere far from Tashkent
I might have a brother or a sister,

Or perhaps even several of them.
At first, I was really angry with my mother
For having abandoned me,
But then, although, not straight away,
I managed to forgive her in my heart,

My beloved Aisha was the one who help me in this.
However, let me tell you everything in order.
Hearing others talk of my father, you might think
He treated our mother unfairly
And abandoned her. This is not the case.

They really had a strong and beautiful love.

It was just that my father, Omar Al-Faiz,
Born a Palestinian,
Had been forced to abandon his studies in Moscow,
To return to Israel and bury his parents.

My grandfather on my father's side so loved my grandmother,
That when she died, he faded away quickly and passed away soon after she did.
My father was left alone and, for a long time,
He was unable not just to continue his studies,
But even get back to the Soviet Union.

However, in 1986, hearing of the death of Mama Lyubov,
He found an opportunity and the funds to come to Russia
And get me.
Only we didn't return to Israel.
For some time we lived in Europe,

In Paris and Prague,
Before moving to Lebanon.
Brother, I can't say I've had that interesting a life,
To relate it like a book.
I graduated from medical college, specialising as a paediatrician.

I got married early this millennium.
My wife's name is Aisha, as I've already written.
She, too, is Palestinian.
James, tell me honestly, you don't see us Palestinians as the enemy do you?
I know we have a long-running history of war, intifada and mutual hatred,

But I am someone far removed from politics
Although, of course, I am patriotic.
However, in our case, it would be foolish,
Having not seen one another for so many years,
To draw a red front line between us, don't you think?

Well, of course, if your convictions don't allow it...
No, James, I choose not to believe that.
I remain confident that on our earth...
On our common earth, peace will one day reign.
Perhaps people like us are the ones to ensure it does, eh?

I had a difficult relationship with my father,
Because he was, you see, an active political figure.
His entire life was devoted to the continual struggle against the occupation.
He tried to teach me from an early age
All about military matters, conspiracies and the law.

He taught me to harden body and character,
But I never got to be a warrior, although I don't regret that a bit,
Because I believe that, by healing children,
I am bringing my people just as much benefit, if not more,
Than the soldiers fighting on the political front lines.

I am not afraid to appear banal, but I will say
That I believe these children will have a different future.
Anya told me
You have an excellent command of spoken and written Russian,

Which is why I have chosen this language for my letter.

Although, as Mama Lyubov told me,
Our grandfather had an incredible grasp of many languages.
She also believed that they should be passed down to us.
I write fluently in both English and French.
But, unfortunately, I never got to learn Hebrew.

I have two sons growing up, less than a year apart.
Their names are Zaidulla and Asadulla.[197]
James, do you have children?
Aisha and I dream of meeting your wife.
When you read this letter, say a big hello from us.

Our home is in Beirut.
We are not going through the best period in our country,
But we can easily meet anywhere in Europe
Or in Russia. Or even in Tashkent!
Well, anywhere's possible; the world is such a big place.

I am writing this letter and I am so excited.
Sorry if it comes across all muddled.
Please answer as soon as you can;
We can't wait to hear from you!
After all, we are now one big familia.

We are leaving Beirut tomorrow –
Aisha wants to visit her father.
She's the youngest;
My father-in-law is really getting on now.
He wanted to see his grandsons

And he wanted some advice from me,
Seeing as I'm a doctor.
On our return, I really hope to get a reply from you.
We won't be away for long, a week or a little longer.
It's just that we are going south, to Bint Jbeil.

It's not the quietest place at the moment,
And I fear there won't be any Internet either.
The Hezbollah people have turned the south into an army camp,
But there's nothing to be done, as my father-in-law can't come to us on his own,
So we'll have to go to him.

But don't you worry – it's quite safe for me.
I am a pretty well-known doctor in my country,
So, there are people in the south who would put a word in for me.
Right, James, time to end my letter.
I won't say goodbye, rather, see you soon!

I'm thinking how best to end this letter.
Looks like I won't find anything better
Than simply writing this:
Brother, now that we've found each other,

---

[197] *Zaidulla* (Arabic) – *gift of Allah*; *Asadulla* – *lion of Allah*. The same as in Hebrew *Nathan* means *granted (from above)* while *Ariel* means *lion of God.*

Let's stay together

Forever and ever and ever.

With love,
Jacob Al-Faiz, Aisha,
Zaidulla and Asadulla.
Beirut.
                    11 July 2006.

Reading the letter, I was stunned.
But tomorrow... Tomorrow the war starts!!![198]
It's images attacked me like wild demons,
With an understanding of *what* had happened
And *how* interconnected it all was!

Who had that man been, who had extended his arms to the heavens,
Weeping over the bodies of his murdered sons?!
How could I not have noticed that fatal resemblance?!
That is who that teacher with no wish to become a warrior had been;
That was whom I had met in the Gaza Strip!

That was who had destroyed my family
And who had died by my hand!
I rose from the desk like a zombie,
Felt for my car keys
And went outside.

I don't remember how I had got to Capernaum so fast,
And why it was I had gone there specifically.
Leaving the car, I wandered over in the direction of the Church of the Apostles, but...
It had gone! It was deserted and quiet everywhere.
Again, like on that weekend I spent with Solomon,

My eyes hurt from the coloured circles.
A bright flash tore through my brain
And I collapsed to the ground, losing consciousness.
The last thing I managed to see
Through the thick mist

Was some strange people,
Bending over me.
'Who are you?' a firm and authoritative voice asked me.
'I am Azrael!' I croaked
And fell into unconsciousness.

****

Well then, James, son of Alphaeus,
What your story is is a prophecy.
Why be horrified that you're hearing about wars and unrest?
Why be astonished when nation rises up against nation,
Kingdom against kingdom?

What's surprising about

---

[198] The Second Lebanon War actually started on 12 July 2006.

376

The treachery of parents, brothers and relatives?
That they will strive to kill you?
Don't rely on a bag to protect you from the rain;
Sell it and buy yourself some clothes!

But then the earthquake will come and your clothes won't save you,
So, sell them and buy yourself a sword!
But then God will mete his punishment and your sword won't save you.
What will you leave yourself then? Your life?
But Azrael will come and you won't manage to conceal your life from him.

So give it to the Lord of Worlds, and don't haggle; thus, you'll be victorious...

Verse 28. Parables

'How do we distinguish the true feeling of our importance from a false one?' some students asked Hodja Nasreddin.
'Imagine a caravan of camels riding across the desert,' Nasreddin suggested. 'Who do you see yourself as?'
'The first camel!' one of the students exclaimed.
'The tail of the last camel,' said another.
'The merciless sun,' uttered a third.
'The driver,' proffered a fourth.
'A dune,' suggested a fifth.
'Allah, who created the desert and the caravan,' uttered a sixth.
'I am me,' declared the seventh student, 'and what have camels got to do with anything?!'

Tales of Hodja Nasreddin

They say that the angels took a dislike for man
For taking a place before the Almighty
Closer than theirs. What rubbish.
Our Beloved Friend told us what really happened.
The reason was laughter!

The angels, archangels, cherubs and other elements of the Heavenly establishment
Possessed all the power even to turn back time,
But the one thing they didn't have was the ability to laugh,
Laugh heartily till they cried,
Have fun, despite the might of thunderstorms, the elements and life's twists and turns.

But Adam could.
It is hard for us now to imagine his first laughter,
But they say he laughed for the first time when he saw
Adonai create the parrot.
'Lord,' he said, 'he mimics Iblis so,

That I will have a merry old time in the next world too.'
Iblis, though, was affronted and said that theatrics would rule the world
When the time comes.
The Almighty didn't understand, for he too didn't know how to laugh.
The second time was much worse.

Adam laughed when Eve the foremother was tempted by the snake,
But the Almighty began handing down verdicts.
Then, Adam laughed louder and said,
'Lord, you are taking a geopolitical decision
That, incidentally, has complex ramifications,

And all because a woman scoffed some fruit.
What's that – a triumph of the royal court?'
And he laughed so infectiously that Adonai
Took serious offence and cast
The human couple down to earth. And Satan with them.

To the same place.

Eve was offended, telling her husband he could have been more restrained.
But Adam replied,
'My dear, if it weren't for joy and laughter,
How would we have known that
Where we lived was actually Paradise?

379

Well, where else can one laugh if not in Paradise?'
'Well, now you'll shed tears here,' Eve said.
'But could you laugh?' However, Adam replied,
'And I'll laugh here too. Let laughter be
Our eternal reminder of that sense of life in Eden.'

When we parted with the apostles to heal and teach,
The Rabbi told us we went, 'Remember those parables
That I told you in our little circle and to others too?
Your task is to find a continuation or an addition to them.
He who find the funniest or smartest continuation

Will be rewarded with a special mission.'
The brothers went their separate ways, to Palestine and across the world
And, when they returned, the Teacher asked them,
'So, you're back after much healing and much preaching,
But have you found a continuation to My parables?'

'Yes, Rabbi,' the brothers replied. 'We found continuations for some,
But not for all, although we've found some new ones.
Do you want to hear them, Teacher?'
'Well,' the Beloved Friend said, 'if they're funny,
Then let's have a laugh.

If they're sad, let's get to thinking and feel sorrow.
And if they are neither one nor the other, well, the pots have long been in need of a wash...'
We had so missed His laughter, that we began vying with one another
To relate our findings, but He laughed
So infectiously that we were afraid

That Adonai might banish us from this paradise of companionship.
Or that some foolish angel, flying past,
Might recall some ancient, cross-species affront.
However, everything passed without esoteric rage,
And I now recall that time with tears in my eyes, but tears from a smile.

'First,' the Beloved Teacher said, 'let's discuss
Why we need to speak in parables at all when addressing people.
Before, I said to you myself
That only you are the ones to hear and understand.
Therefore, it turns out that we deliberately limit

The circle of those who understand; those we can address with parables,
Leaving for everyone else a sermon as straight as an arrow.
The human heart has hardened, you see, but it is not that that's so important
When there were lighter times in human history,
So as not to put the best human qualities to the test.

Another important thing is will hearts, souls and minds continue
Their search for the Kingdom of Heaven and Divine Justice
Or have they stopped and submitted themselves to the rules
That are created by the ruling human pseudo-justice
That is prevalent in today's society at large?

If that is the case, is it not all in vain?
That, though, is too broad a question; let's return to the parables,

The need for them and the timely nature of our coming together
With different people in our Path in life, from different strata and classes
And, incidentally, from different cultures and even times.'

'Allow me to speak first,' Judas said.
'Proverbs are priceless and often more important than those straight-as-an-arrow sermons.
That's because a sermon gives direct prompts.
It's a kind of high-handed, dictatorial address, particularly
When conveying God's will or perhaps interpreting and deciphering it.

Let's class the sermon as pure and formulated knowledge
That appears when a prophet, herald or preacher
Has managed to bring previous experience together,
And I mean not only earthly, but heavenly experience too.
Or when the prophets broadcast the will of the Lord

Either as an interpreted narrative,
Or by being direct mediums of His Divine Will.
In all these cases, we are talking about true sermons,
Not about those that are shackled by the political climate.
Therefore, it is also important who the preacher is.

Generally, pure knowledge has the right to take the form of a monologue.
A parable, on the other hand, means joining
The one you are telling it to
To the eternal, endless search for the Truth,
Elevating the value of the very process of this search.

A parable can present hundreds or even an infinite number
Of interpretations or levels of understanding, but, most important,
It can lead to conclusions that are the polar opposite of those
That were in the mind of the narrator.
This is why the genre is phenomenal and so ingenious.

Take, for example, the story of a certain mullah,
Who was reading sermons in the mosque. One day, the mullah noticed
That one man would always weep during his sermons.
"Such elevated feelings must arise from my words,"
The preacher thought and he asked the man tenderly

Why he wept so bitterly and so sincerely every time;
Was it not for love for the Almighty, brought about by the sermons?
The man replied that he loved and revered Allah,
But that was not why he was weeping. It was just that he had had a quite charming goat,
Which he had cherished, nourished and nurtured.

Recently, however, wolves had devoured his beloved goat.
The man was now looking at the mullah's beard and weeping,
For his goat had had the same beautiful beard
And it had trembled just as delightfully
As the venerable mullah's beard trembled when he delivered his sermon...'

Everyone laughed, but our Beloved Friend the Teacher said,
'That's a wonderful story, Judas, and very instructive too.
It would appear that this could be a lesson for the preacher
(And it is relevant for us, brethren),
That his self-admiration had taken him so far

From the worries of this simple man, that he had basically forgotten
To whom he was dedicating his sermon.
So, how successful was he in his role as a servant of God,
Who should never ever forget us,
While this prattler clean forgot?

However, there is another side to this parable, you're right, Judas,
About the many levels of understanding.
You see, this simple man didn't insult the mullah, quite the opposite:
He called him most honoured and told him his beard was beautiful.
It was simply, perhaps, that this preacher

Was a true master of his craft.
When he spoke of Allah the Almighty
With inspiration, passion and true Love,
He was able to light a true fire of the tenderest and
Most wonderful thoughts in the parishioner's heart,

Which had been looking for an emotional escape
And which, primarily, had wanted to catch hold of certain clear images
That this poor man must have had.
Evidently, this lad was poor and unfortunate,
For his only joy in life had been that goat

Whom he had loved, truly and deeply, alone
In this cruel, wicked world.
The poor man's imagination went through numerous images:
His nagging wife, cruel employer,
His greedy and ungrateful children and his hypocritical neighbours.

It was only the image of his silent, loyal friend
That in all that was worthy of that beautiful flower
That the sermon about our Beloved God, delivered by the master, had aroused.
And is he or the mullah really guilty for this
Poor man finding the true and devoted love of a friend

In a creature as ugly for many as a goat?
And is that mullah not a skilled master if he
Was able, based on psychoanalysis and commendable words
To find that key to Love, of which that poor man could once never even have imagined?
And did his beard not play the wonderful role as that key?'

The Beloved Teacher smiled and everyone applauded.
Some even wiped away tears, Simon included,
Who muttered, *Adonai, so many poor folk*
All across Galilee. And so few prophets
Capable of generating tears, and not from cruelty either.

'I think,' said John, 'that the main wealth in a proverb
Is its understated nature and its semantic *sfumato*, if you will,
Constituting the very essence of Truth; its incomprehensibility
Which, at times, is absolute.
Therefore, a perfect parable must encompass

All levels of understanding of the existent and the transcendental,
Reflecting one of the designs of the Lord,

382

According to which, if He actually wanted
To make everything make perfect sense to us,
He would simply have sat down and told it all to us clearly and concisely.

But He didn't do that and He won't either
Even in the Holy Qur'an, which contains the essence of his lines on the creation.
That's because, with the advent of total expression,
It's not so much the mystery of hidden meanings that disappears
As it is Love, for if you speak about Love in full clarity

That would generally lead to its demise.

Love, like happiness, is a fleeting second of unity with God,
For which we aim and aspire
And after which we ponder and recollect.
So, basically, a parable is beautiful and wondrous
When it is uttered at the right time, in context and in the right situation.

For example, one day, Molla Nasreddin[199] met a friend of his
Who asked if Nasreddin had plans to marry.
Molla then told him how he had been looking for a partner in life.
"First of all, she must be a complete woman in every respect,"
Nasreddin had thought and headed for Damascus.

In Damascus, he had found a girl of heavenly beauty,
But deemed her insufficiently developed spiritually.
And so, he had set off to search some more.
In Isfahan, he had met a most spiritual woman
Who was also of unearthly beauty, but her character had left much to be desired.

Finally, in Cairo, Nasreddin had found her:
An ideal individual, a wonderful girl who was perfection itself...
"So, you married her?" his friend asked impatiently.
"No," Molla replied. "Unfortunately,
She was looking for the perfect man herself.'"

'John, Bravo!' everyone cried, the Teacher included.
'Your story is perfection itself!
How beautifully it conveys the dangers of the mirage
And the fleeting nature in searches for true Love and happiness.
How wonderfully it speaks of the twists and turns in the Path

In the search for Perfection!'
'Someone,' the Beloved Friend said, 'sees in this only the vanity
Of man and woman, who believe that they are worthy of only
The best of the best and, for not one second
Do they have any doubt in their aspirations.

Someone might see an entire story about a lord and master,
Who seeks perfect methods for governing a country,
But who ends up being cut off from his own people.
Another will see their Path to God in everything,
Where the most important thing is not *what* you're seeking, but who *you* are!

---

[199] Molla Nasreddin, Nasreddin Efendi, Apendi, Kozha Nasyr – all variations of the name Hodja Nasreddin, the famous character from Eastern parables and legends. It is generally accepted that the collected tales of Hodja Nasreddin make up the Book of Teachings of the Sufis, Muslim mystics.

Now, this story has a worthy continuation, John.
There was once a man called Toksan-Biy[200], who was a great orator.
He had never known defeat in any dispute. One day his students
Asked him, "Has there really never been a time
When you accepted the arguments put before you?"

The *biy* laughed and told them this story:
His kin had long been seeking a suitable partner for the sage,
But they could not find a bride worthy of this distinguished man.
The women, now on their last legs, often courted anyone
If only to maintain their level of application.

One day, a match was found for Toksan-biy from the neighbouring aul.
The girl was completely unknown, but the judge decided
That he wanted to meet her first, before
The official brokers were sent.
He set off for the next village and asked for the girl to be brought to him.

The lass proved a plain creature who did not correspond at all
To the criteria that the relatives had proposed in the first place.
Moreover, the *biy* didn't take a liking to her at all and he said
He wouldn't marry her for anything and instructed her to get out
In a rather rude manner, angry more at his matchmakers

And the old women for their unnecessary zeal.
However, the girl remained where she was and simply asked
To say something.
"Speak," Toksan-biy instructed.
"You have probably dreamed and asked of Allah," the girl said,

"To match you with a girl
Who was a wonderful person,
Outstanding in something and worthy, is that not so?
Well, I have dreamed of the very same.
Your dream has not come true, but mine has,

And I will not back down, whatever might happen!"

"That same young girl – is standing here before you,"
The judge finished his story with a laugh and
Embraced his wife, who was sitting by his side.
"We have lived together now for many, many years.
And all because, just the once, I was not as persuasive,

While she was.
And my one defeat
Actually proved to be my victory.
Most important, however, was that this victory
Was not something that I had been striving for at that time.'"

'If we set aside the purely loving context of the two stories,'
Levi Matthew spoke,
'And view it through the lens of striving towards a Beloved God,
Then this parable might mean that it doesn't matter

---

[200] *Biy* (Kazakh) – a judge.

Who you proved to be at the start of your Path or how many your sins and errors.

Most important is to be suitably prepared
For the ephemeral moment when you achieve your dreams
So you can display your confidence before the most confident
Become the best speaker before the best speaker,
As was the case with that girl.

And only the sincerity of motives and convictions in this moment
Will tell you *what*, at this precise moment,
Is the most important thing and where the keys are.
Because it is beyond this door of a moment that life diverges
Into a million different directions, only one of which

Is your life that is your own.

And that anyone can do this, not necessarily just those with
Superpowers and the seal of a genius,
And you don't need any special mythical greatness either.
And, against the backdrop of this story, how frightening
Those who are destined to change their dream appear,

Given the simple insignificance of humanity.'

Everyone fell into thought and, for a time,
The silence over our fire was such
That even the usually impudent desert wind
Seemed to have asked permission to pass between us,
But no one granted this permission.

'What I particularly like in the parables,' Thomas said pensively,
'Is that you often encounter an infinite variety of
Logic chains, which often, in their last link,
Turn out to be quite unconnected to the original assertions,
Which, at the beginning of the parable, seemed indisputable.

We are not even talking about a strict logical sequence here,
Rather about a variability in the development of plots,
Which arise both from the situation *after*
The plot of the parable has unfolded,
And from what could have been *before* and in what situational surroundings.

Right here is a real depository for exercises,
Not only for the mind and its ability to think logically,
But for the imagination, able to expand four phrases
Into a picture of the general against a backdrop of the particular,
And not restricting yourself, even in the number of known measurements.

Here is one story I heard:

A scholar once asked Hodja Nasreddin,
 "What is fate in your opinion?"
Hodja replied, "It is an endless sequence
Of interconnected events, each
Influencing the other in a completely unpredictable way."

The scholar frowned, "That is a pseudo-scientific

385

And, I'd even say, unsatisfactory answer.
I am sure that fate has a neat,
Cause-and-effect link,
A logic that is clearly traceable in everything."

"All right," Hodja said, "you see this procession?
They are going to hang a man.
Is it because he is a good singer
And that he was given a silver coin for that?
And that he used that coin to buy a knife

And robbed a grocery shop?
Or is it because someone saw him do it?
Or because there was no one in this society
Who could stop him?
Or is it, all the same, that he's being hanged because he's a good singer?"'

'Quite right, Thomas. Very smart,' the Teacher said
After a pause for thought.
'Modern science and computers based on probability theory
Will very soon prove that the history of this robber
Without doubt, contains a cause-and-effect link.

And the scholar, it would seem, should prevail.
However, taking into account the multiplicity of measurements,
In which this parable was told,
We can boldly state that this story is by no means about the gallows,
But it might be about the society in which poor folk are doomed to the gallows,

However they might see themselves
And whatever the singing talents they might have.
Or perhaps it's about the indifference of people
Who indeed did nothing to stop the criminal.
Not literally, of course,

Rather in the sense that all the conditions are there
Whereby he has no alternative means of finding food.
But perhaps it's about the fact that everyone has a choice
As to where they can spend that silver coin.
Or perhaps there really is no choice at all!

After all, if there is a root to the phenomenon, then what's the difference
What coin he spent on the knife,
Be it earned from singing or, the next day,
From a handout, at a building site or money he's simply found on the street?
Or perhaps he was paid specially to rob a competitor

With the offered coin or with sweet talking that clouded his judgement?
Most important, however, whatever the probability theories
And whatever the supercomputers that predict how events will unfold,
Who today can accurately
Predict all the finer points and the twists of fate?

Although it is thought that the Almighty holds our lives in His hands,
Are all the cause-and-effect relationships
Of everyone's fates really so transparent for Him?
And in any case, logic is the domain of man, what he says and thinks,

Or is it also inherent in the Divine?'

'I heard one wise man once say,'
Interjected Bartholomew.
'Only a fool looks for cause and effect
In the same tale.
Therefore, it is not the logical variability that attracts me in the parables.

The most amazing thing in this genre is
That everyone finds their own Truth in them!
On the one hand, this speaks of the infinite variability of the truth,
While, on the other, that there is in fact only one truth...
Or is that not the case?!

For example, one day, Nasreddin Efendi was standing by a well,
Scooping water, ladle by ladle, into a jug with no bottom.
Scholars drew Nasreddin's attention to the fault in the jug,
To which Efendi responded,
"I am trying to fill the jug,

To see the moment when it becomes full.
To do this, I am fixed on the rim of the jug, not its bottom.
When I see that the water is full to the brim,
I will see it as full.
Then, perhaps, the time will come to think about the jug's bottom."'

'But that is madness!' Peter exclaimed. 'It's an attempt at quasi-wisdom
To form a parable based on pure paradox!
It's outrageous and it has literally no meaning!'
'Calm down, Cephas,' the Teacher said with a cough,
'And don't rush into making conclusions.

You've perceived clear images too directly,
Without stopping to think that this parable might actually be about the jug.
Tell us, Philip, as a teacher,
When you pour the water of knowledge into your students,
Ladle after ladle, are you thinking about the bottom of these vessels?

Do you think that the jug could be filled
In a second by simply lowering it straight into the well?
But is that what the teaching process is about?
And not in looking into the students' eyes, day after day,
Waiting for the neck to fill with water?

And even then, when they leave the *cheder* and then the *yeshiva*[201],
Does the filling process ever end for them?
And who is the central character in this parable? The jug?
The missing bottom or is it actually the water?
Or is it the students who have placed the teacher's intelligence in doubt?

There could also be the following interpretation:
The teacher was indeed deep in thought and didn't notice
That the vessel had no bottom.
He was thinking and this thought was just as bottomless,

---

[201] *Cheder* – a Jewish religious primary school; *yeshiva* – a Jewish religious institution for higher education.

That he had become lost in it,

Feeling total enjoyment from the work of his mind.
The clueless students had interrupted this stream of enjoyment.
The teacher was disappointed that he had not formulated his conclusions
And he reprimanded them for distracting him from his thoughts of the Almighty.
He would find the time for them, only without ever taking him away from God.

And tell me honestly, Cephas, what gives you pleasure
Right now, from this conversation we're having –
The thought that water will pour forever,
Or actually that everything wonderful has a bottom, an end,
Which ensures its finitude?

Or is it, all the same, that you, like Nasreddin Efendi,
Had concentrated on the neck of the vessel,
And the thought that the water would eventually reach it at some point
Would cause you pain of something coming to an end?
So, do you wish for a bottom to our jug?

You see, it is actually a story of Love.
Who ever thinks, when they marry their Beloved,
That they'll ever part or there'll come an end when death will part them forever?
Don't the lovers look at the neck,
Fearfully doing away with the image of the end, as a condition of infinitude,

Relying on the image of the bottomless jug as a symbol of Eternal Love?

That's enough for today, brothers,'
The Beloved Teacher added wearily.
'It is time to sleep or turn to night-time thoughts.
You've told some wonderful stories;
Each of them shall start to live in you and in me too.'

Everyone parted, some wiping away tears, others smiling,
Others going to sleep, another noisily settling down
To get a better view of the stars.
I wished the Teacher a good night and he smiled mischievously
In the dark and said,

'One day, Nasreddin felt
His wife shaking him by the shoulder.
"Wake up," she said.
"Leave me in peace," Hodja moaned. "What you call *wake up*,
Is what I call *go to sleep*."'

*****

The next day, once again,
Everyone gathered round the fire,
Loudly gesticulating and arguing with one another.
However, when the Beloved Teacher approached,
Everyone fell silent in a true tremor of anticipation.

'Brothers, you remember the parable of the sower,
That I told you and the people by the sea.
Behold, a sower went out to sow. And as he sowed, some seed

Fell along the path, and the birds came and devoured it.
Other seed fell on rocky ground,

And only a few seeds managed to sprout.
The few shoots that made it through
Were flattened by the wind and wilted under the sun,
For their roots were not strong enough.
Other seed fell among thorns, and the weeds grew up and choked it

Even though it had reached for the sunlight and fought as best it could.
Only the seed that fell into good soil
Produced grain and gave food to the people.
Have you found parables like this amidst human wisdom?
Have you been able to further and deepen its meanings

While we've been apart?'
'Teacher,' Peter spoke up, 'what you've told us
Is so perfect that could it really require
Addition or amendment?
Is this parable not destined to pass through the centuries as it is?'

Some of the pupils nodded, some murmured
As if disagreeing with Cephas.
But the Beloved Teacher placed
His hand tenderly on Peter's shoulder and said,
'Cephas, whom are you denying development –

The parable? Me? Or human wisdom?'
'I am by no means against creative thinking and development,'
Cephas muttered. 'It's just that the original
Is always much better than the subsequent.
Now, it (the subsequent) always carries a risk of distorting meanings.

Others are so intent on improving the original
That they become more interested in the very process of the transformation
And not the essence of what is being said at all.
This is what one ancient wise man once said:
It is hardest of all to teach three kinds of people –

Those who are delighted that they have achieved something,
Those who, having learned something, have become depressed
Once they realise what their mind had been deprived of before,
And those who are so preoccupied with a desire to progress
That they have stopped sensing their development altogether.

Are these not words of wisdom, Teacher?'
'They are indeed words of wisdom, Cephas, but are they not worthy of development
Of the image of the seed that fell on stony ground?
You yourself used your parable about the ancient wise man
To confirm that an idea that has stopped growing

Is nothing more than a seed choked
By the wind, sun and weeds.
Don't you forget that to feed the people with knowledge
You'll need more than one harvest;
You'll need an hourly operation of body and mind.

Then, rejoicing in the one
Who's become the prototype sprouted seed on the good earth,
Will we forget those whom fate has cast to the stony ground
And smeared across the road of life?
Even if they themselves are at fault?

It will be very easy to deal with those who hear
And those who see, but turn away from and confine to oblivion
The tax collectors and sinners, tyrants and hypocrites.
What is the point of saving the saved?
Do we not go out onto the Road to gather up what's been lost?

Did our Sower not love and care tenderly for
All the grain in the same way, indiscriminately,
Before he began his work?
When all the seed lay in a single sack,
Could He have seen that one would fall on stony ground and another into the weeds?

And should we not, at the cost of our lives,
Take as many of the cleansed and those who strive for the good earth
With us to the Kingdom of Heaven?'
'Now, listen here, brethren,' the Zealot said, his eyes sparkling,
'To what I once heard at an Indian bazaar.

During a flood, neighbours said
To a man with a sack of wheat
On his back, "Discard your useless load
And save yourself!"
The man replied:

"If I discard what seems useless now
But will be the most important thing in the future,
Saving my life loses all value."'
'So you see,' the Teacher nodded, 'the experienced peasant farmer
Knew that only part of the seed would fall onto good earth,

But he was concerned about saving the entire sack of grain.
Thus, the Almighty sows prophets around the world
Not to divide us into four parts,
Dooming three of the four to perish
Among the sands, rocks, sins and temptations.'

'But then,' Thomas said, 'this is what I find hard to understand:
Where, then, is the moment when the seed itself, meaning,
Allegorically, man, makes its decision?
It turns out that we are simply dependent on the hand of the Sower,
Passively waiting for a fortunate chance to miss weed and rock.'

'Oh, I have an interesting parable about this!'
Said Thaddeus, animated.
'One day, Hodja Nasreddin, when he was young,
Studied under one old man,
Who believed he had comprehended the highest wisdom of the universe.

One evening, he gathered his pupils together and declared thoughtfully,
"We should not address Allah in our prayers with requests.
In so doing, you embody your disagreement

With the harmony of the world
In which the Almighty gives everyone what they deserve.

Instead of feeling humbled
In the face of the order of things,
You sow doubt in yourself
In the higher Divine Justice.
And this is a sin of pride and vanity, expressed in

Your demand to have more than you deserve."
Three days later, the wise man had to cross
A frozen river in the middle of a harsh winter.
Hodja Nasreddin was by his side.
Suddenly, the old man fell through an unnoticed ice hole

And cried out for help to Hodja
Who was standing nearby.
"What's with all the shouting, teacher?"
Nasreddin asked the old man.
"Are you not trying to destroy the harmony

Of the order of things with that loud shouting of yours?"
He extended his hand to the old man, who grabbed hold of it right away.'
Everyone laughed, but the Teacher said, 'That's right, Thaddeus.
He who sees life in all its sin and temptation
As the triumph of an unshakable world order

Shifts the responsibility from himself to that world order,
Preferring to slowly sink into the cold ice hole of evil.
Hodja Nasreddin was merely a man standing nearby.
He cannot stand by every ice hole.
But the Almighty is not a man. He can.

And he whose eyes don't agree to see a stone before them
And whose ears have no wish to accept the rustling of the weeds,
Will always extend a hand to save a spirit
And show the way to fertile lands.
Humility and stoicism are notions from a wholly different context.'

'There is one more parable,' Thomas said, grinning mysteriously.
'It concerns grain as grain and perhaps as an allegory too.
One day, Hodja Nasreddin was standing in front of his house,
Scattering grains of rice.
His neighbours approached him and asked,

"Hodja, what on earth are you doing?!"
"I am driving the tigers away," came the reply.
"But there are no tigers here and there never have been!"
The neighbours cried.
"Then it's a very effective solution, wouldn't you say?"'

Even the gloomy Zealot had to laugh.
The teacher, wiping away tears, gave Thomas a poke.
Then, when everyone had calmed down, he said,
'This is such a good story and so much deeper
Than it is funny at first glance,

That one just doesn't want to dispel its charm
Among the nuts and bolts of semantic analysis.
Leaving it without discussion, we would not be making that much of a mistake,
For is a wonderful mood not
One of the aims in cleansing the spirit?

Does the stern and overly serious face of the righteous man
Not inspire more trust?
Even if he is to face hardship and ordeal,
Or perhaps even martyrdom?
Will no one want to see a *passionate*

Desire of young people to live in our laughter?'

Silence reigned over the fire and I shot a glance over the brothers,
Trying to glean what was going on inside them.
And there was much to see: embarrassment, sadness, even fear,
But what had changed after having been apart
Was that no doubt remained.

'You know, Beloved Teacher of ours,'
Bartholomew sheepishly broke the silence,
'You see, not everything depends on the person alone
And his philosophy on life.
Remember your parable about the wheat and tares,

When evil sowed tares
Among the good wheat.
After all, that means that evil isn't simply present when we have a choice;
It is active and decidedly energetic.
You see, in your parable, as many weeds grew

As wheat so that, as the keeper of the house said,
Nothing should be touched for the time being
For fear of pulling the wheat up
With the weed, roots and all.
That means one needs not only an active philosophy in life

But an ability to distinguish between wheat and tares too, right?'
'You know, Bartholomew, my friend,' the Teacher replied,
'Let's leave the discussion about an active life philosophy
To one side for now; it is not quite the thing
That determines those who truly hear and see.

But it is worthwhile talking about the craft of evil.
James of Alphaeus, do tell your parable
About the thief and the little man.'
James moved closer to the fire
And began his tale in detail but with emotion.

'I heard this tale a very long way from here.
This is the story of a little man
Who was such a religious fanatic
That he even saw his short stature
As a Divine reward.

That said, he could not find any use

For his height, however hard he tried.
One day, a stout fellow approached him
And said, "I am the greatest thief in all Cusco,
In fact in all the Inca Empire.

And you are so small; what use have you found in that?
I could turn you into the nimblest acrobat,
Who could get into places
That no ordinary human could ever imagine."
At first the little man was vexed,

Then embarrassed and agitated,
But then he grew more interested in the thief's proposal;
The fanatic's vanity then became
A desire to rise above others and hold them in contempt.
He agreed and the thief began his training.

Day after day, he revealed more and more
Skills to the little man in how
To overcome all manner of obstacles.
The thief skilfully manipulated the fanatic's ambitions,
Using a combination of praise and honest flattery

Making the little man no longer able
To do without the criminal's company.
Time passed and the little man
Achieved such success
That he had no equal in Cusco or even anywhere in the Empire.

The time came for his test,
Which would secure the status quo once and for all.
The thief proposed that, at night,
The little man should rob none other than
The palace of the supreme Inca ruler,

Impossible for a simple man to enter
Without being noticed by the vigilant guards.
However, the objective of overcoming this vigilance,
In the eyes of the little man,
Eclipsed all else, for he hungered to be recognised as the best.

"In the centre of the Sapa Inca throne room[202],"
The thief said to the ambitious young man,
"There is a ruby *Tawantinsuyu* Sun Symbol on a pedestal.
The name of the one who takes it
Will be forever recorded in the annals of history.

The thieves ascended the fortress walls and made their way into
The throne room, but when they drew closer
To the pedestal, where the treasure had stood,
Two lights suddenly lit up

---

[202] *Sapa Inca* (Quechua) – The supreme Inca or, more precisely, the *Only Inca* – the name given to the Emperor of the Inca Empire. *Tawantinsuyu* can be translated as *Four United Provinces* and is the full name of the country of the Incas in the Quechua language. *Ucha lachak* – an Incan secretary or scribe. *Supay* – the god of death and demons, ruler of the underworld Ukhu Pacha.

To illuminate the Throne Room, in the centre of which,

Surrounded by nobles and *willaq umu* priests
Sat the incomparable Sapa Inca himself, who, in a wrathful voice,
Demanded an explanation for the event.
"Your highness," the thief addressed the monarch meekly.
"I would like to remind you that but six months ago

I was granted a pardon by your generosity
After I spoke in my defence
That my poverty and destitution from early childhood
Made me become a thief but that even the most
Religious of men, in whom the dark demon

Supay resides, could too become a thief.
You released me on the condition
That I transform an honest man into a thief
And bring him before you.
I know that you uttered those words as an aside

And then forgot your demand.
I was told this by the head of police, who
Told me to leave while my head was still in its place,
And that no one needed my evidence.
But I didn't forget. For me, this became like

A matter of principle.
And I found such a person,
Who saw himself has the luckiest creation of the Sun God.
Only on the basis that his biography
Began from childhood on blessed and bountiful lands.

And now I have brought him here. Here he is,
Standing and greedily staring at the Holy Sun Symbol.
I persuaded Ucha Iachak in advance
And he arranged this entourage,
To perform everything to the greatest effect,

And to ensure there could be no doubt
That I have fulfilled my promise.
The Throne Room was filled with cries
Of indignation and outrage from the priests and nobles
But, with a decisive gesture, Sapa Inca

Demanded silence and then spoke:
"My friends, I understand your outrage and disgust.
But believe me, this lesson was worth the effort.
After all, it is truly a miracle that this thief proved honest enough
To keep his word, something, I must admit, I had not really demanded.

But this religious fanatic here has proved
Dishonest enough and suitably lacking in spirit
Such that he not only lost his devotion to himself
But, by changing himself fundamentally,
Succumbed to the temptation and became a dedicated thief!'"

'Well, I am prepared to argue,' Thomas said,

When James had finished his tale,
'That this parable, in its meaning, is the same
As the one that the Teacher told us
About the wheat and the tares growing together.

We don't see the beneficial grain here,
Only the interaction of dark forces.
After all, the thief did not shed light on the truth through a clear sermon,
Rather, he applied his black charms,
To destroy, not enlighten another person.

This is nothing but a dispute between a dandelion weed and his fellow nettle!'
'You are mistaken here, Thomas, and you're contradicting yourself,'
Bartholomew said, waving his arms about.
'You said yourself before that parables
Draw you in with the beauty of their conjecture on

What "might have been before" and what "might come afterwards".
Did the thief not teach Sapa Inca a lesson
That not everything is just, safe and well in his state,
Where the destitute and spiritually poor are doomed to a path of crime,
In the face of the direct condoning by conceited fanatics?

Can't you see the stunning image of Ucha Iachak here,
Risking his neck and career
And who was the first (!) to truly appreciate the thief's lesson,
To allow the monarch and nobles to be woken in the middle of the night
For the sake of such an extravagant form of report

About the true state of affairs in his state?!
How could you not see the symbols of the good grain here?'
'I am still thinking,' said James, son of Zebedee,
'That this is an excellent addition to the Teacher's parable
But not so much because of the images of the rulers.

I think that the main meaning and the harmony are in the fact
That far more important in the Path is not so much
Who you are at the beginning, a shoot of wheat or a nettle.
What is important is who you turn out to be in the end.
The householder who forbade the weeding of the wheat at the start

Knew that not every shoot of wheat
Would reach the end of the Path as a slender, full-fledged ear.
The evil spirit of Iblis might enter any of them,
Any of them might stop striving to reach the sun
And start drinking the juice of the neighbouring ear,

Thus transforming into an evil weed.
He knew that not every professional and wise man
Would be able to see the wheat in a green tuft of grass.
Sure, in a professional sense, he would discern the majority,
But doesn't *everyone* have value for the Kingdom of Heaven?

And that it is criminal to speak of admissible and objective losses,
On the Path to Perfection,
As if there is not a soul behind
Every green shoot, although without it, we will not arrive perfect,

For the absence of just one will make us flawed.

Flawed, not because we are missing a finger or a fingernail,
But because we have accepted this loss in our souls.
Therefore, separating tares from wheat should take place
Specifically for the harvest – the Judgment Hour,
When everyone will be either bound and burned

Or placed in the Lord's granary.
As for the methods... Well, they are varied
And what is important is not how you reach your goal.
What is important is that you achieve *it*,
Specifically it.

Here's a parable I heard in distant lands:

There was once a young master swordsman.
He had defeated all famous opponents
And his teacher told him that he could teach him nothing more,
But, if he wished to perfect his craft further,
It would be best for him to find the famous master Miyamoto Musashi.

However, the great master greeted the student coldly.
He gave him a sword and instructed him to go and chop wood.
The lad spent a year doing this,
On each occasion asking his teacher when he would
Teach him the way of the sword.

To this Miyamoto Musashi would say something indistinct in reply.
After a year, the student posed his question
To the teacher more insistently.
The master looked in surprise at the lad,
As if he was seeing him for the first time. He said,

"Ah, it's you... go and fetch me some water."
To carry the water to the house, the student had
To cross a stream over a narrow rope bridge,
Which shook, spilling half of the water from the bucket.
Every time the lad brought anything less

Than a full bucket, the teacher would beat him with a stick,
Each time telling him he was an idiot for bringing so little.
Another two years went by in this manner and, at the end of the third,
The student implored the teacher to teach him the way of the sword.
Then Musashi told him, "Go and cross that abyss over that log there."

The lad went over to the edge, frowned and said,
"I am afraid!" Then the master laughed and told him to sit down and listen.
"The main principle in martial arts," he began,
"Lies in the unity of three principles:
Shin is the mind, *waza* is technique and *tai* is the body.

Upon an encounter, a developed technique beats a developed body;
If a developed technique and mind meet, then the mind will win.
When you had only just arrived, I saw instantly
That your strike was not strong enough but you achieved this
In a year by chopping thick firewood with your slender sword.

Then I saw that your movement technique was weak
And you are not in constant readiness to strike.
Then you started walking over the narrow bridge,
Receiving a beating from me for spilling water.
That was how you trained in both things.

Now all you have left is to focus your mind
And think why you're afraid of walking along a log,
When you've spent the last two years running over narrow ropes."
The student got up, easily ran along the log and then realised
That, at that moment, he had perfected the way of the sword.'

'What a wonderful story,' the true warrior
Simon the Zealot whispered in awe.
'I've had to train beardless recruits in the legion
And you are always aware that any mistake you make
Is a scar on his body or, worse, a funeral for a mother to prepare.

I am willing to swear that to avoid this,
Truly any methods are right if they save lives.
And yes, I will not agree with you either, Thomas,
That the thief's methods stem from some dark forces.
That's not because any methods are good,

For otherwise we'll say that the end justifies the means,
And this is outright cynicism. It's not about that.
It's just that monarchs and school masters have been described here.
They are indeed well-versed in the arsenal of influencing minds.
And yet, at first, it was all about a poor thief.

Here's a question:
How come this poor soul,
Who'd lived his life in the embrace of evil,
Knew of other methods? Who taught him?
However, the moment his honour was on the line,

He realised that this was the only way to redeem himself.
He gathered in his fist everything he had and took the risk.
After all, this fanatic could have handed him straight over to good people
Like a decent, upstanding sort.
But the baseness in him was too overwhelming and he turned himself into a lowlife.'

'All the same, I believe that there have not been enough arguments just yet
To draw a line under the matter of methods,'
Levi Matthew joined the discussion.
'I am talking about when you place yourself
At the centre of a situation with your aim,

While making another the instrument
And the means for your own purification.
That's one side of the matter.
The other is this: what if the little man had not met the thief on the way
Who then exposed him

And displayed what he was actually like on the inside?
What's important in the story of the thief and the fanatic

Is that the little man believed himself to be a full-fledged member of society,
Perhaps even a part of its foundation.
This took place because Satan, living in his heart,

Remained invisible to others and,
Therefore, inaccessible, enabling the Greedy One
To carry on with his dark deeds for years at his leisure,
Hidden behind the mask of a wholly decent, common man.
As a rule it is they who make up the majority in society,

Exchanging their feigned decency
For the right to be a right bastard inside.
And society tolerates them, of course it does.
Well, they might have views that are a bit radical,
They might be a little brusque and not that tall.

No matter, we all have the right, you know, and all that.
Only when the concentration of these fanatical shorties
Reaches a certain level in society,
The black swastikas start to appear
And I don't mean the Buddhist ones either.

And then it turns out that there is no need for these trolls
To sport such a decent, bourgeois-looking air.
Not only can they now spit in your face when out and about,
But they can form whole detachments of associates
And pass down orders from on high to destroy you.

And all because, well, because they never met
Such a conscientious criminal on the way?!
It turns out that such behind-the-scenes bastards
Exist all thanks to our benevolent consent
And agreement, is that it? Or should I say appeasement?!

To our conscious reluctance to look
Into that inner world of dragons that live next door?!
And although I'm not prepared to recognise this thief as a redeeming hero,
I will speak out in his favour
And retract the argument about his egocentrism.

Bartholomew is most likely right when he says
That there could have been an "after-story";
I am merely guessing that there was a "before-story",
By imagining which I can assume
That the thief spent a long time searching for a man

With true darkness in his soul,
Whom not only could be, but had to be
Exposed, but punished, too
For his evil and conscious cultivation of Satan
In the soul – in the field that God granted to you.

After all, it is behind such sophisticated mimicry
That the poisoned ears of wheat are hidden,
Outwardly the same as cereal crops, but in fact, just weeds.
You detect that not when you're gathering the harvest,
Rather when you eat the rancid, poisonous bread.

And talking of egocentrism... It's all much simpler;
Here's a short parable for you.
One man, in his self-improvement, had reached a point
When he was prepared to part with all his property
And become a wandering dervish, devoted to the Road.

He went out, found the first person he met –
And this was a beggar by the Central Mosque –
And he gave him everything, even exchanging his decent robe
For the rags of that unknown vagrant.
And then he set off, happy and content.

He wandered for many years until he reached Khurasan
And saw a white silhouette of Al-Khidr[203] himself,
The dervish, delighted to have met the Ideal Interlocutor,
Who would be the crowning glory of his quest,
Rushed toward the old man in white.

However, the nearer he came,
The heavier and more unsteady his legs became.
And when he had but three steps to go,
The poor man collapsed, devoid of all strength
And wept bitterly.

"What is the matter, my son?" Al-Khidr asked him.
"I have only just realised, oh, wise one, that, many years ago,
When saving myself, I killed another," the dervish replied.
And, through the bitter veil of tears, he failed to see
The prophetic old man disappear in the mirages of the desert.'

'Speaking of methods, you recalled only the thief's methods, Levi,'
Philip interjected and stirred the coals in the fire with a stick.
'But you forgot the methods of Miyamoto Musashi.
When I was listening to the story about him and his student,
I was tormented by doubt:

Why did the Master conceal from his pupil what he wanted him to achieve?
Why did he not make him a conscious participant in the process?
The same goes for the thief – did he have the chance to talk
That little man round?
Influence him again with a sermon

And call on the last of the good
That perhaps remained in his soul?
After all, you have just sentenced one man
To final obduration – is this the work of our hand?
And what about the fact that the Lord values each and every one of us,

Like grains in the sack of a peasant, fleeing the flood?
You see, our Beloved Teacher spoke about the Judgment of God,
But here we have applied our own judgment.
Do we actually have the right to decide who is worthy of
Entering the Lord's granary and who is not?

---

[203] The righteous servant of God possessing great wisdom or mystic knowledge.

It turns out that we are like Nasreddin Efendi in one tale,
When a friend asks him to borrow money
And set a time frame for its return.
Efendi replied that he wouldn't lend him money
But that, because he was a friend, he would not set a time limit.

It turns out you're saying
We will fight for every sinner,
But, at the same time, he should not be one.
I understand that we are talking about the deluded and the certain.
About those who have erred and those who've chosen Satan.

I have to admit, however, that I've seldom seen
Those who are certain followers of the Greedy One.
At least they declare publicly
That they are a weed, a nettle or a dandelion.
But those who are hidden, like our fanatic,

Always hide behind the rhetoric of the public good.
In the case of the little man, we are talking about religion.
So, what are we to do? Even if society has not judged him,
But we take it upon ourselves to do so.
Will it not turn out that there are so many such people

That it is not the granary that'll be full,
But the fires to burn the sheaves of tares?
After all, if there were so many sinners
The Lord would not then have sought us,
Rather he'd have sought Noah, right?'

'Philip, quit the sophisticated wordery!' Cephas exclaimed.
'You're like Dan Shen[204], feeding first the wolf, then the hare,
Before deciding he had no interest in it!
It's just the other way around – he at least, at one moment,
Decided to feed someone.

You must understand – it's not we who judge this fanatic,
Rather he found himself
Face to face during the harvest
With a weeding sickle
With no argument in justification.

To a certain extent, the illuminated Throne Room
Is an allegory of Judgment Day, when the Lord and the Angels
Ask, hey, people, why have you climbed up here like thieves?
And then he will have only one thing to say to God
And, perhaps, he will deserve forgiveness, even though he is a thief.

The other one will all the same be left standing with his trousers down,
Awaiting his punishment for his brainless downfall.
After all, what objection could he possibly raise against what Sapa Inca and the thief had said?

---

[204] The parable of the zen buddhist monk Dan Shen. When Dan Shen went out into the world, he saw a wolf chasing a hare. He killed the wolf and saved the hare. Soon, he saw another wolf, chasing another hare. He caught the hare and fed it to the wolf. Then he saw a third hare and a third wolf and said, 'I cannot save all the hares or feed all the wolves. I have tried both and I have no further interest in it.'

400

None, of course. He had come with sinister intent. Himself!
Even if he had concealed the fact, he would soon have been exposed!

If we do the same as Dan Shen,
Then we'd do what he did in another parable.
One day, Dan Shen met a man
Who had long had an arrow protruding from his shoulder.
He was so afraid to touch it, that he had almost come to terms with the pain.

Dan Shen went up to him and decisively pulled out the arrow.
The man rebuked the monk and walked off
But, after a while, he returned
And showered him with gratitude
That the pain had gone and that he was feeling considerably better.

Then Dan Shen said, "I don't need your gratitude,
Just like I didn't need your abuse.
I did what I thought needed to be done
But it is up to you if
You die or get better."

And so, Philip, you need to decide on something,
And not simply babble on. The little man is still a man and he also has value.
As they say, he has a right to a personal life,
To be himself and it's not for us to judge and bla-bla-bla...
Pull out the arrow first!!!'

Cephas cried out so loudly that everyone shuddered,
But then they all laughed, so marvellous was his outburst.
Philip grinned at Peter
And Peter, glaring from under his shaggy eyebrows,
Shook a fist at him, But then they embraced.

The Beloved Teacher watched us tenderly
And then, turning to Philip, said,
'You know, brother, you noted something very important:
What if there is a prevalence in today's
Society of the morals and ethics of the weeds,

While we are just a little seed, threatened with choking and death?
I'll tell you truly, if we are like the mustard seed,
We will grow into a large tree,
Where the birds of the skies will all hide,
And against which the nettles and dandelions will be powerless.

And we'll not only defeat all the weeds around,
But we'll clearly be visible from afar.
And travellers from far and wide will remark, there's a tree.
How did it grow here in the desert?
Where there is no fertile land,

Just roads, sand and rock.
How come the sun has not scorched it or the wind not torn it down?
How have the weeds and other useless grasses not choked it?
Who helped it survive if not the power of the Heavens?
If not its own strength, helping it grow up to the Heavens?

Clearly the enemy failed to see it when the tree was but a seed,
Failed to cast it to the rocks or feed it to the birds.
Clearly, the enemy was unable to realise and distinguish
What he could ignore
And what he really needed to worry about.

And for precisely this to happen, we ourselves need
To see the essence of the grain from the outset, so we can understand
What specifically will grow from it.'
'That is truly the case!' Andrew smiled. 'Allow me, Teacher,
To relate a parable that I heard in the bazaars of Baghdad.

One day, Hodja Nasreddin
Loaded his donkey with bales of salt
And took them to the market to sell.
At one point they needed to cross the river.
Once they had done this, the donkey started jumping about with joy

Because the load had grown noticeably lighter.
Nasreddin, was obviously furious.
Another time, Hodja packed the donkey with sacks of cotton.
On this occasion, having crossed to the other side of the river,
The donkey shuddered from fatigue, for wet cotton

Is considerably heavier than dry!
"There you go!" Nasreddin exclaimed.
"Let that be a lesson for you not to forget
That not every time when you cross the water
Will you come out a winner!"

Well, what is the connection of this with the parable of the mustard seed,
You might ask?
I believe the connection is the most direct
Wheat and mustard grains, salt and cotton
Have the identical, positive essence

For man, even though they are entirely different.
People too are basically identical in form,
But in essence they may differ fundamentally,
Both in the path they choose in life and the side they take,
The values that shape their life's path.

Do we really need to be a mustard tree in the forest
If it gets lost among the redwoods and eucalyptuses?
Do we really need to salt the water for
One to die of thirst out at sea?
Are we really going to stuff the mouth of the starving man with cotton?

It turns out that we need not only to distinguish the power of the little grain,
But also the notional timeliness
Of its being here, at this time and in this place.
Is Pilate really interested in discussions
About the qualitative signs of the Mashiah?

More likely, he will react energetically to
Whoever is defending Rome's interests in this satrapy.
Will the high priests really want a public

Discussion of who will sit on the throne of the Jews?
No, they'll probably leave this question for people to whisper about in their kitchens.

However, as for matters of the Jew's communication with Adonia
And the qualitative signs of the Saviour King –
This is something to which they'll dedicate maximum attention and judicial zeal.
What will Herod find of interest in the messianic problem?
Most likely, his bored mind

Would want to see a real miracle like walking on water
Or turning water to wine.
But again, exclusively because of some indolent depression
That has subjugated his young conscience
Under the roof of a benevolent lack of authority on the part of the Romans.'

The Teacher thought about Andrew's words a while and then said,
'You're right, brother mine. That's such an interesting slant
You've given to the parable of the mustard seed,
Going much farther than just the question
Of the all-conquering principle of the Kingdom of Heaven,

But continuing the thought, right? And at the expense of what?
For, otherwise, we'll be like something evil,
Something that missed the sowing of the mustard seed,
By being too engaged in the destruction of other grain
And the sowing of tares amidst the neat rows of wheat.

We don't want to be like one wise man
Who the king elevated to the top of the pile
And made his prime minister.
This wise man was walking in the garden and saw the royal falcon.
He thought he'd never seen such

A strange dove before. So, he fetched some scissors
And carefully trimmed the falcon's talons and beak
And clipped the combat-ready wings with the words,
"Now you look like a proper dove,
Clearly you have not been taken care of before."

That is basically an answer to you, Thomas, to your
Earlier question of whether goodness has an active beginning
Or if we are simply passively pursuing the destiny we have been determined.
Should we not protect our mustard seed,
Our salt, wheat and cotton?

Yes, but intelligently and not rushing headlong without thought.'

'Teacher, I have been saying all along,' the Zealot said, his eyes lighting up,
'That our education lacks a fighting spark.
Why then should you speak of
Bringing Your sword into this world?
The question is who, then, should pick it up. Me?

After all, goodness should have decent fists, right?'
The Teacher laughed and said, 'Our strength is not in
Standing by the road, field or crossing with a sword in our hand.
Rather that our reason should always come to the aid of our heart.

James, tell us your parable about the master swordsman.'

'Hm...,' the elder of the Voanerges muttered, moving closer to the fire.
'One day, while cruising Lake Biwa,
The famous swordsman Tsukahara Bokuden
Met a cocky young samurai,
Trying his best to challenge the master to fight him.

"So, what schooling have you had?" the lad asked him arrogantly.
"The school of winners without getting one's hands dirty,"
Master Bokuden replied coolly.
Now, to get the blustering bully of his back,
He suggested they fight on a small island in the

Centre of the lake, so that the other passengers wouldn't get hurt.
The moment the boat neared the island,
The young tearaway jumped first onto the shore.
Bokuden took up an oar and pushed the boat off the shore.
"That is the school of winners without getting one's hands dirty,"

Bokuden calmly explained to his fellow travellers,
For he had no desire to see that whipper-snapper
Shed blood for no reason.'
'Spot on,' John exclaimed, 'for in the thick of
Our discussion of parables, should we not

Avoid distorting our own teaching
About the essence of things when we say
We must love our enemy
With all our heart? So, what sword do you speak of, Zealot?!'
'Calm down, John,' Simon replied,

'You have been given reason to realise
That turning the other cheek without thinking
Is also not the point, because, otherwise,
We'll be like Hodja Nasreddin from this other parable.
Listen up: one day, Hodja was attacked by thieves.

They robbed him of everything he had,
And then took to beating the wise man, to which he cried out angrily,
"What are you beating me up for?!
Did I not pass here at the right time for you or not bring much?!'"
The brothers laughed, but John turned to the Teacher, affronted:

'The line between love for one's fellow man
And actively protecting one's views,
One's mustard seed, salt, wheat and cotton
Is so fine. So how, oh, Beloved Teacher,
Are we to demonstrate to others our understanding of this line?

Should we not give reason a chance to judge
When to love our enemy
And when, under some guise of security considerations
To enter into battle against him, even without a sword?
Can there really be double standards when fulfilling commandments?!'

'Quite right, brother John. Here, I think,

We need to return to the original parable about the mustard seed,
I mean, to the interpretation that will subsequently
Be deemed canonical.
The grain is, after all, an allegory of the Kingdom of Heaven,

Destined to grow in a man,
If the sower has planted this grain in him.
And so, our active stance lies specifically in
Placing this grain into the human soul,
Which will unavoidably grow there

So that he will actively protect this Kingdom within.
Nevertheless, we have still not deviated from the subject.
After all, the matter of choice between the commandment of turning the other cheek
And an active defence of one's beliefs will
Bring confusion into people's minds for centuries to come.

So, where is the line between open-heartedness and a lack of will?!
As the Son of Man, I have no straight answer,
At least not now, not today.
The one thing I can say with certainty is this:
We will prove what choice is right

Through our destiny, brother John. Our destiny.'
On saying these words, the Teacher stroked the poet's head.
'After every chapter in life,' He continued, 'known as *Say*,
Comes a chapter known as *Do. Accomplish*.
It is only with a combination of such chapters

Will the Great Book come to be.
We'll rest today and return to our further
Discussion tomorrow.
After all, sleep, too, is to a certain extent a fair judge
That can clarify many judgments and correct many errors of reason.'

****

The following evening, the Teacher began the conversation:
'John, you asked what would enable us to
Complete our path so that people would understand our views
On the line between our actions, worthy of the Kingdom of Heaven
And the path that closes its gates to us.

I replied that we would demonstrate through our lives
What this fine line is but allow me to focus your attention
On the need for you to be fully prepared
For your own path, so as not to err
And fall among the pitiless tares of history.

That's right, we are led by the Almighty Father to our destiny.
But are we the first or the last?
And who knows if there are those, destined from above
To become righteous on the Path,
But who turned out to be but a grain that fell on the road?

I told you the parable about the Kingdom of Heaven
Being like a starter culture that a woman

405

Places into three measures of flour until it has all soured.
So, is our reason not this starter culture?
I am not talking about reason just being the capability of the brain,

Rather I also mean the reason
That comes from deep in our heart.
I am talking about the experience that has been immersed into this heart
Through sincere feeling about what has been experienced.
Including what's been experienced by others.

Without reason and wisdom,
Guided only by righteous emotions and impulses,
The path to mindless fanaticism is so short,
The doors that shield from the path
To the fate of weeds are so weak.

Fanaticism is terrible and wicked,
But the path of scholasticism and dogmatism is no less terrible.'
'Yes, yes, Teacher, and allow me,'
Philip said, entering the conversation, 'to relate one story
About a conversation that our now much loved Hodja Nasreddin

Had with one who thought himself a wise man.
During a discussion, this wise man
Presented evidence to Nasreddin, foaming at the mouth,
That every person should behave in the way
He wishes that others would behave.

He meant that your heart should wish for others
The same as it wishes for itself.
Hearing this, Hodja replied to the wise man,
"There once live a bird that ate poisonous berries,
But which caused it no harm whatsoever.

In fact, the berries were delicious and the bird took great enjoyment from them.
One day, in a most positive frame of mind,
The bird gathered a whole sack of these berries
And fed its friend the horse,
Who proceeded to die very quickly..."

Brothers, you see, I think this tale
Really accurately conveys the idea that reason is a starter culture,
Only I'd like to add that reason
Also facilitates the notion of responsibility
On the part of the sower over that of the one who cultivates and keeps.'

'Aha,' Andrew grinned wickedly,
'You often see a person either has feelings
That run ahead of his thoughts, or vice versa.
Rational reason and a desire to keep a low profile
Are what restrict good intentions.

There's the story of one chick who
Loved running about the mill, pecking at the grain,
But who was terribly afraid of the fox
Who prowled nearby
And could gobble him up at any moment.

One day, the chick prayed
To Allah to turn him into a fox
And the Almighty granted this wish.
Now he had nothing to fear
And could run about the mill to his heart's content.

However, when the chicken-fox got there, to his dismay,
He realised that, being a fox, he would never be able to
Peck at his favourite grain.
I believe that these two stories
Are pretty much about the same thing.

After all, in the first instance, the bird had good intentions,
While the chick had a fairly understandable wish
To get one over on his predatory enemy.
However, given that they were deprived of reason,
The outcome of their actions was an obvious evil.'

'What's the point of teaching,' the Rabbi uttered
Seemingly to himself, 'that fails to disclose to a person
What is good and where the line with evil actually runs?
Where are the limits of stupidity and kind-heartedness,
A love of freedom and irresponsibility?

What's the point of sermons and stories
If they don't lead one to
Find treasure, pearls and kind fish of gold
Amidst all the complexities of the world,
And lose the Kingdom of Heaven in all the hustle and bustle of evil?

I sometimes think that wealth and the complexity
Of the religious ritual are basically called upon
To mask the loss of fundamental meanings,
And specifically the loss by defenders of the faith
Of the ability to distinguish good from evil.

Then they dish out poisonous berries
Albeit with good intentions
But, still, inevitably leading to our deaths
Or to the loss of original meanings and values,
As was the case with the chick.

The priests and the rabbis will say,
But it's still a good thing, little chick,
That you became a fox. This is a bit of an evolutionary leap
Up the food chain. You know, that's undoubtedly positive.
And then, a leap like that

Will remain the key goal for this creature,
Which, over time, will cease to be
Either a chick or a fox; it will lose its name.
In our case, the name *Human*.
So, what will it become then? Into what will it transform?

And, at the end of the day, has it not transformed already?!
Do we still have the ability to see

Those original meanings that
Lie hidden beneath those multiple layers of civilisational development
And centuries of religious dogma and scholastics?

No, no, not even scholastics, just basic traditions,
Customs, at the end of the day?!'
'Do you know, Teacher, what a wonderful story I heard
From this scholastic priest,
Who in an instant ceased to be such after what happened?'

Cephas said as he poured tea for his brothers.
'One day a mullah was strolling along the river when he spotted a boy,
Happily turning somersaults on the dusty bank.
However, when he saw the holy man,
He rushed to him and greeted him most respectfully

And asked what the right way to perform a *namaz* was.
Was it not like he was doing over there in the sand?
The mullah rebuked the boy in irritation for being so forgetful
And showed him how to read a prayer
And perform the required number of rak'ahs.

A couple of days later, the mullah was walking again in that same spot
And he caught sight of the boy once more,
Only he was playing on the other side of the river.
Seeing the mullah, the boy rushed over to him,
Greeted him and expressing his respect.

Once again, he asked the mullah to teach him how to read a prayer in the correct way
Because he had forgotten it again. However...
He ran to the mullah not over the bridge,
But directly across the water, so naturally, as if he had always done this.
Seeing this, the mullah was taken aback, scratched his beard and muttered,

"You know, boy, you pray as you see fit.
That's right, pray any way you want, just be sincere."'
'I could relate a similar parable,'
Levi Matthew joined in animatedly.
'One day, the guru Marpa, the teacher of Milarepa,

Came to see a wise man and confided in him.
The wise man lived under the benevolent charms of copper pipes,
So when Marpa asked him what to do,
He brushed him away and replied, "Simply repeat my name as a mantra
And that will be all you need to do."

There and then, Marpa went to the river and set about dancing,
Singing and running over the water.
His teacher was staggered and asked,
"Marpa, but how do you do that?"
Marpa replied, "Just like you taught me, teacher!

I simply repeated your name."
The wise man rushed over to the river and tried to do the same,
But he quickly sank to the bottom.
When his students had dragged him out, he caught his breath and said,
"I am no teacher, rather I'm just a sham.

And you, Marpa, know this: it wasn't my name that worked,
Rather your faith in it. The faith that I have long since lost."
Saying those words, the wise man gathered his things and left to become a hermit.'
'Friends, hold on a minute,' Philip interjected.
'Of course, I understand that this is all conscious hyperbole,

To depict the boy and Marpa walking on water.
But won't this lead us to a situation
When only the contemplation of a miracle is capable of returning a person
To an initial understanding of values or to an understanding that
New people have appeared, on whose lips they will sound fresh and new?'

'You're right, Philip,' the Beloved Teacher replied.
'For example, remember the parable about the sovereign and his slave.
The slave was unable to see the miracle of forgiveness and trust
In the deed of his ruler. He could not transfer this miracle of goodness
That had been directed his way to one who was in his debt.

On the contrary, he treated him cruelly and viciously
For which he was punished by the king.
So what will happen when both parties are blind?
Who will lead whom and to where if they
Cannot teach, hear or heed a lesson?

To the Pit of Tartarus, Hades, Gehenna? But is that the most terrible thing?
To live in a world where there is no fertile land,
No wise rulers, breeding or people with vision,
Where mustard seeds perish and crops are choked amid the tares –
Now that is a terrible punishment. Is there any more terrible?

To a world where everyone knows everything, wants and receives everything
In exchange for a universal equivalent but that equivalent is not faith.
To a world where a Master sends his lieutenants
And then his own son, but he is killed
But this bypasses the public eye

And the information and entertainment cauldrons of the television,
Bypasses the press hounds who rush to fulfil any wish of
The one who has long since agreed to exchange their pearls
And treasure for a dead infotainment fig tree that no longer bears fruit.
What will the Lord of Worlds do with them on the birthday of the new Kingdom?

So, has it transpired that the quantity of denarii
Has become a measure of justice, after mixing the first and the last,
The called and the chosen, violating all notions of good and evil
And preserving just the proportions and principles governing the distribution of benefits
And sensitively safeguarding their fundamental nature?!

What will become of the world where values have been turned on their head?
How can we live in a world that exists simply in expectation of the next punishment?
Whose name will be voiced by people who want to walk on water,
But see it as nothing more than a virtual diversion?
And how, brothers, have we allowed all this to happen?!'

'Let us, in our repentance, to be like that son of the wine grower
Who erred but nevertheless repented.

409

And what you, Teacher, told us in one of your parables,'
Judas timidly raised his hand
And continued hesitantly.

'You ask how this all happened?
How did the change in notions come about
And the fundamental upheaval in the field of values?
I'll tell you one parable that might just shed light
On the logic and absurdity of what has happened.

One day, Hodja Nasreddin was boasting to his neighbour
That he was a very rational and clear-headed man
And that he was extraordinarily proud of the fact.
When they met again a couple of days later
Nasreddin appeared very downcast.

"What's the matter, Hodja?" his neighbour enquired.
"I have a problem with my faith. Today, I saw
A mouse sitting on my Qur'an and I questioned,
If the Qur'an cannot handle a regular mouse,
How on earth could it possibly protect me?"

"Forget it," his neighbour said, but Nasreddin would not calm down:
"I'm a rational man and I cannot let this pass."
"Then it would be logical to start worshipping that mouse,"
The neighbour laughed. Hodja, though, took this at face value
And became a mouse worshipper.

A week later, the neighbours met once again
And Hodja looked simply awful.
"You see, my faith is now forever subject to new trials.
Six days ago, I saw a cat eat that mouse.
I had to start worshipping the cat

Until my dog chased it from the yard.
I had to become a dog-worshipper until
My wife beat the cur with a stick.
So, does that mean my wife is the mightiest of all creatures?!
But I can't force myself to worship her!"

"Nothing doing, Hodja," the neighbour said, barely able to conceal his laughter.
"As a rational man, you have to be consistent."
Nasreddin looked depressed but then he suddenly brightened:
"But I don't have to be subordinate to my wife herself,
Only her image! I'll order her portrait and will worship that instead!!!"

Another five days went by and Hodja Nasreddin's
Frightened wife came running to the neighbour for help.
"Hodja has locked himself in his study
And he's been in there three days!"
The neighbour ran to their house and this is what he saw:

Nasreddin was standing naked before the mirror
And was quite clearly worshipping... himself!
"You see," Nasreddin began explaining to his friend,
"I came to a logical conclusion.
Three days ago I was angry with my wife,

410

I beat her and I realised that, as I was stronger and mightier than she,
That meant it would be more logical to worship myself!'"
There followed much noise and laughter, but Judas went on:
'It's a funny story for sure, but I think
That such an inversion of meanings is precisely

What has happened with the majority of people today.
Only I don't know why. Either it's from too much rationalism,
Or from the triumph of the cult of consumption,
Which is essentially the worshipping of oneself, isn't it?'
'There is a parable,' John spoke up, 'which more precisely

Reflects what you've been saying, Judas.
I found it when I was looking for a continuation
Of our Teacher's parable of the ruler
Who had invited everyone and their brother to his son's wedding feast.
This is how my story goes:

Every year a caliph from Baghdad
Would set a sumptuous feast and every time
The festival's main dish had to outdo the previous festival's
Main offering many times over.
On this occasion, Hodja Nasreddin found himself at the feast by mistake.

After all the dancing, singing and ceremony,
Hundreds of dishes were brought in,
Each adorned by a beautifully decorated
And wonderfully prepared
Roast peacock!

The dish had been designed so beautifully and to such effect,
Glistening in caramel decorations,
Sweet cream and multicoloured spices,
That everyone gasped from the sight and the smell
Of this true culinary work of art!

The silence was broken by the cry of the dumbfounded Nasreddin:
"Let's eat this peacock right this minute,
For the more I look at its beauty,
The more I am overcome with doubt
That the food among us is it and not us!"'

'There it is – the mirror of that inversion you were talking about,' the Friend said.
What is unclear today is if mass culture
Is running ahead of the sophisticated consumer
Or if sophisticated consumption is dragging people behind it
Who, in any event, have been converted to that contemptible faith of the age of new slavery.

So, what are we saving them from now?
Who are they, today's sufferers of spiritual poverty?
Is it only the rich who can now
Overcome the test of the camel and the eye of the needle?
Where is our fertile land now, that foundation of our faith and our Kingdom?!'

And that was how another evening of dialogue and parables came to an end.
When everyone had gone, I asked the Teacher,

'Tell me, at the start of the conversation, You
Reproached Cephas for, as they say, preventing people and parables from growing,
We are preventing ourselves from learning, is that right?

So tell me this, *Does the Lord also learn?*
Does he too absorb our forever varying experience,
Thus improving His very essence?
Or is it that He is Absolute and, hence, is not subject
Even to divine dialectics?'

The Teacher closed his eyes, as if deep
In a search for an answer to all the intricate puzzles of the Universe,
But then he spoke: 'This question, my friend,
Strange as it may seem, requires no answer at all,
As it is, in itself, the process of faith.

Remember the parable about the bottomless jug.
The thing is, if you find a negative answer to the question,
As well as a positive one,
It will destroy your faith in exactly the same way.
So, don't think about the bottom of the jug, rather about the finality of the process.

Leave enough room in your heart for agnosticism
To the extent that you don't become a fool or a fanatic.
Leave room for rationalism, too, only be sure to stop in time;
Rationalism demands insistently that all the answers be found.
This is basically the essence of the scientific worldview.

Here I got to thinking that
Judgment Day too, after which all definitions, sentences
And awards will be announced
For centuries, for millennia, forever,
Carries really too much certainty.

So, my friend, leave certain doors open.
You remember what one of our group said during our conversation:
If Adonai wanted maximum certainty in everything,
He'd have simply come and explained it all in detail. To everyone.
Each and every one. No riddles or code, just chapter and verse.

He alone can really do that. For now, go to sleep. We'll continue tomorrow...'

****

However, the following day there never was
A full-fledged discussion of the parables, as usual.
Event after event
Proceeded to overwhelm our little community,
Accelerating the flow of life all the more,

Inevitably and inexorably directed
Toward its end...
However, I still need to tell you something
For otherwise the picture
Will be not so much incomplete as, I don't know, unfinished.

This took place on the shores of the Sea of Galilee.

The Teacher had walked off to pray
Where the waves crashed into the sky
And the clouds were reflected in them,
Laughing and twirling like children at play.

We were sitting around the fire and Cephas and Thomas
Had got into one of their customary arguments
Where all of us, slowly but surely, became involved.
'So, you're saying,' Peter said heatedly, as always,
'That it's the complexity and the multiple layers

Of the story's main concept that gets you, right?
But you don't lose the most important thing,
The simplicity and the accessibility of this idea for a great many others?
Don't you place the pretentiousness of reasoning
Above the mission that we place in the parables?'

'Cephas,' Thomas argued, 'stop treating the parable
As just propagandist material
For our views and convictions.
The parable lives its life, regardless of whether
Prophets wander this earth or not!

It is not supposed to serve for the formation of ranks
Of all manner of religious and political organisations,
Just to help find solutions to difficult things in life;
Help find answers to topical questions;
Help acquire knowledge and experience!'

'There's no need to make my position appear so primitive, Thomas!
I quite understand that a parable is not a political poster.
It's just that it has to correspond with the context,
And I mean the context of a specific time and specific people.
That means us in this particular instance.

Otherwise it'd be like in the story of the ferryman,
Who takes the wise man across the river.
The wise man asks how many books he's read
And hearing the reply "several", he says
The man has lost half a life.

The ferryman asks if the wise man has learned to swim.
Hearing that he hasn't, he tells
The wise man that he risks losing all his life,
Because the boat has started sinking.
So, you see, Thomas, if you stand on the battlefield,

There's no point reciting poetry to the enemy.
You should be in the context of the event
In which you find yourself.
Therefore, why waste time on some empty-headed discussion
About tales that have no bearing on our reality?!'

The quarrellers failed to notice that the Teacher had quietly returned
And was standing to one side, listening to their debate with interest.
'You, Cephas,' Thomas went on, 'in your striving to dot every *i*
And cross every *t* in defining your goals,

413

Are actually going round in circles,

In your attempt to tarmac the Path of Life.
Why don't you want to come to terms with the fact
That both what we need now and what appears trifling
Might be equally valuable
And, what is most important, simultaneously?

One day, Hodja Nasreddin was asked
How to unite egoism and altruism.
He replied that it was very simple.
"Look at the Earth, revolving around its axis
And, at the same time, around the Sun!'"

'You know, Thomas, having no love for the specific
Really borders on being outright lazy,
All hidden under an idle veil of pseudo-sophistication
Behind every instance of vague wording
Lies a real lack of purpose in life

Or even outright stupidity.
Just like in the story with the same Nasreddin, wandering along a road
And turning to Allah with the words,
"Oh, Almighty one, riding on horseback,
One would make it home far quicker!"

After that he felt someone
Jump on his back.
In desperation, Hodja cried out, "Oh, Almighty one!
You have been my Allah sixty years now,
Yet you still haven't learned to work out my requests!'"

'Allow me to interject, brethren,' the Teacher suddenly spoke,
'But by no means to pass judgment
On which of you is right and which of you is wrong.
I just remembered promising at the time that
I would award the one who tells the most

Interesting story with a special mission.
Well... What I can say is that you're all
Wonderful storytellers and researchers
And, clearly, the winner will be determined by history and time,
If they deem it necessary to do so.

It is hard to call this award,
For it is more likely fate that has bestowed it, not I.
Certainly not I...
The choice has already been made for us
And not on this dune-rich land.

All that remains for me is simply to point a finger,
State verbally what is destined for you
And there is no special gift of foresight in this.
The stories that each of you brought to our soirée
Serve merely to confirm the paths that you have chosen.

It is all just like this because, by a certain age

414

Almost all the letters of fate will appear
On the body of any man.
And there is no fatalism in that at all,
Just the consequence of that man's choice.'

Thus spoke the Teacher and everyone sat round,
Broke bread and poured wine with particular care.
'Few remember that the tradition of soirées
Arose specifically when
The wings of the birds of fate swished

Over the heads of our little brotherhood,
A fate that by that time was almost unavoidable.
And yes, all that remained was to experience it, pass through it.
Shout, sing, cry,
Laugh, speak, perform a deed

And return to the beginning...'

Everyone quietly warmed the wine in the simple cups with their hands
And a kind of peace descended upon us,
Despite the fact that just a moment ago
There had been heated discussions
And lightning flashes of strong masculine emotions.

'I still cannot see all the paths,' the Beloved Friend said quietly,
'But something has already been revealed to me
And, once revealed, has drawn every tear from me.
For the path you have chosen is not an easy one.
For the hundredth time I blame myself for not driving you away, but...

Even I will not dare to deprive you of the right
To your own destiny. So, let's begin...'
He took out a bundle and placed it on the table.
For you, Bartholomew, Philip and Levi Matthew.
Here is gold, frankincense and myrrh.

The time will come when we will part, but we will meet again
And you will need to understand that this meeting has taken place,
To recognise Me and make it known to everyone of My return.
To you, James, son of Zebedee, Thaddeus and James, son of Alphaeus,
I give my staff. You will have to protect the Road.

Remember, our Path, our source of Truth
Or perhaps simply of the joy of friendly conversation,
And love, must never dry out;
Let us continue our eternal Path,
Even when we remain motionless...

To you, Simon the Canaanite and Andrew,
I give the sword and the law.
To you, Thomas, I will tell something strange and secret,
But the time for that has not come yet.
John, I give you a stylus.

You know what to do with it.
You, Judas, in the most difficult moment in my life,

415

Will gift me a brotherly kiss of support
And of your and My fate
And hope, that everything will occur just as it should.'

'And me, Rabbi?!' Cephas cried out impatiently.
'What do you bequeath to me?!'
'You, Cephas...
Here is stone, some clay and paint.
The time will come and you, please, build us a Home...'

****

Before turning in, still under the effect of the soirée,
I said to the Teacher, 'Tell me, Rabbi,
Well, if we preserve our loyalty to one another,
Our power of persuasion, the gift of healing
And the Kingdom of Heaven in our hearts,

Then we'll be able to win the hearts of millions
And gain ultimate power in the world,
The mightiest throne and crown; perhaps even Roman.
We can rule and govern as
Our convictions dictate and our dreams depict.

Don't we have everything we need already?
Did the fates of those who, under the shade of Your blessing,
Might not only bear news but also stand up to an enemy,
Not form a single, bizarre mosaic?
I recall a parable:

They say that one day, Mullah Nasreddin complained, saying,
"I dreamed my whole life about making halva,
But it never worked for me.
When I had flour, I didn't have butter
And if I had butter, there was no flour."

"What, so in that time
You couldn't get hold of butter *and* flour?" he was asked.
"When there was butter and flour, I was not around myself,"
Nasreddin answered.
Teacher, look at our brotherhood today.

Do you not have at your disposal the butter and the flour,
And the individuals to erect a new, mighty throne?'
The Beloved Friend fell silent,
Customarily and, somehow, quite mundanely and without ceremony
Coughing and smiling sadly.

'Yes, my friend,' He said quietly.
'I indeed now have the butter and the flour.
I have friends and this is enough for a happy life,
And a life that doesn't need to be vested with the power of thrones or crowns,
Simply one shaded by the village olive trees.

The circumstances, ingredients and destinies have all combined into one.
You're right, only we're not destined to enjoy
Cooking halva to sweeten our lips.

416

Tomorrow, when the neighbour's donkey disturbs the morning with its cry once again,
We'll head for Jerusalem.'

End of Book One

BOOK TWO

Verse 29. The man living in time-stood-still

'Tell me, Philip, about your Path to this day.'
Right... Well... It's hard to remain taciturn
In your company, friends, even if remaining silent
Is the key trait of your character.
Although, Allah is my witness, when silent,

I never interrupted one of your conversations.
They always flow through me, oh-so quietly,
Like the waters of Acheron, the eternal, quiet witness,
Watching souls descending
Inexorably into the depths of Hades.

Thank you for never seeing me as morose.
I couldn't stand such a definition
From people I am close to.
Not because it's not true,
Rather that being taciturn is an acquired trait of

My character, one that appeared not that long ago.
You see, before, I was different, because...
Well, I was following a different profession,
That melancholic types are really not that suited
To given its professional standards.

I am a pedagogue. A schoolteacher.
Not a Teacher with a capital T,
Just a common soldier in the ranks of educationalists,
Working every day, every hour
Nurturing future generations

Of marshals and TV hosts,
Prophets and date sellers,
Poets and bank clerks,
Film directors, gangsters and police officers.
Basically, all those whom the secondary education system

Casts every year onto the employment market,
To institutes, the army, prison and sports clubs.
Boys and girls with burning eyes,
Walking through thorns in search of paths,
That stretch toward broad roadways,

Cherishing dreams in the search for combining the incompatible,
The beautiful, young, ambitious and frightened.

421

Those who believe that the horizon is something attainable,
While a dream is but a computer program,
Setting algorithms of what is sure to happen to them.

I am someone who naïvely believes
That I am the creator of human destinies,
The architect of personal foundations,
And only on the grounds
That I possess the time of children

Handed over into my almost unlimited authority for a long time.
On the grounds that this pool of time
That a child spends at school
Is immeasurable more than that which they spend at home
With their parents, who have given their offspring over to school discipline.

On the grounds that we are the first totalitarianism
That a child encounters in the world.
The first system, the first army, the first disciplinary castigation
Before the silent ranks of their brothers.
The first kings, tyrants and stewards of alien blood,

That they have not chosen for themselves.
You ask why I describe school in such dark tones,
Mixing truth with bitterness every other phrase?
I'll tell you that, no, I am not being dark at all.
I am being objective. You might think that I'm bad-mouthing

My colleagues on the shopfloor, like a child,
Ground down by school, like a misfortune.
Hm... that's just one side of the story.
The other is that school
Cannot be totalitarian

Only on the basis that childhood
Is not a divine creation.
God never created children and He didn't program them to look like Him.
He created adult people from the off, in the form of two individuals,
Who had never known what childhood was.

Of course, God never created the lion cub or the baby rat either,
But He didn't impute the lions and the rats
To think about having a likeness to God and to build nations and temples.
He created a self-reproducing fauna from the off.
With people, however, things turned out differently...

After expulsion from Eden, the humans had children
Who had never seen paradise and had no idea what it was.
They were placed in collective institutions:
Kindergartens, schools, boarding schools and technical colleges,
Which teach the human offspring to bite from the poisoned apple.

And this means teaching them specifically to grow
And then bite into it, without a second's hesitation,
Like Eve the Foremother had hesitated before the serpent of temptation.
This army of cute, naïve creations,
Under the guidance of wise, evil, kind and cruel shepherds,

422

Solves problems by the hour, problems that God refused in this time.

And you can keep to yourselves your comments that
With approaches like that I am no teacher and that
Me and my thoughts should be kept well away from children.
I see the angry faces of the educators and parents;
As psychologists have written in their notebooks, Freud's crowd.

My tale is by no means about, well, first of all,
Who children are essentially and what the education system really is.
Second, from the outset, that is not how I thought.
Now, these are not the reasonings of a humble teacher from Chorazin...
Rather of the Stone Thrower. Who is that? Listen and you'll find out.

Many years ago,
A young graduate from the Jerusalem Pedagogical Institute,
Inspired by a dream of selfless devotion to teaching,
I decided not to remain in the capitals.
The walls of the Holy City and the gardens of Caesarea didn't tempt me.

I was determined to fulfil my mission
In a small provincial school
Where I thought I'd be more needed to my Motherland
And its educational ambitions.
In an attempt to start my journey completely from scratch,

I didn't return to my native Bethsaida,
But set off to the cosy and traditional Chorazin,
Which was not that far from home,
While, at the same time, it was far from my many relatives,
From the increased attention from the army of my uncles and aunts.

I would have had to teach not pupils, but a crowd
Of nephews, my neighbours', friends' and classmates' children,
Each blessed with a worried Jewish mother I knew,
Prepared, however, petty the reason,
To launch a war of Judgment Day.

And, like a regular Jewish mother,
She would certainly win and with a convincing beating,
In this case, of yours truly. Then I'd have to deal with my relatives.
Alahi, what I'm telling you, you already know;
What it feels to be intoxicated from the feeling that a new life lies ahead!

And it was with this feeling that I entered by first class,
Looked into the eyes of my future pupils
And I became so overcome with emotions at that moment
That words of prose can simply not express;
Such feelings are worthy of only poetry.

You're all waiting to hear me say that disappointment then came?
Not at all. I was lucky with my team, especially its leader.
The head, Zinoviy Melamed, was an exemplary teacher and parent.
Exactly that, because, having no children of his own,
This man was the father and mentor to the teachers

And a strict yet kind grandfather to the kids.
So, why was he a father to us? Because we had a young team.
All of us were recent graduates,
Great friends and the best kind of specialists,
Who were not afraid of innovation or a regular routine.

And the children? Well, the children were like children everywhere:
A wonderful symbiosis of angels and little monsters.
Creatures with a wholly unpredictable algorithm,
But on other occasions quite the contrary: diligent and disciplined.
Sometimes even rebels, but on others, the source of naïve and pure tears.

There were even times when a conflict might arise
And you'd be left alone to face the head in his office,
Proving you're right, as a professional or a human.
You're oppressed by the fear of an unequal battle with the system,
And you come in the next morning for the slaughter and

There my class would be standing at the head's office
And, with fists clenched, although desperately scared, and with lips resolutely closed,
They prove to Grandfather Melamed
(the nickname of my mentor and boss at the time)
That they would never leave me and, for me, they'd even sacrifice everything for me, even...

Oh, God! Even a Sunday trip to the seaside!
Grandfather Melamed would have a grumble, bash the table
With a mighty knuckle and then say, well, the bright lot have turned out all right!
Off you go and have a think, eh? And (oh, the horror) tomorrow, I want
All the parents here (another knock of the knuckles) in my office!

That concerns you, Weidman! And you, Katseva!
And don't you hide yourself there, Melamed Junior,
I'll deal with what your father's teaching you there myself!
This is his nephew and everyone knows he won't deal with his brother;
He didn't have that kind of upbringing. Joseph Melamed is the most famous hazzan[205] in town,

And, most important, he is two years older than Grandfather Melamed.
Or rather, this is not the most important thing; Joseph never actually has time to deal with his son,
Preferring instead to trust his brother with his upbringing.
Does he kick over the traces? Well, go and work it out, this is a school; it's your turf.
In the synagogue, he is the meekest of the meek, so you work out what you can.

What is most interesting is that he won't call his parents either.
Why? They stood up for the teacher? Well done, them!
As for the teacher... Be so kind as to come to see me, my good fellow...
He'll make a bit of noise and then he'll say, 'You know, Philip,
What you propose is a great innovation,

But trust my experience and start it in a year.
You can't do it now, at their age, when it's all seething inside.
For now you should deal with their balance while loading them like that…
Well, in a year, they'll come to you and all you'll have to do is

---

[205] *Hazzan* or *chazzan* (Hebrew) means the person who leads the congregation in prayer at the synagogue. He sings the prayers which are then repeated by the congregation. The Hazzan is elected from among the members of the community, while, according to the requirements of the *Halacha*, he must have a thorough knowledge of the liturgy, have a decent, strong voice, a suitable appearance and impeccable behaviour.

Support *their* initiative.

Going to the seaside – that's a wonderful thing!
And you keep them together as a team more often.
On their own, they find it harder to cope with those new emotions.
And keep an eye on Weidman –
He's the kind of lad that if he takes the wrong path now,

Nothing will shift him later.
He'll have nothing inside;
He could even be an outstanding criminal,
But society... well, all right, *we* need him
To become a positive man who'll live a long life.

But *on the other side*, people don't live that long.'
Only once did the Old Lion get terribly angry.
When we missed the war that broke out between the lads from our school
And those from the boarding school in Chorazin.
Oh, now that's another story that really needs telling!

This war quietly came to a head away from our eyes.
The town still remembers it as the *war with the legionnaires*.
What was shocking was not so much the cruelty of the teenagers,
As what had provoked it:
The irresponsibility of the adults and their political games,

Which had instilled hatred in the immature hearts of those boys.

I'll tell you later, that the very appearance of that Chorazin boarding school,
Two years before the *war of the legionnaires*,
Was itself the precursor of these events. But more on that later;
For now, I'll return to the telling you about Grandfather Melamed's anger;
After this incident, he became known as the Old Lion of the Desert.

The boarding school went up fast, *in the Roman way*, as they used to say.
The thing was that, not far from us, in Tiberias,
Antipas continued to build his grand residence,
And that meant there was a surplus of gangs of builders and materials.
However, there was also another reason for the high speed of the building.

After the death of the ethnarch Herod Archelaus,
The Romans were in no hurry to hand his provinces over to the Israelites,
No matter what Antipas's wishes might have been.
The authorities in Caesarea and Jerusalem
Found themselves completely in the hands of the procurator.

For the people of the Land of Israel, this was not a simple question of politics.
Our life began to change, slowly but inexorably,
The life of the simple people of the land of Canaan.
Earlier, Rome's military problems were something remote for us,
No more than newspaper headlines.

Now, our men and boys were being enlisted into the army in droves,
To supplement the ranks of the Roman columns and sometimes the legions.
With the Empire's expansion, Rome needed more and more
New people, not only to safeguard their lands,
But also to engage in military action in Germania and on the borders of Parthia.

But that is not all. Our women and young girls too,
Under a ruling of the Jewish procurator,
Or rather, in the interests of the Roman magnates,
Under various pretexts, or sometimes simply by force,
Were regularly sent to the metropolis,

Where they became slaves, concubines
And labourers on the Roman *latifundia* estates and *collegia*.
As a result, entire families suddenly began to disappear,
And a typical story would be
Of the breadwinner dying on the battlefield under a Roman standard.

No one could speak for the mother
And she would be taken away to Greece or Rome,
Leaving the children literally on the streets.
The authorities started building these boarding schools
All over, where they gathered up all the homeless children.

You think they did this from humanitarian considerations?
Not a bit of it. First, it was so they wouldn't spoil
The new, white cityscapes of Caesarea and Tiberias.
Second, the schooling in these institutions had a distinctly military flavour,
Designed to ensure these boys would go on to supplement the legions of Tiberius.

Let's return to the teenagers' war... From the off, we basically guessed
That something like this had to happen.
At first, the municipal authorities resisted the construction
Of the boarding school in town as best they could,
Which had a reputation for being a quiet, traditional and relatively prosperous place.

The high-ranking officials often visited the capitals
And had seen crowds of ragged urchins on the streets.
Therefore, any thought of these gangs,
In large numbers and in an organised manner,
Coming to their beloved Chorazin, filled them with utter horror.

The town sent delegation after delegation.
They say that even in Caesarea, the people doubted the reasoning behind the construction
But everything was decided by a visit of the Melamed brothers to the capital.
They returned with tears in their eyes
And announced to the townsfolk that they had seen these unfortunate children.

The speech that Hazzan Iosif made to the council
Called fervently upon the descendants of Moses to remember
Their abandoned children and it melted the people's hearts.
You cannot remain indifferent faced with the dying future of your people,
And our duty is to become their new home, he said.

However, when the first detachments of boys
(A shelter for girls was built in Acre)
Arrived in Chorazin and we saw these little grown-ups,
We felt not only a sense of pity and sympathy,
But an understanding that the concerns of the town's fathers had not been unfounded.

What we saw in the eyes of those wolf cubs
Was how a cruel life could cripple children's minds.

We saw that spiritual poverty
Had set them firmly on the only possible path,
And that was the path of struggle for survival at any cost.

However, lost in righteous feelings about setting up the school
(And literally the entire town played a part in fitting it out)
These concerns faded imperceptibly into the background.
Then there was even an illusion that our
Bourgeois fears of these snot-nosed little boys was groundless.

The fire broke out unexpectedly and rapidly.
On the morning of that day, entering the school entrance, I ran into
My excited colleagues, headed by Grandfather.
The entire crowd of them were rushing somewhere.
'There's trouble,' the physics teacher whispered to me on the way.

We ran as far as the provincial amphitheatre.
Entering the arena, we saw crowds of policemen,
Soldiers, doctors and scurrying journalists.
A terrible sight met our eyes:
The field, like a gladiators' arena, swayed

In waves of a rushing throng, where it was impossible to make out
Who was where. Gradually, though, the essence of what was happening dawned on us.
An hour before, the pupils from the school and the boarding school,
Having lined up to face one another with wooden sticks in their hands,
Had been exchanging insults and claims

After which, with a wail, they had rushed into battle, like real troops.
We got there just when the police
Had rushed in to pull the two mobs of lads apart.
The commotion was down to the fighters continuing to thrash about,
Despite the decisive police charge.

Here and there, pockets of attack continued to flare.
A few seconds later, I could distinguish our lads from theirs,
Despite the fact that the boarding school pupils had no uniform.
Our boys were yelling *smash the legionnaires!*
While the *legionnaires* fought silently and ferociously, only growling.

There were clearly more natives of Chorazin, but there were more losses among them too.
Boys were lying here and there, tending to their bruises
While others, to our horror, lay motionless.
Doctors and parents were now scurrying about them,
Gathering up the beaten and carrying them to ambulance carts.

The police were evidently not as effective.
After all, in its lifetime, the town had never witnessed
Such a fight, so out of the ordinary it was.
They ran about and did their best, but the battle showed no sign of subsiding.
And then we heard the Lion of the Desert for the first time.

'Enough! Stop right there!' He screamed in such a terrible roar
That everyone teetered back, as if struck by the wind.
'Schoolboys to the right! Boarders to the left! Weapons to the ground!
Now!' After a funereal silence, which lasted an eternity,
We heard the clatter of sticks and chains falling to the ground.

'Belferman! Line your boys up!' That was addressed to the boarding school's head.
Then he addressed our lads: 'Get in two lines! Hands out front!
So I can see them!' In silence, the police then came to their senses
And quickly divided the crowd into two camps.
A minute later, the children were standing in line before their heads.

An hour later, the head of police reported to the town's fathers
In detail about what had actually taken place.
In so doing, he did not conceal his dislike for the *legionnaires*.
It stood to reason: he was one of the most vehement
Opponents of the boarding school being built in the town.

The nickname *legionnaires* had come about almost the same time
The new boys had arrived in Chorazin.
It made sense, too, for the fathers of the vast majority of them
Had served or died in the army of Rome.
I think that another major role in this

Was that, at first, the new lads had moved about only in formation,
Whenever they went into the town from the boarding school.
And what could they do; their teachers were mostly officers,
Commissioned from military service.
Well, and I've already told you about the objectives of their teaching.

Over time, they assimilated into the town
And the locals grew accustomed to them too, and to their navy-blue uniform.
The cadets generally behaved in exemplary fashion,
If we don't count the odd couple of minor skirmishes and
One teenage booze-up, which was funnier than it was dangerous.

Once they taunted someone, then felt the rabbi's hand;
Once they hit on some girls
And again felt the hot hand of the same rabbi.
Basically, the usual boys.
The most interesting thing was that there was not a single theft,

Not even an apple, despite the fact
That they knew all about the meaning of hunger,
And the food at the boarding school was, well, far from plentiful.
Evidently, they took very seriously
The giant inscription at the boarding school gates:

Thank you, residents of ancient Chorazin,
Which we had seen as some formal kind of propaganda.
Anyway, according to the chief of police, 'this pack'
Had unexpectedly 'gone wild' and had picked indiscriminately
On innocent boys in the street and beaten them up.

'I believe,' Police Chief Barzilai had said,
'That these wolf cubs at first simply hid out of sight,
Only now their stray essence has come crawling out into the open.
They need to be severely punished, put behind bars
And sent to do community service, 'to ensure none of

Those punks, who are still to come here,
Would ever think to torment and bother the fine folk of Chorazin.'

The majority of the town's fathers nodded with their beards,
As if to say, quite right, so they'd never think of such a thing,
While at the same time looking reproachfully at the Melamed brothers.

Grandfather Melamed remained silent and said nothing.
Iosif, however, with a voice that would stand no objection,
Interrupted Barzilai and the town's bigwigs, saying,
'First, let's investigate everything in detail,
And then we'll decide. If it's to punish them, then so be it, if they deserve it.'

And on that note, everyone parted for the evening,
Only a cold wind of hatred blew over the town.
Thanks to Allah, everyone was alive. However, many lads
Had been seriously injured,
And two from the town were still fighting for their lives.

The fight had been deviously brutal.
We had arrived on time and that had ensured no one had been *finished off*.
Although both sides had cried out to *take no prisoners*,
Which meant *to the death*.
Until the point of elimination, loss of consciousness and total incapacitation.

Naturally, that wind of hate was the parents' doing;
They didn't want to wait for an investigation,
Preferring to *put the squeeze* on Barzilai,
Demanding that the matter to taken straight to the local Sanhedrin court,
Whose members included many of the victims' parents.

The town demanded the blood of the *wolf cubs*.
No phrases like 'sons of Canaan' or 'family of Moses'
Could stand in the way of their retribution.
The temperature turned right up
When Barzilai read out his report to the town council,

Where he stated that the instigators had been
Senior class prefect Yeshua Magidson from Gush Halav
And another twelve lads from different provinces.
The senior police officer demanded that they be put away
Into the town prison, while a couple of dozen other lads a little younger,

Should be given a year's community service.
And if those two from the town don't make it.
Punish a dozen with their leader with execution and mutilation
By chopping off their hands, like thieves,
Or by branding their foreheads.

It goes without saying that the more sober-minded thought
That execution and mutilation was simply too cruel.
And, it seemed, that's how the majority thought.
However, strange as it may seem, it turned out not to be the case.
The majority, for some reason, had no issue with the ferocity of such a sentence.

Feeling the cold breath of the wind of hate.
The *legionnaires* barricaded themselves in the boarding school
And, it turned out, in good time, because that night, a crowd of irate parents
Surrounded the building with blazing torches,
Although they decided against storming the place.

First, because the boarding school's walls were imposing,
But more because a note was sent out from within,
Bearing but a few words:
We'll fight to the death for every last one of us.
The crowd made a fuss but, after three hours, went on its way.

This, however, did not mean that they had all calmed down.
The boarding school was literally under siege.
If the cadet boys went to the market
Or simply to the municipal wells,
They always risked running into angry parents.

That's right – parents! It was as if everyone had gone mad!
However, one thing stopped the crowd from the lynching.
One specific feature of Chorazin. It was this...
Well, I'll call it as it is:
Our Galilean intelligentsia,

Which we'd always been so proud of,
And which today is only a memory.
Back then, though, it was a powerful social force,
The object of our universal pride.
You see, in other dialects of the Land of Israel

No such word even existed.
It appeared only in our Aramaic dialect.
It's now said that Aramaic is the language of the poor.
To a point, that is correct, but our intelligentsia intentionally
Preserved its language like a tradition and took pride in it,

Emphasising its difference from other provinces
Of the Kingdom of Judea.
Then, they would say, *The high priests from Judea,*
The kings, from Edom, the magnates, from Samaria
And the intellectuals, from Galilee.

If all we Galileans are traditionalists,
Then Chorazin was the heart of the *old regime.*
I am sure that every resident of the town,
Perhaps in a little-used room, but still in a place of honour,
Secretly kept a Hasmonean[206] flag.

We were very proud of our intelligentsia.
Even the town's council was half-comprised of representatives
Of the *smart* professions – poets, doctors and teachers.
This pride allowed us to look down on our neighbours,
While they responded with the contemptuous *Syrians.*

But they never said that to our faces,
Only as a hissed retort as we walked away.
But we weren't shy or afraid

---

[206] In 37 BCE, King Herod the Great, who came from Edom, engaged the help of Roman legions and overthrew King Antigonus, the last of the Hasmonean dynasty, who had ruled Judea from 167 BCE as leaders and, since 145 BCE as a royal dynasty. Herod created a new, Herodian Dynasty.

To call our neighbours either Greeks, or Bedouins,
Or even *Jewish-Romans.*

Naturally, Grandfather Melamed was one of the most respected
Representatives of the town's intelligentsia.
I sensed that it was specifically thanks to his active work
That that base cruelty never came to the surface,
The advent of which in fellow citizens

Would plunge us into extreme, genuine confusion.
There was a feeling that from somewhere in the depths of labyrinths,
A monster had emerged on the surface,
A monster raised by another's hands
For our edification, or perhaps as a punishment.

And Grandfather's work really was active.
Earlier, he would file sedately about the school's corridors,
Chatting with parents
On elevated themes of philosophy and art,
Or on the rudiments of national pedagogy.

Now, though, like a true lion, he would rush into school for a short while,
Call in the parties involved in the incident, then the witnesses.
He would question them in turn, draw out the details,
Then rush away with his heavy leather-bound notebook,
Returning only nearer to evening, tired but focused.

He would often take me by the arm
And, leading me into his office,
Where it seemed that total chaos reigned,
With scattered papers, photographs and video cassettes,
Portraits of participants and a host of various scribbled notes,

He would ask me to help him in
Reproducing a complete picture of what had happened.
Grandfather pursued his own investigation.
Despite the fact that Barzilai had already gathered reams of papers
And was ready to hand the case over to the Sanhedrin,

The chief of police understood that dealing with the Melamed family
Would be more trouble that it was worth, so he held back on the charge.
Moreover, by that time,
The town's intelligentsia was recovering from the confusion and fear
And had declared its position unequivocally,

Stating it would never permit raving terror
To be meted out on the boys from the boarding school.
Now all three Moirai of fate had come together
Around a single, fateful object –
Grandather Melamed's thick, leather-bound notebook.

So, when the Lion of Order and Enlightenment
Had gathered all the information and gleaned all he could
About the *war of the legionnaires,*
We locked ourselves away with him for several days
In his office, asking that no one disturb us.

Step by step, we began reconstructing the events,
Endeavouring not simply to recover the chronology of the incident,
But to understand the undercurrents
That had led to such an outburst of wholly inappropriate cruelty
On the part of the teenagers and the adult residents of Chorazin alike.

Grandfather Melamed was sure that there were such undercurrents.
And what picture arose in the end?
The essence of what had happened shocked the both of us;
I now understand that if there had been no investigation,
I would never have got to the bottom of the subsequent events.

In terms of the chronology, it all began
When the cute and quite harmless Josik Gabay
Came home one day with a broken nose
And a bruised face, like when you get hit right in the middle of the forehead,
As the bruise spreads over both eyes.

Everything would have worked out not quite as badly
If Josik had come home just a little later,
But he walked up to his home right at the time
When his father, who was not just anyone, but Isaac Gabay,
The head of our synagogue,

Was standing out front with all five of Josik's brothers.
They had just returned home from a meeting
With the high priest from Jerusalem.
Incidentally, these meetings are worthy of special mention,
For otherwise it would be impossible to grasp the full background.

These meetings were an event in themselves, as they used to say
In the cultural life of Chorazin.
And some, for none other than the
Recently appointed High Priest,
The young and energetic Joseph Caiaphas would come to them.

The nature of these events was made all the more exclusive
Because Caiaphas was a *Sadducee*,
The first of the Jerusalem high priests
To come to the very heart of the Galilean *Pharisees*,
As our quiet university town of Chorazin was seen.

He had already held five meetings by that time.
And he planned another three.
It has to be said that this young high priest
Was an outstanding propagandist
(And it is hard to pick another word here).

His fiery speeches on free will[207]
Caused unrest among the priests and intellectuals,
But were met with warm approval

---

[207] One of the key differences in the three main currents of Judaism was that the *Essenes* preached divine predestination; the *Sadducees* – absolute free will, that a man's fate is entirely in his own hands; while the *Pharisees*, on the other hand, asserted that, 'although man is given the freedom to choose between honest and dishonest deeds, the predestination of fate also plays a role in this'.

By merchants and small businesspeople.
There were no magnates in Chorazin at that time.

However, most of all, the local elite were not worried by speeches
On the potential successes of an entrepreneur,
Evidencing that God is entirely on his side.
What caused the most alarm was the somehow overly tempestuous,
Irreconcilable and radical anti-Roman sentiment.

Given that the nearest Roman we had
Who one could meet was no nearer than in Tiberias,
And that the high priests in Jerusalem lay themselves out before strangers
In this slimy, affected, politicking,
This propaganda appeared more than a little odd.

The intelligentsia and the clergy immediately realised
That the aristocratic Sadducees were not averse to raking the heat
Using the hands of others. But did we actually need that?
It happened that Antipas and his *oprichnik* guards had never
Got further than Tiberias into the ancient land of Galilee.

However, for some reason, these speeches had had a
Mesmerising effect on the young people.
The elders would leave the meetings with mixed feelings,
Huddling by their homes and speaking in whispers
That new, troubled times were evidently not far off.

Fathers would come to the meetings with their sons as they were supposed to,
So that the sons, from an early age, would grow accustomed to religious discussions.
The Chorazinians were not afraid that Caiaphas would change anything
Fundamentally in the children's upbringing; the Pharisee traditions were too strong
And the roots of the intelligentsia were too powerful.

They weren't afraid but how wrong they were. And they would very soon realise this.
That said, it was already clear
That some of the young people who came to the meetings, secured
The Sadducean sign of the cross in the form of a Roman X to their clothing –
The symbol of the chalice and the sword.

And this craze seized not only the young people.
Many merchant's stores, somehow unnoticed,
Became adorned with an oblique Sadducee cross as a sign that
The owner of the given company
Was accepting a new view of life and a new meaning.

But let's return for now to Josik Gabay, who had loped home
At the wrong time. It was wrong because
Isaac Gabay had to deal with his son,
To ascertain what had happened, in the eyes
Of a dozen heads of families and in the presence of their children.

He could have simply learned about it on the quiet,
Gone and sorted things out with the offenders,
More likely, with the parents.
And what of it? This was just a fight between lads.
It would certainly not be the first.

However, what was unusual was that those offenders were the *legionnaires*.
Having heard this from Josik, the men, of different ages,
Began murmuring and raising their voices, saying things like,
Can you believe what those legionnaire *squirts have been up to?*
It's right what Caiaphas said: an alien culture has got into the heart,

Diluting and dissolving the integrity of the Galileans,
And immersing them in a cruelty
That is not inherent in the sons of Moses.
Here, the elder looked at them in ire
And shouted, 'You'll be baying for blood next, you sons of Chorazin,[208]

The way that Jerusalem epicurean has got you going!
We'll deal with this ourselves; there's no need to take the behaviour of rowdy kids
And dress it up as something it's not – politics.
Khalfan, Glazerman, you want to tell me you never got into fights in your childhood?'
He stopped short, for the first time encountering stubborn rejection.

The elder went to the boarding school and, having weeded out the offenders,
He brought them outside, to work out what had actually happened.
(In the presence of their teachers, of course.)
It turned out that Josik had been hit by the cadet Tsakhi Amir,
And the reason was that

Three times a week, Josik attended the music school,
And his route there took him past the boarding school.
(That was basically why, on that fateful day
He had missed his father's and brothers' trip to meet with Caiaphas.)
Near the boarding school, there were always cadets milling about,

Taking a break from their studies or for whatever other reason.
One day, Josik was stopped by a tall lad in a blue uniform
Who screamed, 'Hey little Gabay, show us your violin!'
It was Tsakhi Amir, the ringleader and comedian.
Josik stopped in fright; there were a good dozen lads there,

And they could put the heat on him good and proper.
Those things were rare but they did happen.
However, here was the thing:
Since early childhood, Tsakhi had dreamed about playing the violin
And had even managed to teach himself at home in Bethlehem,

Until his father died and his mother drowned
On a slave trader's trireme.
Then he had no time for the violin, which he swapped for some bread.
There followed two years of begging in the slums of Bethlehem,
Before he had come to the Chorazin military boarding school.

Every time he would stop Josik on his way from school
And take his violin to pluck at it a little,
Much to the delight of his classmates.
Of course, this was hurtful to Josik,

---

[208] A fundamental difference between the teachings of the Pharisees and the Sadducees concerned the attitude to the death penalty. The Pharisees did not recognise it, while the Sadducees did; the latter were in favour of the harshest possible penalties for religious infringements and crimes.

But then he even grew accustomed to it all.

If he would stand there like an idiot at first, shuffling from one foot to the next,
Waiting for Tsakhi to finish his exercises,
Later, he would even sit down next to the cadets
And play *nozhichki*[209], thinking, to hell with that violin,
That he hated it and would have been better to have had binoculars instead.

However, after ten or fifteen minutes of fun, emitting
Awful sounds from Josik's violin, Tsakhi Fmir
Would carefully replace the instrument in the case,
Sigh and with a hard-to-conceal yearning, he'd return it to Gabay,
Saying, 'now beat it,' to conceal his feelings behind his rudeness.

That is how this symbiosis existed for a time –
Josik happily missed every other music lesson,
While Tsakhi distracted himself from his military drill by plucking away on the strings.
However, this was not destined to last long
Because the music teacher complained to Monsieur Gabay

About his son and the father gave Josik a stern
But fair talking to about his education.
Josik refrained from mentioning Tsakhi, simply saying
That he was hanging about with the lads from the neighbourhood.
He said nothing to his brothers either,

For they would soon work out where he'd actually been hanging out.
It seemed that everything should fall into place,
But there was still the music-loving cadet Amir.
It is unknown what would have happened
Had Gabay junior simply told him everything as it was.

But Josik chose a different path.
Rather, he was pushed into it by a new propagandist,
Who had arrived from Holy Jerusalem.
I mentioned that Caiaphas's fiery speeches
Had lit a dubious fire

In the hearts of the Chorazin boys.

On the eve of having it out with Tsakhi Amir,
The brothers had secretly sewn the Sadducee cross
Onto their shirts so their father wouldn't notice.
The younger ones, to be honest, had done it more out of mischief,
But the older ones were really quite serious.

The eldest brother, Elimelech
Said to Josik, 'Well, brother, when you grow up, will you become a zealot?
And beat the Romans in your native land?'
'I will,' the boy mumbled.
'First, though,' Elimelech went on, proud of himself,

'We'll destroy all the hangers-on and cowards in our towns and cities,
To ensure the sons of Israel won't find it repulsive
To get weighed down by those foreign colonialists!'

---

[209] A divide-and-conquer game, drawn in the earth with a penknife.

It was pretty much in this context that Josik had set off that day
To sort things out with the music-loving cadet.

Josik spent the entire journey convincing himself, 'I'm no coward! I'm no coward!'
He prayed that Tsakhi had been placed on duty that day,
Or even for a week. No, forever! *I hope he's been enlisted into the legion!*
He's a legionnaire, right? Yes, that's right, the bastard's a legionnaire!
He is evil, violence, one of Rome's henchmen!

But I'm a Zealot! I'm a hero! I am David, slayer of Goliath!
I am the spark and the fire of uprising!
I'll end this shameful, slave-like lack of resistance
Once and for all, as is befitting a hero!
As is befitting a fighter against foreigners and barbarians!

Josik drew nearer the boarding school with these thoughts,
When, from round the corner, with a great big grin on his face, came Tsakhi.
'Hi, little Gabay, give us your instrument!
The sprogs are waiting for their game of *nozhichki* with you.
They're sentries today, and they've been given their guards' daggers.'

The *sprogs* waved to Josik from beyond Tsakhi.
The cadet, stretched out for the music case as was now customary...
But Gabay flinched away as if he'd been stung.
'You!' he suddenly roared breathlessly,
Breaking hysterically into a squeal.

'Get your hands off! You won't have my violin anymore!'
Tsakhi's eyes widened and his voice betrayed surprise.
'Gabay, what's the deal? What's got into you?'
'Get your hands off,' the boy persisted. 'I'm not giving you anything!'
The *sprog*-cadets watched the scene unfold motionlessly.

'Jos, take a look at these daggers! Come and play *nozhich...*'
One of them started to cry, but then stopped.
'Don't you dare come near me again!' Gabay went on,
'You Roman henchman. You foreigner!
You son of a Roman washerwoman, you *legionnaire*!!!'

Tsakhi's eyes suddenly fell on the new badge,
Sewn onto Josik's sleeve. Cadet Amir's eyes darkened
And turned as grey as steel.
He put his hands in his pockets and turned,
Silently walking back towards the boarding school.

No one saw the scenes that swirled before the lad
Like a swarm; scenes he had seen not so long ago.
The shore, a jetty. Soldiers taking women onto a boat.
Suddenly, one broke away and started running
But exhausted, she fell at the feet of a bearded man in white.

'Save us, Rabbi, save us!' she croaked with the last of her strength,
Stretching out her arms.
The man recoiled in horror
In a way that almost toppled his turban
With the letter X on it, like a cross.

436

'Don't you dare touch me, woman,' he muttered,
Hiding behind the backs of Roman soldiers. 'Don't you dare!'
One of the soldiers bent over the woman
And gave her a proper clobber on the head with his baton.
She wheezed and fell limp.

The soldiers picked her up and tossed her
Into the dark, hungry belly of the boat,
From which songs could be heard,
The likes of which others would hear many years later
And thousands of kilometres away.

A boy then walked up to this man
In white with his turban marked with a cross,
Grasped at the hem of his robe and, oh-so quietly,
Barely louder than a murmur of the sea breeze, asked him,
'Please sir, save my mummy! *She has done nothing wrong!*'

From the unexpectedness of it all, the man dropped the coins
The fat ship's master had counted out to him.
He frowned and nodded to the soldier standing nearby,
As if to say, *get that off me.*
The soldier kicked the boy and, after that, it all went quickly black...

It was images like these that had forced Cadet Amir to hunch over
As he wandered over to the Chorazin boarding school,
Leaving behind him a little part of the dream
That, to be quite honest,
The occasional squeaks on Josik's violin would not have saved.

A dream that was not destined to come true,
Because all that awaited him was war
For foreign goals and ideals,
A foreign home and foreign landscapes.
What awaited him was the legion.

What? That was it? Josik had fallen silent in surprise.
So where was the heroism? Where was the battle with the superior forces
Of the colonial enemy? Where was the fight? Where was the gallant deed?
In three leaps, Josik flew like the wind to the cadet *sprogs*
And, snatching a dagger from them, rushed after the offender.

The scream of one of the boys
Made Tsakhi turn just in time.
Thanks to his training in the homeless struggle,
He was able to step to the side from the boy's attack
And thrust his own hand forward.

Gabay slumped to the ground, Blood flowing from his nose.
Tsakhi looked in astonishment at his fist
And then at the *sprogs.* He said, 'Take him home.'
Then he turned, spat maliciously and, glancing once more at the cross, said,
'Sadducee idiot!' And went on his way.

The cadets resolved not to accompany Josik home.
They took him to the yards and, shaking him down, sent him on his way.
Then, like a silent flock of ruffled sparrows,

Ran to the protection of the boarding school's walls,
Evidently sensing the start of something not good.

So, that is the story that father Gabay heard
When he came to sort things out at the boarding school.
He demanded that the teachers bring Tsakhi Amir in,
And he looked him over with a long stare,
Before saying sternly and gravely,

'From now on, don't you dare offend the little ones!
If I find out you have, you'll have me to deal with!'
And that was it.
The incident might have run its course there,
If Josik's brothers hadn't learned about all the finer details.

Where from? Well, the world is not without good people,
Prepared, with good intentions,
Quietly to do some slimy evil deed.
Two days later, five Gabay teenagers
With crosses sewn onto their sleeves

Ambushed Tsakhi Amir by the western wall of the boarding school
And executed their cruel reprisal against him.
They might even have beaten the lad to death,
If it had not been for his training in the slums of Jerusalem
And, most important, his cadet comrades who appeared in time.

Grandfather Melamed wearily wiped his eyes behind his glasses and said,
'Philip, we have, like you, encountered a host of fights between boys.
There is a point of vengeance, after which
It is in everyone's interests to disperse, lick their wounds
And put a stop to mutual reprisals.

The reason for this is that
Not one of the opposing sides
Has any interest in
Adult forces getting involved in the showdown.
If there are too many fights,

Then wait for Barzilai in your backyard.

This is a completely different thing.
These were not face-offs in the style of *an eye for an eye*
Or a struggle for control over three park benches.
This was an ideological war,
On whose banners quite different meanings were inscribed for us.

The *legionnaires'* ire was not kindled because of the lynching of their comrade,
Rather the fact it had been done by the youngsters
With identical Sadducee crosses on their shirts.
The cadets had their own scores to settle when it came to this symbol.
Each one of them.

I interviewed the kids from the boarding school,
Asking what lay behind their terrible dislike
For people of the clergy. Didn't it sound like nonsense?
And what does faith have to do with any of this?

The picture that formed from the kids' stories was this.

Faith and religious hair-splitting have absolutely nothing to do with anything.
The Sadducees are not just a religious movement;
They are a powerful and far-reaching aristocratic clan.
When Archelaus died and Judea and Samaria found themselves
Without a sovereign, under the control of a Roman procurator,

The Sadducee clans decided to seize control
Over all the financial and trade flows in these provinces.
They reached agreement with the Romans, that the latter would not
Poke their noses where imperial authorities had no interest.
They agreed only to regular tribute payments,

Control of tax collection and maritime shipping.
The most important thing that the clan leaders obtained
Was the return of the right to hold court.
All the Romans left were crimes against the Empire
And the imposition of death sentences.

The Sadducees wanted to keep the latter for themselves
And the Romans actually had no serious objections.
However, the Pharisee communities came out strongly *against*;
And they still had considerable influence in these parts.
They forced the Romans to take the death penalty upon themselves.

The Epicureans[210] gradually cleared the Sanhedrin
Of its enemies, and this body
Then received almost unlimited power
In Judea, Samaria and Edom.
The Romans demanded a high price for the right to hold court.

The Sadducees had to pay tribute in human form –
By replenishing the foreign-based Roman legions
And for delivery to the slave markets of Italy and Hellas.
Incidentally, our compatriots in the local Roman
Units served with pleasure as it was;

The pay was good and the social status decent,
Only no one wanted to die somewhere, a thousand parasangs
From the Land of Israel.
Not only that, but our *peregrini* were certainly not flavour of the month
Among the Roman soldiers for their involvement in crushing the rebellions of legionnaires.

So, our children from the boarding school are the victims
Of this monstrous deal struck by our compatriots
With the official authorities of the Empire.
Now you understand, Philip, why Tsakhi was so influenced
By the patch on the sleeve of that simple Chorazin boy Josik Gabay?

You remember that Barzilai spoke about,
You know, those *legionnaires*, running amok, beating everyone up,

---

[210] In his book *The Jewish War*, Flavius Josephus presents analogies for an accessible explanation of the Jewish teachings, using some of their similarities with Greek teachings: the Sadducees with the Epicurians, the Pharisees with the Stoics and the Essenes with the Pythagoreans.

Following no system, indiscriminately and quite ferociously?
Well, it was all the other way round.
The day after Tsakhi was beaten up

(And that was a weekend, so there were few officers around)
Groups of cadets were hammered together and hit the town,
Capturing lads with cross patches and
Beating them up
The thing was that Tsakhi Amir was beaten very badly

And would lose consciousness from time to time, while telling
Who had beaten him up and why.
Therefore, the cadets didn't know they had to look
Specifically for the five Gabay brothers,
And instead performed a diligent cleansing of the entire town

Of those *Sadducee idiots*.
Fights would break out here and there.
Back then, our Chorazin lads didn't really understand
Why someone would want to sew on a horizontal cross and,
To the cry of *they're beating up our lads*, everyone rose up.

Near to Severny Boulevard, the Chorazinians gathered
An impressive cohort,
Which then moved decisively to meet the boarding school cadets.
The *legionnaires* retreated to their lodgings
And, by evening, the town was quiet.

The townsfolk then swore to have their revenge on the outsiders,
But, to prevent others getting in the way,
Everyone swore an oath to remain silent about what had happened.
You recall when we tried to get to the bottom
Of the bruises that Weidman and Botvinnik were sporting?

Back then, we decided that these must have been regular yard fights.
Yet not one of them said a word!
I'll go on. Everything was unfolding pretty much according to the typical scenario
When street gangs have their usual showdowns,
Only the events sped off in a completely different direction.

The series of meetings of the townsfolk and Caiaphas was coming to an end.
The young high priest, it turned out,
Really wasn't counting on the power of persuasion alone.
The last meeting was choreographed as a complete triumph
With what at first seemed to be foolish ceremony,

Elements of showmanship and theatrics.
But whatever, with the showmanship.
During the meeting, Caiaphas turned word into deed,
Offering our merchants proper contracts
For the supply of goods to the central provinces,

And offering lending terms of
Banks in the capital to finance these transactions.
He did this at the beginning so, by the end of the performance,
The eyes of the citizens burned with a fire of anticipation
Of new horizons in benefits from trading with the Centre.

440

The Sadducees didn't forget the young people either,
Inviting them to form so-called
Free-Will detachments,
And engage in enhanced patriotic training,
As he put it, "for the great battles of the future."

Naturally, there was no mention of what kind of battles these were.
After all, all that was needed was one stooge
And the Procurator of Caesarea would quickly place
A young, high-handed type as high priest.
However, the propaganda was so sophisticated and patriotic,

That no one even reported on the agitator.
Although I do think that the inherent decency
Of the residents of Chorazin was still very much alive.
After this meeting, the merchants and artisans went home
To dream of the fates of magnates and oligarchs,

While some of the young people gathered in the central park
Where they held a vociferous meeting
And resolved to create the *Chorazin Free Will Union*.
In so doing, every new member was handed
Patches and insignia, which Caiaphas had prudently prepared in advance.

Then something interesting happened.
When the lads got together the following day,
To plan their act of vengeance against the boarding school cadets,
They witnessed a fundamental split in their midst.
Some of the lads demanded that the retribution

Be the first military operation of *Free Will*.
However, the majority of the teenagers, in no less decisive terms,
Demanded that the new and for now
Not totally clear ideology not be mixed
With the knightly code of the lads from the streets of Chorazin.

Moreover, the greater part,
In light of their traditional, Pharisaic upbringing,
Decisively rejected all notion of
All the lads automatically becoming
Members of the new organisation.

The New Sadducees threatened their fellow countrymen
That, in any case, they would enter battle with the society's insignia,
And whoever disagreed would be declared an accomplice
Of the *legionnaires* from the boarding school and, through them,
Of the Roman occupying forces.

They recalled that it had been specifically
Lads with insignia who'd been beaten on the streets,
So they had every right to declare to everyone else
That this was purely a matter between cadets and the *Free Will* members,
And that everyone else could get lost.

The contradictions were so strong
That the participants went on their way without even deciding

441

When Josik Gabay and the *New Sadducees* would be avenged.
In addition, those not included in the Union
Considered themselves insulted and rudely sidelined from the matter.

As for the Union members, without waiting for a common decision,
Arranged a torch procession the following day
From the central park to the boarding school gates,
Where they shouted threats and, as yet,
Poorly formulated slogans, all in unison.

They ended their march by shoving a sheet of paper under the gates,
Onto which, in blood from cut fingers,
They wrote the date when the cadets were called to fight.
Those not accustomed to torch processions
Didn't really understand the young people's enthusiasm

And chose just to ignore them, thinking,
Well, they want to march, so let them,
Perhaps it's some paramilitary patriotic game or something.
As the boys couldn't really explain
Their crude slogans and appeals,

Everyone chose to brush them aside; some even praised them,
As if to say, the lads were right and speaking plainly.
The lads not in the Union,
Despite not being united under the banner of one organisation,
Still had their backyard warning system in play,

Using which they quickly spread the decision
That, since they were not being considered and that the others were taking advantage,
So be it. Let the *New Sadducees*
Deal with the cadets themselves; after all, indeed,
They did beat up the lads with the insignia.

You see what a complicated story this is,
And one that could have been called protracted,
Had it not unfolded quite as rapidly as it did.
And what did you learn about that boy,
The cadet leader Yeshua Magidson[211] from Gishala?

How did he come to the fore
And what is his role in all of this?'
'Yes, headteacher, sir, what I can say
Is that the line of conduct of the lad in all this
Is also wholly unusual.

The thing is that Yeshua enjoyed authority among the cadets
Not only because he was one of the oldest.
Magidson hailed from an Essene family or,
To be more accurate, a community,
And he was trained in its traditions from childhood.

---

[211] All surnames in this verse have a meaning, describing either origin (profession) or a descriptive image. For example, *Melamed* means primary school (*cheder*) teacher, *Weidman* is a hunter, *Katseva* (*Katsev*) is a butcher, *Barzilai* means iron, *Belferman* is a junior schoolteacher, *Magidson* is a preacher, *Gabay* is the head of a synagogue and so on.

You know that this odd people of foreigners from Judea,
Hanging out in the caves of our deserts,
Finds marriage unacceptable and often adopts other people's children.
So, Magidson is not even a surname.
It might even be a nickname.

So, since childhood, this lad had this certain *je ne sais crois*
That clearly distinguished him from the crowd of waifs.
Our excessive love for our Hasmonean home
Even led to all manner of speculation
And myths about the boy.

The officers from the boarding school even saw a kind of royalty in him,
But by no means from a desire to command.
Remember how at the very beginning of the boarding school's operation
The newspapers kicked up a fuss about the awful, cruel customs
That were established among the pupils?

About the humiliation of juniors, the bullying of the little ones
And the endless fights and beatings during the night?
Anyway, all that came to an end when Yeshua arrived.
Somehow, he managed to instil in all the lads that they were
All part of a single whole, a brotherhood,

Who, against their will, would have to put their heads together
The next day, so there was no need to fight one another.
In fact, quite the contrary, do everything to help one another out.
Very quickly, criminal news from the boarding school
Dried up and we teachers

Saw it as a natural outcome of the educational process.
In reality, however, this was the result of the work
Of a seriously talented young man of unknown origin,
To whom not only friends came to resolve things,
But often the officers from the boarding school too.

And so, in the heat of the *military* action,
Having learned about the formation of the *Free Will* Union,
This Yeshua and his twelve cheerleader friends
Took a desperate step,
Which I can't get my head around.

In any event, I recall nothing of the kind,
From all my experiences in life.
Forgive me, but I also grew up under the harsh laws of the streets
Of my native Bethsaida. Well, it makes no difference where;
The lads' knightly street code is pretty much the same all over.

So, what was Yeshua planning?
Having learned about the location of the *Free Will* meeting,
He went there with his twelve companions.
What was most surprising was that the lad's charisma was such
That, at first, the *New Sadducees* didn't even lay a finger on him,

But heard him out for at least an hour.
According to witnesses,

The majority of the boys even began to doubt
The need for a retaliatory battle,
For Magidson's words certainly hit a nerve.

Not only did he call for an end to that day's fighting.
But he spoke of there actually being a need
For a struggle for justice and liberation,
That the *great battle* would take place not in the strife of boys,
But on the fields of other conflicts, before which we would need

To preserve a true sense of brotherhood and love for one another.
"You see," he said, "perhaps we and you,
Gabay and Weidman,
Will stand shoulder to shoulder
On the same side of one Holy Army?"

Naturally, I am giving you the gist in my own words.
We have to remember that the boys were faced not with an Essene monk,
But a weathered warrior of Jerusalem street fights,
From where he had been brought to the boarding school by Antipas's soldiers.
The only thing is that every organisation

Has its leaders, who dislike it
When people come from outside and take for themselves
What is most important: control over the hearts and minds of their allies.
While many still doubted,
The leaders, who incidentally included Gabay Jnr,

Had arranged an execution for the cadets.
What was most surprising was they were afraid to beat them.
They needed to achieve something else – moral humiliation,
A trampling over the principles of the kids and their grinding into dust,
To force them to renounce these same principles.

They brought the cadets to their knees
And, mocking them, shaved their forelocks.
Then they painted their bodies and faces with the word *peace*
And, having drawn a broad Sadducee cross of their chests,
They sent them packing.

Initially, there were plenty of opponents among the boarders
To the peaceful campaign of Yeshua and his comrades.
What's there to say? They included those
Who were not happy with calm and just practices,
As established by the lad from Gishala.

When the humiliated leaders of the *legionnaires* returned to the boarding school,
The adversaries skilfully turned the indignation
To a ferocious battle cry for the cadets.
However, Yeshua had the last word.
He held back with his decision for a day,

Remaining alone and deep in thought.
The next day he entered the barracks and announced his verdict:
"We've been slapped across one cheek.
Having suffered such humiliation, are we really going to present the other?
Let those who don't wish for peace, receive our swords!"

444

And so, a couple of days later, on the appointed day, the massacre took place,
Of which, headmaster, sir, you are fully aware.'
'No, my dear colleague, not everything,' Grandfather objected.
'The doctors at the hospital said that two boys
In the gravest condition

Are most likely doomed not to recover and that means
We are on the eve of a new round of hatred.
Alahi, who can explain what is happening?!
What's the point of all these ideologies, insignia and torch processions?!
They are just children. *Our children!*'

What could I say to Melamed in response?
I also sensed that the algorithm of our lives
Had suddenly begun to be controlled by some terrible machine,
Extending its grabber-feelers from within,
Invisible and yet relentless!

Sensing how powerless I was, I didn't know
That this was only the beginning of events to come...
Suddenly, the door to the office swung open
And we saw Hazzan Joseph standing there.
'Bad news, Zinoviy, the boys died in hospital this morning...'

Headteacher Zinoviy Melamed shook his shaggy grey
Head like a mighty lion. His eyes flared a fierce fire.
He jumped up, took his leather-bound notebook and,
Snatching the notes from my hand,
Rushed out in the direction of the town square.

This is how the events then unfolded:
Grandfather Melamed demanded an emergency calling of the town council.
And just in time, for an enormous crowd of people
Had moved in the direction of the boarding school
With a wholly unambiguous desire to lynch the cadets inside.

The council gathered swiftly.
First of all, the headmaster forced Barzilai to give the order
For the police to cordon off the boarding school in a tight circle.
The head of police conformed reluctantly but he did give the order
To his idly watching officers to surround the building.

The council sealed all the doors
And then the search began for a solution, destined to take many hours.
Onlookers, journalists and parents
Could only hear, from behind the heavy doors,
The loud, low voice of Grandfather Melamed.

I walked with the crowd towards the boarding school.
It was not for nothing the cadets had received military training;
The building had been barricaded according to all the rules of a siege.
The gates opened only once, and just for a moment,
To let the training officers out.

They emerged with placards attached to their chests, reading:
He who is not ready to die of his own will

445

Will not die. Some tutors had wanted
To stay but they too were unceremoniously
Thrown out the door.

Everyone was waiting for the decision of the council and Sanhedrin.
The police cordon did its job.
The crown began, little by little, to cool down and disperse.
However, its aggressive core continued its menacing
Hustling of the silent ranks of law enforcement officers.

Having calmed down a little, I suddenly noticed
That the ranks of the most zealous,
Decorated with their *Free Will* crosses,
Contained an ever-growing number of adults and even women.
At the time, I still couldn't explain this.

The council was in session for several days.
The entire town felt like it was under siege.
Despite the changing time of day,
The exalted *New Sadducees* continued
Their siege of the boarding school.

The council doors opened only at the end of the second day.
The haggard fathers of the town emerged
But everyone could see that, despite their fatigue,
Their eyes were aglow with a particular determination,
Which told us that,

In reaching a decision,
The people had grown above themselves.
Their fatigue merely told us
That this growth, over a very short period,
Had come at a very high price.

To our surprise, the town fathers
Did not announce their decision loudly,
Rather, they dived energetically into the crowd
And each of them, gathering people around,
Proceeded to explain the situation.

The people listened attentively and, to my satisfaction,
They mostly nodded their heads in agreement.
I instinctively felt that the right solution had been found.
So, praise be to human common sense!
And, praise be to the Chorazin intelligentsia and the clergy!

One thing still bothered me.
The ranks of the *New Sadducees* had been joined by those town fathers
Who had also sewn a horizontal oblique cross on their coats.
This was the only thing that did not overshadow my mood.
Who knows what views people hold?

After all, we live in a town of freedom of belief.
That is the strength of the Galilean Pharisees –
The ability to find compromise
And the ability to listen,
Without infringing on their freedom of expression.

446

The solution actually exceeded all my expectations.
The Melamed brothers had persuaded the council
That the trouble had begun because
Our children had been divided
By an invisible, alien hand.

But they had no guilt in that;
They were all children of our people.
Therefore, the town fathers were now on the square, convincing the residents
To resolve the matter fundamentally and...
House the cadets among the families!

Naturally, this concerned those who could afford it.
To my surprise and great pride,
The people's anger rapidly changed to compassion.
Everyone was clearly overwhelmed by conflicting feelings
During these difficult times.

Somehow, from out of nowhere, tables appeared,
Taking the names of those wishing to adopt cadets.
The expressions in the people's eyes quickly changed too.
The *Free Will* activists suddenly seemed confused
And slowly, reluctantly, they shuffled over to the tables.

Half an hour later, it was a completely different crowd.
Gone was that animalistic magnetism of marches, cries and slogans.
It even seemed that the people of the town had gathered for a holiday,
Because smiles and joyful excitement were now at the forefront.
Here and there, people went up to the town fathers

And thanked them. But for what?
I quietly went over to one group of townsfolk,
Who were surrounding the Melamed brothers
And I was shocked by what I heard.
'Thank you for giving us back the real us,' they said.

The families of the lads who had perished said to the priests –
And Adonai's part was plain to see here –
That, having failed to save their own sons,
They were being given the chance to give happiness to other boys,
Whom they would bestow the additional name of Nathaniel.[212]

However, one problem remained.
All this time, the boarding school stood with walls of a Masada-like fortress.
How would the cadets themselves react to this solution?
The Lion of the Desert headed the delegation to the boarding school, of course.
Well, and I got myself into the small group.

The gates opened before us and we went in.
I saw the boys' faces – they were frightened and wary.
Some clutched at daggers,
Others peered out
From behind the backs of comrades.

---

[212] The name Nathaniel means *God given*. A name from the Tanakh.

Others conducted themselves in military fashion,
Quite unusual to see in teenagers;
Adjusting weapons in a business-like manner
And looking us over indifferently,
They continued their watch from their posts.

We went into the school sports hall
And the first thing that leapt out at us
Was that, tied up in one corner
Were Yeshua and his twelve comrades.
However, there was no time for our indignation to rise,

As it was explained that they were tied up because they had wanted
To offer themselves up in atonement –
Go out and be mauled by the crowd and thus save the others.
The cadets, however, wouldn't allow them to do that.
When we told them the problem had been resolved,

They untied them there and then.
I saw that as soon as a cadet sergeant untied Yeshua
The latter gave him a clip round the ear that appeared to end
A dispute that we hadn't seen.
The sergeant merely grinned mischievously. Kids!

Of course, the council of boys accepted the solution cautiously,
Silently and with distrust, actually.
What did they want from these unfortunate homeless children?
What grounds did they have to trust us adults?
What if it were another trap?

However, glory to Adonai, everything turned out well.
In a week, all the children were found homes.
There were even arguments over who would take more.
I was so proud of my people,
For my town, the warm-hearted Chorazin.

They say that, from that time, there was a tradition in the Land of Israel
Not to erect shelters for orphans, but give them to families
To preserve the seed of the tribe of Moses,
So that no tribesman would be broken
By the lot of a homeless orphan.

The town's fathers had reached another decision too.
That was that no one would ever try to restore the group of boarders;
Late one night, unnoticed, the school was set on fire and
Not a trace remained of that imposing Roman building.
Any recollection of the *legionnaires war* was gone.

Of course, a commission of Roman commissioners arrived
Along with messengers from the Jerusalem Sanhedrin,
To investigate a case of deliberate arson.
However, as one, they simply shrugged their shoulders
And said it had caught fire all by itself.

And what was there to say? It was so hot, that there was little wonder.
But where were the children? Who knows, perhaps they'd fled to the Essenes.

Everyone must have fled before the fire.
What, you didn't take them into the legion then?
We thought you must have and we weren't worried.

They tried counting the children,
Counting how many the townsfolk had and how many there were now.
After all, this was essentially the theft of Imperial property (kids)!
Here, our Galilean breeding didn't let us down.
So, how many kid's does Sema's family have? Five or six.

No, it's seven. Definitely seven! Or perhaps it's six...
I don't know for sure. I'm not even sure how many I've got.
I personally heard how the Romans screamed and shouted:
'Herod was planning to hold a census
And never got it finished. Now try counting those hooknoses!'

Those in Jerusalem also shrugged, saying
How do we prove that kid is not so-and-so's?
Who knows whose children those Essenes have,
So, what, we have to change our traditions, is that it?
Upon hearing the word *traditions*, the Romans immediately saddened.

We really got to them with our traditions.
In short, they gave up on the whole idea, closed the matter
And went on their way.
Incidentally, do you know the most interesting thing?
Tsakhi Ami was taken in by the family of Gabay the prefect!

That same Yitzhak Amir, the great violinist
Who we saw on the posters in Tiberias,
Is none other than Tsakhi the cadet! How's that for a story?
Today, Josik is champion boxer of the state police.
They say he still can't stand the violin.

The town came to live a life of its own.
And so did I. Year after year, Seeing kids graduate and move on.
I became immersed in my school days.
Glory to Allah, I was never bored
Thanks to the active life of a shepherd of children.

Oh yes, there was one important thing I forgot.
Yeshua Magidson lived for a while with Hazzan Joseph.
Melamed Senior really loved the lad.
He told him a lot about the scriptures.
They often spent the nights talking about things we don't know.

One day, however, Yeshua left and disappeared without a trace.
Since then, no one has seen or heard anything of him.
He had come to see me one evening before he disappeared,
And we chatted at length over a cup of tea.
If only I had known that the next day he would leave the town!

I don't particularly remember our conversation.
The only thing I do remember was the sadness
In his terribly grown-up eyes
When he told me that he had realised one thing:
'There is no power in the sword that slaughters many.'

449

I objected, saying that if not the sword, who would stand up for the weak?
He replied, 'Am I not culpable for the death of the innocent?
For it was me who proclaimed the need to fight,
Even if it were for an idea that I thought was right?
Even if everyone around me recognised it as right?'

I replied, 'But didn't that lead to an outcome
That was to the benefit of your companions?'
'Yes,' he said, 'that is precisely what I'm talking about.
After all, it was the decision of the town fathers that
Was a model solution for a *war without the sword*, right?'

'You know (I have to admit, I was not ready for such a conversation),
Yeshua, you know, judge for yourself,
But if it were not for the death of those boys,
Could the town fathers have reached such a ground-breaking solution,
To adopt the children of the boarding school?

Perhaps, and Adonai forgive me, but the lads' death
Was the sacrifice that had to be made
To awaken the fundamental essence
In the hearts of the townsfolk
Of, and I'm not afraid to say it, their main duty to the people and to God?'

I was so preoccupied in checking the exercise books
That I admit I wasn't able to concentrate fully
On the conversation with the young leader.
Therefore, I was taken aback by the tear that suddenly
Ran down his cheek bearing its early man's fluff.

'So that's a sacrifice, nonetheless,' he uttered.
'So, only that, not a word, a song or a poem
Are able to make people return to their essence...'
'No, no, Yeshua,' I hurried to turn the conversation back on track.
'No, of course not, only, then, we couldn't find

The right songs, words or verses.
But that doesn't mean they have no use.
It all happened so fast,
And no one could gather their thoughts when the fateful time came
To take decisions, and we missed an awful lot...'

His eyes dried at that and took on a decisive expression.
'The time is of no consequence,' he said gravely.
Let it repeat itself over and over in its cycle.
But, up above, that one will always
Look down through a lens of sacrifice,

That is clearly the price of returning
A man to his very essence.
It remains for us to understand if
Sacrifice is always so effective
As we think it is, according to our human canons of logic.

Perhaps there are other ways
Where there is no sword and no crucifixion?

No torture to the death or worse, no doubts?'
'What crucifixion, my friend?'
I could not raise my eyes from the exercise books.

'What crucifixion, for everything turned out for the best, didn't it?'
The young man stood up and shook me firmly by the hand.
'I will return to Chorazin, to the place,' Yeshua said,
'Where I saw the essence of man in all its glory,
Where the Greedy One broke his wings

On the power of human love, only not of one man,
But an entire society, which suddenly realised it was an integral whole.'
'You said an integral whole. Perhaps you mean a universal whole?'
I mumbled. (Oh, Adonai, what's with the hair-splitting?).
'After all, the unity of the diverse is not integrity, rather it's entirety, right?'

He chuckled. 'That's correct.
However, in conversation with the Almighty,
You shouldn't bargain with Him, saying *each to his own*,
That diversity is wonderful and the world is beautiful
Thanks to the multitude of faces, cultures and outlooks.

If we cannot be integrated in essence,
Then one person needs to become integral
And answer for everyone on the specified day.
And this will go on until
That unification actually takes place,

Which will enable us to speak as equals not only
With the one we call the Almighty,
But with the one we know as Greedy.'
'Hold on a minute,' I perked up,
'Do you want to say that there'll suddenly

Come a day when the Roman will be the same as
The Galilean, the Hellene or the Kazakh?
That everyone will transform into a single mass,
Losing their traditions, race and name,
And forgetting the geography of their origins? But that's nonsense!'

Suddenly, his head dropped and he wept:
'If only I had known it would be like this!
If I had the knowledge, the books, the upbringing.
If I had not seen the lies of the authorised translators
Aiding communication between humans and God!

If my heart had not burned with a strange pain,
Inexplicable, cruel,
Gained from no one knows where.
Would I not have drifted down that magical river of life
Like everyone else, cheering on your oar strokes with a song?!

A song in a specific language, of a specific people,
Of a specific family, specifically mine?!
Would I not have sought my happiness
In the smile of a Galilean girl,
In the guttural dialect of my own nation?!

I want, I really want to be a level-headed
And kind-hearted citizen,
Who cherishes his children and respects his elders.
I want to be Melamed, you, a Galilean, a Jew,
A Spartan, a lawyer, an artist, an old man when all's said and done!

But it burns right here and never lets up...'
I was taken aback by such a storm of emotions.
To be honest, against the backdrop of a steady flow of the river of life
It seemed to me to be not just superfluous,
But frankly anomalous, verging on a disease of the spirit,

Like, you know, when you meet something
That goes beyond your consciousness,
And something starts to ache in the solar plexus,
Rising up to the head
And sending a shiver throughout the body.

That's what I felt for a moment,
Sitting there in front of this weeping boy.
But then I regained my self-control.
'Yeshua,' I said like a teacher,
'The most important thing you need to learn from your experience,

Is that humans possess a truly limitless
Potential for finding solutions and an ability to find meanings.
They are always intuitively oriented
To find solutions that are both good and well-balanced,
Even if critical situations sometimes arise.

Never mind situations, even wars arise!
But you know, the crowning moment of any war is peace.
And we are given peace so as to display our best qualities.
And, Allah be my witness, we are able to consider and elevate these qualities
Above the stirrings of evil, arrogance and callousness.

We are all destined to become old men; I don't understand the essence of your regret...'

I don't know if I managed to convince that strange
Messenger from the north or not.
However, the next day, he disappeared from Chorazin.
Josik Gabay was the last to see him.
He said that early that morning,

As he was walking to the boxing gym,
He saw Yeshua standing by the western wall of Chorazin.
It seemed to him that the lad was weeping
And laughing simultaneously. Yeshua had waved to him amicably,
After which all Josik's suspicions had dissipated.

They had smiled to one another and this smile
Had seemed both warm and even jolly to Gabay,
And he had gone on his way, further inspired with dreams of the ring.
For some reason, on this early Chorazin morning,
The boy had thought that everything in his life would work out.

452

Hm... I'll go fetch the kettle and grab you a blanket, Thaddeus.

There you go. Right, now I'll continue.
Where was I?
Ah, yes, about that strange conversation with the boy,
Which instilled a certain anxiety into my general outlook.
In everything else, life continued in Chorazin as before,

Carrying the waters of life like a giant river.
I had a strong feeling of inspiration
After that humanistic feat that
Our town had performed,
And this had a positive impact on my work,

On my attitude to it and to my profession in general.
One day, during a regular class trip
To the shores of the Sea of Galilee,
After the last of the rascals had calmed down and gone to sleep,
I went down to the shore in complete and contented solitude.

I looked at length at the moon's reflection on the water and I thought:
There's the sea. It's like the fate of a teacher.
Children and childhood are something beautiful, bottomless and tender.
The waves are the faces, always new,
Of classes, leavers and next generations.

New children, like these waves, are identical
In the tasks they face and their problems,
And they are so different in their manners, characters and events.
It would appear that, day after day, year after year,
The waves of the generations roll so identically,

But behind every splash, there is an enormous album of memories.
They come and they go, diving into their adult lives...
While, standing on the shore for the fifth, the tenth, the thirtieth time,
We hear the buzz of the leavers' last bell
And the headteacher's speech, barely ever changing,

About the fantastic opportunities that study reveals,
And about the horizons to which the leavers will strive once they've gone.
I suddenly remembered that mixed feeling
We have when we see off the latest class.
I sensed the tremor of the new stage in life

That you feel when you open
A register for the first time, with its new names and last names,
And you cast an experienced eye over the scared faces of first-year pupils.
This eye never fails to pinpoint
That, indeed, we're going to have big problems with Zucker,

Or that the Gabays will have a girl only once in a blue moon,
Or that Weidman looks nothing like his brother,
So fat and absent-minded.
I stood on the shore and thought
That school had given me not only the joy of my profession.

It was here I had met my Hanna,

My strict and principled partner,
My passionate and long-desired,
The one who is so perfect in everything
That even her burnt eggs are perfectly inedible!

I was full of pride for the memory
Of the incredibly humanistic act
That the town had performed with the orphans.
Adonai, protect the Chorazin intelligentsia, I prayed.
Preserve the spirit of this town and let me be a worthy part of it!

So, that is how I stood there on the shore,
In harmony with my work, love and Motherland.
And I still feel that salty taste of happiness,
That I was given that night by the most wonderful of all lakes –
Our warm Sea of Galilee.

****

Mummy, mum! It really hurts, mum!
Those blows from all sides sting like fury!
My whole body stings, my nerves, eyes and bones are all done for!
They're killing the child you brought into the world!
When will he come, mum?

From where will he come, mum?!

That blessed and merciful one,
Bringing calm and flight
From this unrelenting cruelty and injustice,
Inflicted by the skilled and generous hand of release,
The last, deadly throw of the stone..?

So why, against the backdrop of such a blissful image of the sea
Did I suddenly recall the prayer I'd once heard
Of the man sentenced to stoning?
Well, because our life went on to be like how
That lad felt at the moment of his execution.

How do you imagine hell?
What is the key word for you in all that?
Torment, torture, humiliation?
No, the key words in the definition of hell are
The close interweaving of Eternity and Hopelessness.

The misfortune that wields the ultimate form of evil – war,
Epidemic or severe cold is not the most terrible;
Nor is it the misfortune that comes in one go,
Carrying within the clearly defined image of the enemy,
The clear and understandable direction of resistance.

Most terrible is the misfortune that envelops you
In a tender embrace, year after year,
Coming and going, getting a good look, striking, but not to the death,
As if protecting you like a field of self-realisation,
Without which it would cease to exist itself.

It was this misfortune that, slowly but surely
Came to our cosy little university town of Chorazin.
I told you about the black seeds
That Caiaphas had sown in our hearts,
When, like a new, enticing wind,

He had confused our youth, the merchants
And even the clergy and the intelligentsia.
At first it had all seemed awfully progressive –
Our money changers, businessmen and artisans
Gained untold advantages

From trade with the capitals.
The slogan *Free Will* grew logically into free market.
Everyone welcomed this too.
Of course, why wouldn't they?
The whole world lives on the fruits of its enterprise!

Why should Chorazin stay away from this horn of plenty?
Our townsfolk, the young, adult and the experienced
Are hardly poor in intelligence, skills and education.
Couldn't you convert this level of intellect
Into wholly tangible benefits of human progress?

Most important is that money and opportunities arose.
Not only for the money changers, but for the learned too.
How many people found funding
For their research, which once lay idle on the shelf
Or progressed by a spoonful a year at best?

No, now they had gained an unprecedented start, speed
And an intensive development dynamic.
The world around us stopped flowing like the monotonous current of the Jordan
And transformed into the boiling rapids of the Terek,
Washing away the coast and the cliffs!

Our own magnates began to appear,
A phenomenon hitherto unknown, not only in Chorazin,
But in Capernaum, Magdala, Bethsaida
And basically anywhere else in blessed Galilee!
And what's wrong with that, you might say?

Quite the contrary, the basis of society's thinking
Was the notion of *initiative*, that vein of entrepreneurship.
Some of our magnates
Actually gradually reached the heights of trading with Rome
And the well-to-do Athens!

For once, the Eternal City and the cradle of antiquity
Would learn of our master craftsmen!
Was that not something to be proud of?
Well, of course, not everyone would enjoy success;
That's a normal thing in competition.

Let the intelligentsia grumble from time to time,
That financial success is not a measure of morality.
Excuse me, but is poverty moral?

If not, is wealth not its opposite?
Is success not God's reward for us? Is *Free Will* not its cornerstone?

So, in this way, slowly but surely,
Innovation, progress and modernisation
Swept through our society with business-like enthusiasm.
Only Grandfather Melamed, equally slowly but surely
Suddenly began dipping into some incomprehensible yearning.

This, however, was attributed to his conservatism and backwardness.
Therefore, to add to his nickname of Lion of the Desert,
He was also bestowed the epithet *Old...*
I didn't hesitate to join
That fresh current of popular initiative either.

We opened a consultancy company
For specialists in various fields
Could easily be found for subcontracting
In the university town of Chorazin.
Now, everyone was drawn to money and how to make it.

My Hanna, too, was very much up with the times.
She opened paid tutoring classes
And a centre for psychological assistance for children
Who have suffered at the hands of street thugs
And from beatings by their peers.

Generally, life bubbled along in a new way.
I barely had time to fulfil my teaching duties.
To be honest, I even began to feel bothered
By the rigid nature of the learning process,
Devoid of unexpected emotions and the unpredictability of competition.

The town was also undergoing gradual change.
The council now had fewer representatives of the intelligentsia and the clergy.
Instead there were energetic *Free Will* representatives.
Not only that, but the town's fathers, too, gradually
Began to feel their importance in addressing business issues.

Only on one occasion did a group of rabbis
Arrange a decisive demonstration
In front of the synagogue, demanding clarification
As to the extent to which the new trends
Correspond with the ancient letter of the Law.

However, a quite new feature of the Pharisees appeared before me.
Earlier, this teaching was an unshakable sentry,
Watching over our antiquities and strict rituals.
Now, however, the prosperous top brass
Had suddenly became imbued with ideas of progressivism.

Back then, the entire town would follow the discussion
Of our clergymen.
Unfortunately, many of the intelligentsia were not
Actually admitted to the debate.
People say that this happened because

A recommendation had come from Jerusalem,
Calling on representatives of the secular classes
Not to meddle in religious affairs.
To the residents of Chorazin, this seemed like utter nonsense,
Because the discussions covered universal, ethical and behavioural norms.

Incidentally, the greatest opposition came from a section of the conservatives
Who stood firm in their belief that the discussion should be open.
But here, in all its glory,
There came the notion of a new term into our consciousness:
Lobby – the representative defence of another's interests.

When the votes were counted,
It transpired that the majority had decided to limit
The purely theological side of the discussion
And, therefore, the intelligentsia were politely shown the door,
And it was forced to come to terms with that.

And how else, for the voting procedure was flawless!
Only evil tongues continued to whisper at length
That the majority at our Sanhedrin
Were already the beneficiaries of major corporations,
Pulling in their branches to the centre of Judea.

However, the people of Chorazin formed their opinion swiftly.
The voting was fair and the unity of views
Was but a conservative relic of the past.
Everyone, as they say, has the right
To his own opinion.

The discussion was actually about just that.
Where is the line between *free will* and social values?
Why does an individual, a bearer of freedom,
Have an absolute value,
But a community does not?

And when a dispute arises between a community and an individual,
In whose favour should the value assessment fall?
The verdicts of judicial and arbitral institutions were not implied
And nor, the application by the representative bodies
Of the delegated decision-making right,

Rather it was the value relation to a given precedent
That was discussed here!
Do you, for example, recall how long has it been since
There have been discussions of value categories in your town?
I think it has been a long time, probably even never.

So, glory to our town!

The little Essene community of Chorazin
That had been present at the discussion, was categorical.
Basically, they said, the question had not been put correctly in the first place.
It is not the institutions that form consciousness,
Rather the value-based system must form the necessary institutions.

Equally categorical, only in their own way,

Were the representatives of the *New Sadducees*,
Who had asserted that God had created man free,
And the legal system must protect his freedoms,
His property, accomplishments and himself from the pressure of the community.

The Essenes said, 'You are so obsessed with the abstract individual,
While, naturally, reflecting the interests of specific individuals,
That you have not thought about the most important:
We launch all legal forces to protect the individual,
While this individual might well turn out to be a total nonentity!'

'Okay,' the Sadducees objected,
'So which value system should be used to assess people?
You see, everyone has their own!'
'Why,' the Essenes replied, taken aback,
'If everyone has their own value system,

Then what is the use of our ancient laws?!'
'Let's take a look at progressive thought in the world,'
The Sadducees persisted.
'So, is Roman state law not an example of
Modernised development for you?

Is it not at the heart of Rome's frenzied commercial and financial might
Where this legal system lies?
And, if it is an indicator of success,
Is it really so ungodly
And unworthy of emulation?

Look at Phoenicia and Greece.
They have dynamically fallen in under the new world order.
Take a look at Jerusalem, Judea and Samaria.
Even at the neighbouring Tiberias.
What, so, we are to trail forever at the back of world progress?

Leave the regulation of domestic relations to religion.
Observe the ancient law in the circle of your nearest and dearest,
Imagine yourselves as a community at the synagogues,
On traditional holidays
And during the mass singing of hymns.

What you should allow to enter the value system
Is what moves world progress,
And that is the right of the individual to absolute individuality
And immunity from restriction of enterprise
On the part of abstract moral philosophising of the community.'

'In other words, everything
That, of course, is beneficial to one,'
The Essenes went on,
'Should be taken for granted by the community,
Even if it is of no benefit to everyone else?'

'And what right does everyone else have,'
The Sadducees objected, 'to a man having earned something
From his own abilities and skills?'
The Essenes: 'But what if, in doing this, he breaches the moral and ethical standards

And, under the protection of this right,

He conducts a profligate lifestyle,
That facilitates his enrichment?
If he, once rich, turns his neighbour into a pauper?'
The Sadducees: 'Why would he be the one to blame
For another becoming a pauper?

The pauper had to work himself and
Eventually beat the former in competition.
And what's so bad about wealth?
In the consumption of what you deserve, what you've earned?
Why should one worry himself over the problem of another who is lazy?'

The Essenes: 'You have an incredible system for substituting notions;
You believe that equality before God should be ensured
Not by the word of God, but by the primacy of the individual over the community?
But that is absurd! That will increase social differences
And, in the end, will grow into the egoism of entire nations!'

The Sadducees: 'And when were people ever equal?
Never. Doesn't your doctrine say, submit to the will of God?
So, submit to the fact that, according to His will,
There is a difference between the enterprising and the stupid,
Between the successful man and the loser.'

The Essenes: 'We still don't understand how one can be happy
While contemplating the poverty of one's neighbour.
Well, okay, let's speak in terms of your categories.
Entrepreneurship is often associated with
The position occupied by the powers that be.

After all, power is also a subjective thing: whom to give advantages,
And from whom to take them away.
Or perhaps, based on your logic, one should simply
Make money successfully by stealing
From the town's budget. What then, if not ethical standards,

Should there be to stop such people?'
The Sadducees: 'Well, judicial protection of competition, the statutes,
The presumption of innocence,
The evidential basis and the collective means of bringing a verdict.
Sensitive public control, parties, the press once again.'

The Essenes: 'And all that, just to
Prove that a man is a scoundrel and a blackguard?!'
The Sadducees: 'Why a scoundrel? He's just guilty.
Everyone has their own understanding of
What a scoundrel is, and a what a blackguard is.

So, these notions will disappear from the legal vocabulary.
He will be either guilty or not guilty.
If guilty, then in something particular:
If he killed, then he killed; if he stole, then he stole.
Receive your punishment, because you overstepped the rules.'

The Pharisees observed this dispute

459

Closely and silently and they saw
That the Sadducees had the logical and systematic understanding,
While the Essenes had only emotional definitions
And clung to the community, meaning to the past.

But they understood something else, too,
That the ancient Law was being replaced
By a wholly new system and a new set of values.
And that this system
Would enable the Sadducees, once and for all,

To do away with a moral assessment of deeds.
Conduct, the running of affairs and even municipal management.
They even saw further than this,
That, in time, under the auspices of this new system,
A new morality would arise or, more precisely, a new understanding of it.

Despite the discussion being completely closed,
The details still managed to seep out,
So, when the building of the Sanhedrin was opened
For a public announcement of the decision,
Everyone didn't just know what was going on,

But they had split into different camps.
It wasn't that hard to understand
Who was defending which position.
What surprised the townsfolk was not the split,
Rather how and under what principle it had taken place.

People were governed now not by strength of character,
Upbringing, family tradition or temperament,
Rather by the benefit any given verdict would bring.
This criterion of benefit had a drastic effect on people.
Some would say to each other,

'Sim, look me in the eye. You know, that thing – that's low,
You know exactly what I mean.'
And those Sims would reply, 'I get it, but it's better for me
If this opinion passes,
For then I can get my bank fully off the ground.'

'Have you no conscience?' 'Well, you don't need to exaggerate like that.'
'Sim, have you no shame? Tomorrow, you won't
Lend to me, your neighbour; you're only interested in your return,
And that's not according to the Law, Sim.'
'What,' said Sim indignantly, 'you think I'll stop honouring the Sabbath,

That I'll start eating pork or stop going to the synagogue?
I'll stop giving my daughter away in marriage according to custom,
Or that I'll forget my prayers and national holidays?
Or what, trade was invented just today?
Corporations and banks too?

You see, it's not about that, it's about that stupid levelling up.
Why do all of us in the community have to be the same?
And anyway, if I'll be rich and happy,
You think I'll stop being a true believer?'

'Now, that's the question, Sim...

Don't you lie to yourself, my friend.
You're ashamed to talk like that.
It's just that you saw an alternative morality
And realised the benefit of manoeuvring between
Two value systems.

But can you actually serve two
Masters at the same time?'
'You see, I'm not against community;
If I'm rich, I'll be able to help you all.
I could help build the stadium,

That's been standing idle two years now, like an eyesore.
I'm currently opening a branch office in Bethsaida
And I'll build this stadium three time faster
Than the community could manage it.'
'And didn't you think, Sim, that the stadium should go up

Precisely at the time when we were ready for it
In our own eyes and in the eyes of God?'
'Well, excuse me, but that is some pretty ignorant reasoning!
In your opinion, if current trends help
To erect a Temple faster, is that not God's providence?'

'That's the whole point, Sim. It's for us to build it
And if it is destined to be built,
That is a matter for God. Not one technology in the world
For accelerating the construction tempo could tell you
If we are currently worthy of a Temple or not...'

It was these arguments and others like them
That sprang up all over Chorazin.
Of course, everyone waited impatiently
For the decision of the Sanhedrin.
But most important, though, was

That no one was afraid, rather they were sure
That our Sanhedrin was wise enough and suitably enlightened.
To reach this decision,
Which would put paid to the disputes once and for all
And return to us a sense of stability and unity.

No one ever, whatever the trends going round,
Would ever dare to argue with the Sanhedrin,
Because this was not simply the collective and consultative mind of the town;
It was the bearer of the Law and tradition,
Meaning it was the guardian of our virtuous future.

Even Sim, if a decision were to be passed that wasn't in his interests,
Would sigh and not proceed to open a branch office in Bethsaida,
Because it's not worth making money on your brothers in one place
And pretending to be righteous in another,
Bearing no relation whatsoever to the loan interest.

Later, everyone will come to understand that Sim lost a lot of money,

461

But they'll come to support him.
And when the holiday comes
They're sure to present him with a new donkey,
The one he had wanted to earn himself.

But they'll give him one because they know that that was his dream,
And everyone in a community always knows each other's dreams.
It makes no difference that with a new office in Bethsaida
He could have afforded to *buy* a hundred donkeys.
What would be the point? He was dreaming about one donkey.

And that is what he'd get. And he'd be well pleased, too.
And he'd shed tears; Sim would always shed tears when he was happy.
As for the ninety-nine hypothetical donkeys,
Well, they can go and look for ninety-nine
Hypothetical Sims.

We also felt a sense of security
Because, despite the energy of the Essenes and the Sadducees,
The Pharisees still enjoyed an overwhelming majority.
And these people knew and understood the feeling of the balance
That enables us to bring all that is new into our society

With the necessary degree of graduality.
After all, only a fool would poison a pear with fertiliser,
Place it into an unnatural environment
And hurry its ripening,
Only to poison oneself and one's neighbours with its artificial flavour.

The wise man simply waits
For it to ripen at the will of the Lord,
And he knows that when the pear is full of its sun-drenched juice
And becomes edible,
Then he too will be ripe and ready to eat it.

We knew that for the protection of our souls and consciousness
There was the phenomenon of the thousand-year-old *Pharisee breeding*.
And we were not given the ability to foresee
That this notion would transform before our eyes
Into something quite the opposite.

Everyone brightened up because they'd noticed
Old Hazzan Melamed, majestic and noble,
Making his way through the crowd to the building of the Sanhedrin.
Only recently, he had stopped playing a part in the courts.
He would say he was old and that the young ones...

And yet his voice remained quite marvellous.
The years could not change him,
Because the right to announce the decisions of the Sanhedrin
And the town council too
Always remained the domain of the old hazzan.

And everyone knew that Joseph would enter the building
And spend at least an hour and a half there.
That was also a tradition of sorts. It was associated with the fact that
The judges needed to immerse Joseph fully in the problem at hand

And the essence of its solution, so that when it was recited

Everything would appear as if he were relating it to the people from the heart.
Basically, that is what would happen.
And this was a very wise step,
Because could anyone really believe someone
Who didn't understand what he was talking to the people about?

Joseph emerged an hour later and everyone could see his confusion.
To be honest, this had never happened before,
And this was an alarming sign for us all.
The hazzan's beautiful voice suddenly shook in the air,
Like the rustling of the trees, doubting from whence the wind was blowing.

The decision was such that it pulled the ground from under the feet of many.
It sounded something like this:
'Are Divine Predestination
And the free will of the individual
In direct and uncompromising contradiction with one another?

Apparently not, and life proves this to be the case.
Was it not Divine Predestination that led to
A new doctrine for viewing the world
Being brought to our town, not by a pagan or some barbarian,
Rather by our compatriot and the High Priest at that.

That means that the world really is changing at the will of God
And He is giving us a signal
So that we will not lose ourselves as a nation in the ocean of other countries,
So that we might strengthen ourselves to fulfil the Lord's will
And bring this world into the Almighty's embrace.

However, we must come to Him renewed and strong.
And who else, if not the strong individuals with their energy,
Directed for the good of society,
Are capable of leading the people
Through new dunes of new roads and thorns?

Does a pack not have leaders?
Does an army not have commanders?
And can there not be people in society who
Who would voluntarily harness themselves to the yoke
That drags us to prosperity and well-being?

That means that we must do everything expected of us
Not only to push new leaders to the surface,
But to become these leaders ourselves.
This is the notion of *Free Will* –
Will you be the flame that leads others in the dark

Or will you remain behind the guide,
Blind and in the dark?
You see, it has basically always been like that –
Divine Predestination truly does decide
Who is born enterprising and who, talented;

Who, a leader and a torch of progress,

And who, doomed to the pitiful existence of an outsider
And a loser, dragging our society back
To slavery, Egyptian executions, flight and the search
For one's place in this world, for oneself and one's impoverished tribe!'

And then, something incredible happened (For no one would ever dare to interrupt the hazzan),
A voice came from the crowd: 'Excuse me!
Did our community not have leaders before?
So, who are you? And why should it be others?
After all, by leadership you mean a desire for wealth!

And in the past, did you not unselfishly determine our fates?
Why should our fates now be decided by those,
Whose criteria is simply growth in consumption
And a striving to elevate themselves
Above those they once saw as brothers?

Who will he now consider them to be?
It seems like casuistry to me!'
A hum spread through the crowd and it was one
Both of approval and of displeasure.
Hazzan Joseph stopped short and fell silent.

At this point, one of the Sanhedrin members intervened:
'Don't you worry! We had a community and so it will remain
The main bearer of the criteria of morality,
Mutual assistance, brotherhood and solidarity!
By no means are we abandoning our ancient traditions of collectivism!

It's just that collectivism and individualism
Will now coexist,
Not interfering, rather supporting one another!'
Incredulous laughter broke out from the crowd.
'So what happens if they quarrel, Rabbi?'

'Everything here is so incredibly interesting,'
Another Pharisee from the Sanhedrin interjected.
'We will not stand for any threats to our traditions.
The Sanhedrin performed just court before
And it will continue to do so!

It's just that we are introducing new and very progressive procedures,
When proof of the degree of a person's guilt
Is not a matter of vague and obscure moral criteria,
But specific norms of violations of the laws of fair competition,
Which clearly determine the culpability and its value.'

'Rabbi,' someone suddenly cried out,
'What do we need more laws for?
Is our Ancient Law not the only law,
That came to us from the depths of time,
And are you not its guardians?!'

The Sanhedrin member with the cross on his turban suddenly became angry.
'No one has abandoned anything; we are simply expanding
Our understanding of justice.
So, how were you to plan on proving the rightness and moral qualities

Of any given person?

Through the usual synagogue whispering,
The shaking of heads and complaints to the rabbi like before?'
'But what's wrong with that? What was more powerful before
Than our traditional whispers and head-shaking?
What was more powerful than the public condemnation of greed,

Foul deeds, base behaviour and deceit,
Which, when brought to the surface
From under the secret covers of scoundrels' lives,
Burned like chips in the fire, shaming those who
Committed these deeds, so incompatible with the townsfolk's morality?

What was more powerful before than public shaming,
When people fled to the desert,
Unable to bear such shame?
What was more effective than public penance,
More powerful than lashes, because each condemnation

Contained an enormous amount of forgiveness?!
Does punishment really make people better?
Does it not actually awaken the worst in people?
When repentance surely appeals to
The very best qualities? Or is that another example, you think, of vague morality?'

'Don't worry,' the clergy leaders remonstrated with us.
'All our traditions will remain in place.
It's just that we need to use new formats more energetically,
Create parties to be better heard,
Write to the press, expand the electoral space.

Rotate various posts with greater frequency,
And basically create a competition of views and opinions.
That's because the most dangerous thing is when one person's opinion
Suddenly finds itself unheard because of the joint opinion of the community.'
'But what if that voice is that of a creep?' someone said and everyone laughed.

The crowd and the clergy continued bickering for some time
But, by the evening, the arguments had dried up and the voices had faded.
The vague words of the Sanhedrin had failed to generate
A response in the hearts of the townsfolk
And everyone had gone home, scratching their heads.

No one could understand the meaning of all the talk
Or all the in-depth analysis.
It looked like someone was up to something
But, behind all the foggy religious and legal discussions,
They had cleverly hid the most important part.

Everyone was sure of one thing, however:
We, our Law, our traditions and our lives
Had been entrusted to the Sanhedrin members
And the town council – our best representatives,
And they would somehow get to the bottom of what was what.

However, this was a misunderstanding.

The clergy, intelligentsia and the *new leaders*
Had become mired in religious and dogmatic discussions,
Which had spilled over into newspaper articles,
And which had suddenly become more and more voluminous.

Disputes became the norm in our lives.
There were those who agreed and those who disagreed,
Those who opposed everything and those
Who were perfectly happy with everything,
As long as the matter never concerned them.

However, the majority said to themselves,
If everything is now in my hands and mine alone,
Well, I am smart, educated, experience and skilled enough
To achieve success and become just a little wealthier.
There is no sin in this, quite the opposite.

Did the Rabinoviches get richer? So, that is a godly thing.
How else could it be? Then the members of the Sanhedrin dressed up
And became like the metropolitan establishment,
And not some small-town rabbis, like they were before.
And now it is a pleasure to see!

Have the Friedmans become poorer?
Well, no one cancelled Divine Predestination, did they?
You get what you deserve –
The equivalent of success, which is equal to what you are actually
Worth in this world, all pulsing with all that's new.

All manner of partnerships, companies and firms have appeared,
New goods, services, and from all corners of the world.
Spices from India? Here you go!
Silk from China? But, of course!
Thermal baths from Rome, private bacchanalia and chariot races.

Statute books with spicy illustrations from Hellas,
Wonderful wines from Colchis and Armenia.
Graceful steeds and expensive weaponry from the kingdom of the Huns.
All this began to paint our life in new colours.
And new fires were kindled in place of shepherds' torches.

This was the age of directors and presidents –
Everyone, who was previously just Izya the neighbour,
Shlomo the scholar or Sima the tearaway became one.
Everyone was buying, selling, exchanging and spending.
This was a time when time flew so fast,

Unlike any creature on earth,
Including even our Chorazin swallows.
Incidentally, the swallows had gradually all disappeared.
Either because of the power station with its enormous chimneys,
Built where the residential districts of the Essenes had once stood.

Or was it... what, was I talking about the Essenes?
They disappeared unnoticed, in any case against the backdrop of the hubbub
That the newspapers generated because of various events.
However, no one wrote a thing about their disappearance,

As if their fate was of no interest to anyone.

The only thing that received a token mention in the news chronicle
Was an article about some beggar falling under a bulldozer.
The bulldozer was knocking down the town's slums,
A source not only of disease and microbes,
But of heightened criminality too.

They knocked it down and what of it?
However, it was later revealed that they had knocked down the Essene districts
That I so loved for their quiet and cool,
Emanating from the cosy gardens and irrigation channels.
Back then, I thought,

There is no criminal danger from the Essenes, is there?
That was absurd, a contradiction of their teachings.
But then I simply forgot, for in place of their districts,
Directly opposite the shiny gates to the power station,
They built this amazing shopping and entertainment centre,

Without which, no child could imagine surviving their childhood.
And the Essenes? It turns out, our children could happily imagine their childhood
Without them, just as without the swallows.
The town's appearance, as you can see,
Had also begun to change at pace.

The old synagogue disappeared.
A new one was built nearer the outskirts.
It was huge and, to be honest, not pretty.
In place of the Song of Songs Gardens,
The lights of the Scipio theme park now shimmered.

Right in front of my house,
A three-level intersection stretched out,
Thanks to which I could get to work far faster,
Only the cries of charioteers and the roar of chariots
Prevented me from getting to sleep at night.

Everything was flying forwards
Or spinning in a mad whirlpool.
Only one man didn't change one bit
In my eyes.
It was as if he was living in time stood still.

This was the Grandfather Melamed you are familiar with.
After that story with the *legionnaires*
And the discussion within the Sanhedrin walls,
He somehow gradually lost his lion-like standing,
Although he didn't lose a shred of his dignity.

I almost never appeared in school now.
After my consultancy business took off... Eh?
Why didn't I go? It's just that I had been bought out for a modest price
By the representatives of a major Roman brand,
Well, and out of politeness and so as not to get under anyone's feet.

Anyway, back then, I opened a small publishers.

I printed Russian *byliny* folk tales, a Turkic epic,
Greek tragedies and comedies.
From time to time I would look in on Grandfather Melamed,
To discuss what might have been interesting for the Chorazin reader.

The eyes of the Old Lion of the Desert lit up for a while,
When we discussed literature.
Then, they went out beneath the shaggy grove of his brows,
If we switched to a discussion of our present life,
With its new morals and trends.

'I get the feeling,' he said,
'That we have lost something incredibly important.
But believe me, colleague, I am not smart or intelligent enough
To understand specifically what.'
What could I say to him in response?

If he wasn't smart enough, what could be said about me?
Everything seemed to be in its place: a brain, ambition and fantasy.
But my business was becoming more and more
A kind of altruistic project;
What else could one call my risible profit-and-loss balance sheet?

'I'm not talking about the problems of our Chorazin businessmen,'
Grandfather Melamed went on pensively,
'That is all as clear as day.
You think you are sufficiently enterprising and energetic?
It's not that at all. It's just that you are in a knowingly losing position,

Faced with the giant Krusenstern publishing house.
First, it has an international business across the Empire.
Second, a good half of its profit share is held
By the office of the Procurator himself and, third,
It has long been fattening the town council and the *New Sadducees* from the Sanhedrin.

That was why it received the town budget's order
For propaganda posters, leaflets and brochures,
And you didn't. That means it will quickly build up its book market
Right next to your little shop under your publishers
And it will send you to the wall, as a major monopoly always does.'

I choked up. What was there to be surprised about?
I knew myself that this would happen sooner or later.
'I'm not talking about that, my friend,' Grandfather went on
Calmly, as if he had not passed down a sentence to me just then.
'You're a young and sophisticated man,

So, tell me, why didn't you hand out bribes to the department of culture?
Why didn't you go to Caesarea and take the procurator's secretary
To the baths and bacchanalia, like Krusenstern did?
After all, you definitely knew for certain
This this would bring you fabulous dividends, right?'

'Well, probably, but I...'
'Stop right there, Philip, I know the answers to these questions too.
But what I don't know the answer to is this:
Who are you? A lost past or a mysterious future?

You are what will be irretrievably lost,

Like a relic of some uncompetitive archaism,
Together with your publishers and your home
Which will go under a bank's mortgage bond.
Or are you something that needs to be saved for the future,
When this bacchanalia of self-interest comes to an end?'

'Well, time will tell, Mr Headteacher, time...'
'I have stopped time for myself, my son.
For what is the point of this time
If it has suddenly started moving backwards?
And what is the point of its movement, if it is moving in the wrong direction?

Why should I rush forwards where there are no people like you?
And if everything moves in a spiral
And time will return to normal,
Why run around in circles,
When it is perhaps enough to take a step to one side,

To the neighbouring branch of the spiral?'
I left Melamed utterly bewildered.
However, I still didn't think
That the old man had gone mad and drifted into melancholy.
Something told me he was right about something

But I had no time to delve into the reasons.
Gradually the enthusiasm and initiative of my generation
Began transforming into a kind of emergence from a hangover.
While teachers, scholars and poets did their *directoring* and *presidenting*,
Schools, institutes and Houses of Writers stood empty.

And when most of them were a fiasco in business,
There was almost nowhere for them to return to.
Why most of them and why the fiasco?
Let's leave to one side the argument that everyone
Should focus on their own affairs and their own professions.

This is no universal axiom.
Dozens of teachers, scientists and poets
Have become businessmen and chairmen of companies,
And many of them, in their professional fields;
They opened their own university or House of Writers.

However, the majority did alter their profile;
Banks, oil and information technologies
Somehow present far more opportunities to achieve enrichment.
We are talking about the majority of the overwhelming minority.
The majority in a company cannot be rich,

Or the minority poor. This is historically and rhetorically nonsense.
Behind the mass fiasco was the illusion that enrichment was obligatory,
Stemming from the illusion that everyone has the same opportunities at the start,
Which the *New Sadducees*, foaming at the mouth, try to prove is the case,
Saying, *look, we began as equals but now look at us.*

Unfortunately, things are different:

469

Are *you* able to become the Krusenstern
Who takes the secretary or even the procurator himself
To the baths or the bacchanalia,
In order to essentially correct these so-called *equal opportunities*?

But no, there was another thing:
Are you not a son of Krusenstern or even of the procurator,
And, since childhood, have frequented the baths and bacchanalia
At others' expense,
Which, one day, will logically prove or at least seem to be your own?

Alahi, what a wonderful coincidence
Of free will and Divine Predestination!
How then did the Sadducees so wonderfully come up with everything
So that, in the end, there'll be so many people
Deprived of both the former and the latter?

Forgive me, though, the doctrine of the *New Pharisees* likewise
Has no tradition of placing the responsibility for one's troubles
On someone else's shoulders,
Even if, at one time, they had been responsible
For the justice and piety of the community.

It was only that, even though I didn't share Melamed's stances
On the means of handling time,
This time, began suddenly to stick,
Not only in my eyes,
But in the feelings of many others.

All right, then the business wasn't a success.
We'll tell ourselves that it's not for everyone.
Many were even delighted to return to their vocations.
True, many were ashamed for
Succumbing to the charms of a fast buck.

We gave it a try but we came back.
Time would hardly slow because of that, right?
Wouldn't we carry on being young,
With our blood boiling and our eyes sparkling?
Are we not the same children of our age, like everyone else?

Almost all of us came back –
Thanks to Grandfather Melamed for that;
Once again, he gathered us together in our quiet, cosy staff room.
Almost all of us, apart from three.
One was a PE teacher, who had died at the dawn of the new age.

They say it was during a shootout
With gunmen, hired by the *New Sadducees*.
Another, previously a young teacher,
Who had become the head of major advertising agency,
Was found at home, hideously contorted from a drug overdose.

The third was Belferman, former head of the boarding school,
Who was accompanied at length by geyser bursts and the burlesque of success.
He had become an outstanding entrepreneur and, judging by the newspapers,
He'd not only acquired several firms,

But had become the co-owner of several banks in Samaris and Edom.

He had even been introduced to the court of the Emperor Tiberius!
Later, however, he had disappeared for good.
Some say he was seen in Chorazin before disappearing,
Haggard, but with a feverish glint in his eye,
Either buying horses from the Turks or leasing a boat from the Phoenicians.

He had once been so close and familiar
But was now so distant, impetuous an unintelligible
That no one could keep up with his fate,
And that meant that no one could keep up with his soul,
Which he had taken away, or hidden or lost without a trace.

We returned to our cycles of time:
The school hours, semesters, graduation classes, new faces and old subjects.
It seemed that Melamed's spiral had returned us to our former state,
But it very soon became clear that
This was merely an illusory return.

When others label you a loser,
You can disagree or even fight it;
Or even not give a damn about the opinion of others.
However, not everyone had the courage to speak about this with themselves
And this epidemic of sick vanity

Came to the classrooms.
Many couldn't forgive society for the way it had shocked
With bold horizons, waved before their noses,
Only for them to take away, so they thought,
All their prospects, through insidious deceit.

The people began to mete their revenge. On themselves, their colleagues and the children.
Moreover, these were no longer the same children
From that legendary school and boarding establishment.
Krusenstern's children appeared in the classes,
Encrusted into the layer of the community's simple children.

These symbols of Divine Predestination
Became a major irritant for the deceived by *Free Will*.
However, this was not the worst thing;
That was the awful inversions to which human
Consciousness can be subjected.

You think that they took to wreaking vengeance on God's chosen children?
Far from it. They would fawn and grovel before them
But they'd wreak vengeance on those who were overlooked;
Those who were their mirror image,
In whom they saw themselves, pressed into a corner of the spiral of history.

I thought it was a temporary illness,
Perhaps even a generational thing.
Those who had endured a fiasco would leave,
Cast back into the majority,
While new people, regular and proper, would come.

Perhaps this would all have taken place

Had the school been an island in the midst of the society.
However, the Chorazin society as a whole
Most certainly did not return, like we did,
To its natural cycles.

This was our time, which, having played and raged,
Had returned to its measured, flowing sands
Of the duration of lessons and breaktime.
This could not be said of Chorazin.
The town needed new sacrifices.

The time had now come for the infernal millstones of politics.
Before, we had never shied away from politics.
After all, everything in our town had been done with the active involvement of the people.
We had been spoiled by the fact that both the council and the Sanhedrin
Needed both our opinion and our voice.

However, politics was like a noble river,
Decorating the ancient urban landscape as it went.
A river that people knew flowed peacefully and nobly,
Bringing us fish and coolness in summer.
But no one ever thought of changing its course.

Why? Is it not the Almighty who determines the way it flows?
And is it not He who, through the power of the eternal Law, one day, once and for all
Determined its course?
Now, however, such an understanding of politics had disappeared.
This river had simply become terrible and had come to every house.

Was it in the form of a discussion, or a conviction,
Or in the search of a voice, given to a historical decision?
No – it had come to every citizen's house in a frenzy of campaign hysteria,
With tentacles of manipulation.
However, it burst especially brutally into the teacher's house.

I have already told you that the rivers of politics seethed like the rapids of the Terek,
All around us, although we would have happily kept our distance.
However, a sense of protest began to build in the town
Against the consequences of that famous Pharisee decision.
Some of the citizens were unhappy

With things returning to how they had been,
And they began enquiring as to the true reasons for what had happened.
What is more, in the end things had become clearer and clearer,
That the word *loser* could be attached to the forehead
Of pretty much any resident of Chorazin, apart from a hundred or so of *God's chosen ones*.

Then the authorities launched a terrible and cynical wave of propaganda.
So, what was the role of us teachers in all this, you ask?
Well, we had, *en masse*, become its free and unrequited instrument.
Have you even once seen a magnate or an oligarch
Who, having public money at his disposal,

Ever spent his own?
This was unlikely, at least for us in Chorazin.
By that time, the town had seen some fundamental changes.
The town council had slowly but surely been cleaned of all

Members of the traditional urban intelligentsia.

You would no longer have seen Grandfather Melamed there.
The *New Sadducees* celebrated behind closed doors,
When the town council was completely rid
Of their representatives and their low, ornamental hangers-on
From among the wholly bought-out intellectuals.

But their joy was short-lived.
The Jerusalem Sanhedrin in all the provinces
Set out to destroy the local Sanhedrins with great energy.
This was called *a delegation of authority*.
And, just six months later,

You could see these broken elders,
Clutching staffs in their trembling hands
And peering out from under turbans with faded Xs on them
At the building of the Chorazin Sanhedrin,
Which housed the new Galilee Commodity Exchange.

Now, the court was presided over by three representatives of the Jerusalem Sanhedrin,
Whom Caiaphas had appointed personally from among Judea's residents
And whom, by way of covering expenses,
Were gifted enormous estates,
Slapped down where there had once been public urban gardens.

While, so that the local intelligentsia and the clergy didn't kick up too much fuss,
Detachments of *Free Will* were recreated in the town
Branded, well, how do you think?
As the *historical traditions of Chorazin!*
However these detachments were a far cry from what had come before.

These were no longer crowds of indignant Komsomol members.
They were the *Sturmabteilung*, marching out in quick time,
True to Caesarea and the Jerusalem Sanhedrin.
And this was no youth organisation.
Free Will had become a full-fledged police structure,

Capable of charging, prosecuting, sentencing and punishing.
You think they became the subject of popular hatred?
Far from it.
Who was it cleansed Chorazin of its beggars and small-time thieves?
Free Will.

Who brought order to the town's market,
When migrant speculators from Syria had taken over all the trading?
Free Will and its *Sturmabteilung.*
Who got rid of the killer doctors, forever dissatisfied with their lives?
Free Will again!

And who do you think supported them most of all?
The Pharisees, Sadducees and businessmen?
Hm. No. Let's put it this way: the majority of my colleagues
From among the losers of the business boom,
To my great surprise, were part of the intelligentsia

Which was in favour of evicting the enterprising

Samaritans and Edomites from the town and,
In so doing, for some reason, stopping that *Essene infection* from getting in.
Oh, Adonai, what on earth is that *Essene infection*?
It turns out that this was Enemy Number One of the Divine Will,

Bearers of the ideology of evil, levelling up and the vow of poverty.
What vow of poverty could there be in a prosperous society?!
Well, all right, they would play at being the nation's saviours,
As long as they left the normal people alone
And refrained from interfering in professional affairs with their stupid slogans.

At first, this was what it was like.
I was talking with Barzilai Junior.
I told him: 'Look, so you'll do in all your enemies and then what?
You'll come for us?'
They said , 'Come on, but you're our teachers!

How could I possibly dictate any terms to you?
You, the people who raised us?'
Less than a year went by, and a fat official from the department for education,
With a *Sturmabteilung CB* badge for some reason,
Brought us subject instructions,

Which were now to be mandatory.
It was called *A Free Vision of the World*.
The one who had drawn it up was an idiot from *Free Will*
Whom Grandfather Melamed had once turfed out of school
For having absolutely no knowledge of his subject!

And he didn't know, because, being a *child of Krusenstern*,
He had preferred to sit all his exams in their monetary equivalent.
And for this alone, he had gone to Tiberias,
To the Herod the Great School, where morals flourished
For which they would once take the birch to you in Chorazin.

This was no subject, rather a total mess,
Consisting of paganism, PE and stupid chanting,
Bearing no relation to freedom or to
A vision of the world.
Nevertheless, this subject was introduced and,

Even though Grandfather Melamed had tried to resist, saying *Over my dead body*,
They decided to introduce it 'gradually',
Adding to it and adjusting it, to make it somehow correspond
Either to notions of science
Or to notions of faith.

This gradual approach soon ended, when Grandfather was taken to hospital
And remained there for a month.
The stormtrooper-like official appeared at the school and, taking a red pen,
Entered the subject into the curriculum himself.
And he chose the moment when there were no male teachers at the school.

At first we resisted and stonewalled things quietly,
But after one teacher,
A man as pure as the driven snow,
Was put away for molesting teenagers,

With all the teachers trumpeting the fact with no little relish,

And another was, for some reason, beaten up near his home
By Essene thugs who'd wandered into town,
We all realised that resistance was futile.
The most amazing thing was that they quickly found plenty of enthusiasts!
How inscrutable, the way a human personality can transform!

Then there was the grim story of the town council elections,
When we were included in the electoral commissions.
At first we set about our task with enthusiasm –
For this was a worthy role, representing the most important
Democratic institution in town!

Then, however, it all gradually descended into farce.
I don't want to go into what happened,
How the young female schoolteachers wept after being forced
To alter ballot papers in favour of candidates
From *Free Will.*

At the same time, we oldies just stood and stared helplessly
As the elite of our future profession were broken down.
It was we who, slowly but surely, had begun to bring time to a standstill.
Where was it flowing if it was leading nowhere?
Why would it tick by, if the absurd had become a constant value?

Only once, in a fit of feverish protest, did I
Rush to Grandfather Melamed with eyes aflame,
To tell him, 'We must stop putting up with this – we have to fight!
We can't let all this happen!
If we let our moral values slip through our fingers,

How can we deem ourselves enlighteners and the intelligentsia?!'
'Pulic servants,' the Lion of the Desert said quietly.
'What?' I said incredulously, looking at him bemused.
'There are no enlighteners or intelligentsia;
We are now simply public servants, parasites of the public purse,'

The old head explained calmly.
I slumped onto a nearby chair.
Of course! Public servants, of course!
We had been defined not through the value-based vision of our role,
But simply through the universal equivalent, meaning finance and money.

Later, elections were held for the school's headteacher.
There were no more eyes aflame or enthusiasm for the struggle.
I wafted about the school like a sleepwalker,
Calling members of the parents' committee,
Who were taking part in the voting.

I persuaded them to cast their vote in favour of Grandfather Melamed.
And here, the Old Lion made a mistake.
He wrote an open letter to the town council
And the *troika* of the Sanhedrin Sadducees, who, by that time,
Held all the power in the town.

The council had remained like this, merely for the sake of appearances.

Zinoviy Melamed filled six sheets of paper
To give all the new orders a fundamental dressing down
And this, it seemed, put the wind up all the old-school townsfolk,
Who recalled the old spirit of true freedom, and not *Free Will*.

Like a fierce beast of the desert, the Old Lion,
Using the mastery of his great and mighty Aramaic language,
Smashed down the foundations that had eaten away at Chorazin like leprosy.
However, the most important thing he attacked at the end of his letter
Was the very latest judicial innovation,

The right of the Sadducee Sanhedrin to pass the death sentence.

This had really crossed the line!
We are an old Pharisee town that would never accept
The politics of punishment. After all, our slogan was that
Punishment has no power; repentance has power.
The worst sentence of all was always banishment from the Motherland,

For, what was life for if your Homeland has cast you aside?
However, even this could be reviewed after a special process of repentance –
One that was public, on the town square, on one's knees, before one's father
Or before another elder relation,
To whom an oath would be spoken,

Or not even an oath, rather words of repentance:
Abba, Abba, lama sabachthani?[213]
Father, father, why have you forsaken me?
To which the father or other elder would reply,
'My son, my son, you have suffered enough

And your torments have cleansed you for good.
Your father has not forsaken you,
Your town has not forsaken you,
I accept your repentance,
So, return in peace!'

And no one would ever dare repeat their deed!

Even despite the fact that the words *I repent* had been mercifully dropped
In this oath. And here they were with a death sentence!
The Romans limited the right of the Sanhedrin to pass the death sentence.
The *troika* could consider only execution for those
Who had violated the Law, and more in its day-to-day part.

Melamed, angrily and passionately,
But with scathing reasoning at the same time,
Destroyed all the Sadducee ambitions
To get their hands on the divine right
To take the life of another human.

Chorazin stirred and murmured,
And Caiaphas's people and those from *Free Will* sensed it.
They had nothing to say in response to the Old Lion of the Desert.

---

[213] Jesus Christ's dying words on the cross in Aramaic, translating as 'My God, my God, why have you forsaken me?'

Then they invited him over one evening for an event
That was meant to conclude after dinner with a discussion.

Zinoviy Melamed didn't let them off the hook there either,
But then the unthinkable happened.
After that evening, Grandfather suddenly fell very ill
And, by the time the doctors arrived, he was already unconscious.
Two days later, the Lion of the Desert passed away having never regained consciousness.

All Chorazin gasped in horror.
Not only had they lost an old enlightener;
They had irrevocably lost an entire era,
The golden age of the Chorazin intelligentsia,
And the golden age of the entire town altogether...

As if in an act of mockery, the Sadducee *troika*
Took care of all the funeral arrangements.
With truly Jesuit hand-wringing
And with tragic speeches, they played out a spectacle of mourning
Before Chorazin, which had fallen into a stupor from such treachery.

Everyone understood that the town's last defender had gone,
The father of all its children, children we had once been.
Gone was that last bastion of resistance
To the madness
That the *colonising compatriots* had wrought on us.

They had killed him.
However, the investigation adopted the hypocritical stance
That Grandfather had died from exhaustion from overworking,
From which his heart had failed.
'Colleagues, why didn't you take better care of our treasure?!'

The Sadducees, investigators and judges
Mocked us blatantly.
And we... we couldn't even grind our teeth any more.
We lowered our heads and our hearts dropped
Faced with this overwhelming, treacherous force,

Handed down to us either by Divine Predestination
Or the freedom of our own will.
And it was then that I brought my time to a stop.
One day, I simply refused to turn the sand timer over
And it froze there and then.

You think I fell into a depression or a social coma of sorts?
Not a bit of it. I simply switched off the thing inside
That enabled me to fix
Ballot papers on autopilot,
Not just once, but many times; well, what the hell difference does it make how many?!

I took part in fake parades,
I took it upon myself to teach *The Free Vision of the World*
And I spoke enthusiastically about Chorazin's fabulous achievements
Under the leadership of the current government,
About how we had overtaken and outperformed Bethsaida and Capernaum.

I became an exemplary agitator and illuminator of the Sadducees.
I angrily denounced the Essenes and mocked the Pharisees,
I regularly thanked the authorities that we had more than enough for bread and cheese.
I praised with gusto the distant authorities of Caiaphas
And Annas, his wise and just teacher.

Incidentally, Annas came to visit us once.
I was among the loyal activists,
Who had been invited to dinner with him.
Oh, the joy we had, jostling and giggling
By the richest-ever smorgasbord, laid out at this event!

Once, during an event, I spouted something
To the applause of my colleagues, sweating from either the admiration
Or the excitement.
It was then that Annas gave me a long, hard look,
As if he were looking right through me.

I could see or, more precisely, I could sense with the instinct of a jackal,
That there was something he didn't like.
Suddenly, he stood up and approached, very briskly for an old man.
'I don't see a Sadducee cross on you for some reason.'
He squealed in an unexpectedly nasty voice.

'I, I, I am not yet worthy of such a high...'
Annas interrupted me with a gesture and extended trembling hands
To the turban on my head.
With eyes askew, I saw him trying to attach
A Sadducee oblique cross.

I raised my arms and applied it myself with all my might.
'Well done,' the former High Priest smiled
And jokingly threatened me: 'Wear it proudly and don't take it off!'
I was amazed at how utterly sincerely
I managed to portray limitless joy, embarrassment and pride!

Annas viewed me closely for several moments more
And then, seeing me smile so happily and hold the cross in place,
He suddenly closed his eyes.
When he opened them, I saw disinterested
And undisguised contempt.

He walked off. Everyone rushed over to congratulate me.
Have you ever seen such a thing: a cross from Annas himself!
The almighty father-in-law of the High Priest Caiaphas himself!
I stood there, happily smiling
And I was amazed at how *sincerely* I was acting.

Later, I came in blind drunk
And shouted some loyalist rubbish.
And then I argued with my Hanna for the first time,
Had my way with her like some shameful hyena,
Humiliating his nearest and dearest while being unable to attack a lion.

These bouts of drunkenness then repeated themselves. As did the arguments.
Once, someone told me that they'd seen her
Kissing the Rottenführer from *Free Will.*

And how did I react? I didn't. It was more like I took it for granted.
Then she left although it must be said, she wept sorely before we parted.

But I just didn't care.
I revelled in my insignificance.
More to the point, I didn't even feel it.
Feelings are like streams:
They engulf you but move past you.

They move, do you understand? Time.
But there was nothing moved in me that one could call feelings.
You think I'd lost myself to the booze?
Far from it – hyenas are more resilient than you might think.
One day I got up, had a wash and threw all the booze out of the house.

I came to the school and looked at length at the children.
So, I'll disfigure them and nothing will bring me
To feel an ounce of remorse.
How much has already been said and how much whinging there's been in the staff room,
That we are being pushed around, belittled, exploited.

And what comes of it? What comes of it is that tomorrow
We'll continue our monstrous mission to disfigure our future.
I wasn't worried about when this would all end and how.
What worried me was what there might be beneath this low point.
When I can justify almost everything,

Whatever I might have done.
After all, I would ask myself, what's my way out?
I'll get the sack; I could hardly dare to resist
That monstrous machine,
That would swallow me, this little grain of sand, without even noticing.

And I'd... just die, I'd degrade from malnutrition and poverty.
As such, I'm a prosperous merchant,
Not just someone observing evil passively,
But someone who is a direct conduit for it.
And not just anywhere, but right into the defenceless souls of children.

It was then that I became... Became what? I've told you – A Stone Thrower.
The thing is, as I told you earlier,
The Sanhedrin had gained the right to execute,
But the Romans had kept the privileged forms of execution, like
Crucifixions or hanging, for themselves.

We were left to make do with
The ancient tradition of our ancestors – stoning.
And then, one weekend,
I went to the square and saw a procession,
Heading to execute two lovers,

Accused, by all accounts, of adultery.
I quietly joined the crowd
And when the execution began, I grabbed a stone and threw it at the lad.
He groaned and his head dropped in a deathly convulsion.
The girl screamed in a terrible voice,

But that wail of fear never reached me.
I heard the roar of approval from the crowd – *what a hit!*
Did I experience a thrill from the killing?
No. It was a legitimate killing and my hand
Had been driven by justice; what do you want from me?

I started attending all the executions that took place
Mostly at the weekends, to ensure there were more people.
Gradually, do you know who began to recognise me?
The execution regulars,
Who weren't simply onlookers,

Rather, let's say, connoisseurs of the process.
All week, I span in a whirl of training,
Propaganda, flyer distribution for *Free Will*,
The compilation of inflated lists of voters,
And reading poetry of the Sanhedrin's eternal glory.

Only at the weekend I did my favourite thing.
What are the finer points of stoning, you might ask?
It's that your hands hold not just death,
But the whole drama of the process.
How you should throw so as not to kill instantly,

To extend the victim's torment.
For example, when a suspected paedophile was being executed...
Why should I care if his guilt was proven or not?
I don't think it was, but the charge enabled me to think
That he was guilty.

At first the crowd chucks stones anyhow,
And at the end, too, once the person has been killed.
In the middle, however, it's not just theatre that begins,
But a proper stone-throwing contest,
Where each throw is given the crowd's due appraisal.

We stoned one 'paedophile' for a long while
And the one who inflicted the killer blow was deemed the loser.
The winner was judged to be the one to receive
Not only most of the crowd's cries of admiration,
But the most wails from the unfortunate victim too.

Where's the interest in chucking stones at a dumb body?
Neither the crowd, the soldiers nor I got any enjoyment from it.
There were other times when the crowd
Displayed sympathy for the victim
For some reason or other.

I didn't care for the reasons why;
Most important for me was to capture the mood.
One of my competitors, laying claim to be the best,
Actually ended his 'career' this way,
Not realizing that the victim had to be killed quickly.

With boos and hisses, and even with anger,
The crowd removed his leader's crown
And placed it on my head...

After considerable practice
I had perfected my crowning technique –

The so-called *mercy square*.
This was when the victim needed to be killed quickly.
You have no idea of the subtleties in this technique.
The *mercy square* technique was an intricate thing,
Something I had worked on many times.

It would be the blow that the crowd was waiting for.
Of course, if they felt sympathy for the victim.
This was how the *square* would play out:
First of all, you take four different stones,
Different in size and shape.

I would spend long evenings out in the desert,
Looking for stones of the right configuration
And setting them by for future executions.
I remember always being accompanied by boys,
Who were awfully proud if they found me what I needed.

There were no problems with the executions.
It was as if the Sadducees had been let loose
For there were executions pretty much every week.
Perhaps it was from this that the Sadducees became
Renowned for being such stern upholders of the Law.

In fact, this was a hypocritical masquerade, a distraction
From the crimes they were committing themselves.
If the people knew what they did during their time in power,
They would understand that this was incompatible
Not only with the Law, but with simple human reason, too.

A great many were executed,
But I was indifferent... Rather, I focused passionately
On honing my skills...
Anyway, the *mercy square*.
You wait for the moment when the crowd's desire to show mercy

Has reached its peak.
I don't know how, you just sense it; the moment just arrives.
You hold a short pause,
During which the young and inexperienced throwers,
In error, launch a couple of cruel throws at the victim.

The crowd starts to roar and get indignant.
And that is where I come in.
The square is four different stones that you throw
With great intricacy and calculated strength,
Because each of them plays a role.

The slightest delay and you fail
And the victim's torment would be amplified threefold.
Judge for yourself. The first blow is a medium-sized and hard pebble,
Which flies into the victim's head in a way
That strikes the upper part of the forehead

And forces the victim to throw back his head,
Revealing the neck. The second stone, a cutter,
Should be launched at the neck, so the cutting edge presses against
The carotid artery.
It shouldn't pierce the neck, which is not possible anyway.

It becomes possible when you launch the third, large pebble
At the next, only a little lower, almost at the Adam's apple.
The victim instinctively lowers his head
And, in doing so, presses the cutter tight against the neck.
From this sudden movement, the skin on the neck will even start bleeding.

But still this is not enough.
You take the fourth, large stone from the *mercy square*
And literally drive it with great force into the carotid.
You pierce the artery, the victim loses consciousness, relaxes
And bleeds out fast. A masterpiece.

Often, the crowd will even chant:
'*The Mercy Square! The Mercy Square!* '
Once this is done, no one bothers to finish the victim off,
Unless they're some maniacs.
As for me, I'm carried aloft to the town centre,

To cries of 'Philip the Merciful! Philip the Merciful!'
And the strangest thing is that I felt a strange pride,
With no joy and no feelings. Just this wicked sense of self-satisfaction.
In fact there were many different master-strokes,
But I won't insult you, brethren, with a cynical description.

Everything had gone. All the ideals, the children, the school.
Memories of Hanna and Melamed grew hazy.
Hanna openly despised me and shunned me.
I later heard that she was expecting my child
And had died giving birth. The infant too.

But I felt nothing.
All I remember was that I had performed the *Mercy Square*
For the first time that Sunday.
And insignificant little me even thought
That Allah was compensating me for my pain by granting me this skill.

Friends, it is in this state that you found me,
When they wanted to stone that girl from Magdala.
Beloved Teacher, you said then
Let him who is without sin,
Cast the first stone.

I remember that, while the execution was being prepared,
Judas Lebbaeus, for some reason, was staring at me
With piercing eyes and a mysterious squint.
You think I succumbed to this propaganda trick of
Let him who is without sin? Give me a break.

All subjects of tyrannical rule, especially those who serve to support them,
Are simply convinced that they are without sin.
This is what distinguishes them from free and,

482

Therefore, doubting people.
I was one hundred per cent sure I was without sin.

It was just that at that moment I had popped to search
For suitable pebbles for my *mercy square.*
When I returned, I saw only one thing.
I had always had a feel for the crowd and its mood.
I sensed that something was not quite right.

You and the brothers had turned and were making to leave.
But I... something evil came over me with a resentment for absolutely everything.
I decided to destroy that hated woman,
As beautiful as a lock of God's hair,
And, hence, so contrasting with the ugliness of my soul.

The rest you know. Brother Lebbaeus, never taking his eyes from me,
Walked up and shouted loudly at me, 'Philip!!!'
At the sound my name, something exploded inside me.
I fell to the ground and wept.
The people had already dispersed, but I continued to sob.

You remember when Brother Lebbaeus disappeared for three days?
He was tending to me at home.
I wept all those days, sobbing dark black tears
When I saw that it was not only my brother wiping my tears,
But that girl from Magdala as well.

I didn't simply continue sobbing,
I was dying and rising again, dying and rising again.
When Judas Lebbaeus and Maria had left,
I got up and went to the old, shabby parts of the town,
Where I found the old and blind Joseph Melamed.

I fell down before his feet and said,
'Abba, Abba, lama sabachthani?'
The blind hazzan shuddered, hearing those old, forgotten words
Of age-old repentance,
He found my head and said,

'My son, my son, you have suffered enough
And your torments have cleansed you for good.
Your father has not forsaken you,
Your town has not forsaken you,
I accept your repentance...'

Then he was silent for a while, before adding,
'Don't return to Chorazin,
It is not your town, not your Kingdom.
Search for the one who will show you your town,
And then return to it in peace!'

Verse 30

Watchful are the Gods of all
Hands with slaughter stained.

Aeschylus

Our greatest ability as humans is not to change the world, but to change
ourselves.

Mahatma Gandhi

It was the first day of our journey to Jerusalem.
At noon, the Beloved Teacher
Interrupted one of us,
Shuddered as if from the cold
And then smiled, sadly and tenderly.

'It's time,' He said.
'It's time.
But I am afraid. I won't go there alone.
Accompany me, brethren.'
We all jumped up, ready for anything.

Perhaps today was *that* day?
'No, brethren, not today.
It's just that the time has come
To speak with the heavens
In one language.'

We went off towards the mountain,
Whose name will be invented by our descendants.
Our sandals stepped with ease,
Only we felt no such ease in our souls.
'What can we do for You, Teacher?'

'Not for Me, brethren. Not for me.'
Boys and girls suddenly ran out onto the road.
'There they are,' the Beloved Teacher said.
'Whatever happens to me there, promise
That you'll give them what God deprived Adam and Eve: their childhood.'

'We'll do everything, Teacher, only how?
How can we become fathers to the whole world
When we are not the whole world, just a small part of it?
When we and our fates are but an episode in a great epic,
Created by Allah for centuries to come?'

'There is no need to be fathers of the world,'
The Beloved One said.
'Just be Good, Kind Men;
That will be enough
For children to want to follow suit.'

'But You said that what is destined for us
Was not something You'd wish for Your own sons.
Are they too to be doomed to the same fate?
Should they not be in a state of bliss?
Should not roses bathe them in their fragrance?'

485

'Yes, when they're children.
But not when they're husbands and wives.
In life everyone will have their mountains and lowlands.
Let them climb then to be able to descend;
You will be but their guides.

You will just walk beside them and shed tears,
To ensure they shed fewer tears of their own.
You will weep so that they might weep less.
You will suffer so that they might suffer less.'
'And what about You, Teacher? You are speaking like you're saying goodbye.'

'Brethren, why the greeting when we've seen each other before?
Why the farewell, if we'll never be apart?'
'You're crying, Teacher! Are those tears of grief?' 'No, that's just the dew.'
'You're smiling, Teacher! Is that from joy?'
'No, that's just a recollection.'

'Your hands clasp your staff
As if You're clinging to the fabric of the world. Is that regret, Teacher?'
'No, that's just fatigue.'
'Teacher, You're so pale! Is that excitement?'
'No, that's fear.

Go back, brethren. I'll go on alone from here.'
Dejectedly, we turned and walked away.
'No. wait a minute... Why don't you,
Cephas, the Zealot and John, come with me?
I...' 'No words needed, Teacher. We're coming.'

I trudged behind them,
Quills, papyrus and parchment in my hand.
I also felt afraid.
The brothers wrapped themselves in their robes as if from the cold,
Although the way was warm, bright and wonderful.

The sun was enormous and beautiful.
Tiny birds, with their shrill chirping
Flew up into the air here and there.
Let it be a journey of trials, we thought,
Let it be a journey of anger!

Let it be a journey of searching and doubt!
But we... we are friends!
We are friends and it is wonderful
To be a friend to the one
We call the Good, Kind Man,

Who came to us we kind of know from where,
But then we don't know this simultaneously.
Well, by and large,
Do we even know where we're from?
There's the Sun! But it has no friends.

And what's there in the heavens, then?
Who is your friend, Adonai?

You invented our friendship, but who is Your friend?
If someone's a friend, that means they're someone equal.
You invented our loneliness but did you invent your own?

Does our likeness to you
Only ever occur in loneliness?
When we are happy with our friends
Does that mean we grow further from You, from Your original plan?
Does that mean that if we are happy with someone, we are violating something

That You once established for us?
And if we're happy in love?
Happy when we're not alone.
Does that mean we are defying You?
When we are with lovers

In bed, in the kitchen, on our travels or at war?
When we give birth to small children who are like *us*?
Incidentally, Adonai, were you ever little?
Hardly.
That means you are *Ahad and Wahid* – the loneliest one?

'Tell us, Teacher, it turns out that Allah
Is the loneliest of all, is that right?'
The Teacher laughed and His fear subsided,
Revealing to us the Beloved
Friend we were so used to.

'How do I know?
Who do you take me for?'
Suddenly, everyone stopped and fell silent.
'What?' the Teacher asked somewhat flustered. What?'
'You... You are our Teacher and Friend,' Cephas said.

The Teacher smiled: 'That's right, Cephas!
Whatever happens today,
Please, always deem Me as your friend.
As for Teacher, I don't know... Were we not walking the same path?
But as a friend... Don't leave Me...'

'No, no,' John interrupted him passionately,
'We will never leave You!'
The Teacher suddenly felt sad and embraced each of us in turn.
I can still feel that embrace.
Do you understand?! *I can still feel that embrace!*

He said,
'I don't know what awaits us up there.
I don't know if we'll come down alive,
And will it even be *us* who come down from the Mountain?
The only thing I know is that I am heading for that promised

Second meeting.'

Twilight knows how to extinguish emotions.
The grey world enveloped us,
And only the silhouette of the orange mountain,

The last thing to say farewell to the Sun,
Shone in a bright spot up ahead.

We climbed to the top in silence.
As always, Cephas busied himself with orders
As to who would go where,
As if we were simply preparing
For another evening prayer.

We quietly observed the falling of the Sun
Beyond the edge of our Galilean world.
Deep in our thoughts,
Each of us saw in the night in our own way
And the quiet that accompanied it.

Suddenly, something changed in the air.
A shrill wind picked up, suddenly cruel and hot,
As if it were echoing fires far away.
The Teacher jumped up in agitation
And went over to the edge of the precipice.

John ran over, attempting to hold Him,
But Cephas, with a sharp motion of the hand, held him back.
Our hearts slowly began to fill with
The fear of the unknown, a fear we didn't understand,
Which was rapidly expanding the chasm between us and the Teacher.

The wind grew stronger and stronger. The sky became filled with clouds.
Something strange was happening in the heavens.
Occasional flashes could be seen,
The storm clouds bothered by rare and anxious lightning.
The air became filled with strange smells.

And then came the rumble.
It came from all sides.
It ruffled the Beloved's hair,
And made us huddle together in our fear.
The sky shook!

Have you ever seen the sky shaking?!
A terrible thunder then suddenly seemed to split our heads.
Dark shadows swept around the top of the mountain;
Ears exploded in pain; faces were contorted in terror.
We were afraid, as people should be.

But what is the fear of *people* –
The expectancy of terror, of death?
Did He have these notions at that moment? I don't think so.
The Teacher stood motionlessly on the on the tip of the peak. It seemed
That the world, afraid of His motionlessness,

Had yielded and was now spinning around Him,
While we felt this rotation with all our bodies.
The whirlwind around the mountain top
Became akin to a mountain mudslide,
Through which not a thing is visible.

Suddenly, amidst the terrible noise, it seemed to us
That an enormous, awful, laughing face
Had emerged from the whirlwind's dark depths, and we heard
A hoarse, hissing voice:
'No, boy, that is beyond you! Ha-ha-ha!'

At that moment, the Teacher's profile turned
Into a monumental column.
He lowered his head and jerked an arm to the left,
As if pointing a tamed hound
To its place.

The face responded with an awful howl,
It cast out a swirling stream
At the Teacher, like a blow from a mighty giant hand.
Only at that moment I saw something amazing.
Cephas jumped up and, drawing his Hun sword,

That Simon the Zealot had once given him,
He chopped off that monstrous arm!
Oh Allah, what courage!
The face of the Greedy One (you know him, right?) howled
And the whirlwind began slowly to crumble and fall,

Until it had collapsed at the foot of the mountain.
The Teacher turned and nodded to Cephas,
He laughed and cried out through the hurricane's din:
'You see – it's not just me! Thank you, my friend!'
With that, he turned to look to the heavens and the horizon.

This blow had taken all of Cephas's strength away and he collapsed with us.
We pressed up close together,
Trying to shelter from the hot, howling wind.
And our fear was no more.
We looked out.

Suddenly, we heard a voice: *'Look!'*
It struck us right in the brain,
As if it had come from inside us.
It ripped through our ears,
Like it had entered our heads from outside.

John pointed to somewhere in the North.
A lone horseman was rushing in through the whirlwind,
Crying, 'Kalagia! Kalagia![214] You have been called!'
Beneath him was a white steed while the horseman's head bore a wreath.
He held a vessel with water from the River Jordan and a shining shield,

Bearing the inscription,
There is no true power, there is only Faith!
He flew up to the top of the mountain and brought his wheezing horse to a stop

---

[214] *Kalagia* – In Shambhala Buddhism, there is a legend where the world is controlled from the heavenly *Shambhala* and the earthly *Shambhala*, where seven disciples reside. When they decide to assign someone a special mission, this person hears the summons, *Kalagia, come to Shambhala!*. This calling is reported by four horsemen, or one of the four messengers of those running the affairs of the world.

Immediately in front of the Teacher.
He dismounted, walked up to Him and embraced Him.

We heard the Beloved's sigh of exclamation:
'Eliyahu! Is that you?! You're alive?!'
We recognised him as the Forerunner.
'Is there death indeed?' the horseman asked with a smile.
'Hello, ben Joseph!'

'Hello, John, son of the tribe of David!'
The Beloved replied admiringly.
'Is that even possible?
But you were executed and now, what, you're alive? Or...?
Or you are indeed the Great Forerunner and I... I...'

The Forerunner laughed and his sparkling laughter
Eclipsed even the noise of the mountain wind.
'Brother,' he said, 'is it not you who carry the understanding of
What is death, immortality and time?'
'No, not Me,' the Teacher replied confused.

The Forerunner laughed again:
'That's because You haven't been able to make a choice yet
And you grasp at your human essence.'
'What do you mean by *grasp*? And who do you think I am?'
The Teacher asked somewhat perplexed.

'This is what we will learn today.
I have a message for You, look.'
He unrolled a piece of parchment,
Bearing the inscription,
You...

That's right, I took a good look at this inscription,
Despite the fact that we were afraid to get too close.
But what did it mean?
'Look West! West!' we heard John cry out.
And a hurricane rose with renewed vigour over the mountains.

We caught sight of a horseman rushing from the West
At full pelt on a black horse. He was shouting, 'You have been summoned!'
We saw the black wind of the Greedy One
Endeavouring in vain to throw the rider from his horse,
But he inexorably continued to draw nearer to us.

We heard an inward/outward voice, saying, *Listen!*
An instant later and the horseman flew up to the mountain top.
And there he was, right near to us.
What was this old man? In one of his hands were the scales of wisdom,
In the other, a shining shield,

With the inscription, *There is no true Victory, there is only the Path!*
He brought his horse to a sudden stop right in front of the Teacher
And the mighty old man dismounted.
'Sholom, son of the Road,' he said
And embraced our Beloved Friend.

'Hello, Father of the Path! Hello, Rabbeinu[215], oh, Great Leader!'
The Friend wanted to kneel but the elder would not allow it.
'Arise, for it would be improper for one who has heard the Voice
To bow before an equal.
Or perhaps for a superior? I don't know.

This scroll bears a message.
It is not for us to know what is written there;
We are allowed to open and read its contents only in Your presence.
The only thing I can say
Is that there are only two options.

Either the King or...
Well, read it!'
The Beloved One opened the scroll,
And all that was written there was,
You must...

'You... must, you must what?' the Teacher whispered.
'Look East! East! Look to the East!'
The young John announced once more.
Amidst the swirling winds of the Galilean desert,
We caught sight of a third horseman, crying, 'You have been summoned!'

He rode atop a hot red horse of the desert,
Whose name was Burak[216].
He rushed like lightning and the desert receded from his divine gallop.
The rider held a curved Arabian sword in his hand.
The pen is mightier than the sword! Was the inscription on his shield.

The thunderous voice from the heavens then announced,
Read! [217]
And the echo of this command
Spread across the surface of the sea,
Over the mountain tops and shook the world under the ground.

With a mighty roar, the red beast
Cast terror among the djinns, demons and peri
Who surrounded the mountain.
And he scattered them over the expanses of the Galilean desert.
The Great Warrior dismounted on top of the mountain,

Walked over to the Beloved One and embraced Him.
'And so, we meet,' the Great Arab said excitedly.
'As always,' the Teacher said with a smile.
'This time it is not I who bring you the decision of Allah the Almighty.
I hold only part of it in my hand!'

He extended his scroll to the Friend.
With an embarrassed smile, the Beloved One unrolled it.

---

[215] *Rabbeinu* (Hebrew) – our Teacher, the nickname given to Moses.
[216] *Burak* – a horse or a fantastic creature on which, according to Muslim legend, the Prophet Muhammad ascended from a rock in Jerusalem to Allah in heaven.
[217] *Read!* – *iqra* (Arabic), the Prophet Muhammad's first divine revelation, from which the Qur'an, the sacred book of Islam, derives, where *Qur'an* means *reading*, or *the search for knowledge*.

Again... was the inscription.
He dropped the parchment.
'No! No!' the Great Arab cried.

'Never, ever, ever
Will I admit if, once more...
I will once more be forced to betray my dream
For Divine Will!
And that is the only thing I can say for myself in the Book,

Violating my obligations to heaven!
Oh, Almighty Allah, answer me,
Who has the power to stop this?!'
With endless love and tenderness,
The Beloved One closed the lips of the Great Warrior with two fingers.

They looked one another in the eye.
They both were tearful
And those tears masked centuries. And an eternity.
'If this is a dream,' the Beloved One said,
'If this is a dream, will *He* not let you have it?'

'Look South! South! Look to the South!'
Cried John, losing his strength
Everyone turned to face the fire
That had flared up like a false dawn
Over the tormented sands of Galilee.

The rain fell on the earth, the sand and the rocks.
Through the grey, steel ranks
Of military divisions of the night rain
Arose before us the profile
Of the fourth horseman.

This wasn't exactly a horseman, for,
On an enormous steel chariot,
Harnessed to a pale Horse,
An enlightened Prince
Drew nearer, exclaiming, 'Kalagia! You have been summoned!'

Heaven and earth trembled from that terrible voice.
'Feel it!' he announced.
Was it the thunder from the rain?
Or was it the clatter of the horseman's shining shield
Adorned with the inscription, *When you suffer, God suffers with you.*

'What's that in his hands?!' The Great Arab and the Great Leader cried out.
'A shroud or a crown?'
Yet the hands of the fourth horseman were empty.
The chariot came to a halt with an awful screech
Before the mountain top.

The Enlightened Prince came down.
He didn't approach the Beloved One, he just stopped
And everyone could see his tears.
We couldn't understand a thing,
But the horsemen understood it all.

They guessed *what* was in the fourth scroll.
The Prince walked slowly over to the Teacher.
'It was just a shroud that wasn't handed...'
He said and his weeping interrupted his words.
All five of them embraced, but the scroll slipped from

The Prince's hand and rolled over to me,
Damaged by the drops of rain.
Peri... I could make out.
I snatched it up and hid it in my breast.
You... must... again... peri...

Alahi! Alahi! But he is so young and handsome!
What have You prepared for Him?!
If we disciples and companions had understood
But a fraction of
What had now happened!

Who were these horsemen? What were these scrolls?!
Where did it all come from?
Cephas, John, Jacob and I
Gathered together and shivered in fear,
Weeping from the sense that

Something awful had just been decided,
Perhaps something cruel, perhaps just,
Perhaps divine, or perhaps simply a consequence
Of our mass madness.
However, we had also changed;

We now possessed knowledge, only we knew nothing;
We had seen events, but we did not understand their logic.
What could be done? What were we to do?
What now depended on us?
Were we, the sons of man, now losing or gaining?!

Suddenly, from the thundery sky,
Now infinite and deep,
All-encompassing, sovereign and commanding,
All-merciful and gracious,
Like a sigh of heavenly pain, came the word,

Love!

For a moment everything froze.
The roar of the skies, the emotions of the brothers,
The gestures of the horsemen and even the face of the Greedy One
Against all that was going on up there.
There was only Him, washed by the torrents of rain,

With his arms outstretched like a Tengri cross,
The Eternal Blue Sky,
Or some other symbol.
He smiled somehow fatefully.
Bursting from him were flames of faith, death, hopelessness, suffering,

Visions of childhood, joy, happiness,
Doubt, fear, danger, struggle, hardships of a journey,
The fires of wisdom, knowledge, sympathy and mercy,
Generosity, devotion, decency, will
And love.

For a moment, we saw Eternity too.

With an expression both stern and sad,
The horsemen said their farewells, looking into each other's eyes
As if they were saying goodbye for evermore, but not forever,
As if they would meet again and many times over,
But only Eternity would determine the time and place of such meeting.

The Teacher stood there, lashed by the streaming rain,
Beautiful, Beloved and Doomed at the same time.
The four horsemen, though, stretched out their hands to him,
But more and more spray
Now separated them, pushing them further apart.

They were *returning*.
The white horse snorted,
The black horse neighed its love for its master.
The gilded Burak frolicked under the mighty Warrior.
The pale horse called its master on its way.

At the last moment, the Enlightened Prince suddenly stopped
And gestured for everyone else to pay heed.
He went to the chariot and took out
His shining shield, which bore the inscription,
When you die, your God dies with you.

The Great Arab burst into tears and, spurring Burak, he
Shot off into the darkness, whispering, 'Until next time, ahi.'[218]
The Great Leader tenderly wiped raindrops from the Friend's brow,
He nodded, closed his eyes and jumped onto his horse, disappearing in the swirling storm.
The Prince joined his hands in prayer and, touching the reins,

Drove his pale horse into the sky.
Only the Forerunner remained at length, embracing the Friend
And patting him on the back.
Only once did this patting
Give rise to sobs on the Beloved's part.

The Forerunner slowly took to his white horse.
'*He* has yet to decide when that day will be,'
His words, like heavy stones,
Fell from his lips, down the mountain and beyond:
'But You know how *He* loves You.'

The white steed roared, anticipating a wild leap,
And it soared into the skies, leaving behind
Sparks from its feet, splashing up from contact
With the electrified air.

---

[218] *Ahi* (Arabic) – my brother.

In a moment, all that surrounded us

Was just the Palestinian spring rain.

Verse 31. The King

'Tell me, Bartholomew, about your Path to this day.'
Brothers, I don't like it when you call me by that name...
You see, I once acquired a new name –
Nathanael,
And that is how I always want to be known.
...

What? You want me to relate everything openly?
Do you need me to tell you absolutely everything about my life,
My torments and my aimless wanderings,
About my search for the truth and understanding of history,
What is happening now and what is destined to come to pass?

All right, if you insist.

I am Bartholomew, Bar-Tolmay!
My full royal name is
Ptolemy XV Caesar Philopator Philometor,
Last Pharaoh of Upper and Lower Egypt,
Nicknamed Caesarion,

Officially not of the living, but killed
On the orders of my half-brother
Who was actually my nephew,
Gaius Julius Caesar Octavian Augustus, Emperor,
Pontifex Maximus, Tribune and Pater Patriae.

What, Thomas, the dates don't match?
Indeed, if time really had total power
Over my life, then I would now
Be about seventy years old.
But that is not the result of some miracle or spatial distortion.

It could actually be the other way round.
Of one and the other.
And why? Well, that's something I'd like to learn with you.
Many people who know history wonder why, when I had
Such a wonderful opportunity

To flee to India with all my riches,
Did I return to stand before
My cruel half-brother.
No, I wasn't counting on mercy because he was a blood relation.
I wasn't really counting on anything, to be honest...

That's right, I just walked to meet my own demise,
Because it was predetermined.
It was then that Octavian uttered the words
Too many Caesars is not a good thing,
And I understood the meaning of this like no other.

Back then, on a ship that carried
The years and generations of a calm, comfortable life

In a foreign land, that did not know me
And had no wish to either,
I asked the priest Roban, my tutor,

If I had chosen the right path,
In deserting my people and my kingdom to be
Desecrated by new people, placed to rule my country.
Roban was silent for a long while but eventually he answered sincerely:
'How do I know, sire?

After all, it is you who are anointed by God to rule,
And I am but your shadow.
It is you who stands between God on the one hand
And your people on the other.
Who could possibly act as intermediary in such important decisions?'

Back then, brothers, I didn't know we were talking
Not just about the position of sovereign
And all the benefits that come with it.
We were talking, no more and no less,
About the *Greatest War of Man* –

The war for monarchy.
The war for the right to decide the fate of people or peoples,
Determined for you either from birth
Or afterwards, when the previous ruler
Departs from this world, leaving you with the power,

Which will determine your fate for ever after,
Regardless of whether or not you have succeeded in ruling.
You are anointed into this kingdom by the will of God,
And that means that, even if you lose this power,
Its anointed seal will never leave your head.

I ordered the ships to turn around
And sail back to blessed Alexandria.
What moved me to do that? Vanity?
And what did I know of vanity at fourteen years old?
What did I know then about the power of the crown of a king, tsar or pharaoh?

Perhaps I was moved by a desire to command people unchallenged?
But what did I know about absolute power at my age?
Perhaps I was moved by a passion to become the richest man in the country?
Hardly, for my wealth is right here, with me.
I could be happy in a foreign land,

Possessing countless Egyptian treasures,
That I might have taken from my own people.
I could console myself with the thought that these riches were rightfully mine.
That it was not created from a myriad of tears and droplets of sweat of my nation,
And that this reflects the true will of the Almighty.

You might say I was moved by foolishness. So be it.
After all, the swords of legionnaires awaited me,
Not reasoning as to who would be truly good
For my people and who would not.
I, a young and foolish monarch, reasoned as follows:

King is not a position and not just a pretty word.
Tsar is not the ability to trample over nobles and subjects.
Khan is not wild merriment, servility and glory.
Sultan is not the ability to take and alter fates
As one pleases.

Pharaoh is the concentration of a nation's honour and its true destiny.
Something more elevated than simply the well-being of one's subjects.
Monarch is the responsibility and readiness
To answer for one's actions directly before God.
Who stands more exposed before the Almighty

Than a monarch?
The priests who speak with the One in the same language?
Hardly. They don't have such a level of responsibility for everything.
Let them speak with God, sure, but on whose behalf?
But a king... on whose behalf does he speak with God? His people.

So, what is a king without his people?
To whom does he carry the will of the Almighty?
Perhaps God will not disappear when man disappears,
But when his people disappear, a king
Transforms into meaningless dust on the road of history.

That is how I reasoned at that moment.
I thought that only the deceitful and cowardly usurpers
See the throne only as an opportunity, not a seat of responsibility.
However, imposters with only selfish and base desires
Use the throne to meet their own mean needs.

I am anointed by God, and I am not like that.
I won't hide behind a wall of seas and mountains
From pursuing ferocious Roman mercenaries.
I will return to my nation
And I will stand before it in all the glory of my defencelessness,

But, nevertheless, in the belief that there is no one other than me

Capable of answering for its fate before the Ruler of Worlds.
My tutor Roban cried and sobbed.
I said to him, 'You are weeping like a human,
Like a millionth part of a nation.
You weep over death, which means something different

To me than it does to you.
You will just disappear from imperial records.
I will hold close and care for
The tender, wounded falcon that personifies
My beautiful, proud people

Who, apart from me, will see in no one a decree of future fate.
If I, like a hare, just try to save my own skin,
Then I'll lose that right to protect the hardy bird.
But what else do I have apart from this?!
What will my life be worth if it's deprived of its very essence?'

With tears in his eyes, Roban said, 'But you're only a child!
And your fate is worth no more than mine purely because
It is just as vulnerable to the Roman spear
That inevitably awaits us
On the very shores of our glorious Fatherland!

You know no more about the monarchy than I do.
Or maybe even less!
You are first and foremost responsible for those
Who have forced themselves to forget the smell of their native land
And have rushed after you to foreign lands, wishing to save not only their lives,

But yours too, Pharaoh, for the sake of their future aspirations!
You won't just kill yourself, my boy;
You'll wipe out the last stronghold of faith in you, you'll see!'
I pondered this and ordered my ships
To dock at an island in the middle of the mighty Indian Ocean.

I wanted to ask the people myself what I should do.
How should I act when the dynasty's blood says one thing,
While the logic of reason and expediency
Says another?
Let my people answer the question that the young lad cannot.

A fraction of my people came ashore.
We lit fires and indulged ourselves with memories of our Homeland,
To give us strength to make the most essential
And perhaps the only, final important decision
In my life.

One evening, after hymns and prayers,
I addressed the last subjects of the true Pharaoh,
Driven away by the winds of the Indian Ocean:
'Here is the choice. Here am I. Here is my power over events. Here is yours.
What should I do?'

The women, old folk and the children wept and wailed,
'Oh, Pharaoh! Oh, the beauty of Upper and Lower Egypt!
Oh, the might of the pyramids and the leader of ferocious Nubians!
Oh, bearer of the eternal faith and the heir to the Great Empire!
Life is the only source

From which everything springs:
History, glory, victories of the past and victories still to come.
Save your life and ours too;
We will serve as the foundation,
So that our people might become numerous again

And, returning home, set the enemy running
From the borders of the Sacred Nile, the river of the Gods!
We will bear sons and daughters, and we'll build new ships,
Which will berth on Egypt's shores at the sacred hour
And fill the country once more, like the sand fills the desert!'

The merchants and the town's commoners piped up,
'There are many ways, oh, Lord of Egypt,
To restore the Homeland to its former limits!

We will master new trading routes,
We'll set up a government in exile,

Whose authority will be a thorn in the side
Of the Roman invaders and usurpers, causing
Excruciating pain!
We'll convert many to our faith who will fill our ranks,
And we'll buy warships to carry our new army

Into fierce battles around the sacred Sphinx!
And the ranks of this army will be supplemented
With mighty regiments of numerous mercenaries,
Whom we'll pay with our own funds.
And victory will shine in your crown, just as it did before!'

The priests and philosophers all sang in harmonious unison,
'We will announce to different countries that
Egypt lives and its Pharaoh lives!
We will gather many allies,
Who will help us not only through the power of words and support,

But with their armies too, weapons and the advantages
That the military alliances and unions will provide.
We will choke Rome with the force of diplomacy when needed
And with the force of our arsenal when needed!
What is needed from you for this, young monarch?

Only to be, to be alive and personify legitimacy.
Let it be in exile but preserve that image of the true throne all the same!
You will grow up among educated elders,
In the circle of attention of the wealthiest subjects,
And among beautiful virgins, but most important,

This wealth will be enough for a long time to come,
To ensure you grow into a mighty warrior
And then send out to the sands of Egypt
Countless armies with Indian elephants in their ranks,
With ferocious nomads on their finest steeds,

With Chinese engineers with their incredible design genius.
And while this is all accumulating and coming together,
You'll get a taste of the benefits of what no throne can do without,
The riches, luxury and the beauty of ceremonies,
Which are what will shape the true Pharaoh,

The bearer of the way of life, the values we associate with enjoyment and philosophy,
Without which culture will become
Only the leisure pursuits of a rough and ready military camp!'
Stern and morose military men also spoke:
'We, descendants of the mighty warriors

Of Upper Egypt, Nubia and Macedonia,
Address you, oh, Pharaoh and God's Anointed One!
The words of the commoners, the women and the eunuchs doubtless
Carry the seeds of the sensible, logical
And, to a point, the undeniable. And yet!

What are we dying for on the battlefields?
For honour, for glory, for land allotment and a quiet pension?
To some extent, yes, but this isn't the main thing for us.
The main thing is the sense of an eternal continuity
Of tradition and the power of the throne.

So, what does this mean for us?
Not just a royal ritual and award trinkets.
What it means for us is *a continuity and constancy of values*,
Which must be unalterable.
You see, then, death too becomes meaningful

And noble in its inevitability.

Continuity for us is the reliable realisation of
Where, when and *for what* we would not have died;
The Motherland will be eternal and will ensure
That our families and our children will remain valuable to society.
Our sons will grow up with their own sense of pride,

That the sacrifices of war are not in vain,
Even if they themselves become victims of future wars.
Debt remains unaltered through the ages, like an oath, and this means
That the Path of warriors, both the living and the dead,
Will always be honoured and glorified.

And no one will permit our death to be interpreted
To suit the changing whims of politicians,
Tradesmen and their weak and calculating women.
Or our military prowess to be trampled to dust
By the reproaches of ideological deserters and cowards.

We don't see this power of continuity today
Because the core value of our outlook itself,
The thousand-year power of the Pharaoh, is under threat.
That means only one thing:
As soldiers and officers of our noble kingdom,

We must either perish in defence of the throne,
Or bow our heads to the new powers that be.
As you can see, we didn't follow the second option.
That means the only thing left to us is to die.
Yes, the commoners and priests are probably right

When they say a new army can be created.
They could probably reinforce it with mercenaries and foreigners
Which is basically correct from a military point of view.
One thing is wrong, though: what is the strength of a soldier
When he does not stand on his own land?

There is none.
So our word, the word of the military class is this:
Why dwell in shameful contemplation of
Foreign armies arriving in Egypt
To liberate what is alien to them but lucrative,

When it is better to die now, alongside our monarch,

Holding in contempt, as befits warriors,
All the boons of a happy and successful emigration.
Only then will our children stop being the army
Of Upper Egypt, Macedonia and Nubia.

Only then will they grow up, realising what it means and how
To die for one's Homeland, casting aside all other benefits.
Only this is a guarantee of the restoration of Egypt's glory,
While the other route... well, it's likely, but unacceptable all the same,
For our thousand-year-old warrior's spirit.'

I pondered this long and hard and asked my people
For a little more time, until the next morning,
To reach a decision,
Which would be right, not in human terms,
Not only for the duration of our lifetime,

But right in monarchical terms,
To see the unity and the inviolability of our power
For thousands of years ahead.
That night, I sat in my tent for some time,
Unable to find a single point of support,

On which I could confidently lean.
However, it was still up to me to decide.
I might be fourteen years old and I have yet to taste
The sweet taste of a peacetime administration,
Fair judgment, construction and creation.

So, I might be just a boy,
Cast by the winds of the Indian Ocean to the deserted shores
Of some unknown island.
I am the Pharaoh; I am part of God's plan on earth;
I and no one else is destined to decide

What I will arrive at eternal life with;
The label history ascribes to monarchs –
A coward, visionary, sycophant, warrior or child?
Or even a monarch about whom the information is so insignificant
As if I never even existed in the time of my nation.

I retired to my tent
And I wept. Oh God! After all, I am really nothing but a boy!
I don't even know the scale of the decision
With which I was faced!
I knew not what linked phenomena, not criteria nor boundaries

Between true greatness and royal tyranny.
I prayed to the One and Only God!
Only to Him, for, as monarch, I knew
Whatever games the priests might play with the pantheon,
Up there, in the heavens, there is One King,

The decision-maker for everyone and everything.
I prayed for a long time and only my tears
Stopped me seeing straight away
That I was no longer alone in my tent.

His messenger had been sitting behind me for some half an hour.

He sat there with a smile, observing my helpless pleas.
Then he spoke, loudly and in a familiar tone:
'Pharaoh! I have been sent to you by the Almighty.
He has a weakness for people like you,
So he has instructed me so that,

On the night the decision is made, I give you
What you are so missing:
Great historical experience.
He loves Egypt, I don't know why.
You see, He can't stand your polytheism! But it's not for me to judge.

And here I am, and we have a journey to make,
After which you'll reach a decision.
What is it? Personally, it makes no difference.
Soon, there will be war in Heaven and He will understand
That you are incapable of deeds other than the selfish and base.

Get ready, whatever He thinks,
I have no intention of challenging his orders.
At least not now.
'Who are you?' I asked, frightened, wiping my tears and runny nose.
'There is not much my name will tell you,' the angel replied,

'At least not yet. Are you ready?' 'I'm ready.'

Brothers, I will never forget
What I experienced in the next moments.
It was more a case not of moments rather of a darting eternity,
An eternity that moves through time and down the river
Of human history, as seen through the eyes of monarchs.

Only not the monarchs sitting safely on their thrones,
Rather those who found themselves, sooner or later,
One on one with things like that
Which I had to do.
The fact that time is one of the conventions

Of our human life on earth
Is something I understood then, but there was something I didn't
And that, at the same time, is
One of the greatest abstractions
With which you either come to terms with or you don't.

It all depends on what
Categories you'll leave for your mind
And which, you won't.
I thirsted for the experience that the angel spoke about.
Therefore, in the following moment,

I flew, ripping up the boundaries we can see,
With both mind and body,
But which we are unable to overcome.
I saw Constantinople and the fall of the Komnenos dynasty.

I was wearing purple boots[219], but my authority was already burning with the flame of death.

I was the great warrior and adventurer Andronikos,
Standing before the tomb of the Emperor Manuel.
My eyes burned, but my lips said,
'I will avenge you, my persecutor, on all your kind,
Who will pay for all the evil harm you have done to me!'

And there I was, trampling on the corpse of the young Emperor Alexios,
Knowing that there was now nothing between me and the Byzantine throne.
I rejoiced in the extermination of thousands of Latins,
Drowning in blood and choking on the ashes of fires.
There was the crown on my head – I was the saviour of the Empire!

There was a crowd of Constantinople's residents
Praising me and telling me I was the best of the dynasty!
He is the saviour of the Empire! He will return us our strength and glory!
But... That same crowd was killing me,
Tearing me to pieces and screaming,

'Look, he remains as bloodthirsty as ever!'
Because blood was gushing from my arm,
When I raised it to my face without its severed hand,
To cross myself.
'What on earth is going on?!' Came my cry, addressed to the angel.

The angel, though, just smirked and said,
'That is *vengeance*! *Vengeance* has eaten away the great Andronikos
From outside and within.
It was vengeance he sought when destroying the House of Komnenos,
And vengeance returned to him in that dreadful form.'

Then we flew with the angel over the seas and cities.
There I was, that handsome and slender prince of the steppe people,
Presenting his sword of loyalty to the Manchurian throne of the Qing.
I was Amursana, the last Dzungar Qong Tayiji,
Who had only just received an army at his disposal,

To remove the rightful ruler Deveci from the Oirat throne.
I bowed my head before my enemies, anticipating
That I would deceive them later and bring the entire might
Of the Dzungar and Kazakh armies crashing down upon them,
Upon my age-old and cunning enemy, the Chinese Emperor.

However, the picture was changing, with the Chinese methodically
Slaughtering my people, from tent to tent.
The women, the elderly and the children all fell,
Great warriors all cast to the dust and dirt
Of the steppe roads, never to recover.

There I was, dying in the remote Russian land,
Using the last of my strength to wipe the blood and pox
From my face and my wounds – punishments of my own God.
I was dying and I recalled the moment of betrayal,
But I just couldn't understand, even on my deathbed,

---

[219] Purple boots were a symbol of the power of the Byzantine emperors.

Whether this moment was the rise or the fall of
The one endowed with truly imperial talents,
To raise a shaking empire from oblivion,
Once more pacify the Kazakhs and, subordinating their people,
Rush out against the powerful and age-old enemy and crush him.

'What is it, oh, angel? Where's the answer?' I cried out again.
The heavenly messenger smirked and said,
'That is *envy*, my friend, *envy* as black as the pox!
When you are smart, energetic, talented and noble,
You think that he who bears the drops of the Divine Seal

Is not worthy to be ruler and only you, Amursana, are worthy!
Then envy devours both you and the empire
That you wanted to serve,
And which has to fall, prostrate
At the feet of your genius!

In the end, there is no Komnenos nor Dzungar Khanate!'
The angel laughed and cried out to me through the noise of its wings,
'Look over there, what do you see?'
'I see myself!' I cried. This time, I am the King of France!
I am Philip IV the Handsome, but why,

Instead of enjoying the pleasures of festivities,
Do I turn my gaze to the execution stake?
Who is it there, at the stake? Any why does the Pope himself
Bless this cruel execution?'
'Look carefully,' the angel screamed, 'and listen.'

And then, at a certain moment, I began to realise what was going on.
The man at the stake was the last Grand Master
Of the Knights Templar Jacques de Molay!
Before death forever sealed the Templar's lips,
The valiant knight exclaimed,

'Not a year will pass and you will die,
That's you, you deceitful and greedy monarch and you, Pontiff!
Days flashed past before my eyes and there was a different picture:
I was still the king, only I was as helpless as a child.
My body was paralysed

And I was lying but two steps from my bed.
Before me I could see the death of Pope Clement six months before
And the horror of the Templar Knight's prophecy.
'So, what happened, angel?' I cried out to the heavenly messenger.
The angel smiled meaningfully

And, spreading his wings, took me away from France.
A little while later, he cried out, as if in triumph,
'That is *greed*, Bartholomew! Insatiable *greed*;
That is what did for the great king,
Who had been the first to gift the States General to the French!

He had wanted to get his hands on all the treasures of the Templars,
And found he was unable to stop, incessantly confiscating, robbing and executing.

Power always presents such a test,
When you realise that, since you are the most important,
Why shouldn't you be the richest as well?!'

Further and further the wings of the mighty
Angel carried me, overcoming not only distance,
But the shackles of time too.
There was another great country and there I was within it.
A strange feeling came over me.

It was like a sense of a triumph of justice.
As if I had experienced much humiliation and deprivation,
But I had behaved so nobly and honestly
That I had deserved from God and the people...
That... I had become Emperor Dmitry I Ivanovich,

The true owner of the Russian throne!
And I was no Grigory Otrepyev and no False Dmitry!
But the son of the Sovereign Ivan IV, who had won his crown
From the vile Godunov hordes!
I could see myself in full royal attire, but...

A second later and everything changed; there was the maddened crowd
Around the royal chambers,
And I, Tsar Dmitry was in nothing but my underwear, a halberd in my hand,
Defending myself and crying out that I was the true tsar.
However, with cries of 'Smash the Polish whistler!' the crowd

Was killing me and tearing my body to pieces.
'What is that all about, messenger?
How did Dmitry, the restorer of justice, so displease the Russians?'
'That is *lust*, Bartholomew!' The angel replied.
'*Lust and oppression through passion!*

Which overshadow the king's mind, placing him at the mercy of women
And not only bringing traitors to the Homeland,
But handing it over for yesterday's and tomorrow's enemies to desecrate.
And, while the monarch is busy with his *passions*,
The noble gentry roam the Homeland, violating its self-respect.'

We flew further and I could see
Young soldiers, falling under volleys of buckshot,
Their eyes burning and their lips exclaiming,
'Long live the Revolution!'
I am Bonaparte at the Battle of Marengo,

Bringing the light of French Enlightenment to Europe
Along with the ideas of the French Revolution,
After which the people will forever cease to be slaves
And dumb puppets in political processes.
However, moments later,

I transformed into a Great Emperor,
Imprisoned in the shackles of an island prison
And living on memories of the Great Army
And its great victories.
'What is this story about, angel?!'

The Almighty's messenger grinned:
'This is a story of *the substitution of ideals*, my son!
When the idea of freedom, equality and brotherhood
Transforms into *large-scale military aggression*
And the restoration of the Empire.

Oh, and there will be many more examples like this,

Perhaps even ones that are more characteristic,
But, my young friend, there aren't enough
St Helenas in the ocean for everyone
To imprison all those who
Replace high ideals with the more base!'

We returned to the Pharaoh's tent in the morning.
The angel was in no hurry to leave, as if he wanted
To be there when I made my decision.
'Angel, it seems to me that you haven't shown me everything.
Don't the fates of kings decide

Such things as simple stupidity
Or a lack of luck?'
The angel nodded and replied,
'Yes, there is much that decides the crown's future.
It is personal qualities, combined with absolute power,

That give rise to the dependence of the fates of a family
On one person,
On how he sees his own fate
And how much he identifies it with the fate of his state
And his nation.

It is this that holds that part of the god-like nature
That is contained in such despicable creatures as people,
In that part of the people who are to become
The leaders of these creatures.
We angels, for example, don't have such qualities.

Therefore, we are but blind guides
Of Divine Will,
Although that requires considerable effort on our part,
To observe how you little people are still given this right
To decide fates and hold the degree of responsibility

That you deem royal.'
I asked the angel, 'But what about those
Who were *elected* leaders?
They say that some nations have such a practice;
The Hellenes and the nomadic barbarians, for example.'

'Oh, Pharaoh, stop playing so smart!'
The angel flew up to the top of the tent,
Flapping its wings.
'The process of election merely brings power down to earth,
Giving the electorate some illusory sense of just equality.

But who, say, elected you?
All right, let me clarify that. Why are you monarchs chosen by God,
Even though there are still little clashes over descent
And legacy in royal houses?'
'No one, it's God's Will,' I replied hesitantly.

'So, then, act in accordance with this will!'
The angel yawned and folded its wings.
'But how will I see this will and this future,
Which will follow any given deed of mine?'
I cried out in desperation.

'What if my step also leads
To a substitution of ideals, a triumph of greed or envy?'
'You don't know how or you don't want to decide,'
The angel answered calmly.
'Renounce responsibility and go spend what you've made.

You think the throne is the main human prize?
No, my dear young man, that is not the case.
How many have there been, are there and will be
Who have taken fright and fled from the weight of the crown?
How many have placed it on their heads

Only to weep from its weight?
I have given you examples, perhaps not all of them...
When people have erred but have still not shied
Away from now having to communicate
Not with the simple human categories of

Family, wife and home,
But carry their royal burden,
Keeping in mind only the notions of *God* and *People*.
And carry this burden, not weighted down by the feelings
I described to you, and which are key to their downfall.

Remember, young man, there is only one concept of *True King*.
It is hard to find, but easy at the same time;
It is what God gifts to the people,
But, at the same time, what the people gift to God.
And, by the way they talk with each other

You can understand w*hether this conversation is taking place or not.*
And, Pharaoh, it makes no difference if you've been elected or chosen by God.
The question is for whom will they die – the warrior, the commoner and the woman
Who brings her children to the sacrifice.
You! Can you take on responsibility for everything

When you're in the middle?!
Can you not fall into all those vices I have shown you
And make it so that God and the People
Arre not separated from one another?
Or perhaps you'll find a king who is not afraid

To stand between God and all people in general?!

Today it's your war, Pharaoh,

509

And no one cares how old you are.
This is your war, of *your* Egypt.
You see, before you gave the order to move towards India,
Egypt was still *yours*, right?'

'Egypt will always be mine!' I exclaimed passionately.
'Then that's agreed then,' the angel said with another yawn.
'And I have done what I came to do.
So, you now have something to compare with.
And how to imagine your deed.

Anyway, I'm out of here.
We will have our own war soon,
Up there. In Heaven.
And I don't care what you do.
Just remember, you cannot see into the future,

So, why the hell are you called a king?
Perhaps, they have now come to Egypt,
Those people who are certain of the future, eh?
And you just come to terms with it and emigrate yourself.
Raise children, explore a foreign land.

Farewell, Bartholomew. Perhaps we'll meet again.
Perhaps not.
What's the point in another meeting with the one
Who has a kingdom but doesn't know how to rule it?
So, go and rule! Even if you've been removed from power.

The elected leader is given to be humble,
But have you seen God's chosen one ever humble himself?
After all, it is around the thrones that your
Largest and most important war is raging.
What then, against this backdrop, has true meaning?

To what, then, shall we devote the rest of our life?
Recollections, regret and memoirs?
Gardening, raising grandchildren,
For whom anointment will remain a closed door?
Most important, what will you speak with God about and with one's abandoned people?!

Farewell!' The angel waved and was gone
Like a white cloud in the bright sky.
I gazed after him for a long time,
But my thoughts were already far from this island and my conversation with the angel.
I saw the shores of the Sacred Nile.

Oddly enough, when we were disembarking,
We did not encounter Octavian's patrols
And we calmly headed in a north-westerly direction
Towards the capital of Alexandria.
The frightened Roban explained the lack of Romans as follows:

'They say that Octavian is most likely convinced
There has long been no trace of us in Egypt.
Because he could not even imagine
Such an insane step as the one

I was taking, returning to the country.

I didn't listen to my kind old tutor.
He had already passed onto me all he knew about the world's values.
What the angel had told me
Would never descend to the mind of a priest,
And would remain simmering in the heart of the last Pharaoh alone.

The lack of Roman troops on our journey
Gave us the opportunity to equip our caravan in such a way,
As was customary for a monarch
On a campaign;
With all the attributes that befit a monarch.

We moved inland,
And the familiar landscape slowly
Pushed the anxious thoughts that had reigned in my cortege
Into the background.
Only a small detachment of guards was constantly on the alert.

Three days later we overtook a large Roman detachment,
Stationed in an immaculate encampment
Near an unknown source.
Our procession boldly approached the camp's temporary gates
And Aristarchus, head of the Macedonian Guard

Demanded that they be opened before the sovereign's palanquin.
The Romans obeyed but it was clear
That they were surprised and stunned by this.
I realised that this was the detachment, whose mission was
To accompany us to the ocean shores and then

Return to Alexandria to report that
The last Pharaoh of Egypt Ptolomy XV
Had left the country
And departed for distant lands,
Forever losing touch with his ancient Homeland.

We advanced through the rows of military tents
To the camp's central square.
I could already see a surprised centurion
Running out of the central tent
Donning his sword as he went.

I saw his adjutants hurrying to report to him,
Pointing fingers in our direction,
That they had sent messengers to Octavian too soon
With news that
The one and most important political problem in Egypt

Was no more, by the will of the gods and the cowardice of the runaway sovereign.
The centurion approached my travelling throne.
Roban, standing next to me, announced loudly,
'On your knees, soldier, when you face the Son of Ra...'
But I decisively stopped the priest short.

I knew that the centurion had a secret order,

Secret but already known to every subject in the country,
That if the Pharaoh failed to depart to distant lands,
He would be put to death as an enemy of Rome.
Why put a soldier in such a position

When, still respecting Egypt's legitimate authority, he
Nevertheless sees an enemy of Rome before him?
What choice would he have, when ordered to kneel
Before the one he was supposed to kill,
If his escape were not swift and nimble?

I knew that if I showed any fear to this angel of death,
Which everyone who knew of Rome's sentence
Must have... was obliged to experience,
Without a moment's doubt, he would give the order
To capture the caravan and kill me outright.

That meant that fear was the one thing
That this son of Mars would not see that day.
'What is your name, soldier?' I asked the centurion in a calm,
Even friendly tone.
The soldier hurriedly donned his *cassis* and,

Saluting as was required,
Barked loud and clear,
'Marcus Cassius Lentulus, Your... M-Majesty!
Centurion of the Third Legion of Cyrenaica,
On a special mission for the Senate and People of Rome!'

'Do you know who we are, Marcus Cassius?'
'Yes... Your Majesty! You...'
I saw a bead of sweat running down the military commander's cheek
And, with a wave of a hand, indicated that he could stand at ease.
'We have a request for you, centurion.

They say that these deserts
Are teeming with robbers and the enemies of both Egypt and Rome.
Escort our caravan to the capital,
If that does not conflict with your special mission!
We will leave at dawn and set up camp

Here, next to you, where the valour of the world's greatest army
Will make us feel both comfortable and secure!'
The centurion saluted sharply and replied,
'Your Majesty, you can count on my humble
Assistance all the way to Alexandria!'

Oh, Amun-Ra! How wonderful those Roman warriors are!
How eager they are to rush into battle
And how truly they hate it when the might of their legions
Is mixed with the filthy muck of politics!
And yet they are so disciplined when it comes to military regulations

And their meticulous fulfilment!
The centurion had no clear order on what to do
If the daft Pharaoh of Egypt
Would turn his ships back

512

And calmly and assuredly

Sail to meet his death.
That meant I still had time.
But for what? To delay the hour of my death?
No. Going deep into the expanses of my Homeland,
I breathed it, lived it and for the first time I felt

I was a true King, anointed by God.
And I acquired this right to feel
This way, only after dooming myself to death.
We moved through the immaculate ranks of the Roman camp
In total silence.

The soldiers and officers pointed at us carefully
And stealthily,
So as not to offend our royal splendour.
However, they knew all about
The special mission for the Senate and People of Rome.

The silence was so tense and dense as cotton wool
That when this sharp exclamation was emitted
By three dozen powerful male voices,
Roban, my entire cortege and I shuddered involuntarily,
While Aristarchus even reached for his sword.

After a second, however, the fear was replaced
With a triumphant realisation
That my return was not simple tomfoolery,
Dooming us to a pointless death.
Right then, we entered the territory occupied by

The Nubians, assigned to the detachment of Marcus Cassius.
They stood to attention and saluted us,
Shouting with every ounce of their military prowess into the silent sky,
'Glory to you, Great Home, Golden Mountain, Son of Ra,
King of Upper and Lower Egypt, Lord of the Reeds and the Bees!

We, your warriors of light, salute you!'

I saw tears glistening in the eyes of Priest Roban,
I saw tears that the head of the Macedonian Guard was trying to hide.
I saw tears, frozen on the lips of the Nubian soldiers.
I heard their farewell to the Homeland
Which for centuries had been the embodiment of the throne of the Pharaohs.

However, no one saw *my* tears.
They flowed down the folds in my banner.
They watered the hieroglyphs of the age-old history of my Home.
They washed the valleys and oases
And, flowing into the waves of the Eternal Nile, they disappeared forever...

When we settled down for the night
By the camp of Marcus Cassius,
Roban silently pointed to something in the sunset.
I caught sight of four riders on swift Arabian horses,
Racing into the distance to ask the mighty Octavian

What our further fate had in store for us.

Our caravan advanced slowly
Towards the capital.
It was becoming bigger and bigger as it went.
Many people greeted us with wreaths and palm branches,
Welcoming the Pharaoh upon his return to the Homeland.

Even the soldiers from the legion of Cyrenaica
Had a share of this joy and happiness,
When they were adorned with garlands and they were fed like sons.
They were embarrassed because they understood
The full ambiguity of their presence in my caravan.

We set up camp on the Sacred Nile Delta,
In an inconspicuous location,
Surrounded by scraggy-looking groves.
By this time, Marcus Cassius had become a regular guest in my tent,
And the young women in my cortege shot smiles at the bold Roman soldiers.

Roban fussed about as usual, ensuring the due hospitality
And the remnants of royal protocol.
Aristarchus argued laconically with the Romans
On why the Macedonian phalanx was better than the maniple.
However, I was plagued and tormented with doubt.

Why? Why was I doing all this?

To gratify my monarchical ego?
I spoke to Roban and Aristarchus:
'Ask all these people who have joined us on the way
To leave this instant.
What can I give these simple people as king?
Can I provide for them by reducing taxes and tribute?

Can I feed the poor and house the homeless?
Can I manage and rule to create all conditions
So that they would be able independently to achieve their dreams?
Is their freedom in my hands?
Is it in my power to pass fair judgment upon them?'

However, Roban and Aristarchus replied,
'Only a foolish and presumptuous tyrant thinks
That people are just a mob, thirsting for nothing but material gain,
Wishing only for prosperity and a predictable, comfortable life.
Only a worthless dictator believes

That only money, riches and benefits stand between him and his people,
That he rules and exists only thanks to a treaty
Stipulating that he can drown in luxury
In exchange for regular handouts to his populus,
Festive medals, performances and bread.

Don't deny them their dreams, sire!
You think they don't know you're doomed?
You think they don't know they too are doomed

By glorifying you and singing of your disappearing Home?
That's right, they won't be warriors capable of protecting you

And they'll scatter like lambs,
Frightened by the swords of foreigners,
When your destiny catches up with you.
But know this, sire, your death lies on the edge of Octavian's sword,
But your immortality lies in the hearts of these simple people.'

Finally, the expected day was upon us.
Messengers came riding from the Great Empire
Bringing with them the news of my fate.
My tent stood on a raised platform
From where it was clear to see

The goings-on in the Roman camp.
New divisions had appeared of another legion,
The Legio XXII Deiotariana,
And they had rapidly surrounded the detachment of Marcus Cassius and his Nubians.
There was the centurion, on foot and without his helmet,

Standing to one side and clearly protesting about what was happening,
Only no more than he could afford,
Being a well-disciplined Roman military leader.
I saw those divisions advancing rapidly towards our camp.
Roban understood everything and began fussing about,

Ordering all those who had no cause to die to flee.
Aristarchus gathered his Macedonians,
A few veterans who had stuck around
From the armies of Egypt and the Nubian tribes,
And busily gave out combat orders.

The time had come for me to prepare
For the key moment in my short life.
I donned the red and white Atef[220],
And Horus spread his wings above me.
My head was crowned with the silent cobra-uraeus,

Burning through Egypt's enemies with its eyes.
I took the golden crook in my spear hand,
And the gilded flail in the other[221].
At that moment I sensed
There was someone standing by my side.

I turned and was shocked to see
That angel-messenger had appeared, although I had not expected him.
I smiled to him and was amazed at how calm I was.
'Hello there, messenger of the heavens.
With what have you come at this odd hour?'

We stood there, quietly chatting,

---

[220] *Atef* – a double crown of Pharaohs, which had two colours. The skittle-shaped part (white) represented Upper Egypt, while the cylindrical part, decorated with a feather (red) represented Lower Egypt.
[221] The crook (*heka*) and the flail or flabellum (*nekhakha*), are two of the most prominent items in the royal regalia of ancient Egypt.

As if we hadn't noticed the noise of battle drawing nearer.
Roban, standing like a Theban column,
Was struck down by Roman swords.
The shining helmet was knocked from the head of Aristarchus,

And ten Syrian arrows struck the body of the leader of the guards.
The angel smiled and said,
'It turns out, you're an impudent and self-confident boy, eh?!
What you've done has given you the right to an answer
To two questions from Heaven.'

'What two questions?' I asked, brows raised.
'Surely, everything is now clear, on the verge of my death?'
'No, not everything,' the angel yawned and took his foot from the place
Where the mighty Nubian veteran had fallen,
Pierced by a legionnaire's spear.

'Look there,' the angel said, pointing to a small oasis,
Near which the last Pharaoh had set up camp.
Centuries from now, a city will stand here,
Whose name will be Al-Mansur, the *Conqueror.*
And near this city

Your descendants, the sons of free Egypt
From the House of the Mamluks,
Will trample the dreams of the Latins into the dust,
Just as the Latins are trampling yours today.'
'And what's the second question and its answer?'

I enquired, tilting my head a little,
To dodge a Roman dart.
The angel smiled wolfishly again and soared into the sky:
'You'll only hear it after
You stop being a Pharaoh.'

'Then we'll meet again after my death, angel!'
I cried out after him and looked around.
My Macedonian Guard and the veteran defenders
Had been killed for the most part,
While the survivors stood, breathing heavily,

Facing the closed ranks of Roman soldiers,
Prepared for an imminent death
And praying to Heaven about one thing only:
For that death to be worthy of true warriors,
Protecting their young sovereign.

With a slow, regal gesture, I
Placed the staff and whip onto the throne behind me,
To stop these symbols of authority from being soiled by the dust,
And I took out the final symbol,
The sword of the Lords of the Nile.

Shouting, 'Be eternal, noble Egypt! Farewell!'
I rushed to meet the stunned enemy.
The veterans howled like hounds of the desert
And rushed forward onto the Latins' swords and spears.

Receiving a terrible spear wound in my side,

I fell to one knee, but still I tried
To strike the nearest Triarii[222] soldier with my sword.
However, a dull blow to the head
Threw me backwards, to the base of the throne
And I lost consciousness where I collapsed.

****

I saw a deserted temple,
With an enormous hole in the floor, leading underground.
I saw that it would be easy to get down there
Along the edge of the pit, now collapsed due to its age.
Going down was frightening,

Because scared and unfamiliar shadows were rushing about there.
For some reason, however, I *had* to go down there,
And so, down I went.
A moment later, I found myself facing a giant corridor,
Gaping in a cyclopean void.

The corridor was huge, the third of a stadium[223] wide
And a third high.
The void, stretching into the distance, was so majestic and endless
That the squally wind that roamed there
Seemed both insignificant and shy.

The corridor was dark, but rays of light made it
Through every other stadium distance.
I needed them to see the four giant hounds,
The guardians of the underworld, approaching
In silence from the gloom towards me.

The hounds drew closer and, for a time,
They played, making no sound, as if they were wolves.
Then, they sat around me,
Fixing me with their terrible eyes.
I could clearly see that they had human eyes.

They were as black as the black
In which, in this world, you can never see a thing.
'Give your name,' one of the hounds said.
'I am Ptolomy, son of Ptolomy,
The Last Lord of the Eternal House.'

The hounds fell silent for a while and then the second of them said,
'Name the place and the hour of your death.'
I replied, 'It was noon on the fifth day of the fourth lunar month,
At the Al-Mansur oasis,
In the Sacred Nile Delta.'

There was silence again, just the howl of the wind.
The third hound then spoke: 'You have given the incorrect name.

---

[222] *Trarii* – heavy ancient Roman infantry.
[223] An ancient unit of measure.

You won't come here with this name.'
A terrible howl burst out from the tunnel depths;
Only eternal pain can make a creature howl like that.

But the hounds paid it no heed.
The fourth then said, 'You name the place and time of your
Death wrongly.
Before coming here,
You have to see several earthly kingdoms

And two heavenly kingdoms.
You will see the Armenian and Georgian kings,
Then you will arrive at the borders of the Persian lands
Where, in the city of Albany, near the tower,
You will create your real Eternal Home[224].

And now away with you.'
The hounds got up and only then did I realise
That they were the size of Bactrian camels.
Quietly and without a word, they walked away, deep into the endless tunnel,
Leaving me alone to puzzle over what my future life would be like.

****

Brother's I'll spare you the details of
How the simpler of my people
Brought me back to my feet and concealed me from persecution
From the predatory and domineering Octavian.
All I'll say, however, is that thirty years had gone by!

For thirty years, I wandered the lands of different peoples.
Until the coming of the new era.
Which era? Don't you know?
Well, any Egyptian astrologer or Persian magus
Will tell you when the era of the past ends

And a new era begins.

That's right, it was in that year
When the sky is torn asunder by the unearthly beauty of the light
That you call the Star of Bethlehem.
In fact it is a planet
That is called the *Meeting Place*.

You have heard about it from those madcap gossips,
Brilliant scientists and exalted Bohemian ladies.
It is Nibiru, the devil's planet,
Which appears quietly, mysteriously and unavoidably
In our sky, and which we think we know all about.

Those of the brothers who are older

---

[224] According to legend, the Holy Apostle Bartholomew (Nathanael) was put to death in a city called Al'ban, Alban or Albanopol, by the Persian King Astyages. Orthodox tradition believes that this is the city of Baku, where an ancient basilica was found near the Maiden Tower and until 1937, there was a chapel of St Bartholomew there. The *Eternal Home* is a direct translation from the ancient Egyptian word *per-o*, which actually means *pharaoh* in Greek transcription.

518

Will remember its appearance thirty years ago,
When it appeared in all its glory
And altered our sky's customary landscape.
True, most of you hadn't actually been born at that time.

I, however, had already reached the age of forty-four –
Either the age of maturity or the age of
Fatigue, I'm not sure.
At that time, thousands of astrologers, prophets and soothsayers
All screamed simultaneously,

Shouting about the advent of the incarnate will of the Lord,
About our death and the beginning of the Last Judgment.
You know, there is some truth in there somewhere,
Because its advent was to be followed
By new trials for humans.

This expectation of new trials
Is already an excellent opportunity
To revisit the state of your being
Before God and before yourself.
I then found myself in the environs of Jerusalem,

Dressed according to the vows of the ancient order of Sufis
In pieces of fabric, reflecting all the countries that I had visited
And also the diverse ways in which
These countries communicate with God.
You can see from my story that the content of this communication

Quite often doesn't depend at all
On the faiths to which these countries adhere.
Then there was a great panic.
Scholars stated that the star would fall on us
And destroy every living thing.

Others would say that Nibiru would pass us by,
That the Almighty as it was had plenty of ways
To return his children to the original path.
Others still said that it was only an omen
For the advent of a true and universal King.

Foolish Herod reduced everything to a vulgar *war for the throne*.
According to his understanding of the question,
It was simply that a Hasmonean son would be born,
Who was destined to drive the Edomites from the throne of Israel.
He gave no thought to God and his conversation with the people.

No one's fears were confirmed.
The planet never went on to kill anybody.
It broke into the Solar System,
Rushed past the great planets,
Named in honour of the idols of the Latin usurpers

And quietly and sedately drew nearer to Earth.

It came so close
That we could see its reliefs and the pure blueness of its atmosphere.

Yes, Thomas, you might laugh and say
That the surface of any body that breaks into the Earth's atmosphere
Will burn with a thousand degrees of heat.

But, you know, brother, if the Almighty so desires,
He will take into account all the conventions of
What is happening, at least to ensure this planet
Approaches the Earth untouched and alive.
It was an amazing sight to behold!

Not only did Nibiru not destroy anything on Earth,
Like even simply the Moon could.
It approached us so smoothly and *tenderly*
(You know, brothers, I cannot find another word
That so accurately illustrates its appearance in the sky),

That it caused no catastrophe or tsunamis on Earth,
No displacement of the Earth's axis,
And no other apocalyptic nightmares
That a person who classes themselves
Among the implacable enemies of nature likes to imagine,

And therefore, who invariably awaits a holy war to come of it.
A huge body appeared in the sky,
Overshadowing the Moon and the Sun with its beauty.
Persian and Babylonian astrologers
Gave the people the following explanations:

Nibiru had lost speed as it drew nearer to Earth.
It had gently entered our atmosphere
And acquired its own rhythm of rotation,
Positioned in such a way as not to obscure the Sun from us,
Just slowly moving along with the Earth.

It will rotate in a way that shares sunrises and sunsets across the Earth,
Only in the opposite direction.
Therefore, it will slowly pass alongside our planet,
From East to West,
And then begin to lose its gravitation pull.

And in about thirty years, it will gradually start to drift,
Until it breaks away again and is carried off into an unknown space.
However, astrologers have named two of the most interesting things.
The first is that our eyes don't deceive us;
We really do see on Nibiru

A blessed climate, much like on Earth,
Not only that, it is visible to the naked eye.
The second is that Nibiru is so close to us,
That its gravitational pull begins to act somewhere really close,
Near the peaks of Earth's great mountains.

In theory, this creates an incredible phenomenon,
Whereby, if one were to jump from a mountain top
When Nibiru is in its immediate proximity,
One wouldn't fall, but come under the influence of its gravitation.
Therefore, one is carried upwards when you start

Falling onto this planet!
If one can devise a way to slow this falling,
Resettlement on Nibiru
Would become a genuine reality!
As always, the dynamic Hellenes

Came up with a theoretical device
That consisted of an enormous piece of fabric,
Which was capable of slowing the fall.
If you believe the Babylonian astrologers,
The lion's share of the land on Nibiru

Is all seas and lakes,
Landing or, more accurately, splashing down onto which,
Increases the survival rate many times over
When embarking on such a risky move.
Of course, the Hellenes, who value the life of the individual

More than anything (they call it democracy),
Simultaneously devised a host of legislative restrictions
For its citizens to risk their lives
With no legal protection.
Put simply, they made a move to Nibiru

Legally possible only for the wealthy,
Who would be able to afford the risk.
As for those countries that are not that bothered
By the financial or legal side of things,
Or to put it simply as the Asiatics do,

'If you want to die, then knock yourselves out',
Then it turned out that it was the poor, the losers
And adventure-lovers that strove to the new planet from these countries,
As they were able simply to buy or steal
The large piece of fabric that they would have use for only the once.

Given that Nibiru was moving alongside the Earth,
From East to West,
The people of the Far East were the first to reach the mountains.
Names for them appeared immediately –
The first settlers were called *People of Fuji*

For the simple reason that they jumped
From the top of this great mountain on the Japanese islands.
Of the *flyers-over*, as the new colonists were called,
No more than thirty per cent survived,
But even this was enough for the people to continue *flying*.

Then came the time of the second wave –
The *People of Tibet and the Himalayas.*
The majority of these perished, judging by the fact
That they were actually counted only occasionally
And then, for propaganda purposes, hushing up the true losses.

Of course, the Phoenicians and Hellenes
Quickly set up *take-off stations*,

Making big money on it
And forcing the new colonists to sign a total waiver
Of responsibility for their survival during landing.

Then came the turn of the *People from the Pamir Mountains and the Hindu Kush.*
Why were the colonists divided by *take-off point*?
Because they claim that once on Nibiru,
They would immediately begin forming colonies based on common origins.
However, this is so typical for the children of Earth, so why the surprise?

The appearance of a new planet per se
Led not only to a wave of *flights*,
But a global shift of consciousness as well.
It was impossible to recall a newspaper, TV channel or forum
Where the question of Nibiru wasn't discussed.

As always, the kingdom of Israel came alive
With the advent of dozens of new prophets and messiahs,
Shouting at all quarters that
Adonai had sent the Kingdom of Heaven incarnate,
Where only people, cleansed of their former earthly sins, might enter.

Actually, a whole mass of new religious doctrines came about,
For which the common notion was
This very Kingdom of Heaven incarnate
And, accordingly, the absolution of sins for those
Who enter there.

Indeed, what else was there to devise,
When every evening, slowly
And with dignity, an enormous
Alternative Earth appeared up in the sky,
Frightening and enticing with its beauty.

By virtue of the fact that few returned
From Nibiru,
Legends and myths continued
To flourish in vivid colours about it.
Of course, the authorities tried to control

Over the peaks, at the very least to have some regulation of emigration.
But it was useless.
Why? Have you ever seen the Pamir Mountains or Tibet?
Or their submission to the human mind and its organisation?
Probably never.

Time passed and the new wave came to be known as
The *People of Altai, Tarbagatai and Khan-Tengri.*
Nibiru came close to the Caucasus,
And four small waves appeared, united into one –
The *People of Ararat, Elbrus, Kazbek and Demavend.*

Time passed some more and striving upwards
Came the *People of Sinai*, inspired by ancient legends
And new hopes.
Amicably and in business-like fashion, forgetting old feuds,
The children of the deserts, ancient kingdoms and the Great River *flew* to Nibiru.

Then came the *People of Olympus, Vesuvius and Mont Blanc*,
Who had carefully prepared for their flight,
And the last thing it now resembled was the search for a new life,
Rather, the search for new opportunities,
Which is why they *flew over* in an organised and well-planned manner.

The last to rush to the *Meeting Place*
Were the *People of the Andes and Cordillera,*
Known for their pure spirituality
And love for nature,
Of which they saw themselves as a part.

It was right at this time that I found myself
On an open square before a small tavern in Jerusalem,
Where I was sitting and admiring the majestic coming of Nibiru
In the yellow Palestinian sky,
Sipping coffee and mulling the fates of kingdoms.

Hearing a slight movement by my side,
I raised my eyes from the ancient book I was reading.
I recognised my guest, smiling at me
As if the thirty years of my wanderings and search for meaning
Since our last meeting had never been.

'Hello, Bartholomew!
I won't call you Pharaoh for now,
Although this title is for life.'
'Hello, messenger from Heaven,
And what do you have in store for me this time?

Can it really be, that in his colourful dervish's robe,
The King, devoid of power, Home and subjects,
Is still of interest to the Almighty?'
'Specifically looking like that and specifically now... Pharaoh!'
The winged messenger grinned.

He fell silent, threw his hands behind his head,
Spread his wings, to warm them in the heat of the setting sun,
And his gaze fell on the mighty beauty of Tayanar.[225]
We said nothing, having no particular desire
To break the peace and quiet of the Jerusalem evening with words.

Finally, the angel broke the silence and said,
'That's enough. All anyone ever talks about is this planet.
It even hurts to think that our Earth has been shunted into the background.'
'This is *our* Earth, angel!' I smiled.
'Of humans and djinns, but not you angels who reside up there in Heaven.'

That's true,' the heavenly messenger said, seeming sad.
'However, for us heavenly creatures, the Earth doesn't cease to be
A source of worry and anxiety.'
'Go on, say it,' I said, slamming shut my book
And demonstrating my determination to listen to him attentively.

---

[225] *Tayanar* (Nibiru) – the Sumerian and Babylonian name of the 12th planet. In Altai mythology, the planet is named Tayanar.

'After all, I am in your debt!'
The messenger looked at me in amazement:
'You? In my debt? What gives you that idea?'
I laughed: 'Oh yes, angel, I forgot
That human worry and emotions mean nothing to you!

That said, I am all ears!'
The winged messenger shrugged and chuckled,
As if to say, *so how can we understand you sometimes?*
But a moment later he went on, as if nothing had happened:
'The entire problem is up there,'

He said, pointing up into the sky,
'Only not exactly up there, rather in those who... have *flown* there,
As you so vulgarly and foolishly put it.'
'What's so bad about those *flights*?'
I asked.

'Don't people receive the Kingdom of Heaven right now,
Genuinely, without any mysticism or esotericism?
Is this not a chance to begin a new life,
Giving up everything
That soiled our spirit here, on this long-suffering Earth?

I have seen many *flyers*.
They believed sincerely that there, on Tayanar,
They would have an opportunity to start afresh,
Based on that natural purity
That is inherent in man.

And everyone believed it was possible because
Over at the Meeting Place, there was no need to store
All the old baggage of one's conventions,
Which serves down on Earth as a preserving environment
For vices, sins and their repeated reproduction.'

'Yes,' the angel said wearily, as if he had heard it all before.
'Yes, you're right, that is how it was and continues to be.
However!' The messenger turned towards me so sharply,
That he knocked over my coffee with a wing.
'But then something started to happen,

That the Master of Worlds could neither understand nor explain.
And when He cannot explain something,
It would be best not to appear in Heaven, believe me;
You could seriously find yourself in a little Armageddon!'
The angel's eyes seemed to penetrate right through me,

And I believed him; more, I sensed his fear.
'And... so what is going on there?' I asked somewhat sheepishly.
'Well, that is what you have to ascertain, Bartholomeo!'
'Hm...' I grinned mischievously,
'The heavens need a spy, is that it?'

'No, Pharaoh! You won't be going there on reconnaissance;
That can easily be done by others...

524

By flying creatures!'
The angel waved his arms about like wings and his eyes bulged
Humorously.

'You'll go there...' He stretched his arms to the side theatrically
And made a funny bowing motion, 'As a king!'
Only my long self-restraint of a dervish
Helped me from losing my temper.
I clenched my fists and narrowed my eyes.

'What is this...' I said, my voice becoming unexpectedly hoarse,
'Some new kind of mockery of a former Pharaoh?
Have I somehow angered the Master of Worlds?'
'No, of course not,' the angel fussed. 'Come on. Of course not!
This really is very important.

Judge for yourself. There are interesting things afoot.
You know that all the... erm... *flyers-away*,
Who depart for Nibiru, took the texts of divine commandments with them.
And they took them all, regardless of
What their confession was on Earth.

So, the Chinese methodically gathered together all the Holy Books,
The ubiquitous Turks, for some reason, studied the Oral Torah,
In their turn, the Jews got in a twist,
In their attempt to pronounce the ten disciplines of the Hindus,
While the Russians, in addition to the Testaments,

Squeezed in the teachings of Confucius and the Great Yasa.'
'But these are earthly laws, right?' I objected meekly.
'Yes, quite,' the angel nodded, 'earthly and human,
But, you must agree, they're the same as Hadith and Halakhah.
All this, my friend, is a kind of corpus of case law.

However, this law always originates
From the Divine understanding of the organisation of society
And it comes from the Divine Books or views of the Lord of Worlds.
No one, Pharaoh, no one took
A single constitution or charter with them!

Not one body of laws, created by secular states!
Not one book, created by way of civil compromise!
Not a single work of Aristotle, Hegel or Feuerbach!'
'So, what so surprises you, angel?
Don't they go... sorry, *fly*,

In an attempt to build the Kingdom of Heaven
According to those same heavenly laws?
What is so surprising and alarming
That so worries the Ruler of Worlds?'
The angel looked at me like a student looks at a stupid schoolboy.

'A-ah, I think I'm beginning to understand you!'
I suddenly saw the light.
The Lord was faced with a need for revisionism
As regards all that
He Himself had sent out in different languages and at different times!'

I laughed, but the angel's eyes flared in anger:
'What are you laughing at, Pharaoh? What's so funny? I don't understand.'
'I am laughing because there is basically nothing new in what I hear.
Are you saying there wasn't a period in the history of Earth,
When no secular law existed,

But the people happily went around smashing each other's faces in
And destroyed people in their thousands *on behalf of*
Different *names* of the One and Only?
Perhaps a new planet will give meaning to the Organiser of the Creation,
So that He now might unite all doctrines into one?

But not like He did with the Muslims,
When he told them that their teachings were final and generalised,
While He forgot to inform everyone else.
As a result, what we got
Was everyone continuing to fight one another as equals,

Believing that something was more valuable, the older it was,
Not acknowledging that the newer
Might actually be truer.
At the same time experiencing
Wholly justified indignation –

How can that be? For thousands of years there was one Word of God,
And then it was suddenly different,
But we were never notified of the fact?
But the Arabs did for some reason?'
'You blaspheme, Pharaoh!' the angel screamed.

'No, not I!' I had also lost patience and started shouting.
'No, angel, I am not blaspheming!
Kings, tyrants and metropolises expend incredible effort
To rule over the vanquished,
Separating them and thereby weakening them.

They do this so that hatred toward them is not focused in one place.
However, we, angel, we people don't hate Our Father!
So why separate us?!
Why bring our heads, our tongues and Books into conflict?
We love Him, we want to love and that's what we'll do,

Come what may!
Even though, between us and Heaven's Eternal Home
Tyrants, dictators, fat merchants and money changers have long been idling!
Tramping over the spiritually poor and transforming them
Into common-or-garden rabble!

Now, when there on Nibiru
The people are trying to build something different and new,
You are sending me to become a tyrant there?!
Among people who took with them the only thing
They consider to be the Word of Truth – books and commandments?!'

The angel was silent and leaned back in his chair,
As if to let me know than we both needed to calm down.

Past the tavern, jostling excitedly and noisily,
A group of people walked past,
Pulling huge pieces of fabric to ensure a soft landing.

I noticed that they had next to no belongings with them,
But I did see an old Jew in a hat and side-locks,
Clutching the Qur'an and the Mahabharata
As if he were afraid of losing them.
Oh Lord, where did he get his hands on the Mahabharata here?!

'All right,' I said in a conciliatory tone,
'What does the Heavenly Secretariat
Expect of me on Nibiru?'
'You don't have to travel there as a king; that's not the most important thing.'
The angel's voice contained a hint of affront,

But he was calm now.
'You can go there as a wanderer.
Most important, we got wind of a new trend on Nibiru,
The origin or the essence of which are something
We simply cannot understand.

However, it causes us no little concern.
What you have to do is grasp this trend, and get a feel for this new mood.
And there we'll be able to see for ourselves
All that will become the future for the
New colonists, their Inevitable Future.'

Suddenly the angel sharply bent over the table
And fixed his piercing gaze on me:
'Bartholomeo, are you really not interested
In what is happening there and how, eh?
You see, there's a *genuine* Kingdom of Heaven there!

Perhaps that new society is being created there
Which will become a prototype for people on Earth.
Don't you want to see the Golden Age with your own eyes?'
I also leaned forward and brought my face closer,
Really close to that of the winged one:

'I want to,' I said. 'I really do!
When do I leave and how?
Via Sinai or Fuji?'
The angel gave his now customary grin and jolted me in the shoulder:
'You really are fools, you humans!'

He spread his mighty wings.
'Pharaoh, you don't need a parachute!'
'A parachute? What's that?' I asked, confused.
'Ah,' the angel replied with a wave, 'then ask Thomas –
He was friends with Leonardo and he'll tell you what it is.'

'Thomas? Leonardo? Who are they?'
But the angel was no longer listening.
He wrapped me in a steel embrace
And then soared up into the cool of the evening over Jerusalem,
His wings slicing through the air over the Holy City.

In less than an hour, I was already standing on the green grass
Of the Great Gondwana of Tayanar,
Stretching from the Eastern Ocean to the Western.
The angel circled over me, crying out,
'All the best to you, Pharaoh!

You only need to think of me
And I'll appear!
For now, though, farewell, you pilgrim of the Kingdom of Heaven!'
And, as always, lile a weightless cloud,
He disappeared into the unfamiliar sky.

****

I am used to wandering,
But the roads on Nibiru were both easy-going and safe.
I landed near the lands of the *People of Tibet and the Himalayas*.
I instantly fell into the joyous embraces of their hospitality.
I realised that it was impossible to be a spy in these lands.

Why ferret and nose about?
The people were open, welcoming and polite,
And they were happy to tell me anything I asked,
And not without a sense of pride, either.
The residents of Tayanar had plenty of reason

To feel pride and joy, too.
First, they were all industrious, but work for them was no torment.
This was primarily because Gondwana
Spared them with its nature from what
Had so complicated life for the Earth dwellers back in their Homeland.

In the lands of the Chinese, no monstrous rivers burst their banks,
There was no flooding, locust swarms or hurricanes.
The Indians were not met with clouds of midges, heat
Or exhausting, incessant rains.
The Turks forgot their *dzhut* famine, drought and snowstorms.

The Russians even missed their severe frosts,
Not that they really hungered for them to appear.
The Armenians found fertile soil,
The Jews – green valleys and mountain lakes.
The English forgot the smell of the fog and smog.

The children of deserts, Tuaregs and Arabs,
Grew accustomed to abundant bodies of water and forests.
'What about states and governments?' I asked the people of Tayanar.
'What do we need them for?' They replied in surprise.
'A government keeps track of people,

To punish those who break the law,
But we don't have people like that.'
'Why?'
'Every inhabitant of Nibiru knows by heart
The commandments of their historical faith

And everyone else's too,
And, let's say, they barely differ from one another as it is.
Therefore, everyone simply adheres to them.
We have no theft, so what use do we have of one?
Just ask, and you'll be given,

Especially on the first days after arrival.
Everyone understands, there's no gain in having poor people nearby.'
'Sorry,' I persisted, 'I get what you say about theft,
But people are different;
Some are more industrious, some, lazier.

Do they really live the same?'
'That's a good question,' came the reply,
'And, let's be honest here, this was not easy to resolve.
However, it was resolved, and for one simple reason:
We simply wanted to find a solution that was Good and Kind.

You see, Bartholomew, there's no such thing as lazy people.
There are those who are forced to do things
They don't want to or don't know how to do.
Take, for instance, the story of Zhang Bao.
He *flew* into a farming community

And for a long time he couldn't start work and grow rice.
He couldn't grind it, wash it, or fry it.
He simply didn't want to!
To be honest, seeing the way he approached the task, we really
Didn't want him anywhere near the harvest as it was.

But we fed and watered him,
We came together and helped him build his house, because we knew
That, sooner or later, he would find his feet.
At first, Zhang Bao took it all for granted,
But then he came over all shy and developed hang-ups.

And when he couldn't find himself a bride, well, who needs an idler?
He became despondent and went out into the field.
There he remained for some time, crying and complaining about his lot.
He even became angry and envious of us.
Then, one day, all his envy, bitterness and dissatisfaction

Spilled out into a powerful and beautiful song!
It turns out that Zhang Bao had a divine voice!
It was such a joy and so easy to work to his singing
That we went to him in the field and said,
"Zhang Bao, you don't need to plough or sow,

But just sing to us while we gather the harvest
Or plant the rice.
Your singing is of far greater value than any other work,
For you alone can help everyone in one go!
And we will share with you what we have!"

That attractive house on the outskirts,
Where all those children run about,
Is the house of Zhang Bao and his lovely wife.

So, Bartholomew, what is most important is
To prevent even the smallest sprouts of evil feelings

From taking root in people's hearts.
The idlers, tricksters and loafers
Will soon grow tired of their boredom
And will find themselves a place in the community.
All you need to do is ensure that the sense of love for others never dies in him.'

I was surprised but still I took this story to be a special case.
When I came to the *People of the Pamirs*, I asked them,
How it was they could live without authorities,
After all, it wasn't just seekers of the Kingdom of Justice that *fly* here.
There were those who'd heard that

Naïve and foolish people lived on Nibiru,
That there was no government or police.
That meant they could easily be deceived and robbed with impunity!
'Right, Bartholomew,' the *People of the Pamirs* replied,
'Moscow wasn't built in a day.

Take the story of that thief and trickster Bobojon.
He had come to our town with precisely this objective
That you're talking about.
Using deceit he stole food, belongings and clothing,
Showing no mercy on women, widows or families with many children.

Having deceived many folk in our town,
He moved on to the next
And there he caused many kind people to suffer.
To be honest, we itched to teach him a lesson,
Even give him a good beating, and make an example of him.

But you know, Bartholomew, we know the commandments of all nations by heart,
And nowhere have we found the word *force*.
Even if it were written that someone had committed an evil deed,
It was simply said that he *must* do something, pay, compensate.
But who is in charge of this *must*?

Of course, back on Earth, it is the police or the authorities,
But we don't have any of that.
However, we decided that still we would not deviate from our principles.
At first, we just bided our time
And kept an eye on Bobojon.

Okay, so he would steal something or obtain something by deceit.
What next?
We don't really have any money.
It's money that depersonalises crime,
Because when you spend a depersonalised equivalent in coins,

You never think about where they came from.
No one ever keeps two piles of money separately,
Saying this pile is honestly earned and this one, from the sale of stolen goods.
With things, however, it's different.
They need to be carried and used for all to see

530

And every time you recognise that you came to have it by means of deceit.
Humans are burdened by this knowledge
And they start to hide and conceal things.
But what happens with the stuff they've hidden?
That's right, it simply stops being something you need.

What's the point of it sitting in a cupboard?
That means the thing loses its original value
That it had when you stole it.
Bobojon was tormented over this for a long time.
Then, one fine day, we had a feast;

We invited the thief and swindler and we said to him,
Bobojon, there are different kinds of people.
There are those who don't need much and those who need a lot,
But they can't always afford that.
Clearly you are someone who needs a lot.

You only had to tell us that!
So, we've brought you lots of gifts, so help yourself!
Take these furs, these coats and carpets,
Don't be shy; all of this now yours.
If you need more, just let us know.

Hmm... Bobojon paced about for a good while
Before he gave it all back.
He was proud and didn't want to admit openly
That we had made him feel terribly ashamed.
That was why he returned all the gifts and the stolen goods

As if they were gifts from him.
However, no one condemned, castigated or gloated.
One day, Bobojon gave everything away.
He sat in front of his empty hut
And sang a sad song.

Then we went to see him and said,
"Don't be sad, Bobojon.
You're so good at telling false tales
And without the slightest embarrassment,
So, we'd like you to come and entertain us at our feasts.

You'll be our entertainment
And we'll give you presents in return,
But this is not all.
A swindler has *flown* into the next town
And he thinks he's the first of his kind here.

So off you go, be a good man, and put him onto the right path,
But, in so doing, you teach him, not in a way that riles him,
But so that he understands the foolishness of his ways."
Bobojon took heart at this,
For we were able to see in his wickedness an ability

To prevent such wickedness taking place.
He didn't even have to change,
Just redirect his skills and abilities

For the good of the people.
From that day on, there have been no swindlers or thieves in our towns.

Most important, however, there is no police
With the powers to mete out punishment.
But there is Bobojon, who so diligently protects all the good people,
That he already has organised a club
For reformed swindlers and tricksters.'

I was amazed by these stories.
So, what stopped us from doing the same on Earth?!
Are these people really so different?
Now, the generations of those born directly
On Nibiru had not yet grow up.

When I arrived in the lands of the *People of Altai*,
I heard another story, one that was quite different.
I asked the Altai people, 'You know, it does happen
That idlers and fiends
Tend to find one another and unite in gangs.

How do you deal with them?
Surely, over all that time, someone has killed someone else, right?'
'Yes, Bartholomew, we have sad tales too,'
The Altaians and the children of Khan-Tengri replied.
'Take the story of the *Bandi*[226] Nasharvan.

One day an entire group of young *dzhigits*
Flew into our steppes in one go.
At first, they diligently studied the commandments of all nations
And they helped the villagers to graze and raise cattle.
However, one day, laziness and an unwillingness to learn got the upper hand

And their leader, Nasharvan, said,
"Why have we been given youth and strength,
Masculinity, dexterity and intelligence?
To become *malshy*[227], like these new fellow clansmen?
Let them break their backs, but we will take from them

What we deem necessary.
Who can stop us here on Tayanar?
We want to be free, wealthy and without a care.
Otherwise, what do we need this Heavenly Paradise for,
If we have to go back to work there?

They then gathered together a desperate gang
And began terrorising all around,
Even wandering at times onto the land of the *People of the Pamirs*,
Defenceless against their powerful warhorses and clubs.
They also knocked about the lands of the *People of Kazbek*

---

[226] *Bandi* (Kazakh) – misspelled from *bandit*, a thug, robber. In the 1920s and 1930s, this word did not have an unequivocally negative connotation for the Kazakhs, during the uprisings against Stalin's regime. Often it meant something along the lines of the *Maquisards* on Corsica, guerrilla resistance fighters against the government.
[227] *Malshy* (Kazakh) – farmhands, meant here in a disdainful, hierarchical sense.

Among whom they found *abreks*[228]
The *aqsaqal* elders tried to do everything they could to stop them,
Shaming them, exhorting, even bestowing gifts,
To ensure they were well fed,
But it was all in vain.

Not one of the Good, Kind means of persuasion
Had any effect on the thugs.
Someone even talked of a people's militia,
To use decisive force against these robbers.
"Kindness must come with fists," they would say.

The *aqsaqals*, however, refused, saying
"We might disperse this gang today,
But another will come tomorrow, perhaps not to us, but to our neighbours.
They will seek help from our militia
And then it will be impossible to stop.

Then we will need a punitive, not an advisory court,
Police, guards and then a khan.
Would it not be simpler to return to the earthly steppes
And continue living there, like we lived for centuries in our Homeland?
What, then, will become of our dream of the promised land of *Zher Uiyk*?[229]

We need to find a solution."
And so they sat down to think.
Three days and three nights they sat thinking.
But other than the use of force,
They could think of no solution.

Then, Umai-apa, the wisest of women, entered the meeting yurt.
She said something to the *aqsaqals* and the men there.
At first, cries of indignation and protest were heard
But, then, in silence, all the men gathered at the edge of the village,
Gathered together their bows, arrows and lances

And left somewhere to the North.
The following morning, Nasharvan's gang, at a fair trot,
Rode up to the fat herds of the Altai people,
Rubbing their hands in anticipation of an ill-gotten gain.
They emerged onto the hill and froze in bewilderment.

Before them, prancing on lively horses,
Were the beautiful daughters of Khan-Tengri,
Dressed in bright outfits, decorated with silver and owl feathers.
Seeing the gang of thugs, the girls rapidly gathered in a huddle
And began teasing and laughing at them.

"Hey there, Bogatyr Nasharvan!
Why have you frozen still, like a steppe idol?
Come on, let's fight.

---

[228] The word *abrek* is a North Caucasian term used for a lonely warrior fighting for a just cause. much like themselves.
[229] *Zher Uiyk* – a mythical Promised Land, a land of eternal bliss and justice, sought by the Kazakh sage Asan Kaigy (Asan Sad) throughout his life. The archetypal Golden Age in the Great Steppe. Often used in the same way as *utopia*, an unattainable, naïve dream.

Take our livestock, why don't you?
Or perhaps you'll find something more of interest?"

The girls jumped but Nasharvan gnashed his teeth:
"Hey, you stupid women, where are your men?
Are they hiding behind their women, like cowards?"
"Why cowards," the girls replied brazenly,
"They're off hunting for wolves and tigers

And to fight with real men,
Protecting their lairs and their children!
Tigers are no slackers like you lot;
No, it is worthy battles that await our men.
Why would they waste their fighting fervour on nonentities like you?"

And again the girls laughed boldly.
Nasharvan grimaced in annoyance, looked around at his men
And he was stunned to see their eyes had not a trace of fighting prowess left.
The lads' eyes shone from excitement of another kind.
The *bandi* grew angry and screamed at his men,

"Why are you standing and staring at these women?
Drive the cattle out and pay them no heed!"
But that is not what happened, oh no!
The girls gave a whoop, grabbed their bows
And showered the *batyr* "heroes" with blunt arrows coated in dung.

"I'll show you!" Screamed one of the thugs
And he rushed after the girls.
The daughters of Khan-Tengri scattered easily across the steppe.
Hard as the thugs tried to catch them,
They escaped their would-be captors with featherlight ease.

The moment the gang approached the cattle,
Those Amazons would reappear
And shower the lads once again with their dung-coated arrows.
The gang would race after them again.
Instead of ferocious cries, nervous laughter would now be heard.

"I'll catch you! I'll get you, you'll see!"
"Come on then, *dzhigit*. You riding a cow
Or a fine horse?"
But however hard the gang tried, they couldn't catch a single girl.
Nasharvan spat angrily, somehow gathered his young men together

And began driving away the herd.
Only this driving rapidly became a real nightmare for them,
With that combination of female derision
And the stench of dung arrows.
Rumour soon spread across the steppe

That Nasharvan's "fine *batyrs*" were fighting girls.
The *bandi* decided from then on that he would send scouts,
So as not to come up against those gutsy gals.
The daughters of Tengri soon received from all over the steppe
Light, swift horses that were impossible to catch.

Every time the gang approached the herds
They would be met with audacious tongues and arrows of dung
From the daughters of Altai and Tarbagatai.
Nasharvan became more and more furious,
But there was nothing he could do.

The thug realised that he had lost his key advantage –
The fear and confusion among the steppe dwellers.
On the contrary, he had begun to sense acutely
The laughter and mockery at the markets and squares.
This awful story even reached the *abreks* of Elbrus.

One insolent fool was even subdued with a blow of the club.
This ensured that the *bandi* had even fewer friends
Near the lands of the *People of the Caucasus*.
The worst thing that had happened was that
He had noticed a change in behaviour among the ranks of his own gang.

The young men would disappear more often for a couple of days
Returning not with bounty, as before,
But with burning eyes and flaming cheeks,
Smiling at something only they knew.
Once, during a raid, the leader lost his nerve.

Paying no attention to the herd, he ordered his men
To attack the village.
They burst into the settlement but, to their horror,
They were met not with fear and fright,
Rather by old women riding bulls and donkeys,

Waving wooden sabres and shouting,
"*Batyr* Nasharvan! Come and fight!"
Now no one even bothered to run away.
Quite the contrary, one old woman on a horned bull
Came right up to the leader of the thugs

And screamed at him: "Come on, show me how you deal with a woman!
You're no good in the field, perhaps we should retire to the yurt?"
Restrained laughter was heard even behind his back, after those words.
And when the steer boldly butted Nasharvan's *Argamak*,
The thug whipped his horse and, black as night, sped away.

It's a terrible thing, contemptuous, black glory, in the steppe.
It's like air: you try to stop it,
But it instantly takes up all the free space around.
One by one, the *dzhigits* began to desert Nasharvan
And it was obvious in what direction they went.

Is it really possible to resist the dashing beauty
Of those steppe Amazons with their pearly teeth and coral lips?
And that was how that famous gang of Nasharvan
Slowly faded away to nothing...'
'But why,' I asked, 'did you say that this was a sad story?'

The steppe folk looked at each other and one said,
'Okay, Bartholomew, we'll tell you everything without hiding a thing.
In the end, there were only seven men left

535

In Nasharvan's gang
But they were out-and-out scoundrels and violent thugs.

Nasharvan realised he had lost his war
But he had no wish to make his peace with this
And his bastard accomplices wouldn't allow him to in any case.
They decided to mete out bloody vengeance
And make the people pay for the indelible disgrace.

One day, they waited until the men from one village
Had left to hunt onagers and ferocious boars,
Whereupon they flew like a whirlwind into the helpless village.
They set fire to yurts and tents,
Destroying everything they could get their hands on,

But the worst thing was that they killed several women and elders.
Having completed their reprisals, they headed West,
To the towns and villages of the *People of Mont Blanc and Olympus*,
But they never actually made it there.
Everywhere they went, they were met with lead-coloured, condemning eyes of the women,

Who shouted after them, "Nasharvan, you're a murderer of old women and children!"
They turned their horses around and swept across the steppe,
Never finding peace or shelter.
Wherever they went they were chased off with spit and cursing
Back to the place where they had committed their terrible crime.

And so, when they again reached the lands of the *People of Altai and Khan-Tengri*,
They were met by a huge group of silent but stern horsemen.
The thugs fled
But they ran into pursuers wherever they went,
Who weren't chasing them, simply slowly but surely closing the circle.

Up ahead were some women, loudly singing a *zhoktau* farewell.
The thugs slowly began to lose their minds,
A wild, bestial fear grew in their hearts,
Although they knew for sure that none of those horsemen
Would raise their weapons against them, simply because they didn't have any.

The enclosing circle pushed them nearer and nearer
To the slopes of Mount Tayanar-Tengri.
And when the thugs saw those sacred slopes,
They realised the only thing that they could do.
In a panic, they abandoned their horses by the slopes

And, making it to the mountain top,
They launched themselves up, meaning down as well,
To meet not the warm embrace of the Homeland,
Awaiting the return of their sons,
Rather towards an inevitable death.

They say that when their corpses were found on Earth,
They had already been thoroughly cleaned by looters and thieves,
Warming their vulture's beaks
Under the scorching Turkestan sun,
Along the routes of the Great Silk Road.'

536

I paused and allowed myself to ask:
'Was it not possible to push the thugs up to the mountain,
Forcing them to flee back to Earth?'
'That is the right question, Bartholomew, but, still, it's a question for an Earth dweller.
You talk and think about execution,

And the right to perform it.
What we are telling you about is
How people deprive themselves of paradise,
Where life becomes unbearable for them.
And it becomes unbearable when

Society is both united and mature,
When it is not indifferent and, in unison,
Creates this unbearable state
And demonstrates a moral rejection
Of such violations of *dharma*.

An Earth dweller might even think
That our men are weak and timid
But that is not the case.
It was they who showed that terrible fortitude,
Which did not let revenge, war and violence into our lives.

As for the dead old men and women...
We speak with their souls and they answer us,
Saying that they were happy to make the necessary sacrifice
For all of us. Bartholomew, do you know what the most important thing is?
They did something that now everyone is prepared to repeat.'

Incidentally, brothers, let me remind you of one important comment.
You mustn't think that such names
As *People of Altai* or *People of the Himalayas*
Fully correspond *ethnically* to those peoples
Who reside near these mountains on Earth.

That would be a fatal mistake in understanding the history of Nibiru.
From an ethnic point of view, the *People of Fuji*
Were for the most part Germans, Latins and Africans.
Of course, there were many Japanese there too,
But it wasn't they who determined the appearance of the new region of Nibiru.

The *People of Tibet and the Himalayas* were not only Chinese and Hindus;
There were many Latins, Greeks and Turks, too.
And the *People of the Pamirs and the Hindu Kush*
Had barely any Tajiks or Iranians at all;
They had flown to Tayanar together with the *People of Olympus*.

So, the information that had been spread among us, proved to be incorrect.

What was the language or languages of the residents of Nibiru?
In what dialect did those who
Honoured the commandments of all peoples and religions communicate?
This is also interesting.
The main thing was that there were no countries

And that means, there was no political geography.

You could speak Latin or Hebrew anywhere
And find people to talk with.
I was amazed that the languages were so mixed up
That it was impossible to find their source.

The languages ceased to divide people, only unite them.
How is that possible?
How can it be that no language
Came to play a dominant role?
I don't get it. This can be explained only by the fact that

The societies had only begun to form in political terms;
Trade and a common information space
Had only started to take shape.
And then a wholly earthly question began to plague me:
Perhaps that's how things should be?

I could see how the workers of the global information systems were snorting.
What now – the news had to be translated into everyone's own language?
That is not practical, economical or effective.
Not economical – that's not the way questions were raised on Nibiru.
Effective – equally so. And what was the hurry?

Was there not an eternity ahead?
That wouldn't be practical. And is it practical to stop respecting
Another because doing so wouldn't be expedient?
I have to admit, many issues that Nibiru's residents discussed
Had me puzzled. I told them about this

But they just told me to think it over, take a break
And then come and talk some more.
Puzzles are created to
Teach people to think without hurrying, carefully,
And not to rush into actions

That might then divert one away from the main goal.
And what is the main goal?
The Golden Age, brother. And that alone.
There is a unity in the different and sometimes, the opposite.
But why do they need to fight?

If you want to fight, go (*fly*) back to Earth.
There, you'll have enough fighting for many years.
There, fighting is the essence of all that's going on.
Conflict between fathers and children,
Conflict with a mother, a child, with friends,

Conflict in a close circle of colleagues.
Global and regional conflicts.
It's as if the Earth was created for this.
Why drag it all here?
There is only one reason to abandon one's sacred Homeland

And that is to gain the chance to start building
One's Golden Age, one's Kingdom of Heaven.
Even back on Earth the *emigrants* think that way.
You talk to any of them; what will they reply?

First, that they are ridding themselves of the network of their Homeland's conventions,

That they want to leave behind them when in the new country.
Second, understanding that their lives will be a struggle,
They dream of their children living without these
Conventions and systems of coercion
That exist back in their Homeland.

Third, loving their Homeland, they try to bring all the best from it
And immerse it in an alien system of values.
And what comes of it? Well, nothing, that's what.
Not the first, the second nor the third.
Either you become enslaved in the new system of the new country,

Or your children grow up to become the fruits of your inferiority complex,
Which was the result of your rejection of your own self.
That, or your community finds itself in conflict
With the local views,
Seeing you as an outsider, and alien and, therefore, historically superfluous.

Well, that's doesn't happen on Nibiru.
Well, so the *People of Mont Blanc* arrived later
Than the *People of Altai*, but no one shouts at them.
That they weren't here before.
From the off, everyone wants to share what they've managed to achieve for themselves.

There are no words like *indigenous* or *aboriginal*;
Who could be called that on the Great Gondwana of Tayanar?
However you look at it, it looks like Campanella's *The City of the Sun*
Or Thomas More's *Utopia*.
Only not a *utopia* that people laugh at

But one that captures the imagination.
And you start to think
Why did everyone laugh at the *Utopias* and *The Cities of the Sun* back home?
If you had the imagination to dream them up,
Why wasn't there the will to create them on Earth?

Napoleon said, *Ability is nothing without opportunity.*
Does that mean our human genius of the mind, heart, soul and love
Are enslaved by a lack of opportunity to realise
Our dreams?
How, when and why did it come to be

That the base has become the eternal and the almighty,
While the wonderful is just for dreamers, idealists and prophets?
That means that something once radically deprived
The human genius of the soul of these opportunities?
Does that mean that our everyday life must be stifled and we have to be happy with that?

Why is it generally accepted that politics, a contest of the mind,
Is something dirty?
Can communication and a competition of intellects for the good of the world
Not be something wonderful and sublime?
What is it that has come between us and ourselves?
Why do we need floods and the advent of Nibiru,

Meaning with the advent of opportunity
To start everything afresh,
To see the chance to start living the right, noble way?
To do Good and Kind deeds?
Surely the Greedy and Bloodless One is more industrious

Than the Beloved and the Only One?
If on Earth the opportunities for talent
Are not in the hands of the Good and the Kind,
In whose hands are they?
What is *actually* happening on Earth?

That was my reasoning as I travelled through the heavenly Shambhala,
Not mythical but truly real,
Which was filled with those same Kyrgyz, Zulus, Germans,
Turners, cyclists and musicians,
The sanguine, the *hikikomori*[230] and the disabled.

I asked the *People of the Cordillera* and the *People of Sinai*,
'There is still much that I don't understand.
The conflict of people with people
Is so complex
That you cannot get by with one set of Commandments alone.

For example, your current social relations
Say that the Tayanar societies are
At a fairly primitive stage in their development.
So what about the scientific and technological progress and its end products?
You see, they create new principles

Of social differentiation, don't they?
But this is not the most important thing either – they create an additional product,
Based on which new social strata arise,
Which exist as a result of this product.
And we're not talking about dumb consumption in the form of some beneficiary *rentier*.

We are talking of an additional cycle of goods circulation,
Which is not connected directly with food production
Or consumer goods, right?
You see, these are layers of *upper consumption* of production surpluses.
What, and then you have new professions, new relations

And new principles to govern consumption?'
'That is a very important matter,' the *People of Cordillera* answered.
'Indeed, the scientific and technical progress
Does create new principles and kinds of employment, but
Here on Tayanar, the Scientific and Technical Revolution doesn't create new principles of consumption.

You've got to agree, Bartholomew, consumption
Is a fairly limited concept,
If it's not artificially heated up.
The statistically average person cannot eat more in one dinnertime
Than another, and that's a fact, but this is the basis of the principle of consumption.

---

[230] *Hikikomori* (Japanese) – young people who voluntarily withdraw themselves from any form of social contact.

If you're raising the question of quality,
Then you mean not so much the question of quality,
Rather the matter of its exclusive consumption,
Just as it takes place down on Earth.
We have this one artist, Leonard Wilson.

He really wanted his house to be enormous
And decorated with Doric columns
And 19th-century furniture from back down on Earth.
Why did he need it?
Well, because it was in such interior that inspiration came a-visiting.

We had a discussion and realised
That this was not an idle question of dumb consumer aesthetics.
We are talking about an atmosphere, where he paints his pictures
Which, in turn, decorate our own lives
And ensure it is spiritually rich.

We built him such a house
And everyone played a part.
Leonard Wilson now has the house
That enables him to work creatively.
He now has the opportunities,

Without which the geniuses on Earth are so limited.
However, he didn't start eating more
Or putting on more clothes.
However, Bartholomew, we understand your question is not about that.
The question is not whether we have achieved

Scientific and technical progress,
Rather, it's a question of how we distribute what we've achieved.
On Earth, any invention means an advantage
For a community, nation or district over others.
When you take from your worldview

The question of *the need to achieve this advantage*,
Then you have only one question left:
What to do with the energy, the effort and the talent,
The working hands, after all, of those
Who are socially released from the labour process

Due to the advent of robotisation and new technologies.
Society always has a crowd of people
Who don't like sitting in offices,
Standing my machinery,
Or bending double in the fields for the harvest.

In the language of the Middle Ages, they are either nobles
Or idlers.
We have no nobles. Well, we do, but they are only children of Earthly traditions,
Who are fully in line with Tayanar's social relations
And who don't violate them.

So, Bartholomew, the question relates to the idlers.
But, you know, there are few classical idlers.
They are often people who don't agree with the traditional professions

That their family, town, age or anything else force upon them.
Therefore, we took drastic steps.

The first principle is that
Any scientific or technical achievement
Should be a universal achievement,
So as not to be the exclusive domain
Of any given society.

But how could this be achieved?
That is why we need many different agents,
Who would distribute these achievements and introduce them,
Gift, teach and spread over all the Gondwana of Tayanar.
We value any labour. Someone knows how to teach,

Another studies the intricacies of an invention,
While another is even able to set up production.
And someone, Bartholomew, can simply talk about it beautifully.
You think that's not enough?
Well, go and tell the traditional deer herders

About the factory-scale slaughterhouse
Or the dam builders about the virtues of new explosives!
You need to relate not only the technical aspect
But also make this invention part of their worldview!
You need considerable talent for that.

There's really not much that's difficult here, Bartholomew.
Everyone goes to work and then rests.
Who will write the books for their leisure time?
Who will make series and shows for them to watch?
There's a lot of work. Is it just that the main thing is

What will your reward be?
The silent money of Earth –
The symbol of your independence and self-sufficiency?
Or is it the love of the community
Which might build you a house with Doric columns

Simply to ensure you work well?'
'Please, please,' I said, worried.
'Are you saying that there's never been a case
When the desires of, say, a *Bohemian*, were not
Inappropriate to what they gave back to society?

Has there not been an instance when a person has demanded the community's attention
Only to later give it nothing in return?
That would be unnatural!!!'
My companions laughed heartily
And their lashes and eyelids glistened with tears.

'Sorry, Bartholomew, we don't want to offend you with our laughter,
It's just that the logic of Earth dwellers is still so familiar to us.
First of all, we see the inordinate egos of the Earth dwellers,
Wanting a result right here and right now,
Without a thought for whether

The changes might take years, which are also a sacrifice.

Answer me this: how prepared are you to
Live a new way?
Establishing new social relations
Is a matter for *the future*, which you need to love genuinely.
Remember the discussion in Britain

About whether policemen on the street should carry weapons.
What choice did the nation make?
Right – you need to think not about *how you'd punish*,
But about *what you'd be encouraging!*'
'But Britain isn't the entire world!' I cried.

'It's just one episode!'
Then, the elder from the *People of Cordillera*,
Hailing on Earth from the Sioux Lakota tribe, rose to his feet:
'My friend, look at the people of the Great Gondwana of Tayanar!
We are all British; we are all Lakota,

We are all Turks, Armenians, Basques and Venetians!
What makes us different from the people of Earth?
Well, nothing! The same people, the same historical memory,
The same traditions and their fundamental difference!
However, the difference is in the one most essential thing:

Our understanding of private and public property.
Social relations, even under capitalism,
Under feudalism or in a post-industrial society
Might be built not based on what you have that's *yours*,
But on what you have that's *ours*,

The moment you say *here is my exclusive knowledge –*
Technology, a song, a scientific discovery, oil,
A brand, an invention or creativity.
You are just like the children on Earth,
Who, whatever formation you present them,

Will always divide everything in it into the *mine* and the *not mine*.
We won't conceal all the difficulties on the path we have travelled.
Of course, in addition to Zhang Bao, Bobojon and Nasharvan,
We have encountered many of those conflicts
That Earth has brought us.

But when you have a clear vision of the future,
Its outlines and meanings that fill them,
You realise the key motif that forms the relations
To which you will eventually be striving.
This represents the key criteria for assessing what is happening.

To a certain extent, things were easy for us –
We don't remember who that great ideologist or prophet was
Who instilled as the basis of our new society
The notion that we must honour and fulfil the holy commandments
Of everything invented on Earth.

You can become beautiful and sacrificial.

You might not ever have to face sacrifice,
But in every moment of your life
You must be prepared to sacrifice *yours*
For the sake of *ours*.

What could be simpler, Bartholomew?
You think the entire population of Tayanar
Does nothing but make sacrifices?
Initially, there was a lot of sacrificing
But not anymore.

Now we have formed the necessary tone for public relations,
Which are pretty easy to follow.
The main thing is to *love*, not *crave*!
Give and not *take*! You'll find this simple recipe
In the commandments of any people.

You can subordinate any phenomenon,
Be it capitalist, feudal, pastoral or idyllic,
To whatever you want.
It's just a question of what you actually want
And what you bring to those *on whom realisation of this desire depends*.

You can rob them and deceive them,
You can rule over them or lead them astray.
You can even kill them!
But you are a part of this world,
And it will give back to you precisely what you once sowed.

That's why I'm proud of my compatriots
Who one day, shivering from cold
And a lack of oxygen at the foot of the great mountains,
Said, *What shall we take with us to Nibiru?*
And what should we leave here on Earth?

No one talked about belongings, property or technology.
Everyone said the same:
'Let's take with us
What unites us. As for what divides us,
We'll try not to let it into the New Kingdom of Heaven.

You see, Bartholomew, what we left behind
Is the main paradox of earthly humanity –
Governments.
Their essential function was initially one of unison and compromise,
But then it changed fundamentally.

We left them behind
Because it turns out that they had
No real unification of people, neither within, nor without,
No real sense of compromise,
And no real love either.'

My heart was beating with excitement
Like a blacksmith's hammer.
Was there really a human society
Where all the base features of its essence were suppressed

And where all that was lofty and spiritual reigned supreme?

I wandered the Great Gondwana of Tayanar
And took in this new life.
Thousands of dialects had ceased to be an alien environment for me;
They had become my wealth instead.
And yet one thought tormented me:

What was the wormhole that the heavenly messenger had spoken of?
What was it that so had frightened and alarmed him?
Perhaps, as is befitting an angel,
He attributed uncharacteristic features to people,
To once more blacken them before the Lord of Worlds?

But I couldn't find anything
That could have clouded my vision
Of this new human civilisation.
Moreover, I thought that
This new understanding of the world

Would pour from this Divine Ark like grains of buckwheat.
Man always strives for the best,
Which means it can't be long until the day
When the rays of a bright understanding of life pour down from here,
Capable of changing all of humanity on both planets.

And this was a feeling sensed by all Nibiru's residents.
Slowly but surely, they began to speak about
It not being very fair to leave one's Homeland in the abyss of evil.
There is a certain egoism in this, and some.
After all, many had left families, relatives and friends down there.

It turned out that Earth hadn't forgotten Nibiru either.
Rumours about the Kingdom of Heaven increasingly captured the minds
Of the real children of Altai, Mont Blanc and the Caucasus.
One day, I actually got to feel
That source of anxiety of mine and of the angels.

Somewhere on the border of the lands of the *People of Mont Blanc*
And the *People of Ararat*,
A small community appeared.
It was small but had arrived from Earth in an organised fashion.
At first they were no different from the colonists.

They honoured all the commandments of all confessions,
And they shared everything and became part of the common whole.
However, I sensed an unknown organised nature in them,
A certain excessive purposefulness in all they did.
And no one could quite understand what it was.

They studied the commandments so carefully
That everyone began to suspect they had a different objective in mind,
Rather than simply studying.
They also raised the flag of love,
But they proclaimed it in a strange way.

They devised favourite commandments that were equal to others

But which were still their *favourites*.
No one objected as such, as if to say, you want to love, then love.
There were only a few wise men, who said,
'Don't go looking for the exclusive where everything is equal between you.'

This was seen as casuistry and was quickly forgotten.
Generally speaking, the commandments more or less coincided
With those that were in any case the beloved ones on Tayanar,
So no one saw the need to object to the new *flyers*.
However, things did not turn out quite as simple.

Someone called them *stonemasons*
Because they stoically opted for the hardest labour;
Someone called them *apprentices* because they liked
Being hired in big groups to building sites,
Where they showed themselves off in the best light.

They called themselves *The Watchers*,
Because everyone had an eye tattoo on the palm of their hand.
Everyone was happy to accept their wish
To live in a closed group
With their own particular ceremony.

First, because they very quickly invented
A great many things and shared them generously;
Second, because they emphatically and zealously
Fulfilled all the commandments known to the people of Earth and Tayanar.
No one suspected any danger or threat in them.

Only one thing bothered them –
That was those proverbial exclusive, favourite commandments.
But no one could put into words why this was bad,
And so they had no right whatsoever
To pass judgment.

I am the former Pharaoh of the Great House,
I knew what this symbol meant, but there was no point
In suspecting The Watchers of adhering to
The old 'Earthly' interpretation.
Everything on the Great Godwana was new.

The time came when there were a great many Watchers everywhere.
Given that building work was happening everywhere,
There was also a lot of work.
There were no boundaries or principles to restrict movement
And no one ever kept track of this.

Conversations sprang up
About the *People of the Eye* hoarding,
And this was a really serious rebuke on Nibiru.
However, these idle rumours were quickly dispelled,
When they gave generous gifts to all their neighbours near and far,

And continued bestowing new inventions on the world,
Which improved over time in their small, closed community.
In so doing, they simply amazed the residents of Nibiru.
However, everyone who shared was highly respected here,

And any industrious type was doubly respected.

And yet I still felt a certain unease
And so I decided to find out
How their favourite commandments
Shaped their worldview,
And where that source was of all that alarming rumour and suspicion.

However, no espionage was needed.
Any *stonemason* would always say openly
That their favourite commandments were these:
Do not store up for yourselves treasures on earth, where moths and vermin
Destroy, and where thieves break in and steal,

But store up for yourselves treasures in heaven, where moths and vermin do not destroy, and
where thieves do not break in and steal,
For where your treasure is, there your heart will be also.[231]
Well, what could be purer than these thoughts?
What else could be more in line with the worldview of the people of Tayanar?

Another favourite commandment was:
But I tell you, do not resist an evil person. If anyone slaps you on the right cheek,
Turn to them the other cheek also[232].
Basically, these are the main commandments of all residents
Of the Great Gondwana of Tayanar. What is anti-social about them?

Quite the contrary, I thought,
It even smacks a little of fanaticism.
However, given the Good, Kind mindset
Of the Tayanar residents, it was worth assuming
That this excessive fanaticism would soon be overcome.

After all, the planet's residents aren't really that fond of fanatics.
But they do love the conscious, devoted and enlightened
Following of the world's commandments.
Evidently, these were simply illnesses from the recent *flight* over.
These things happen with all pilgrims from Earth.

Actually, only a few had suspicions.
The people of Tayanar continued to envelop all recent arrivals
From Earth and those they sincerely
Believed needed attention and friendly help
With love and attention.

Nevertheless, I settled near one of the Watcher communities.
It wasn't that I was observing them or anything;
I just wanted to get a handle on something and put my mind at rest.
All the people of Nibiru strove for harmony.
I also strove for this, overcoming an unnecessary anxiety in doing so.

The Watchers were no different from those around them –
They also worked and sought things for their idlers to do.
The number of these idlers had evidently increased,
So, they had settled near various communities

[231] Matthew. 6:19-21.
[232] Matthew. 5:39.

And each expressed themselves there in their way.

And what of it? It was not only supported,
It was even encouraged on the Great Gondwana!
Most often, these *idlers* didn't sing and didn't paint.
In the evening they would gather the community's residents
And discuss with them that they have two key, favourite commandments.

Who would object? No one.
Only once, during a meeting with the Watchers' *idlers*,
I asked why they would single out certain,
Specific commandments.
Were they not all our values simultaneously?

The Watchers replied modestly
That these two were key in the worldview
Of Nibiru's residents, so why not remind themselves of this once more?
The people applauded them because they
Not only spoke

But even gave colourful examples and told stories.
Most important, to what could I object?
And why?
Only once did I have a thought
Like a former Pharaoh:

Oh, were I a king now, with my apparatus of state,
I would send several counterintelligence agents
To learn from the inside
What actually lies beneath the ideology of these stonemasons.
But I quickly rid myself of that thought.

That's the phantom pains after the loss of your throne talking,
I told myself,
And the traditions of a lost Homeland.
Down on Earth that's what they do.
But what's the need here?

However, a scandal broke out a couple of years later.
Several people from the *stonemasons'* community fled.
They told us it wasn't right at all
How the Watchers perceive the commandment about
Hoarding in the Kingdom of Heaven.

They take it literally,
That this cannot be done on Earth,
But that here, in the Kingdom of Heaven, it's no problem,
And that this is stated in the Divine Commandments.
According the escapees, the Watchers

Had accumulated such untold riches
That they could put not only the surrounding communities to shame,
But the entire population of the Great Gondwana as well.
Then the elders of the *People of all the Great Mountains* gathered
And brought their complaint to the Watchers:

'Tell us, is it true what the fugitives have told us?'

548

The leaders of the *stonemasons* came out and fell to their knees before the *aqsaqals*.
'It is true that we have accumulated certain values
In one place, but you ask why?
You think it's for us?

Take a look at us, sirs,
What poor beggars we are.
It is customary on this planet to help, give and share.
We only wanted to gather things so we could then hand out to our neighbours.
All of them.

That is our sole objective here.'
'Hold on,' the elders objected,
'Assistance and a desire to share
Should not become something systematic and organised
And should certainly not have hoarding at its heart.

You see, every man shares what specifically he has.
And this is where the true act of friendly, sincere help actually lies.
It's not that you give *something*, rather that you give *from yourself*,
While completing the main ceremony of understanding
Who you are and with whom you can share sincerely.'

The *stonemasons* fell to the ground, snivelling and tearful.
'It's all true, sirs,' they said,
'But our community is so poor and we are so poor.
See as us not being able as individuals
Even to give a friend a broken spoon,

But, by gathering something, crumb by crumb,
We can at least offer someone the help they need without humiliating ourselves
With a realisation of our own poverty!'
However, the elders weren't fooled by this casuistry:
'Even a broken spoon, when gifted sincerely,

Will warm a man's heart no less
Than an enormous cooking pot. Quite the opposite,
Such an insignificant sacrifice as a spoon, evidences
That you are prepared to share the last thing you possess.'
The *stonemasons* bowed before the elders once again:

'We have realised our mistake
And all that we have accumulated will be handed out immediately.
Only permit us, so we don't humiliate our brothers in the community,
To hand it out to those who have only just arrived on Nibiru,
For they are needier than everyone.'

The elders nodded their beards and agreed
And, with my king's perverted and corrupted mind,
I suddenly thought that if we could not control the hoarding,
How would we control all the handing out?
Should we not appoint accountants?

I said this to the elder Vazgen from the *People of Ararat*,
But he interrupted me angrily, saying,
'Don't go sowing mistrust, it's dangerous.
Didn't you see the sincerity and the desire to atone

In the eyes and faces of those people?!'

I was embarrassed and stepped to one side.
Indeed, riches then flowed as if from a horn of plenty.
Everyone *flying* in would receive a special package,
Decorated with the image of an eye.
No one saw anything wrong with that either.

The Watchers continued to hand out gifts, and to members of the community as well.
The people who gave out one of only three cups
Or one of only two spoons, or who handed over their only mirror
Felt most uncomfortable
When the *stonemasons* gifted horses and brocade, wine and paintings.

No one could understand what was unacceptable in this embarrassment.
What wormhole was hidden there?
Everything appeared to be correct – they ordained and they handed out.
The people began to suspect themselves of envy
And tied themselves up in knots as a result.

You see, thanks to these handouts,
The number of the *stonemasons'* supporters grew considerably.
At the same time, not one of these supporters was a member of this
Closed society, but in disputes and peaceful conversations
They heatedly defended them for some reason and told everyone they were right.

Then came the time to realise
How the Watchers saw the commandment about a slap.
Perhaps you thought that Nibiru
Was an emotionally sterile planet?
That it never seethed with jealousy, resentment and anger?

Far from it. There was all of that.
However, you have to understand the abyss in the transformation of consciousness
Experienced by the passionate Caucasians, vengeful Corsicans,
The Russians with their heightened sense of justice,
The Turks with their culture of fighting spirit

And every other people, part of the culture of whom
Involved a cult of revenge.
There were fights, man-to-man combat,
Clashes of justices,
Basically everything that makes one raise a hand to one's neighbour

In response to wrong-doing.
However, on Nibiru, they understood the main thing:
You have to see how it all ends
And know what you really want.
Everyone wants peace and harmony; they want to understand and be heard.

They don't want to be the object of injustice.
So, when something happened that was out of the ordinary,
Everyone expected the offender to come forward himself and ask forgiveness.
He would choose his own penance and punishment,
Without asking anyone whether or not it would be sufficient.

Because the highest level of justice

Was seen not to be the satisfaction of society
That a guilty party has been punished,
But the fine day
When he awakes and sincerely feels that he is forgiven.

There was a time when the brave Japanese
Fostered their traditional ritual of *seppuku*,
Until, one day, an elder from the *People of the Andes*
Stopped a samurai descendant in his tracks with one question:
'Okay, so you'll die now, but who will answer me

If justice has been done or not?'
The strict adherent of the *Bushido* moral code was taken aback
And, the next day, he adopted all the children
Of the warrior he had killed in combat.
And five years later, seeing one of his new sons

Galloping about on a horse and singing a foolish song,
He somehow felt with all his heart and realised what his father's spirit
Was telling him that he was forgiven.
This was indeed one of the basic commandments
That became a well

From where all the residents of the Great
Gondwana of Tayanar drank pure water.
So, what was wrong with the Watchers' interpretation?
How could such a commandment
Become anything other than something good?

Once, I became involved in the art of calligraphy.
I liked to draw hieroglyphs with water,
Seeing their disappearance as a symbol of the world's frailty.
I wrote down the poems of Saadi and Hafiz in a divine *Nastaliq*[233].
I used to love meticulously writing Gothic letters,

Each like a small temple.
I would copy the bizarre curvature
Of the Georgian and Armenian alphabets.
However, this wall of beauty still failed to save me
From the disturbing news from outside.

One of my students, with whom I had copied some
Forty ancient Greek codes, bounded over to me
And reported to me on events that were very strange and hard to explain.
Simple folk seldom notice the turn of the key
That alters world events so fundamentally,

But they do have an acute perception of the events
That are their consequence,
When they affect their own town or home.
Now, too, the people had failed to see who had turned this key and when,
But now, they were noisily and vigorously discussing the consequences.

The Watchers, preaching about the might and the glory of the slapping commandment,

---

[233] *Nastaliq* is a beautiful Arabic-Persian script, based on the instantaneous depiction of the correct and harmonious writing of text.

One day demanded that society
Must actively display its loyalty to this commandment.
'But how do we do that?' Asked the elders of the mountain Homes in amazement.
'It's very simple,' the Watchers declared.

'We need to form a corps of emissaries,
Who will periodically check to ensure
The strength of the people's convictions,
Performing this literally.'
'How?!' the elders exclaimed in horror.

'Like this: if our convictions are strong,
The emissaries will select people they deem necessary
And give them a slap round the face
To check their unwavering devotion to the commandment.'
'But that is just absurd!' the elders objected.

'A man's devotion to the commandment is proven through his life,
His deeds, his attitude to everything in society and the story of his life!'
'No, no,' the *stonemasons* retorted.
'Our task is not only to go with the flow,
But also to foresee where the rapids come.

And anyway, what could possibly happen
If this custom is repeated only occasionally?'
The Russians, Turks, French and Anglo-Saxons all grumbled,
'Why not let us break them up, these guys,
And dissolve them into the communities?'

But their voices were instantly drowned out in the midst of their compatriots,
Dressed in brocade and cloaks, bearing the eye symbol,
'What's the problem? Why not?
If everything we have is common, why should those
Hidden thoughts that some might conceal not be common either?'

'But there's the presumption of guilt!'
The members of the community and the hunters said in outrage.
'And then, what are the criteria for selecting
Someone worthy of a slap?'
They took the discussion off on a foolish tangent,

Partially recognising the legitimacy of the cruel checks.
Immediately, the eloquent supporters of
The Watchers rushed forward, waving their arms
And babbling, 'Don't worry, we'll make all the procedures
Transparent and honest!

No one will suffer among those
Who have never been questioned.
You can trust us!'
'But why you?' the elders objected.
'Well, we have organised units everywhere for that.

Do you?'
Everyone admitted that there were none as organised as the *stonemasons*
And... they gave them this right!
Although they scratched their head and whispered

That this was all probably absurd, they still said

That the majority wanted it
So that meant there had to be a grain of truth
In the need to check the least trustworthy!
However, the elders put the freeze on the decision
Using the strength of their authority.

However, somehow befitting the occasion,
A series of incidents unfolded
Across the Gondwana of Tayanar.
When the calm and reserved members of the community
Not only responded in kind to the offending slappers,

But even found a reason to give them a good beating.
The neighbours and relatives would say that
They had been provoked long and hard.
They were well brought-up and upstanding heads of their families!
It's just that they had been deliberately harassed by certain external forces!

The Watchers said, 'You see
What might be hiding in the hearts of even the decent-looking people?
Just think what's going on with the less respectable types.'
With that, the elders' patience finally ran out:
'What external forces? How absurd!

What daft world conspiracy theories are you talking about?
Everything is transparent and open in our societies,
And no one can be suspected of concealing thoughts!'
They nodded to the Watchers: 'What must be will be,
So form those emissaries.'

And here a truly unregulated wave rose up.
Every day, the newspapers controlled by the Watchers would write,
Across the entire community of Johannesburg Jnr
A hundred miscreants have been exposed,
Concealing their vengeful tendencies!

In Paris Jnr, even the community's leader
Was unable to control his emotions and punched the emissary in response!
An entire village in Beijung Jnr
Beat up an emissary for his quality preaching!
But we did it! And it was a success! A great success! A great success!

Regiments of these emissaries dispersed in a solid wave
Across the Great Gondwana of Tayanar,
Encountering criminals wherever they went
But handling them successfully wherever they went!
Many even swallowed the story that before, it turns out,

We were stupid lambs, believing
That we were living in a prosperous world.
But take a look now!
In Moscow Jnr alone there are entire communities of avenging conspirators,
Destroying our holy commandment!

Thank you to those emissaries!

They're our true hope!
What would we do without you?
How would we have preserved the true purity of the commandments?
There were occasional voices heard, saying,

'But before all these checks
There were never any conflicts!'
Strange, but the communities reacted aggressively
To such assertions:
They yelled and screamed at those saying those things; they even beat them.

Worst of all, though, they reported to the local emissaries
That this was where the potential, hidden enemy was to be found
And that he should be given a good slap round the face!
The culprit would receive a resounding slap in the face
And would crawl away home, losing what was left of his pride.

I listened to my student nervously.
And I scrawled the second inscription.
'Is that it?' I asked.
'No, teacher, now comes the most important thing.
One day, two elderly men,

A Jew and an Arab, were playing backgammon in a tavern
When in walked emissaries.
They dared to criticise their methods,
For which they were mercilessly beaten
And both of them later died at home, unable to bear the shame before their communities.

Their two sons swore to bring justice,
But not seek revenge or violate the accepted principles.
They went out onto the square during a boisterous festival
And approached the two largest emissaries.
For all the crowd to see

They gave them two hard slaps round the face,
From which the bells rang over the entranceway.'
'Well done!' I cried excitedly,
'I suppose those two retreated and everyone saw what was what!'
'Quite the contrary,' the student retorted gloomily.

'The *stonemasons* got them and beat them to death,
Screaming that they were terrorists and destroyers of the foundations of the world,
Only because these founding principles state
That only a certain group of people
Can hand out slaps with impunity, not just anybody.

And those who are against it
Are lowlife, contemptuous barbarians and terrorists.
The crowd gasped at such hypocrisy
But what was most surprising was
That many reacted with approval to the execution!

Now the *People of the Great Mountains* were divided in two.
They gathered weapons and prepared for war.'
I howled like a wounded animal! There it was, the angel's warning!
There it was, the true essence of man, risen to the surface!

War again! Again the armies, attacking one another with walls of men!

I saddled my horse and flew like the wind from the mountain
Where my calligraphy school stood,
Forever leaving behind
The tranquillity of the Golden Age.
Several hours later, I arrived at the *People of Altai*,

Where I realised I was too late!
War was raging all around!
People were killing each other in the hundreds and thousands,
And no commandments could ever stop them.
For a moment, the king in me awoke

And I asked a Sious Lakota elder I knew,
'Where is the front line of battle?
What is our potential?
Do we have men in reserve?
Who deals with provisions for the army,

Ammunition and uniforms?!'
The old Lakota looked at me
And replied sadly,
'There is no front line, son.
This is a different kind of war.

When we flared up and came out onto the square,
It turned out that the Watchers had for years been accumulating
Not only jewels, trinkets and things.
They had been importing and manufacturing
Weapons on a grand scale that had never been seen on Nibiru.

What can we counter them with?
What can our shit-smeared arrows do
Against their tanks, their guns and their planes?
So, we sharpened our lances and sabres
And set about killing them everywhere

We found them,
While they declared it a sacred battle against terrorism,
To protect our own commandments and values!!!
They're right: we are terrorists;
I mean, we're hardly soldiers, are we? What do we have for war?

We're not at war with the enemy, rather with the one
We have wrested from our belly ourselves
With our naïve and helpless beliefs,
Which, it turns out, can be deployed in way
That makes heaven and hell change places.

We've lost this planet too, son.
But we've lost it not to the Watchers and the *stonemasons*,
We've lost it to ourselves,
To our sacred commandments,
And our faith in the Kingdom of Heaven.'

I looked down from the top of Tayanar-Tengri

At all that was going on down below and what I saw was terrible.
Someone was trying to stab two or three *stonemasons* with lances.
Someone was endeavouring to resist
The metal tanks and huge weaponry

Which cannot be called military devices because
They struck the enemy from a distance without ever engaging.
What kind of warrior are you if you defeat your enemy with a bow
Only from a distance?
Any commandment will say that you're not a soldier, just a technological coward.

But what importance did my thoughts have?
I saw the majority of people running towards the Tayanar mountains,
To take off in a panic into the abyss and fly to Earth,
Saving themselves from the planet that had become a treacherous hell for them
When it could have become the Kingdom of Commandments.

You think the Watchers had seized the planet
And instilled their own procedures and flourished?
No, far from it.
They destroyed all resistance
And prepared to reign supreme in a kingdom of their own harmony.

They had everything for this:
Accumulated riches,
A close-knit community
And a sense of just victory.
They even had their own brief, yet military history.

I didn't flee with the first wave
That escaped from Nibiru,
To watch the drama unfold to the end
To this end, on a daily basis
And sometimes even twice a day,

I had to put up with slaps from emissaries of the state
And say nothing in return, losing my dignity.
The *stonemasons* accounted for everything but one thing:
The selectivity of the commandments played a wicked trick on them.
New arrivals had nothing sacred in their souls.

They either became emissaries,
Or they simply lived by the laws of the jungles of stone,
While the Watchers could no longer restore
Rule over people using the commandments;
This was no longer possible.

Once abandoned, there would be no going back.
That is why only two commandments remained:
Mad hoarding and slaps round the face from the state,
Which you just had to put up with,
To create a semblance of being honest citizens.

The number of *stonemasons* dwindled and dwindled;
All manner of rabble began to arrive from Earth,
Already informed about how everything was now taking place and why,
And accepting just one law:

There is only you and your right either to survive or not survive.

And there are but two opportunities:
You either hoard or you beat up those
Who don't have such a legitimate right.
In the end, this rabble came to fill all of Gondwana,
Applying pressure to the might of the Watchers.

At one point, the majority realised
That there were so few commandments
That you had no need to restrict yourself in your behaviour at all,
Especially if you bear some relation to the
Class of hoarders.

The lower circles simply began to eat one another,
Consuming, in every sense of the word.
The upper circles, despite trying to preserve their status-quo,
Also absorbed the vices of the rabble,
Killing, raping and creating idols for themselves.

The people pissed in the streets,
On ancient inscriptions with commandments,
Thinking they were simply an antiquated column design.
Consumption of everyone and everything
Became the only coherent system for regulating

Public relations.
At the same time, however, no one ever forgot the regular slaps in the face,
The origin of which no one could remember any more,
Thinking that it was just part of the civilisational plan.
Fragments of the ancient *People of the Mountains* remained,

Who were locked up in zoos
And put on show for the amusement of the rabble settlers,
For them to laugh and see
To what turning away from daily slaps round the face
Might actually lead.

Then I heard a rumour from the pyramid of the Watchers
That they had begun to devise something truly grandiose,
In a fit of admiration for their own might
Or, rather, stemming from the hopelessness of their spiritual impasse.
They forged a new doctrine,

And it sounded something like this: Earth is the source of the rabble
And nothing good comes from it,
Which means you need to gather all the weapons you can on the devil's planet
And destroy the Earth once and for all!
It might seem to you now that the idea is grandiosely absurd,

But believe me, if you ever have to
Live in a society that has once betrayed the commandments,
You will understand that this is a society
With an inferiority complex
That will never let you forget about it.

Like a crazy, sick person

Who tries to rid himself of a headache
By butting a wall,
A sick society will strive to beat up everything external
To distract itself from the pain inside.

But...
Then I thought.
And he appeared, the messenger from the heavens.
I told the angel everything, in every detail
And with the conclusions that my royal mind allowed me draw.

He listened attentively and at length,
Frowning, nodding and without interruption.
Then, he said,
'It's all too serious
For me to decide for myself.

Wait for me here, I'll be right back.'
He disappeared, but returned a moment later,
His eyes burning with a flame of ill determination.
'Nibiru is leaving Earth's field of vision,' the angel said to me,
'But it will soon be back

And will arrive in two thousand years, whatever the astrologers might say.
It will rise from the West
In what will be a symbol of Judgment Day.
But for its current inhabitants the Last Judgment
Will come today.

And woebetide Earth if in two thousand years
It repeats the fate of the civilisation of Tayanar!
Now, Pharaoh, you will stand on the White Mountain,
The Lord's earthly throne in the Altai mountains,
And you will witness the downfall of all

Who now live on Nibiru.
This is our gift to you: to see vengeance for everyone.
And another thing – the Lord of Worlds and the Heavenly Secretariat
Are grateful to you and are prepared
To fulfil your wish, so speak!

I thought for a moment and then replied:
'After I see the downfall of the House of the Watchers,
I would like to see the true King,
The real Master of the Kingdom of Heaven.
That is my only wish.'

The angel shuddered and frowned,
Before asking, 'Are you sure?
This path will not only be the fulfilment of your wish,
It will require a sacrifice on your part too,
Which you'll hear from that King.

Tell me again: Are you sure?'
A tear ran down my cheek
And my voice trembled, but I remained firm:
'If this King returns to me the Kingdom of all the Commandments,

Then I have no need for the House of Egypt.

I want to see the House of Tayanar once again
In all the glory of those
Who created it with love.
And if there is no such King and never will be,
Then leave me here on the *Devil's Planet*!

I will die broken here!'
The angel raised his eyes to Heaven, as if looking for a response,
But then, receiving it, he said,
'There is such a King,
Just look at the punishment of the Planet Nibiru

And then go!'
A moment later, I found myself on the White Mountain of Altai on Earth.
From there I saw the angels rise up
And crush the unholy palaces, pyramids and temples
Of the doomed House of the Watchers and the huts of those

Who had allowed themselves to be their subjects.
Two mighty tsunamis rose from the Eastern
And Western oceans,
The soil shook and the Great Gondwana droned.
A light wind blew

But I couldn't find any of the faithful,
Those with a pure heart and mind.
In a few moments, the civilisation of Nibiru was finished
And the wandering planet,
Having seamlessly counted down its hours,

Began to move slowly away from the Earth,
To return again thousands of years later
And put us and our commandments to the test.
Quite agitated with the destruction,
My familiar angel dropped down,

Picked me up and carried me over the ground.
When I began to suffocate from the lack of oxygen,
He cast me down into the Valley of Canaan.
There I learned that, from the moment I had taken off from Jerusalem,
Not much time had passed in a linear plane, which had kept me young.

And there I was, wandering through Cana of Galilee,
And this young man walked up to me and asked,
'Do you know anything about commandments?'
I laughed and walked on, grumbling,
'What the use of talking about the commandments at noon?'

The lad kept pace with me and, looking back at someone behind us,
Asked again,
'What have you heard about the Messenger from Nazareth?'
I answered him wearily,
'Oh! What good is there from Nazareth?'

But the lad persisted, saying,

Do you want to see the Kingdom of Heaven and its King?'
That was the last straw for me. I stopped and said,
'I'll give you what-for, you idler
And I'll like to see how you and your King will respond –

With reciprocal beatings or with eternal friendship?
And right then I heard a voice that seemed familiar:
'Here is a true Israeli without a shadow of guile!'
I turned and replied,
'I am no Israeli and, as for guile, you would know,

If you were the true King!'
Before me stood a Good, Kind Man,
The like of which I had not encountered from the time of Tayanar.
He smiled: 'I know who you are and I know you are not a son of Israel!
You're Bartholomew, aren't you? Master of the Great House?'

'I am Nathanael,' I said to the Man and I smiled back.
'And won't You show me my House?'
Then I heard the voice of the black Dog of the Abyss:
'You gave the correct name...'
'I'll point it out,' the Man replied. 'With Me, you'll see your Bright and Eternal Home!'

'Then I'm coming...'

Verse 32

(30) Say, 'Have you considered? If your water drains away, who will bring you pure running water?'

Qur'an. Surah 67, 'Sovereignty'

(1) The Reality.
(2) What is the Reality?
(3) What will make you understand what the Reality is?

Qur'an. Surah 69, 'The Reality'

After what happened with our Friend on the Mountain,
We were horrified and dismayed.
Who was He now, a survivor?
Who had we now become, the witnesses of everything
And those come down from the mountain?

Our Friend, our Teacher, walked, staggering,
As if he'd drunk burning wine
That had intoxicated his mind and then left him
Alone with a severe hangover.
He walked, wrapped in a blanket,

As if that could save Him
From the streams of rain, transforming with every drop
From warm and tender
To fierce and cruel.
A downpour of reality.

The Friend coughed badly and His shoulders trembled.
Everyone tried to give Him an item of their clothing,
But, with a sad smile, He refused.
Then John tried to embrace the Teacher
To warm Him.

'No, brother mine, no,' the Beloved One said.
'My fever is not from the cold of the deluge.
Thank you, brother.'
'But your cough is as dry as the cracking
Of a dying Lebanese cedar,' we implored.

'Let's stop and get a fire going!'
We stopped and the ubiquitous Cephas rapidly
Got a flame going,
Which had hitherto been hiding
In the midst of the dry twigs.

After a short while, we heard
The tramping of many feet.
Was that the enemy coming? A robber perhaps?!
Cephas grabbed his Hun hero sword.
No, it was the rest of the brothers running in.

It wasn't the flame that warmed us, but their arrival.
We were together; who could tear us apart?
Even the Palestinian rain
Hissed in the fire

And disappeared, running back up into the sky,

Leaving behind a moist, fragrant trail.
We were just frightened that our Beloved Friend's cough
Had become worse and worse.
Has an illness not befallen You?
Is it not fatigue from the eternal Road? No...

What is a fire in the desert?
It is a beacon that attracts
Not only the random traveller,
But the beast in the darkness too,
Whispering a song of fear, of his and of the human.

First, the elders emerged from the darkness,
Wise, eminent, yet humble too.
They turned down our dirty blankets,
But then thought better of it when they felt
The desert cold and they covered themselves.

Then the modest Galileans came
Who, bowing to the elders,
Crouched shyly by the fire,
Looking fearfully at the Pharisees,
For they were the Pharisees, the guardians of ancient truths.

Then came travellers from Samaria.
The Jewish elders kept their distance from them,
But we sat between them
And everyone agreed to share this meagre flame
Even with strangers and despite their prejudices.

Then a young man emerged from out of the darkness,
Dressed in rich brocade.
He was a decent lad, well brought-up.
He shared his foreign halva with everyone there
And quietly settled down next to the fire.

Then the Greedy One came,
Sat deftly down by the fire, pretending to be a traveller.
We didn't recognise him,
And he ate and drank wine
As if there was no tomorrow,

Until the Teacher recognised him and said,
'The time will come when you'll have your fill of my blood.'
The Greedy One guffawed but stopped
His foul gluttony.
Pointing a finger at the Teacher,

He hissed haughtily and satisfied,
'He knows! He sees!'
At that, the wealthy young man asked, 'What,
My dear and most wise Perushim[234],
They say that somewhere in Galilee

---

[234] *Perushim (Parush, Parushi)* – the Hebrew for *Pharisee*.

562

A pretender to Herod's throne has appeared.
He seems to be a descendant of David,
And he will demand the return of the Hasmonean throne.
What is more, Judea now has
Neither a sovereign or an ethnarch, is that not right?'

The Pharisees whispered among themselves:
'Yes, it would appear so. There are those rumours going around.
But we're actually heading to Jerusalem to say
That there's no such thing in Galilee
And we have not noticed it ourselves.

There's this one strange chap, however;
There are all manner of rumours about him,
That, you know, he heals and performs miracles.
But he's as elusive as a ghost.
Wherever our spies might go,

All that was left was quiet hearsay,
Like the faint sound of the wind after a storm.'
'No, no,' the lad persisted,
I have heard that he was anointed by God
From an early age to rule,

That he displays, by the will of the Almighty,
That his power not only heals,
But banishes demons too,
And even raises from the dead!
Is this not new information for you?'

The most senior of the elders
Angrily interrupted the young man:
'You speak most provocatively.
If this proves to be true,
Civil war will not pass our people by

Again, like it did before.
Once again, kings, and warriors
Will clash in fierce battle but, most important,
They will attract into battle
Either the sons of Ishmael[235],

Or Roman legions,
Having placed our faith,
Our Temple and our independence in jeopardy.'
'Oh, get you!' The Greedy One interjected hoarsely.
'What, and you have so much independence left now, do you?!'

The elders fell silent.
The demon had hit them right where it hurts.
'I also heard,' the young man went on,
'This pretender to the throne,
Has an entire army, the *militia Christi*,

---

[235] The Sons of Ishmael – Arabs who are deemed the descendants of Ishmael, son of Abraham. An intimation that the Arab king Aretes was involved in the civil war of Hyrcanus against Alistobulus.

Who could destroy whole regiments
Of Edomite usurpers
With a single glance.'
The elders shuddered, as if they'd been caught
In an act of state treason.

'No, no, you pious young man,'
They chattered, interrupting one another.
'And there is certainly no army!
Herod could suppress any
Major unrest from Tiberias,

So, those rumours are groundless.'
'I see… If Herod can drag himself away from his concubines and his boisterous feasting, that is,'
The Greedy One laughed, lobbing a twig
Into the nervous, trembling flame in the fire.
'Who are you?' One of the elders enquired, frightened.

'Let's put it this way: the one you have to fight,
But who you decide not to mess with,
Preferring instead to kill the innocent,
Or, in this instance, the innocent
Who you have doomed to death!'

And he laughed again.
We said nothing; was it not for the first time
We were present at a dispute
About us, carried by the Lord's Wind
Across the land of Canaan?

Especially since the Beloved Friend
Had dozed off, exhausted, on John's shoulder
And was not involved in heated debate as usual.
We took this as a signal not to butt in, rather to listen.
Perhaps we would learn something new about the mood in Palestine.

'They also say,' the young man said, lowering his voice,
'That he is not just a king, but actually the Mashiah sent from on high.'
One of the Perushim could stand it no longer and he jumped up:
'What's this nonsense you are spouting, young man?
Have a sense of what is permitted, when all's said and done, eh?!'

'Permitted by whom?' The Greedy One cried out drunkenly.
'By you, the court of Herod or the Romans?
Or perhaps the Tzaddukim[236] that trample you
In your indecision?
In your ambiguous views and cowardice?!'

The one who had jumped up, set his eyes on us
Imploringly, wearily listening to what was happening.
'Is there not a true believer among you
To calm this insolent beggar,
Who so insults this hearth of hospitality?!'

---

[236] *Tzaddukim* – the Sadducees.

'There is,' came the quiet voice of our Friend,
Broken by his tormenting cough.
'There is, Perushim, but my intervention
Is unlikely to cheer you up.
The demon knows that I can calm him,

But is that what you need if it is I who do it?'
The Greedy One jumped up and span abut
In a drunken, reckless dance around the fire
And singing a ridiculous song:
'La-la-la-la-la! Op-pa!. La-la-la!'

As if anticipating some entertainment he was sure to enjoy.
'I can drive him from the fire,
Is that what you want?'
The Teacher asked quietly and wearily.
'No, no,' the Pharisees said with concern.

'It's not good to drive anyone from the fire,
Whoever they might be.'
'That's all you are,' the Beloved One said,
Turning away and concealing his face
In John's embrace.

I thought that they were basically kind, traditional folk,
Who were not prepared to drive the Greedy One from the fire,
Just in order to preserve their reputation;
Prepared to accept grave evil,
Just to ensure the harmony was not broken

In their right to God-loving hymns.

'Aa-ha-la-ha-la!!!
La-li-la-li-La-a-aii!'
The Greedy One began screaming blatantly,
Continuing to dance about in circles.
The Pharisees shivered under our dirty blankets and said nothing.

The wealthy young man took out an expensive cigar
And lit it in the fire,
Waving his arms about insincerely,
Demonstrating he didn't want the tobacco smoke to reach
The sacred noses of the Pharisees. He went on.

'Now, I think that since the Mashiah has been predicted,
Eliyahu must be before him,
And that means it looks like everything will be coming true!
Elijah is that crazy righteous bloke down by the river,
Who Herod recently executed,

And who now hails as if he's some king, right?
Isn't that the case?'
'Well, something like that,' the Pharisees agreed by way of a compromise,
Glancing at the Beloved One and then
The Greedy One apprehensively.

'Something like that.'

'But then there have to be clear preconditions for that.
What are they?' The young man perked up.
'Do you expect him to defeat the Romans
And gather together all the tribes of the descendants of Moses?'

'Yes-yes, of course. How else?'
The Pharisees had now perked up. 'Now look, young man,
The Law has provided for all the formalities
And conventions, under which we know *exactly*
The circumstances of His advent.

You see, this knowledge shapes our nation in its own way,
Defining us as God's chosen ones!
After all, it is we who possess the precise parameters
Of what, how and when this should happen!
And that we must safeguard this knowledge

For new generations to come!
So, where do you find grounds for doubt?
Are you not a Jew?'
The young man yawned, as if to show
He was sufficiently educated

To avoid using the obvious wording.
'Look,' he said, rummaging through his richly embroidered
Saddle bag and pulling out a flat plate
The size of two hands.
Look, this is a tablet, an iPad.

Imagine this: I enter a global network
And I receive the message: *I am IHVH and I am speaking with you.*
What do you think I should write in response?
Naturally, I reply that they shouldn't mess me about and should prove it.
But he sends me a link... there... an earthquake in China.

And again, I say I don't believe him,
And back he comes with a train crash in Germany.
And you watch the television
And, you know, no one expected or knew
Why it had happened...

So, do you think I should carry on sitting
And waiting for a Jew to emerge on the square in a crown
Or an Arab about forty years old
To announce the end of the world?!
All while not believing in the links that this

Secret correspondent has been sending?!
I can choose not to believe, but...
But, you see, it was *I* who asked him (or Him) for proof!
Perhaps it's *my* fault, what has happened
In these countries unknown, eh?'

The Greedy One fell to the ground laughing.
The Pharisees were outraged
And began noisily pointing at the tablet.
The lad lazily hid the iPad away and moved closer to the fire:

'I know, I know. You'll have a little think

And you'll find an explanation for this too,
By rummaging about in your knowledge of *The Law*.
I was raised in a pious Jewish family,
And still my reason forces me
To believe you.

The only thing is to what extent can all this be explained and predicted,
To do the right thing when encountering the unknown?
To what extent is God's imagination
Limited to what he's already published?
Why do we deny Him the right to change something,

In what he said before?'
The Pharisees began shouting loudly and berating the lad.
The Greedy One laughed his head off and behaved himself
Like an absolute clown and jester.
He yelled and, approaching the Friend,

He poked him in the chest and shouted,
'Hey, have you seen? Have you? I told you so, right?!
A Jew in a crown is one thing, but what if we get a Dutchman in a crown?
Or a Tuareg in a crown?'
The Greedy One yelled wickedly at the elders,

'They'll kill Him!!! They'll tear Him to pieces!!!
They'll stone Him and connect
Electrical wires to Him!!!
They are mine!!! Scholasticism and dogma doesn't get any better than this!
Oh, my goodness!' Then he made a face, looking up into the sky.

'And You placed them above us?!
And You gave this Man your Word,
Thinking you wouldn't be condemning Him?'
Suddenly, he gave a terrible howl of pain.
The Beloved One had grabbed him by the hand and had pressed him to the ground.

'You are foolish and helpless,'
The Teacher said quietly and His cough had gone completely,
'Only in that you couldn't predict your downfall.
And you couldn't compete even with the weakest of these elders,
Who are at least strong in their faith and *The Law*,

Which they observe
When protecting people from you!
At least because they limit you in this world
They are worthy of respect
Around the fire, where you are merely permitted

But not invited.'
'What, you're not kicking me out?' the Greedy One howled,
Rubbing an aching wrist,
And brazenly settling down by the fire again.
'No, I won't,' the Beloved One said with a sigh.

'You forgive me, you fool,' the Greedy One grinned wolfishly.

'So what, you'll forgive Adolf the Austrian
If he appears by the fire at night?'
A ringing slap in the face deafened everyone sitting around the fire.
'It is not for you to judge and predict my actions,'

The Teacher said, his eyes flashing angrily.
The Greedy One whined but did not retreat into the darkness.
Here, we recognised the Bloodless One, but the elders and other people did not.
For a while it was silent.
Then one of the Samaritan women spoke to the Friend:

'Tell me, Kind man,
They say that if the Mashiah comes,
Everyone will know about it
Or, more precisely, *everyone instantly* will know and follow Him
For their salvation.

And you, elders, answer me this: is that what will happen?'
The Pharisees grew angry again, but so did the Galileans.
It was unseemly for a woman, and particularly a Samaritan,
To address a man, especially with such a question,
And they grew angry and cursed the heavens,

Without addressing the Samaritans directly.
The Greedy One perked up again:
'You say it to me, woman. I will interpret.
It has been like this and always will be,
That when peoples have no wish to speak to one another,

I'll be their interpreter.'
Cephas then silently took out his Hun sword
And he glared at the Bloodless One.
The latter recalled the previous night
And shut up.

'No, my dear woman,' the Friend said, 'it will not be like that, alas.
No announcement will appear in the sky
Or a global network, saying
Here comes the Saviour,
And the people would simply say,

Well, *at last*.
You know the most important thing is not to read of His appearance
Based on the dogma of books and the precise arithmetic of predictions.
The most important thing is not to determine His age,
Ethnic nationality or distinguishing features.

The most important thing is to be *ready* to see Him.
What does this mean?
It means that the advent of the Anointed One
Will not become a guessing game for priests,
Rather a test for those meeting and awaiting.

Perhaps it will take place in conditions
That violate *every* possible dogma,
But isn't the Lord of Worlds the greatest playwright?'
'My dear sir,' the woman objected politely,

'Then why should these dignified elders

Follow the letter of *The Law*, if everything can change
In an instant? And against their instructions?
Why would the Lord of the Universe destroy the authority of those
Who have served him all these years and millennia,
From generation to generation, truly and faithfully?

How can that be fair on His part?
Is He not the bearer of justice?'
The Teacher smiled and said,
'I know, my good woman, that you have a jug of water.
Please let us take a drink from it.'

The woman was taken aback
And, taking out the water, offered it to everyone.
No one said no.
'Look,' the Teacher went on,
'Water is *The Law*, and we know it is the same for everyone.

However, everyone will drink of it themselves, alone,
For if we all dived into the jug at the same time,
We'd smash the jug and spill the water.
One would take a gulp and pass it to a friend,
Another would let an elder drink first,

And a third would greedily drink more than the person next to him.
And, before the Lord of Worlds, we will stand alone
On Judgment Day.
Now imagine that this vessel is held by the elders
And these elders are being begged to give water to drink,

But they hold it and state that,
No, the day has not come, when one needs to drink,
And that someone should come forward to establish a queue.
At that time, someone dies of thirst,
Another waits patiently and a third rises up and takes the jug by force.

These are cruel dogmatists who have frankly lost touch with God.
They keep *The Law* as sacrosanct
But will they save the people?
Let's take another example: the elders are not so scholastic
And they give water to those who thirst for communion with the Lord.

But water has a tendency to run out.
Who will fill the jug after that?
And Someone will come and say, 'Let me fill the vessel',
But he will be told, 'No, this water is sacred
Because water has been added to it from the Zamzam Well.

Another kind would not do, for the consistency would alter.'
That Someone will say, 'But my water is sweet-tasting,
I'll offer it to the people and quench their thirst.
But he will be refused,
And people again will die of thirst.'

'But if this Someone comes, imitating the intonations of our Friend with sincerity,'

The Bloodless One said,
'And proceeds to add poison to the jug,
Which might kill those afflicted with thirst,
Shouldn't the dogmatists and scholastics stop him?'

'Yes,' the Beloved One smirked, 'without your comment,
The allegory really wouldn't have been complete.
Initially, the jar was filled by the Almighty,
And the water there was as pure as that flowing in the river through Eden.
Then, however, He passed the responsibility for filling it to the people.

The people were forced to look for clean wells
And top the jug up in small portions,
Opening it up for the innovations of a world that was rushing onwards.
It was here that the Bloodless One got involved;
Under the guise of innovations, unknown phenomena and events,

He took slowly to adding
Various poisons, drop by drop, into the Divine Water.
Do the keepers of *The Law* need to be reprimanded
For allowing this to happen? On the contrary,
If not for them, people would instantly have assumed a demonic appearance,

Having been fatally poisoned by the Bloodless One.
In place of *The Law*, a nightmarish conglomeration of
Evil and vice would rule, worst of all, masquerading as pure water.
And so, these elders abide by *The Law*,
Rushing about, doubting in their impotence but sacrificing themselves

To somehow, in the age of *non-appearance*,
Ensure that *The Law* never ceases to reach the people.
One day, however, there will be so much poison
That the first to drink from it would not simply drop dead,
But reappear as a demon and servant of the Bloodless One.

And these walking dead would soon
Come to fill the entire world.
It is then that that Someone would appear
And say, "I'll drink from the vessel and show you
That it's filled with death;

You'll see it's true, as I'll die instantly."
"No," the elders will reply, "the King must drink first!
And only then, his people and other peoples."
But the Someone will say, "No! The King will drink and then die."
The elders won't believe him,

Then someone will come and say,
"Let me drink, for I am the King!" "Well, seeing as you're the King, then drink!"
So, he drinks and dies, dropping the vessel and smashing it.
Then the elders will curse the man,
Saying he wasn't the King, for which he was punished with death!

But the Lord of Worlds is All-merciful and Beneficent.
He gives the elders a new vessel, again filled
With the original water.
And everything starts over again,

Until the time that God as allotted to the Bloodless One has come to an end.'

The woman gasped and said,
'So, who is He,
Who knows the initial tase of the water
And who is able to recognise poison therein?
Are there many of them, or does the Lord have only one?'

The Beloved Friend looked sad and he shivered from the cold.
John tenderly wrapped a white blanket around Him.
'There are few who know there's poison,' the Friend said. 'They're there and will continue to be.
They will see for sure what's inside the jug
And will tell people precisely

What true water should
Be there in the first instance.
However, if we talk of who is prepared to drink,
To die and convince others, as far as I know,
There is only one.'

'We will,' James, son of Zebedee suddenly exclaimed.
'We will drink Your water with You!
You see, we know now what Divine Water is!
And we know about Your fate!
We have no doubt and no fear!'

Then the Galileans and Samaritans kicked up a fuss
And pointed over at the Beloved One.
Then, the woman from Samaria stood up
And, approaching the Friend, bowed before Him:
'We recognised you, walking the mountain path,

You are the Mashiah, our Victor!'

The fire flared up in an ominous hue,
For the Greedy One had jumped in, irate.
'You stupid, reckless people!' He screamed from within.
You don't have to bow your head and follow the elders
Without trying to find changes in the world!

You foolish, primitive creatures!
You doom yourselves by believing!
You doom Him to an inglorious death!
Never, ever, ever
Will the sages recognise His royalty!

And they'll never recognise conformity to *The Law* in Him!
And you will never be able to
Keep your faith in Him
Under pressure not only from dogma,
But your own base doubts and cowardice.

What are these empty hopes even for?
Why this shameless waste of emotions?
Merely to plunge your sword into my wounds?
I'll pursue you across the ground like a hovering kite,
Drive you round corners and through ditches, feed you to lions and hyenas!

You'll know only about the consistency of God's water,
But the composition of my exquisite poison, too,
Hidden and wonderful, delicious and enticing!
You'll regret a hundred, a thousand times
That the *word* has sounded again today!'

The Greedy One flashed a thousand sparks and was gone.
It was only then that everyone realised
Who had been singing the awful songs round our fire.
The woman brimmed all the more with faith
And now said firmly,

'I mean no affront to the elder and the accepted norms,
And I do not deny the earthly thrones and their masters,
But in the name of our last hope
I say: You are the Mashiah!
And if you refuse your mouthful,

Hide from us, flee to distant lands
So that we might never see you,
But just deliver us from the news that you refused
To accept your fate and fled,
For what will we be left with

But hunger and injustice,
But darkness and time stood still,
But kings who live in concert with the Bloodless One,
But our own vices to which we succumb,
But our children, born without faith and that *non-appearance!*

But the expectation of a new war,
But the feelings, tagged with monetary value,
But flight into intoxication and the twilight of consciousness?!
All that you see as so constant
In this world, changing and yet unchanging?'

She finished speaking and burst into tears.
The Pharisees were indignant and moved away from the fire,
Along the road to be further from the heresy that had been spoken.
But they stopped somewhere in the darkness and spoke.
After a while one of them returned.

'My name is Nicodemus,' he addressed the Beloved Friend.
'I was sent by the Galilean and Jewish wise men
Whom You offered
Your hospitality by the fire.
They asked me to relay this to You.

We will close our eyes to that heresy
We heard about the Mashiah,
That rebellion You are staging,
Against the authorities,
Pushing the people into recognising You as someone

Who perhaps You are by family or tribe,
But who you cannot become through lack of strength

And political will to fight
The Edomite and Roman usurpers.
We will not report You to the authorities or the high priests,

But on one condition:
Stop your free-thinking and leave.
Emigrate, buy yourself a house in the Alps,
Write your memoirs, but leave the long-suffering land of Canaan alone.
It hurts us too much

What you are awakening so cruelly in people,
Seducing them with illusions and empty hopes.
As an alternative, there is another suggestion:
Come to Jerusalem before Passover,
Come to the Temple and stand before

The Tzaddukim high priests,
Relate Your family tree to them and then,
As patriots of our Homeland, we'll create a secret order,
Who will, to start with, overthrow the Edomite usurpers
And then the Roman authorities, when the time comes.

You see, Hasmonean royal blood
Is such a find for us.
If you knew that the burden of empty hopes and expectations
Is not only the prerogative of the poor and disadvantaged,
But also those whose minds can embrace the depths of injustice.'

The Beloved Teacher fell silent
And said, 'Go in peace.
You will learn about My decision from the news of people.
Thank you for your patience and wisdom.'
And Nicodemus departed into the night after the wise men.

We were not accustomed to seeing the Teacher like this,
And in this situation himself.
'Why didn't you destroy them with your inspirational power?'
Peter asked. 'Why didn't you say, like always,
The sevenfold *woe unto you*?

Why didn't you get into a heated argument with them
About the interpretation of *The Law*?
Why didn't you cast them into despair, as You've done so many times,
Challenging their conservatism and inertia?'
The Beloved Friend coughed and spoke calmly:

'Every day presents a lesson.
There it is, that *Pharisee breeding*.
Beware of it.
After all, what did that wise man just say?
"We are kind," he said, "But You must not be Yourself."

What does that mean?
It means that both these notions
Constitute *their* conversation with themselves.
They tell themselves that they are kind,
And what I must do according to their understanding.

But what do they leave Me, you or others?
Nothing. What a wonderful skill it is
To give people a choice
Without actually giving it to them.
You know what's most important?

Most important is they themselves were thrown into doubt,
Forcing them to rush about from pillar to post,
Seeking an advantage between their own hopes
That force them to see what's actually happening
Outside the jug that awaits the thirsty

And the desire to preserve the status quo at the same time,
So as to have the opportunity, in case of failure,
To return to one's previous, quiet way of life
And pretend that nothing has happened
And that the water that the Lord has not replenished is inexhaustible.'

The Samaritans also bowed to Him and went on their way;
Anxious but high spirits reigned among them.
The Galileans bowed to Him,
Saying, 'and we have drunk from his jug,'
And they disappeared into the dawn haze.

Only the wealthy young man remained and he asked the Teacher,
'If I give you *a third* of my riches,
Can you ask God for salvation for me?'
'We have no need for your riches,' the Beloved One replied,
'But are you prepared to see *a third* of God?'

The young man was embarrassed, but went on:
'How will I know how much I need to give?
Perhaps You could ask Him for me?'
'Haggling with God through an interpreter
Is the same as a camel going

Through the eye of a needle,'
The Friend replied with a smile.
'Why don't you ask Him yourself?'
'But how will I know that He will answer me?'
The lad gaped.

'But how did you find out what He is asking?'
The Teacher answered calmly.
The confused rich lad
Took to his horse and rode off into the night, apparently thinking
That chance meetings are not that good for one's peace of mind.

'And now, brethren, tell me this,' the Beloved One turned to us,
You heard the choice that the Pharisees gave me.
What should I choose?
Even if the fate of your Friend is foretold,
No one can take away My choice.

Do you want to become close to the King of the Jews?
Rule the country and distribute the benefits,

574

Without forgetting your trunk in the process?
Do you want peace in distant lands,
Dedicating the rest of your life to telling stories about our interesting past?

Who am I for you? That's for you to decide.
Don't fear the wrath or the censure of My Father,
Who showed Me My path.
Man's choice is the thing
Against which any power of the Heavenly Throne is powerless,

Because He rules not by decree, rather by Judgment.
But let me warn you, if you come with me to Jerusalem,
You will drink your fill from the sacred jug.
So, I say: only one will remain alive
And he will carry the burden of *The Word* for all of us and for himself.'

'You are the Mashiah,' Cephas said,
Replenishing the water of the Lord's spring.
You are the One we are waiting for, but not to reign
In the lands of the tribes that we know.
You are the master of the Kingdom that comes to us in our dreams,

And which will soon meet us in the flesh.
We have no need for earthly thrones; we abandoned them
When we were in different lands.
We do not wish to be courtiers there,
Where my sword will become an instrument of persuasion.

And then, well, we all know about the cycle of time,
Repeating the inevitable every time.
You might say that we have a choice,
This is not a choice of convictions or, thus, of actions either.
May that which is preordained repeat itself many times over.'

'Answer just one question, Rabbi,'
Thomas stepped forward.
If he is the Only One and Omnipresent,
And You call Him Your Father,
Who are You to Him – the Son of God? Or are you God?'

The Beloved Teacher smiled and said,
'I knew, Thomas, that it would be you who would ask that millennial question.
What answer do you expect from Me?
If you expect a *yes*, then it's yes.
If you expect a *no*, then it's no.

Now listen to what I want to ask.
When I ride on a donkey, who am I – God?
No, I am a son of man, just like you.
When I eat bread and honey with you, who am I – God?
No, I am the same as you – soul clothed in flesh.

And you, Thomas, when you gaze at length at the sky,
What do you see?
First, you see clouds, then your fantasies, then eternity.
And then you see yourself!
But am I there?

What you are in fact asking is not who I am,
But how I differ from you, Thomas, isn't that right?
Imagine there are many people in the synagogue,
And suddenly a fire breaks out. God is in whom?
In the one who opens the doors and *saves* everyone.

So, I am the door.
But tomorrow it might be you standing next to the door and saving everyone.
If people seek but cannot find, pondering and in despair
And someone comes and tells *The Word*
That gives them an answer to what they seek, in whom is God?

So, I am *The Word*.
But tomorrow, Cephas might say *The Word* and *save* the desperate.
So, many people have gathered and they seek the truth;
One person comes and shows them
Something they haven't noticed; in whom is God?

So, I am Truth.
But in a year, James will be the one who found the Truth and gave it to the people
So, it is not only who I am that's important,
But when I am? In what moment?
When I was tormented by doubt and fear, who was I?

Thomas, and you, brethren,
Don't try to give shape to something
That has no shape.
Don't try to put something into words
When that something is what defines us.

We are all Sons of Man
And we are all Sons of God.
If you say that, since God is in every person
And there are a billion of us, that means I have a billionth part of God in me.
Well, if you want to be a billionth part, you be that.

Just remember, that young lad who was just searching
Refused to see just a third of God.
He will try to comprehend Him in His entirety.
And what about you?
Are you willing to accept less?

Tell me – I will try many years
To explain God; I will study many sciences,
I'll read a lots of scientific evidence
And, in the end, I will come to
Some final, logical formula.

Well then, if you *believe* this formula,
You are welcome.
But take a look around you –
Will you demand that your beloved provides
Logic-based, scientific evidence of her love for you?

Maybe it's easier just to wake up one day
And realise that, looking at you, God sees you as a son,

576

Just as one day you realise that
This is your greatest love, this, your fate and your door to earthly love.
What's stopping you finding your door to heaven right now?

What's so hard, you might ask?
Why won't a billion people wake up one day
And say that they believe?
Then the Golden Age would return.
Then, the Bloodless One would stop adding poison to the jug.

O, the difficulty is that
When you say, *I am The Word! I am The Truth! I am the door!*
When you say to Him, *I am your Son!*
When you say to the people, *I am the Shepherd!*
Will that be true?

Not true in the sense that you are deceiving,
Engaging in wishful thinking,
Substituting notions – this means nothing.
The Lord of Worlds will see through any deception in an instant
And return this knowledge to you;

You will get your fill of this returned understanding that you are lying.
That means you will serve another master,
The master of deceit, substitution, falsehoods and hypocrisy.
Only when it is true and you say *I am The Truth!*
Will it be *The Truth.*

Only when it is *His Word* and you say *I am The Word!*
Will it be *The Word.*
How does one understand, realise, guess or sense
That this moment has come?
Who should you ask? Who will send a sign? Who will explain

At what moment shouting *Ana al-Haqq!* would be heresy,
And at what moment God will acknowledge you as his true son
And give you the Shepherd's crook, The Word and The Name?
And give you Love, The Mission and Confidence?
And give you a jug of water to be cleansed?

I don't have clear answers to this question.
There is only the life that we lived together,
The Path that we walked together.
If we judge on their basis, two things are enough,
Which have brought us closer to the door.

This is the Road,
Taking which, we say *we are searching!*
And that is being Good, Kind Men.
Calling themselves that one day and not changing this;
There is a sure way to that night which one day,

When the Palestinian rain falls, we can say to ourselves,
I did not turn off the Path that twists on earth,
But goes straight in the sky.
I did not deceive myself, being a Good, Kind Man,
And a Beloved Friend for my friends.

In the deeds I did and in making decisions,
I spoke with Him and He answered me.
I spoke only with Him; I wouldn't agree to anything less.
He inspired me and I accepted my fate.
So, the day will come and I will say *Ana al-Haqq! – I am The Truth!*

And this will prove to be the truth, even if, in the next moment,
My Heavenly Father were to take me from this world.
And I will leave it with no regret.
That's because, he who has one day told himself *I am Him*
Assumes the burden of His solitude and immortality.'

'Tell me, Rabbi,' Judas Iscariot said,
'Such a solution, at first glance, appears too simple –
Being a Good, Kind Man.
Isn't that what a lot of people think of themselves?'
'Quite the opposite, Judas,' the Friend replied.

Going out onto the road, doing nothing
And teaching everyone to be smarter is simple.
But being a Good, Kind Man – that is the hardest thing of all,
Especially if it's not *you* assessing it, but Him.'
'But how do you know how He assesses things?

And how does this assessment differ from mine?' Judas did not let up.
'Just ask yourself honestly, with whom have you just been speaking,
With Him, or with yourself?
And you'll see that you cannot hide the true answer,
Even if you really want to.

And if you deceive yourself,
The Almighty will find a way to convey His assessment to you.
But if you dig your heels in and close your eyes inside,
Very soon you'll find yourself a different friend,
Sitting nearby in Bloodless form and biting his nails.

So, listen and hear what I say, my beloved friends!'
The Teacher's cough had disappeared and his voice was now
Like Gabriel's Horn, so powerful and so... beautiful.
He stood up, spread his arms like a Tengri cross
(Back then, we didn't know what else it was like):

'Truly I say to you,
Everyone chooses his own Kingdom;
If he doesn't, then others will choose for him.
Everyone chooses his own Shepherd;
If he doesn't, then others will choose for him.

The Shepherd is chosen merely to
See which Road to follow.
You have to speak with the Almighty Father yourself,
To be Good, Kind Men
And daughters.

Don't ask him for anything, just one day,
Just one moment,

When you can say, *I am Him!*
And, in doing so, remain true to Heaven,
And not to the earthly judges, including yourselves.

He who says *He was Christ!* says,
"He's the one to answer; I'm off to bed."
He who says *He is the Mashiah!* says,
"He's the one to fight the Dajjal;
I'll join the victor."

He who says *God, besides me, he's there!*
Has drunk the Bloodless One's poison.
He who says *God is not me!*
Says, "I am not here either, and nor is my soul."
He who says "I do not acknowledge Him as my Father!

For I have a natural father,
Here he is,
And he gave me my name and surname!!
Loses both.'
'But how can that be?' Thomas exclaimed.

'Surely, we can say "I am my earthly father?!"'
'That is why,' the Teacher answered calmly,
'People are given old age and the infirmity of parents,
So they might understand that this too is possible.
So that we might understand there is no true primary and secondary.'

'And if someone has never seen a father or mother,'
James, son of Alphaeus asked, perturbed.
'If they have been deprived of paternal and maternal affection?
The path to love for them must be many times harder.
Surely, the fear of loneliness is stronger in them?'

The Teacher's head dropped to his chest,
And sadness clouded his brow:
'That, then, is a child,' He said quietly,
'Already doomed to the Road as their choice of Path.
That means, he speaks with God from the outset.

Therefore, anyone who offends an orphan
Has been affected by the Greedy One's poison.
And he will never, ever, ever enter
Even the open door of the Kingdom of Heaven,
And he will remain deaf to the calls of the Shepherd.'

'And if a man is faced with a choice,'
John exclaimed,
'To act as his natural father says
Or in a different way, as the Heavenly Father says to him?
And if that choice is to wrong an orphan

But save thousands?
And if the choice is to become evil and bad,
But protect the Fatherland?'
'This is precisely that moment, that choice,' the Teacher replied.
'It is that existentialism, that anguish

When, perhaps, that moment comes,
When you go straight up to the peak
That enables you to cry out *I am The Truth!*
And to be *The Truth* as your choice.
To give yourself to Him completely without condition,

To take Him into yourself entirely, not agreeing just to a third,
To be true, open and in love.
To be vulnerable, strong and cruel,
To see eternity, the loneliness in choice and the fear of doubt,
To be completely Him and completely yourself!

There, let me tell you truly, brethren.
The day is near when I will have to say,
Ana al-Haqq! *I am Him!*
The world will again be put to the test to see if there is peace there.
It will kill Me, but I am destined to conquer the world.

Not killing it, not wounding it with arrows of ire,
But striking it with rays from a mirror
That reflects his very self back at him.
They will say that He is higher than us,
Let them therefore humiliate themselves.

Others will say that He is beneath us,
So, let them revel in their greatness.
But none of them can say,
I am Him!
And neither can you straight away.

I told you that one of you will stay alive
And will say *I am The Word!* and they'll not be lying.
But I will not say who that will be.
This is not for fate to decide
But the man himself. And he will say *Ana al-Haqq!*

And show people where the poisoned waters flow
That they must seek on the Road.
You will all do that too,
But I say to you truly: he who gets to the end,
Will be presented at a feast

With the jug of the panhuman soul
That seeks cleansing of the Bloodless One's poison.
And he will drink from it.
And I will be in it.
And he will be Me.'

'No, no!' the warriors Peter and the two Jameses cried.
'How can we allow You to be killed?
This will not happen!
You said there is a choice. Here it is:
We won't let a hair fall from Your head!

May the Great Messengers send You messages,
That Your fate is foretold.

But who asked us if we were prepared
To bleat like cuddly lambs and watch over the death of our Friend
At the hands of those who are not worthy of a hair on Your head?!'

The Beloved One suddenly appeared weary
And he back sat down on the ground; John carefully covering him.
'I say truly to you,' the Teacher said
Quietly and coughing again,
'If I don't go now,

Then I will deprive you, too, of your moment,
When you are destined to become True ones.
If somehow I can decide about My life,
I cannot when it comes to yours – everything has already been done.
I don't want to be the one to take that moment from you,

When you are able to say *I am The Word!*
I no longer have this right.
But I'll say one more thing,
To stop a sense of doom reigning in your souls
Instead of the triumph of conquering the world.

Together we learn not only a lesson of death,
But one of immortality too.
After all, without immortality, what is the point of exclaiming
I am Him? There is none.
I don't know how things will turn out.

But our Path of knowledge has not ended yet.
You see, the cup of the Path of our deeds has not yet been emptied.
So, in concluding the conversation, I will say to you, Thomas,
There is nothing that distinguishes us from one another,
But for today, everything does.

Nothing, because my day already sees me and I, it.
And you have to see the same day, only your own.
And *everything*, because I already see my door,
And you will still cry out for my *salvation* here on earth
When I speak to you about *salvation* everywhere.

And forever.'

Verse 33. The Great World Revolution

'Tell me, Andrew, about your Path to this day.'
The landline rang so obstinately
That it was actually able to wake me.
It was an uncomfortable ring,
As, for many years, I had only answered my mobile.

There were two options:
Either Mum had forgotten how to use her mobile,
Or the state was calling.
I had not the slightest wish
To speak with the state –

What could they say to me that was good?
What could they talk to me about
As part of my system of values
And in my language?
Right, nothing.

We live in different worlds.
The only difference is that, before,
Those who departed into their cave
After losing to this world,
Felt weaker than it.

This was not the case with me.
They are slaves to ancient analogue customs.
I am master of the digital world.
Well, all right, not exactly master,
But I can still ruin a hundred breakfasts and dinners for them.

Even their understanding of themselves as the state
Is something I find funny.
I can imagine how frozen stiff that poor border guard must feel
As I pass by him,
A light symbol of the intangible: a number, a formula.

But he just stands there freezing,
Thinking he is this insurmountable barrier
Between the expanses of two countries.
He is the personification of this old state,
Built according to the analogue customs of empty realities.

Perhaps it's even me, this border guard,
Cut off from the worldwide web,
His hair cut, a uniform donned
And placed in the middle of the forest-steppes
To preserve the peace and quiet of some stupid, conservative bureaucrats.

So, where was I? Ah, yes. The landline.
I raked through a heap of papers, stickers
And leftover pizza boxes,
Before eventually finding the telephone.
Incredible, I thought, that

The battery hadn't died. A miracle, in fact.
Raising my head above the pillow,
I looked to see if the modem light was flashing
As I'd set the computer to reboot,
Because I'd wondered for a while whether the monitor was off or the whole computer.

Realising that the computer was fine and only the monitor had gone to sleep,
I calmed down.
I picked up the phone apprehensively, making
My voice sound clear and awake,
So I wouldn't need to explain to Mum why I was sleeping during the day.

'Hello, Andrew, hello!'
The receiver yelled suspiciously optimistically,
While the voice was not Mum's at all.
'Hello, Andrew? I didn't wake you, did I?'
My brain searched for that language bar in the corner.

Tap-tap. Ah, right. English. 'Yes? Who is this?'
And why did I need to be polite?
'Andrew, it's me, Raj!
Rise and shine, Moscow! Come on, wake up!
I urgently needed your brain

To understand what I had to tell you.'
Raj... he had been on my course at Lumumba.
'Hey, Raj, I'm not asleep.'
A lie as always but this didn't bother Raj on the other end.
'Allo, Andrey,' he switched into Russian.

Damn. That language bar again. Tap-tap Russian.
'Andrey, can you come to LA?
And as soon as possible.'
What the hell? LA – where is that? Out in Chukotka? Buryatia?
'Andrey (there followed an intelligible student-hostel tirade in Russian).

Get a flight to California right now!
The tickets are already booked and paid for.
Those meeting you are footing the bill for everything.
Basically, there's this project – you'll fricking love it!
It's pretty much what we were dreaming about at uni.

All you need to do is get off your arse
And get over here, you hear me?!
In a word, give yourself a reboot, have a wash,
And I'll be waiting for you in Los Angeles.
And don't you dare protest

Or I'll send *rakshasas*[237] and a hundred thousand viruses!'
Unbelievable, what can I say?
It was only as I began to wake up that I thought,
Yeah, right, Rajpal Maninder Singh!
California! No invitation, no visa, no passport!

---

[237] *Rakshasas* – evil demons in Hinduism.

At that moment, the doorbell rang.
I opened it, doing my best to conceal my cornflower blue underpants
And the interior of my hovel they called home.
A smiling young man stood on the doorstep,
Of a Central Moscow nationality I couldn't place.

'Andrey? Hello! Are you Andrey Sergeevich First-Called?[238]
A package for you – a passport, invitation and much more besides.
Please come tomorrow at nine hundred hours
To the US Embassy for an interview.
Good bye.'

What a turn up! What would I tell Mum?
Although she wouldn't really be hearing anything new.
What has this country of evergreen tomatoes ever got?
Everything evergreen apart from a regular
Human salary?

A country where projects are launched with pretentious fanfare
And then rapidly peter out to nothing once there's nothing left to steal?
Where the customer comes in two types: the Neanderthals,
Who stubbornly refuse to understand that it's not me but they who need it
And kindly chaps who instantly hand you a document

With *recognizance not to leave* for five hundred years.
No thank you.
It'd be better dealing with the hard workers from Bangalore
And the big heads from Silicon Valley
While gumption still permits.

And while you still have friends like Rajpal.
But... there are *chaps* like these in any country,
From all manner of awful intelligence agencies
Who, smiling with cowboy teeth, draw you into bondage
Which, over the ocean there, really

Didn't appeal to me, as a Russian.
We have plenty of that promised land over here.
However, judging by my intensive correspondence with Raj,
He always worked specifically in business projects,
Doing his best to avoid the state's warm embraces.

I don't like rules I don't understand.
All the same, the way I saw it was that
No one was stopping me going
And finding out about everything once there.
Again, it's not every day you get to travel to

Yankee-land at someone else's expense.
There were two reasons for me to go. One,
I wanted to find new and interesting things to do,
Which would require dynamic and contemporary solutions,
And not like over here where they either rush ahead like madmen

Or sit around for six months waiting for funding,

---

[238] *Andrey Pervozvanny* refers to Andrew the Apostle, also known as *First-Called*.

Which depends on some slippery customer
With ambitions of a post-industrialist slave owner.
The second reason was that I'd spent an awful lot of money lately,
And my prospects at home were all rather wishy-washy.

All right, I'll square with you –
I have a dark side to my character
And I can't get along with just anyone,
Especially when it comes to ambitious assignments,
The implementation of which depends on stupid bureaucrats,

Who think more about their dress code
Than about the search for
New and interesting solutions.
I've had so many conflicts
That, naturally, ended with my defeat.

Hammering away at bank databases
Was not for me.
It's not that my freedom is worth more,
It's just that the Russian *zone* is the death knell,
The death knell of what I'd like to have been doing my entire life.

And another thing: a big dream of mine
Was to create or be involved in a project
Not necessarily one to make a name for myself in the world,
Rather that, in my own eyes,
I'd appear a titan of thought and the mastermind of a technological breakthrough.

Emerging at the gates at LA International,
I was met by my good friend
Rajpal Singh, my best mate,
Who usually grinned white teeth
Through a dark beard,

In his ubiquitous turban,
That never-ending butt of student jokes.
My body and mind were still tormented
By the drastic change in time zones,
But after just five minutes of noisy, chummy embraces,

I was listening attentively to Rajpal,
Who, incidentally, had picked me up in an amazing limo.
'Well, spit it out, Raj, what's this project?
First of all, why Los Angeles and not Frisco?'[239]
'Hold on, Andrew, one thing at a time.'

We reached the hotel and dropped of my things
Before sitting in some boring café.
'Basically, Andrew,' said Rajpal, looking me in the eye,
'We're in Los Angeles because this is where
The selection process for the project is being held.

I'll say right from the off – thanks to me, to a certain extent,
You have no competition.'

---

[239] Frisco – San Francisco, the Californian city closest to Silicon Valley.

I ceremoniously held out my hand to Raj and made a mock bow.
He responded with equal play-acting.
'But why, might I ask?' I enquired.

'Is it because it's a secret Sikh conspiracy project
For world domination an you're the Grand Dragon?'
Rajpal laughed, but then turned serious.
'As for whose project this is, Andrew,
The customer, how can I put it more accurately, is the United States Government.'

Wowzer! Seeing me frown,
Raj hurriedly grabbed my hand.
'But that's not all. Hold off with the face pulling!
Of course, it is those same *theys* who are the customer here,
Sleek chaps, the kind you can't stand, but...

The project doesn't belong entire to the USA;
Twenty countries have joined forces here.
I hope you've heard something about the G20?'
'Yes, of course,' I muttered and pulled out my hand. 'I'm not a complete idiot, you know?'
'So,' Raj went on, 'Our Russian chaps

Have full representation in the project
And your bloody Russian anti-Yank patriotism
Can rest easy –
Your Homeland wants you here too,'
He shrugged his shoulders. 'And mine wants me too.'

Haha! And there I'd been wondering,
How, by some miracle,
I had suddenly found myself with an international passport.
That lad who had brought it, too,
Had looked nothing like a travel agent...

'All right, Raj, let it be your way,
Although, you know, if there'd been anyone else other than you here,
I don't know how I'd have behaved.'
Raj nodded in satisfaction, although he was already focused on his ice cream.
'So, what's this project about?'

Rajpal nodded, his mouth full,
Then he carefully wiped his lips
And looked for an age for white drops of ice cream in his beard.
I wanted to joke as usual, but I held back, just smiled.
Finally, my friend finished his beard preening and swallowed his ice cream.

'Now this, Andrew, is something I shouldn't tell you.
At least, for now. There is all the same a certain regime of secrecy here.
But you won't have long to wait.
Let the selection process run its official course,
And you'll learn all about it for yourself first hand.'

I must admit that the selection process
Did indeed pass as a pure formality.
And then a few days later,
Those who had been inducted,
Were gathered in a small, rather cosy room.

Everyone looked round with interest,
To capture those first impressions of the people
With whom they would soon need to work closely.
Attention was drawn to the pleasant, agreeable
And the disagreeable upstarts, too,

Who were overly confident of themselves.
However, this is generally the usual feeling one gets in a new environment
Among new people.
A smart, elderly man entered the room,
For some reason dressed in military uniform.

'You can call me General Johnson.
Easy to remember and not too far from the truth,'
The military man began.
All right, a general – that was promising.
Apparently, a certain indication of the project's importance.

'Congratulations on having been accepted
Into the ranks of those destined to put in practice
One of the most ambitious projects
That humanity has ever set its sights on!'
Sporadic applause broke out in the room –

As always, the Americans were earnest and energetic,
While everyone else was sluggish and with only just a sufficient degree of politeness.
'Dear friends,' the General said, unceremoniously ignoring his chair
And sitting on the table in the middle of the room.
'I'll begin with some general organisational matters,

And then I'll move onto the essence of why we're here.
So, in this general composition,
You will meet only at the project's third level.
Today, we will divide you into three groups,
Which, for the first two levels,

Will operate fairly autonomously from one another,
Communicating only over networks and using them to
Exchange ongoing technical and theoretical documentation.
As you can see, the project managers are
Banking on young specialists.

Moreover, I will say with confidence, given that I have read the files on each of you,
That no one here has ever been fully immersed
In the essence of the task that lies ahead.
Perhaps some of you have occasionally come close to similar solutions,
But no more than that.

What this choice?
Primarily because the work we
Will have to do
Comes after a huge amount of scientific and theoretical research
By the greatest scientific minds of many different countries.

However, what concerns us most is the practical solution to the task at hand,
Which is often harmed by excessive immersion

In theory, as, unfortunately, this takes us far
From the actual achievement of the final result.
This doesn't mean that you'll be cut off from

Studying the theoretical basis of
What has already been achieved and researched.
However, put it this way, this knowledge will be given to you in doses
As each of the project tasks are completed.
This dosed supply is also conditional,

Because no one will restrict your access
To what the Internet has to offer,
And you, as masters of your craft,
Will still get your hands on the information you want.
Therefore, you simply won't get scientific guides on the given subject.

What you will discover and study for yourselves
Shall be the fruits of your labour.
We consciously apply an approach where,
Possibly, at some point,
You will see only a segmented picture

Of the theoretical and practical research on this issue.
There are a number of excellent theoretical physicists among you,
Also so that you might have the opportunity
To see, perhaps, more efficient and shorter routes
To the goal that we will designate for you.

This is a conscious risk,
Because, by simplifying the initial conditions,
The complexity of the task itself doesn't reduce at all,
Both on the level of physics and mathematics,
And on the level of an interdisciplinary research method.

But this is the risk of the project managers.
Of course, no one determines ceilings for you
Or corridors to follow to resolve set tasks.
A little more about the organisation
And we'll move onto formulating multi-stage goal-setting.

Three groups will be formed: A, B and C.
Group A is the Analysis Group,
B is Technical Solutions
And C is the Synthesis Group.
You will operate over the first two stages in this structure.

A joint group will be formed at the third stage,
Whose objective will involve taking the project to the end.
Group A will be stationed in Silicon Valley,
Where a separate complex has been created for its work,
Specially equipped for the group's tasks.

The Technical Solutions Group will move to Boston tomorrow.
Why the Group's base is to be located there
Is something, I think, that needs no explanation.
The Group C complex is located in Aspen, Colorado,
In the immediate vicinity of SCI, the Santa Fe Institute on Complexity.

At the third stage, the joint group will move
Directly to Santa Fe in New Mexico,
Where it shall complete work on the set objectives.
And now, please listen to the lists,
To learn what group you're in.'

The boring process of listing unknown last names
Took some time.
So, there were three items of use and which I understood:
The team was so colourful and multinational,
And that made me believe what Rajpal had told me.

The second thing was that I was in the Analysis Group.
The third, that my friend Raj was in the Synthesis Group.
What did that mean? For now I was completely in the dark.
However, I had the patience:
The situation was becoming all the more intriguing

And that meant it was interesting.
General Johnson waited patiently
While his assistant, a large girl in glasses,
Called out names, learning as she went that she was unable
To pronounce the majority of them, and answered
A number of basic questions.

Then, with a nod of thanks to his profusely perspiring assistant, he continued:
'Today we have our first and last initiation conversation
For everyone simultaneously.
Therefore, please listen carefully to everything
I am about to say.

If we have to meet again like this,
It will be only because the project has entered a crisis
At the very first stages.
I don't wish this for you or for myself.
However, I sincerely hope it won't come to that.

Moving on. At your respective locations
You'll be introduced to the group curators
With whom you will have to address other questions
And find answers to them.
Now, please dim the lights for the presentation.

The age of supercomputers has presented humanity
With incredibly wide-ranging opportunities.
There is no point focusing on their successful use
In physics, chemistry and even in biology.
Our goal (attention!) is to formulate and solve a *super task*

In the application of nonlinear science and synergetics
On the development of modelling and forecasts
Of historical processes.
Specifically, we have to understand
The conditions and the probable future advent of...
(The General paused before moving to the next slide)
World Social Revolution.'

The audience's reaction was very mixed.
Someone gasped in surprise,
Another was silent and tense,

While a third smirked with open disbelief.
'I understand the scepticism of some of you,'
Johnson went on unperturbed.
'It evidently comes from those who know
Nonlinear dynamic systems, chaos theory and so on first-hand.

Well, let me respond as follows.
First, if we are speaking of existing achievements,
The virtual forecasting of social phenomena
Has long-since been a reality of our present.
We already know how to work with multi-level sets of indicators,

Enabling us to simulate military operations and
Election results, calculate the prospective policies
That have, at a given stage, the maximum potential.
We can also forecast local revolutionary processes
In separate countries.

We have the ability to predict
A pretty accurate development of monetary phenomena,
And, overall, in the economies of entire regions,
For the simple reason that, in these areas
There is a large quantity of deterministic indicators.

Second, in any case, mathematical modelling
Is of interest in practical terms
Only as an additional tool
For analysts, experts and
Decision-makers.

Accordingly, and third, if we get a tool
Albeit for *soft modelling*,
Which, as a minimum, can outline in general terms
The fluctuations that we ought to avoid in future,
To avoid disaster,

Then we would be able to consider the project a success.
However, there are a number of problems,
Solving which is key
For all human civilisation.
For such problems of a truly civilisational scale,

It is not enough simply to use supercomputers
As a simple machine for calculating
The infinite variability of development vectors,
In which there is just no point, because the maximal nature of choice
Destroys the very notion of choice.

We are really counting on the fact
That the mass of experiments we have planned
Will help us achieve a decisive convergence
Of humanities and exact sciences,
And will create the launch pad we need for this.

Naturally, it will need to be supplemented and developed moving on,
But the breakthrough would have arrived and this is important.
We need to expand the *forecasting horizons* decisively,
And start adding clarity to one of the key questions
Of human civilisation –

There are, after all, universal laws governing social development,
Or are there not?
What are the limits of chaos in the development of societies?
When do we see an infinite iteration
Of communities, relationships, cities and civilisations
As only an intuitive vision of the patterns of their development?

Guys, think about this one thing:
King Priam had a dozen solutions for
How to deal with the Cyclopean horse of Odysseus:
Burn it, chop it up, for instance. Or, in the end,
Force someone simply to look what was inside.

But he made the one and only
And simple decision to bring the horse into Troy,
And this decision put paid to hundreds of years
Of the Trojans' Mediterranean power and
Ten years of its courageous defence.'

'But, General Johnson,' we suddenly heard the voice of the smart Rajpal,
'Well, that was a bifurcation point for the Trojans,
Who sailed away to Italy and founded Rome –
A civilisation no less great and even more powerful.'
'I see you are familiar with Toynbee's theory of civilisations.

That's marvellous,' Johnson said, his voice betraying
He was happy with the direction the discussion was taking.
'However! That's if you have somewhere to sail and build a new city!
The global crisis today tells us that
There might be hundreds of *Priam's decisions*,

But the destruction of humanity
Would require but one, am I right?
Well, let's say *might* require but one.
Therefore, a current understanding of basic development algorithms
For what we call human civilisation

Is not simply a dispute between several belief systems.
It is an understanding that the opportunity to model and forecast
Is where the potential for our overall survival lays.
And if we say that common civilisation
Has long-since lost the focal character of individual civilisations,

Then we should also talk about the fact
That we need to have, albeit in general terms,
An understanding of the basic algorithms for its development, destruction,
Break-up, genesis, growth... whatever!
For now, this is an unaffordable luxury

To see one part of the world through the eyes of Confucius,

Another through the eyes of Spengler and a third, through those of Gumilyov.
As if, in the end, one doesn't have to view the world
Through the eyes of the Mitochondrial Eve[240],
Only deprived of all the natural beauties of this world,

Turned by people into desert.
Friends, let's move from the big and the complex
To more mundane matters.
First, about the method.
There are several, as you can understand. Each stage

Has its own characteristic methods.
At the first stage,
This is the method of *The Primitivism of Empirical Analysis*.
So, what are its main components?
First of all, an understanding that history

It is a multidimensional model
Where changes occur
In such multiple dimensions
That, from a mathematical point of view,
They form a nonlinear dynamic system as a whole,

Or chaos, which is extremely dependent on the slightest changes to
Initial conditions.
I think that many of you here are familiar with the concept of the *butterfly effect*.
With such an understanding of history, creating its theoretical models
Is not so much difficult as almost impossible.

This is primarily because, when you analyse,
Splitting events into many typological components,
You go so deep into the wilds of your own knowledge,
That you can't formulate macro-algorithms,
Remaining all the time on an excessively detailed level

Of micro-algorithms, which are often cycles of specific,
Rather than having systemic influence.
With that, the better the specialist,
The more variable and, therefore, the more unpredictable the wilds.
But that's not scary either.

What is frightening is that many initial conditions,
Which are key in historical events,
Are not quantifiable at all,
And, thus, cannot be subjected to any mathematical,
Comparative definition.

What did this lead to before?
To the fact that, on the one hand,
Clever physicists and mathematicians got together,
While, on the other, historians,

---

[240] Mitochondrial Eve – the name given by molecular biologists to an abstract woman believed to be the closest ancestor of all humans of the species *Homo sapiens sapiens*.

In an attempt to reach at least some form of physicalism[241].

In the end they wallow in the things that don't unite them
And separate the exact sciences and humanities into different corners.
We came to one obvious
And one paradoxical solution.
The paradoxical solution is

That which, through effective management methods,
We can attract people
Who have absolutely no experience in any given field of
Exact sciences or humanities,
And sort them into groups of tasks, containing

The need for effectiveness in one instance
And the possibility of conscious primitivism in the other.
Of course, in their purest form it is impossible
To find such people; everyone has an outlook,
An education and, for that matter, the Internet.

Yet this is just a slight deviation from the principle
That is simply levelled by other methods
Of organisation and process management.
This is the paradoxical part of the solution,
Which involves counting

Not on the most knowledgeable people,
Rather those with the minimum of specialist knowledge.
To be more precise, the correct grouping of those
Who know and those who don't,
Depending on the goals of the group or the stage!

But the obvious solution is

That when we set about
Forming an empirical analytical base,
Creating the necessary initial conditions
For the subsequent forecast –
Meaning *systematic* historical information, as such –

We *know the end result* –
The generally accepted narrative of well-known events in history!
In other words, the bloc of the *unknowing*
Have almost no chance of being wrong,
For, in the end, what we might have is that

Rome lost to Carthage,
Wellington to Napoleon at Waterloo,
Reagan destroyed the USA and not Gorbachev, the USSR,
Or within Central America
There will be three Israels or something along those lines!

Put another way, we create a sequential circuit for the experiment,

---

[241] Physicalism – a concept of logical positivism. Proponents of physicalism make the value of any position of any science dependent on the possibility of translating it into the language of physics. Suggestions that do not lend themselves to such an operation are seen as devoid of scientific meaning.

Where the end link tests the one before it
For its conformity to existing knowledge
About the course of history which is basically
Known, albeit in general terms, with a permissible degree of accuracy.

Basically, the key milestones of the historical process
Will play a role for us of strange attractors[242],
To which, at the first stage, we'll
Be forced to give a role of known paradigms,
To isolate the stable features of the chaos of history.

To make it clearer for you,
I'll tell you about the algorithm for work at the first stage.
So, Group A, the analysts,
Is organised in such a way
That its participants have a fundamental historical,

And, no less important, historiographic education
From various schools around the world.
At the same time, these people have been selected
For, by the will of the market, it transpired that they were familiar, not through hearsay,
But on a decent level, with modern computer science.

Group B is formed of specialists,
Who are, for the most part, *pure programmers*,
Although there is a slight nuance here, which I'll cover a little later.
The third group, Group C, is formed from experts of different fields,
Who have skills in the synthesis of obtained results.

What does that mean at the first stage?
I will also explain this in order.
Please show the next slide.
So, the main focus in the first stage
Is placed on the interaction of groups A and B,

Because Group C will
Record mostly the observing functions
And functions pertaining to the control of the final model
To the picture of history that today we
Believe to be real.

Let's follow the path *from simple to complex.*

At first, the Analysis Group compiles and then submits to the Technical Group
Sets of indicators that can be determined.
Primarily, these include
Financial and economic data.
As a whole, we are aware of the dynamic of, say, the exchange rate of the Roman talent,

The stateira, drachma, tetradrachma, dinar and so on,
Which make it fairly understandable
Not only to track the ratios of currencies

---

[242] Attractors – a compact subset of the phase space of a dynamical system, all trajectories from a certain surrounding of which strive to it as time goes to infinity (Wikipedia). Here – certain fixed points that embody change trends in chaos of history towards a certain definition. Strange attractor – an attractor that is not regular. Again, strange attractors are different fixation points of intermediate results of a multidimensional history process.

Over two or three centuries,
But also to see the dynamic of changes.

The same applies to data on
Trade volumes, an understanding of its profitability and loss ratio
And so on.
This also includes indicators of population development –
Without interpretation – simply up or down.

The number of countries, cities and villages,
The taxed population, volumes of tribute,
Contributions, royal pledges,
Harvest indications, the number of dykes, dams,
Aqueducts, factories, plants and much more besides.

We are not starting this work from scratch.
The world's best research centres and universities
Have already provided us with dynamic tables,
Along with accompanying explanations of the qualitative changes
Behind most of the numbers and sets of data.

This entire array, after additional processing,
Is sent to Group B.
From a technical point of view,
The first level of simplification of empiricism is applied.
How does this work?

Very simple: the final material
That the Tech Group will forward to the Synthesis Group
Is... a fundamentally primitive model,
Based on game theory.
To put it even simpler, on the platforms of computer strategies,

Such as the games *Civilisation*, *Julius Caesar*, *Pharaoh*
Or military strategies from the *Total War* series.
The latter appears preferable,
Because it combines two fields:
A vision of the Great Map of the Theatre of Historical Events

And a platform for local historical events
That is exclusive when viewed in terms of pure probability theory
And an understanding of the fluctuations that occur
As a result of the active impact on the change of events,
In this instance, of individual wars and battles.

However, this principle can successfully be changed;
It is entirely up to us.
Please also note that using the stepwise
Strategy platform
Will facilitate more effective control over the intermediate results.

In future, of course,
We will move to real-time platforms,
But this will be at later stages.
In the end, we will get a primitive model of the course of history,
Visualised as a series of parameters and even key persons.

What is left for the Synthesis Group?
At the first stage, it's tracking conformity
Of the computerised visual model
With traditional historical narratives, but!
The complexity of their work involves

The fact that, in the event that artificially
Created subjects deviate from traditional ones,
They need to draw conclusions as to the reason
Why this could be – a programming error,
An incorrect setting of tasks

Or poorly specified algorithms.
Or in none of these,
Rather in a general lack of information for a given period
Or, possibly, in its incorrect interpretation
In traditional history.

Is that complicated? Yes, it is.
But this is also a process involving the *feeding*
Of known historical narratives
Through mathematical modelling.
At the same time, the reverse process also takes place;

This is where the entire difficulty of the first stage lies.
Here, the main difficulty facing specialists from the Synthesis Group
Is to understand what is testing what.
History testing the mathematical model or vice versa?
Despite this, they are performing the work

Not in some abstract field
Rather with knowledge of the narratives, artifacts, names and how phenomena are linked.
There is hope that at the first stage
We will create a balanced system
That will enable us to move further.

This implies that this wholly philosophical problem
(I'm talking about the *what tests what* problem)
Will also transition to the next stage.
However, at the first stage, we are not interested in the answer,
Rather the balance of the *possibility* of building

A primitivised but *sufficient* model,
Which will lead us to have the ability to implement
The next stages of work and experiments.
So, as you can see,
The aim of the first stage is this:

To determine not the *essential* paradigms and algorithms,
Rather those that are sufficient to give the chaos of human history,
A nonlinear dynamic system,
Certain deterministic, ordered features
Which can be relied on in modelling

And, consequently, in forecasting.
Any questions?' 'Yes!'
A mighty Finnish lad stood up,

Dressed for some reason in Moroccan trousers and a Palestinian *keffiyeh*.
My name is Veiko Himmanen and I'm... er... from the Tech Group.

There's a problem with the adequacy
Of sets of data for different periods of history
That we'll be receiving from the Analysis Group.
The problem is that
Known historical information

Will decrease *backwards*, from modern times to antiquity.
You have to agree, that is an objective fact.
If, thanks to the chroniclers and, to a greater extent, the bureaucracy
We'll have multidimensional information for the 19th century,
For the 10th century, we'll have only fragments.

Does this not mean
That, in simplifying basic algorithms,
We will end up with paradigms of the primitive communal age?'
The General gave an ironic smile, but said approvingly,
'You know, Veiko, your question is a perfect illustration

Of the multidimensional nature of an interdisciplinary approach.
This tells us that, biologically speaking,
We are dealing with *homo sapiens sapiens*,
Who are essentially the subject of the research
And who, for centuries

Have not survived such significant mutations,
To be able to speak about fundamental changes
To our material, emotional and other motivations.
Therefore, there will be many questions like this
In our research.

For example, why did you decide
That it was in the primitive communal system
That the key motivations and development paradigms of
Human development as a global species emerged?
Some believe that we actually became a global species

Only in the age of worldwide information systems.
Therefore, don't look at the primitivisation principle
In such a linear manner.
Perhaps we'll be able to answer this question:
When did human algorithms move from focal to global trends?

It's possible that we'll detect mutations of the species too,
Which are currently only hypothetical
Against the backdrop of urbanisation and technical progress.
Sure, a certain primitivisation will occur,
But we believe it will lead us

To the stable values in chaos
Of which we are currently unaware;
Worse, though, is that we attribute their qualities
To other concepts altogether, that today
Flourish as stable stereotypes about the laws of history.

Remember Hegel's *pastoral idyll.*
No one today can assert with confidence
That the vector of human development is unequivocally directed
Purely in an evolutionary direction.
Perhaps it'll transpire that this vector should be directed back

To the age when man existed in harmony with nature.
You have to find the answers to these questions.
Therefore ,in summarising my answer, I can say
That if such a primitivisation of basic algorithms indeed takes place,
This would not be a flaw in the experiment, rather its specific result.'

Everyone exchanged looks of amazement
But no one objected. It was becoming more and more interesting.
'Another question!' A lad from Ust-Kamenogorsk raised his hand.
'Kairat Kunanbaev, the Analysis Group. Do you not think that the difference in the information systems

Will lead to us building
Not a single, continually developing model of history,
But several models, all formed based on the focal principle,
Dictated by the difference in the availability of information?
Will we not, therefore, obtain

An artificial model of the socio-economic formations
Of Marx and Lenin, only based not on the theory of philosophy,
But on the quality and the quantity of the data?
After all, it will turn out, will it not, that we will determine the primitivity
And sophistication of civilisation by how well known it is?'

'An excellent question,' the General said, snapping his fingers.
'It's excellent because it illustrates
Not only the modelling problem,
But also the shortcomings of the traditional history narratives.
Allow me to split my answer into two parts.

The first part is about focal history.
Here, you touched on an enormous layer of philosophy and historical science,
But, at the same time, you touched directly
On the question of the algorithm of the work of your Analysis Group.
Your one question identified two philosophical systems

For viewing history.
On the one hand, we have Toynbee's civilism,
While, on the other, the Marxist theory of socio-economic formations.
This is the right approach but it isn't enough.
Indeed, both as a result of analytical splitting,

And as a result of mathematical modelling
Based on the similarity of systems,
We can come to a loss of history as a single system
And come to a situation in the end, at the Synthesis stage, where we get
Several different games, as it has been done

In editions of the *Total War* series of games.
However, first, if we are to talk on the level of games,
All *Total War* strategies are built on similar algorithms and,

Second, and this is most important,
When compiling technical specifications,

We will use *all* known systems of views,
That have attempted to see history
As a single stream of development or an action of man as a species.
In other words, this is also the theory of socio-economic formations,
And the views of Spengler, Toynbee,

Mackinder with his *Heartland*, Spykman and his *Rimland*,
Fukuyama with his *The End of History* and
Gumilyov with his phases of ethnogenesis and,
You'll laugh, but we will even take into account
Fomenko's new chronology.

Even understanding these theories requires a titanic effort,
Which only genius or academies of science can handle.
Moreover, I can reveal to you yet another paradoxical feature
Of the organisation of our project:
If any representative of fundamental history or philosophy

Sees our Analysis Group list,
He will unerringly and quite rightly say
That this group of specialists is *not competent*
In its summarising of such a significant layer of knowledge.
However, note

That when I announced the principles behind the setup of Group A,
I placed my emphasis on knowledge not so much of history,
As of historiography and source studies.
In other words, at the first stage, experts need
Maximum knowledge not of *what* has happened,

But of *where* you can find out about it.
Therefore, you have at your disposal any specialists
In any field of history, archaeology, philosophy and source studies.
Gentlemen, what we are embarking on is a *global* project,
So, the question of accessibility to the capabilities of a civilisation

Will be removed with maximum possible efficiency.
Then, you know that history
Is twenty per cent knowledge of artefacts and primary sources
With the rest being a field of interpretations and, what is most harmful for us,
A field of ideological interpretations.'

'I'm sorry,' a small Japanese man said with his hand up;
His hair was bleached and he was dressed in a way
That defied description:
'But it is historians and not historiographers
Who create an understanding of how phenomena are linked!

I mean it is they and not a specific sector of this field of the humanities
That can resolve the matter of building a coherent history,
And not just its focal view!
This is precisely what interpretations are for –
To explain the continuous flow of one complex system

Into another, is that not so?'
'That is right, Mister... erm?'
'Kenji Uesugi, the Synthesis Group.'
'Thank you, Mister Uesugi, for your question!
Because it enables us

To move to the tasks of the second stage
And understand them in terms of their comparison with the tasks of the first.
There is absolutely no doubt that we will work
With interpretations of history
And precisely in the vein that Mr Uesugi has spoken about.

However! What forms the fundamental area of competence of the first stage
Is work, first, with precise and known data and,
Second, with phenomena capable of possessing
Quantitative features.
Moreover, at the first stage, we will

Endeavour as much as possible to see such features
In phenomena that, it would seem,
Cannot possess them.
For example, we will try to see questions of piety
Through the prism of quantitative indicators of priests,

Participants of religious festivities,
By volume of donations,
The correlation of *jizya* and *kharaj*,[243]
And so on.
In other words, we will take

The interpretation method into account
Only when there is a clear insufficiency
For, pardon the tautology,
Filling in *sufficient* links
In order to build the most primitive linear model of history.

Before I finish with the overview of the general tasks of the first stage
I would like to make one small
But very important clarification.
You might get the impression
That the Group B tasks are quite primitive –

You know, accept projects of paradigms and algorithms
And create a primitive computer game.
This would be the wrong impression.
At the first stage, the tasks facing the Technical Group
Will include a completely independent assignment:

The creation of a *system of development obstacles*
Based on *artificial intelligence*.'
'Wow!' someone from the last row exclaimed in French,
'We will be creating a mathematical devil!'
'Mais non!' the General smiled.

---

[243] *Jizya* – a per capita tax in Muslim countries in the Middle Ages, levied on Muslims. *Kharaj* – a land tax, levied on non-Muslims.

Can we really list among the Bloodless One's deeds
The Huang He floods, the droughts in Egypt, the lack of natural resources
Or natural mountain obstacles?
If we fail to consider the esoteric or mystical context,
Then any civilisation has certain limits

Of a natural kind – rivers, seas, steppe,
Population size,
The desires and ambitions of neighbours,
Ultimately, the correspondence of desires and the state
Of technical progress,

As we can see using Leonardo da Vinci as an example.
After all, we know that someone developed the basis
For creating an atomic bomb
And someone consequently put this knowledge into practice.
The reason for such a shift was, at the very least, defeat in war.

We know that there are Italians who want
To discover America,
Only it's not Italy that provides them all they need to do this.
The correlation of where an idea originated
And where it was put into practice

Will interest us from the standpoint
Of why it was not put into practice
Where it arose.
It is clear that the degree of complexity of a task
Cannot be resolved as part of a method

Of the primitivism of empirical analysis.
Therefore, it is continuous for the entire duration of the experiment.
However, I had to mention that right now.
Summarising the comments on the remark,
I can put your minds at rest for now: the mathematical model of the Fallen One

Is not a task for the first stage.'
'But will we get to that in any case?!'
Came the same voice again.
'Well...' General Johnson adjusted his tie.
'Let's move to the next stage and we'll discuss everything in its own time.

So, what do we get from the first stage and the implementation of its methods?
First of all we get two arrays of information,
One of which we have managed to bring into a wholly
Algorithmic and paradigmatic state,
By partially translating them into a linear field of understanding

Based on the principles of synergy.
Ideally, we will be able to see fractals[244] of the historical process,
That act as small, self-organising systems
And which have a direct impact
On history as a system as a whole.

---

[244] Fractals are a complex geometric figure that has a self-similarity property, meaning it is comprised of several parts, each of which is similar to the entire figure taken as a whole.

We may not see the existence of fractals
In endless time
But we can still consider their development
Over long periods of historical time,
Meaning the time of known human civilisation.

As for the emerging primitive model of history,
As I've said before, we get that
In a fairly primitive form.
I'd like to point out that this is not a shortcoming of the system we've created.
As you know, human hearing is not capable

Of capturing all nuances of analogue sound,
Because it reflects
The most realistic palette of ambient sounds.
The same applies to human sight,
Which is capable of perceiving only a certain number of lines.

In other words, we forgo 1,500 lines at the cinema,
625 on the television
And we accept a more primitive, sufficient picture
Of history, the main task of which
Is to show us the film's story to the end,

In one go, without breaking for advertisements or splitting up into episodes.
The second array of information is
That very volume of lines that sits beyond the limits
Of our visual abilities,
Yet it is this array that actually forms the beauty of cinema

That we need for complete and emotional contemplation.
And we understand that it is on the quality of this contemplation
That the depth of understanding often depends.
At any rate on account of the power of the emotional impact.
Therefore, we will try to use the entire array that

Remains behind the scenes during the second stage.
First of all, this is because the lack of depth in understanding
Will create us problems with the study of the full fluctuation spectrum,
Without which, in turn, a high-quality
Forecast is impossible,

Even if it is broken down into probabilistic scripting.
By establishing a paradigm and
Defining the main algorithms, we will further aim
To increase the conceivability of history,
And that means making it as predictable as possible.

Therefore, we are fully aware that
The quantitative indicators might not
Fully explain the formation of development vectors
That have arisen after the bifurcation points.
However, we will be able to see what they have led to in terms of a simple, well-known narrative!

Simply put, we cannot explain *why this happened*,
But we can see *what happened* in the end.
And *how it happened* in terms of how the story unfolded.

We also understand
That the most primitive linear model

Might not arise upon completion of the first stage either.
However, we will see the problem areas
More clearly defined and deterministic in terms of
Mathematical modelling.
The clearest way I can explain this is

Is using the example of approaches to philosophical systems
Of the cyclical and stage-based nature, say,
Of the core logic of history.
In other words, if we consider Toynbee's teachings
At the first stage, in terms of the movement of tribes and

State building,
At the second, we will turn to his notions of Reason and Revelation,
The people who form the Response to the Challenge
And how this is related to the mimesis[245] it leaves in its wake.
If we previously considered Gumilyov's theory of ethnogenesis

In terms of the development stages of an ethnic group.
Now, we are coming very close to an understanding of passionarity,
A quantity that no one has yet measured
Quantitatively.
The same applies to the theory of Marx-Lenin

About the driving forces of the revolution.
Note that we have not
Considered the aspects of faith,
The rise and fall of religions
Or the death or reign of the Prophets.

Yes, we will touch on this at the first stage,
Either through religious civilizations
Or through the concept of the formation of super-ethnoses,
United not by the will of a king,
But by their faith.

In the second stage, we will consider
The emotional and psychological environment,
Which has hitherto only occasionally opened up to us the potential
Of its quantitative measurement.
However, note that here we apply the following methods:

The definition of *Elementary Historicity of Emotion*
And the *Sufficient Constellation* method.
As you can see, the simplification algorithm is also present in these methods,
But we take it as a necessity
That is close to absolute as part of our research.

This stage will also witness another complication
Of the project's interdisciplinary approach,
Primarily by strengthening the psychological component.

---

[245] Mimesis – social imitation, thanks to which the Response, formed within the creative minority, becomes the property of the non-creative majority.

We will look at both psychology of personality
In the historical context

And the correlation of its mutual influence with the psychology of the masses.
You might think that by ordering one area of chaos,
We encounter an equally complex and independent chaos.
To a certain extent this is true, but not to the same extent
That you might have thought at the very beginning.

First of all, this is about what unites these two methods,
Which in turn form two sub-stages for the second phase.
Now our interest will focus on the set of emotions
That influence human behaviour
At the moment the Challenge is accepted and the Response, formulated.

Of course, this might be any combination
Of cognitive interpretations, effects and moods.
These might be love, fear,
Hunger and hate, envy and pride.
As far as logical motivations are concerned,

We can see this as a field
That is capable of determination.
However, if we come up against an emotional process
In the bifurcation point, then we have to be able
To separate predictable emotions from the random.'

'Sorry, I have a question!' A blond chap in glasses in the front row had raised his hand.
'Hm... Jan Pilsudski, Technical Group...
Why are you considering a bifurcation point
As a starting point for fluctuation changes,
When you're not taking into account that, at the same time,

It is also final? A point that displays not only

The logical factors behind the solution,
But the end point of the effect of an emotion?'
'A valid comment, Mr Pilsudski...'
'Just *Jan* if you don't mind.'
'Okay, Jan.

This will take me a little away from what I was planning
By way of my presentation going forward, but this question is indeed important.
Here we are faced, as I have said already, with
The fact that we are starting all our research from scratch.
In some areas we have already made some progress

And have reached certain degrees of certainty.
I will say from the off that during the research,
You might turn away from them and that is perfectly normal.
But for now, at the point we are getting acquainted with the project,
This would be premature.

Nevertheless, thank you for the question;
I will endeavour to answer it.
However, it will probably not be an answer,
Rather a statement of the problem,

Because, if we had the answers, for what would we need this series of experiments?

First of all, we recognise that emotional processes,
Both of separate individuals,
And small, medium and large groups,
Are an integral and, perhaps, even the most important factor
Influencing the course of historical processes.

Second, when constructing a mathematical model,
He need to find a way to count them in
Emotional processes,
Meaning their quantitative features,
Which would be not approximate but as accurate as possible.

Put another way, we can say that, as a result of, say,
Gaining independence, a given nation
Experiences *joy*.
But questions immediately arise: is that everyone? For long?
And how many times will this joy

Form the basis of active deeds?
Then, as regards the vectors of the advent
And existence of an emotion.
We have tried to create a three-tier algorithm:
Motivations and motives > bifurcation point,

As a point of achieving the goal of motivations >
Start of the action of the defining emotion.
You can see that this algorithm is very conditional
And in turn does not solve problems of enumerability.
How many people need to recognise the point when

The goals of motivation are achieved? And, generally, on whom and on what does
The formulation of the finite nature of the motives and motivations stage depend?
What is this – a sensual or rational experience?
Another shortcoming of the three-link model we've described
Is that, in the end, it might turn out to be

Two-tier, but consist of a single-plan process.
We could, of course, say that
After passing the bifurcation point,
New motives and motivations and new interpretations
Of the meanings of activity will begin to form again, isn't that right?

Perhaps we'll be able to remain in the field of motivations,
Such as in Maslow's hierarchy of needs,[246]
Based on his five- or seven-tier
Classification of levels of needs and priorities.
Or in other classifications

That take other nuances into account –
Extrinsicality and intrinsicality,
Individual or group,
Biological and social motivations and so on.
However, through the lens of the motivations of larger groups,

---

[246] Abraham Maslow (1908–1970) – a prominent American psychologist and the founder of humanistic psychology.

Such as ethnos, nation or super-ethnos, for instance,
We will see a large degree of distortion of the theories
That are based more on the psychology of individuals
Than on the psychology of large groups.
And if we begin deliberately to primitivise

Motivational processes to a level of basic algorithms,
We will see that, on the one hand, we'll arrive at
The Marxist theory of interests in class war,
While, on the other, at a hypertrophied role in history
Of a separate, albeit outstanding individual.

The most difficult thing, however, isn't this.
All our assessments of the objectivity of the results
Will again be emotionally interpretive,
And not quantitative, that is, measurable.

And this will happen for one simple reason:
Today, no one will undertake to work out
The correlation of the role of classes, nations, super-ethnoses and individuals
In the implementation of any given historical event.
Even in simple percentage terms.

At the same time, you note, we are still in the field of motives,
Catalysts, almost completely removed
From the pure field of emotional processes,
While realising at the same time that motivations and emotions
Exist simultaneously in a closely intertwining dimension.

However, let's try and find
At least some principles of linearity
In the measurement of the emotional processes
Of individuals, groups and large groups,
And not simply for a specific segment of history;

That would be a fairly understandable and already partially implemented mission.
What interests us, specifically against the backdrop of an endless historical process,
Is what we have here in the form of numbers and classifications.
First of all, we have knowledge of the concepts
About basic emotions.

We know that, according to Ekman, there are seven of them
Or eight according to Izard.[247]
We can even use the wholly mathematical-looking
Periodic System of Emotions of Max Lüscher,[248]
However! Again, they all relate to

A description of qualitative parameters of emotions
That we don't know how to insert
Into the animated model of real history.

---

[247] Paul Ekman – an outstanding American psychologist and Professor Emeritus at the University of California, San Francisco, who is a pioneer in the psychology of emotions, interpersonal relations, psychology and lie detection. Carroll Izard – an American psychologist and author of the Differential Emotions Theory.
[248] Max Lüscher – a Swiss psychologist and the developer of the so-called *Periodic System of Emotions* and the *Lüscher Colour Test*.

Of course, we can set several qualitative parameters
For the historical figures who,

In the model of history that we built during the first stage,
Stride across the Great Map of the World.
This is used with a vengeance in computer games
And even in strategies.
Let's say, according to the decimal system, that

Valour level is 7, Management Skill level is 9.
But, here, we run into a problem, related to
Over-specified artificial intelligence.
You know that if the difficulty level in a game is low,
Then almost any character controlled by artificial intelligence

Will lose to non-standard human decision-making.
Conversely, if the difficulty level is high,
And the character is focused on finding a probable solution
That stems from the theory of the probability of your weaknesses,
Then he will smash you up and beat you until...

Well, until you find a non-standard solution again.
In other words, this means of setting parameters
Is good only when the objects are controlled by a person.
When I say good, I mean in terms of
The imitation of real history.

Then again, since we're dealing
With supercomputers and not household stations,
We can create multi-parameter characters
That could compete with a real mind,
Including in terms of the degree of the non standard search for solutions.

However, in reality, we still end up with an artificial model.
Why, you might ask?
And why did Saladin, after the brutal siege of Jerusalem,
And after the Christians had killed 200,000 Muslims there,
Release the besieged crusaders from the city,

So enamoured was he by their courage and dedication?
Why did Erik the Red
Not return from Iceland to the fjords of Norway,
To take his revenge on his aggressors,
But instead turned his ships to search for Greenland?

Why did False Dmitry, after winning the Russian throne,
Fall to the charms of Marina Mniszech?
We can know the set of motives
That have brought an individual to a bifurcation point,
But we can neither calculate nor anticipate

Which fluctuation vector this individual will consequently select.
What can we say about ethnicity
That encounters the Challenge

And is compelled to formulate the Response[249]
Under the influence of thousands of emotional components?

Hitler immediately after the defeat of the Beer Putsch
And Hitler after the defeat of France
Is the same person
But completely polar emotional portraits.
That means that the individual person is a dynamic system!

So, when we are talking about
Having to fill the course of the mathematical model of history
With an emotional and motivational component,
We assume that we'll have to follow
A path of primitivisation of a known series of emotions,

Selecting from them those emotions
That we very loosely define as *historical emotions*.
In other words, those that are not so much key,
But which are algorithmic in terms of their systematic influence
On a long historical process.

We can see all the shortcomings of this approach
But we understand that the search for the key algorithms,
Performed at the first stage,
Will perhaps help find other approaches. And it will be you who find them.
As for the principle of the *Sufficient Constellation*,

This is also a working definition.
It stems from the need to soften the boundaries
Between the definition of the role of the individual, on the one hand,
And popular masses in history, on the other.
What does this mean?

How do you determine the number of people
Making up the driving forces of war, revolution or reform?
How many passionaries are needed (as per Gumilyov)
To start the great migration of peoples?
How many individuals have to be embraced by

Fukuyama's *Thymos of the thirst for recognition*?
Often, just one passionary figure is enough;
Someone able to stand on the edge of an evolutionary leap
Or, to the contrary, lead Troy to Doom.
But there are also instances where passionaries in society

Might never come into contact with one another throughout their lives,
But converge in one bifurcation point
To implement the choice of a nation and then go their separate ways.
From this distance away, we think
That weighing up the value of roles *of individual or nation* in history

Will fall away of its own accord when we come to the understanding

---

[249] Toynbee's concept of Challenges and Responses, which he disclosed in his works, particularly in his *A Study of History*. A cultural civilisation develops as a series of Responses by the creative human spirit to the Challenges that nature, society and the inner infinity of man himself present to him. At the same time, various different options are always possible as they might be different Responses to the same Challenge.

That an entire people cannot, in a single act and simultaneously,
Influence the passage of the bifurcation point,
While a *lone* person is unable
To formulate the Response vector.

In other words, we will strive to define a particular phenomenon
Which cannot be defined in loose notions such as *elite*
Or *intelligentsia*, ruling *party* or *dynasty*.
For now, we use the term *constellation*,
In the understanding that it is only a working term.

We are talking here about the emergence of separate groups
Who, in unison, are able to formulate development vectors and,
Accordingly, act decisively
In communicating with one another,
Developing common plans and making them a reality through cooperation.

Groups like these are far from definitely being
Representatives of one nation or tribe.
They can be formed of
Completely unexpected configurations,
Where national borders are unimportant.

For example, this could simultaneously be Philip II of France,
Frederick Barbarossa, Richard the Lionheart
And Archduke Leopold of Austria,
Who became passionaries of the III Crusade.
Groups can be formed not only based on

Historical super-ethnoses.
For example, Margaret Thatcher, Ronald Reagan,
Helmut Kohl and Mikhail Gorbachev,
Who united one thing
And destroyed another.

Or that famous trio of Stalin, Roosevelt and Churchill.
And there are many more examples like them.
What led to the emergence of such constellations?
How great is the importance of regular patterns in this
And how great, the importance of emotional compatibility

And simple human affinity?
Let us remember that neither Stalin nor Gorbachev
Knew English or German,
Just as Roosevelt and Reagan knew no Russian.
What does this mean?

Would there not have been such a constellation if not
For the constellations of interpreters and their skill?
Is that the case or isn't it?
Should we take the translation factor into account or attribute it
To general civilisational aspects of development?

This is more or less the same series of tasks
That are to be implemented during
The second stage of our research.
Where the configuration of groups A, B and C

Will remain only they will change significantly

In the sense that they will join forces.
Of course, this joining of forces will take place
Under the auspices of the Synthesis Group where, by this time,
All data will have been collated, on successful solutions,
Problems and, God forbid, dead ends.

Are there any questions on the second stage?'
Someone called out,
'Mister.... oh.... General Johnson!
I would like to say...
Oh, sorry, Patrick O'Gilvy, Dublin. Oh, I mean, Tech Group.

I wanted to say that what you have just said contains
So much that makes simple sense
And much that, at the same time, is wholly unimaginable,
To the extent that, to be honest, at some point
I wanted to get up and make a run for it!'

The hall resounded with liberating laughter.
'Hm, let me go on... But, you know *what* it is
That makes me want to stay?
It's that some of the things you said
Evoke a heated protest and a desire to object, saying,

No, not like that. You can do it like this!
I can't explain yet to which of your
Statements this applies,
But I assure you that such feelings really do arise!'
The hall nodded and murmured approvingly.

The general liked it too.
'Good... Good... That's exactly the reaction
I was counting on.
If you don't mind, let's move onto the third stage.'
There were no objections.

Some leafed noisily through notebooks,
Others opened a new page on their laptops and tablets.
'When it comes to the third stage of the research, I will be brief.
At the project's second phase,
We are only studying what is called a *constellation*

Or a *Critical Constellation*.
We are exploring the patterns,
That have led to the emergence of such groups
And individual passionaries in the past.
However, if you recall the project's main objective,

You will come to realise that we need to send the entire scope of
Accumulated knowledge for forecasting,
Meaning for modelling the emergence of such a constellation,
Which will devise, resolve and implement
The hypothetical project of World Social Revolution.

Let me say from the off that we are leaving out

The emotional and ideological attitude
To this phenomenon.
Like everywhere, there are opponents and supporters of revolutions among you.
But we'll keep that to one side for now.

And for one simple reason:
We don't know and cannot assume what its qualitative characteristics are.
Do you get the gist of the changing approaches in the third stage?
Hm... There will basically be two sub-stages,
In response to different issues:

The first is – *how* and *when* might this take place,
And as a result of *whose* actions?
And *will it take place at all*?
The second is – *what exactly will take place and to what end?*
And *how should we feel about it?*

When it comes to questions like:
Will there be an attempt to prevent this event
Or catalyse it artificially?
Adjust it in some way?
Or simply expect the inevitable in the Taoist manner?

I don't think the search for answers
Falls under the remit of our project.
We'll leave that to the powers-that-be.
Neither you nor I will be given such powers.
However, providing the Fathers of Nations with versions of events and attitudes to them

Is our specific task at hand.'

The general paced back and forth
After a few seconds of silence,
Lost for a moment in his thoughts.
Then, however, with effort, he returned his focus to the hall and asked,
'Are there any more questions?'

Silence reigned, as if before their eyes
The French Jacobins had just rushed by,
Followed by Telman's militants, Kronstadt sailors,
The motley faces of the *colour revolutions*
And the unknown, new names of their leaders.

'Mister General,' an uncertain-sounding voice
Finally broke the silence.
'Fabrizio Borgia, Tech Group.
This is the question I wanted to ask:
I am an automobile-design specialist

And my hobby is historical costume.
IT for me is but a tool.
I can see that the Analysis and Synthesis groups
Contain people with wholly creative professions;
I even know some of them.'

By way of confirmation, someone made as if to wave to Fabrizio.
'What is the point of our being in groups

With such complex, interdisciplinary tasks?'
'Oh, that is a wonderful question,'
The general said, perking up.

'There are two sides to this aspect.
The first is purely functional –
We believe it is impossible to study a historical process
As part of its emotional component,
Without an idea of beauty, art

Or creativity as a whole.
History contains purely creative acts
That have served, without exaggeration, as Challenge points.
For example, Leonardo's paintings in the context of the Renaissance.
Or John Lennon's *Imagine*.

And how many works of art and architecture
Stand at the intersection of the development of creative thought
And the technical revolution?
Like the Eiffel Tower, the Empire State Building,
The Millau Viaduct[250], or the design of the Lamborghini?

Works that evidence imperial might,
Like the Mamayev Kurgan memorial complex,
Or imperial decline,
Like the novels of Erich Maria Remarque.
Who can imagine

Hundreds of years of the migration of peoples in the USA
Without the Statue of Liberty in New York?
There is weapon-art, like Solzhenitsyn's *GULAG Archipelago*.
There is art that challenges the imagination, like Pop Art
Or Malevich's *Black Square*.

Well, and if we get really close to the topic at hand,
What is revolution without the *Marseillaise*,
Without the *Internationale*?
Without the *You fell victims in the deadly struggle...*[251]
Or *Hasta siempre Comandante* about the undefeated Che Guevara?

The second side is this –
Guys, we create our own history, ourselves,
Humanity!
Are we really giving the aesthetic side of our model a wide berth?
How can you think about

What the military genius of Genghis Khan was
When all you see is a dot jerking about on a monitor?
They say that if you don Napoleon's cocked hat,
You can think for two minutes about how Bonaparte thought!
This is a joke, of course, but there is some common sense in it.

We need to create a pictorial solution
That would be illustrative in every respect.

---

[250] The Millau Viaduct in France is considered to be the world's largest bridge.
[251] From the famous Soviet song with lyrics by Anton Arkhangelsky.

So that you might see history not in letters and dots,
But obtain the chance, thanks to the very latest technology,
To see its pulse with your own eyes!'

Everyone smiled, for that was a good way to put it.
'Anyway,' seeing that some of those in the hall had started fidgeting,
The General resolutely walked over to one of the walls,
Curtained with a piece of fabric.
'I think the time has come

To introduce you to our project's symbol.
Now, I hope, you'll have a deeper understanding
Of the meaning in its name.' He pulled off the fabric and we saw the emblem.
'Welcome onboard
Project Constellation, gentlemen!'

****

To say that the work progressed with gusto
Was an understatement.
Although you couldn't use the image of gusto to describe
The processes that were visible on the surface.
Rather, they could be described as volcanic

Magma running into the ocean,
So contrasting did the processes and the results appear.
HR specialists and psychologists
Worked well at the project creation stage.
We encountered almost no problems

With the incompatibility of the characters and styles of the work.
It was incredible, but teams, close to the ideal
Of a positive working relationship, are indeed realistic.
Despite the excellent organisation of advanced time management,
We worked beyond our limits.

I'm talking about both physical and mental abilities.
A saving grace was that every person involved in the group
Was not only an effective link
In teamwork brainstorming,
But also completely covered their field of activity.

I call them *medium-size tanks*,
Capable not only of attacking as part of larger formations,
But independently to perform a full range of combat assignments,
From taking a foothold to outright partisanship.
(Bravo, Marshal Katukov and the Thirty-Fours!).

The role of the group curators was pleasantly surprising.
It transpired that they had no managerial functions whatsoever.
These incredibly knowledgeable specialists
Were assigned more tasks to support our own work
For everyone, at any time and at any cost!

It was they who formed that global sense of the project.
At first request, with lightning speed,
They would organise conferences, consultancy sessions

And open brainstorming with any specialists!
There would even be instances when a question

Could only be answered by one document
That was only in hard copy and only held
In some local history museum in Mongolia!
And if it is needed, it will definitely come,
Either in the form of a clear copy

Or even accompanied by a high-ranking Mongolian official
In a special package with government stamps
And delivered by private jet!
A special system emerged with languages, too.
That's when we remembered General Johnson's constellation of interpreters!

Not only does everything need to be translated into the language of numbers,
Which, incidentally, was developed
Specially from scratch in the Tech Group,
But a standardisation of concepts also needed to be achieved.
After all, they need to be continuous and uniform.

As a result, we obtained a kind of slang,
Mixed together from a multitude of languages.
Of course, the basic language was English.
However, the philosophical terms we used were mostly German.
Where would be without German classical philosophy?!

The verb base and structure of adjectives
Were French, imbibed with the majority of the virtues of Latin
And Russian, enabling us to draw on all the richness of the epithets
Of Turgenev's language.
Greek, naturally, came as default.

However, we preferred to add neologisms
From the mathematically strict potential of Arabic –
There is so much space in there!
Incidentally, if a conflict arises between concepts,
It is likewise better to use the Arabic matrix system.

Encountering different languages, we saw for the first time
How failures occur with many algorithms,
Which we believe are of a continuous, generally historical nature.
The focal nature of history began to unfold as early as the level of languages.
Thus, military terminology from prior to the 18th century

Was preferred in Turkic
And in the lingua-franca (until a certain time).
Then it was German and Russian, having absorbed
Turkisms, Slavisms and Germanisms.
In the 20th century, nothing could be done without English military terminology.

If terms were required, related to sensitivity
And abstraction, we have to dive
Into the depths of Sufi poetry in Persian,
Japanese *haiku* and, sometimes, words
Were even dumbly replaced with Chinese characters.

I can say that, despite the depths of efforts,
The first stage was not as successful as expected.
True, we were able to create an algorithmic model
For the continuous development of history.
Visually, it looked stunning.

No wonder the General spoke of the project's pictorial aesthetics!
We obtained a Grand Map, as the basis,
Onto which information then accumulated
In an endless number of layers,
Differentiated by properties and distinguished by colours.

It really did look like the Grand Map
Of *Total War* strategic games, with landscapes,
Models of climate change
And even a host of lesser characters
Who, if so desired, could be tracked and assessed.

There were hundreds of layers: economics, cities, routes,
The change dynamics in country borders,
Military campaigns, even pretty girls
Featuring among the historical figures –
Cleopatra, Josephine, the Queen of Sheba and the like.

However, there were not many continuous algorithms and paradigms.
Trade was vulnerable to climate change,
Technical progress flitted from side to side across the map,
Religions were spread across basins
And ethogenesis as a whole, given the existing historical views,

Became a paradoxical and unpredictable element of nature.
Only war gave us more-or-less intelligible paradigms,
Because it was waged irrespective of climate or other conditions.
I suppose that troops cross the Alps,
Wander across deserts,

Freeze in the plains of Russia
And battle typhoons off the coast of Japan because they have to.
Elephants roam Europe,
Macedonians roam Samarkand
And Greek fire is invented in three places at once.

A small number of continuous algorithms
Got us thinking that perhaps we really
Were still Cro-Magnons,
And those five or six basic paradigms live in us
That were driven by these primitive chaps.

If, all the same, concessions were made in favour of accepting the *focal*,
The picture of paradigms had already changed.
This then suggested two thoughts: Toynbee was partially correct
When he said that there is no common algorithm;
There is an algorithm of civilisational focal points.

However, it must be said
That we do have a unified stream all the same.
The global civilisation of modernity

Could not have arisen from nowhere, right?
The paradigm of occupying free spaces

And then connecting them together
Went nowhere, in fact it actually developed
Simply on account of the jump in the Earth's population
And the drop in the number of these free spaces.
However, all the same, in our model,

Before a global world, history continued to appear focal
And flared up in a fairly chaotic manner.
Even if we combine Gumilyov's theory of *biogeoethnocenosis*
With global climate models
That demonstrate the change dynamics of the climate in the past,

All the same, after processing the data,
We obtained a subject match
In the attractors of ultimate historical subjects.
Gumilyov's quantitative indicators of sub-ethnoses as
Self-organising subsystems and the *frequency*

Of events in ethnic history didn't help us either.
Although, to be honest, we had high hopes for them.
What is more, the Synthesis Group very seldom
Returned us an assessment of the result,
Saying that we were dealing with insufficient information on its entry.

Errors for the most part related
To an incorrect interpretation at the outset.
For example, chaos in ethnogenesis,
Associated with a lack of mathematical function
Between the *ethnos* set and the *name* set,

Led to a situation where, on the final model,
We obtained five Turkic Khaganates, three Frankish Empires
Or even the emergence of some mythical peoples
With terrible artificial names,
Like Chernogrunwalders or Inco-Czechs.

At one time we thought
That we could find a way out
In Marx's theory of socio-economic formations,
Which combines evolutionism and the *focal* at the same time.
However, this *focal* element was considered in a time-based dimension.

The theory enabled us successfully to include in the set of indicators
Processes of technical progress,
Which are closely connected with evolution in the development of productive forces.
At some point, it seemed
That the paradigms had been found,

But Marx's theory broke down based
On what it always breaks down on –
The so-called *Asiatic means of production*,
Starting right at the gates of Europe,
And onwards, spreading almost everywhere.

Nevertheless, we were able to get a great deal
From Marx.
Primarily, history has a system of
Sequential formations,
Only not exactly those about which Marx was speaking.

Moreover, if we are saying that history
Is not a tangible, existing past,
Rather a system of interpretations of the past,
Even if based on tangible artefacts,
Proceeding from principles of knowability,

We have developed so-called
Information-emotional formations.
What are they?
The further we get from today,
So the information array of precise knowledge

About events in the past sequentially reduces *back*,
Gradually becoming an array of interpretations and conjecture.
The power of understanding the emotional background of events is also weakening,
Transitioning to a level of intuitive emotional empathy.
Have you ever noticed

In the old films about distant history
How people talk in this unnatural manner
And look like total morons with a limited range of emotions?
So, you see, the most interesting thing
Is that people from films about the distant future

Were often depicted in exactly the same way.
These are all the consequences of one and the same process
Moreover, if Cro-Magnon mutations occurred in the past
And they'll take place in the future,
The degree of their mutation into enormous spherical creatures

Is heavily exaggerated. Most likely, in the future
We will be dealing with accelerating mutation,
But it is unlikely to be with a transition from one species to another.
Well, all right, if you insist on the probability of
Mutations under the impact of radiation,

Then I'll ask you to stop right there
And shelve all discussions about the future for later.
We would then be able to deal with the past.
Anyway, I will continue.
Basically, using the fact that we share with the ancient Egyptians

A single nervous and emotional platform,
We can intuitively assume an emotional range,
But getting it exactly right and then anticipating
The subsequent behavioural fluctuation
Is practically an impossible task.

Another thing in our time
Is the printing press and the Internet
That churn out tons of memoirs into space

Which are of value specifically because of the precision with which they reproduce
The emotional range around any given event,

And that exclusive informational highlight
Of which other historical narratives have been deprived.
The development of language also contributes
To the expansion of our understanding of emotional circumstances.
So, by dividing the historical process

Into information-emotional formations,
We have gained a better understanding of system-based algorithms,
That formed the basis of given
Fluctuation changes,
But where we have failed to achieve transformation of the historical model

Into a single, continuous series of events.
However, this was still a definite step forward
Because what became the algorithm was the fact that
The knowledge of the information-emotional historical background
Decreases *forwards* to the same extent as it does *backwards*.

In other words, we were able as early as the first stage
To gain an understanding
About the more or less realistic boundaries
When forecasting moves from the precise
To the intuitive.

We have seen that the exact period
Is sufficiently large and this has already instilled a certain optimism in us.
Because this is already a certain algorithmic vision,
If we take into account that the peak of information-emotional knowledge
Is not constant, but is gradually moving forward

Simply in line with how we are living!
And this system has a tangible degree of constancy.
Another lesson we learned from Marx is that
This is an understanding of the Asian means of production
From the opposing side.

In other words, comparing it with the theory of formations,
We saw not their replacement, as Marx had wanted,
Rather, to the contrary, we considered a huge seam of the constancy of paradigms
Which have not changed essentially over the centuries,
Even in individual regions;

But these are still enormous regions!
Simply in a certain period when we celebrated
Vulgar evolutionism and the theory of modernism,
Many believed that history had left Asia for good.
Today it is already clear that this was a systematic error

By many theorists of the West,
Who, at a time of crisis,
Create a new system of world order
Literally, as they say, *on their laps.*
Well, it's a good thing they have the tools of influence for this!

But let's not digress.
The one thing we understood from Marxism
Was that, despite the development of the forces of production,
Social relations do not always depend
On the nature of relations in the socio-emotional superstructure.

Decent conservatism is identical in both England
And Japan. Why decent?
Because, in the search for constant algorithms of history,
We still rely on these chaps, these conservatives.
And the time to study the paradigms of the rest,

The romantics, reformers, revolutionaries and avant-gardists
Still lie ahead of us.
So, what else has Marx and his Asiatic means of production given us?
That which, from the standpoint of historical paradigms,
Keynes, with his state regulation of the markets,

Told the Europeans what the Chinese have always known.
And so, European factory-conveyor production
Returned to where it came from, China and South-east Asia,
To the countries that have lived throughout history in a conveyor society.
One could even go further and say *conveyor consciousness*.

So, it is unknown if a high-quality German conveyor
Is a consequence of the European mould,
Or actually of the military-Asian type of consciousness.
We cannot ignore one of Marx's main paradigms –
Capital.

Here, too, we saw that the narrowing of this concept
To the framework of a capitalist society
Proved to be artificial,
Because, over the course of history,
It was not so much the extraction of surplus value

That was important
As its permanent objective –
Investment of accumulated capital into authority.
Moreover, the realisation of this objective
So powerfully nullifies the difference between the nature of the extraction of funds

And the nature of their accumulation
That all the specifics of capitalism or feudalism are
Nothing more than an accompanying abstraction.
It is specifically the objective value of a regime
That always determined all related

Humanitarian, legal, structural, organisational,
Military and effective parameters of *true legitimacy*.
What has no importance and never has had
Is what mechanism provides for your throne or elected seat –
Military campaigns and division of booty,

Effective distribution of collected taxes,
Inexhaustible oil reserves
Or an advantage in hi-tech.

If the collective investment into a regime does not conform
To its parameters of what is expensive and what inexpensive,

Then collapse becomes inevitable.
There were objections that, you know, such a model of relationships
Is nothing but a pure formula,
Cut off from the conditions of the country's external environment.
That's because any society

That co-exists in harmony with a just regime
Can always be subject to annexation
On the part of a state with a balance of internal political
Relationships that is less just.
And here we are talking about the wrong interpretation!

We are not considering the paradigms of one state,
Rather we are looking at a common platform of humankind.
Even if a state is not aware of its place
In the global information space.
And is unable to conduct a comparative analysis of investment,

Say, into an adequate army,
Then this does not mean that the regime bought by this nation
Might seem harmonious because of a lack of external comparisons!
To the contrary, the deliberate isolationism of tyranny
That seeks to hide its qualitative characteristics

Is a sign of a regime that is costing the nation too much.

So, should any nation see their regime
In a global context?
This has become possible only when
Geopolitics is the hardest thing to alter.
That much is true. But if I tell you that global knowledge

Arose not because Columbus was eaten up by a passion to discover,
But because throughout history
Nations have instinctively striven to acquire
A global assessment of the effectiveness of their regime,
And it is this that has become the real basis for globalisation of the consciousness.

Can you object? No, you can't. Because globalisation of the consciousness
Is inextricably linked with the export of legitimacy.
If not for this question, then the global association
Would never have referred to the specifics of control.
They're different, you say? All right.

Live how you want, only trade honestly;
That's what the question would have been if at the heart of intergovernmental communication
There was a purely capitalist interest,
One of a mutual and sustainable benefit.
But that is not the question at all.

What is Obama's one-billion election campaign fund?
It is the overstated cost of government services,
The effectiveness of which just isn't worth that.
Therefore, on the one hand, we have a nation

That is obliged to pay this price,

While, on the other, we see a nation that seeks additional funds
To pay all the expenses of its elite.
It is here that the countries are sought
That are able to top up funds for paying bribes to those in authority,
Who are seemingly suffering

From an overstated cost of their own regime.
But isn't it the case that, in the end, a fair price for a regime is being established
In the country of intervention? No!
This phantom cause of aggression was never of interest to the elite,
Who had become too costly for its people.

We have managed to see the algorithm
Where the most aggressive countries are those
With the least just and least effective
Systems of internal control and distribution of benefits,
That they compensate:

First, using external sources to pay for the upkeep of the regime;
Second, using effective propaganda, state bribery and other
Diversionary manoeuvres
That ensure people remain ignorant
To the fact that, every day, they are paying for

An unjustifiably expensive regime.
In other words, by altering the common phrase,
We can say that, *a people is worthy of the ruler*
Whom he pays out of his own pocket.
Everything else that relates to the system of social relations –

They force us to pay, *They give us no choice*,
We have the most expensive but we are the richest,
We don't have it as bad as others and so on –
Are just various interpretations
Around the one basic algorithm

That has existed for centuries
And which has not changed a bit today.
Well, no one has been able to answer the question as to
Why countries with the richest regimes,
Which should be the most technologically advanced,

Always end up with primitive methods
Of fundraising for their rulers:
War, intervention, pressure, slander and spin.
Why is it only weapons that are improved
But not the quality of foreign relations,

Including the communication style of humankind as a collective of nations?
After all, you can educate a person in teams, right?
At the same time, the healthier the team,
The more effective the methods, right?
So why is that the most advanced

Are still the most aggressive?

There is one answer: they have the least effective and the most expensive regime.
And they want others to pay for it too.
Agreements and collective international rules
Do not reproduce cheap capital,

So, there is no fundamental interest in their effectiveness.
Fair enough, you say,
But what about the fact that there are peoples
Who back home pay sixty per cent tax
And only grumble on rare occasions,

While there are others who don't even pay ten per cent
But are ready to take to the barricades?
I take you back to Marx.
Taxes are but the visible part of the cost of a regime
And the smallest.
Systems for extracting payment for a regime are far more varied.

There's the payment by agreement to be poor,
There's the separation from capital and national wealth,
There's the tax on dying soldiers,
There's the removal of freedoms part by part
And so on.

Those who agree to pay high taxes,
As a rule, know
That the other options for taking payment
Are seriously limited on the part of society.
However, if you look at those who

Pay lower taxes,
It will probably turn out that they will overpay elsewhere,
And some.
And with the support of those
Who replicate the model of high-cost regimes around the world.

In other words, we've learned one important and interesting paradigm
When it comes to external aggression.
If, as part of a nation, you have built
A society of relatively fair payment for their regime,
Then wait, and those who overpay will come,

Either in the form of open military aggression,
Or as a totality of diplomatic efforts,
Or in the form of an ideology,
Which slowly undermines the balance you have achieved.
Why do they need a positive example shoved under their noses?

There are those who'll come as a wave of migrants,
Who choose themselves a better price in another country,
Than the one they pay back home.
But in rich societies, you say,
It is not only the representatives of the regime who are rich, right?

There is the beau monde, the business elite and the technocrats.
Right, and we don't mind.
They're just at the accumulation stage,

Which will inevitably lead to the acquisition stage.
Only they are acquisitions not for *us* but for *themselves*.

Do you get the difference?
After all, you know about the system of privileges,
Benefits, using one's fame at elections,
To move into the ranks of the paid.
Authority is not set in stone, after all; it's an ever-changing structure.

And, generally speaking, so as not to drown in the variability and the finer details,
Return in your reasoning to the algorithms,
About what lies at the heart,
What has remained unchanged for years, and get away from the interpretive superstructure.
Reasoning about this is wonderful exercise for the mind. But no more than that.

What I'm talking about here is that the price of power
Is a continuous historical paradigm
That we have been able to consider
As a constantly repeating algorithm
Over the entire course of history,

An algorithm that does not depend on notions of capital, on capitalism
Or feudalism, or a slave-owning system.
The difference is only in the effectiveness of the accumulation
And reproduction of funds, inevitably directed to the purchase of authority.
On its purchase or its imposition on others.

****

You know, the division into groups A, B and C
And using the technique of mutual
Cyclical testing
Bore fruit.
Despite the fact that modern technologies

Have almost put paid to distances,
Geographical distance still had its say.
We learned to build balances and correspondences.
We achieved a certain stepwise performance of operations,
Brought about by an objective waiting time for the results.

Indeed, as General Johnson had said,
We accumulated two enormous arrays –
One was the one we managed to translate into a result,
The other was the one that had not yet been synthesised.
However, it was already fired up in anticipation of application.

Having completed the first stage,
Every one of the chaps from the three groups, with rare exceptions,
Gathered in Santa Fe in New Mexico,
At an enormous complex,
Built specially for our project.

The only specialists who didn't come were those
Individuals with narrow tasks, mostly of a creative nature.
They completed their assignment,
But I know they were not let loose,

Because, with the qualifications they had acquired,

It was no easy matter letting them roam free.
And, as you know, there is always
Lots of work for decent professionals.
We remained in contact with them.
They even came to visit; that was not forbidden.

Generally speaking, the security regime was pretty comfortable,
Which couldn't fail to impress.
Perhaps this is the beauty of global projects like these;
What's to hide and from whom?
Terrorists?

What could they do without data
Without supercomputers?
Without a single vision of the overall process,
The details would look like utter nonsense
Or desperate, foolish futurism.

Actually, the plan had been for the groups
To join forces a little later,
But the assignment had proved to be so complex
That General Johnson had decided
To gather at one centre.

As you recall, we had already made a Grand Map,
Illustrating the roaming of people, storms, merchants, famine, books
And pretty little morons
Fighting each other,
Establishing diplomatic relations

And getting entwined in official
And emotionless love intrigues.
The second step involved doing the impossible –
Attach the algorithm to emotional processes,
See at least some kind of non-chaotic system there,

To be able to anticipate the direction of vectors,
Emerging after the formulation of Responses
In the bifurcation points.
Well, what can I say?
We tormented dozens, even hundreds of doctors of psychology,

Trying to find these signs of the historicity of emotions.
We engaged in live simulation,
Becoming guinea pigs,
Taking it in turns to wear Napoleon cocked hats
And bear the sceptres of Prince Charles.

But to no avail.
The effect of Priam, selecting the most ridiculous solution
Of all possible solutions,
The Caesar's Rubicon effect,
The Fair Saladin effect

Could not be classified at all

Or subjected to any intelligible systematisation.
Incidentally, everything worked out much simpler with motivations.
We actually united them with the concept of
Interests and the paradigms we achieved were pretty clear.

But, friends, when we talk of revolution,
Where just one word might mean everything –
We could do nothing about this.
How could General de Gaulle,
With one radio station in London,

Manage to achieve a situation
Where the suppressed and, essentially, non-existent France
Became a full-fledged participant
In the post-war division of the world?
How did Stalin's single phrase –

Life has become better, life has become happier, comrades
Change the post-war rhythm of life in the USSR
From the sacrificial heroic
To one of total creative optimism?
And all that against the backdrop of the GULAGs still being around?!

What happened to people when one person
Simply appeared and said *I have a dream*?
How did these ragged, hungry and bearded lads
Descend from the mountains and create the New Cuba?
Why did Rouget de Lille, author of the *Marseillaise*,

Become an overnight hero
And then disappear into the abyss of revolution, never to be seen again?
It was at a moment of feverish searching and despair
That our group was formed,
Comprised of me, Rajpal and Hima.

Hima was the Finn Veiko Himmanen.
Perhaps we became close because of our knowledge of Russian;
Hima had lived a long time in Saint Petersburg
With his girlfriend, who...
Well, now's not the time for that.

Be that as it may,
One day we had buried ourselves away
In one of the *burrows* of our complex.
Burrows was the name we gave to the fabulously equipped
Rooms for our brainstorming assignments,

Which were great not because of the equipment and facilities
But because they each had settees, a shower and coffee,
Even a small bar.
Most important, they had excellent ventilation,
So we could smoke.

Basically, we were so happy
That the smoking regime
Was not at all American.
Without all that stupid social nonsense.

Most interesting was that we approached the matter in such a way

That those who suffered from the smoke
Never suffered at all.
That those who suffered without smoke
Likewise never suffered at all.
Okay, I digress.

Hima somehow managed to systematise everything in a really calm manner,
Also helping us to understand
Where the essence of the dead ends actually were.
(I so respect those Finns for their calm, methodical nature!)
Then there were several days of creativity

And one hardcore piss-up,
After which we gathered in our *burrow*
And started yelling that we had had insight
With a massive hangover.
We quickly put together a draft solution

And after three hours, drinking litres of coffee and water,
To the understanding smiles of General Johnson,
We told him
What we *had got to devising there*,
Interrupting one another and dropping papers on the floor.

I was trying to fix my slurred speech
Almost completely.
'General, things aren't as bad with humankind as they appear.
(Stupid questions were a necessary accompaniment for all conversations,
Even the most serious)

First of all, studies have shown
That we don't have one enemy but two.
The first, as you know, the extreme variability of emotions,
Close to complete chaos and complete unpredictability,
If we are talking about at least a hundred individuals.

The second enemy is the so-called causal attribution,
Which means we attribute
Role-playing emotions for historical characters.
And this means that if we work with quasi-emotions,
We fail to get a picture of the true emotional state

Of the historical character, right?
Is there a baseline level
To which one could descend without losing the essence
And the objectives of the field being studied,
In which individuals are completely different from each other,

But where they play key roles?
Nothing worked out with the basic emotions,
However many of them there were in the classification system.
You know that.
If there are two of them, the variability will all the same

Tend towards infinity.

Most important, we will still remain
Alone with the qualitative features of our emotions.'
(I drank a huge glass of water
But the General waited patiently for me to continue.)

'Where can we see a different understanding of the basic nature of emotions?
If we take Freud or Jung,
We still run into the individual characteristics of the individual,
And given that we have millions of them, this is no use to us.
Then (Rajpal clicked his mouse and turned the next page of the presentation),

Then we came to the two-factor theory of Stanley Schechter.
According to this theory,
Emotions arise in the form of a quantitative component –
The functions of physiological arousal
And the qualitative – the interpretation of this arousal.

Of course, Shechter has another quantitative section in mind,
But what interests us is that,
If we accept
That emotions are basically identical in origin,
Then we can extrapolate that to all people!

And, accordingly, we get another quantitative parameter,
Only the one that we need.
Obviously, the emotions of all people at once
Is a hypothetical thing,
Which might be typical

Only for the age of the global information space.
Therefore, we must define the unit
That will play the role of a fractal of the entire historical process.
The problem with modern psychology is
That it sets out the psychology of the individual wonderfully

And isn't bad at systematising the psychology of the masses.
However, the masses are viewed more often in the form of temporary connections,
Like a crowd on the square
Or during the storming of the Winter Palace.
Psychology is good at defining group behaviour in small groups

But when it comes to an understanding of large historical groups,
They are actually doing pretty badly.
Perhaps the reason is in fundamental history
Which itself is unable to define
What it is, even a provisional fractal of humanity

And which of them possesses the greatest number of the module's features.
We had to find an acceptable understanding
Of the fractal of human civilisation,
As a group, the characteristics of which
Humanity as a whole possesses.

Races won't do; there are too many of them
And worse still, there are too many transitional forms.
The superethnoses won't do either;
Their boundaries are just too arbitrary.

We have already come undone with ethnogenesis;

You know that.
There are no clear boundaries and that means there is a constant
Overlapping of phenomena.
Vytautas is whose hero – pure Lithuania's or Byelorussia's too?
Historically, is Genghis Khan Mongol or Turkic?

And so on.
When we analysed what the group underlying humanity as a whole
Should be in terms of the effectiveness of the research,
We concluded that this should be the mean group.
Again, as we understood it,

Based on the empirical nature of the research,

Not from the standpoint of a sociological or psychological
Scholarly vision.
Well, you know, you have to take risks.
So, in terms of group participants, there should be
No more than three hundred.

Where can we find such a classification?
Nowhere, but we could see it
On our own Grand Map
And the principle of the group's vision is quite obvious.
We take the countries of the world as a group.

Clearly, their size is not a constant, but
We will proceed from the number of nations as of today
As a starting point,
Going *back*, and changes to country borders will not play
Such an important role for us.

Today we have 193 countries,
Acknowledged as subjects under international law,
12 that are not recognised,
3 in the form of territories with an undetermined status
Plus 62 dependent territories.

In other words, this is precisely the scaling of groups that we need.
Moving on.
Now we need to choose an emotional fractal.
With the unification of emotions into one physiological group
This has become easier to achieve.

All that is needed is to assign
Standardised features to the emotions.
We adopted the following parameters –
Seeing as we are talking about the emotions of a country as a group unit,
Then we take the first parameter,

Which is a nationwide event.
Such events might be accession to the throne
Of a new ruler, the release of a critical legislative act,
Completion of the building of a town or temple;
Generally, there's a lot of purely specialist technical work here.

The first question that arises is:
How is war marked if it concerns two subjects at once?
Here, as in classical diplomacy,
There are bilateral and multilateral relations.
If two subjects are involved,

Then we mark both of them.
If the interests of several subjects are affected,
We then enter the notion of the *continuous* or *network* emotion,
Where we mark as epicentre points
All those who, one way or another, are involved in the conflict.'

The General fidgeted in his chair:
'Wait a minute, so, in choosing a state, how are
We moving away from the ethnogenesis platform?'
'By giving the event the semblance of a mathematical function –
One event, one physiological emotion, one place,

Marked on the map as an epicentre point,
Which means that it makes no difference which ethnos ascribes
That historical event to itself.
We label the overall involvement in a completely different fashion.
The functional approach is the most important thing.'

'But the degree of involvement of different countries isn't the same, is it?'
'That's right, but you are already touching on qualitative characteristics.
Allow me to return to the continuous or network emotions.
We assign to every network emotion a numerical
And a letter-based code,

And we assign a separate layer on the Grand Map to each.
That way we can see the super-ethnic or regional
Distribution of the emotion as a physiological flash.
Global emotions obtain another level
Of numeric and letter-based classification,

Where the letter defines the type of event,
The first number, the mode of repetition,
The second, third and so on – any quantitative characteristics.
Now we introduce another stable quantitative indicator –
The time duration of an emotion.

To do this, we take the Russian quaternary classification of emotions,
Which are divided according to the duration
Of their impact over time.
Specifically: Affects, Emotions, Feelings and Moods.
These concepts also differ in their intensity,

But their essence is simple: over time, we see a drop in their intensity
And impact.
In the graphic solution we simply apply
The living factor of the time the emotion existed
By calculating the average empirical duration.

As a result, we see the following on the map:
First, the emotional epicentres arise,

Then emotion, with a certain coefficient
Of the speed of information movement
That is characteristic for the given age,

Shall be distributed as networks outside the state
Or remaining inside it as a conditionally pulsating point.
Thanks to the measurability of the time parameter,
These emotions exist throughout
Different periods of time and then just disappear!

We have obtained a completely calculable quantitative field,
That is not only measurable but one that can also be visualised!
Now for the qualitative characteristics.
Yes, indeed, as you move away from the epicentre
Emotion can weaken and have varying degrees of intensity.

Moreover, the distance factor is not necessarily the most important thing;
For example, Japan, which is located
In the immediate vicinity of the USSR,
Most probably reflected less on the fact of its collapse
Than Cuba, which lost a buyer

For its sugar cane,
Imports of which to the USSR
Made up the lion's share of its national wealth.
One way or another, as regards the quality of emotions,
We can assign a conventional impact scale to it,

For the sake of credibility, some 90-ary scale,
To account for the maximum number of nuances.
The power of impact and reflection
Is something we can denote in the form of light differentiation
and take Max Luscher's approach as the basis for this,

Adapted to the maximum to the psychology of nations.
We have already carried out a number of practical experiments
With the Grand Map of Theoretical History,
And we have revealed a number of remarkable features of the method.
First, according to the intensity with which the epicentres arise,

We can see indirect confirmation
Of Gumilyov's theory of passionarity, where we can visually see
The difference in activity in the akmatic phase
From the behaviour of a nation in homeostasis.
We see that the intensity might not decrease,

But the colour difference evidences
The increasing power of conservative trends
And their dominance over the active-reformist
Or military trend.
The map of network emotions

Allows us to see certain confirmation
Of the priority of mutual interactions
Of the states of Heartland and the crescent of Rimland.
We really can visually see
The emotional link of many geopolitical axes.

631

We can say the same about the ideas of Spengler and Toynbee.
Once again, in conditional real time, we observe
Confirmation of many civilisational views.
However, the most valuable is that we can consider
Their more systematic adjustment.

In this way, by initially entering emotions
Into the system as a vulgar physiological impulse at first,
In the end we can, by building up the qualitative characteristics,
Come to a maximum measurability
Of interpretations for the broadest range of emotions.

We can even add layers of causal attribution,
To see different versions
Of emotional fluctuations of individuals and nations,
Or we can simply fantasise;
The layers of artistic conjecture can always just be removed.

At the last stage, we made a model
For growing motives and interests
And we could observe if it was the case
That in the algorithm we were proposing,
The system of complex enhancement of motivations

Actually leads to the advent of an epicentre of a surge of emotions.
And, oh, what a miracle! We achieved an almost 80 per cent
Match of fields.
However, this combination of fields will require more time
To allow us to clean the experiment as much as possible

From random coincidences.
Now we have to formulate
The rudiments of the approach to error rates,
But this seems to be a daunting task
As it will mostly require the work of a machine.'

The General suddenly stood up
And said, 'I want to see all this on the Grand Map!'
We knew that, despite the fact that
We had showed him in great detail
All the animated fragments and illustrations,

Nothing is better than viewing the hypothesis
Directly on the Grand Map.
Why? You've guessed it!
Who can resist the opportunity,
Albeit for a moment, to become godlike?!

****

The General was truly shocked by what he saw!
The animated map not only moved mechanically.
On the surface of this artificial earth
Nations and characters lived, felt, loved,
Suffered, died in anguish,

Sang triumphal marches,
Kidnapped princesses,
Suffered from leprosy,
Challenged others to duels,
Shared money and power.

He saw feelings being born,
Hatred growing and glory subsiding,
Messengers spreading the news,
The Fuhrer smashing his fist on the table in a wild delirium
And Stalin wheezing in dying delirium.

The memory of heroes disappearing
And new heroes emerging from the ashes.
He saw Alexander's mighty phalanx,
He saw the Romans' horror before Hannibal's elephants,
He saw men crying out *La garde meurt et ne se rend pas!*[252]

The Sioux perishing on the banks of Wounded Knee
And bombs flying to Nagasaki.
There go the Soviet students to virgin lands.
There rests the Chaka Zulu, with his assegai on his knees.
There flows the dark blood from the head of Lincoln!

Johnson, clearly in a state of shock,
Turned silently and left the room.
In the corridor he stood and barked,
'You three – do nothing for three days, just rest;
That's an order!' He left the complex in a quick march.

That evening, exchanging barely a word,
Each of us hung a portrait of the great Poincaré
Over our desks,
With the quotation underneath: *A reality completely independent of the spirit
That conceives it, sees it, or feels it, is an impossibility.*

****

However, it so happened
That we started our work not in three days
But a little later.
One of the reasons was that
General Johnson,

In order to fulfil the tasks of the third and decisive stage,
Reorganised the groups.
There were three of them again,
But each of them were given
New objectives.

The first group was given the name
Event Series Synchronisation Group.

---

[252] *The Guards die but never surrender!* The phrase uttered by General Pierre Jacques Etienne Cambronne at the Battle of Waterloo, when the fate of the battle had already been decided. The remaining battalions of the Imperial Guard were told to surrender, to which Cambronne replied with this legendary phrase. In response, the British destroyed the guards with volleys of buckshot.

We immediately gave the group members the nickname *Archangels*.
The thing is that, dealing with the past,
We had brought events to a period that was now two years old.

The group now had to:
A - Catch up with current events;
B - Synchronize events happening now,
With the Grand Map life algorithm.
In other words, for the Map to settle in

Perfectly in sync with real life,
With a time delay of half a day.
This algorithm was linked with the process for accumulating information
And with the time lag in the USA.
All the while, it was American time

That gave us the advantage
Of the most accurate reflection of the real picture of the day.
At first this group was
At the top of a giant global network
For the systematic collection of data,

Until it came to addressing Task C –
Bringing the process of receiving information
And introducing it into the mathematical model of the Grand Map
To a maximum state of automation.
In this way, the world of the Grand Map

Became an almost completely automated
And self-existing system.
The name *Archangels* hadn't come about by chance:
We saw that our colleagues were
Like messengers of heavenly will,

Between them bringing the world of
The real into line with the world of the ideas of the demiurges.
The second section was called
The *Modified Changes Group*.
As a joke, we also called them

The *Subjunctive Group*, and here's why.
As you know, history doesn't tolerate
The subjunctive.
In reality, there can be no *if that it were* and *if that it weren't*.
But this does not apply to the opportunities of the *Constellation* project.

We can, we want and now we have the opportunity
To model episodes of the past
If peoples and individual characters
Had acted differently
In the bifurcation points.

In essence, the work was extremely interesting
Because even our limitless imagination
Is not able that often to issue such twists in historical events
That would have occurred, had historical figures acted
One way or another, but on the plains of the Grand Map, anything was possible.

However, we shouldn't think that the group was engaged
Solely in this most entertaining of scripts.
The guys' main task was
To train, test and prepare
The principal player for predicting the future –

Artificial intelligence.
If you specify modifications
Of historical development vectors
AI should not be overly passive
Or overly aggressive.

It should be natural and *relevant*,
Forming the functions of resistance, assistance,
Accompaniment, confrontation and counter-initiative.
It should have a certain flexibility in decision making,
And imply a degree of emotional involvement.

And much more besides.
In other words, our colleagues actually created
A mathematical demiurge.
However, the nickname *demiurges* never
Really stuck with the guys from the group,

But the nickname *Demons* did,
Thanks again to that lad from France
(His name was Roger Clemenceau),
Who, during our first conversation,
Said we would have to create a mathematical devil.

Our group, which, in addition to me, Rajpal and Hima, included
Another nine people,
Were originally given the nickname *Gods*,
Because we had to do the most important thing –
Everything that had been realised and systematised in the past

Had to be taken and deployed for predicting the future.
Figuratively speaking, we had to lift the rails from behind us
And place them in front to continue moving.
Then, essentially, we had to see this future,
As if we were soothsayers, prophets or someone like that,

Vested with the gift of prescience.
That said, the nickname didn't stick,
Either because it was overly pretentious
Or because of the advent of some new oddity
Among the members of the *Constellation* project;

Somehow, everyone imperceptibly acquired the features
Of some anxious unction.
It wasn't a case of total canonical religiousness,
But blaspheming
Or making risqué jokes

Became outright bad manners.
Therefore, a little later, the group

Acquired a new and not so controversial nickname –
Zwölf meaning the twelve, the number of group members.
It was accidentally given by our lead analyst,

Peter Blucher from Germany
And easily picked up by everyone else,
Because, if you remember,
We had been communicating for some time now
In a multilingual slang that only we understood.

And so, after some time,
That the other groups needed to perform their basic assignments,
We set about studying the holiest of the holies –
Modelling the main question of the research –
The World Social Revolution.

It has to be said that certain changes had begun
To appear in the atmosphere surrounding the project.
The first of them was
The significant intensification of secrecy.
This happened after General Johnson,

Behind closed doors and without us
Presented the first developments to the project's Fathers.
It has to be said, this was a serious matter.
Just imagine, the Demons, you see, not only simply modified
Whatever historical events they wanted –

Of course, they were primarily engaged in revolutions.
Therefore, we received huge arrays
Of event-based variability from them
Of all the more-or-less famous revolutionary events,
From the palace coup of Tutankh-Aton,

Who became Tutankh-Amon as a result,
To the Arab revolutions of the 21st century.
We included a conventional time accelerator
On the Grand Map, set a mass of algorithms
And gave the expanses of AI to this uncompromising demiurge.

So far we had taken only national and short-term approximations.
What started happening on the Grand Map
Defies any description.
We observed such twists and turns in the clashes of characters,
Real government leaders,

Their peoples, political systems and so on,
That we had no need for any futurological cinema.
Before your eyes, we could change the initial parameters
And calm evolutionary development
Would transform into a whirlwind of fateful events,

Leading to default, collapse,
The disappearance of whole nations and the destruction of international law.
Checking the short-term forecast was ridiculously easy.
All we had to do was implement one of the set
Risk parameters (and I won't lie, this was done often),

And those same interconnected phenomena,
That the day before had been but a puppet model
On our Grand Map, began to manifest themselves
In real life.
Events began to move confidently toward those attractors

That we had anticipated the day before.
A one-hundred-per-cent match of results
Brought the Fathers of the project to a state of mystical horror,
And we were locked in our complex
Like prisoners.

Only it wasn't this change that proved the most disturbing.
The most disturbing change concerned us,
And it involved the fact
That we didn't suffer at all without the outside world.
The eyes of the chaps in the *Demons*, the *Archangels*

And, most of all in the *Zwölf*,
Those with the maximum knowledge and information,
Began to burn with a most unhealthy fire.
This now whiffed not only of fanaticism,
But of serious psychological shifts.

Two months later and we had already completely exhausted
All the variability of the short-term forecast
And the modelling of local revolutions.
The time had come to search for the time and place
Of the key worldwide collapse.

And here we encountered unexpected
And systemic obstacles.
However many predicted configurations of events
The chaps from the *Demons* suggested to us,
The supercomputer began refusing to issue the final model,

Issuing the stock answer *insufficient information*.
We modified scenarios through it all:
Hunger, world war or fundamental climate change.
One we even entered the parameters of a worldwide catastrophe
Of a cosmic nature – asteroids, Nibiru and all that.

But AI clammed up, most often transforming
The wonderful Grand Map
Into a colourless, animated, dumb cartoon.
The voices of sceptics grew stronger,
Saying that perhaps this was evidence that

Such an event would simply never come to pass.
That it just wouldn't happen.
And that we were dealing merely with a complex manifestation
Of causal attribution,
Ascribing role-playing behaviour to all of humanity.

The behaviour that, as such, it
Wouldn't be able to, would not want to and would not implement.

However, General Johnson would not rest,
And, incidentally, neither did the majority of the *Zwölf* Group either.
If such events as world war,

The reconsideration of all state borders
Of all countries in the world or the advent of a single ethnogenesis
Were being designed, then why wasn't the World Revolution?
Everything could be anticipated - even the advent
Of an alien civilisation and consequent human behaviour,

But why was it that World Revolution
Led to a system crash?
After all, it was an obvious crash!
So, what mysteries was *this* event actually hiding?
We had no doubt that it was mysteries it was hiding.

Nevertheless, many hours of brainstorming,
Variative modelling of events,
Bordering on insanity and a total loss of logic,
Failed to reveal any more-or-less suitable
Explanation for the phenomenon that had arisen.

One day, sitting in a tired and fateful atmosphere
Of the fruitless collective searches of the *Zwölf* Group,
The General suddenly said something incomprehensible:
'We need John!'
We shuddered from the unexpectedness,

Trying to understand what we had just heard.
Who do we need?!
It transpired that our inflamed minds had affected our ears.
'We need Juan, Juan Bolivar!'
Johnson said, now clearly, loudly and confidently.

We realised what this meant literally the following morning
When into our main consultative *burrow*
Strode this tall lad with a bushy beard
And long, curly hair.
He was dressed oddly, but the strangeness of his attire

Was not something that would easily surprise us;
By the way our creative types dressed
We could boldly predict the arrival of aliens.
However, the strangeness of his clothes involved something else –
Either he was a hippie or some separatist.

The mysterious Juan Bolivar
Was evidently an old acquaintance of General Johnson.
It wasn't just his clothes that were strange, for
He himself was extraordinarily pale
And he leaned on a bamboo stick.

'Hi Tango,' Johnson said with special tenderness
That had us all seized by envy.
Juan smiled and his smile was so radiant
That it was in sharp contrast to his wan, emaciated appearance.
'Hello, Major, how many times do I have to tell you,

I am Cuban, even though I live in Argentina!'
This was evidently a customary ritual of theirs,
As the General quickly forgot about it,
Jumped up and personally sat Juan on a chair.
Is he a drug addict or something? was the mean thought that flashed through my mind.

'Well,' Juan said, looking over the group with a smile,
'What did you steal me from the hospital for, Gringo?'
'Gringo? What's with the familiarity?' came another jealous emotion.
Johnson began to explain
The essence of the problem.

At some point Juan closed his eyes
As if he was tired, but then he interrupted Johnson,
Placing his hand on the General's.
'I see, Major... oh, who are you now, Gringo?'
'General,' Johnson said, taken aback.

'I see, General, so you've gone for this all the same!
You decided not to listen to me then?'
Johnson suddenly grew angry, but in a grumbling way,
Like a fussy old man.
'How did you want things to go, Tango?

You think a man invents an axe
To place it in a museum and take pride in it?
You think man invented the television
To buy it and admire its design?
No, chum, everything that we have invented

Must, simply must, work for our good, Tango,
For your good and the good of our children!'
Juan coughed rather helplessly
And cast a somewhat vapid glance at the General.
'I don't have children, Gringo. And you know why.'

The general stopped short, but then went on,
Although his cheeks were flushed:
'Well, others have children! Come on, Juan, you do admit
There are children in the world, don't you?!'
Juan turned to us, as if the General were not in the *burrow* at all.

'You know, he set fire to me and my men in Bolivia, in the jungle there.
I was left on my own, but I can't have children.
I don't mean physiologically,' he said and beamed,
As if he were telling a story.
'It's just... like someone told me not to. And, anyway, when would I have been able to have
them?'

'Listen, Tango...' Johnson was about to say,
But Juan interrupted him, continuing to address us:
'But I am alive thanks to this Gringo.
I don't know what drove him, but it was your boss
Who pulled me from those dungeons

That, it seems, don't actually exist in America.

You go in, but you never come out again.'
The general was silent and appeared embarrassed.
'Come on, Tango, why are you telling the lads here?'
'Trust, Gringo,' Juan said weightily.

'We want to work together and achieve something, right?
So, there must be trust between us.
And anything left unsaid simply destroys it.
Go on, Major... oh!'
'Oh come on!' Johnson waved a hand and, relieved,

Continued telling Juan about the project.
Juan appeared to listen but simultaneously looked
Over each of us attentively
Giving each of us a smile,
As if to say, yes, *and you're a good chap too!*

We'll cooperate just fine.
'All right, Gringo, don't rant and rave!
It's just what we've always talked about
And what I've always warned you –
If you seek to predict everything

That a man might do,
Then that means what God can do too.
After all, he leads us, right?
I don't need details, just that back then,
In my youth, I told you that idiotic idea...'

'Yes, but,' the General said, a little affronted.
'So much time has passed since that day
And technology has come so far...'
'Don't be offended, Gringo. I'm not reproaching you for anything.
You always were and always will be a great soldier.

So, tell me, why then,
When I lay before you,
You didn't empty the magazine into me, eh?
Why did you hand me over to the CIA
Only after healing and patching me up?

Is that not a crash of the base algorithm?
After all, you always were the best soldier, right?
What will happen if the best soldiers
Deviate from their functional paradigms?
After all, back then, *there*, there was only me, you and the jungle.

What, then, might happen if there's lots of them there,
And all with crashed algorithms, eh?
You're awfully quiet, Gringo!
Let's suppose you've calculated the variability of the manifestation of emotions,
But by averaging them, is it people you're dealing with?

Now, show me what you've done on your Grand Map.'
He got up with difficulty but politely refused
Hima's help, leaning on Johnson's arm.
We went through to the central demonstration hall.

For several hours, Juan silently observed the processes

That the *Archangels*, *Demons* and representatives
Of the *Zwölf* Group showed him.
Juan said not a word, but later signalled to Johnson
That it was time to return to the *burrow*.
There, he asked for a glass of water and, glancing guiltily at me,

Saying, 'It's medicine – I can't go without it,'
He drank down some pills.
I noticed that there were many of them.
Juan's face was now veiled in a curtain of sadness.
He paused and then asked everyone,

'And what, do most of the predictions really come to pass?'
'Yes!' We all blurted out together.
Bolivar shook his head and looked at Johnson.
'Major, let's cut to the chase:
What do you *really* want from me?'

The general jumped up and paced around the room.
'Tango, you're the son of the Revolution;
You know first-hand
What that is. *What* people feel and sense,
What they do when, step by step,

They make it by themselves.
You had a brilliant future, after all, didn't you?
An education, a family, people around you.
What did you feel when the colossus of the regime
Seemed enormous and unshakable?

What did you feel afterwards,
When you saw his vulpine fear and helplessness?
How, Juan, how?
How does it work?
I know all there is to know about war and partisans, you know what I mean...

I know what it's like to be an official, a citizen,
A solider and a taxpayer.
But... to rise up against the current order?
When the front line passes literally right through your apartment,
Where your dad is a royalist, your brother a loyalist

And your mum was brought up in the spirit of not fighting evil with violence?'
'No, no, Major, I'm not asking you
To what your duty as a soldier, official,
Taxpayer and project leader calls you to do.
I am asking why do *you*

And these lads need it? And in the end, Gringo?
To whom will you impart strength? To those who,
Tomorrow, getting your results and their own,
Will chase over jungle and desert after people like me?
Humanity has plenty of excellent inventions,

But are that many really

Designed to do good?'
The General looked at us and said,
'You know, Juan, even at the initial stage,
The guys and I agreed

That we were creating a project but we would have
No relationship with its results.'
'Marvellous!' Juan exclaimed, slapping his hand on the table.
'You agreed! Tell the truth: you demanded that
And there was nothing they could do but agree to it!'

The General looked at us anxiously,
As if to say we shouldn't be privy to this conversation.
'Major, don't you be shy in front of the guys.
Perhaps it is in the absence of meanings that that
Crash of the paradigm that led you down a dead end is hidden?

I agree that, at the first stages, you might have been driven
By purely professional ambitions,
But when you got to the point where you had to assess
Human worldview values,
How could you remain indifferent? Tell me!

You ask me about the Revolution?
Anyone could do it, do you see? Anyone!
The only one who *cannot* do it
Is precisely the one who is indifferent,
Unconcerned and intent on consuming the end result.

A social animal who is happy with
The price paid for him and how much he has to pay for power!
Revolution for him is the nightmare of instability and deviation from the rules;
And you think there are high values behind such deviations?
Not one! Believe me, not one!

Only fear, cowardice, self-justification and self-abasement!
People like that don't need to be belittled,
As they will do that themselves, and all because
They don't think about how to *live through* it, the Revolution,
But what will come of it and where the personal benefits are hidden!

So, tell me, isn't what you're doing a Revolution,
At least as far as technology is concerned?
Is all that you've modelled
Not able to model the Golden Age?
For those who live *there*, on that map?'

'Listen, Tango, what, you're trying to give a soul
To these electronic models that roam about this model?'
'No, Major, I'm trying to stop you taking away the soul
From those who have created this quasi-world,
And have to formulate a moral belief for themselves

In respect of this.'
'Well, you know,' the General said, turning to the window.
'If anyone else were here instead of me,
He'd say that this was not a professional approach.'

Suddenly he turned sharply and, narrowing his eyes, snapped,

'Or perhaps, Bolivar, you want me
To turn these guys into revolutionaries, is that it?
To make them *want* it, right?
And model it, well, for themselves, for the future?
Then to go and complete it in reality?!

And what do you think the Fathers of the project should say to me?
Ah, no, I'll tell them we are just role-playing,
That we love revolution only for technical reasons.
And they'll say, of course, Johnson, Why ever not?
Well done, keep it up! Is that what you think?!

What, you think that the Fathers of the project are a bunch of fools?
That they don't understand this is all...'
The General waved at the papers, slides and laptops,
'... A weapon?
A weapon against those who want to undermine the foundations of peace?!'

'Gringo,' Juan said weightily.
It's *you* who's modelling the Revolution.
You're already the bastard
Who's trying to see the benefit you can get from its outcome.
Do you know what those who wait indifferently

For revolution and those who plan it for others
From their cosy, warm offices,
As your friends have done so brilliantly
Not only in Langley, but in London, the Tuileries,
The Kremlin and God knows where else have in common?

What they have in common is that they don't care
About those who are destined to *live through* it, lose their social status,
Relatives, friends, peace and quiet and their customary way of life,
While retaining their soul in the process,
The freedom of their soul before Heaven and their Homeland.

Now, though, on this electronic boilerplate,
This is your Revolution, Major!
You live through it.
Perhaps then you'll understand its algorithms and paradigms,
And perhaps then you'll find it in you

To participate in the process where the decisions are made
As to who will reap its sacred fruits!
And you share that with your guys,
For they are not simply working for you;
They are *living* their lives here.'

He tapped the floor of the *burrow* with his stick,
'Not to teach these electronic impulses to walk,
Rather to give everything they are doing here
A certain higher meaning.
And if they don't know it yet,

You are not just their boss, you're their mentor!

So, teach them that, General Johnson.
Then you'll see how secondary the importance
Of finding a technical solution to that impasse
That you found yourself in.

And I'll... I'll help you, so be it.
I am in your debt, after all.'
The General was about to raise his hand, but Juan interrupted him:
'Don't object – I need to repay my debt to you for my sake,
For the sake of what I'll say to the Lord when I meet him.'

To be honest, we didn't fully grasp everything that the General and Juan
Had spoken about.
It was obvious, however, that the conversation
Was a continuation of some other dialogue,
That they had started a very long time ago.

Starting literally from the following day,
Juan immersed himself into the work.
At first he listened attentively to all our calculations
About where the problem might lie
And how we had tried to resolve or get out around it.

He listened very attentively.
He would nod or interject with brief comments,
As if to ensure we were talking about the same thing.
He spent a lot of time
With the Demons, asking them to demonstrate

Certain revolutionary subjects,
After which he would fall silent and thoughtful.
After one of the sessions of variable changes,
His eyes were tearful for a long while for some reason,
As if he regretted something or was experiencing something in a new way.

The *Zwölf* group had a very warm, friendly
Relationship with him.
He was never as tough on us
As he sometimes was with the General,
But, still, it was with him that he

Had a special relationship.
In time, we came to understand
That he was seriously ill,
So much so that his condition deteriorated before our eyes.
One day he even appeared with a nurse

And then in an automatic wheelchair.
He was fading away, that was clear,
But Juan's smile, oddly enough,
Was always radiant and literally rejuvenated
The dedicated recipient.

And we needed rejuvenation
Because we were running ourselves ragged.
Our rooms were opposite,
So it fell to me most often

To take Juan out for a walk along the alleys

That stretched all around our complex.
We would chat during these walks.
Juan did not talk about himself, and I did not pester him.
As such, all conversations, one way or another, were about work.
Sometimes the only conversations went like this:

'Andres, what would you never give to anyone?'
'Well, I don't know, er, my Homeland,
The right to be myself... Mum...
Juan, hey, I'm still young and I don't really have anything –
No wife, family, no big house or money.'

'And what would you do if someone tried
To take all that away from you?'
'Ha... You're waiting for me to say I'll grab my gun
And storm the barracks of Moncada?
Hardly. I dodged the draft.

You're probably looking for heroes among us.
We're for the most part programmers, historians, nerds, basically.
Even if they've spent six months
In the mincer as part of *Delta Force* or *Counter Strike*,
They'll faint at the sight of an unloaded Makarov.'

'You're wrong, Andres, everyone has their own citadel,
Which they're prepared to defend to the death.'
'Well, maybe you're right, I don't know...
Only where can this courage be applied?
Unless it's to fight back against louts on the street,

But... there's not much point in that.'
'How do you mean?'
'Well, there's always a crowd of them; the outcome is obvious.'
'And what do you normally do in such instances?'
'What do you mean? Scarper the heck out of there.'

'I don't think you're any different from Jorge Manuel.'
'Who is that?'
'Well, this lad. The son of the chemist.
I remember, we always used to duff him up on the street
And take his pocket money to buy cigars.'

'And?'
'Well, nothing. One day during a fight,
He ran between the hills as a messenger.
He was told to at least take gun with him,
But he just said that he wasn't afraid.

Once, though, he took a grenade.
We saw him from a distance away, standing calmly,
Waiting for them to approach in greater numbers.
He looked exactly the same as when we used to beat him up –
He stood there, his eyes squeezed shut in fear.

And then... *Venceremos!*

And he pulled out the pin.
Those twelve soldiers probably weren't enough then
To do us all in in those hills...'
'Juan, well, I don't know.

Somehow, that is all so unlikely for me.
Or perhaps I don't know what I am capable of,
But I don't really want
To get into a situation
That forces me to find out.'

Bolivar nodded in silence
And then we just talked
About the principles behind algorithm selection
And other professional nonsense.
To be honest, with him everything seemed calmer.

That mad glint in the eyes had gone.
It had the best possible effect at work too.
We worked keenly, thought clearly,
And everyone sought each other's advice: *Juan, what do you think?*
Tango, and what if we go in like this?

Hey, and what if we change the principle itself, the very approaches?
He liked phrases like these most of all.
He was a revolutionary even in the little things.
He even use to smoke contraband cigars
Behind the doctors' backs!

Where on earth did he get them from?
We later learned, of course: he got them from General Gringo!
Sure, he would swear for appearance's sake,
Saying, 'Come on, you were high yesterday!
We agreed – one, and no more!'

Then we'd catch sight of them both on the secret bench
Behind block three, sitting, puffing away
And laughing about something.
The General would straighten his blanket,
Check the wheelchair was standing firm.

That's how they lived. And the work?
It was here that things became really complicated and interesting.
One day we brought representatives of all three groups together,
For a brainstorming session
On the causes of revolution.

An enormous table was created,
With motives, reasons, interests,
Capital, grievances and conspiracies.
Juan listened at length and then said,
'You are all discussing this

Not like the organisers of a revolution, rather...
The organisers of some advertising campaign:
One lot want this, others want that.
Remember, those who organise and plan a revolution

With cold hearts

Are enemies of your Homeland and they are not part of it.
What we are looking for is a continuous, universal algorithm
To get the heart racing,
Making revolution a career for life,
Life itself, right?

Forget all those permanent revolutions of Trotsky,
The lumpenproletariat
And Bakunin's Social Revolution movement –
They are just theories,
But not paradigms.

Why don't you answer this question instead:
What do you think the primary thing in a revolution is –
Revolutionary action or a sense of freedom?'
Opinions were split,
With some saying the motives come first,

Then action, followed, depending on the success,
By a sense of freedom.
Others objected, saying that first come the motives,
Then, simultaneously,
A sense of freedom and actions.

Juan listened at length and finally said,
'No, guys, it's not like that at all.
You can gather motives all your life,
Speak about them, feel outrage,
Present arguments and then go off to sleep,

To return sedately the next morning
To public service.
Actions cannot go first
Because revolutionary actions are akin to crime;
They are something unlawful,

From which only a criminal can feel satisfaction.
Let's just say that a revolution has plenty of criminals too.
Only it is not they who constitute its essence.
The most important thing, guys, is the sense of freedom!
When one day, contrary to logic,

Fear, prejudice and even your own safety,
You say, I am free!
I am different now! I can see and feel a new life!
There is no going back to the old ways for me!
No way,

Because it has ceased to be my reality.
My reality now is freedom!
You might be a hero, a warrior, a girl or a boy,
Yesterday's pen-pusher, a police officer
Or a simple boy from the yard,

But you change from just the understanding of this word –

Freedom!
And then nothing can stop you.
You can be broken, killed, trampled into the dirt,
But once you experience this new *feeling of oneself*,

You will never forget it!
Even if you suffer defeat,
Even if it takes years
But you will never go back to your former self
Never, ever, ever!'

Everyone fell silent, until Rajpal asked timidly,
'Tango, we can now see the universalism of this feeling,
But how do we turn it into a part of the mathematical model?'
'I don't know,' Juan said with a seemingly indifferent shrug.
'Let's do this:

Let's get into groups and hold
Separate meetings
Where everyone will remember
If they had such a sense of freedom,
How this happened and why.

If there wasn't such a sense, write *none*,
Don't fabricate anything.
And if there was, try to experience it again,
Remember it and then tell us
About your feelings!'

Everyone dispersed, scratching their heads,
But no one wanted to admit that there was no technical point
In such an idea,
But the fact it was just interesting –
This was clear in any event – it was no different with Juan.

A couple of days later we gathered
All the results in the *Zwölf* Group,
And we were horrified!
Only a third of the recollections came from
Events having but a semblance

Of social colour to them!
The rest were about stealing sweets that parents had prohibited,
Nicking the neighbour's motorcycle,
Playing truant from kindergarten and buying ice cream
Or trying on their mum's makeup!

'Juan, this is a failure,' Hima said sadly.
Bolivar by this time had become really gravely ill.
He was now coughing badly and often, not like before.
He had to give up the cigars
And even the walks became shorter.

However, during the brainstorming sessions he was invariably calm
And smiling, despite the fact
That he was really suffering.
'No, no, I say, Veiko!' Juan said.

'Just no.

We have already reduced such an extensive
Multiplicity to a single attractor!'
'Yes, but,' I objected, 'if we enter this sense of freedom
As a regular physiological impulse of emotions,
Even with several quality characteristics,

This will still give us nothing;
We've already tried that!'
'Uhuh,' Rajpal agreed, 'even if we
Place the impulse everywhere.
The mathematical model will not be able to recognise *what* it is.

It will react in the same way
To the tsunami in Japan, the beginning of the Iraq war,
An Afro-American becoming US President
Or Spain winning the football World Cup!
What should distinguish this impulse from others?'

'Right,' Juan sighed,
Okay, shall we try to work with unknown factors?
Suppose there is this Factor X,
Which leads, say,
To the simultaneous emergence onto the square of many people.

Even if this is not really the same as a revolution.
We can still determine certain boundaries
Or contours of the impact of Factor X,
Which will first bring people onto the square,
And then, say, force them to dance or light fires.'

This was a familiar task for us
And we went off to our *burrows* and laboratories.
Now the algorithm had become pretty simple –
Motives > Factor X > Sense of Freedom > Emergence onto the Square.
Or something like that.

Before we went off, Juan asked me
To take him into a room.
To be honest, I was worried about him.
I was pushing his wheelchair along a corridor
When he unexpectedly grasped my arm.

'What do you think, Andres,
If we step away from all that technological nonsense for a moment;
Does this search for Factor X not remind you of anything?'
'N-no...' I mumbled.
'What is it supposed to remind me of?'

'Well...' Juan coughed heavily.
'We know that something will happen,
That something will take place
That will change the world;
We've found predictions –

So, can we give our mathematical model a name?

But then again, we don't know what to do with all this
Only because we are not properly ready
To see the future that we seek.'
'Tango, I have so much in my head,

That I just don't know
What to answer you...
But I promise that I'll find the time to think about it.'
Bolivar squeezed my hand hard:
'Promise you'll find the time, okay?'

'Okay.'
'Because the conclusion is near.' Juan looked me right in the eye.
'You mean the project's conclusion?'
I asked, not able to understand.
'Just promise!' 'Well, okay, I promise.'

I didn't understand anything
That Tango wanted to say to me,
But, to be honest I had no time for that.
My head was full of formulae
And various combinations of solutions.

The conclusion really was too close.
A week after working out combinations
With the unknown Factor X,
We entered the data into our supercomputer
And waited to see the result.

****

On that bright Sunday afternoon
People all around the world
Were getting ready for the festivities,
Preparing to visit friends
And dressing up for the occasion.

From the morning, we had gathered by the lead car.
Everyone was in high spirits.
General Johnson arrived in full parade dress
And revelled in hundreds of compliments.
Only Juan remained silent, chuckling to himself,

His expression making the General blush.
Rajpal sat at the computer
While I began my upbeat report:
'General, application of the principle of the intermediate unknown
Gave us the opportunity

To study the phenomenon of the Decisive Factor,
Without examining what it actually is,
But still to determine the degree of its impact,
Its contours and, most likely, its main characteristics
That, with the aid of a simple visual

Analysis, will help us determine
What it is.

Whether or not it is a phenomenon, the result of the work of a separate group
Or perhaps even of a particular individual.
We don't know this yet

But indirect pictures of the results of calculations
Demonstrate that the machine has found answers to our questions
And we have found ways out of all previous impasses.'
Someone applauded and the General nodded approvingly,
But Juan had closed his eyes for some reason.

'So, General Johnson,
Give the command
And we will launch the visualisation of the X phenomenon.'
The General ceremoniously glanced at his watch and nodded.
Rajpal opened up the Grand Map.

An image of multiple layers came on.
A picture appeared with a model of humanity in the present.
My lord, how beautiful it was!
It might have been artificial but it was still a living world
We had made with our own hands!

Everyone gradually began to grasp the sense
Of the extraordinary significance of the moment.
Then the conventional time accelerator was turned on.
Rajpal began to enter activation keys for
Factor X.

The camera jerked into action and glid across the map.
Aha! So, it wasn't a total phenomenon,
But more likely a local factor!
A subject or a group of subjects!
Suddenly musical sounds were heard from the machine

And several of us exchanged glances.
The music got louder and louder.
'Raj, turn that music off!'
But it grew louder! I suddenly recognised it
As *Confutatis* from Mozart's *Requiem*.

'Rajpal, I said, turn that music off!'
Hima was not shouting.
'But it's not me!' Raj cried.
'The machine is generating the music itself.'
I looked over at the General,

Who was shaking his hand impatiently
As if to say, *hah, let it play!*
That's not the important thing right now!
The view focus was increasing
And zoomed us into a point on the map.

I was sure no one had time to figure out
Where it was, what the country.
Closer and closer it went. And closer!
Then we could see a vague spot.
One moment longer And we would see what it was!

Suddenly, this awful interference passed across all
The enormous screens.
Everyone was talking at once.
The music reached its climax and filled the hall
Imperiously.

Right at that very moment,
When the focus was making its final adjustment,
An enormous word appeared, filling the screen:
Irratio.
What was it? What did it mean?!

The General twitched and leaned tensely forward.
The next word then popped up like a glowing scarlet flame:
Nomen.
Everyone started screaming.
Only the General remained silent and we saw

His iron jaws moving.
The next work shot out in a flame of blue.
Ratio.
Panicking, Rajpal tried pressing
Some buttons.

'Don't touch anything!'
Johnson suddenly yelled terribly,
And we didn't recognise him.
Seeing such an explosion of rage for the first time.
Rajpal rapidly removed his hand from the keyboard

And looked over at me, frightened.
The next word then appeared, in an ominous black frame
Immortalis.
'Does anyone understand what is going on?'
The General yelled again.

From the corner of my eye, I saw Juan Bolivar
Slowly wheeling his wheelchair to the door,
As if preparing not to let anyone out of the room.
Suddenly, the screens flashed
And displayed a date,

With the prefix y.b.,
Which evidently was indicating someone's year of birth.
Once again the screen seemed to lose its mind
And flashed opened another window,
Which also began to focus in

To a different place.
We could see the camera closing in on another silhouette.
In the next window along, the first silhouette
Was beginning to acquire a more clearly defined outline.
In yet another new window a new word lit up.

Magister.
'Someone write this down, God damn it!'

The General screamed again,
But there had been no need,
For Himmanen had recorded everything.

Homo.
Lit up in orange.
Requiem was already playing at full pelt.
Deus.
Was the next word from the machine to cascade

A new wave of interference and musical chords.
Inauguratio.
The screens all flashed
And everyone was overcome by a sense of mystical terror.
But the machine once more issued a birth date.

Rajpal suddenly let out a cry,
His hand pointing at the screens.
'I've got it! I've got it!
The first four words...
I've got it!!!

The first... Look at the first letters!
It's INRI!'[253]
'Oh!' everyone exclaimed.
'Factor X is... is INRI!
The date of birth... That means... That means!

And the second, what does the second abbreviation mean?'
Rajpal jumped up and, still pointing,
He cried, 'The second abbreviation is MHDI!
That stands for Mahdi[254]
And His date of birth as well!!!

That means they are already here!!! They are born!!!'
At first not everyone realised what had happened,
But at that moment the General rushed like a hawk
At Himmanen and snatched the sheet of paper
He was holding with dates and abbreviations.

With the paper in his hand, he headed for the door,
But he was stopped short again by a cry
That burst from all our throats
Once we had seen the word
Zwölf on the screen!

Once again, the General screwed up his eyes predatorially,
Scanned us with an unfamiliar, alien gaze
And went decisively for the door.
However Juan was there, in his way.
'You're going nowhere, Major!'

Bolivar said coldly.

---

[253] IESVS NAZARENVS REX IVDAEORVM, or *Jesus of Nazarus, King of the Jews.*
[254] According to Islamic tradition, the joint appearance of Isa (Jesus) and Imam Mahdi on Earth means the eve of the Day of Judgment, when Isa and Mahdi will have to fight the legions of Dajjal (Antichrist) and defeat him.

'Get out of my way, Juan,' Johnson growled.
'You're going nowhere!'
Juan repeated decisively.
For a moment the General lost his resolve.

'Tango, we urgently need to inform the Fathers of the project;
They have to take action.
This... this needs stopping right now!
They... they need stopping right now!!!'
But then Johnson saw the icy cold in Juan's eyes.

Then he pulled out a gun
And pointed it decisively at Bolivar.
'No!' I cried and rushed between them.
'Johnson, don't shoot!!!'
At that moment a shot rang out

And I was thrown against the wall.
When I opened my eyes I saw the General
Striking Himmanen across the jaw with the gun in his hand,
After the Finn had also tried to stop him from leaving.
Juan's wheelchair lay on the ground,

While Bolivar himself was crawling helplessly to the door.
Johnson, however, kicked him back and ran out.
All the same, Juan did succeed in snatching the piece of paper,
And the General did not risk coming back for it,
Knowing that all the data was in the supercomputer.

He stopped in the corridor
And, shaking his fist at us threateningly, he sped away.
The bullet had struck me in the chest and I began to lose consciousness.
Before me was the face of Juan.
'INRI, INRI,' I muttered, falling into unconsciousness.

'What... what is your... full name?'
'Yes, yes, Andres Yes!
My name is Juan Bautista[255] Bolivar!
Yes, my friend, you've got it right!
Raj, help me, help me!' he called into the hall.

I heard Hima groaning somewhere under the table.
Rajpal ran up and fussed about, trying to raise
First me, then Juan.
'No, no!' Juan cried out. 'First, do this!'
And he extend him a memory stick.

'What is this?' Raj asked in astonishment.
'What's in there... will kill all the data and destroy the Bloodless One.'
Rajpal's eyes were like huge saucers.
'What? Destroy everything we've been working so long on to create?
With our own hands?!'

Peter Blucher came running over
And, saying 'give it here' to the indecisive Singh,

---

[255] Juan Bautista (Spanish) – John the Baptist.

Snatched the memory stick from his hand.
He calmly walked over to the table
And inserted the stick into the port.

He raised his hand, froze, looked around and asked,
As if he were talking about a mere cup of coffee,
'I hope no one objects?'
'No, no, no one! Go for it, Peter!!!'
Blucher resolutely pressed a key and activated the memory stick.

Juan exhaled and collapsed on the floor in exhaustion.
'Farewell, Andres!'
'Farewell, Bautista!'
He closed his eyes and, once again, his
Famous radiant smile reigned supreme.

I was coming in and
Out of reality.
At one moment, I saw soldiers dressed in black
Bursting into the hall
Peter stood proudly in front of the machine, looking defiantly at Johnson.

In a second, the general understood what had happened
And in his desperation and rage, he fired a bullet right between Blucher's eyes.
Peter collapsed to the floor without even changing
The proud look on his face.
Rajpal Maninder Singh cried out militantly

And, taking his Kirpan[256],
He launched his attack on the soldier.
A second later he was mowed down by a machine-gun burst.
He fell and his last movement was an awkward,
Childlike attempt to hold onto his turban.

Fabrizio Borgia grabbed a paper knife from the table
And, with the defiant cry of *I am free!* plunged it into the throat of the black uniform.
Falling back, the soldier shot a round through the lad.
Like a raging bear, Himmanen
Grabbed the General from behind and began choking him

Only he too was struck by a bullet.
Roger Clemenceau remained unperturbed and continued to destroy the data.
The general yelled at him to stop,
But he snapped angrily
Back at him, 'La garde meurt et ne se rend pas!'

And pressed the button to launch the final operation
And laughed in Johnson's face.
The bullet struck him right in the throat.
Patrick O'Gilvy and Kairat Kunanbaev
Fiercely fought off the black uniforms with chairs,

Until they too collapsed to the floor dead.

---

[256] From the five items (Five Ks) that all Sikhs must carry. They are *kesh* (unshorn hair, hidden beneath his turban of *keski*), *kangha* (a comb for the *kesh*), *kara* (a bracelet, usually made of iron or steel), *kachera* (a white undergarment) and *kirpan* (a small curved sword or dagger).

Kenji Uesugi and Jan Pilsudski
Had rushed at one soldier
And fought him with their bare hands.
The commander of the black uniforms walked up

And shot them both in cold blood.
Looking round and seeing that the others
From the *Zwölf* Group were also dead,
He muttered into his radio,
'The terrorists are destroyed,

The site is clear. All groups – out!'
Then he stopped, inclined his black-helmeted head,
Looking over the dead lads,
And muttered,
'Fuck's sake, they're just kids!

What is going on?'
And he walked towards the door
With a sense of accomplishment.
Across the hall, through the traces of battle, like a mad elephant
Staggered General Johnson,

Muttering strangely,
'The paper! There must be a piece of paper!
They probably didn't manage it.'
Then, leaning over Juan,
He caught sight of a corner of the sheet

That had recorded what
Could now have given meaning to everything.
He noticed it on the beard near Bolivar's mouth and understood everything.
Then he sat down on the floor, his head in his hands,
And howled like a wounded animal.

I wasn't brought back to reality
Rather, it was like I was pulled from oblivion,
Tugging on my shirt collar.
I choked on the air rushing into my lungs
And I heard the conversation:

Is that him?
Yes, it's him, the first one. The First-Called.
I'm not yet ready to take responsibility for others.
Well, now's a good time to start.
So, farewell. I've done everything for You today.

I made out a silhouette through the mist
And vague features, somehow familiar.
Ah! I remember! The Grand Map!
Then I remembered everything else
And the pain of lost friends

Dragged me back into unconsciousness.

Verse 34. The Angel

'Tell me, Thaddeus[257], about your Path to this day.'
'I'm going to shoot everyone one here to hell!'
'Wait! Wait! There's someone you know here,
Who really wants to talk with you!'
'Martinson! Hello, you old rogue!'

Martinson neighed with nervous laughter:
'Ah-h-h! Is that you, Levi, my black angel?'
Then came over all hysterical again:
'You'll answer for all this, you filthy, vile Pharoah!
For all those years you destroyed in my life!

For everything, you hear?! For those stinking cells,
Those lustful ni***rs,
Everything! And this very day! You dirty bastard!'
'Martinson! Hold on, hold on. Calm down!
Today you win. Take a look around, you're an old hand, right?

You see, you have everything under control!
The entire space in front of the building is lit up.
You have total control over the situation, right?
Take it easy. Now, calmly, nice and easy...
What is it you want? And I personally will make sure you get it!

I say again, you win. But what are you going to do
With this advantage, eh?
Drop dead or what? I'd only be too pleased, you know!
So, calmly list what it is you want.
Nice and easy!'

'Hm... I...' 'Speak up, Martinson!'
'I demand...' the thug yelled.
'I demand five million dollars!
Put it in an armoured Group 4 truck!
And ensure me a corridor to Mexico!

These slit-eyed creatures are coming with me!'
'How many people do you have there?'
'Five! A family of *chinks*! Levi, their kids are so-o-o little!
And you can kill them today...'
The thug gave a triumphant laugh.

And that'll be the end of you, you sonofabitch!'

'That's enough, Martinson! You've won, I've already told you!
Don't think about me, think about what you'll do with your victory, eh?
Look, I'll pass on all your demands
To Captain Lebowski. You'll take care of everything, captain, won't you?'
'Yes, yes,' came the reply over the megaphone.

'You hear that, Charlie? It's all in hand!'

---

[257] The name of the Apostle Thaddeus is often given as Jude *not Iscariot* or as Jude Lebbaeus.

'You've got twenty minutes, cop!
And then you can come and pick up the brains
Of these Chinese fuckers!'
'Charlie, I won't manage to get five million together in twenty minutes!'

'That's your problem, Levi!'
Martinson shouted with a grimace and shook his sawn-off shotgun at the window.
You see that? I'll send you all to hell!'
'Hey, Charlie! That's something new. What's that – a sawn-off shotgun?
Since when have you been walking about with them?

Go on, show me again!'
'There! There! Take a look, dickhead! I'll blow those little *chinks* away –
There'll be nothing left, you hear? You hear?!
Anyway, where are you, Levi? I can't see you!
Tell them now to cut one of the spotlights!

I want to see your arrogant face!'
'We're cutting it now, Charlie.
You know, I've changed my mind.
Kill that bloody Chinaman,
And then the State of California will sure as hell send you

To the gas chamber
And I will never have to think about you at all!'
'What did you say?! Come on, show yourself, you swine!'
'Martinson, you look out and you'll see...
That I'm...

Right behind you, you bastard!'
Martinson turned sharply and froze in surprise.
That moment was all Detective Levi needed
To carefully snatch the sawn-off shotgun from his hands
And smash the butt into the thug's jaw.

The surprise remained in Charlie's eyes
Even when they began to cloud over.
The detective didn't deny himself the pleasure
Of leaning over him and, pointing out the microphone headset,
And shouting, as Martinson's consciousness faded:

'Technological progress you stupid Neanderthal!
You see, you cretin? You'll never get the better of me!'
The following second, with his foot on the thug's throat,
Levi quickly but carefully passed the hostages
Straight into the hands of trooper standing behind him.

Outside, Levi was beckoned to the radio.
'Yes, Michael, yes, go ahead!
Got it, I'll be there in forty minutes.'
'Who's this Michael?' his colleague George Lee enquired.
'From the Department?'

'Eh? Ye-es... From the Department...
Georgie, have you got it from here, eh?
I've got to shoot off... to the Department.'
Hearing the *okay* in response,

Levi got in the car and put it in gear.

As usual, Michael was sat at his cyclopean table
In his monumental-looking office.
'Michael, you do love erecting such mansions
For yourself in any country, don't you?!'
The detective said instead of a greeting

And made himself comfortable in a deep, comfy chair.
'And why do you angels,' Michael retorted,
So love turning into doctors
And policemen on Earth, eh?
What, there aren't enough other professions doing good?'

'You've been told a hundred times, Michael,
That you feel the pulse of life in these professions,
In the fight for human life,
When they stand on the boundary between life and death.
We angels, you see, are deprived of that...'

'You could have been a soldier; there are so many more boundaries there.'
'Oh no, after the Great War we tired of
Those bloody stumps and spilled innards.
And after the Second War of the Angels,
We got really sick of all those military manoeuvres.'

'Haven't you got all sentimental when in among the people?
And when you're with your Arkhovites,
You treacherously struck our rearguard
And we lost thousands and thousands. You ever think of that, eh?'
'Hey, enough of that already.

You know full well that was no act of treachery,
Rather a skilled bit of deceit, set up by Asmodeus and Belial.'[258]
'Uh-huh. Well, yes,' Michael grimaced.
'Thank Metatron[259], for not including you in these...
For, otherwise, you'd have been rushing about like dark shadows...'

'Well, okay,' Lebbaeus said with an impatient wave of the hand.
'What have you got there?'
'The mission only appears simple at first glance,'
He said, tossing a thick folder to Lebbaeus.
We need to find these people.

Incidentally, your experience as a police officer will really come in useful.'
The archangel chuckled and began lighting his pipe.
Lebbaeus carefully flicked through the folder
And looked at the back cover
As if trying to find some kind of catch.

'Is this serious?

---

[258] Asmodeus and Belial are two of the four so-called Kings of Hell, the others being Lucifer and Astaroth.
[259] In Kabbalist teaching about angels, Metatron is the highest in the host of angels and in the world of incorporeal heavenly forces. He has no equal and stands directly before the throne of the Creator. The light emanating from him surpasses the light of all other heavenly beings, and no angel can do anything without his permission. A part of the radiance from the Heavenly Throne has passed to him, and he knows all the secret decisions of the Father, Who is in Heaven. In Kabbalah, Michael and Samael are deemed two aspects of Metatron.

Is this some kind of coincidence? A misunderstanding? Or a joke, perhaps?'
'No, no,' Michael replied, as if he had expected such a reaction from the angel.
'No jokes, no coincidences. Everything is as it is.'
'Perhaps it's some symbolism, eh? And what are these iconic names?'

Lebbaeus still couldn't believe it.
'Listen, there are no jokes there!' the Archistrategos said, knitting his brows.
'Look *for whom* you're looking for them and *to whom* you have to hand them over.'
He jabbed his finger at the first sheet in the folder.
'I don't understand a thing!' Lebbaeus muttered pleadingly.

Michael chuckled smugly, but still scratched the back of his head,
As if demonstrating that he, too, did not really have a grasp.
However, it was not the done thing to discuss
The Heavenly Secretariat's assignments, as it was clear who was handing them out.
And peppering Metatron and begging him to ask again

Was altogether a waste of time.
'Maybe... Maybe this is The Beginning? The Beginning of the Days of Judgment?'
Lebbaeus shifted in his chair, agitated.
His heart was beating fast but he kept himself together.
For some reason, Michael was looking at him very attentively,

And responded only after a lengthy pause:
'No... Most likely not,' he said, getting up from his chair
And pacing softly across the room.
I have managed to have a word with Jibrail,
And you know that this is not an easy thing to do these days...'

Lebbaeus nodded in understanding.
He knew that after the Second War,
The angels were not recommended to communicate
With this mighty Archangel.
The Lord of Worlds had instructed him henceforth

To communicate with people, of his dissatisfaction with whom
He had spoken carelessly and in a fit of temper during the Second War.
We understood the Archangel's irritation –
For how many souls had he devoted himself entirely during the war!
And these mortal creatures on Earth

Just kept on falling
Under the spell of the Prince of Darkness,
Giving him strength both in Heaven and the Tartarus,
From which our brothers continued to perish
On the heavenly battlefields.

However, the Lord of Worlds is extremely sensitive
To what others say about his favourite creation,
Which is something we have witnessed many times...
Gabriel was now called by different versions of his names,
In order not to be suspected of circulating

Good News to the Lord.

Therefore, upon mention of his fellow brother,
Michael's eyes betrayed a genuine sadness.

But, praise be the Lord of Worlds, this sadness was not *eternal*,
Although, had He so wished, it certainly could have been.
'Anyway,' the Archistrategos went on,

'He said that this was hardly a signal for the Beginning,
Because in this case he would have been given an order,
Where his predicted role was written.
And he would not have hidden the truth,
For the Beginning simultaneously signifies the end of his reprimand.'

'And what about the other Archangels?'
'They are busy putting Heaven and Earth into order,
And they have no time for the finer ins and outs of human lives,
Not least because they are now mostly under the jurisdiction of Jibrail.
Raphael is busy pacifying the djinns

Who have spoken against us.
Uriel is rushing through Hell and returns the punished
For their punishment.
The rest... well, you know they'll only shrug
And nod upwards, to show they have enough on their plate as it is.'

'Strange, because, one way or another, this concerns everyone...'
Lebbaeus shook his head.
Michael waved his hand dismissively
And his sleek, snow-white wings
Fluttered with the trembling of thousands of exquisitely crafted feathers.

On Earth the angels would conceal their wings,
To stop people from seeing them
When they were not supposed to.
However, in each other's presence, such a need disappeared
So, they happily spread them out,

Stretched and folded them back comfortably –
After all, hiding one's wings all the time was physically difficult.
'You know what I thought,' Michael went on,
Gently pacing about the room.
'Couldn't it be that He

Decided to give people an understanding of the Circle of Time?
You see, they had almost come right up to it themselves –
The science, imagination and all that...'
'What's the point? What's the point of giving mortals
A notion of cyclicity and, most important, of Infinity?

What if it pulls their consciousness apart?
Suddenly plunges them into *jahiliyah*[260] or simply desperation?
And then start everything all over again?
Unlikely, I don't think so...'
'Don't you go rushing to conclusions!'

Michael said, returning to his chair,
Only without sitting down.
'And what if the Lord of Worlds

---

[260] *Jahiliyah* (Arabic) – the age of ignorant paganism and polytheism in Islam.

Decided, how can I put it, to soften the choice for people?
Make it not so rigid,

As it will be on the eve of the Great Day?'
'Well, then... Well, then that is easier!
Let him tell Jibrail,
And he will then bring the Good News!
Why complicate the process and repeat the process of understanding

Through the minds of the people?'
The Archistrategos looked at Lebbaeus with displeasure
And sat down in the chair.
'It's immediately obvious that you haven't conversed with Gabriel for a long time.
I always said that it was impossible to do this with him...

Well, anyway, what am I saying?
You haven't conversed with him for a long time,
But he would tell you what the cost would be to him and the Lord of Worlds
To build confessions on Earth, step by step,
To ensure they become sustainable systems.'

'Really?' Lebbaeus's eyes twinkled.
'And the fact that the fastest-growing confession today
Is basically non-confession doesn't bother them?
The fact on Earth has different forms of
Theism, deism, agnosticism and practical atheism,

And there are already more than a billion of them isn't a problem?
Perhaps there wouldn't be a problem
If the Son of the Morning[261] hadn't climbed into these holes,
Dragging with him *jahiliyyah*, declining morals
And the worship of money, dope and insatiable consumption!'

'Hmm...' Michael thought, looking into the distance.
A few moments later he focused his gaze once more
On Lebbaeus. 'Only bear in mind
That there is contradiction in what you say.
On the one hand, you complain of growing faithlessness in the people,

While, on the other, you're surprised about why they should be given
A notion of the Infinity of the Circles of Time.'
'Well... there is that...'
'Who knows, Lebbaeus, perhaps this is not a contradiction at all,
But a reflection of the real state of affairs,

And that means a certain statement of the task at hand,
What do you think?'
Michael got up again and went over to a beautifully decorated safe.
He fumbled in his pocket and, retrieving a key, he opened it.
'Take a look here,' the Archistrategos said solemnly.

'This should tell you that this
Is a very serious task.'
Shimmering in the dark half-light of the safe

---

[261] *Son of the Morning* is one of the nicknames or a translation of the name Lucifer, literally meaning *Bearer of Light* (Latin).

Were a lustrous crown and a three-tailed whip.
'If you complete your task successfully,

You are promised the return of the symbols,
The return of your status and your name.'
Lebbaeus was speechless, swallowed convulsively
And looked pleadingly at Michael.
'Yes, yes, Jegudiel[262], temporarily bearing the name Lebbaeus

As punishment for his error during the Second War.
You will return to the rank of Archangel
And receive your crown and whip.
This is not my word, but the word of Metatron.
And that means *His Word*.'

Lebbaeus rubbed his face with his hands,
As if trying to dispel an illusion.
Michael closed the safe and returned to his comfortable chair.
'Brother, I am confident you'll manage it.'
The Archistrategos's voice was warm

And wished to inspire and hearten his friend.
'Here, take a look at these bios.'
Lebbaeus, still under the influence of what he had seen in the safe,
Pulled himself together and opened the folder.
Michael continued in a quite businesslike tone:

'It appears that these are the same people as before,
But if you look at their lives, they clearly are not.
There are two options: either they are forming their own, new cycle,
Or they are being viewed through the Circles of Time.
The former option is dubious,

Because it is so contrary to rudimentary beliefs,
Which will inevitably meet with staunch resistance
From the zealots of the faith.
What is there to say – from the majority of supporters.
That's because if these are new people,

That means we're talking about a new *shekinah*[263] as well?
And that is another couple of thousand years of awareness, resistance,
Theories, disputes, interpretations and so on.
So, it is unlikely that this is the case.
In any event, you don't immediately need

To formulate your theory of the
Decision of the Lord of Worlds.
You see, there is a specific, certain mission,
Which is to find and track down these lads.
And seeing how scattered they are across the entire continuum,

---

[262] Yehudiel (Laudation of God) – one of the eight Archangels in Orthodox tradition: Michael, Gabriel, Raphael, Uriel, Selaphiel, Jehudiel, Barachiel and Jeremiel. The golden crown and three-tailed whip are symbols of Yehudiel in Orthodox iconographic tradition.

[263] The Hebrew word for *dwelling* or *settling*. In Judaism, the term denotes the presence of the Lord, including in the physical aspect.

Let me tell you, this really is not a simple task.
But while you're busy looking for people,
You'll realise what and *whom* we're dealing with.
You remember how the stories go and that means
You'll meet more than once with Jibrail.

Don't be afraid to watch him – it's not forbidden.
If you get to talk with him, so much the better!
But be careful.
But not just because of the commands –
Gabriel's power on Earth is limitless.

If he is powerful in the heavens, he is three times stronger on Earth.
Don't allow him to suspect us of the doubts
We've been discussing here.
In the Heavenly Secretariat
I'll try to find something out from Metatron –

So we two can form a full picture of
What the Lord of Worlds wants this time.'
'That's why it's always like this,' Lebbaeus said with resentment.
'Why is it that, often, neither we nor people
Have an overall picture of the plan.

Why are things left unsaid like that?'
'Easy now, Jegudiel,' Michael said, tiredly closing his eyes.
Remember that such questions have
Started all wars in Heaven.
Well, on Earth too.

You know only too well that we are not given to know His will,
Because we are but his instrument,
His heralds and messengers.
We even implement management in the Heavenly Secretariat
According to His sole will.

And the people? Well, you know that as well.
They are given a soul and that means *the right to choose*.
The right to choose is *the right to err*,
Which is something we don't have.
You also know *who* maintains that balance of sins and errors.

You will have to meet Him,
As soon as you find the first lad of the Dozen.
Incidentally, if you want, you can get to know him before that;
His location is specified there.
Let Metatron see how zealous we are.'

Michael stood up decisively,
Which signified the end of the meeting.
Lebbaeus also jumped up and gathered his folders.
The angels ceremoniously spread their wings
And completed two ritual flourishes.

'Oh, and another thing,' the Archistrategos added.
I will assist you in your search in every possible way –
I'll send you what I can find out

About these lads,
Scattered here and there throughout history.

We can't really drag things out here, all right?'
'Marvellous!' Lebbaeus smiled and saluted the Archistrategos.
'All the best, brother,' Michael said as they embraced.
We miss you here.
You'll finish the assignment and tell us where you were after the War.'

****

Brothers, you ask why I told you about this conversation
And where I could have heard that conversation of angels?
Remember how and when I asked you
To call me Thaddeus,
And what I was called before that?

The first occurred after we had all got together.
And the answer to the second question – Jude Lebbaeus, you remember?
So, I am that angel Yehudiel-Lebbaeus,
Sent to bring you together and bring you to the Beloved One.
That is where the explanation lies as to why you always

Saw my face first
And only then, the Teacher.
It also explains why Andrew remains as First-called,
Even despite the fact that when he appeared,
I was already by the side of the Beloved Friend.

I was not counted back then, you understand?
There's no need for those eyes of surprise,
As if you've seen a living angel in the flesh.
First of all, that's not the case;
Second, in order to understand,

You'll have to listen on to my story.
There's a lot you'll have to believe before
I tell you about the essence of that reincarnation
That took place in me,
And then you'll understand how I know everything.

First, I'll tell you about the Second War in Heaven.
It is known alternatively as the War for Meanings.
You know about the First from legends –
It differed from the Second in that
It took place exclusively among the people of Heaven.

Back then, people were only a reason for discord,
When Iblis would not acknowledge God's creation
And refused to bow before him.
The Son of the Morning was sent along with his army
To the place he shall remain until the Day of Judgment.

It turned out that everyone had become involved in the Second War –
The angels, djinns and peri.
Even heroes had to be raised from Earth.
It all began because Iblis,

Having lived for many years among the people,

Had learned from them about the deceitful
Practice of making war not oneself,
Rather by stirring up confusion even among the most righteous.
You think it's only Iblis who teaches people evil?
Far from it. How did an angel get the ability to manipulate choice?

The Fallen One had never had it.
He could seduce and debauch but exciting a choice
As a source of doubt was something that had always been difficult for him.
Only by understanding how it works in people
Was he able to bring this nightmare to Heaven.

It all started when everyone's favourite Gabriel
Asked the Lord of Worlds,
'Why are people and djinns given the right to choose?
Would it not be simpler to implement the will of the Almighty,
Without giving rise to discrepancy and disagreement?'

This question disturbed many, especially the angels,
Who were never subject to doubt
As to the instructions of the Lord of Worlds
Because this contradicted their very existence.
However, the Almighty does not create programmed machines,

So the dark shadow of dispute and discussion
Slowly began to spread across Heaven.
The Lord of Worlds heard of this
And was enraged!
He decided to punish Gabriel

But Michael and Metatron discovered
That the Son of the Morning had secretly got to Gabriel on Earth
And, before his very eyes, subjected the entire population of Ashur
To *jahiliyyah*, after which it was mercilessly destroyed.
Gabriel felt pity for the noble Assyrians.

He saw that their thoughts were not so unclean,
And that, had a little more time passed,
They would have found their righteous path.
Pity is not really a feature of the Archangels;
I am just telling you in human terms,

To make it easier for you to understand.
The Archistrategos was driven more by a sense of expediency, I suppose.
When so much effort had been expended on Ashur,
What can be said about Babylon?!
To scatter the enlightened people like this in an instant

Across the boundless lands of the Oecumene.
And so he asked this question, not suspecting
That he had become the subject of Lucifer's manipulations.
Note that it wasn't hatred and dislike for people,
Rather a desire to preserve them

Until the Hour of the Great Choice that drove Gabriel!

Having heard what Metatron and Michael had to say,
The Almighty still decided to punish Gabriel,
And he was forbidden at first from participating in any Heavenly affairs.
The seraphim, cherubim and angels were overcome with confusion and doubt!

This gave rise to disorder in their affairs too,
For Gabriel had been in charge of an enormous sector
In the Heavenly Secretariat!
The Fallen One made full use of this
And began slowly to raise his armies against Heaven.

The heavenly troops failed to notice
Lucifer's armies capturing the stronghold
Of Heavenly Jerusalem,
Which for a time turned from Light to Dark.
However, the forces of the light overcame their helplessness in time

And, gathering a no less numerous army,
Besieged the Heavenly Jerusalem.
After the first assault, it was clear
That the angels were losing the battle against the forces of darkness,
Primarily because Lucifer's army

Was comprised not only of demons of darkness.
Its ranks included not only angels but Ifrits[264],
Black peri and, the horror, the most invincible warriors –
The dark heroes from the tribe of humans!
It was with these that the angels were unable to cope.

It was then that the Lord of Worlds ordered Michael
To summon into the Heavenly Army
The white djinns and the peri-warriors.
However, to summon human heroes,
He needed Gabriel.

It was then that the Almighty altered his punishment
(It is customary in Heaven to say *reprimand*)
Whereupon, from that time on, Gabriel would not have
Duties to perform in the Heavenly Secretariat,
But he would be assigned all interaction with people,

Both in the war for their souls and in the relaying
Of Good News to them.
In a short space of time, Michael and Gabriel
Gathered an even more mighty army
And advanced once more on Heavenly Jerusalem.

I was involved in that last battle.
I remember the city, covered in black ash
And devoured by flames,
Against the backdrop of which we could clearly see the silhouettes
Of the burning Temples of Holy Books.

---

[264] *Ifrit* – a black djinn. According to Islamic legend, djinns, like people, populate the earth, only in a parallel space. Also like people, they have the right to choose, so they are divided into black djinns (*ifrits*) and white djinns. The marids are also different; unlike regular djinns, they are sexless and do not create families. It is believed that while humans have blood running through their veins, the djinns have fire.

Our jaws were clenched from our powerlessness
And hatred of our enemies
Who had allowed such atrocities to take place!
A mad and terrible scream was heard.
Two mighty ifrits has emerged and issued a challenge for single combat.

Two white djinns stepped forward from our ranks.
For several years they fought each other with fiery clusters.
The white djinns defeated one ifrit,
But the remaining one struck down both his opponents
And emerged triumphant.

Then two angels of light came forward and challenged the dark demons.
They fought for a hundred years, and only one angel of light survived,
But two demons were vanquished.
And yet the angel of light also fell and perished.
Then came the turn of the ferocious peri warriors with their terrible spears,

Challenging the black peri to battle!
However, both black peri crushed the whites
And triumphed!
Then two mighty heroes of darkness stepped forward
And, in a booming voice, challenged our heroes to single combat!

Michael and Gabriel realised
That the last defeat might prove decisive
And they looked up into the starry sky,
Endeavouring to learn the name of the certain victor.
And they began calling, 'Come out, Qazi Muhammad!'

But the ranks remained silent; there was no such warrior among us!
Then the angels saw a rather plump and modest-looking lad,
Standing in the ranks of heroes, clutching a spear.
'It's you, they said, come on out!'
'But that is not my name,' the lad replied.

'Go, hero. Here is your sword!' The angels told him
And handed him a sword, forged in Heaven.
The confused young man went forth and raised his sword.
Another hero stepped out to join him
With a giant mace in his hand.

They fought for three hundred years until the bright hero with the mace perished,
Leaving the warrior named Qazi Muhammad.
He looked weak and timid before the mighty
Black, steel-clad heroes.
But then the unexpected happened,

For the lad turned and ran!
Everyone gasped, but this turned out to be
An ancient tactic, deployed by the Horatii against the Curiatii.
One of the black warriors lagged a little behind the others
And the bright-clad warrior brought his sword down

On the soldier following him,
Before calmly dealing with the straggler!

With a sense of a just victory,
Our army descended upon the walls of Jerusalem!
We broke through the city's defences from different sides.

And then something incredible happened.
Our squad, with me at its head,
Entering the city from the south,
Was preoccupied with pursuing the enemy, manoeuvring cleverly
And, with all our might we came crashing down

Onto our own men who were rushing towards us!
All the bright-clad warriors had been showered with black ash
So it was difficult to recognise them in the heat of battle.
This was a regiment of bright-clad heroes
But my angelic cavalry

Crushed it to dust in moments.
Only one warrior remained standing, still fighting,
Falling to his knees from centuries-old fatigue.
When I looked at him, I saw
It was our saviour Qazi Muhammad.

I halted the angelic cavalry, but it was too late;
The brightly-clad earthly heroes had perished!
It later transpired that Lucifer himself
Had commanded this cunning move
And had made me kill my own men.

But it was too late.
And so, I was punished and settled on earth,
To understand better
What is unknown up in Heaven,
But which on Earth has long been practised in the form of military guile.

We recaptured the Heavenly Jerusalem
But we chose not to speak about it,
So as not to show people that Heaven
Can succumb to the united cunning
Of the minds of the Fallen One and his dark allies.

And there was no one on earth to tell
Because my cavalry, blinded by hate,
Had destroyed all the heroes on Earth.
For this reason, there are fewer and fewer heroes among the people.
Quite the contrary – the black heroes, descending to their homes,

Came to use the knowledge of djinn and angel weapons.
Now they do not engage in single combat,
Rather they prefer to destroy the enemy from a distance,
Afraid of even drawing near
And meeting death face to face.

The only thing, they say, is that Gabriel and Michael
Hid the modest lad known as Qazi Muhammad
Until a time when the warriors would cease
Focusing their efforts on infighting for foolish earthly reasons,
And only when needed for the decisive battle,

Where this lad might help the true forces of light,
Unburdened by interhuman strife.
And he will become the support for the Saviour and the Forerunner,
Standing modestly in line with the soldiers,
Without drawing attention to himself and his heroism.

Later, however, he will bring us a decisive victory
In the predicted battles.
Gabriel knows Earth best.
He said that this lad was not so unknown,
That someone would dream about him.

Well, we are unaware of that, of course.
What I do know, however, is that I saw that sword, forged
In the best angelic smithies!
And seeing as I had never met him anywhere else,
He must be kept next to his master,

So as not to take part, based on temptation by the Fallen One,
In fratricide or some other unrighteous deed.
That means he will return, the Great Hero of the forces of light,
Whose new name we don't even know;
Yet Gabriel and Michael, the most powerful,

Will find him a suitable name for sure!

****

So, there's the story of my angelic life,
So different from the stories of your lives,
Not only because some may say it has few events,
While others may say it has many.
Your stories, in their essence, are of the Earth.

Mine, however, is from another world, the Heavenly World.
I remember how I found Andrew...
A young man, standing before the Friend and me,
Both bloody and
Devoid of dreams.

How could the angels, with their endless lives,
Understand what it's like to have no dreams in one's youth,
When life is finite?
But it might not end at the time
When death touches your brow,

But when your life's work collapses
Irrevocably and forever.
I remember finding Cephas when he was doubting
Whether to leave down a new path in life
Or not.

Would he be able to come alive again?
I remember your birth father, Cephas,
And yours, Andrew, by confession,
When he didn't ask you the question *why?*

670

Rather, he simply wished you to find your meaning,

For without that, what other meanings do people have in life
When they have that priceless, Divine Gift –
The gift of choice?
I remember preventing the explosion
In which Simon was supposed to die.

I knew then that he had a different fate,
Than simply perishing, martyred by some terrorist.
I knew this not through human knowledge
Rather according to documents from the Heavenly Secretariat,
But I hardly made your choice for you, did I?

I doubt that.
I remember you, Levi Matthew,
Trying to repay the debt of your conscience.
But I knew then that this was not how you would return it,
And nor would you return it to the same people

Who taught you a lesson.
You remember, Judas, when I met you,
Wandering on the verge of insanity
On the shores of the Sea of Galilee,
Whispering, 'I'm ready! 'I'm ready.'?

Remember James, son of Zebedee,
When you heard the call, insistent and foreboding,
That your Path would not end
Among the fishermen,
Peacefully gathering in their catch?

Remember, Thomas, when you were looking feverishly to the heavens,
Trying, half-mad, to see
The foundations of your temple in Heaven?
Remember, Philip, before the coming of Cephas
And the girl from Magdala,

Whose wings deprived you of peace at night?
That is why we were created angels,
To bring you the will of Heaven at the moment
When your strength is running out and doubt rules your mind.
However, let me tell you one thought of incredible importance:

In a moment of despair and ruination,
It was not my voice that called you;
I merely drew your attention,
So that you would listen!
I diverted your attention just a little

From the vanity of vanities
That prevent us from seeing the most important thing
Behind the curtain of the everyday flow.
The true voice that called you
Belongs not to me

But to our Beloved Friend.

What struck me the most was not
What He did by calling you,
But *how* He did it!
What would I have done, an angel?

Well, I would simply have roared in the night,
Man, here's your command!
And do you remember what He did,
Our Beloved Friend?
Do you remember?

I do. He said,
'You have lived your life, seeing it through the lens of yourself.
And you want to see it
Through the lens of all people?
And I saw that you agreed,

Not because you were driven by some cynical curiosity,
But because you were prepared
To pay the highest price for it.
What price? You didn't know it then.
But, knowing it now, you didn't leave.

Thank You, our Beloved Friend,
That You have made me
Who I am today!
Thank you for the laughter
That resounded when I demonstrated to You

What a foolish angel is capable of in flight!
Thank You for the time
That we spent together
And when You said,
'Or perhaps we should leave *them* alone?

Perhaps, let them live a normal, quiet life like everyone else?'
Oh, Beloved Friend, You understand so well
That people have no peaceful life!
That those whose calling is to be by your side
Are but grains of sand among billions of human fates!

These people are a grain of sand,
But you have given them an understanding
That even a small pebble
Can form the basis
For the Great House of Heaven.

You remember you told us
What death is?
It is simply what every person
Has to *do* in life.
That death is but one of a series of regular

Human deeds,
No more than that.
But as for *how* to do it –
To what it should be dedicated and to step aside for a moment

672

From this objective – *that* is the most important lesson of all.

****

I remember that sunny day
As I flew over the plains of Hind,
Weary from my search for the Twelve.
My thirst forced me
To examine a well down below.

I dived down from the heavens,
Anticipating the coolness of the earthly water.
Having sated my thirst,
I decided to rest a while
In the shade of the grove of a small oasis in the middle of the desert.

Suddenly, I saw, a small, old man
Walking slowly towards me
From behind the trees.
His head was bald
But wise, penetrating eyes

Were hidden behind round spectacles.
The man's smile was inclined to conversation
And, having helped him quench his thirst,
I invited the elderly traveller to sit with me
On the bench, caressed by the midday shade.

At first we were silent, unsure how to start the conversation.
After all, the traveller was a wise old man.
Then I made up my mind and broke the silence.
'My name is Lebbaeus,' I said.
'And how should I address you, *aqsaqal*?'

'Call me... Call me Mohandas[265],'
The old man responded and leaned his staff against the bench.
'I see a young man with a Biblical name,
And that you have a question you would like to discuss
With a stranger, am I right?'

In an instant, I was won over by rays of light
That seemed to shimmer in the old man's eyes.
'Why specifically with a stranger?'
I feigned surprise, although I must admit
It was precisely this that I had sought.

'Because when a man stands on the threshold
Of some big decision in his life,
And I can see that this is what is happening in your soul,
Then he awaits a signal from outside.
From the outside often means a conversation with a stranger,

For everything else in your social circle
Has evidently exhausted every possible scope for argument and

---

[265] Mohandas Karamchand – the name of Mahatma Gandhi. Mahatma was a nickname that he did not particularly like given his modesty. The symbolic meaning of the word Mahatma is *Saved in life* or, literally, *Great-souled.*

673

Logical and emotional conclusions,
Isn't that the case?'
'It is,' I replied, surprised. 'It certainly is...

I really do have one question
That I would not want to discuss with anyone
That I know.
Not because there is not enough wisdom in my social circle.
Quite the opposite.

When you encounter something truly important in life,
Something rudimental, you inevitably face a choice
Of whether or not to become a part of this important thing
Or simply pass it by,
Having completed your mission and placing it

Among your memories which might be the best and most wonderful things,
But they're still just memories.
The choice is essentially about
Who to be: the witness of events
Or a participant in their making?

Experience it or limit oneself to happiness,
With the knowledge of what has happened
And only the right to talk about it in graphic colour?'
'That is a very serious choice, my friend,'
Mohandas said and, picking up his stick, drew a circle in the sand.

'However, for all the seriousness of this choice,
I see that it is something else that torments you,
Rather than the choice itself.
I think there is a question,
The understanding of which lies at the basis of your Deed, am I right?'

I turned sharply to the old man
And I had the feeling
That I had encountered something in his face
That was not destined for me up above
Among the host of angles and the population of Heaven.

'You... you are indeed perceptive, Mohandas.
However, to be honest, even I do not know where to begin...
How to begin, so that you might understand what I have in mind.
After all, you don't know me at all or my essence,
And the question specifically concerns my essence...'

'Don't worry, young man.
Whoever you might be, two travellers will always find
Those points of mutual understanding
That arise specifically by wells in the middle of the desert.
And, please, don't talk as if only *you* want to learn something.

Who knows, perhaps this conversation for me, too,
Will be a voyage of discovery, all right?'
I nodded and thought for a moment.
I don't think that the fundamental issue
That the traveller had spoken

Had completely formed in my mind,
But one thing was clear for sure:
There was indeed something that was troubling me
When communicating with the Teacher and His friends...
Alahi! My Teacher and my friends!

I was with them, I shared my Path and lodging with them,
My stories, conversations and the pain of the universal understanding of what was going on.
However, there was something... something that traced
This inexorable line between them and me.
What was this line? What was keeping me apart?

The fact that I am an angel and they are people? That is obvious,
But that is only a superficial difference,
Because I felt in harmony,
A part of this society, a part of this friendship,
Sanctified by a tender and rather touching purity.

With one exception...
'Mohandas, what is death?'
The old man raised his eyebrows, astonished, and he looked at me.
At that moment, I felt the depth of his perception
Allowed him to see the feathers from the angel wings

Secretly folded beneath my himation[266].
Mohandas suddenly burst out laughing and said,
'Listen, young man, take a look around you.
This is India!
Here, any person will tell you about *samsara*

And the immortality of the *purusha* soul
That transforms from one image to another
Depending on
Your karma!'
'No, no, that's not what I mean,' I interrupted passionately.

'What does it feel like for people?
What does it feel like? How do people come to terms with their mortality?
What is its essence and the main role
It plays in human life?
What place does it take in personal and mass world views?

I understand that there are Hindus and Buddhists,
That there are Muslims and atheists;
There are scoundrels, fools and the fearless.
But what is it in the universal sense?
For everyone, regardless of their religion or system of values?

Is there some understanding
Or is it really so fundamentally different
In the human perception?
Where does this line run?
Is it between confessions? Or between good and bad?

---

[266] A *himation* was an outer garment in Ancient Greece, a length of fabric worn over a tunic called a *chiton*.

675

Between different ages or genders?
Or does it depend on one's level of education and life experience?'
Mohandas thought for a while, leaning on his stick.
He was silent for a long time. I looked up at him and saw
Scenes coming to life in his deep eyes,

Either of a life lived or visions of heavenly forces.
I didn't hurry him though. What is time for an angel?
He was in no hurry either. What is time for an enlightened person?
What is time, spent on a step,
A step of at least a pace's length closer to the truth,

Closer for me and, I began to realise, for him too.
'One way or another,' the old man broke the silence,
'Death for anyone is basically a matter of fear.
One way or another, man is doomed
To live in constant fear of this death.

He will always count the remaining years
He is destined to live out by virtue of his genes
And his attitude to a healthy lifestyle.
When children discover for the first time that they are mortal
They are horrified at the thought of what it will be like.

One day I'm there, the next I'm gone! Forever and ever and ever!
No feelings, no thoughts,
No sight, no sense of touch.
The body will burn away or decompose,
Transforming into filthy ashes.

No one and nothing can break the vague emptiness,
Into which your consciousness will transform.
There is nothing! Simply *puff*, and nothing but oblivion!
You see those who have come to say their goodbyes to you,
But then you realise that your vision will be gone to you.

You hear people talk about how sad it is you are dying,
But then you understand
That your hearing will be gone to you too.
You stretch out your arms in a final effort,
But you realise that your limbs no longer do your bidding

And you no longer have a sense of touch.
Forever.
You're gone! In the full sense of the word!
Gone! Never to return!
And this will last an eternity, no less!

You can't wake up,
You can't come to your senses,
You can't distract yourself from thoughtfulness and absent-mindedness.
The mind fades, fading in a matter of minutes,
Disappearing forever.'

Mohandas stopped and drew another circle with his staff
In the sand and a huge great dot to one side of it.
At that second, a stupid bird anxiously squawked.

Had it sounded at any other moment,
No one would have paid it the slightest attention,

But now it sounded particularly ominous somehow.
At that moment, from the grove at the oasis,
A young man appeared, covered in dust from the road.
He was dressed in a khaki shirt
Which markedly jarred with the noonday peace and quiet.

He quietly approached the well and, quenching his thirst,
He cast curious and studying glances
At me and the enlightened old man.
'There is also fear,' Mohandas went on,
'Before this transition to the other world is made.

There is death that is
Gradual, peaceful and expected.
But if it comes with terrible pain,
Tearing apart the body, which was once the repository of life,
Affecting the mind with its unexpected nature and lack of logic,

When death comes from a mortal wound,
Murder or torture,
When it is so insidious
That it destroys all understanding that you have accumulated over life
About how incredible and well-balanced the world is in places,

Such a death flies in with terrible violence,
Not only when you face the fear of your pending absence of this world,
But it ultimately destroys all that is wonderful
That you once knew about the world in your delusion.
And before you meet that transition into the unknown,

That dying moment destroys all sense of good
That you had before,
Confronting you with the nightmare of human madness and cruelty,
Far beyond the thresholds
Where everything else remains. Everything. Everything that refused to accompany you

In your final parting moments with life.'
The unknown man, having quenched his thirst, approached and greeted us politely,
Asking our permission to join us.
'You see, I recognised you,' the unknown man broke the silence.
'There are a great many people who'd have liked to meet with you

By a well,
Without a crowd of admirers and onlookers.
You are Mahatma!'
The old man smiled and interrupted the lad in khaki:
'Please don't call me that, young man, if you don't mind.'

'So, what should I call you?'
'Simply call me, well, as *bhai*[267]...'
'All right, *bhai*, tell me,

---

[267] *Bhai* (Hindi) – brother. *Hindi rusi bhai bhai* is a political slogan used in India from the 1950s to the 1980s that was officially advocated in India and the Soviet Union. It means *Indians and Russians are brothers.*

I am from round here, unlike...'
'Lebbaeus. My name is Lebbaeus,' I responded.

The young man nodded and went on,
'So, tell me, *bhai*, if I understand it, you are talking about death.
But our faith tells us
That we are essentially immortal.
Why frighten a foreigner with images of nothingness?

And how can you speak of dying suffering,
If not all of our life is like this?'
Mohandas smiled and replied,
'My friend, we are not talking just about people of our faith,
Rather about all people on this earth.

Can a person, Good and Kind,
Discovering a cure for a disease
Really brag to others that he has the cure
While others do not?'
I shuddered when I heard the words *Good and Kind*

And I looked closer at Mohandas.
Had there been an error in the calculations of the Archistrategoi?
Had they overlooked this son of India
When drawing up their lists?
However, the old man seemed to answer my question,

While continuing to address the lad in khaki:
'My friend, there is no need to cast blame on those
Who found answers for themselves and opened the gates to faith for many.
Is it not too much to ask that, in our current lives,
We can bring peace to the hearts of all humankind,

Every day, by uniting them as one?'
'Sorry,' the lad said, plucking a blade of grass and fiddling with it nervously,
'Why should we save everyone when we
Can't even save our own during the course of our life?
Are we not the sons of our own people?

Let others be the concern of their own wise men and leaders!
We'll save those who are already closer to the truth
And that, perhaps, will be an example for others!'
Mohandas looked attentively at the lad,
Squeezed his staff tight, closed his eyes and then, opening them, went on,

'You see, my young friend,
What is death? I was telling Lebbaeus about only its elementary sense.
Christians, Jews, Muslims, just like us,
Talk about one thing – there won't be a vague emptiness,
An absence of everything. Something will remain in life that will survive.

Believe me, this is where our views differ slightly
From those people who do not belong to our faith.
However, the question isn't really about that at all.
We share the same understanding
That if you are righteous in life,

678

In a future life you will be reborn as something new,
Isn't that the case?
You are focusing on the differences,
While the respected wanderer Lebbaeus and I...'
Mohandas nodded in my direction,

Are currently talking about the things that unite us.
Can it really be wrong to view such a fundamental thing
As death together as one,
When in life we are, alas, so divided?
We are talking about death in a slightly different plane,

About its role in the sum of all things for basically everyone.
We can touch on doubts too, can't we?
Aren't morality, conscience and righteousness
Elementary divine blackmail
Based on our fear of death,

On our orthodox ignorance of

What follows:
Will it be reincarnation into something else,
Or a thousand-year wait
For awakening during the Last Judgment?
That morality and conscience, a desire to be Good and Kind

Are no more than a derivative of the fear of non-existence,
On which they are based
And, therefore, they carry nothing positive
Because they cannot carry any *a priori*,
As they are a secondary animal sensation,

Enhanced by the human imagination?
Can they, at the same time, be the positive feelings
That are based on one negative,
Yet total sense of horror,
Which actually pervades a person's entire worldview?'

'Right,' I went on, 'whatever the certainty
Of people of different faiths that the spirit is immortal,
I still think that death involves
A monstrous act of separation, parting and estrangement from what is most dear.
I won't believe that all people feel the same about this;

It's no wonder that many think
That this is a key criterion,
A factor of the total fear of people
Who believe that death is
An absolute evil,

The creation of dark forces
Because it doesn't just happen in the life of any person
But, during that person's life,
All it does is
Take irrevocably away from the living, from those who continue to live.

Separating them forever and ever and ever.

In other words, until a person reaches that threshold themselves,
It shall raise its head dozens, hundreds of times
In the form of grief for the loss of loved ones, the passing of strangers
From news reports of disasters, wars
Or simply in the form of a soldier's funeral.

Some people believe that death is an evil demon of separation.
Something people are punished with,
The ultimate form of punishment.
Death is the ultimate act of retribution,
Which applies not only to the dying

As to those who cherished this person during their life.
Even if, in your religious understanding this is indeed
A transition to another state
According to the laws of *samsara*,
This is still the most orthodox parting

That could be imagined.
It is a loss, however people may hide behind
Religious teachings.
You know, Mohandas, is it not true
That all the world's religions,

Twirling in their doctrinal dances,
Still prance around one thing –
The answer to one question:
What is there after a person
Breathes their last breath?

Only materialists and atheists assert
That death is the end of everything,
Comforting themselves with only a notion of honour in the hearts of others
As compensation
For a lack of an immortal soul, is that right?

This is your most total and eternal
Disappearance as such, right?
The disappearance of your unique individuality? Your spirit.
All the rest – all morality, conscience and other such nonsense –
Is given only to supplement this notion,

Which simply has to survive
Come what may.
So, the rest simply comprises the reasons for a simple, natural act,
This terrible, vague emptiness
That reigns forever, is that it?

Pretty much every religion in the world
Is essentially focused on trying to answer
This sacramental question of what is death.
You see, this fear lies at the heart of all religions in the world,
So as to convince a man

That there won't be a sense of losing all senses,
Rather that there'll be a certain transition of

What lives in these senses
Into a certain, different state,
Which will actually replace it.

Right?'
'Well, no,' our new companion exclaimed,
'Everything you say, Mr Lebbaeus,
Appears disrespectful to human beliefs
And, primarily, to the faith of my ancient people!

You are talking about merely a textbook understanding of life,
Which we see in the suffering in the shackles of *samsara*.
You talk of the *jiva*, or whatever it is you say about the soul,
Which exists in the embraces of sensual illusions,
The main obstacle to enlightenment.'

'Hold on there, young man,'
I said, trying to cool the fire that I sensed
In the lad's words.
'We are trying to talk about some common understanding,
In an attempt to piece it all together

From different faiths, because...erm... er...
It is not interesting just for people.
I am just trying to understand what formed the basis of the understanding of death
For a given civilisation;
Does the cultural layer of different beliefs

Have a process for manipulating the notion of nothingness,
Which overstates the significance of this sorrowful act?
Has man not become the victim of a key mistake
Which has found its way into everyone's worldview,
Thus clouding the true picture of life?'

'Hm,' the lad said suspiciously. 'Personally, I reach the following conclusion:
Everything you say doesn't simply influence my thinking
Here and now.
Our conversation is an extrapolation of
How another's worldview dissolves the consciousness of an ancient nation,

Of which we, the Indian civilisation, are one.
You are young, your civilisation, so you insist on the notion
That you are given but one life,
After which you go into some storage facility,
From where it is unknown when you'll emerge

As a result of some divine act of justice,
Which is called the Last Judgment.
What does a civilisation that preaches
A once-only time in this world bring with it?
Only that you will inevitably

Strive to get everything you can and right now
And specifically in *this* life.
And that means you will come (well, you actually already have)
To the understanding that everyone is worthy of
Both power and wealth,

Voices too, the appeasement of all wishes
And in *this* life too!
That which is meant to cleanse you,
Will inevitably enslave you until
Until you realise

That the *moksha*-liberation
Is not some reward for exemplary and sinless conduct,
Rather a true release from the insatiable *ego*.
You will come up with all sorts of formulas
When bargaining with your God and, you're right, Lebbaeus,

You will live forever in a physiological fear of death,
Because it will still mean a failure for you
In realisation of your desires, dreams and aspirations
That you have cherished your entire life,
Seeing the world through the eyes of your *ego*.

Having made everyone equal from birth
From the outset in your mind,
Paying no attention to the fact that this birth
Was preceded by years, centuries and perhaps even ages of the Karmic path,
You will reveal paths to power to any old scoundrel

And you'll reveal paths to money to any old blackguard,
By creating common rules for them only based on the fact
They were born a *homo sapiens*.
And you will still protect these rights with the sincerity of fools,
Saying that the life of the individual is sacred

Only based on the fact that you gauge everyone
By the sameness in physiological acts –
In birth and death!
It is from here that we get the ochlocracies,
Forced to listen to the opinion

Of those who will be reborn
In a future life as a rat.
You will defend the insatiable consumerist syndrome of those
Who, in their next reincarnation will appear as pigs.
You will despise monarchs, believing that they are the equals of

Both rat-people and pig-people.
You will kill the enlightened ones,
Believing that it is not fair
That people born equally can be given different things in heart and mind!
And envy will overwhelm your consciousness.

And what will you do? You think you'll avoid class division?
In word, yes.
But when you encounter the impossibility of the anthill,
You will divide people into the successful and the unsuccessful.
What do you think these groups are, if not new *varnas*?

That is precisely what they are: *varnas*, castes that create new pariahs.
But what can you give these new pariahs in return,

If you have no understanding of *samsara* and *karma*?
Nothing. So, all you have left is the fear of death
And the fear that your *ego* will not get its fill before death comes!

In fact, you are the same – you despise the lower classes,
The proletariat, the rabble and the latter-day untouchables, the losers,
And only because, for you to love,
You need a vision of
Whom to hate.

So, let me tell you, Lebbaeus the traveller,
Continue your journey away from India.
Don't bring anything here that will make my people
Fall ill with diseases that are not indigenous.
After many centuries of colonisation and humiliation, the people here

Understand who the outsider is!'

I was dumbstruck by the lad's heated words,
But Mohandas broke my trance.
'I recognise these words,' he said to the lad calmly,
As if he had not been witness to his hot-bloodedness.
'I encounter them every day in my life,

And let me tell you this, young man.
You cannot reproach me
For ignorance of our faith, isn't that so?
We have recently lived through a tragedy.
When our Homeland was divided, split into parts.[268]

Is it not the despair that we cannot live together
That has divided us?
Surely, in twenty years from now, people born
Who played no part in this division
Will ask why we did this?

Did we Indians take advantage of the fact
That, as they say, we are wiser and our teaching is more ancient?
No. We did the same as everyone else
As our *egos* ordered us at that moment.
What were we supposed to do?

If our teaching is stronger, of which you are sure,
Then why has its light not overcome the darkness?
Why did the British leave peacefully,
While we parted ways with our brothers, sowing blood and tears?
Why did we persuade those far away with *satyagraha*,

But told our own brothers to *get the hell out*?
What is the strength of our knowledge and faith,
If we couldn't even sort our own house out?
Doesn't this tell us that we are different in our faith,
And that, in our actions, we have forgotten about God and Faith?'

The lad's eyes flashed with anger and he threw his blade of grass to one side:

---

[268] This refers to the division of India into two states – India itself and the Islamic Republic of Pakistan in 1947.

'I was... er... happy to meet you, *bhai*.
I am sure it is not the last time.
You were unable to convince me –
You speak with the voice of a stranger.

You have spent too long, *bhai*, in the company of infidels,
For your enlightened view
To remain unclouded.
But no matter. Life will judge us.
And perhaps what you have discussed so passionately with a foreigner, too.'

He got up and headed decisively down the path.
'What's your name, *bhai*?'
Mohandas called after him.
The lad stopped, looked up to the sky in doubt, made his decision
And, turning, he replied,

'Nathuram, *bhai*. Nathuram Godse.'
With these words, he walked resolutely away.
I must admit, I was dumbfounded by the outcome of the conversation,
Which had initially promised me
A stream of wisdom and reflection,

But which had transformed into an uncompromising dispute,
Whose beginning had arisen not here and not now.
I could sense it.
Moreover, I was upset that the conversation, seemingly inevitably,
Had turned to politics and away from matters of faith.

'Don't worry yourself like that, my dear Lebbaeus,'
Mohandas's voice pulled me from my troubled thoughts
And returned me to the bench at the oasis.
'I understood immediately why you asked the question about death.
That said, however, I don't know the ultimate goal for you needing this knowledge.

You're not a human, are you? You're a deva[269], am I right?'
The sun played mischievously in the rays around the old man's eyes.
'But what... what if I were a *rakshasa* –
Would you still talk with me?'
'Of course. The only ones afraid of the dark forces are those

Who have given into their fear.'
'How difficult it is with people.
Even an understanding of such universal things
As life and death
Has so many interpretations for them

That it is able to split them along real borders
Of countries, towns and even districts where they live.'
Mohandas signed and patted me on the back:
'Don't despair, my friend,
You're immortal, after all; why do you need the twists and turns of earthly discord?'

At that moment, I suddenly became acutely aware of how I differed

---

[269] *Deva* (Sanskrit) – in Hinduism they are divine beings or heavenly angels. The opposite, demonic beings, are known as *rakshasa*.

684

From my new friends.
I felt that, for me, death would always be
A one-sided loss, a parting farewell.
I dropped my head into my hands.

'You see, Lebbaeus, Nathuram is right in many respects.
I understand that his emotions are nourished from the pure source
That is his love for his Homeland,
Through which the bloody wound of demarcation has passed.
Well, his righteous anger is not only because of this, of course.

This fear lives in me, too, not only because
Of how I have lived my life, but because
I am unsure if I'll complete all that I dream of
In the time that is left for me.
Can I, even for a short while,

Help people overcome the boundaries,
Not only of countries and nations,
But so that the boundaries disappear in their wonderful hearts and souls.
So that mutual hatred ceases to be the main impetus
In their deeds and way of life.

Most of all, I dream of
My ideas and not my mortal body
Were able to conquer death and the fear of it.'
'But how, Mohandas?
How is that possible – conquering death?'

'I don't know, but it is evidently when
You dedicate not only your entire life,
But your death too, to love, peace and the dream.
So, let me tell you, my dear Lebbaeus,
There are times when people give up their entire lives,

But when Azrael comes,
The monstrous *ego* of fear calls to them
And, in an instant, turns an entire life's work to nothing.
I forbid my nearest and dearest from calling me Mahatma,
Only because I don't have a final answer to this question –

Am I really him?
However, it will become known for certain at a *certain* hour.
And so, my friend, death
Is also an Act of the highest category of self-sacrifice,
Which can often say more about you

Than a hundred years of life.
In essence, one's entire life, from birth itself,
Might be devoted to it, and all because
The Path of many is impossible to understand, comprehend
Or even love,

Without knowing *how*, *with what* and *for what* they have gone to another world.
This can probably be called a victory over death,
I don't know.
Someone once said how can one speak of death

When it's *not behind* you.'

We parted there, by that peaceful well.
I have to admit, I had a feeling
That I had never really got the answer I was expecting.
However, to be honest, for now the essence of the question
Was still something vague for me.

Didn't I know that people know about death,
And what its religious contradictions are?
It's just that, earlier, this knowledge was
Cold, indifferent information for me,
And which in no way ever affected my angelic tranquillity.

There was something else. But what?
I immersed myself into the dusty clamour of the cities of India.
I spoke with *sadhu* ascetics, dervishes and wise men,
But these conversations failed to reveal
Anything fundamentally new for me.

One day, in one of these cities,
I encountered... the Fallen One.
It happened like this. I was walking down the street
And approaching a house
With its yard full of people.

I walked past when suddenly an explosion went off.
People were panicking and running in all directions,
But I caught sight of one figure who remained motionless.
The Bloodless One was standing by a wall and his only eye
Was glowing with triumph.

I became invisible and approached him, rudely asked him,
'What are you doing here and whose fields are you ploughing, you traitor?'
The Fallen One chuckled and replied quite brazenly,
'Well, I'm doing your job, you idlers!'
'What job do you possibly mean?' I asked incredulously.

'I saved the life of a righteous man,' he replied and scratched himself grossly,
'Some fanatics wanted to kill him, but I stopped them;
I scared the bomber to death
By showing him one of my faces.'
'Since when do you save the righteous?' I asked.

'Well, I'm just having fun really!
When people's logic is all confused,
They quickly lose their conviction.'
He laughed and spat his betel onto the ground.
'Well, of course,' I said calming down and smiling coldly,

'And there I was thinking you had stepped onto the path of light!'
The Fallen One hissed like a vicious cat
And looked at me with hatred:
'Be on your way, Yehudiel, you don't belong here.
You know where we'll meet.'

'Oh yes, I know. Farewell... you bomber-scarer.'

The Bloodless One quietly disappeared after first fixing me with his gaze,
Full of malice and contempt.
However, there was something I could see in those eyes –
Perhaps it was some anxiety?

I spent several days at different ashrams
And returned to Delhi several days later.
I was sitting in an open-air tavern and looking out onto the street.
My gaze fell on an old newspaper lying on the floor,
With the headline reading, *Failed assassination attempt on Mahatma Gandhi!*

I remembered my old companion at the well with his radiant eyes
And kind smile and I picked the newspaper up.
While I was reading, a dark shadow swept past me.
Raising my eyes, I saw the Fallen One again,
Rushing somewhere, preoccupied with his own goal.

I followed him unnoticed
And we flew once more to that same house
Where I had met the Bloodless One several days before.
And then that conversation with Mohandas about death
Flashed through my mind like a lightning bolt!

Guided more by feeling than by reason
And a complete understanding of what was happening,
I launched myself at the Fallen One with my Archangel might.
We fought for two weeks,
Naturally in angel time and remaining invisible

To prying eyes.
I continually reminded the Dark One of the provocation in the Heavenly City
And much more besides.
I finally got the better of him by knocking out his fangs.
He angrily spat blood and sped off,

Hissing at me as he went,
'Now go back to where you came from, you stupid fool
And admire your handiwork,
Guardian of good, my arse!'
In a flash, I was back at Mohandas's house

And I realised I was too late.
The irreversible had happened:
I only managed to hear the three gunshots
That pierced Gandhi's body.
I saw my old acquaintance in the khaki shirt.

That's right! It was that same Nathuram Godse Gopal,
Standing with the smoking gun!
I saw as the little wise man slowly fell
And suddenly... He gave the murderer a sign of forgiveness,
Before crying, 'Oh, Rama! Oh, Rama!'

And falling dead.
I remember what followed as if in a haze.
Screaming with anger, I rushed at Godse,
Burning with a desire to turn him to ash, but...

I suddenly saw the confused look on his face,

Which told me what he understood in that second
When he had received the signal of forgiveness.
He realised that he had shot at Mohandas Karamchand Gandhi,
But it had been Mahatma who had died before him!
The light faded in my eyes.

I soared up into the sky and rushed towards the nearby desert.
There, I slumped to my knees and sprinkled earth on my head.
The sobs shook my whole body, despair tormented my mind.
Then I sat down on the ground and shut myself off from the world,
Into my own torment, as if tearing at my heart and brain with my own hands.

A long time passed before my thoughts
Began to take shape properly.
After that, slowly but surely, I came to
Understand.
And realise what had actually happened.

How did it come to be that the Dark One had prevented the death
But I had contributed to it. What was the point?
Finally, I understood it all and, rising slowly up into the air,
I flew to the land of Canaan.
Before, I hadn't properly understood the human phrase

I'll give my life!
It seemed that this was just about dedicating one's life.
Only now was it clear to me, an immortal angel
That, in saying this,
People actually mean, *I will give my death for you.*

I can overcome all the fear and terror of nothingness,
Beyond which no one really knows what awaits –
Reincarnation, purgatory,
Or the blessed gates of Eden.
There is only faith that this sacrifice will change the world.

Well, for a moment at least. For an hour.
Or perhaps forever.
And the immortal devil is powerless before such a sacrifice,
This last great sacrifice,
Which he, the Fallen Angel, doesn't even have at his disposal.

Therefore, he hangs around where the righteous go to the slaughter,
Therefore, he is powerless before the Lambs.
Therefore, he rules with the fear of death,
But he is terrified
Before those who are capable of such self-sacrifice.

I realised how I differ from my friends;
They had dedicated their lives to our eternal friendship.
Now we are talking about
Giving the last thing a person has at their disposal,
And that is where they differ from angels.

We winged ones don't and never could have

Such a supreme form of self-sacrifice.
And that means...
The fact that I would give up my life, my death in the name of my friends
Was something I already knew.

But who would teach me to give it up for everyone?
Muslims, Hindus, plebeians, patricians,
Losers, *vaishyas*, *bogols*, outcasts,
Serfs, kings, lepers and warriors?
I know the place where they'll teach me all that...

****

And then the following happened.
I told you that Michael had promised to help me
Look for you all, you remember?
I would often visit him
And he would reveal to me more and more

Pages from your biographies.
Here, all my time
Was devoted to speaking with the Teacher.
So, one day I came to see the Archistrategos and saw
Him weeping (!), studying all the ins and outs

Of your path in life.
I asked, 'Wow! So what has made
The Mighty Archangel
Surrender to human weaknesses?'
He answered,

'I look at these boys, Yehudiel,
And I think to myself, how badly has fate tossed them around in life?
But my emotions are not driven by empty sentimentality;
Who knows how many human fates I've seen?
This is what I think – their fate is predetermined,

But they were still able to be reborn
And, knowing that their demise is inevitable,
They stick with the choice they made one day.
So, tell me, Yehudiel,
You're talking there all the time –

Who are these people?
What makes them choose to die over and over,
When they know nothing of Infinity?'
I then sat in front of Michael in an armchair and said,
'Brother, now listen to me carefully.

Can you fulfil my request?'
'What request?' the Archangel replied in surprise.
'You could also speak to Metatron,
But I know that you can do this yourself
And then tell the Lord of Worlds.'

'Well, speak up then!'
'I want... well, I want to become a human

And one of them!'
The Archangel jumped up from his chair and stared at me:
'Are you out of your mind?!

Perhaps the Fallen One has got to you with his evil-doings?!'
'Hold on, brother. Calm down.
I understand that I am one of the youngest Archangels,
But still, I am not guided by childishness,
Rather, this is a mature decision.

I know that I will relinquish my immortality.
But, unlike these people,
I know precisely what should happen to us and how,
Even my Friend spent a long time in search of the knowledge
Of what is unavoidable.

I, you understand, knew it all from the very beginning.
And... I want to share this fate.
I am an angel but I want to become a mortal man
And make my choice,
A moral and, most importantly, human choice.'

'Hold on a minute, brother,
Perhaps you're driven by a sense of guilt for the beating
Of human heroes during the War?
Well, this is just a simple miscalculation of military tactics!
That's why He wasn't so strict with you!'

'No, no, brother, that is not my main incentive.
You know, how can I put it?
It all comes down to him, this Good, Kind Man.
I suddenly realised... I don't know how to put it exactly...,
Basically, for me to communicate with the Lord of Worlds,

I don't need any Metatron,
A crowd of cherubs or angels of the throne.
I get the impression
That... I am actually communicating with Him as it is!
Although he is so frail-looking and... human!'

Michael jumped from his chair and, as was his custom, took to pacing the room,
Only his steps were not soft;
He marched loudly and jittery, and his wings
Knocked over the trinkets in his exquisite interior,
But the Archistrategos paid them no heed.

'You see,' he said excitedly, wringing his hands.
(I had never seen him looking so agitated.)
'You see, that's not very fair on your part.
These people... well, those eleven others...
They didn't know straight away what awaited them,

But you knew in advance!
It seems you missed the main process, eh?
You have a different essence of the Path, for you knew everything from the start.
You said yourself – this is some textbook subject, right?'
'Well, yes, I knew. But look, they're gathered here from different times, you see;

What, you think that none of them know
Textbook subjects?
Michael,' I said, leaning over to the Archangel as close as I could.
I get the impression they know about the Circle of Time!
No Jibrail ever taught them that, you understand?

They don't know about it even from the laws of physics
And not from modern science at all.
They have, how can I put it,
An inner knowledge, an inner feeling
Of the essence of the matter!

We angels are immortal and so we don't know
What it means to sacrifice everything!
You can't even say that they put everything at stake;
They're not players, Michael!
They don't gain a thing – so I die, and then everything will be wonderful!'

Michael suddenly jumped up to the safe
And flung it open:
'Take a look! No, you look and look properly!
What is that? The crown and the whip! That's power, that is, Yehudiel!
Power over a host of such events,

For the sake of but one of which
You are sacrificing yourself!
You do understand, right, that Metaron, you and me,
And Gabriel too, without a shadow of a doubt,
We can get together and work together

To drag this human world
Carefully to its inevitable denouement, right?
And then, brother mine, then, after Judgment Day
Eternity will in any case become the common property
Of people and angels alike!

And then, when you were in exile,
You were reincarnated as different people, weren't you?
Doctors, policemen and all that...
What's stopping you from doing the same again?
You can be with your friends in human form

And then return to Heaven, eh?'
'What are you talking about, brother?
That's something completely different, don't you see?
It's one thing to play a role,
But living is quite another! Living a full life,

Realising that it is not forever
And that there is only one opportunity
To dedicate this life to something worthwhile!
And wouldn't it be a betrayal
To break bread with those

Who consciously proceed to fulfil their mission,
Suffering, frightened and doubting,

691

But never grumbling.
Do you have any idea what strength of mind that is?
And you suggest I just spend some time with them

And then disappear like a gentle breeze,
Telling them that angels have a different fate?!
Michael, hereafter, every moment of this angelic eternity
Will become the eternal torment of hell for me,
Which I will doom myself to by betraying my friends,

Betraying my only cause;
In what other Circle of Time
Would it fall to me?
And if these Circles go on forever,
Does that mean my betrayal will be eternal too?!'

'But how can I understand the meaning of your reincarnation *from here*?!
We'll lose an Archangel, a rule of steel
Over worldwide, global changes,
And what do we get?
One little man

Who has gone on about some temporary emotions?
Where is the hierarchy of priorities in your head?!
Take a look at the map; do you see Armenia?
You see how they'll bait you with animals,
Burn you in the oven and then slash you to pieces with a sword,

Like a simple hoodlum?'
I laughed: 'But no, brother Michael mine!
You see, your angelic attitude to death is showing through.
It's not like a hoodlum or thug that I'll be killed,
Rather as the bearer of His Word, you understand?

Archangel, do you realise what the difference is
Between the Word of the Lord of Worlds descending upon you
In the form of an instruction and
When you absorb it into yourself and carry it around the world,
And this is your decision and not that of some bureaucrats from the Heavenly Secretariat?'

The Archistrategos slumped into his chair,
Like a Solomonic pillar.
All-encompassing fatigue was evident on his angelic face.
He fumbled around for his pipe that had gone out
And, like a blind man, began looking for his tinderbox.

'And how do you imagine I'll go about organising this?'
'Very simple, brother. Tomorrow Thaddeus will die,
The beloved brother of my best friend
James, son of Alphaeus.
He cannot be saved; I did everything I could.

I will simply move into his body
And that's that. Only, you know what?
I'll have a soul!
I went to see Thaddeus and asked for his consent;
He made his choice.'

The Archangel was silent for a long time and then... he nodded.
We remained silent for a long time, each deep in their own thoughts.
'Oh, by the way,' I said, breaking the silence.
'About your mission.
I completed one part, so Metatron will be pleased.

He doesn't care who, just as long as all twelve
Are gathered around the Teacher.
As for the second part, this is what I wanted to tell you.
We angels see processes that take place with humans
Through the lens of infinity,

At the end of this comes the Day of Judgment.
People, though, feel the world through their short lives,
Something so insignificant from the standpoint of Eternity.
So, every time during their tiny little stages
They are prepared to repeat what we call

The textbook material.
Every time they repeat them in different guises,
So as not to lose their connection with Him.
Maybe if they had the chance
To accomplish a feat, and then rest in anticipation of the Day,

That's what they would do, but!
He who does not have Eternity
Will be forced to sacrifice his life each time
While he who has Eternity, like us angels,
Unfortunately, has no soul

To love the Almighty as they love Him.

So, let me go, brother Michael!
There is so little life for me *there*
To waste it on mechanical angelic doubts.
And so many events lie ahead
To not cherish every day by the side of the Beloved Friend,

Every day of this tiny, but simply wonderful life!'

Michael got up and walked over to me.
He embraced me with the words 'farewell, brother'
And held me so tight that I realised
What was about to happen.
A sharp pain in my back told me that my wings were falling

And something was happening inside me.
Hot blood rushed through me
And my heart began beating in a different way
As it became human.
I felt pain from the impact of stones,

From the pain in my stomach from a heavy meal,
And knees worn out from the hard earth.
I felt I was becoming a man,
Shuddering from the sharp pain of circumcision;

I felt Thaddeus entering his wife

And waste from vital activity accumulating in my stomach.
I felt my head hurt with hangover,
And my hands and feet ached.
Affront, rage and anger burned inside,
And an enormous, boundless sensation rose up – love!

My head was spinning and, in that moment,
The wind struck me in the face from the beating wings of the Archangel
Carrying me somewhere far, far away!
I screwed up my eyes and in a moment
I sensed Michael come crashing down to earth.

In the next second,
I saw myself falling near some desert tree
And some people running towards me, waving their arms.
While they were still approaching, the Archangel stood over me
And suddenly, whispering 'Yehudiel!' he kissed me hard on the forehead,

Leaving a large birthmark in its place.
Then he soared into the sky; the people brought me to a fire,
Wrapped me in a blanket and gave me warm wine to drink.
When I had fully regained my senses,
I caught sight of my brothers, looking at me strangely.

'Can you believe it?!' James, son of Alphaeus yelled, slapping me on the shoulder.
'I told you my brother was a right dreamer!
He never even left his fisherman's hut;
My father and brothers even took the fish to market
Because they were afraid that our little Thaddeus was not very strong-minded

And would get lost out on the road for sure!
But, you know, brothers, I love him to bits,
For his wild imagination and the stories he tells!
Angel of the Heavenly Host, would you take a look, eh?'
He hugged me tightly and for some reason I felt

That, as always, he would always have my back.
As always? Where did I get the knowledge from?
Clearly, I'd got them from Thaddeus.
But enough! I am now Thaddeus!
I have made my choice!

I looked up and met the eyes of the Beloved Friend.
He looked, without taking his eyes off me.
For several moments an Eternity rushed between us
But then it dropped into the fire
And, shooting up hundreds of sparks,

It disappeared forever in the darkness.

Verse 35

Of less value to me still is the title *Mahatma* which I received thanks to these quests. Often this title would greatly sadden me and I recall no one instance when it ever brought me joy.

Mahatma Gandhi

Shortly before Passover
We approached the Holy City of Jerusalem.
It was then that the Teacher said, 'I know and see
Many people have come here from different parts of the Land of Israel,
And each of them have brought their news about us.

Someone brings news of the King and the Kingdom,
Someone merely about a king and a new ruler,
Someone about a healer and a resurrector,
Someone about a prophet who can see what will be,
Someone about a criminal worthy of death.

Watch and there'll be a lesson for you.
I will enter riding a young donkey, as Zechariah foretold.
Then you will see that many
Will judge me not by our deeds
And not by the Word.

They will look at me atop a donkey
And they will judge by the donkey.
The donkey will tell them more than our entire Path of Knowledge.
There it is, the power of the stereotype,
When people talk more to the donkey

Than to Me and He who sent Me.
Their eyes have been blinded; their hearts, turned to stone,
But their mind is enslaved by delusions.'
Thomas smiled and said,
'Do You want to laugh at the people of Jerusalem,

Riding in on a donkey?'
'No,' the Beloved Friend replied,
'I want to give them a choice
In whom they see themselves, in Me
Or in this charming young donkey?'

And so it happened that someone said, 'There is the Messenger
Because he sits atop a donkey.'
Another said, 'There's a prophecy because there is a donkey.'
However, most kind and good people
Said that if there's a king of Israel

Who is so humble and smiling,
Someone who is so close to the simple people;
If he doesn't walk through the people,
Surrounded by Romans, the lies of courtiers
And his own fear,

Would we not honour and love him as our own?

695

We see our hope in this Man,
Our light and our *salvation*,
And we are ready to tell Him that this is what he is:
The true king of Israel!

The Pharisees ran to the Sadducees and said
That He had assented to a plot to overthrow the Herodiades!
He sends us a sign that he wants
To be our ruler, so hurry to open your trunks and take out
His genealogy, hidden away from prying Edomite eyes!

We have found a suitable, controllable person
To drive him as we wish, while he
Demonstrates his vulnerability
Through an irrepressible storm of ambitions!
Is this not the solution we've been waiting years for?

Caiaphas rejoiced and, rubbing his hands, he said,
'That's good luck, sailing right towards us!'
Only the wise old high priest Anna
Remained silent for a long time and then raised his hand:
'That which is created often rises up against its creator.

What has been made often confuses itself with its maker.
The insignificant often destroys the grand.
What do we know about this Young Man?
That he is audacious and disrespectful for the keepers of the Law,
That He allows demons to enter into Himself,

Able to violate the foundations granted to us from on high.
We know that the simple folk marvel at his tricks,
That He has surrounded Himself with chancers and idlers,
Eloquently spreading their primitive teachings
And bringing confusion to the hearts of kindly subjects.

Let's watch them awhile.
Most important is to understand the extent to which He can be controlled;
Is He capable of becoming our weapon?
Will He not become a weapon against us?
What will come out on top in Him – a desire to rule or a desire to shine?'

At that time, we were walking through the streets of Jerusalem,
Thinking that such popular love as this
Was able to protect us from misfortune
And the desire of the mighty of this world to destroy
Our little circle, as they had tried to do so often in the past.

To be honest, we were even overcome with euphoria.
But perhaps the Friend is wrong? Perhaps things are not so dismal?
After all, we don't see evil looks in the eyes of the
City people, with which even our fellow countrymen
Directed at us when they heard the Word.

We will be protected by the kindness of these people,
Their hope and desire to be purer and closer
To the true Kingdom of Heaven.
It will protect not just from death, but from simple affront as well,

From envy, blasphemy and the base conduct of the all-powerful.

The shimmering reflection of palm branches,
Slender and long, played on our faces.
We went deeper into the streets of the Holy City,
Moving closer to the Temple,
Towards reconciliation with our own people.

I saw how happy the brothers' faces were.
After all, what could be more beautiful than reconciliation with one's own people,
Even if the price we paid was to forget
About others?
There can't be that many of you who, in order to regain harmony with their Homeland,

Are prepared not only to forget the entire Path traversed
But to fall to one's knees in ignoble repentance,
Saying that one's people are the criterion for truth?
You can already see the grinning faces of the Pharisees,
The high priests, emerging onto the staircase.

Caiphas standing there, smiling at the grandeur of his own plans.
There were thousands of people around.
They witnessed the approval of the high priests
And became more and more excited, crying out,
The King of Israel returns to announce our salvation!

Right on the approaches to the Temple,
As if from under the ground, the figure of the Bloodless One rose up.
Only he looked sanguine and contented,
But Greedy, as always.
With a sweeping gesture of hospitality,

He invited our procession to march on.
However, the donkey stopped dead in front of him.
The Teacher's eyes lit up in anger
And our euphoria slowly began to transform
Into a fluffy cloud, dissolving in the sky.

'What are You doing here?!' the Friend cried.
'How dare you come so close to the Temple,
You fallen angel?!
Who allowed you to be here,
You, who live on account of My forgiveness?!'

No one could understand what was going on.
Dumbstruck, the Pharisees and Sadducees exchanged glances.
The smiles of the city folk were replaced with anxious shadows and we realised
That only we, and He, of course, could see the Greedy One,
While his image was concealed for everyone else.

'But why are you so surprised,' the Greedy One feigned amazement.
'Why do you see only my treachery in everything?
Just look, I don't step onto my own territory,
But my territory is right here,
Where things will happen as I wish them to.'

And indeed, we could see

That the majestic Temple
Was surrounded by row upon row of noisy
Merchants and money changers,
Selling, buying and lending money.

'It shall not be that the House of My Father
Will hear prayers in the name of anything but His!'
The Friend grabbed the long shepherd's flail from Philip's hand
And brought it crashing down onto the counter of the nearest money changer.
One by one he overturned the merchants' tables,

Expelling the servants of the Greedy One from the Temple.
The agitated Caiaphas then turned to Him:
'What do you think you are doing here, young man?
Why are you expelling the money changers,
For there is a particular meaning in their being here.

We cannot take offerings in coins
That bear the image of Caesar or another monarch.
The money changers were permitted here so as not to offend the Temple!'
'You see,' the Teacher turned to us and the people,
'*How*, drop by drop, the source water has been poisoned

Over many years.
One only needs to open the jug a little to reveal the Greedy One's poison.
Now I only have three days
To show you that there is already poison in the jug,
And I will be given only three days to purify the water.'

One of the Jerusalem inhabitants took fright
And departed there and then from the temple square,
Sensing something new and unfamiliar,
Then terrifying.
Many, however, started laughing and saying,

'At last there's someone
Who will show them their vices,
That they have shielded themselves so long, in the warm embraces
Of the selfish and the enterprising,
From what the people really think about them!'

The high priests and Pharisees kicked up a fuss:
'What jug is this and what is the water?
It can't be that he's being disrespectful about the Temple, can it?
It can't be the Temple, built over forty-six years
That he planned to destroy and rebuild in three days, can it?!'

The Teacher turned His back on the *holier-than-thou* types
To face the people.
He sat on the steps of the Temple.
'Come over,' He said, 'and listen.
There is the Heavenly Jerusalem and the earthly Jerusalem.

The Heavenly city remains unchanged as it is in the hands of our Father.
The earthly city, however, has suffered, struggled and grown weaker
Over the course of many years.
Because the Lord has the Word

While the Greedy One has a thousand ways

Of confusing and seducing even the toughest of us.
So, they think,' He said, pointing at the priests behind Him,
'That they are destined for success in the battle with the Greedy One only because
They hold the office of a priest,
That they are more protected than others from the Bloodless One's machinations.

However, you and I know that the office one holds
Is often no more than a defence of oneself from oneself,
If you fail to see the daily battle for the purity of the Word.
Times and ages change.
People think that something new has come and that it is for now incomprehensible.

And that it can be comprehended only tomorrow
Once we have managed to think things over and comprehend it all.
Our Father has no time and nothing new,
And that means that we don't either; we just need to understand that.
That our enemy is eternal, while the new arises

Only because we ourselves are not eternal.
How can we stand up against our powerful and eternal enemy,
Who each time seeks newer and newer means
To shut us off from Heavenly Jerusalem?
Where will we find the source to give us the strength?

There is only one thing that will deliver us
From the dictate of the novelty of the time
And that is our spirit, our soul, our own clean jug,
Which is filled every time someone is born
With the original water.

If we understand that the soul is a part of the Eternal One,
That Eternal is what it is,
Then the Bloodless and Greedy One will be powerless
Before us, because he is omnipotent over changes,
But powerless before the Eternal One.

Jerusalem! Jerusalem!
You are Me! And we will drink together from the poisoned jug!
Such is your fate and Mine as well!
And you will shudder and fall, writhing and in pain,
But your immortal soul will lift you up!'

The Teacher stretched out his hands:
'Here are my hands; the fates of Chorazin, Capernaum and Bethlehem await them!
Earthly forces will destroy them, but the heavenly forces
Will revive them, when time returns to the place
From whence it began!

When you hear from the mouths of the powerful and the uncompromising,
I am the Messenger of My Father!
I am the one who is expected and who has appeared!
I reign not in palaces but over time!
I am you tomorrow! I am what you are looking for!

Rise up, Man, Son of Man!

See clearly, son of the earthly and heavenly Jerusalems,
Extend your hands to Me and call me your Friend!
And then worlds will be united when, looking into My eyes,
You will say, I am You!'

Hastily looking around in confusion,
The Pharisee and Sadducee priests entered the Temple.
There is no longer a planned royal dynastic conspiracy.
This Galilean is talking about something quite different,
Something strange, blasphemous and dangerous.

The Sadducees rebuked the Pharisees, saying,
'Why did you assure us that this Young Man was manageable?
Now that He has been initiated in our plans,
He mustn't live because this threatens to expose us.
This Galilean is worthy of execution, what do you say?

The Pharisees were taken aback and said,
'We cannot accept execution; our teaching does not condone such a thing.
And it's not within the power of our court!
The court process itself will be dangerous for, during questioning
This man possessed might spill the beans to the Roman authorities!'

The Sadducees fell into thought, but the elderly Anna then spoke:
'Be calm, Perushim, for we have the means
To tame headstrong minds.
In moments when you meet something irrational,
There is nothing better than providing it with the power of the *ratio* in all its glory.

After all, what's the difference between romantic faith
And what we concisely call *religion*?
Faith is blind, gullible and irrational,
While religion and its priests must differ in that
They can control the power of the *ratio* too,

Especially in critical moments.
This is our power, our experience and the constancy
For which those disappearing pagans so envy us.
Off you go and don't worry about a thing –
The new King of Israel will find his place.'

Meanwhile, covering the Teacher with a blanket,
To protect him from the provocateur priests,
We hurriedly fled from the city,
Thinking that by leaving Jerusalem behind,
We would be leaving the danger too.

Three days before Passover
We gathered around a table,
Together as before, only this time with a sense of celebration.
Again, we talked and listened to one another's stories,
Indulging ourselves in reflection and revelling in our companionship.

Only our Beloved Friend wasn't his usual self.
His cheeks burned with an unfamiliar blush,
He was absent-minded with us yet concentrated on his thoughts.
However, he would laugh and smile with all of us.

We sensed that sweet feeling of those previous times on the Road.

A woman came in and, taking some myrrh,
Washed His head and feet,
Like he was a monarch or a Roman.
Judas Iscariot became angry with her and exclaimed,
'No, no, we're not who you take us for, woman!

We are but travellers and seekers, and certainly not
Those who should be worshipped by humiliating oneself!'
The Friend then flared up and shouted at Judas, which was most unlike Him:
'What you call subservience and humiliation
Has nothing to do with what this woman has done!

Why can you all not distinguish forgiveness from worship?!'
We were silent and our celebratory mood
Disappeared in an instant,
So unusual were our Friend's passion and short temper.
We found it unfair that he had said *you all*,

When only Judas had spoken.
Then the Teacher appeared confused and he stood up.
He asked for a basin of water to be brought to Him.
A woman brought it for Him and He bent over
And began washing Judas's feet and, drying them with a towel, he said,

'Forgive my lack of restraint, my friend!'
Judas became scared and tried to refuse,
But the Teacher stopped him, authoritatively and tenderly
And completed the task he'd set himself.
Then he moved onto Cephas,

Who refused loudly and fearfully,
Asking instead for his head to be washed,
But the Teacher smiled and said,
'When I called you in Galilee, your feet
Were not damaged or cut from the Journey.

You want me to restore them to their original appearance?
As I am responsible for everything.
However, I will not wash your head, for the mind is yours
And the choice is yours too.'
Then Peter and the other brothers calmed down, saying,

'No, we don't agree
That you should return our feet to their original state.
We fear that with the wounds and blisters,
We will also lose what we gleaned
During our joint Journey.'

The Teacher washed our feet and only then said, laughing,
'You're such fools – wisdom isn't a matter of blisters rather of the heart.
Blisters merely hurt to torment the mind.'
We laughed in response to that. All this time, though, I could see
Tears of tenderness flowing down the Beloved One's cheeks,

When he touched his friends.

701

I wept too...
All the same, it was a joyful evening!
Therefore, Judas regaled us with stories, Andrew with jokes
And Thomas with pointed remarks.

The Teacher was especially tender and attentive that evening.
Sometimes my heart ached when I recalled
What He had predicted about His death.
I hoped it was just an allegory.
I could see that the others felt the same as I did.

The Beloved One broke the bread and said,
'This body is Mine.'
We replied, 'Are we actually eating you?' and laughed out loud.
He smiled as if agreeing that it was a joke.
He poured us wine and said, 'And this is my blood.'

We laughed again: 'Surely we're not pagans to be drinking blood?'
He laughed too.
Then, however, He said,
'And yet one of you shall betray Me,
And the one who does will receive a special fate.'

At this point we fell silent and realised this was no joke.
Many of us thought, *He said that one of us would survive
And acquire the Word.*
Perhaps this is the destiny of the betrayer?
Perhaps the betrayer will indeed have a special fate?

'Why is this, Teacher? Why would we betray You?'
Cephas asked, tenderly touching His hand.
'And how do you think I can reach that jug,'
The Beloved One asked calmly,
'Of the poison in which the whole world must be told?

How do I reach out to the suffering and seeking?
To those in spiritual poverty and those reigning too?
To the atheists, fools and scientists?
The Muslims, for them to acknowledge Me as *Paygambar*?[270]
To those on the threshold of death and on the threshold of life?!

You think I was talking allegorically about death?
No, brethren, death is terrible and physiological.
And drinking from the jug, I will drink the contents along with the Greedy One's poison.
You think the Bloodless One can be handled with poetry alone,
With arguments about the frailty of the world

And the relative nature of good and evil?
No, brothers, he is powerless only before
Those who have said to themselves and to others,
I am Him!
Before those whose hour has come, and to say this confidently.'

'*I* will do this!' the brothers cried. 'I will!' 'No, I will!'

---

[270] *Paygambar* (from the Kazakh *Пайғамбар*) – Prophet, from the Persian for messenger or prophet. In Islam, *Isa Paygambar* means the Prophet Jesus.

'The one to do it,' the Beloved One said,
'Is the one who was created for this.
Who will repeat what has always been repeated,
Even if he wants to avoid doing so.'

We parted that evening in sadness,
Everyone thinking, trying to understand who it might be.
For one cup contains devotion and faith,
While the other, however you look at it, contains betrayal.
But betrayal in the name of faith?!

Everyone went to bed and asked themselves,
Am I capable of such a thing?
Everyone was faced with a choice and if this was indeed the mission,
That would save my life
Would I be bestowed the Word?

The following evening we moved to the wonderful,
Languid Garden of Gethsemane.
I saw that, along the way, everyone was asking themselves,
Am I the traitor.
Am I destined for life? Will I escape death?

In all our worrying about moving and cloaked in a shadow of thoughts,
We failed to notice that Judas Iscariot had disappeared.
Only I noticed that the other brothers,
Each in their own time, straightened their shoulders after completing
Their long, painful dialogue, and I said to myself,

No, even if this is the path to the cherished primordial water,
Betrayal is still betrayal.
And if our Father looks at us, then He sees
That we are making our choice in favour of honour.
Or perhaps we will all die and it is the Friend who is actually destined

To remain alive? Most likely this is
The most correct answer.
None of us yet have the Word, but He does,
And that means that it will remain with Him. And He will survive.
And we will not step onto the path of betrayal, even if our lives depended on it.

We heard the rustling of the branch of the first Gethsemane tree,
Welcoming us into the halls of its palace.
Another tree took up the greeting
And then they all rustled, as if to say,
The ones we have been waiting for and who have always come to us, have arrived.

They recognised us after years,
Even though we were in this garden for the first time.
We quietly set up our customary pilgrim camp,
Without lighting fires
And without disturbing the trees with any undue noise.

The Teacher walked back and forth
And it was evident that He was restless.
He was clearly expecting something.
Hours had passed before the Friend asked,

Cephas and Voanerges, come with me into the thicket,

Don't leave Me alone this evening.'
Peter and James jumped up,
Taking swords and knives with them, as if they sensed a threat,
While John took blankets.
Well, I trudged after them, cursing the dew that had ruined my quill.

We moved away from the camp
And became immersed in an innocent silence and darkness.
After a time
We reached a glade, where the Beloved One
Asked us to remain while he stepped away.

JUDAS GOES TO BETRAY THE BELOVED ONE

He ran and the branches in the garden
Tore his poor clothes.
He strove on
And Heaven saw his striving.
He was hurrying but then he suddenly stopped, as if rooted.

What am I doing?
This is all so familiar;
It's simply a betrayal!
'Don't go,' came the ingratiating whisper
Of the Greedy One, who was loitering nearby.

'Don't go. What is the point of such a foolish achievement?
Don't go. Everyone will remain alive,
And will roam Palestine for many years to come,
Illuminating the path for the lost and the desperate,
And you'll put a stop to all this.'

'But there is someone among us,'
Judas objected,
'Who will escape a violent death
And the Word will be given to him.
He said so Himself.

Surely that is the price of
What I'll now do?'
'No,' the Bloodless One whispered, 'you are but a stupid instrument.
Why did your brothers not resolve to do this?
After all, everyone had the choice; He addressed everyone!'

'Because they are foolish and self-assured,'
Said Judas, suddenly growing angry.
'They follow Him like lambs, applying no will or reason of their own.
Wasn't that what He was talking about,
That, without reason, faith is blind and foolish?'

You're right to think that, Judas,'
The Bloodless One went on,
While the sound of the trees displayed the anger of the Garden of Gethsemane.
'Don't go, come back.'

'No, no, I say!' said Iscariot, his fists now clenched.

'I will go and earn my life.
What is a righteous man without life?
How will he prove his devotion to the idea?
If he dies, into whose irresponsible hands
Would the mission then fall?

Life and its security
Are the guarantee that you are active,
That you are fighting and, most important,
That you can see the fruits of your struggle.
And without seeing the fruits of it in this life

What's the point of this struggle and these ideals?
Is it not the one who survives and wins
Who will be the bearer of the Word and the Mission,
As the ancient Law tells us?
Surely, the one who survives the death of losers

Will be the one to become the true ruler of thoughts,
Hopes and aspirations of the people of Israel?
Should not the sacred mission
And the symbols of its victory
Be passed to the victor?'

'But Judas, do they really open the doors to the Kingdom of Heaven
With the key of betrayal?
Is this the act of the Good, Kind Man?
Is there an exchange rate between faith and crime?'
No, that's wrong. It is stupid fanaticism,' Judas objected.

'The victor always survives
For how else can it be understood that he has won,
If he does not reap the fruits of victory himself?
Is a one-sided sacrifice what is needed
And not one for which something important should be gained?

Think, Judas, about whom your betraying,' Iscariot said.
'Him or yourself?
Not Him, not yourself,
And not our common mission either.
He said himself that it is destined, so, that is what shall be.'

Judas had failed to notice that the Bloodless One was already no longer close by
And that he was arguing with himself.
The Bloodless One remained a long way back,
Standing there and smiling,
And not even looking at Judas.

Agitated, he knocked at the gates to Caiaphas's house,
Shouting through *the door that opened*,
'I'll betray the Galilean to you!'
Excited, Caiaphas took Judas through to the room
Of the most-wise Anna.

The sage looked at length for his glasses to study

Judas's eyes closely and read what they were saying.
The old high priest gazed at them long and hard.
Caiaphas was choking with joy,
Saying that he had come of his own accord and was prepared to betray them.

'This is how we'll catch that Galilean
And quietly put him to death.'
Anna was silent and paid no attention
To the elation of his son-in-law Caiaphas.
Then he got up, took out seventy tetradrachms,

Thought a moment, counted out thirty and, giving them to Judas,
Simply nodded in silence.
Caiaphas took this as a command.
He called the guards and began to get dressed.
Only Anna stopped him and said,

'I don't want a hair to be touched on the troublemaker's head, you understand?'
'But why?' said Caiaphas, taken aback, 'it's night;
Anything could happen to a vagrant out there.'
'You don't get it at all, sonny,' said Anna, turning angry.
'By killing him quietly and with your own hands

You will make him a hero and a legend for the common people.'
'But what should I do then?' said Caiaphas in desperation.
'He who must be silent and forget afterwards
Shall sentence and execute him,'
The old man said with weight, adding, 'don't you go there for now.'

The guards quickly rushed off into the night, the traitor at their head.

THE BELOVED FRIEND'S PRAYER

Abba! Abba!
Here I am before You!
Here is the You that speaks within me!
Here is my I, dissolved in you,
Here is Your voice, while I have none.

Here is my pain, for I still do exist.
Abba! I did everything as You said.
Here is the Word, here is the Book, here, my Path.
I beg of You, stop the Circles of Time,
Change the essence of all that's happening!

The fate of them all hurts in me when they hurt.
Their joy is *mine* when they feel joy!
Their life is *mine* when they pass along their path in life.
Their sins hurt within me,
And the wounds continue to ache.

Surely things must change some time?
Surely the Greedy and Bloodless Prince must cease to rule?
Surely one circle of time
Must repeat the circle before it?
Why is my blindness getting worse?

Why is my anger growing stronger and more sophisticated?
Why are we the same as we were before,
Only we're more and more prone
To doubt and fear?
Why do you continue to give us over to tyrants?

Abba! I see a young man in the future, suffering
Just like me. Is that me?
I see lads, Good and Kind,
Dying but not changing.
Is that You?

I see those performing the crucifixion, laughing and celebrating after the execution.
Is that us?
I see wars, tears, poverty and injustice.
I see the earthly Jerusalem divided,
I see the heavenly city appearing in my dreams and my delirium!

I see a body torn to pieces by hawks,
Birds that have not yet been born!
I see countries carrying their thrones
And building a new Babylon!
I see drops of ill rain – they are Your silent tears.

Abba! Who are these peoples who arise in the Circles of Time?
Who are these hypocrites, leading them along the Greedy One's paths?
Where is the song that can stop the killers
From sneaking into the hearts of those who know you?
How many new names will you give the punishers?

And how few names will you give the righteous?
When is this Day and how long will it last?
How many more generations will think
That they won't live to see the Day?
How many different priests will die in asceticism,

And how many will just play the role?
How many false prophets must walk earthly tracks
For them to collapse beneath them
And open the gates of Hell?
Where are the clocks that tell the true time?!

How long must we live in *non-appearance* and expectation?
Look – these are the machines that replace the mind.
Look – these are the machines that replace an achievement.
Look – these are machines that fight for warriors.
How much has changed, Abba!

But at the time... nothing has changed.
There she is, crying – her son chose the Bloodless One's dope.
There he is, crying – his daughter will never see where heaven is.
There they are, meeting the zinc coffins together
And here I am, crying – because I see them all!

Look, Abba, there's a country
Where all they produce is slaves.

There's a country where all they produce is rulers
And consumers of the country
Where the slaves are.

Abba! Look how many Caesars are on the coins!
Look how many people they've replaced You with!
How often I don't want to be here.
Does that mean You don't want to be here either?
Show me where the neck of the jug is!

You know, the worst thing is
That humankind is so smart and so sophisticated
And knows so much about how the world goes round
And yet it has been unable for centuries to find this jug neck,
From which I must drink my fate!

Abba, I often think that no one wants
That primordial water, that everything has been forgotten.
The Bloodless One's poison has become so sweet, though,
That no one even needs a pure source!
The jug was never lost; it was consciously hidden from sight.

Abba, look!
If people come speaking in the name of religion
About what we used to call the Path,
Then what they fear most of all
Is one day to say to themselves *I am Him!*

While the one who dares to say it
Will be destroyed, wiped from the face of the earth and chased by dogs.
Doesn't that seem strange to you, Abba?
What I think is that they are not given the right to speak, but sold it
And they have frozen in their anticipation of the surplus value from that.

How does one love, Abba?!
Not just giving someone your feeling,
But to actually be Beloved?
Not loved, attracting universal attention
And universal worship,

But Beloved,
Vulnerable and weak,
Able to stand on both sides of love,
To love truly,
Dissolving not only in time, but in its circles, too.

Why is love today only *in spite of*?
How do we save ourselves, Abba, without becoming *antisocial*?
How varied is today's enemy, whom we need to love?
How does someone close become someone distant,
While the adulterer is acknowledged by society?

Here I am, Abba, naked before You.
I know You are in me now, but today I'd like to
Speak with someone who is not part of me,
So that I am not speaking with myself,
For that is frightening. It is always frightening to speak with yourself.

Where are you, Abba?
Reveal me at least some image of yourself:
A dove, an angel, a song or a poem.
After all, you promised another manifestation of Yourself, didn't you?
There's not much left. Will you make it?

What I wouldn't give for a sign from Heaven!
What I wouldn't give for reliance on Eternity,
When the temporary requires support.
What I wouldn't give to rely on something,
And what I wouldn't give for Eternity so as not to fear living in time.

And now, Abba,
I hear a noise behind me.
That's my destiny rushing towards me.
Allow me one forbidden luxury if you will,
To make one request of you.

No, no, it doesn't concern me.
An inevitable circle of time has spread over me again, you see.
I'm asking You about my brothers.
The boys will do everything themselves; they will find You on the Path.
Simply...

Don't let me forget their names.

****

Look, look!
The guards are rushing to seize the troublemakers!
They've got into the Garden of Gethsemane.
They've seized Thomas Didymus;
He's laughing, saying, 'take me to the enemies, for I am Him!'

But the Beloved Friend is running over
To stop the error of fate in the new circle of time.
Cephas and James, son of Zebedee are also rushing over,
Unsheathing *two swords* in readiness to fight
And stop those meting the punishment.

Judas is flying around and sees the Teacher;
He approaches Him and kisses Him, saying,
'My mission is complete, so grant me Your prediction of life
And the Word!'
He points to the guards and says, 'There He is, the Transgressor of the *Law*!'

The guards seize the Teacher
But Cephas struck one of them with his sword,
Chopping off his ear.
The Beloved One cried out, 'No, Cephas!
No, James, sheath your swords now!

Forgive us, guard, for you are part of My world!'
In saying this, the Friend healed the soldier's ear and said,
'Here I am! Take Me.'
The dumbstruck soldiers bound the Teacher,

Doing their best not to tie him too tightly.

The Friend turned to Judas and said,
'You are right, brother, your mission is complete.
But you ask yourself if the Word is with you?
Is there life for you?
If it is, then take it.

I must admit, I didn't think it would be you.
But seeing as it is you, I give you and your betrayal
Not only life but also, in this circle of time,
That which you did not expect: the eternal memory of the people and

Immortality.

Verse 36

'If You, our Beloved Friend, won't allow us
To protect You from these people,
Who have come as if for an animal with their spears and stakes,'
Cephas said, incredulous at the spectacle
Of the healed ear,

'Then let us at least deal with the traitor!'
Cephas and James seized Judas,
But the Teacher, raising his hand, stopped them:
'Cephas, what do you know about betrayal?!'
He exclaimed angrily,

'When, before the cock crows,
You will deny me three times?'
Peter was taken aback and released Iscariot.
'But how, Rabbi? You mean I'll betray you too?
Then it would be better for me not to live, but to die right here!'

'I speak not to accuse you,'
The Beloved One said sadly,
'But so that you will not forget
What we deem our worldview and our teaching,
That he who does not judge should not be judged.

Cephas, our time of judgment has not come,
So, brethren, sheath those swords and go.
Here I am!' The Beloved One said, this time to the guards,
And they left the garden.
And they came to the house of the high priest Anna,

And the Friend stood before the old Sadducee.
Anna looked for a long time and in silence at Him,
And then asked where Caiaphas was.
At that moment, Caiaphas appeared, dressing himself as he went.
He nodded at Anna and studied the Teacher with some interest:

'Are there any witnesses against this man?'
'Yes, yes,' came obsequious voices from the crowd,
'He said that the trade around the Temple is the Devil's work!'
Anna grimaced as if he were in pain,
But Caiaphas, noticing this, proclaimed once again,

'Is there any other evidence concerning Him?
Well? Speak up!'
'He spoke of a certain Kingdom in the heavens,'
Came a voice from the crowd, this time not so assured.
Anna's chin dropped to his chest as if in despair

From the human stupidity and uselessness.
Caiaphas was already worried, looking at the old high priest.
Then, from out of the crowd, someone pushed
A toothless man with shifty eyes.
'Speak, you dog,' someone unseen whispered.

The toothless man chuckled and announced,
'This man said that he'd destroy the Temple
And rebuild it in three days!'
In despair, Anna covered his head with his hands
And rocked from side to side.

Then, glaring angrily at the crowd and the toothless man, Caiaphas
Literally screamed at the Beloved One,
'Who are You? And who are Your disciples?!'
The Beloved Friend calmly answered,
'Did I not speak with the people in the temples

And were My disciples not by my side?

Did we not have conversations and arguments with you?
Be a little bolder, Caiaphas, and do what you are destined to do!'
At that, the guard struck the Friend across the cheek:
'How dare you speak to the high priest that way?!
Don't get smart, you outcast, and answer politely!'

At that, Anna stood up from his chair and said,
'Let us adjourn until the morning,
And would *you* be so kind as to come with me?'
He was addressing Caiaphas, his son-in-law,
Both angry and frustrated.

Everyone knew that he used the polite *vu* form
Merely to pull the wool over the people's eyes.
It was night when the guards led the Friend
Into a temporary dark cell, past various people,
Among whom was Peter.

'Hey,' one of the guards called out,
'Aren't you one of them, eh?'
This was not an accusation as such
And the crowd just laughed,
As there was no real threat in the guards' voices.

'No, not I! Not I!' Peter mumbled and slipped away.
The crowd laughed more and continued
Accompanying the Teacher to His holding cell.
'Yes, he's, you know, one of them,' muttered an old woman
At the back of the crowd.

'No, no!' Cephas cried and ran as fast as he could
As if the earth beneath his feet was alight.
He came to us at the Garden of Gethsemane and told us everything.
We decided that those holier-than-thou types had no accusation to make,
So there was no need to fear the high priests' judgment.

Only I crept closer, ever-so quietly, to the Friend's cell,
Not to rely on the word of others but use my own observations
To describe everything as accurately as possible.
The next morning, a carefree crowd had gathered again
At the door to the Friend's temporary confinement.

712

Yawning and having fun, they shifted from foot to foot
As they waited for the show to begin.
After all, the next day would be Passover,
And what better entertainment could there be
Than the execution of some robber to mark the Passover?

And here they had a real treat:
Some prophet or other, a psychic or a communist,
Against whom they couldn't find a proper charge.
What was not to like? Was this not proper showbiz?
What could be more entertaining?

There were those who gathered that day on the square,
While others glued themselves to their television screens,
Irritated by the volume of ads during the breaks;
Everyone was waiting to see how this fascinating tale would end,
A tale that Jerusalem's producers, no doubt, had dreamed up.

There were some who sympathised, women in particular,
For wasn't this lad still quite young?
What could he have done that was so bad
To warrant being led from prison in chains like some murderer?
At least that is how they reasoned while flipping the morning omelette for their husbands

Who were rushing off to work,
Equally glued to the television screens and spilling mayo onto their ties.
Some had gathered near the Sanhedrin from early morning,
To get a good view of the show first-hand.
Journalists were also jostling, and policemen too.

Everyone was fussing about, but they had their phones
Ready and were recording everything to later
Post it all onto the global networks in exemplary fashion
Under such headers as, *Execution of a Madman! Cool! You've gotta see this!*
Or *Priests screw up! The crowd goes wild!*

Or *Prophet from Galilee gives it to the Senate Committee – LOL!*
And so on and so forth.
Peter was coming and a policeman
Grabbed him lazily by the elbow, saying,
'Something suspicious about your face, mate. You're not with them, are you?'

'No! No, I am not!' said Cephas, all on edge.
At that moment, the cock crowed,
And he ran to his brothers as fast as he could,
Not from fear this time, but to tell them,
'It was a true prophecy, brethren!

And since His prediction about my denial came true,
That means the Friend's death is unavoidable!
We've really underestimated the authorities here!
I reckon they won't let anyone off for being so helpless yesterday!
Run! Run! Perhaps there's something we can do!'

There was such crowd and with no way through!
'No, sir!' the guards said calmly and politely,
'Sorry, sir, but entry to the court show through here

Is by special invitation of the Sanhedrin only, sir!
There's nothing we can do to help, sir!'

'But this isn't a show! The fate of our Friend is being decided there!'
'Sorry, sir, but we are only acting according to the powers vested in us,
By the state of Jerusalem, so, please be so kind
And step away from the barrier, sir!
There is a special procedure for holding festive events

And we will adhere to it.
You can challenge our actions with the procurator tomorrow if you wish,
But for now, please clear the way, sir!'
'But tomorrow will be too late! It will be a catastrophe tomorrow!'
'Sirs, please let the press through and step away from the barrier.'

Silence suddenly fell over the square,
In front of the Sanhedrin.
Anna, Caiaphas and everyone else emerged, dressed in court attire.
They also brought out the Friend, roughing Him up and pushing Him.
The multi-million TV audience froze

And reporters in all corners quietly began murmuring.
I did manage to get closer to the action.
God, how small and frail He looked, our Beloved Friend!
Above him hung the emblems and insignia of justice
With which all the world's justice authorities like to adorn themselves!

How helplessly he coughed and grimaced
Under fire from the camera flashes and television lighting!
Then He caught sight of me
And he drew the sign of a circle in the air,
Meaning the repetition of the circles of time.

I realised that the inevitable had begun.
That which for centuries has been locked in a cycle of the inevitable,
That people are doomed to inevitability
That, despite His words and deeds,
We have made it all fatal and inevitable.

But He still remains as before; how can you still not realise that?!

THE CASE OF BARABBAS

Many things that happen
Don't originate from things we can see.
The visible part of phenomena
Is actually prepared long and meticulously
Behind the scenes, out of our field of vision.

And all this for the sole purpose of making the show we see
More effective, without flaws in its organisation.
And a much more important thing in this invisible preparation
Are the webs of human interests
That have an impact hidden, imperceptibly but inevitably.

So, shortly before the Teacher was captured,

These conversations took place within the walls of the Sanhedrin prison.
Do you think only prophets predict the future?
No, note the wise old men
Who sit quietly in the corner during the show

Weaving their secret intrigues but, most importantly,
Possessing the power of political foresight.
Well, put another way, with the power of understanding
Of how what is happening now
Will have a bearing on what happens tomorrow.

Note these eternal Sadducees.
They are smart, prudent and cold-blooded.
They'll move a hand, an eye or a brow
And this movement alone will see insurgents crucified,
Or armies rush into the desert to destroy entire peoples.

Their strength and might is so impressive
That generations will say that they are the rulers of the world!
Others will want to get into their ranks and this is the dream of many!
They are the core, the foundation and *the soul* of the modern world!
Hey, Babylon, what powerful priests you have raised over the centuries!

And so an unseen part of the theatre
Was played out in the Sanhedrin prison several weeks before Passover
By two ingenious *lawyers*. They had been instructed
A very sensitive matter, which it was essential
To conclude with a successful outcome,

For which they had been promised big money.
The lawyers requested the prisoners' case files
And laughed at length when they saw that they included two of their namesakes:
Gestas and Dismas[271],
But nothing suggested to them that there was any symbolism in that.

'Here,' said Gestas, 'here's a funny name – Yeshua,
A hardcore villain and robber
And leader of a gang including your and my namesakes.
Let's take his case.'
'Agreed,' said Dismas. 'After all, justice

Is only a matter of luck for some, but grief for others.'
This Yeshua was brought to them.
'Crikey, what an ugly mug!'
One lawyer whispered to the other.
'You wouldn't drink honey from that face, for sure,' the other grimaced.

'Listen here, my good man, they say
You've stolen a lot of jewellery and money
That was to be donated to the Temple. Is that right?'
Gestas asked the robber with a fox-like tone.
'I'm not guilty, your honour!' The robber blinked,

'I don't have anything! This is a lie!'
'All right,' the lawyer said with a lazy yawn.

---

[271] Dismas and Gestas were the names of the two robbers, crucified together with Christ.

But then, like a vulture, his colleague swooped into
The robber: 'You godless creature!
If you have nothing, then what is our interest?

Pray tell, for what would we pull your sorry
Jewish arse out of prison?!
Get out of here!
If you have nothing to pay, then you'll die on the cross
Together with the other lowlifes! Guards, take him away!'

'No! No! Wait, wait!
I... well, I have a little left, that I hid
For my little children and my family,
So they wouldn't go hungry... Have mercy, sirs!
There is really very little there.'

'You're lying, you dog,' Gestas went on, lazily,
Twirling his ballpoint pen in his hand.
You've never had a wife or children.
And you've never recalled relatives either
Throughout your sorry life.

So, how much do you say you have left?'
The robber gave in: 'Just thirty mina[272], perhaps...'
'Half a talent!' Dismas whistled. 'But you're a rich man!
Well, I reckon that if we value your sorry skin at
Half that amount, you won't object...

I can't hear you!' Dismas yelled again.
'Yes, yes, yes! Good sirs, I will honestly...
I will definitely...' the robber Yeshua mumbled.
'Good man!' Gestas said,
His enthusiasm suddenly waking.

'So, where do you say it's hidden?'
'Yeah...' the robber grinned through the remnants of black teeth.
'Of course, so I tell you where it is,
You take it all and forget all about me.'
'You idiot,' Gestas drawled good-naturedly with another yawn.

'You think we're magicians or something?
No, my dear, this money will not be spent idly.
It all constitutes the budget for your release.
What you give a witness will determine how hard he'll try for you.
The mood of the judge

Will depend on how heavy his pockets feel
And that will dictate the concessions you receive. Understood?'
'Yes, and listen here, you little shit!'
Dismas began yelling again,
'Someone must be crucified to keep the Passover crowd amused!

You think others are less guilty than you?!
We drop our guard, we don't have the right inspiration
And we don't do our job properly

---

[272] A unit of measure in Ancient Greece and the Middle East. 1 talent = 60 mina; 1 mina = 100 drachma

And someone else will be spared the cross, not you.
Let's say it'll be my namesake or that other one, what's his name? That madman from Galilee!'

Gestas nodded lazily but never took his
Hawk eye from the robber.
'Well, all right...' Yeshua the robber gave in,
'I'll give you a tip off,
Only there is only part of the amount there!'

'Good man!' Gestas perked up again.
'You're the robber here, while we are just doing an honest deal.
So, don't you worry, we won't let you down.
If we let down people like you
Who would ever look to use our services?' and they both laughed out loud.

'All right,' Dismas said, rolling up his sleeves, 'let's get started.'
Gestas also opened his papers and gave Yeshua a big wink.
'First of all, your name!' Dismas said, pacing up and down.
Yours will not do, for it reminds me of something.
What did that, erm, prophet, broadcast out there?

That he's the son of the Heavenly Father? Aha, we'll make this one
The son of an earthly father, closer to the people
And as far from the unknown and the mystical as possible.'
'Excellent!' the second lawyer reacted
And jotted something down in his laptop.

'Therefore... Therefore, you'll be Bar-Abba!'[273]
Thereafter, the newly-named Bar-Abba became wholly confused.
'May I have a cigarette?'
The robber asked,
Grinning his black grin.

The lawyers looked at him in surprise,
As if they'd only just noticed him.
'Smoke away,' Gestas said with a laugh, extending him the pack,
'Partner...'
Both lawyers laughed loudly once more.

Several hours sitting around
Wore Bar-Abba out. He drifted off
And, half asleep, he could hear the lawyers speaking indistinctly,
And they appeared to him as fish in their native
Sea of Galilee.

'We need the high priest to tear his robes off'
Gestas said, waving his pen about.
'Yes, indeed,' Dismas agreed. 'Quite right.
That'll mean that the discussion is over.'
'Well done, my man! Look at us go!'

'And what do we do about the crowd?'
'Well, we follow the usual route,' Gestas winked to his colleague.
'He's not a robber, but... a zealot! A Canaanite!
But he didn't rob anyone, rather... he saved donations!'

---

[273] *Bar-Abba* – literally *son of the father* – the Biblical Barabbas, who, according to legend, was also called Yeshua.

'So, we write: a journalist's investigation,

Two talk shows with Sadducees and Pharisees,
Reporting from the scene...'
All that was left was for the laptop to catch fire,
There were so many bright new ideas
Pouring from the lips of these diehard professionals.

Long after midnight, Bar-Abba woke up from a sharp jolt
To see Gestas's grinning face in front of him:
'Hey, phony zealot, get up!
Off you go and get some sleep; we need you nice and fresh
To play a role, you defender of your Jewish Fatherland!'

The following morning, Dismas appeared
At the door of the robber's cell.
He was sullen and downcast, like the deathly day outside.
'Hey, sans-culotte! Nothing doing, sorry partner...'
'What? What do you mean nothing doing?!'

Bar-Abba had had his first proper night's sleep and that's what had come of it!
'There's a snag and it's a really big one.'
Dismas scratched his ear with a fingernail
And then examined the nail
As if there could be nothing more important in the world.

'A witness has come forward, who saw
You phffft that Roman...'
The lawyer ran his hand across his throat.
'So, farewell, my good man. Sorry, but there's nothing to be done.'
He moved decisively for the door.

'Listen,' Bar-Abba said, jumping up.
That bird of freedom was slowly melting away in the Jerusalem sky.
'Listen, is there really nothing that can be done? Nothing at all?'
Dismas shook his head helplessly.
'And can't you... you know... that witness...?' the robber persisted.

'What are you suggesting?!' Dismas yelled and, as if he'd been scalded,
He rushed from the cell but... somehow slowly.
So slowly, in fact, that Bar-Abba managed to grab him by the sleeve.
'I don't mean *that*! Perhaps, you could... partner up with him?'
The robber whispered, looking beseechingly with festering eyes

At the lawyer.
'You're quick off the mark, you son of your father!'
Dismas suddenly smiled broadly
And a sheet of paper appeared miraculously in his hand.
'Write down where the rest is!'

'Leave me some... Something at least,'
Bar-Abba whined, already scribbling.
'And your life?' the lawyer asked indifferently,
'That not enough for you? Perhaps we can agree that you'll survive,
But this hand of yours...' he grabbed the thief's right hand tight,

'And chop it off so you don't go sticking it where it doesn't belong, eh? EH?'

Bar-Abba pulled his hand away in horror,
As if the lawyer could have chopped his hand off right there.
'Okay, okay,' he babbled in fright, his hand now firmly behind his back,
'I've given you everything. We're partners, right? Partners, right?'

'Partners, you bet,' Dismas replied with a yawn, placing the paper into his folder.
Gestas will come this evening and tell you what to say,
So, if you mess anything up, it'll be on you.'
He threw a thick wad of newspapers onto the bunk and laughed:
'There, so you don't get bored, you can read about yourself, you fricking hero!'

The next day Gestas brought in some clean clothes.
'Get dressed, you victim of Roman terror.
We're going to the preliminary hearing.
Just bear in mind that you won't be pardoned today,
So don't go off on a tangent, just keep your mouth shut and nod.

You can cry if you can make yourself.'
While Bar-Abba was dressing, Gestas leafed through
The latest newspapers he had brought.
'You watch the television yesterday?' the lawyer enquired.
'Yes,' Bar-Abba said, rather bewildered.

'Did you see yourself? A defender of widows and old men?'
'Uhuh,' the robber responded sullenly.
'That's right... And bear in mind that we don't just need to make
An angel in the flesh from you,
But also mix it with the shit of a decent man.'

'What man?' Bar-Abba asked in surprise, combing his hair at the mirror.
'Well... a prophet or some such... I don't know...'
Gestas stopped to think about far away.
'What are you doing?' Bar-Abba's reflection took a liking to him in the mirror
And allowed himself to mock:

'But aren't you serving the good of justice?'
'I'll give you justice,' Gestas said, suddenly turning angry.
'You sonofabitch, why didn't you tell us about the money
You hid in the spinstress's attic, eh?'
Bar-Abba dropped the comb in his fright.

'Off you go and don't you start any nonsense!
Remember, *carbonari*, we've got you in the palm of our hand, got it?!'
'I got it, I got it,' Bar-Abba said, raising his arms
And smiling apologetically through black teeth.
Once there was a deal in place, he somehow felt more at ease.

When they reached the Sanhedrin,
The place was noisy and overcrowded.
With a broad smile, Dismas greeted them at the doors
To the main hall where the court was in session.
A guard poked Bar-Abba painfully in the ribs

Indicating that he should stand near the column
And not show himself until called.
Dismas went inside and Gestas sat down on a bench nearby
And busied himself in the pages of some tabloid paper,

Picking at a fresh pimple on his chin.

Bar-Abba craned his neck in an attempt to see inside the hall.
Every now and then, through the barrier of
Hundreds of heads, he caught sight of the majestic Caiaphas,
Pacing to and fro and broadcasting something out loud,
To which the crowd responded with a roar of approval.

From time to time, Bar-Abba caught another, much quieter voice
Which made him feel decidedly uneasy.
He was unable to see who was speaking
And was about to give up in his attempts to stretch out his neck,
When he saw a man with a fish-like face emerge from the crowd and yell,

Pointing his finger at the man who Bar-Abba couldn't see,
'He said He was the Son of God!'
Hearing that, Caiaphas threw up his hands theatrically
And began tearing at his clothes, yelling something about blasphemy.
Bar-Abba shrugged and, turning to the guard,

Gestured to him for a cigarette.
The guard gave him one, not taking his eyes from what was happening inside.
The crowd trembled and moved out onto the street.
Amidst the crowd Bar-Abba at first saw a strange man,
Being led by the guards.

He was strange because, meeting Bar-Abba's eyes,
He smiled at him, as if they were old acquaintances,
Although the robber would have sworn
He had never seen Him before.
Then his gaze picked out that man from the crowd

With the fox-like face who had shouted something about the Son of God.
Now Bar-Abba was ready to swear
That he had seen this man before and more than once,
But when Dismas approached him
And shoved a couple of coins into his hand,

Bar-Abba grimaced and lost all interest in the fox-faced man.

The crowd subsided
And then Gestas and Dismas quickly brought Bar-Abba inside
And led him before the court of high priests.
Caiaphas, it turned out, was completely calm, despite the fact
That several moments earlier,

He had been tearing at his clothes, quite possessed by righteous anger.
The high priest had changed into new clothes
And was impatiently, even fastidiously pointing out to the lawyers
That they needed to approach other high priests.
The lawyers, the guards and Bar-Abba approached

The old man with the eagle eye
And hurriedly began talking to him,
Pointing at Bar-Abba.
The old man nodded absently but approvingly.
Then the newly attired Caiaphas approached and the entire Sanhedrin

Moved after the crowd, which had gone somewhere
After the strange man who had recognised Bar-Abba.
Dismas and Gestas accompanied the priests to the doors
And then returned to the bewildered robber.
Dismas gave him a thumbs up, to indicate all was well.

'Well, and what are these, preliminary hearings, or what?'
The robber asked sullenly but restraining his joy.
'What did you want,' Gestas said with a grimace,
An hour and a half's discussion of your worthless life?
Who needs you anyway, you child of the revolution?

But don't you go letting your guard down,
The best part is still to come:
The opinion of the community, as concentrated in the will
Of the powerful jurors,
Known among us as the best representatives of the ochlocracy!'

'Eh?' Bar-Abba grunted, his mouth open in confusion.
'Go on, off you go,' Dismas said, shoving him in the back, and off they went
To meet historical justice and
The triumph of systemic professionalism,
Honed to diamond-like perfection and invariability over many years.

Bar-Abba was now completely lost
But, despite the fact that a certain anxiety
Still gnawed away at him, he was calmer than before.
Even a thieves' showdown took longer
Than their wise meting out of justice.

By all accounts both systems were governed by the same laws
Which before were simply *take it away*,
But were now more intricate, known as *hand it over voluntarily*,
Although the essence had barely changed –
Whoever you might have been, much would be decided by people with foxlike faces,

With whom someone, in a link of a single chain of intent
Had become a mutually beneficial partner at the right time.
And they didn't have to be false witnesses either.
They could be anyone at all,
Into whose good judgment such pros as Dismas and Gestas

Had wormed their way in.
'And now, dear partner mine,' Gestas joked with a grin,
'You'll see the best creation of management science and practice.
You'll see how the all-powerful
Becomes a hostage of its own system

And turns out in the end to be a fool.
Meaning in a position
Into which they are placed by the likes of us –
The angels of modern justice.
And note this, you Al-Qaeda mercenary, there will be no direct control at all!

There will be influence from a host of indirect circumstances,
Which all place the powers that be in a situation

When they need to act *humanely*,
By virtue of their convictions,
But the system forces them to act as *members of the system*.

You will witness their helpless writhing,
The desire to maintain their *I*, but, at the same time,
Maintaining *themselves within this system*, without losing any of its benefits!
You'll see the beauty of choice, when man struggles
Between the notions of *I am me!* and *I am them!*

He growls, grinds his teeth and wrings his hands in despair,
Saying that they're forcing him, but that *I am not them!*
I am me!
Because he loved himself before and cherished the thought
That it was *he* who was using the system for his own benefit,

And not the other way round.
That *he* is trying to improve it,
Not that *it* is turning him into a monster!
However, the moment will come, you believe it, Red Army Bar-Abba,
When the system will deliver its bill.

And then!' Dismas and Gestas spun each other round
As if in a parody of a minuet.
'And then your choice is brought out onto the square,
Where your action darts about between the righteous
And a non-entity like you, partner,

Before everyone's eyes and the TV cameras of Eternity!
And, you know what happens in a person's heart in this instance?
Instead of fighting and dying,
Like this sorry Galilean will die today,
You persuade yourself that this isn't Eternity before you!

That you will still handle the system
And you'll show it the middle finger of victory.
That today is just an episode, one of many,
And the thing you've scuppered is just circumstantial,
And can be forgotten.

You are conversing with yourself
And you are losing the argument,
Not because one point of view is stronger and another, weaker,
But because you have already lost your entire self once and for all before!
You lock up Heaven above you

And wash your hands.'

THE JUDGMENT OF PONTIUS PILATE

He was not handsome, but extremely well-tailored.
He was smart, perceptive, able to listen
And, it seemed, he adhered to the advisory principle of management.
There was not a single key decision
That he wouldn't discuss with the priests.

In so doing, he would listen prudently to their reasoning,
Nodding in agreement and not afraid to argue a point before them.
He was like a set of scales and not because he was infinitely fair.
Simply he was as dangerous as he was considerate.
He never, as they say, *broke a situation over his knee*;

He was a master dramatist.
What else could you call it when he decides
To bring images of emperors into the Temple,
And then, after meeting with the high priests,
He repents for having been so inconsiderate, after which he calls off his soldiers?

Well, and so what that the Temple had
Roman inscriptions and Doric columns.
Well, and so what that the high priests were themselves
Now drawing borders in their own city
For where they could go and where Romans could go.

He would emerge the victor in any situation.
He and the Empire.
He could reproach the residents of Judea for the barbarism and foolishness in the country,
But in Rome he would publish notes
That he had seen a great, inimitable culture in Judea.

He objected with dignity when the Emperor
Demanded that taxes be raised for the provinces of Israel
Using fire and the sword,
But then he gave the high priests the right to collect tribute,
Who themselves brought the requisite amount to him.

He collected works of art,
Shamefully concealing them from the zealots of the faith.
He built bridges, roads, aqueducts and social facilities,
Reinvesting the funds raised in this same country
And sometimes even at the expense of the Empire!

He argued that the mutual tolerance of cultures
Was the highest level of harmony in the colonies,
For which he gained respect in the lands of Israel.
And when the question arose of electing an ethnarch to replace the late Herod,
For some reason, the delegation of high priests in Rome said

There was no better ruler for the domestic scene
Than this diligent and prudent Roman official.
Many people in the Israeli provinces
Even began to say that this could hardly be called colonialism
If they were being treated so considerately.

Could it now be that Romans, Israelites,
Hellenes and other peoples now lived in friendship
Together within the Land of Israel?
Was this one-sided exploitation,
When our merchants and money changers

Were allowed into the markets of the Metropolis?
Were not the culture of management,
The culture of good conduct, economic growth

723

And other achievements of civilisation
Not brought to us by people such as him?

The patriots gnashed their teeth in their powerlessness,
Stating insistently and foolishly
That it was non-freedom that was true slavery
And, worse than that, the reproduction of the slave consciousness
Under the benevolent guise of enlightened colonialism.

What could these unfortunate types object to
Faced with the sensible and calm reasoning of the Israeli elite,
Who had sensed not only respect from this man,
But a strong feeling of stability too,
Allowing progressive development and the implementation of plans,

Of the implementation of which he personally was the guarantor?

He was always neatly dressed and every fold in his toga
Spoke of the latest trends on the streets of Rome.
He arranged festivals and feasts for foreign visitors to the country,
But, most of all,
He paid heed to the Jewish festivals.

This was the best example of colonialism,
Which the Empire had created for the triumph of its power.
This was a man who knew how to live in wonderful harmony
With those of other faiths,
But who lived by his side and made his bread.

He emerged to the cries of the admiring crowd
From the building of the praetorium, to politely pay his respects to the Jews
Who were not allowed to besmear themselves on the days of Passover
By visiting a pagan administration,
And he sat himself on the *Lyphostroton*[274], erected especially outside the building.

And so, in the moment when he was to be immortalised,
Emerging ceremonially onto the stage
Where the fate of the Good, Kind Man was being related,
In complete harmony with himself, Rome and the colony,
Came the Procurator of Judea Pontius Pilate.

'There will be no complicated cases today;
Everything is perfectly clear.
There are these three bad eggs, Gestas, Dismas and some Yeshua,
Who need to be crucified for the amusement of the crowd.
These Jews arere strange folk,' Pilate thought:

'They have so few names that you are often confusing them.
Gestas and Dismas, for example;
Those are the names of the district's best lawyers and, there you go –
The names of two thugs today.
Yeshua... reminds me of something.

Who knows what when half of Galilee has that name?

---

[274] *Lyphostroton* – the *Gavvatha* in Hebrew, is a special stone throne-seat, erected outside the praetorium (the Roman court) and from where court proceedings were conducted.

Every other one of them is a Simon, every third, a John.
There's something wrong with the people's imagination. We'll have to think about that.
It's also a good thing that this Yeshua, the most diehard of the thugs,
Has been called Bar-Abba by the press, so it'd be easier to remember who we're talking about.

There's this other troublemaker, a prophet, psychic or something.
But I think he'll get off with a couple of lashes.
So, there it is – no difficult cases.
Passover is my favourite holiday
Because the more the people are slaves,

The more they know how to have desperate fun.'
Pilate benevolently handed out several awards.
The list of recipients had been compiled very cleverly:
A couple of Romans, three Hellenes and four Jews.
Then the children played some awful production,

Depicting some bloodthirsty local myths.
Pilate surveyed the crowd – there was no sign of Herod Antipas's palanquin.
'He'll miss the trial again and will show up in the evening
With round eyes and rich gifts, the idler,'
The procurator grimaced in annoyance.

'If he doesn't bring me four Arabian horses,
He'll only have himself to blame.
And anyway, there's little point in him in court, that schemer.
The last time, I asked that righteous Essene
To walk on water; that's hardly an argument for a court case, is it?

Then I went and executed that unfortunate John.
Who was he bothering?!
I can imagine what would become of the Hellenes
If I executed their Diogenes or Socrates.
Two... no, three legions would have their hands full for five years

Bringing order to Achaea.
I also executed the Baptist at the request of some woman...
Oh, how long will it take to teach these people the imperial grasp of governance?
And is it even necessary? Look how briskly and merrily they prance about.
No, no, imperial thinking is a great thing and not many have it.

For most nations it is a secondary idea;
The pain of the memory of oppression.
It is not the man who has legally ceased to be a slave who rules,
But he who would give his life not to be one,
Simply because he sees it as beneath his dignity,

Without any inner bargaining or thought of personal gain.
It is *always* an advantage to be a slave!
You bear no responsibility and make no decisions.
He who doesn't want to be a slave and is unable
To assume *responsibility for another people* –

Well, someone else will take on that responsibility in their place,
For there will always be someone on this earth.'
When the dancing began,
Depicting the eternity of love and harmony

Between Israel and the Empire,

Pilate became visibly bored and asked for the papers
On the criminals facing his judgment.
'Okay... everything is clear here. The high priests have done a good job.
There's an inquiry and there's the findings.
But this? What is this?'

Pilate signalled to his secretary,
As if to say, 'Where is the condemned Galilean?
Bring Him to me in the praetorium;
At least I'll have a little fun,
For this obsequious display of loyalty is getting on my nerves.

I'll hear out this Young Man.
These Jews are always interesting sorts.'
Waving to the crowd
And nodding to the high priests, as if to say 'I'll be right back,'
The procurator withdrew into the shadows of the praetorium's columns.

Pilate stood in the pleasant darkness and coolness,
Stretched his neck and then sensed
That someone was standing behind him.
He turned to see
Our Beloved Friend.

'So-o-o-o,' the procurator began the conversation with interest.
'Of what do You stand charged, Galilean?
How have You so angered the venerable Anna and Caiaphas,
That they had the look of angry camels?'
The Friend did not respond in the same familiar tone of the Roman, he simply coughed.

However, he still deemed it impolite not to answer the procurator:
'What can I say to you? What the high priests are saying,
What I think or what you simply want to hear?'
This was already interesting, Pilate thought, and came closer.
'They say You are subverting the people and calling Yourself

King of Israel, is this true?'
The procurator's voice was stern and insistent,
Although this was no reflection of how he really perceived himself.
'I could be their King,' the Friend said quietly, 'if they so wished,
But they prefer to be who they are.

Could that destroy the Kingdom
I am talking about? No.
That means, in Heaven it's time will come,
And I am merely the messenger who has been given the Word about it.'
He coughed as he said this, for prison had had its effect on him.

'All right, Galilean, then tell me,
How does your mythical kingdom differ from the Empire?
Look beyond the columns – do you see joy and satisfaction?
What other joy and harmony are you seeking?
What else can you give to the Jew at Passover?'

'My Word is not only about the Jews, but about all peoples.

726

How happy is the oppressor
When surely the oppressed is his mirror image?
How happy is the ruler
When surely the trampled beneath his feet are his reflection?'

'Interesting...' Pilate said, a little taken aback.
'You mean to say that the greatness of the Empire is nothing,
Only a reflection of the subservience
That the defeated peoples bestow it?
Are you out of your mind, Galilean?

Have you seen the greatness of Rome
To have the audacity to compare its might and power
With what is happening in the colonies,
Taken not just by fire and sword,
But by the will of the Olympian gods too?'

The Friend replied, 'The same will that will trample Rome to dust tomorrow, you mean?'
'No, actually,' Pilate said, a little angry now.
'At least not in my lifetime!'
'But weren't we talking about Eternity, procurator?'
Pilate was startled by this and turned show as not to show

How this question had caught him unawares. Then he gathered himself and said,
'Your words speak only of the pain of injustice
That your people are enduring, nothing more.
Why should I listen to this?
The whole world is built on the premise that someone rules and another is a slave.'

Pilate turned sharply to the Beloved One:
'If we switched places
And you were the representative of the Great Empire,
And I, the people you ruled,
Would your rhetoric not change?'

'No, because here I represent the true Greatness
Of the Kingdom of Heaven,
While you represent only that which emerged from ashes
And which is heading to become ashes.'
Pilate's pupils narrowed and he jabbed a finger into the Friend's chest:

'Nothing makes sense if
It is outside the scope my life.
In my life I have been given the power to govern,
Do my will
And bring the greatness of the Empire to other peoples.'

There was a silence, which, after a while,
Was interrupted by the Beloved One's coughing:
'Tell me, knight, how do you settle accounts with the world?
If it brings you pain,
You respond in kind, am I right?

If it brings you war,
You don your sword.
If it brings you joy,
You drown in your merriment.

727

If it brings you sorrow,

You respond with resistance, right?'
'Right,' the puzzled Pilate replied.
'Then where is *your* true greatness, procurator?
What makes you stand taller than that which comes from outside?
What makes people stand taller than that which comes from outside?

What makes the citizens and rulers of Rome stand taller
Than that which comes from outside?
Isn't that what your genius of governance calls
Secondary behaviour, a response to circumstances
And an inability to rise above them?

Imagine that you've become the king of all kings,
The emperor of all empires.
What will change in you
That in essence, does not distinguish you from a slave,
Oppressed by the governance of the outside world?

Now answer me this, procurator,
What do you have besides
That which reacts to the external governance of the world?
It is not... you?
Do you have yourself?'

'Hold on, hold on,' Pilate said, now completely confused,
'Let me complete a couple of formalities
And I'll prove to You that what You have said
Is just causistry and a playing with notions,
Quite unsubstantiated by the truth of life.'

Energetic and as elegant as always,
Pontius Pilate came out onto the *Lyphostroton.*
He raised his hand and confidently but hastily
Said, having waited for complete silence:
'People of Jerusalem!

Based on our eternal tradition,
I give you your sacred right
On this wonderful holiday, known since ancient times,
As Passover, to pardon
One of the prisoners sentenced to death by crucifixion.'

Suddenly, a terrible shockwave struck the procurator,
Terrible in its unexpectedness.
Free Bar-Abba, our ruler!
Save Bar-Abba from death!
How could this be? Pilate was dumbstruck; it had to be a mistake.

He quickly surveyed the square,
And, again, he couldn't see Herod Antipas's palanquin
That he could exert pressure on
And quickly rectify the situation.
This was unthinkable. What was this?'

What was this unexpected and unpleasant departure from the plan?

Pilate gestured to the crowd to wait a moment
And left for the praetorium again.
The Beloved Friend was standing and smiling sadly.
'What surprised you, procurator?

Is it not that there is so little of you in actual fact?'
'You!' Pilate suddenly yelled,
'It's *You* who speaks of the promise of a certain Kingdom
To this mindless ochlocracy?
The people, who have rejected You?!'

'These people reject Me,
But will I respond in kind?
No, not to these people or to anyone else.
Not those who reject Me openly,
Or those who pretend but reject Me secretly.'

Pilate was now really angry: 'Your life is in my hands.
What I say is what will be.'
The Friend replied sadly,
'It is not in your power to change my fate,
And you won't change your own either.'

Then the procurator ordered the soldiers
To bring their lashes and beat the Teacher in front of the crowd.
The knight spoke to the people, but his chin trembled:
'You see, I am punishing Him.
I deem this punishment satisfactory, for He bears no guilt.'

The soldiers ripped the clothes from the Friend,
Placed a crown of thorns and a purple robe on him
And then, yelling and laughing, saying they'd thrash not just anyone
But the King of Israel,
They beat Him and threw him to the procurator's feet.

The procurator thought that, hearing the name of its nation,
The crowd would have mercy and change their minds,
But the words 'Crucify Him!' carried across the square.
Pilate sensed that he had no power
Over what was happening.

He cried out, 'You will remember one day
Who *this man is* but it will be too late.'
The crowd, however, paid no heed to what the Roman had to say.
'We don't want chaos and revolution,'
They cried.

'We don't what the collapse of our foundations!
He brings only trouble and the fear of these foundations disappearing!
Let Him die. Anyway, why do you need any change, Roman?
What will you lose and what will you gain by asking us for Him?'
Pilate asked that the Friend be dragged to the praetorium.

He poured a glass of wine but grimaced when he drank it,
So akin was it to blood.
The procurator lowered his head and ordered himself
To calm down a little.

729

Why was his approach so sincere and sensitive

To that case of this basically
Quite random vagrant?
Sure, the land of Israel sees a good dozen
Such messengers every year,
All trying on the guise of the Mashiah for size.

He went over to the Beloved One,
From whom blood was flowing onto the praetorium floor
In ragged dark streams.
Frowning, he asked,
'How should I truly act now?

I know how to act correctly,
And I know what to do for the best advantage;
How to act cruelly, I can also imagine.
But what would a deed
Of true greatness look like?'

'Look at Me, do you see the greatness?'
The Teacher said, pointing with his bloody hand
At his joke crown and purple robe,
And at his mouth, full of spit and black blood.
'No-o,' Pilate shuddered from disgust.

'Then don't try to make the beginning of the Path
Its end,' the Teacher said.
Do only what you are supposed to do
Specifically on this day.
And when *your day* comes, you will know the Truth.

Then you will know yourself.'

The procurator lowered his head
And saying, 'I know myself, but *whatever is Truth*?'
Again, he emerged onto the square,
But this time he no longer strode quite so elegantly.
'What is it you want?' he cried, irritated and tired.

'To crucify the one who might be the best king for you?
After all, you should not judge his calling by his attire and a rich throne?
Who else could love you like this, people of Israel?!'
'Crucify Him! Crucify Him!' the crowd persisted.
'Are you not killing the deliverer King?'

Pilate added, his voice flagging.
A stronger voice came from the crowd:
'We have no ruler stronger than Caesar!'
So, my system has caught up with me,
Was the thought that pierced the procurator like cold steel.

With his experienced eye of a ruler
Who had governed Judea for several years,
Pilate caught sight of Gestas and Dismas,
Conducting the hecklers with gusto.
He saw Caiaphas, waving his arms approvingly in front of a choir of screaming elites.

He saw Anna, who looked straight into the procurator's eyes,
As if to say,
'Well, Roman knight, I see you are unhappy
With what the system has yielded for you today,
A system you yourself had created, right?

Well, and are you prepared to smash this system in one fell swoop?
Are you prepared to oppose the harmony
That you've built before your seniors in Rome?
Come along, Roman, for us this is a matter of faith and stability;
For you it is but a whim of God-seeking.

Come back to the traditional and stop trying to be a hero.
I know that you will make it up to yourself tomorrow for this defeat
Anyhow, but we are prepared for this.
We are happy to pay you this price,
Because we know the full extent of its importance.

But today be calm,
We don't need you to be *yourself.*
What we need is for the system that you represent
To make an important, necessary decision.'
Pilate objected, but no one heard the conversation:

'And what price are you willing to pay for Him, old man?'
'This one,' Anna replied with his eyes and nodded to Gestas.
In turn, Gestas waved to someone else.
At that same moment, a man with a fox-like face
Yelled out across the entire square:

'His blood will be on us and on our children! Crucify Him!'

Verse 37

Look to the right – the mountain is wailing!
Look to the left – the walls are wailing!
Look down – His Mother and the women are wailing!
Look to the side – there are John and I,
And we too are wailing.

John asked that He be crucified the following day,
To give Him at least a day, as there was much
That his golden lips might utter,
Even in such a short time!
But the high priests refused;

The following day was Saturday and it had to be done *precisely* on that day
To ensure no customs were disrupted!
'How wicked you are, you people of Israel, and so savage
That you cannot give Him a day.
Why such wickedness?

Is this not the best of your sons?
Is it not He who will bring glory to your cities, Israel?!'
The priests laughed in response: 'Look around you, John!
This is no longer Jerusalem!
It's no longer the Land of Israel!

Another land will execute Him!
The wind of history has taken
The great execution to other lands, but nothing's changed!
Was that the Procurator of Rome, you think?
Were we speaking about that Empire?

No, son of Galilee, we also see
That this is another circle of time!
But you – you are his disciple,
So, are you ready to reconcile yourself with this,
Or will you insist that this is

The Land of Palestine?
Will you not scream and shout yourself
That this couldn't happen in another land?
Are you not a slave, therefore,
To those *precise* customs that you're so angry at now?

Look, there are those who say
"We don't believe",
And there are those who assert "He won't die".
There are those who are full of scepticism saying,
"That won't happen here!"

There are those who honour the Empire
And there are the slaves of that Empire!
Are we talking of Rome today?!
Is it really Israel standing accused?!
What is it you know about *times*?!'

'The first charge was placed against you,

His blood will be on you and on your children!'
'Then why, John, this talk of eternity?
Where is the truth? Only in the past?!
Why then the immortality?
What is its meaning if one day it started,

Only for *one day* to end?!
Surely, before determining
Whom to *save*,
You had already determined
Whom to punish?'

I was by His side,
As was John,
And I saw, that stupid, impudent robber
Bar-Abba hanging about nearby,
Looking stupefied and stunned by the entire experience.

He had got what he wanted, so why was he still here,
When You, so tormented, had to carry Your own cross?
Why did he insult the last moment
Of your life, the *bandido*,
Having taken Your place?

The Beloved One fell and dropped his cross, completely exhausted.
A centurion prodded Bar-Abba with his stick
And said, 'Hey, you! What is your name?'
'Simon,' Bar-Abba lied fearfully but habitually.
'Take His cross and carry it for Him,' the centurion instructed.

The robber reeled in horror but still went over
And took up His burden.
I asked, 'Should he not be deleted from the story?
After all, he took Your place of salvation.'
'No,' the Beloved Friend replied,

'Everything is in its place, but *salvation* is a long way off.
Write about him, for repentance in one person
Will be a Kingdom for many tomorrow.'
I saw Bar-Abba dragging the cross,
And his eyes didn't move.

'Walk *freely*,' he said to the Friend.
'To gain my freedom,
I gave away everything; I lost everything,
And yet I feel like I have gained.'
The Friend blessed him, saying simply, 'Thank you'.

Could there have been a more powerful blessing?
Have you ever heard anything
Like that in your life?
Here is the Path from sentence to death.
And here I drink in every centimetre of it.

Or is the Path drinking me?
Bar-Abba was strong but John and I
Didn't want him to go so fast.
However, the Beloved One whispered,
'Don't steal time, for it is pointless.'

There was Golgotha
And Gestas and Dismas had already been raised on their crosses.
I saw that they looked just the same
As the two lawyers, but this was
Probably just my mind playing tricks.

They laid Him on the ground
To nail Him to the cross.
'Tell Me,' He said to me,
And His voice was shaking from fear and terror,
'I was promised

That the third time He will come...
He will come... to say goodbye to Me?'
At that moment the nails were driven into His hands
And he let out an awful scream,
Not like a dying warrior,

Rather like a suffering Young Man,
Who was feeling the pain.
When the cross was raised,
He screamed even louder
And I closed my ears so as not to hear that pain.

From up on the cross, He spoke to John:
'There is my mama; look after her.'
When His Mother heard these words,
She stopped her weeping and wailing
And simply said quietly,

'He has never called me Mama.'
At that moment, something happened to her.
What? I don't know.
Only she was no longer crying or wailing.
She placed a veil over her head

And froze, staring into her Son's eyes.
She disappeared from this moment
And, between her and her Son
There was not eternity
But a quiet, tender pain and the music of angels.

And He smiled.
Has anyone ever heard
How quails howl when they are killed?
How the eagle squawks and the crows suffer awfully
From the methodical expectation?

When death is so long and agonising
During crucifixion,
You can hear them too.

The high priests grow bored
And the soldiers sit down to play dice.

But you are left one-on-one with your
Pain and His.
My head throbbed
And it was all so hurtful for my heart.
How dare you, body of mine, make yourself known

When something like this happens?!
How dare you, even a little,
Take my thoughts away from what is going on,
Reminding me that my hands and feet are not hurting,
But they see this pain in His body?!

Suddenly He turned to me and said quietly,
'To describe all this
Determination and inspiration alone will not be enough.
There'll come a moment and you'll realise
That you will have *to dare* to do it.

If you ask yourself then
How to write about it
And you hear the answer *precisely and diligently*,
Cut off your hands,
And head for the Road without them.

If you ask yourself
How to write about it
Honestly and unbiased?
Crush your mind
And head for the Road a madman.

If you ask yourself
Who will help you
And you answer, *your friends*,
Tell them about true evil and let them turn away from you,
So that you walk the Path alone.

If you ask yourself
Will it be *today*, this year?
Smash your clock and walk away from time,
You will hear the cursing and ridicule of the rulers and your family.
They are ruled by time, not you.

Then ask yourself,
Has *your* day come?
And when you decide that it *has*, you will hear My voice,
Telling you to *take your pen*.
So, then, grasp that voice and go.

What else do you need besides this?'

Words of response were stuck in my throat.
All I could do was bow my head in sorrow.
Let time and its circles repeat themselves,
But could it be that what was happening with the Beloved One

Could really become habitual?!

'To you, John,' the Friend said,
Blood and spit running from his battered mouth
To the ground like wine, frozen in time,
'I give to you the power of the burning Word.
Light it up, if it is meant to burn,

Pour it out if it is a river.
Discard it if it is a burden.
Spit it out if it is bitter.
But tell not of our songs,
Rather of what His last Day means

For all of us, both *living and dead.*'

Then he said, 'I am thirsty!'
A merciful soldier extended a sponge moistened with vinegar
And wet his lips.
The Beloved One smiled,
But it was not this thirst that tormented Him.

His strength had left Him.
He was fading away,
Only, all of a sudden, from where did he find such power of voice?!
He cried out to the heavens,
Alahi! Alahi!

Then, quieter and with greater penetration,
Abba! Abba! Lama sabachthani!
And then I heard the response from on high
That tore my ears and mind apart:
My son, my son, you have suffered enough

And your torments have cleansed You for good.
Your Father has not forsaken You,
Your town has not forsaken You,
I accept Your repentance for everyone,
I accept Your cleansing for everyone,

So, return in peace!

I understood – He had returned.
I understood – He had been accepted.
This was the end of the Path.
This was the end of the circle.
And for now we are blind to see the beginning.

And He died.
And I died.
Everything died
That
Had no wish to remain alive.

Verse 38. Alpha and Omega

On the day we saw the *omega*
In the Jerusalem sky,
A terrible earthquake occurred.
The roofs of houses collapsed,
Burying beneath them

The righteous, the poor and the rich alike.

My brothers and I rushed to help the people of the City,
Who were unable to withstand their limitless
Human grief.
It had doubled.
You see, we were weeping over the loss of our Beloved Friend,

Could we have done any differently?
Would the Teacher have approved of our action,
If He had seen us passing indifferently
By the weeping fathers who had lost their children,
By the mothers buried alongside their own mothers?

We had not slept for several days and nights,
Retrieving people, both alive and dead, from the rubble
And the caves created by the quake from the wreckage of houses;
Houses that just the day before had been a reliable and warm refuge,
Only now to have become a place for grief and tears.

Only occasionally, through that fog of human despair,
Did we cast anxious looks towards Golgotha
As if asking the Friend for forgiveness
For not being able
To commit His body in worthy fashion to the ground.

From time to time one of us would go to the site of the execution,
Continuing our search for a body or simply for any information
About what had happened to the bodies of those who had been executed.
One day, James came and said he had been told
That a certain Joseph, struck by the courage of the man so put to death,

Had taken the body from the cross and taken him to a grave
Which he had prepared in advance for himself,
Saying, 'I didn't know You when you were living,
And now there is nothing I can give to You in life,
So, accept this gift from me now, when it is the only thing You need.

We searched for the route to this grave
But every time we were stopped
Along the way by human grief
And the need to help people in need.
Once again we became immersed in this hell of human torment.

On the second day, Thaddeus, who had been sent to search,
Walked in and tossed someone's belt before us.
Spitting through his teeth, he said,

'The traitor is dead. Judas is dead.'
We cried out in horror,

'Thaddeus, did you kill him?!
Could you really have departed
So fast from the Beloved One's commandments?!'
Thaddeus raised his eyes and spoke hoarsely and sharply:
'Not me, how could you think such a thing?

I saw Judas on the outskirts of the city.
He was walking along like he was drunk, waving his arms about
And seemingly talking to himself.
I might have taken on a human essence,
But I haven't lost the ability to see my former...

Well, I saw the Bloodless One circling in a black shadow
Around Iscariot's head.
People who had suffered in the earthquake
Stretched their hands out to Judas,
But he was deep in his own thoughts.

Then I cried out to him to stop
And ask him where he was going.
Judas turned around and, quite drunk,
He was unable to recognise me.
He shook a finger at nothing at all

And suddenly began running towards the top of the hill.
I had almost caught up with him and saw
Him throwing a rope over the bough of a tree
That hung over an abyss,
"What are you doing?!" I screamed "Stop!

You don't bear the guilt that you ascribe to yourself!"
Judas yelled back, "What do you understand, you idiot?!
Leave me alone!"
Seeing that the shadow of the Bloodless One was firmly
Stuck to Iscariot's ear,

Whispering evil will to him,
I once more tried to stop Judas by shouting,
"It was Him! He specified it Himself, naming Himself,
So that His death would be pure
And would not lead to anyone's downfall!

Your kiss is nothing without His recognition!
His will alone determined who would be executed!"
It was here that I realised it was useless persuading Judas,
While the Greedy One was sitting on his shoulder like a black owl.
I rushed towards them and attacked the demon.

I was so afraid that the loss of my angel's strength
Would render me helpless against the Son of the Morning,
But, to my surprise,
I was able to tear off the demon and choke him hard.
Of course, I had the power of soul and faith inside!

And what is there in that ethereal spirit
That has no heart?
We fought for a few moments
Until the demon broke free and, coughing and spluttering, rushed away into the sky.
He laughed wickedly as he flew off and I couldn't understand

The reason for his cruel joy.
However, when I did realise, it was too late –
Judas was standing over the abyss and looking right at me.
Weary from the battle, all I could do was silently extend a hand to him
In desperate helplessness.

Without taking his eyes off me,
With a gaze that was suddenly both sober and cold,
Judas croaked, "When the day of your *Step* comes,
Don't allow your heart
To dive into the abyss of bargaining with Heaven."

He plunged downwards, the rope squeezed his neck and he was dead.
I jumped up and tried to prevent his death,
But Judas was hanging over the gaping mouth of the abyss
And I couldn't reach him.
I cried out in my helplessness,

But in the next moment I heard the voice of
A passing Roman:
"Friend! There is an urgent need of water to put out a fire!
Can you help, friend?"
Weeping and reproaching Judas for the last time

For what he had done, I rushed to help those
Still alive and I sought salvation
From the earthly fire. I knew full well
That someone had abandoned my efforts forever,
By preferring to remain without *salvation*

In the embraces of the fire of the black abyss.'

We listened in silence
And, without saying a word
We returned to our rescue work.
I saw that each one of the brothers
Were remembering Judas and praying to Heaven to save his soul.

Sometimes, one of us would lose it,
Like once happened with Simon the Zealot, who exclaimed,
'Why are we helping these creatures?!
Is this not Heaven's punishment for betraying Him
And delivering him into the hands of death?!'

However, Thomas grabbed him by the collar and said coldly,
'How dare you say that
Our Friend is capable of such petty vengeance?!
You have to understand
That this earthquake is just the powerlessness of the Bloodless One

Because he could not prevent

The day of His might!'
'But is this not the Heavenly response for
This City recognising that His blood is on them
And their children?!' Simon persisted.

Then Cephas took Simon into his mighty embrace
And, calming him down like a child
And stroking the Zealot on the head, he said,
'Look, Sima, just look at these children.
Could our Beloved Friend

Really wish them so much evil and deprivation?
Only three days have passed
Since we parted...
Have we already begun to lose
Our feeling of *community* with Him?

Grab a shovel, brother, and carry on digging.
When thinking about saving souls,
Never pass by an opportunity
Simply to save a life.
After all, that is our Path, ours and His, right?'

Simon wiped away his tears and tried to respond,
But at that moment a scream rang out; from beneath the rubble
Someone was crying out! There were people alive there!
We forgot about our disputes and rushed to rake away the wreckage of the building.
That same evening

John came rushing in, extremely excited.
First, he grabbed the jug and drank feverishly from it,
Before starting to speak,
While we watched him in tense expectation.
'Put us out of our misery! Speak, speak!'

'The women... the women have seen Him...'
'Seen who? John, who have they seen? Joseph?'
'Not Joseph... They've seen the Teacher!'
'How?!' we all yelled in unison. 'Where?! Why?!'
'They came in the morning... but the tomb was open...

And there was no body inside!'
'This cannot be! Who needed to steal the body?!'
The Zealot and James, son of Alphaeus cried out,
'Perhaps the Romans or Sadducees wanted to
Erase all memory of him?!

We won't let this happen!'
'Hold on a minute, will you?' Thomas said, cooling the brothers' ardour.
'John, what is it are you saying?
Tell us in more detail.'
'I don't know any of the details!'

John yelled in desperation.
'I don't know the circumstances either!
I was near the tomb
And there was this panic and confusion.

742

The Sadducees came, some Roman guards...

They were yelling something and waving their arms about.
The Friend's Mother and the girl from Magdala
Were sitting there as if they'd lost all connection with this world,
Just smiling blissfully.
They've probably lost their minds from the grief, I don't know...'

Thomas scratched his head and looked over at Cephas.
'Do you understand anything of this?'
'You remember...' Cephas began recalling tensely.
'You remember when were out in the desert...
And he said that he'd tell us about immortality?

That we were destined to learn a lesson not only about death,
But about eternal life too?
At the time, we thought this was just some allegory.
Perhaps, though, this was not an allegory at all?
Maybe this was a direct prophecy?'

'No, no, hold on, Cephas,'
Thomas said dubiously,
'What then is the point of a sacrificial death
If it is not the crowning event?
After all, was this not the main mission?'

Cephas was upset and exclaimed in desperation,
'I don't know, Thomas, I just don't know!!!
If only I knew for sure!'
'But we heard ourselves when He spoke about immortality,'
Andrew murmured.

'And that cannot be a simple allegory.
Then we'd need to see all his prophecies
As allegorical, wouldn't we?
What would we do then with accurate predictions,
Like your three-time denial, Cephas?'

Peter gave Andrew a fierce glare
But then sadly dropped his head: 'Quite so, brothers, quite so.'
'We need to go there, to the tomb,' Philip said decisively.
'We'll try to figure out what's what when we get there.'
'But that's dangerous; after all, the guards and the Sadducees are there!'
John objected.

'Let them be there,' Philip said, getting up and dusting off his clothes.
'You can't escape fate
And there is no point at all
In fighting the call of the truth.
Let's go, brethren.'

The brothers hurried to the tomb.
They arrived to see some people sitting there,
Modestly burning secret fires
And whispering to one another.
The Friend's Mother walked among them,

Offering some water to drink
If they were a traveller
Or quietly relating something
If they were a seeker of knowledge.
We ran up to her

But she greeted us with stern words:

'You friends of my Son took your time to get together.'
Peter then spoke in confusion:
'The earthquake and people's grief
Held us back.
But we'd never really abandon our Friend.'

'Don't worry about it, son!
Who could be closer to my Son
Than you?' she said and embraced Cephas,
Before pushing him to the cave opening.
'Go in and take a look.

And then tell me what you see.'
With shaky legs, leaden from the fear of the unknown,
Cephas walked to the grave and saw
That the stone had fallen away.
Perhaps from the earthquake?

Peter approached the entrance and looked inside,
Frightened of seeing something
That would blow his mind.
Seeing the shroud in which the body of the deceased is wrapped,
All neatly folded,

As if a Jew had broken some ancient Law,
By touching a dead body,
He gasped and covered his mouth with his hand
From the shock.
Impatient, Thomas and John

Pushed Cephas out of the way, shouting, 'Our Friend!
Our Beloved Friend!'
They ran into the cave
And ran about inside,
Like birds, frightened by unexpected thunder.

Thomas grabbed the shroud and, also realising
That it had been carefully folded,
He said in surprise,
'Either some pagan savage has stolen the Beloved One's body,
Or... Or...'

He walked out slowly and, looking up,
He saw His Mother. He ran over to her and,
Embracing her, burst into tears, saying and sometimes shouting,
'What? What does all this mean?'
The other disciples also ran over to the Mother,

Embraced her too or bowed before her,

Weeping like frightened lambs.
The Mother also wept, stroking their heads,
But then she suddenly picked up Thomas
And sternly said to him, looking him right in the eye,

'Look inside yourself and you will see there
What you must now do.
Be courageous, like He was on the cross!
Be as I remember you –
Bright, strong and amicable!

We saw angels
Standing near the tomb,
Chatting indifferently amongst themselves,
As if they couldn't see the grief we were experiencing.
From their lofty position, they said,

"What's with all the noise, women?
Don't you know He is on his way to meet His Father?"
"We all return to the Creator,"
I said to the angels. "But where is my Son's body?"
I turned back but the angels had already gone.

My maternal heart does not deceive me, my children.
I know things are not that simple.
Be on your way; your Path is not completed yet
And don't be like an untended herd,
For there is someone to look out for you,

Even if it's from the Path of Heaven.
And if you do come to understand what has happened,
Send one of you back to me
To calm this mother's heart,
Which somehow has this feeling

That there is no death near here!
And this strange separation
Causes me great suffering...'
We promised the Friend's Mother
That that is what we'd do, and we headed off to the Road.

We wandered along, full of sorrow,
To Galilee, in the deserts and the paths of which
We had spent our happiest days and nights.
The Teacher often appeared to us in our dreams,
Sometimes to each of us individually,

And once, at a hostelry,
To all of us together.
Waking up, we embraced, wept
And consoled one another,
Begging our hearts to come to terms with the loss.

But the Friend's Mother was right,
For we did not sense death
Was by our side,
Although we could not explain this feeling.

Once at the bazaar at Chorazin,

We saw a man who looked like the Teacher
And we rushed over, shouting and calling,
But he disappeared in the crowd.
In Capernaum the following happened:
We had gone to a shop to buy bread and wine

And when Thomas the Twin had gone inside,
The owner and mistress ran up to him
And said, 'It is so good you've returned, Kind Man!
For we didn't have the chance to thank you
For healing us from our longing and hopelessness

With your Good, Kind Words!
Please accept this food as a gift!'
A blinding idea flashed through Thomas's mind.
He cried out, 'When? When did He...erm...I leave?!'
'Well, it was only just now,' said the shopkeepers, taken aback.

Thomas rushed out onto the street
And rushed about, weeping and wailing quite desperately:
'Our Friend! Where are you? Where are you, our Beloved One?!'
We all immediately understood and hurriedly began to search,
But again we found no one...

However, one day, when we were casting our nets
Into the waves of the Sea of Galilee,
To catch ourselves our customary
Fish for our dinner,
The following event took place.

At first we had enjoyed no success at all
And we had no fish in our net.
Then, Cephas recalled the prayer
That the Friend had once taught us
And he began reciting it, quietly at first,

Then louder and louder.
Cephas's voice filled with strength and faith
And we friends picked up the prayer and joined in.
When the *Amen* had resounded over the lake's smooth waters,
James Voanerges screamed

For the net had jumped from his hands
Under the weight of so many fish!
Laughing and joking with one another,
We hauled the fish into the boat
Which almost made the vessel sink into the water.

Happy, we moored up on the shore
And lit a fire in anticipation of our supper.
Philip then noticed a man
Standing a distance away and smiling,
As if he too were happy along with us.

Philip invited him to join us

746

And the man readily agreed.
When we were eating the fish with our bread and wine,
The traveller happily joined in the conversation,
Freely laughing and joking with us.

Somehow we all felt warm inside
And we sensed something familiar in everything.
'You have caught so many fish!'
The traveller marvelled.
John explained to him, 'You see, we simply recalled a prayer

That a Friend of ours had once taught us
And which is addressed to our Eternal Father,
The Lord of Worlds,
And He filled our hearts with faith,
And our net with shiny, fat fish.'

It was then that the traveller, as if it were nothing, said,
'Yes, it is wonderful that you keep in your hearts
All that I taught you, my beloved brethren,'
Continuing to chew the fish and drink His wine.
A deathly silence reigned around the campfire.

The only sound was
The dropping of cups and food from our hands,
Everyone stared at the traveller,
How the crumbs from the bread had become stuck in his beard,
And drops of wine had decorated the corners of his mouth.

'Teacher!' John whispered. 'Is that You?'
The traveller was silent, but grinned so mischievously at us
And winked, that all our doubts dissipated there and then.
As one, we all yelled like madmen and rushed over to Him,
But then the sharp cry from Thomas: 'Stop!'

Brought us to a halt.
We turned to Thomas in amazement
And he repeated, 'Stop! Stop!
If... If You are You, then... then...'
'I know, Thomas, what you want,'

The traveller replied calmly, for it was foretold.
Come here!'
He raised his himation and chiton beneath it
And we gasped when we saw the wound on His side.
Spellbound, Thomas approached the traveller

And touched the as yet unhealed wound.
Blood stained his hand.
He brought it up to his face so he could see better in the dark.
Thomas's eyes widened in amazement.
He fell to the traveller's feet and brought his eyes closer.

When he saw the black wounds from the nails,
Thomas lost all self-control,
His head span and he began to fall to one side, saying in a broken voice,
'Forgive me, my Beloved Friend, for doubting You!'

The Friend grasped him and pressed him to his heart.

'No, no, my dear Thomas. It's all right,
Don't be troubled, brother, and don't go troubling my heart either!'
Now there was nothing to stop us
Shouting out across the desert
And rushing to embrace and kiss the Teacher.

He too wept for joy
And didn't hold back his feelings either.
The entire evening we laughed, joked and reminisced,
Just like in the good old days.
Only one question, from time to time,

Would show in our eyes with slight anxiety
And I noticed this in each of us in turn.
However, we pushed this question away,
As if touching on it
Would instantly make this happy reunion disappear.

The Kinnereth fishermen
Who had lit fires nearby,
Were evidently put out by our rampant joy,
Believing that we were celebrating something.
John, carefully nestled against the Beloved One's chest,

Was gently feeding Him carefully selected pieces of fish,
Stopping Him from speaking, although He raised no objections.
Only once, he lowered his face and
Looking straight into the Poet's eyes, he asked,
'You still can't believe it can you?'

John frowned and shook his head:
'No, I can't. I just can't believe my luck!'
But the time would have to come
When one of us
Would pluck up the courage to ask how. How had it happened?

How, after His ascent to the cross,
Could He be here, alive and laughing like before?
Even coughing like before...
Well, before... Before Jerusalem.
I noticed that Cephas was building himself up,

Knowing that he bore the responsibility.
He was readying himself and
Had breathed the air into his lungs in readiness
But the Teacher, as if anticipating the question,
Beat him to it: 'Tell me, Cephas, am I

Your Beloved Friend as before?'
'Yes, Rabbi...' Peter breathed,
His resolve evaporating.
'Are you ready to tend to my flock?'
Peter raised his eyebrows in surprise

And muttered again, 'Yes Rabbi...'

A warm moon rose up, turning our night-time camp
Into a Home we hadn't had for many years.
Once again, Cephas gathered his resolve,
Raised his head and said, 'Teacher...'

But the Friend closed his lips with two fingers
And, pressing His finger to His lips, He whispered,
'So, are you ready to tend to my flock
And do you know what that means?'
Suffering appeared in Cephas's eyes.

This time he just sighed and, nodding, said nothing.
When the Teacher was relating a
Very funny and informative story,
While we lay around him, as always,
Cephas, whose agitation had not subsided,

Walked off nervously into the desert
And there he paced back and forth,
As if he were talking to himself,
Occasionally casting desperate glances
Over at the camp fire.

A convenient moment arose
When someone went off to collect firewood
For the fire that had nodded off,
Another had run to the boat
For some more shiny, plump fish

And someone had gone to see the neighbouring fisherman
To ask for a little wine.
The Teacher quietly went over to Cephas,
Placed both hands on his shoulders
And said,

'Do you still see Me as your Beloved Friend?'
'Yes, Rabbi,' Peter replied,
His eyes sparkling confidently. 'Just answer me this...'
But the Teacher didn't let him finish.
'Then you'll tend to my flock!

Is there something else you want to ask
That you and the brethren would like to understand?
So listen: here,' and He pointed at Cephas's heart,
'There is enough knowledge both for the mind and the soul.
Here is the strongest thing! Here is your Faith! This is the first sword.

I gave Thomas the Secret Knowledge – about
What happened and will happen, and *how*,
Because Thomas was and is the Lord of Doubts.
The Secret Knowledge is the second sword.
They are not swords of punishment, but swords of power.

You will build us our House,
And Thomas will keep the Secret Knowledge.
Faith will always be stronger than doubts,
As the power of the spirit will always be stronger than the power of the mind.

Only one day the moment will come

When grey, sticky doubts
Will envelop the world in their thick, cloudy embrace.
Then you will find Thomas
And you will reveal the Hidden to the world.
The main thing is not to miss this day

And not let doubt destroy human souls,
Not let them pass *the point of no return,*
Because after this
The swords of faith might become swords of punishment,
And then Love will cease to rule the world!

Like you caught your fish today –
Did knowledge of the place to fish make
Your nets full?
No. It was Faith and the power of its sword.
Only one day Faith will be put to such a test

That, whatever the prayers, it will be weakened by doubts.
Then hunger may set in and this is not hunger from a lack of food.
Such hunger is capable of many things!
Such hunger will destroy everything!
Don't you and your brothers allow this hunger to spread!

Only then, you simply call on Thomas
And you will get maps of those places
Where the fish was hiding from you,
Sensing that Faith was no longer controlling you.'
The Teacher ran his finger over Cephas's finger,

Drawing an invisible sign, and he said,
'But all the same I will explain one thing to you.
You know what it is? It is *alpha.*
What did you see in the Jerusalem sky on *that* day?
Right. *Omega.* That is the essence of it.

That is the meaning of immortality
That I spoke to you about before.
Remember, what is the true miracle of life,
That is destined forever to strengthen our Faith?
That, by passing the *omega* point in your path,

You return once more to *alpha*,
Repeating not only the Cycles of Time,
But the Cycles of Fates, too,
For so it is foretold.
This is precisely how we humans become party to Eternity,

Despite the fact that we are mortal.
But this is our strength faced with everything incorporeal
And eternal.
We *live* our Path by choosing it.
We *choose* our *omega* and we live it,

Even if we die in the process.

And then we begin a new Cycle.
And so on, until we reach the Biggest Day,
We are fulfilling the duty that we chose
And we are living in it.

Will we really find peace, Cephas,
By rushing to the heavens and hiding there,
Waiting for everything to resolve by itself
During the Biggest Day?
Will we really leave the lambs for which we are responsible

To one another?
And each of us, to all of them?
No, Cephas, there will be no rest for us from our duty,
From the Road, from crucifixions and executions,
From the horror of every time we approach the *omega*,

As long as the people are in danger of hunger,
Not of the physiological kind, but much worse –
A hunger that is borne by the Ever Greedy One himself.
So, you and the brethren have already chosen your *omega*.
Go to it, for so it is foretold.

But don't think that repose awaits.
In your farewell, say again *Peace be with you!*
I am returning to my city!
I will seek you out anew,
But first you will find Me once more.

Then we will be together again,
We will part and, again,
I will find you.
And, again and again, you will find Me.
Let's go, for I have told you enough.'

Only now did Cephas breathe out
And he trudged after the Teacher,
Passing everything he had heard
Through the pain of his heart and mind, sensing
That it was taking possession of him completely and forever.

The night became our regular night of Awareness and Insight.
We lay down around the fire,
Listening, arguing, laughing and casting
Twigs and branches into the flames.
The Teacher began telling us something,

And a happy drowsiness overcame us blissfully,
And then plunged us into a joyful sleep.
After a while I opened my eyes
And I saw that the Teacher was no longer there!
Gone was the cosy, quiet night!

A warm but strong wind picked up,
Making a din and playing with currents of dark air.
Suddenly, with a powerful gust, the wind
Awoke the smouldering fire

And its flame rushed up to the heavens with a roar.

The great noise woke everyone up and we all jumped to our feet.
There was not a trace of the peace and tranquillity.
Everyone took to crying out and calling for the Beloved Teacher,
But he had disappeared!
However, slowly from out of the fire, an enormous

And majestic silhouette began to appear!
Several moments later we watched
It transform into a monumental-looking figure.
'Be careful!' Thaddeus yelled through the howl of the wind.
'Don't get any closer – that is Jibrail!

The Bringer of the Holy Spirit!
He will scorch you, so don't get too close; just listen!'
The figure grew larger and we could already make out the powerful features
Of the Heavenly Messenger.
The Archangel was manifested in all his glory

And laughing, he cried out,
'You sleeping again, people?!'
His mighty voice made us frightened
But we made no attempt to hide from him in fear.
The Archangel's gaze pinned us to the spot.

The Heavenly Messenger seemed to be looking at each of us
Individually with hard, strong-willed eyes.
Then he began slowly to raise his hands,
Clenched in a fist,
Until it had assumed the outline of a Tengri Cross.

The wind's howl grew stronger and stronger,
Instilling horror and awe in each of us.
Suddenly the Archangel cried out over the desert
And the lake surface,
Raising his head high to the heavens:

'I am Gabriel!
By the Power and the Will of our Father,
The Lord of Worlds,
I am doing what
Has been foretold!'

The next moment he lowered his head
And, turning his awful face to us,
He blew an invisible flame onto us with some force,
Which then burst into our lungs,
Our hearts, souls, sinews and blood-filled veins.

We screamed and fell to the ground.
The next moment everything had disappeared –
The noise, the wind, the flame and the image of the Heavenly Messenger.
As one, we opened our eyes and seemed to waken from a deep sleep.
The day was already bright

And through the midday heat, we could hear

The chirping of the grasshoppers and cicadas.
The lake rolled lazily onto the shore.
The occasional gull broke the silence with a distant cry.
We started to get up and rub our eyes.

Suddenly we were all simultaneously overcome with horror –
Had this all been a dream?
Had we not seen the Teacher?
Or the terrible might of the Archangel?
Had we simply... been sleeping? Sleeping?!

In our confusion we cast our eyes over the camp,
Trying to find some evidence that
We had not all dreamed the night before.
But there was nothing! Absolutely nothing!
That just couldn't be! We wrung our hands in despair

And swallowed salty tears.
At that moment, Thomas yelled out, 'Brothers!'
We turned to him and saw
Him sitting and gazing stunned at his hands.
They were covered with traces of blood... His blood from His wounds!

At that point John exclaimed in surprise,
For his tunic also had
Barely noticeable traces of blood,
Which had remained after
He had been lying, snuggled up to the Teacher's chest.

At that, Thaddeus gave a croaky laugh,
Taking a long, scorched feather from the fire –
A feather from the angelic wing he knew so well.
Andrew then pointed to somewhere on the shore
And we saw the footprints left by his sandals,

Leading off into the distance.
Cephas suddenly bulged his eyes
And began madly pulling his clothes off
To get a look at his chest.
Yes. There it was. A barely noticeable trace of His hand. *Alpha.*

And then everyone understood and recognised it all!
We began laughing and slapping one another on the back
And warmly embracing!
After that, slowly but surely, we began to sense
A new feeling growing inside.

A wave of warmth seemed to flow right from the heart
And reached right to our fingertips.
John sang a saucy song;
We hadn't heard his poems and songs for ages.
Cephas seemed to have transformed in an instant.

He was now upright and proud...
I actually wanted to add *sadly*,
And even somewhat *resigned.*
But there was no fear or doubt in this resignation.

There was just an incredible strength of mind.

Cephas looked around and resolutely marched
Over to the fishermen working nearby.
We watched him from afar.
He took a young lad by the hand
And led him over towards us.

Some old man rushed after them,
But didn't do anything untoward,
Just embraced the lad (he was evidently his son),
Tenderly stroked his head
And then pushed him towards Cephas.

They approached us and Cephas said,
'This is Matthias. From now on he is our twelfth brother.'
'Shalom aleichem, Matthias!'
'Aleichem shalom, brethren!'
'Can you tell stories, Matthias?'

'Probably not... Before I got in with the fishermen
I was a regular doctor.'
Everyone suddenly burst out laughing
Which embarrassed the poor lad.
'Come, Matthias, there's nothing to be embarrassed about;

You'll understand everything in time.
We also have a lot to tell you.
Would you like some wine and fish?'
'Yes, please.'
After dining, we carefully cleared away our camp,

Gathered our scant belongings
And slowly headed towards the Road.
John was lagging a little behind.
He stopped.
He was a little sad,

Looking at the lake's calming waves.
Then he let out a sigh,
As if afraid to spill out something inside,
And he smiled his Kind and Good thoughts.
He picked up a pebble from the shore and launched it far out into the sea.

Then he looked back and saw young Matthias's
Father in the distance,
Anxiously looking out
With his hand covering his eyes.
The poet waved encouragingly at the old fisherman

And he waved back.
Then John checked himself
And, with his knees jolting upwards,
He rushed off as fast as he could after the brothers,
Whose silhouettes had already begun slowly to disappear

In the haze of the weary Galilean desert.

Verse 39. The Poet

I, John, poet of the Circle of Twelve, testify to you
About my thoughts, visions, revelations:

My heart aches with a universal pain.
My reason rejects what I see, what I've managed to perceive.
My sleep is disturbed.
My body cries out from the burden it carries,
The shards of a suffering soul.

There is time for merriment,
But no room for genuine joy.
There is happiness, a fleeting illusion,
But can a man be happy
Given other men's fates?

One can isolate himself from others, saying,
'I control only my fate, what is theirs to me?'
And one can say,
'Thank You, Alahi, at least for
What I have right now,'

Not asking what my neighbour has,
Or what people have far away.
My dreams are no longer a sign of repose,
But a sign of my destiny, that I must see
What I have never wanted to see.

My world has lost its edges.
My past remains my own,
And my future slips from my hands,
As if to ask,
'Is it to you it now belongs?'

Everyone thirsts to know, to know in advance, what will be.
But seeing even a portion
Of the total picture of the future...
Can they retain their senses
And their capacity to remain as men?

Perhaps even Good, Kind Men?
How do you go on,
When you've seen past the edge?
Seen through space?
And time?

Looked through the mirror, and found another world?
Or maybe there's nothing though the mirror at all?
Maybe there was nothing in Heaven either?!
Yet the point is not what your eye can see
But what your *Soul* can behold,

A soul doomed to the solitude of knowledge,
To senses higher than simple human instincts.

What now, Alahi?
What now, now the Word burns in my heart
And beats so hard within,

And has power over me,
A power out of the reach of even the world's most powerful tyrant.
I sing songs, but why aren't they about laughter?
I read poems, but why aren't they about joy?
What have You done to me, Father?

Who am I now? An ordinary man?
That would crush my understanding about those ordinary ones
Who enjoy the cool currents of fate.
And at the same time, I am ordinary.
But in which of the Circles of Time am I so?

They say, go and look –
The world is how it is;
Did the Almighty not create it?
Is it not at His behest that
The established order of things exists?

I say, all who go and see
Will find their moment to Choose,
Will find their day to Act.
They say, you look, too.
Destiny will erase from its map all who move

At cross currents to the river of life
Forever and ever and ever.
What is left of them?
Only the memory of a neighbour or two,
Receding into the past in a month or two.

The age of the Prophets who spoke with all men at once
Has gone for good and is unlikely to return.
Others now speak with all men at once,
But are they Prophets?
No, but now their time has come.

Are they Antichrists and fundamentally evil?
No, they're just people, vested with power.
Then with whom is your war, my friend?
Are you fighting with yourself inside?
Or has another force lacerated and pervaded you?

If so, then whose force is this –
The force of light or of dark?
Or did they both rise together?
I turned the thin pages over and
Smoothed out the thin parchment.

I sharpened my quill, burning and eager,
I lit my rush lantern with its dying flame,
I looked at the heavens to find myself there;
I looked at myself
To find the heavens.

I walked to the very edge of worlds,
I stretched out my hand and my fingers
Were dyed in blood.
The blood was not mine,
But from the wound that had split Reason and Eternity.

I remember walking toward people,
But they reflected me back,
Like a mirror,
Leaving me only my reflection,
But making me whole,

While they splintered into a thousand shards.
I gathered up the shards,
But now it is my blood that's spilling,
Running in ribbons over my palms,
Along with my soul, love and reason.

I closed my doors and windows tight,
But thoughts, signs and revelations,
Like drops of boiling magma.
Streamed from the gaping, quaking womb
Of the yawning abyss of my essence.

I had rejected the calling,
Praying for worldly joys
In the embraces of the calm lake of life.
But night inevitably always comes,
Banishing the day and the calm of tranquillity.

I consoled myself with imaginary missions;
After all, this world has so many Trails, Roads and Crossings!
I acquired knowledge, experience and property,
Gave of my labour to tyrants and despots,
But just an arm's length from success,

The boundaries of worlds began
                    Bleeding inside me again.
And all over again it became clear to me,
That, like an unhealed wound, not only do space and time
Exist outside me, but they divide me inside too.

And once more, slowly, painfully rending
The frail membranes of my body that envelop my soul,
Through the spasms of my throat and then my face,
Rising to my brain, then falling sharply to my hands,
Onto fresh papyrus emerges the Word.

****

And on that very night,
I saw in my cell another light
Through the dim light of the rush lantern.
I lifted my head and through it I saw
A silhouette so familiar it pained and shook me.

Jibrail, Bringer of the Holy Spirit
And Messenger of the Heavens
Was sat in the pose that seemed his habit,
Reading my codices and dropping scrolls on the floor,
Trembling a little, but not so much

That his eternal angelic calm
So much as swayed.
To avoid troubling my human mind,
He had taken the form of an old man, whiter than white,
Who looked like al-Khidr or Aaron.

'Peace be with you, John, heir of Insight and the Word!'
Jibrail said calmly.
I poured a full glass of wine and drank it down.
The Archangel frowned,
Seeing this as a clear sign of my weakness.

'What is it this time, Heavenly Messenger?'
I said with a degree of disrespect in my voice,
Though I knew he had only to slap my cheek once
And a bloody mark would remain
Forever ensconced on my nervous face.

But the Archangel saw no need
To pay heed to my petty human manners.
He sighed and he stretched,
As if he'd had a difficult day,
And come to me, weary, at the end of it.

'The time has come to speak of Revelation,'
Said the Archangel so matter-of-factly
As if the word hadn't made thousands of harps
Resound with heavenly marches
In my brain, so tired from the silence.

I dropped my quill and rubbed my face.
'Didn't we finish this before?'
I asked, uncertain, lifting my eyes timidly.
'You and I did, but the race of man has not.'
Jibrail's voice was laced with mild reproach.

'And where do you see any of my fault in this?'
'Nowhere,' the Messenger said, all business-like
And suddenly stood up, making it known
He did not intend to sort things out today,
As his goal was much more serious.

'You see, John, the thing is...
You and I gave people a picture,
Realising there are Circles of Time, right?'
I nodded, and swallowed two more gulps of wine.
'But it turned out the people aren't that capable of understanding,

If they don't encounter the concepts of *yesterday*, *today* and *tomorrow*,
And if they don't see a strict sequence of

758

Events that portend the Great Day, that is.
Either they put all these images into a sequential line,
Or they get lost in the logic of how events develop.'

'You want us to clarify and explain everything?'
I asked him, and looked into the Archangel's eyes.
'Oh, no. That would achieve nothing, my dear friend, nothing at all.
A certain uncertainty always preserves
That sense of Divine purpose in people,

What gives them the right to make their own choice.
Unfortunately, if you give a man certainty,
Other qualities entirely and not love for the Almighty,
Begin to surface within him.
It's a rare thing indeed when a man who knows exactly

The dates and events of predictions
Resorts to the highest meanings.
Such things can happen, yes, but mostly
Something completely different occurs.
This is all a consequence of knowing one's own mortality

And not knowing what awaits one across the boundary between worlds.
Most often a man says, *Well, come what may,*
I'll live out this life of mine,
I'll go the whole hog, what will be then will be,
And he becomes easy prey for the Greedy One,

Without wanting it, or even suspecting.'
'But isn't that a choice, too?
According to which a person is destined, after the Great Day,
To take his proper place
Either in Paradise at the right hand of God,

Or in hell, to be trampled by the Fallen One?
What's the point of artificially interfering
In this process, ordained by the Great Books?
Surely man has already been told enough
In words from the Scriptures and the prophets

About how he is meant to live his life?
Why return back to revelations told before?
Surely they contain plenty of certainty and meaning?
Surely the Scriptures have all that is needed simply to follow,
To avoid becoming prey to the Greedy One?'

Jibrail jumped lightly to his feet
And, with his arms tucked behind his back,
He walked around my cell,
Stopping from time to time
To pick up and examine various items

That I kept on my numerous shelves,
Or to open and leaf through some of my books.
'John, I'll tell you two things,' he said.
'First: well, *precisely what qualities*
Will the Lord of Worlds assess

In the Last Day's Judgment, do you think?'
'What?' I asked, surprised. 'Righteousness.
Knowledge and adherence to the Prophecies, Traditions,
The Rituals... and a person's own qualities, too,
When his deeds are measured,

Both good and bad, isn't that so?'
'It is, John, that's exactly right.
But can you define that precisely, in just one word?'
'Well... Did he manage to live out his life
As a Good, Kind Man?'

Jibrail started laughing and slapped shut the book by Hugo
That he had been looking through, nodding, and smiling in satisfaction.
'If everyone were Good and Kind,
Then this wouldn't be a world of people,
But a world of monks and priests,

But you think the Almighty welcomes only them?
No, John, the matter is that he loves you *all* –
His own... nontrivial creation!'
'And?' I said, not understanding what Jibrail meant and staring right at him.
He ran his hands over the spines of Dostoyevsky tomes

And, turning abruptly to face me, he said,
'In a word, John, the Lord of Worlds
Will judge you all by a single criterion:
By the one key choice
That each of you must make in life!'

'Each of us? Must?'
I asked Jibrail in disbelief.
'Is that really how it is?'
'Are you going to object?'
Jibrail's eyes filled with steel.

'No, no,' I hurried to assure the Messenger,
'But there is something I don't get.
It's clear when a man reaches a Rubicon in life,
But millions somehow live out their fates
Without crossing rivers of major decisions.

Or at least, they're invisible, for most of us.'
'For you, *Homo sapiens*, they are invisible.
Even if human life is like
An even, smooth-surfaced river
Carrying its waters forever in one direction,

This choice is always there,
And he makes the choice, even if nobody sees it.
But there, in Heaven, we see it, believe me!'
'But doesn't that mean that a ruffian
Who has only performed evil deeds in his life,

Can one day do something
And be forgiven sooner

Than a priest, who lived his whole life righteously,
But just once broke the *kashrut*?
So where, then, are the criteria of the conformity

Of consistency and a single deed
To the criteria of good and evil?
How do we know what righteousness is
When these are the rules?
After all, then many will carry on any old way,

Telling themselves, they'll do some deed and this will reconcile matters.'
Jibrail was leafing through an album of pictures
Called *Cathedrals of the World*, smiling, snorting at some things,
Nodding his head or shaking it in obvious displeasure.
'John, you're reducing the idea of the choice

To some sort of one-act understanding.
That's wrong.
If that's how it was,
Then somebody could decide, after a Good, Kind deed,
That he's done enough,

And can carry on any old way.
Remember, the Lord of Worlds forgives sins,
He is All-Merciful and Loving,
But He does not hand out indulgences
Not at the end, not in advance.

So that choice must be made by people
Every day, every hour, or even, you could say,
Every second.
And only the Almighty can decide, in the Court on High,
Which of those choices were decisive.

He hands down His verdict, and –
There can be no doubt about it –
We'll execute His will and His sentence!'
I swallowed and then nodded.
'What else? The second thing you meant to tell me.'

Jibrail put all the books on the shelf
And sat down right across from me.
'Tell me, John, Sovereign of the Word
And Heir to Revelation.
Do your best to recall

What you and I told in the Prophecy:
But what has not been read right, would you say?
And not just in our case, yours and mine,
But in a majority of the others?
Is it in there, but, due to a lack of emphasis,

For some reason, as a rule, it remains misunderstood?'
I shrugged, and answered,
'Am I to judge the imprecision of phrases
When I, as a poet, see the beauty of lines
To be in a certain uncertainty?'

Jibrail smirked and picked up an old quill on the table.
'And that was the goal, wasn't it,
Of that revelation of yours, hmm?
Have you guessed?'
I spread my arms wide and looked the angel straight in the eye.

The Messenger met my gaze with a steely cold,
But after a moment the rays around his eyes
Softened this standoff.
'We always talk about men's individual choices.
We always talk about how each one, on his own,

Will be responsible before the Almighty.
But rarely, importantly, very rarely,
Do we speak of obligations of the whole human race.
Certainly, there was the flood and Noah,
The destruction of Sodom and Gomorrah,

But! Never has the question arisen
About how you're actually a mistake of God's creation,
And we ought to get rid of you once and for all.
Completely.'
I shuddered and lowered my eyes.

'You and I always said, John,
That the Lord of Worlds loves you.
And so His punishments were always intended
To make peace and teach lessons, but they could also destroy
The bad that you have accumulated inside,

Having given the chance of salvation
To those who are Good and Kind.
Thereby saving your race as a whole, right?
Take Noah, if you will.
The most telling example.

When the Teacher arrived in your world,
He also talked about how
Those who choose salvation for themselves.
Would be saved.
He tried to bring everyone together,

Taking all your sins on himself.
So that a forceful, powerful wave
Would wash all that's black, bloodless and evil
From the face of all humankind,
And let everyone start out once more

On the path of that choice every minute
And always make that choice toward God, isn't that right?
And the Great Arab spoke of that, too,
That there is your chance, so cleanse yourself,
Begin your life from the beginning.

The door to the Kingdom of Heaven is open to all!
And this chance is not just for everyone individually,

But for everyone together!
After each execution committed against people,
He always had hope...

And you think, John, that he can't feel hope,
As He's not an individual in the human sense of the word?
Paraphrasing the words of Muslims, I'll put it this way:
If there are those who hope, then He is most hopeful among them.
Isn't that the case?

So what do we have?

What we have is that we *sometimes* fail in the daily,
Hourly, minute-by-minute choices that men make,
But almost *always* we fail in the choice
Of all humankind
On the path of its common, single choice.

The entire human world has already transformed
Into something *resembling a whole*,
But what has not happened is its unification
Into *wholeness*.
The wholeness of the combined human spirit,

Able one day to make
The combined, most important, key choice.
And that, sir, is important simply because
At the Eternal Court there will be no first in line,
No first man to be judged;

They will first of all stand together.
Well, maybe not at first, rather at the end.
However, after ruling on each of them,
The Lord of Worlds will pass judgment on everyone together.
And will say, for example, to Metatron,

Basically, does this race deserve life on Earth?
And what do you think the angels will say
Who have always been envious of men's kinship to God?
What will the djinns say, who never could wait
To take over the world from men?

Then Michael or I will step forward, and we will say something like:
O Heavenly Father of ours!
The human race is not monotheistic and is dying in ignorance, *jahiliyyah*,
Even blatant paganism.
You see, if you look at them from above, as a whole,

You'll see they are ruled
By rites that divide them, not rites that unite them!
Everyone says that You are one,
But as soon as the topic of oneness comes up
Various cults, ceremonies and traditions come into play

And separate them all again
Until they worship different forms of dialogue with You.
And what is this dominance of form over meaning?

Shirk itself,[275]
In its most terrible expression.

So, if we take each denomination individually,
They would seem to be dedicated to One God,
But if we look at the human world as a whole,
Then the presence of even two or three ritual systems
Speaks of polytheism reigning in the human world.

Lord of Worlds, look at what happens
When they assemble together!
Not one of them will budge an inch in his view of how
It is best to honour You.
And nobody, *nobody,* has ever once said

What are we, in our strong,
But still tiny convictions,
Compared to the greatness of the One Everlasting?
Here at the general meeting, I place this and that
On the altar of unification, and expect the same from you.

Ha!' Jibrail laughed and rocked on his chair.
'Giving! John, do you understand?
The very simplest choice of each person, individually,
To take or to give –
Doesn't function on a level of all humans as a whole!

Joining together? All well and good, but only by my rules!'
The Archangel laughed more and finally broke the quill
He'd been waving around in his tirade.
Putting the pieces neatly in a corner of the table
He materialised a new one and placed it before me.

'But listen, Messenger, things aren't all that bad.
Why not take as a start either the oldest of the old,
Or the youngest of all of the teachings,
And join together on the basis of that?'
Jibrail cast a bored gaze round my cell,

As if searching for anything else interesting there.
He rose and picked up one of the Great Books
And carefully blew the dust off it,
Then caught sight of my bookmarks
And opened the Book, intrigued, at one of them.

The Archangel's voice mocked me a bit when he spoke,
But not enough to offend me.
'John, you know everything about the Circle of Time.
Why bring up the oldest and youngest of teachings,
When we're speaking of the Messages of the Lord of Worlds,

Who is eternal and has every right
To have not the slightest notion of
What came before, and what after?'
'But angel! We live in time, after all!

---

[275] In Islam, *shirk* is the ascribing of co-creators to Allah; in the general sense, it is polytheism.

For us, all that has meaning,

Even if only because all of these Messages
Were meant precisely for us.
How would you have me choose between one and another?
That will always be an affront
To one of the Divine Revelations!

Are *we* truly the ones to blame,
For the fact they're so widely dispersed across time?'
Jibrail looked at me, over the Book.
'If there's one thing I like about people,
It's the way you transfer responsibility

So easily, just like that, to the Almighty,
Saying, "You figure out what's right,
And what's wrong."'
I leaned into the back of my chair, quite overcome with indignation.
'What? We never blame –'

But the Archangel, not letting me finish, spoke coldly.
'Careful with those confident assertions, Homo.
Do not forget that I am Gabriel.
I know everything that *all* people say and think, every last one.'
For several minutes I held my tongue,

While the Archangel flicked through the Book.
Then I muttered, less sure now,
'But today there are different teachings about unity.
They may be young, but we too, once,
Were nobody.'

Jibrail spoke without lifting his eyes from the Book.
'Enough with your empty words, Poet.
How can you ever share something
That does not belong to you?
That is merely the mission that these young faiths assign themselves.

Perhaps they even think it through, soberly.
The Choice and the Deed must be made by those
Who actually are responsible
For the fate of the Teachings.
Only then can we speak about the potential for a wholeness of Spirit.

But these? They're just a small contribution
To worldwide *jahiliyyah*.
Deeds are not done by masters of thought or of the abstract idea.
Deeds are done by masters of dogma.'
Finally he put the Book aside, and rose easily again from his chair.

'What do you think? Is it possible to unify
These two things, the ones I spoke of a moment ago?'
I shrugged, not for lack of thinking about it.
There was still protest smouldering inside me
Against what the angel had said about men.

'John, it's very simple.

You and I have been engaged in long dialogue,
By my time, for three days,
By yours, two millennia.
How to combine an individual's every-second choice

And the concept of everyone's universal responsibility
Before the Lord of Worlds?
Logically, it makes sense that it's based
On the understanding of that every-second choice
Of all humankind as a whole, right?

I can tell you that the holistic world
Is already taking particular steps on the path to wholeness.
For now, at the level
Of economic practicality.
But note, I did not say

A thing about a peaceful or danger-free life,
Although assertions of the sort are everywhere.
Until you all have universal values,
Questions of calm and peace and security
Will be resolved quite differently.

Well, at least because everyone has
Quite different ideas about them.
The material questions, on the other hand, are almost identical for everyone.
And that's a matter only of scope, standards, style and quantity.
So then, *what* is keeping people, in the end –

Even after reading the Revelations, yours and mine –
From understanding elementary things?
I think there are three reasons,
And one is very dangerous.
That is the thought that the Lord of Worlds

Has condemned them all, unavoidably, to perish in agony.
This may not apply to everyone,
But, to be honest, there's a majority
Inclined to think they'll never make it
Into those hundred and forty-four thousand

To be given guarantees of physical survival
Through the horrors that we have described.
That might repel people from the Almighty.
They think of it this way:
If He's cooked up *that* sort of thing,

Then what forces could possibly
Prevent the horrors of the Apocalypse?
Fatalism, my friend, is one of the most devout foes
Of letting people advance on the Path
That leads to the Ultimate Choice.

The second reason conceals itself in the constant search for certainty
In these prophetic writings.
People here are divided into two camps.
One camp presumes that much has already been done,

Drawing historical analogies with the events described.

The other camp presumes those analogies are contrived,
And that it will all come to pass in the future.
Both these camps inevitably arrive
At a partial loss of responsibility,
Because, in one case, it's that fatalism again,

In the other, let's call it *fatalism postponed.*
This all occurs in an environment with the biggest group of all,
Which believes this is all utter nonsense,
Or, there are some more pious among them,
Who think the Lord would never abuse them that way.

Which is to say, essentially, it's still utter nonsense.
We could also summarise the thing by saying
We have created a phenomenon
Of fatalistic ambivalence
Among people as individuals

And among humanity as a whole.
Still, we've already spoken
That absolute certainty
Can grow into a fatalistic "Who really cares?
Apres nous, le deluge."

And actually, overall,
People who have seen in their own time, who know from history
And modern-day television,
Think more or, more precisely, more often,
Only about their personal survivability

Under Apocalyptic conditions.
I mean, they think like this: *we live far from the ocean,
We live far from earthquake zones,
We have a sturdy house and we have our guns,
Stocks of provisions and things like that.*

Hardly anyone has given any thought, John,
To whether anybody will help them, be it the state,
The police or their neighbours?
Even less, my friend, do they think
That the many castigations of Heaven

Can in fact be prevented!
There's no escaping the Court on High,
But escaping war of everyone against everyone?
Sure thing.
And angelic vengeance for human deeds? That too.

To say nothing of the fact that you can avoid joining
The side of the Dajjal, the Antichrist,
And not fight against the true believers, you know?'
I nodded, not knowing where he was going with this.
'What's at stake is the mass survival of humanity,'

The Archangel continued.

'The race of man, *Homo sapiens*, beloved of the Creator,
As a rule, never stands before anyone!
The reason you can escape the angels' wrath
Is not that the prophecies are untrue,

But because you people have a choice!
Think about it. The Almighty will pass judgment on each and every one,
And then He'll say:
Find for Me in this whole multitude
Just one man who has sacrificed dogma

For the sake of the communion of men,
And I will save this race!
That's the sticking point, Poet!
Everyone thinks a cold wind will blow
And the righteous will find themselves *without fail* in eternal life

In the Golden Age!
But no.
How many lovely, self-sacrificing people
Have there been, are there now, in your race?
And only one of them answered for *everybody*.

But He himself will come to hold Court!
Then will we find enough of the righteous
To protect the whole human race?
Where the unifiers of the world will act outside of politics,
On the basis of the Communion of the Soul?

For then the prophecies will come to be, Poet, yes?
Tell me, have you been in all those Seven Houses,
About which we spoke before?
Where are they now?'
'Many corrected their Path,

Many are gone from the face of the Earth.'
'Right.
But you know, they're not gone for good.
They've only moved elsewhere in time
And geography.

You know. Where are the Seven Houses now,
The ones you'd turn to today?
What would you say to them?
You live in a confined space,
Not seeing that *jahiliyyah* and *shirk* rule the world.

And how will they receive that?
The same way they always do, of course,
With armed crusades and jihads
And *Hindu Mahasabha*,[276] setting fire to the House of the Almighty, right?
Only our path is true; everyone else's means ruin!''

---

[276] *Hindu Mahasabha* is an extremist Indian organisation that agitates against Mahatma Gandhi's call for a 'united India' and against Muslim-Hindu integration on equal terms. It was responsible for the murder of Gandhi on 30 January 1948.

'But why, then?' I wrang my hands in desperation.
'Why then should the Lord of Worlds
Not send to us here in the world
One idea to unify us all?
A Common Book?'

Jibrail looked at me, tilting his head,
And squinting his eyes.
'Poet, what are you talking about?
You know very well that
When that Common Book is opened,

The Final Circle will begin.
And you know if it's opened by the Lamb,
Then humankind will be on the path of war,
A war that He will lead,
And there your sentiments will have no sway!

Sorry, but you humans have received the *right to choose*,
And you must exercise it *before* it happens
That the Great Final War comes about,
And sentence shall be passed
On everyone without exception.

John,' Jibrail said, leaning closer to me,
'John, I'm an angel. I don't care about your fate.
I've spent so much effort
To drive the Bloodless One away from you all,
Because He, Our Father, commanded me to.

What scares me is something else:
Had we angels the right to Act,
We would have used it long ago.
However, we too, even without souls,
Have twice fought our battles in the Heavenly Wars

Together.
The Bloodless One had few of the wayward on his side;
Mainly they were the forces he nurtured
Among men, djinns and peri;
But among the angels, too, there were a few who went astray.

That's the reason I'm so surprised
That you, with all this at your disposal – revelations and Books
And, yes, I'll tell you for the hundredth time – Choice,
You still cannot achieve a communion of Spirit and Faith!
I'm not acting for myself. That would go against nature.

Again I've been sent by the Lord of Worlds,
To undergo with you, little man,
All over again, what
We underwent before, but perhaps overlooked,
For you received the Word not from a tyrant or an angel.

So say it again, now, *do you hear*?'
I lowered my eyes and beheld
How streams of blood dripped on the floor

From my hands and feet.
The side of my tunic was soaked with blood

And it had begun to wet my himation as well.
I was afraid, but remembered the Beloved Friend,
And took this as a sign from Him.
I lifted my head and spoke with assurance.
'Messenger, what am I to do?'

Jibrail stood up.
Now his look was transformed:
He became monumental, gleaming with a metallic sheen
And heavenly rays of light.
'Take all you need, and we will go!'

He commanded, and spread his wings.

****

I found myself in the desert, but not the Canaanite desert I knew.
This one was different.
Far off, there heaved a dying sea,
And all around ships were being tossed,
Deprived of a reason to exist.

I was kneeling, but I rose.
And before me I beheld
The mighty Angel, Jibrail, Messenger of Heaven,
Bringer of the Holy Spirit.
He was immense.

One of his feet was planted firmly in the snow,
The other, scorched by the fire of distant deserts.
Recite! A majestic voice commanded.
Recite what you hear, and speak the words!
I took up my scroll and quill,

And my hand lowered the quill to the empty surface.
I know not what came before–
What it was I wrote,
Or the written words I read.
I lifted my eyes and proclaimed the first lines:

I see!
I see the masters of the Seven Houses,
Wandering the desert.
Saying, *the power is ours!*
But Jibrail, you turn to them, and you say:

'What is your power before the Eternal One?
Bow.
The masters of the Seven Houses bowed and asked,
Only for us to preserve those Houses.
Will that serve us for forgiveness?

'Now go,' Jibrail said.
'You are but the first step.'

The masters set off for the desert and vanished in its dust.
I saw a door up high in the heavens,
I tried to open it, but could not.

Then I looked again and saw
Twenty old men sitting in a circle,
But they sat with their backs to each other.
I asked Jibrail
Why they were talking amongst themselves,

But not looking at each other.
The Angel laughed and answered:
While they do not look at the centre of their circle,
While they speak only with the nations
From whence they came, they will see not the Spirit.

Then a white old man rose from the Circle of Twenty,
Who looked like Abraham, or maybe al-Khidr,
And he said they would still need four more men,
Before they could turn to face one another.
Then they summoned four riders on horseback,

And they said, 'Find us the missing four.'
The horsemen rushed off, but returned emptyhanded.
'Where I looked for the elder for the Circle,'
Said the first, 'sits a tyrant tsar, proud, independent.
He told me his throne is dearer to him

Than the Circle of Elders.'
'Where I looked for the one who was prophesied,'
Said the second horseman,
They were at war, and I could not convince the elder
To leave his tribe and be here with us.'

'The elder whom I sought for the Circle,'
Said the third horseman,
'Is occupied with the material fortunes of his land.
Changing a choinix of his harvest for wine and balms,
And his people are expecting a return.'

The fourth horseman then spoke:
'Where I looked for an elder for the Circle,
Hunger reigns, and the earthly beasts
Are sowing death in that distant land,
And none from that people would deign to come.'

The elders despaired, but a hundred years passed,
And again they sent their four envoys away
To bring those others, the four they lacked.
But again the riders returned with nothing.
Then the white elder rose again and said,

'It will always continue thus,
While we too speak with our own peoples.
Responsibility for them is given to us,
And power over them, and in their name we speak,
Let us turn our gaze to the centre of the Circle.'

771

They turned,
And they saw it was empty there,
But they beheld each other's eyes.
The third time, now, they sent four envoys
And only then did four new elders come.

Then they all saw that in the centre of the Circle
Four wondrous beasts had appeared.
One resembled a lion,
The second an ox,
The third had a face that resembled a man's,

And the fourth resembled an eagle on the wing.
And all of them were replete with eyes
And each had six wings.
And they all said,
'We are created by God and his thought.'

'Who are you?' Asked the elder with Abraham's face.
'We are you,' the beasts answered him,
'We are what you brought with you here,
We are the symbols of various power,
Which you have crafted, within your limits.'

The mighty lion rose and extended his six wings.
'I am the essence of kingly power and of the circle as chosen by the people,'
He said.
The mighty ox then stood, and said,
'I am the power of kings and of the priests to serve them.'

The beast with the man's face rose
And said:
'I am the power of the elected and the first among equals.'
The golden-winged eagle extended its wings and said:
'I am the power of the chosen one and of the chosen circle!'

The elders marvelled at these wondrous beasts
And said, 'What are we to understand with you
And see through you,
Who are made with eyes?'
'Only yourselves,' the beasts responded,

'Only what is behind you, but
That is to understand what is to come.'
The elders then beheld four angels,
Standing at the edges of the earth
And holding back the winds

So they would not topple the mountains.
They protected the forest,
And they left the sea within its confines.
Again the elders marvelled and, exchanging looks,
They began saying to each other,

'That Circle is wonderful.
What else might we see?

We have the four beasts
And four mounted messengers.
There are our four angels,

Watching over the earth
From four sides.
What else would we need to rule the world?'
And they began to say to each other,
'Let us rule the world!'

Then the wondrous beasts said to them,
'If that is so, then go forth and behold!'
And the elders saw seven angels in a line
Blowing on their horns!
The first angel blew his horn, and crashing to earth came

Smoke and fire, hail and oozing blood,
Which burnt the trees and the green grass.
The elders were astounded and they said,
'Oh, our peoples are powerful and strong,
They will triumph over the fire and the hail.'

The second angel blew his horn.
The mountain collapsed into the sea, killing a third of all
The beasts of the earth and the sea; and ships perished!
Again the elders were astounded, but they said:
'They whose lands have seen misfortune,

Ought to save them themselves; we will send those people
Grain to eat, wine and cloth.'
The third angel sounded his horn!
And a third of the waters formed a towering mountain
And the flowering fields

Were transformed to wormwood.
Then the elders exchanged looks
And sent the sons of all their peoples
To help those lands,
That were now suffering.

The fourth angel sounded his horn!
The sun and the stars were overwhelmed
And a third of the stars vanished from the sky!
Then the elders saw an angel, flying
And calling out:

'How have you earthly rulers,
Brought such misfortune
To the cradle of man?!
Such grief to those living on earth;
But is there another way?'

One of the elders then asked
The four beasts,
Who had suddenly changed their image, 'So, who are you now?'
'We are the races,' the beasts said, who were replete with eyes.
'I am snowy-white,' the lion said.

773

Six elders rose up and threw stones at him.
'I am orange-hued,' said the ox,
Another six elders rose
And they threw stones at him.
'I am black as night,' said the beast with the face of a man.

Again six elders rose and they threw stones at him
'I am a hybrid,' the eagle said,
'I am made of those who came together
And of those between the snowy, the orange and the night.'
Yet another six elders rose and threw stones at that beast.

The Circle of Elders looked and saw that the stones they had thrown had formed
A low stone wall in the centre.
And they said, 'This is good,
There is a boundary between us
And the centre of the Circle.'

Then the fifth angel blew his horn!
An abyss yawned open
And out of it swarmed locusts,
Forged in armour, with terrible barbs,
And their swarm resembled a warrior steed,

With faces of men and hair like of maidens dressed to wed.
The elders were frightened and summoned each their people
To war against this terrible attack.
They fought a hundred years,
But only in the last five months did they prevail, together!

Again the four beasts changed in appearance.
The elders asked, 'Who are you?'
The beasts responded, 'Behold,
We are the languages of men.
Northern, southern, eastern and western.'

Each time a beast told them about his tongue,
Six elders stood up and threw stones at those
Who fuelled their dislike.
Then they beheld that a wall the height of a man,
Had risen in the centre of the Circle.

'Well then,' the elders said,
'Now at least we don't need to fear
The beasts in the centre.'
Here the sixth angel blew his horn!
And then the four angels who

Had protected the people from cruel winds and hail
Moved from their places,
And took to battering humankind,
Setting venomous steeds upon them
With armour of flames, hyacinthine and sulphuric.

And they killed a third of all humankind.
And when the elders looked to the centre, they beheld

That the wondrous beasts had changed again.
'Who are you now?' the elders asked them.
'I lead the sons of the Enlightened Prince onward,'

Said the lion.
Six elders stood up and threw stones at him.
'I lead those to the future who
Believed in the Beloved Teacher,'
Said the ox.

Six other elders stood up and threw their stones at him.
'I lead the followers of the Great Arab,'
Said the one with a face like a man.
Six elders stood up and threw stones at him.
'I lead those summoned by the faith of their people,

And those who would not follow any who came before,'
Said the winged eagle.
And another six elders threw their stones at him.
They beheld that the wall in the centre had become so tall
That now nobody in the Circle could see anyone else.

Then a voice came down to the elders:
'Come hither, ascend the mountain
And behold!'
They ascended toward heaven on a cloud, and they saw
That all the peoples had lost hope

That the elders would rule wisely and justly.
They understood their Circle would not protect them
From the terrible wrath of the angels.
Their peoples now searched for their own prophets and witnesses.
Two stepped forward to help and divine the people,

But a fierce beast rose from the abyss and killed them both.
The people were now so frightened
And they despaired from the thought
That their leaders had abandoned them
To the whims of their own pride,

And the prophets, powerless before the talons of the beast,
Were unable to retrieve the bodies of the diviners for three days.
And what they valued was muddled with fear and hunger,
And what had once been evil became an ordinary thing,
And what had been good vanished from their customs.

And the seventh angel blew his horn!
And the elders heard quiet voices, saying,
'What have you done to the land and the people?
For were you not granted the ability
To build a kingdom of peace on Earth?

What did you squander it for?
Where is your wisdom, addressed to the heavens?
Where is your force of mind,
Now overshadowed
By the force of universal power?'

The elders were frightened, and they fled to the desert.
They roamed there a hundred years, then one day,
They met a Bride, at once strange and beautiful.
She was clothed in the sun
And her womb was full; she was soon to give birth.

The elders beheld an immense red dragon,
Near the woman, awaiting the child's birth
And ready to consume it.
The elders were clever men, for all of human reason,
From all races, tongues and peoples

Had been given to them so they might understand.
They realised that before them stood
That which would forever unite them.
And not only them, but the peoples
Standing behind them too.

Six elders stepped forward, and they said,
'We shall give her a dozen stars for a crown,
Our essential wealth,
Only we demand power over half the world in return.'
Here the red dragon moved closer to the Bride

And he attacked her womb.
Six more elders stepped forward and said,
'This matter concerns us all:
We shall give her eagle wings,
So she might escape the dragon's pursuit,

Only we demand the other half of the world in return.'
The red dragon moved yet closer to the Bride
And now it was attacking her throat,
Striving to choke her.
Six different elders stepped forward, and they said,

We now have an understanding of our common fate,
So, we make her a gift of caves
Which will swallow the river
That the dragon will release to conquer the Bride.
Only we demand power over all oceans and seas.

Here the dragon's terrible brow descended
Over the loins of the Bride, intent to swallow
What she bore in her ordeal.
Then came forward the members of the Circle
Who owned the moon, which was ordained

To embellish the Bride and keep her from perishing.
And, in exchange for the moon, they demanded
Power over all that the earth conceals within.
Then, however, one elder arose decisively,
Whose face resembled Abraham or al-Khidr, and said,

'So, when will we gain an understanding
That nothing common can ever be born

Unless we give and not demand something in return?
What are we bargaining for and with whom,
When there it is – our future –

About to be annihilated in the jaws of that frightful demon?
How long will we sit in our unified Circle
But with our backs to one another?
How long will we, turning to the centre of the Circle,
Contemplate the void and the walls?

Is it not time for us to realise that in giving
It's not that we give *to someone*,
But that we give *of our own accord*.
There is no greater happiness in life
Than to possess something of value,

Protect it and gently cherish it,
And then give it away *of our own accord*,
Making it something for everyone!'
The elder approached the Bride
And placed beneath her feet

A young, bold moon,
Which made the dragon withdraw,
Fearfully catching his breath.
Now all the other elders, too,
Gave the Bride what they had promised.

And the dragon fell, slain by their Spirit of Communion.
At that moment, Archistrategos Michael and his Angels
Came to the aid of the elders,
But when he saw that the victory was won,
He was stunned, and bowed to the Circle's wisdom.

And in that instant a cry rang out, like a song.
A child had come into our world,
Born now of a unified tribe,
As proclaimed by the staff in his hand.
How Heaven and Earth rejoiced!

Joyful and inspired, they
Rushed into battle with the dragon,
As the Angels and people had once done together!
They threw him into the pit
Which then became his dungeon.

Then the elders returned
To the same Circle where they had assembled before,
And they saw the wall in its centre had fallen,
And a majestic throne now stood in its place.
And sitting upon that throne was the one

They had been forbidden from seeing before,
When the human world was drowning
In unrighteous *jahiliyyah* and *shirk*.
And the Lamb stood there, offering himself up for sacrifice,
Saying, hello, human!

You have suffered enough

And your torments have cleansed you for good.
Your Father has not forsaken You,
Your Town has not forsaken You,
I accept your repentance,

So, return in peace!

****

'Now hear what I say to you,'
Rang out the Lamb's voice, like a mighty trumpet,
'Behold, how all-powerful we are together:
Human forces,
And the forces of Heaven!'

A sacred book, sealed with seven seals
Then appeared in the right hand of the One on the Throne.
And Metatron called, his voice like a trumpet,
'Who can arise and remove these seals from the Book?'
The elders fell to their knees,

Adoring the gift of the Lord of Worlds.
Then the white elder spoke,
The one with the face like al-Khidr, and said,
'No man among us is able to do it,
Or we will become unequal again!'

Despairing, I covered my head with my hands.
Would the race of man truly be left without the Great Revelation?
Then the white elder spoke:
'O Lamb of God!
Open the Book. Give men light and certainty!'

The lamb laughed and exclaimed,
'O fathers of peoples and tribes!
You have completed the test for communion of the Mind,
And now you are fated to complete
The test for communion of the Spirit!'

Seven lamps now burned around the Book
And seven Angels with chalices appeared around it.
The Lamb opened the first seal.
A many-voiced choir sang in the sky,
An anthem of heavenly forces.

And the world heard a fearsome voice, commanding the seven angels,
Go and pour out the seven chalices of God's wrath onto the earth.
The first Angel poured out his cup
And festering ulcers spread far and wide among the people
With terrible diseases.

Then the elders begged of them:
'Is there really nothing that can change the fate of humankind?
If it disappears, at the behest of the Lord of Worlds,

778

What would be the point of our union
Or even our existence?

Why, then, has this Book appeared,
If those for whom it is intended will vanish?'
The Lamb's eyes flashed in such a way
That the light of Sun and stars dimmed.
He exclaimed,

'Look to the earth!
This is a signal to all humankind,
That what has been prophesied draws nigh!'
And he opened the second seal on the Book.
And the second Angel poured out his cup, and the sea was destroyed

And all that was within it!

The Lamb lifted up his arms, and the elders were carried,
Along with the Circle and the Throne, up high,
And from those heights, He pointed out to them one dark bank.
'Behold, he goes to the Third War.'
'Who?!' shouted the elders, stunned.

'He who divided you and suggested that you take the path of powerlessness,'
Answered the Son of Man.
I watched it all unfold on the shore,
Standing in the ocean sand and shivering from the cold,
Until I noticed

A beast with seven heads emerging from the abyss to the shore.
These heads were inscribed with blasphemous names
And one of its heads seemed mortally wounded,
But it had healed.
The elders recognised the head that they had trampled in the desert,

When they had battled with the Angels
To defend the child and the Bride clothed in the Sun!
The people of earth had seen the power of that beast
Sent forth by the dragon imprisoned in the abyss,
And they bowed before him!

This beast had been given lips
And he spoke with pride and blasphemy!
He said to the elders,
'What is the meaning of your communion?
What is your combined power

If there is no one to rule over?
Rise up, you first six, you second six and you other six,
And enslave those of you.
Whose people are the other six!
Then six, six and six will be the symbol of your might and power!

Or the first six of you can take
All the power of all the mighty kings
And enslave the others,
For whom six, six and six

Will be the symbol of eternal slavery!

Behold! My might has no limit.
Now I will send you a different beast,
With power over the mind and spirit of men!
He will rule in the dragon's name,
And you have no choice but to consent,

Because the people will dictate the law to him
Which no sinner or pious man will
Dare to break, even if he wants to!
Long will he rule, until
His numbers, written on the arms of all people, disappear!'

The elders were troubled.
The beast's words had thrown them into a terrible confusion.
Then the Lamb said unto them,
'What decision have you made?
He is giving you actual power

And much strength for that, to last a considerable time!'
The elders eyed one another with suspicion.
Was there any one among them
Who had already agreed in his soul to divide
Into six, six and six,

Leaving the others to face inevitable slavery?
One of them, however, rose at that point,
With a handsome face like those of all the heroes of the earth,
And he said, 'Now look.
On one hand we have the temptations of the beast,

While on the other, a Book we've neither seen nor read.
What choice will we make?
Either we will trust the dragon's envoy
And start down a clear path, one we have long known.
Is not what he is offering to us

The same as our past fate?
On the other hand the opening of each seal
Which conceals the contents of that Book from us,
Always brings terrible suffering to men.
Upon what must we rely? On what strength

In the search for which decision to make?
In identifying our choice,
Which might prove to be eternal?'
The elder, white as Abraham, responded:
'Yes, brethren, the Lamb was right when he said

That this is our test of Spirit and Faith,
Yet new tests await.
But I know what we need to do. Now follow me!'
With those words, he fell to his knees before the Throne
Risen up in the centre of the Circle,

Before the Lord of Worlds, and exclaimed,

'All Merciful and Compassionate, You must decide
How to deal with all our peoples,
Races and tongues, by which we were sent here to this Circle!
But we believe that, when You brought us the Book in Your right hand,

You brought us a new Revelation,
And that means, our future!
And even though we don't know what is written there –
It could be our own extinction
And that of all humankind –

We still believe in You, the Only One,
And reject all the schemes of the dragon and the beast!
Accept our decision, and if our choice is correct,
Give us strength, for we go into battle with the beast
To defend our Earthly Home from his temptations!

We no longer want
That beastly division between us
Into six, six and six.
We want to be Unified,
In a common life!

But if You decide, nonetheless, to destroy the entire human race,
Which is Your creation, then so be it!
Let Your will be done!
Then we will be unified even in death!'
Along with the white elder,

Everyone fell to their knees and repeated, 'Let Your will be done!'

Again, songs of praise rang through the heavens,
Heralding that the Creator rejoiced at the elders' decision!
Then the Lamb opened the third seal with the words,
'The time draws nigh!'
And the third angel poured out his cup upon the land.

The springs of the earth became dyed in blood,
Resembling the wounds of the righteous and the witnesses of the Prophets.
Then from the lips of the Lamb came the words,
'So, go you to war!
But the Lord of Worlds' mercy is great:

He sends you four Angels to assist you,
To raise people up and imbue them with the strength of Spirit and Faith!
I have dyed the earth's waters with blood,
So that people remember
How many pure hearts have sacrificed themselves

In the name of the triumph of the human race,
So you will not forget to commemorate their names!'
The angels sent to help were the ones who had already
Protected man's world from the winds and the storm.
They swooped across the sky, trumpeting and calling,

'Get ready, all you who have kept the faith,
For a great battle with the forces of the abyss!

Leaders and heroes are gathering!
The Lord of Worlds will give you
The warrior's might and the strength for victory,

But the strength of Spirit and Faith must be your own!'

The elders began descending to Earth,
To lead their peoples into the ultimate battle.
As they went, the Lamb called after them,
'I give you seven months, seven weeks and seven days.
Gather all those who have remained righteous,

Never bowing before the Dajjal or his comrade the beast
And to he who directs their acts from the abyss!
In the last days of the Holy Month
In the Great Arabian City,
Next to Abraham's tower,

You will see someone descend on a cloud.
You will recognise him,
For he will outwardly resemble the Son of Man,
As has been foretold.
That will mean he has come to assist you,

The Great Warrior of Men.
Not only will he help you assemble your army,
But he will brand all of those
Who have sullied themselves bowing to the beast and the Dajjal,
The king crowned by the dragon and the beast.

He will be vulnerable, for he is just like you, a man.
Therefore, you protect him,
For a great battle awaits us all!'
The elders descended to earth
And went out to their peoples, their races and tongues,

Separately, but remaining together,
Because now it was not reason uniting them,
But the unified strength of Spirit and Faith.
Just as the Lamb had commanded,
From Khorasan and Turan, a Great Warrior arose.

He flew around the world like lightning off a sword,
Like the thunder of the Prophets and the righteous.
His voice rang out, here and there, proclaiming:
'Where are you, true believers? Have your leaders
Not called you to a communion of Spirit and Faith?

Behold what the world conquered by the beast has become!
See how sullied you are with your property aplenty!
Vanity and your passion for acquiring has enslaved you
So much so that newly rich shepherds, rather than helping their fellows,
Compete to build the highest towers in the desert!

Where is your knowledge? Why have you given yourselves over to barbarism?
Where is your morality, left you by the Prophets?
You say "Don't kill," so why do you?

You say "Don't commit adultery," so why are you so deep in sin?
Why have you forgotten the words to the prayers?

How could you have sullied yourselves in drunkenness, orgies, depravity?
To whom have you given your earthly thrones?
Behold the men who govern today:
The one-eyed Dajjal, his face marked by malformation!
His power is in everything, not only the laws he has brought you,

But in your souls, your deeds and your desires!
So great is your shame that
The Sun refuses to rise in the East,
And the moon has been split in two!
The earth has been rent by crevasses

And it trembles and weeps with earthquakes and floods!
Why do you honour false prophets and money changers?
Why have you stopped wishing each other peace when you meet?
Take a good look around you, men!
If there is still righteous power within you,

Take up the sword, and the Books and the glory of your fathers
And follow me!
Any who have succumbed to the Dajjal's temptations
Saying, "I have no need for this battle"
Will see the punishment of heaven!

On the restless horizon a vast army
Has already assembled, led by the Dajjal's favourite generals,
Yajuj and Majuj, the valiant warriors of the black army.
Great is their power and their mastery at arms.
But how can the Fallen One reinforce their strength?

What can he give to them, if he is deprived of a soul himself?'
That is how the Great Warrior denounced
Those who still hadn't realised the time had come
To stop looking to the leaders,
And set about making the decisive choice in their individual lives.

With pride and blasphemy, the Dajjal's subjects
Called to the Warrior, 'This summons of yours, to whom is it made?
Which Books do you speak of and which faith?
We're all of different faiths and it's in that where our principles lie!
We are true believers, unlike the rest!

Are we to stand with people of an alien faith?
Are we to share with them their warrior's fate,
When we don't wish to share even a cup of water with them?
And who will repay us for denying ourselves lasting revenge
For those who died defending our faith in the war against them?'

The Great Warrior laughed, and replied,
'You, who have two eyes, in fact have only one,
Just like that leader of yours!
You don't hear the Prophets, nor do you hear the true leaders,
And so your fate is decided!

Pray, and perhaps your dogmas will protect you
From the wrath of the Lord of Worlds!
You are used to having walls in your souls,
Perhaps your walls will defend you from the angels' might
And the power of my sword, and the sword of the Chosen One!'

The time foretold had begun,
And I saw that a vast army had gathered,
A hundred forty thousand heroes, the righteous and people of the Spirit.
Their battle flags fluttered proudly,
And their women, old folk and children

Sharpened their weapons and gathered the soldiers for the Great Battle.
On the second day I saw
Another vast army approaching,
A hundred forty thousand djinns and peris,
Who shared with men different worlds and earthly spaces.

On the third day I saw an enormous army
Advancing from the East,
A hundred forty thousand fair angels,
With the Archangel Michael resplendent at their head.
People, djinns, peris and angels had come together as before

To conquer earthly evil in the form of the False Prophet
And his protectors, born of the abyss.
They awaited only twenty-four leaders,
Still searching diligently, day and night,
For just one more who might be saved.

At that moment, Jibrail summoned me
And pointed to something far, far away,
But I could see everything as if it were happening up close.
I saw the one-eyed Dajjal,
Walking arm in arm... with one of the elders!

Who was he? The leader of one of the most powerful tribes on earth.
I overheard the conversation between them.
The beast spoke to him, and he said,
'You'll see and that will convince you
That I offer you all the power in the world, you alone,

And your people, your race and your tongue.
What you will see has long ruled the world,
Has long been yours, because this power,
Like poisonous ivy, has spread throughout the earth,
And determines every human deed,

And so there is nothing opposing it that could ever win.
They arrived in the desert. The Dajjal pointed the elder
To the Whore of Babylon,
Seated on a powerful, serpentine beast.
The Whore smiled at the elder, as if to say:

'Every earthly king has tasted my flesh, all the moneychangers and lawyers.
They have caressed my body, barely veiled with a blush,
And those embraces have given them a sense of power and strength.

Who can ever oppose beauty and riches such as these,
Draped in porphyry and pearls?

Any who touches me, even just once,
Will never forget it and will always cater to my whims!
I am stronger than prayers and faith, for I am drunk on the blood of the righteous.
I am stronger than any spirit, because I am nourished
With the blood of the witnesses of the Prophets.

I hold the secrets of many men –
Secrets of wealth, procured on the whims of the ignoble,
On their efforts to prevail over their neighbour
And trample him as he languishes in misery and need,
And in spiritual poverty.

Look now, leader, how the world rests in my embrace,
Enveloping all and sundry.
See the nerves react to every trembling of my thighs,
And every stirring of my passionate tongue!
There are kings I have enslaved,

But elevated, too, to the peak of pleasure,
So they do not heed their slavery.
There are tyrants who have forgotten every other purpose in life,
Aside from using my body for their lust.
There are rich men trembling with thirst,

Not thirst for water, but for my power and strength.
I am the entire secret that rules the world.
I am the power that goes unnoticed,
But is stronger than any of these four beasts,
Who are replete with eyes,

From whom tyrants borrow only their shape,
While for them I become all meaning.
Watch how my round buttocks have crushed them,
All the Babylons of Earth, seething on hills and by rivers.
How even the most inferior man there

Is infected with the fever to own me, to have me
At any price, even should they sell, drop by drop,
Choinix by choinix, the seed that lives in their souls.
Watch and see what a dark passion is born in man
To build secret brotherhoods, secret power,

That can guard the secret of the passion of the ignoble,
United as one – in my glorious visage.
My lord, don't be fooled! Carry on the tradition of your people's kings,
Which made them mightier and stronger than all.
After all, you know full well

How hard it is to rule human beings by appealing to their purity and Spirit,
And how easy to rule by appealing to their ignoble interests,
Granting to them, gradually, bit by bit
Small pieces of my body and
The intoxicating wine of coupling with it!

My words are not empty promises.
Here, I have a present for you!
All around the world, among every people,
I have built you a thousand houses
And placed countless symbols of your power inside,

Inscribed with your hand and with your face,
So all will remember who rules the world!
Take this as my gift and come into my embrace,
Embrace me whole, with your arms and legs,
Intertwine with me so we will become a single whole!'

So shamefully did the Whore speak,
Seducing the leader of the most powerful people.
And nearby stood the smiling Dajjal
Nodding at each of the Whore's words.
I was confused, and forgot myself in terror,

Shouting, 'Heavenly Messenger! Stop him!
You have the power to do that!'
But Jibrail crossed his arms coldly on his chest, and said,
'No, Poet, this is his choice!'
'But he's not just an old man! He has his people behind him!

Would they approve of all that, all who came from his land,
Fixed their armour and readied their swords for the Great Battle?
What will become of the twenty-three?
Their communion would be shattered with a single blow,
All due to the error of just one of them!'

But the Bringer of the Holy Spirit was unmoved.
Then I implored him to take me to that desert.
In truth, what could I do alone,
Having no power, no strength and no angelic horn?
Jibrail left me not far from the site of the fateful discussion –

He could not deny me that.
Then I did the only thing I knew.
I took out my harp and began to sing, my voice trembling,
Of how a strength resides in a person
Which no demon or soulless beast can overcome –

That strength is his soul.
The soul, which must be dedicated to what is truly beautiful,
What leads us on the Path to Him,
Who so loves us and who waits for us
In the Blessed City of Heaven!

I could not find words of rebuke, anger or of pathos.
I am merely a poet, not a prophet, not a herald.
But in that next moment I saw
The elder lowering his hand, which had reached for the golden chalice
Offered to him by the Whore.

The leader of his people stopped and wiped his eyes
To rid himself of delusion.
Confidence and power filled his heart.

The Dajjal understood the truth and changed in an instant,
From eloquent and attractive to a pitch-black thundercloud,

Disgorging strikes of lightning.
One of them he launched at me and broke my harp in two.
He cast another over the elder's head, and cried,
'You fool! You sentimental weakling!
For what have you surrendered all your might?

For the frivolous promises of angels?
You deny yourself the true power, worthy of a man
And a ruling lord,
For the sake of slimy gossip of what is yet to come,
Which you can never control, but could have been all yours?'

But the elder was not frightened, and said,
'It has been foretold that all those Babylons and Baal's houses,
Which gave their bodies to be pillaged by the beast, will fall
And his Whore too!'
The Antichrist took aim, but had no time to release his lightning.

Down shot Jibrail, like a fiery eagle
And carried us both away from that desert.
'Didn't you say you would not interfere?'
I asked him, exhausted, as we flew.
The Archangel smiled: 'The choice was made. What more would you ask?'

When we arrived at the place where the Great Army had mustered,
Everyone was in formation and awaiting the call to battle.
'Lead us, Mighty Warrior, and you, Lamb, who sacrificed yourself!'
'No,' the Lamb responded, 'It is not yet time.'
And three times he asked,

'Are all the righteous ones here? Has no one been forgotten?'
'No one,' each time answered the elders
And the leaders of the djinns and peris.
'Any who have decided to remain behind,
Such is their will!'

'Well then,' said the Lamb, and he opened the fourth seal
And said: 'Here is the punishment for sinners,
Brought down not to destroy the human race,
But to cleanse it of the filth of beasts
And the Whore of Babylon!'

The fourth angel rose into the air and poured out his chalice on the Sun.
It glowed, incensed and, rising in the west,
It dried the earth and mercilessly scorched
The people who had remained, despite the summons.
The people began hurling abuse at the heavens,

And everyone said, 'Look! Not a single one is praying for forgiveness.'
The Lamb opened the fifth seal.
The fifth angel poured out his cup of wrath on the Dajjal's throne.
His kingdom took shape, dark and full of gloom,
But even in the gloom none of his subjects looked to repent.

The Lamb opened the sixth seal
And the sixth angel rose over the earth.
He poured out his chalice into the great rivers, like the mighty Euphrates.
Then the beasts rose up and prophesied in lies,
Saying, You are no longer needed by the Lord of Worlds,

Prepare for the great battle,
Whose name is Armageddon.
They began to gather an enormous army,
But the drying Euphrates revealed uncountable treasures,
Over which the knights of that beastly host began to quarrel.

And so, the might of the Dajjal's army began to dissolve
Influenced by its very own mores.
Twice more, it surrendered to internal strife:
When it saw a golden mountain and when it was dividing
What it had plundered from the lands encountered on its way.

The Dragon's Son assembled three formidable armies:
One in the East, one in the West and one in Arabia,
So enormous that the sunlight dimmed in the lands
Carpeted in dust from their horses' hooves,
Like a poisonous, malodorous smoke.

The Dajjal's three armies advanced to a place in the desert
Which they called Megiddo.
Our army, meanwhile, travelled the sky,
Moving on the wings of angels.
From on high, we saw that in the ranks of the One-Eyed Monster

Were many who said that they were true believers.
This perplexed us and we thought, perhaps, we had not called everyone
Under the banner of the Heavenly Host?
But Jibrail calmly explained,
'This reckoning that they are true believers is false,

And therefore it serves not communion, but discord.
The three armies have gathered dogmatic fanatics
Who never tire of scolding each other about the authenticity of their faith.
On the one hand, this pleases the Dajjal,
Because no faith at all is left in these desolate souls.

The ignoble teachings of false prophets have replaced it all.
But also, the One-Eyed Monster is extremely worried,
Because unity and discipline are draining from his army.'
And indeed, from the heavens we saw
How sacred words on the lips of the deceived

Transformed into their own utter opposites.

The day of the Great Battle dawned!
The Great Warrior and the Lamb saddled a steed together
And led their troops into battle.
The Warrior steered their white stallion, while the Lamb
Cut down enemies, one after another.

A hundred years they battled,

And the followers of the One-Eyed Monster perished,
While new divisions joined his army all the time.
And still we could not force the tide of battle to turn.
Then the wonderful moment occurred

When the Lamb struck the Dajjal directly in his only eye,
And then cast him to the ground,
Broken to six hundred and sixty-six pieces –
And so, as he wanted to divide the world,
He ended divided himself.

The following day Yajuj and Majuj,
The beast's great generals, rallied their troops,
And with redoubled strength and desperation
Launched their attack on us
With all the might of their champions, ifrits and black peris.

But they, too, fell at the swords of our Heavenly Host.
What was left of the three armies fled back from whence they had come
To the battlefield of Megiddo.
But they, too, were swallowed up by the gaping earth
In the East, in the West and in Arabia.

Then the Lamb and the Great Warrior took up *eternal* chains,
And bound the dragon, the beast and the Dajjal the False Prophet,
And cast them for time *eternal*
Into a fiery, sulphurous lake on the borders of Hell,
Where they were doomed to *eternal* torment.

Then the twenty-four elders assembled together again
Around the Heavenly Throne.
And the Lamb opened the seventh seal.
Across all the Universe, a mighty voice rang out:
It is done!

The Holy Book fell open,
And the elders beheld what was written there, inside and out,
And they were amazed at the miracle.
They asked the Lamb what it all meant
And the Victor responded:

'The meaning is that this Book is alive,
And is being written even now,
Without end, forever.'
And the sound of a thousand trumpets rang out,
Heralding the start of the Highest of Courts.

I saw the dead rising from the earth and the sea,
Descending from mountains and ascending from valleys.
The living assembled, too, those who had fought the Last Battle.
Each of them approached the One on the Throne
And He judged them by their deeds,

Just as the Holy Books had foretold.
A gentle, good breeze carried the righteous
To the tabernacles of paradise,
And the unrepentant set out

On the long road to the sulphurous lake of Iblis,

To receive the eternal torment they deserved.

After the Judgment came a new Golden Age,
Where there were no wars, for the peoples lived in communion.
Gone were the lawbreakers and tyrants.
The children of earth knew nothing of thieving, stealing or violence;
Even these words had vanished from the languages of the world.

Gone were all signs of corruption, temptation and mistrust.
And faith in the Lord of Worlds came to fill all things,
Like water fills the clean and noble sea.
And any who were asked what they knew of life
Would always answer the same: Happiness, Truth and Freedom!

****

I came to in my darkened cell,
As if jerked awake from a heavy sleep.
Uneasy in the darkness of the place,
I hurried to rinse my face in the basin,
Dashed outside, and froze, unmoving, where I stood.

The afternoon was in full swing
And it stunned me with its noise and light.
It rolled around my silent self
In waves of movement, colours, voices, faces,
Making me the only unmoving element in the scene.

There was a man selling sweets,
Handing out his goods and counting his money with animation.
There were students, winking and laughing at their jokes.
There was an older couple who had stopped in front of the store.
There was a teacher, leading his schoolchildren on an excursion.

I stood surrounded by the whirlwind of real life
And so strongly did I feel my detachment from it,
That I raised my eyes to heaven and shouted, desperately, silently,
'Where are you, brethren, and You, Beloved Teacher?!
I miss you all so much.

How can it be that you have left me all alone?
How much I miss your jokes and your smiles,
Talking by the fire and on the road!
Why have you determined this lot for me,
To long for you all the rest of my days,

And think that my life and the meaning of it
Have been left so far behind?'
Soon my eyes were filled with tears,
But when I tore them from the sky,
I could make out through the film of those tears

That the schoolteacher had stopped and was saying something
To one of his young charges, pointing in my direction.

The very next moment the schoolboy ran right up
And picked my quill from the ground and handed it to me.
I looked at the boy, astounded,

While he just hurried back, quick as a flash.
I lifted my eyes and saw
The teacher and his pupils smiling at me.
They waited for their classmate, then waved a friendly goodbye,
And went on down their road in search of some knowledge.

'Twelve boys,' I counted, and then I understood:
A new Circle had begun.
And in all these many years apart from my beloved friends,
Amidst the noise of life going on around me,
A life I had been torn from by pen, duty and Faith,

For the first time, I felt no pain of loneliness.

Verse 40. Conclusion

(92) This community of yours is one community, and I am your Lord, so worship Me.

Qur'an. Surah 21. 'The Prophets'

Here I stand; I can do none other, so help me God.

Martin Luther

One more, the final record, and my annals
Are ended, and fulfilled the duty laid
By God on me a sinner.
Not in vain. Hath God appointed me for many years
A witness, teaching me the art of letters...[277]

Alexander Pushkin, Boris Godunov
Monologue of Father Pimen

And so it draws to a close,
The story you have probably heard before,
A story passed down from generation to generation.
The story that is passed to us from one of the Great Books,
Which, they say, is greater than anything in the world.

This is the story of the Good, Kind Man,
Who one day gathered his best and closest friends
And departed on a long Path, a Path that was difficult
But incredibly interesting all the same.
This story comes to an end,

But if we are to believe these curious chaps,
As soon as it ends,
Then it will immediately begin again.
And it makes no difference
If it is I who relates it

Or anyone else.
If you ask me to do it again,
Then I will not say no.
I'll just take a little rest,
Drink some water from the jug

And I'll happily start over
From the very beginning.
I love this story.
It's my entire life, you see,
All that I can remember with trepidation

And with no less trepidation
Gift my story to you.
I know that a lot of people tell this story
And not just me, and that is wonderful!
Even despite the fact that

Our tales differ considerably one from the other.
I often encounter them, these other storytellers.
Sometimes we are prone to interrupt one another,

---

[277] The version, rendered into English by Alfred Hayes.

Proving who remembers the finer details better
Or whose version is more plausible,

Whose contains an element of fiction.
But, let me assure you, these are not malicious arguments;
All those who tell this story
Are not simply narrating,
Rather, they carry the testaments of

Whom this story is about.
And this imposes a certain responsibility.
I would even say, a very high degree of responsibility.
Therefore, the other storytellers and I
Never quarrel or bicker,

Just help one another
To recover details and meanings.
Incidentally, remember, those who usually bicker and get angry
When defending their version of events
Were certainly not among their number

And I never saw them.
Because he who has seen
Will never make a noise or display rage.
The only thing is that I have a little secret,
Which helps me convince those who argue,

And I'll tell you about it a little later.
For now, I'll tell you
What I've heard about these
Good, Kind young men,
Who parted on those days

Out in the weary Galilean desert.
They say that Cephas met his *omega* in Rome,
Where the ruthless, merciless tyrant Nero
Crucified him upside down.
Before his death, Cephas remembered all the lads by name,

Bidding them farewell as he named then
And greeting them at the same time.
Andrew, known as the First-Called,
Travelled many countries,
Where he related simple things to the people

That are easy to understand
But often hard to follow,
When you have to relinquish your ingrained fears and dogmas.
Many people remember him
And many see him as their patron.

In one of these countries
Andrew too encountered his oblique cross.
When he saw it before *returning*,
He laughed and fondly recalled Philip,
Who had told so much about such a cross,

Which had become a symbol of the fall of Chorazin.
They say that the ruler Egeat, who had ordered Andrew's execution,
Was frightened by what he heard
Drop from the dying man's lips.
Especially when he saw the sign of *omega* in the heavens.

The king was horrified and wanted to stop the execution
But Andrew had already said his *I am Him!*
Levi Matthew met with the Teacher and his friends
In Ethiopia, where he was killed by cannibals.
The savages had killed him out of fear, not from a desire to eat him.

However, having killed Levi, they abandoned cannibalism altogether
And prayed at length to the heavens, begging for forgiveness.
They say that Levi Matthew, not managing to stand
Before the Gates of Heaven,
Immediately asked the Lord of Worlds

To let him return and forgive the savages,
Which is what he did
Having been granted this wish.
They say that James, son of Zebedee,
Before being beheaded,

Forgave his informer
Who, shocked, decided to accept his own death
Together with Brother James.
I heard that one fine city
Still remembers

When the formidable Shah Astyages of Persia
Put a royal-looking righteous man to death
Because he was frightened of what he had simply related
About the Beloved Teacher and our teachings.
When the shah heard

Bartholomew (for it was him!) saying
'I am the Truth', while on the cross,
He ordered that he be skinned and dismembered.
Oh, Almighty one! What fear and terror
Does the Word instil in tyrants and sinners!

It is also related that when the slaves of the *jahiliyyah*
Were preparing to execute their warrior brother
James, son of Alphaeus,
He simply laughed; the pagans asked him
What he found so funny.

'I am happy,' he replied
'That I will see my friends and the Beloved One again.'
'But how will you see them?' the pagans asked in disbelief,
'You're about to die.'
The eyes of the courageous son of Alphaeus sparkled

And he said, 'He that lives is not destined
To die. And what is dead will never
Be alive.'

'But who is dead?' The pagans asked.
'You are,' James replied.

After that they tortured him for a long time,
But he only laughed and welcomed the moment of his *return*.
When he died, the pagans understood
That they too were dead.
Then they thought about it and said,

'We have killed the one who brought us life.'
They sent a man who was supposed to learn more
About our teaching.
When he returned, reincarnated, they said,
'But how is it possible, when dying, to give life?!'

And, with that, they turned to the true faith.
Would you say that is an amazing, exceptional story?
No, that happens everywhere
Where the Road took my brothers.
Take the former angel Thaddeus, for example,

Who wanted to become mortal.
When he came to the Persian and Armenian borders,
The local pagans offered no resistance
While he healed and delivered them from demons.
However, when he started simply talking to people

And telling them about the Path and the Teacher,
The tyrants then sent a detachment of soldiers
To kill him.
A Persian soldier shot Thaddeus right in the throat,
But Brother Thaddeus found the strength inside to get up,

Spread his arms and embrace the whole world.
At that same moment he was pinned to the wall with arrows.
'Why did you do that to that righteous man?'
The Armenians said in outrage.
One of them got up and drew

An image on their own forehead with Thaddeus's blood,
Making it known that he would be baptised and adopt the new faith,
For there were no rivers or lakes near that place.
Then the Persian commander was embarrassed and said,
'We will build you a city,

Where you can honour this righteous man.[278]
The courageous warrior Simon the Canaanite
Found his *omega* in Abkhazia,
Where the pagans decided to put the strength of his devotion
To his teaching to the test by torturing him in a cave

And telling him, 'Renounce
Or take up your sword and fight with us
For your faith!'

---

[278] Shah Abbas built a separate city for the Armenians, called New Julfa, where he afforded them many privileges and the right to practice Christian worship.

'Can't you see that the battle is being fought?'
Simon asked the pagans, but they didn't understand

And put him to death, leaving his body in the cave.
However, when they returned a day later,
Expecting to find his body torn apart by predators,
They saw Simon sitting on a rock,
Talking with the leopards.

'Are you talking with wild animals?!'
The pagans asked incredulously.
Simon calmly answered,
'But did the people want to talk with me?'
After that, the people bowed before him

And accepted the faith in the One God.
They say that Thomas did, in the end, build
His own fairy-tale temple of his dreams
Where he dreamed of erecting it – in Heaven.
He built it for the Indian King Gundafor,

Who had wished for a temple to his glory on earth.
Thomas distributed all the money that had been earmarked for the temple
To the poor and needy, in the king's name.
When the time came to accept the finished building,
Naturally, there was no temple there on earth.

Thomas was then lanced with spears and cut down with swords.
However, when the king's son died he saw
An enormous, fabulous temple in Heaven.
He asked whose palace it was.
In reply he was told that it was for King Gundafor,

Who had believed in Good, Kind deeds
In regard to his subjects.
The son then requested an hour to tell the king
That a temple had in fact been built,
Only in heaven.

When I heard this story,
I laughed and recalled the bold and smart Thomas,
While Thomas laughed with me –
I could hear him.
According to legend, young Matthias

Was stoned to death in his homeland, in Judea,
Condemned by the same people who had condemned
The Beloved Friend and Teacher.
Only the young and handsome
Poet John escaped martyrdom

Just as it had been foretold.
Just as the Beloved Friend had requested,
He cared for His Mother.
And one day the Word came to him
That has already been spoken of.

All of them, my brothers, found their *omega*,
But they didn't deem it necessary to rest in expectation
Of Judgment Day
And abandon us alone and in fear of starvation,
Just as the Beloved Friend had appointed.

They returned to their city in peace.
So look around – they are among us!
Perhaps that policeman over there is concealing wings?
Perhaps that soldier is holding not an automatic rifle,
But *the second sword?*

Or perhaps that simple teacher
Will tomorrow announce the fate of your Chorazin?
Perhaps the one who took your money
For the state has already set out on the Road?
Perhaps that young man

Is already building his temple in Heaven?
And that uncomely-looking lad
Has already seen his Revelation?
Is it really that hard for you to believe
That the Circle of Time has begun again?

Go and take a look!
There's a sign on his shoulder –
Is that not an *alpha*,
As depicted by the Teacher?
The one you drank wine with yesterday

With the shiny, oily fish –
What was it he said?
And the one laying the stone,
Is he not building us
Our New Home and putting our Old Home in order?

Or that one, rushing and pushing through the crowd –
Perhaps he is rushing
To reveal Secret Knowledge to us,
Knowledge that will return to us the power of Faith
And destroy all doubts?

You ask why I often say the words
They tell, I heard and *they say?*
This is because, after we
Parted back then in Galilee,
I no longer saw any of the brothers

And was not a witness to their deeds,
Achievements or self-sacrifice.
Wait a minute, you might say,
That means you are the witness of everything else
That has been spoken of in this tale?!

Yes, I reply.
But who are you then?! the reader will ask,
Feverishly leafing through the Great Book

798

And running over the ancient legends in their mind.
You're not one of the Circle of Twelve, right?

You see, all their names are known.
The stories have been told.
Perhaps you are one of the Circle of Fifty or the Circle of Seventy
Then what is your name?
Let us find you in the tablets.

Or perhaps you're a woman?
The girl from Magdala who many have also spoken about?
Then why is the entire story
Related by a man?
Perhaps you're a spy or a spook?

Oh, God Almighty!
Or perhaps you're the Greedy and Bloodless One
Or one of his cunning demons?!
Don't instil anxiety in our hearts;
You see, you're not in the lists or the codes!

Who are you? Answer me!!!
I laugh in response and cough a little,
Just as my Beloved Friend had done.
And I say this:
There is no reason for anxiety, brothers and sisters!

The answer is right here, can you not see it?
Haven't you realised?
Who was always by the Beloved One's side,
Never leaving Him for a second?
Who loved and still loves the brethren

And who is destined to meet with them again?
Who has completed the entire Path from the beginning to the *omegas*?
Who has seen the steppes of Turkestan, the docks of Acre
And who loved the children of Chorazin?
Who went up to Nibiru and built the Pantheon?

Who saw Cephas cut off the Greedy One's hand?
Who was on the Mountain and walked on water?
And who saw the Transfiguration of the Beloved Friend?
Who heard His prayer in the Garden of Gethsemane?
Who bid him farewell and then said *Hello!*

To Him once more?!
Who saw the Great Arab, the Enlightened Prince,
The Forerunner and the Rabbeinu in the same place
And at the same Blessed Hour?
Reader, have you still not worked it out?

I am You!

Astana. May 2011

Printed in Great Britain
by Amazon